BARRELHOUSE
BOYS

Joel Williamsen

Library of Congress Control Number 2009911345

ISBN   978-0-615-33316-8

Cover photo courtesy of Ray L. Bellande.

Photos of the Rock Island wreck (back cover) and George Washington Davis, courtesty Nebraska State Historical Society.

Photo of Willa Cather at the Nebraska State Journal, courtesy Philip L. and Helen Cather Southwick Collection, Archives & Special Collections, University of Nebraska-Lincoln Libraries

Unless otherwise noted, other images courtesy of usgenweb.org and wikipedia.org. No copyright is claimed for images or other material in the public domain.

Visit Joel Williamsen at www.barrelhouseboys.com

To Miria

All of this could have happened—

A fair amount actually did.

BARRELHOUSE BOYS

SIDNEY

NORTH PLATTE

OFALLONS BLUFF

LINCOLN

JOURNEYS BY RAIL

ALDER GROVE

SCRIBNER

HOOPER

FREMONT

COLUMBUS

OMAHA

KEARNEY

LANCASTER
COUNTY
MAP AT LEFT

LINCOLN

RED CLOUD

FAIRBURY

FALLS
CITY

NEBRASKA 1894

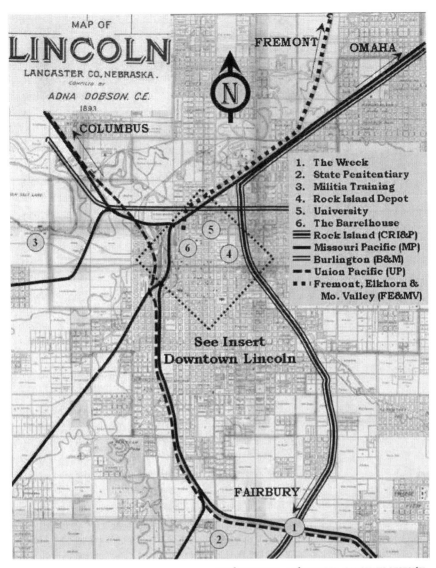

MAP OF
LINCOLN
LANCASTER CO. NEBRASKA.
COMPILED BY
ADNA DOBSON. C.E.
1893

COLUMBUS

FREMONT   OMAHA

N

1. The Wreck
2. State Penitentiary
3. Militia Training
4. Rock Island Depot
5. University
6. The Barrelhouse
≡ Rock Island (CRI&P)
— Missouri Pacific (MP)
≡ Burlington (B&M)
– – Union Pacific (UP)
▪ ▪ ▪ Fremont, Elkhorn &
     Mo. Valley (FE&MV)

See Insert
Downtown Lincoln

FAIRBURY

GREATER LINCOLN 1894

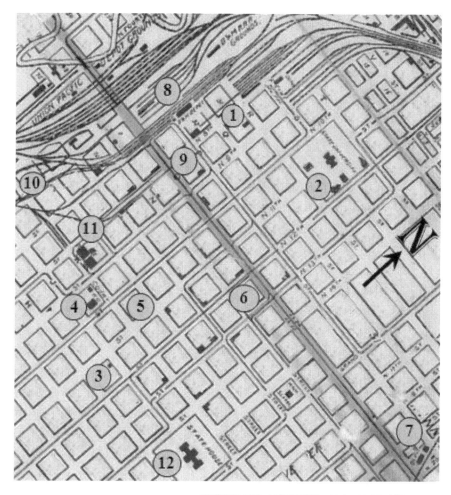

DOWNTOWN LINCOLN 1894

1. The Barrelhouse
2. University Hall and Library
3. The Pack Residence
4. Lancaster County Courthouse
5. Willa Cather's rooms
6. Lt. John Pershing's rooms
7. Rock Island passenger depot
8. Burlington & Missouri depot
9. Lincoln Hotel
10. The Brickyard
11. Lincoln Streetcar Company
12. State Capitol

Gardner Family Tree

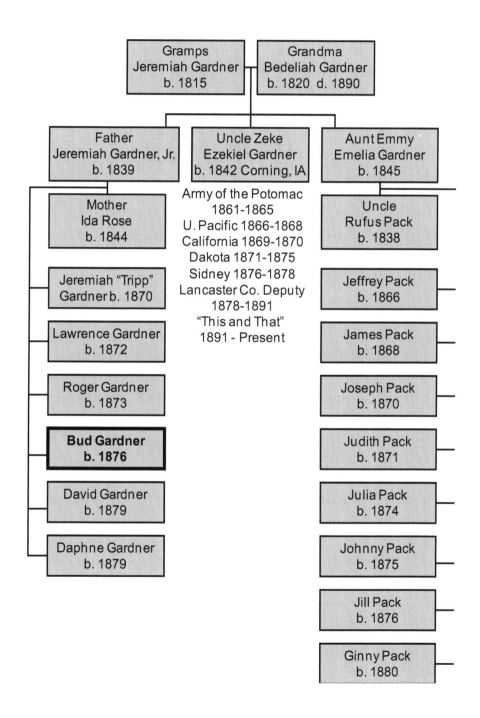

Gramps
Jeremiah Gardner
b. 1815

Grandma
Bedeliah Gardner
b. 1820 d. 1890

Father
Jeremiah Gardner, Jr.
b. 1839

Uncle Zeke
Ezekiel Gardner
b. 1842 Corning, IA

Aunt Emmy
Emelia Gardner
b. 1845

Mother
Ida Rose
b. 1844

Army of the Potomac
1861-1865
U. Pacific 1866-1868
California 1869-1870
Dakota 1871-1875
Sidney 1876-1878
Lancaster Co. Deputy
1878-1891
"This and That"
1891 - Present

Uncle
Rufus Pack
b. 1838

Jeremiah "Tripp"
Gardner b. 1870

Jeffrey Pack
b. 1866

Lawrence Gardner
b. 1872

James Pack
b. 1868

Roger Gardner
b. 1873

Joseph Pack
b. 1870

**Bud Gardner
b. 1876**

Judith Pack
b. 1871

David Gardner
b. 1879

Julia Pack
b. 1874

Daphne Gardner
b. 1879

Johnny Pack
b. 1875

Jill Pack
b. 1876

Ginny Pack
b. 1880

Characters
In Order of Appearance
See Gardner Family Tree for Separate Listing

Name	Home	Occupation
Bud Gardner	Alder Grove	Barrelhouse Boy
Jeremiah Beakins	New York City	Western Union
Robert Harrison	North of Lincoln	Farmer
Roscoe Harrison	North of Lincoln	Farmer's Grandson
Maxwell LeBlanc	Lincoln	Freighter
William "Billy" Tidmore	Lincoln	Ruffian
Franks	Lincoln	Ruffian
Ezekiel Gardner	817 R St., Lincoln	Barrelhouse Boy
"Big Swede" Jorgenson	Gothenburg	Barrelhouse Boy
Amos Aloysius Seville	Lincoln	Barrelhouse Boy
"Bobber" Davies	Lincoln	Barrelhouse Boy
"Professor" Tom Turpin	St. Louis	Piano Player
Eugenia Livingston	Lincoln	"Actress"
Margaret "Maggie" Troy	Lincoln	"Actress"
Miles McGee	Lincoln	Chandler
"Vinnie" Verlucci	Lincoln (via Italy)	Nut Vendor
Fred Miller	Lincoln	Lancaster County Sheriff
Pack Family (Gardner Tree)	1109 J St., Lincoln	Freighters
Willa Cather	1029 L St., Lincoln	Journalist, Student
Anna Marie Vostrovsky	Crounse	Waitress
Frank Crawford	Omaha and Lincoln	Coach
George Washington Davis	Near Lincoln	Farm Hand
J.T. Lynch	Everywhere	Facilitator
Jasper Rankin	Anywhere	Facilitator
Jack Trudeau	Nowhere	Facilitator
Jasper Mooney	216 N. 7th, Lincoln	Restauranteur
C.D. Stannard	St. Joseph, MO	Conductor
Ike dePuis	Council Bluffs, IA	Engineer
William Craig	Fairbury	Fireman
Harry Foote	St. Joseph, MO	Brakeman
Clive Masterson	Lincoln	Grocery & Supplies
Eloise Moseman	Crounse	Farmwife
William Jennings Bryan	Lincoln	U.S. Congressman
"Manny" O'Manion	Fairbury	Hotel Clerk
Nathan Brockhurst	Fairbury	Stationmaster
Lt. John J. Pershing	1213 O St, Lincoln	Corps of Cadets
James H. Canfield	Lincoln	Chancellor, NU

Characters
In Order of Appearance (Continued)

Name	Home	Occupation
Frank and Lewis Ryan	Lincoln	Schoolboys
Ransom Reed Cable Jr.	25 Erie St., Chicago	Jr. Executive
Ransom Reed Cable Sr.	25 Erie St., Chicago	President
Peter LaRue	Chicago	President Asst.
Charles G. Dawes	Lincoln	Lawyer
Hezekiah "Heck" Kohlman	Lincoln	Lawyer
Col. Charles J. Bills	Fairbury	Militia Commander
Jay McDowell	Fairbury	Toady
Fred Scott	Horton, KS	Baggage Master
Charles H. Cherry	Kearney	Postal Clerk
George and William Saxton	Lincoln	Wreck Rescuers
Walter and Lew Seidell	Lincoln	Wreck Rescuers
"Crazy" Charlie Raymond	Lincoln	Hackman
Robert Malone	Lincoln	Chief, Fire Dept.
Frank Malone	Lincoln	Police Detective
Leonard K. Johnson	Omaha	Crane Operator
Scott Low	Lincoln	County Court Clerk
Ignatius W. Lansing	Lincoln	County Court Judge
John Langston	Fairbury	Sheriff, Jeff County
Stephan & Lukas Vostrovsky	Crounse	Farmers
George Flippin	Lincoln	Football Player
Henri Flint	Chicago	Pusher
Charles Cheevers	Chicago	Pusher
Peter H. Cooper	Lincoln	Chief of Police
Wendell Evans	Lincoln	Reporter
Fred Lonsdale	Lincoln	Davis' Employer
Piotr Rémy	Lincoln	Half-Czech Worker
Pavel and Alexi Svoboda	Lincoln	Czech Workers
Andryev Malý	Lincoln	"The Czech Giant"
Charles Flippin	Lincoln	Physician
Eduard Novak	Omaha	Union organizer
Doc Connelle	Fairbury	Physician
Russ Hazard	Fairbury	Farmer
Colonel Philpot	Lincoln	Lawyer
D.B. Courtenay	Lincoln	Lawyer
Leonard Truett	Chicago	Ex-Army Seargant
George Jay Gould	New York City	Railroad Executive

NEBRASKA STATE JOURNAL

LINCOLN, NEBRASKA   AUGUST 10, 1894   NUMBER 382

DEATH BY FIRE

Eleven Lives Go Out in a Rock Island Railroad Wreck

THE HOLOCAUST CAUSED BY FIENDS

A Crow Bar Found Nearby and Tell-Tale Marks on the Rails

HEARTRENDING CRIES OF DYING

Heroic Rescuers Work in Blinding Heat and Flames

The Injured Number Fifteen—Anxious Friends Hunting for Missing— Unknown Dead Leave No Identification Behind

The incoming Rock Island Train was wrecked and burned at 9:20 last night. A partial list of the dead and injured is as follows:

The Dead.

C.D. STANNARD, conductor, Council Bluffs, perished in the flames; family.

WILLIAM CRAIG, fireman, Fairbury; family.

IKE DEPEW, engineer, Council Bluffs, crushed; family.

UNIDENTIFIED, grain man of Fairbury.

ABOUT SEVEN UNKNOWN.

Injured.

HARRY FOOTE, brakeman, leg broken.

C.H. CHERRY, postal clerk, terribly cut about the face and head.

F.T. SCOTT, express messenger, back injured and cut on head.

O.S. BELL, Lincoln traveling man, internally.

A fearful wreck, involving the loss of eleven lives, one engine and two cars, occurred on the Chicago, Rock Island, & Pacific railroad where it crosses on a high trestle the tracks of the U.P. and B.M. railroad at 10 o'clock last night. All indications point to train wreckers as the cause.

Train No. 8 drawn by engine 213 is an accommodation called "Ft. Worth accommodation" and is due to arrive here at 9:40 p.m. Last night it was about 10 minutes late and was making up time when it struck the trestle that crosses Salt creek about four miles from the city and two from the penitentiary. When it struck the trestle the rails immediately spread and the engine drawing the two cars after it went thumping along over the cross ties and then with a crash it fell forty feet to the bed of the creek below. The engine burst and glowing coals spreading ignited the wooden supports and the coaches behind it, and in a few moments the bridge dry as tinder due to its exposure to the sun was one mass of flames. The coals falling upon the coaches lying in the ditches set them afire, and...

Prologue

Saturday, July 7, 1894
6:48 p.m.

Matthew Averman was doing his best to get quietly drunk, although no one could honestly say that Pullman City, Illinois, was quiet anywhere today, even in the small bar in which he had chosen to cloister himself. A half dozen disheveled men—all Union brothers—were similarly immersing themselves in alcohol, some not as quietly as Averman. It was a private establishment, however, unlike most of the "company" taverns, which were owned...*like the houses, like the stores, like the church building itself,* Averman grumbled...*by Pullman. Pullman's factories. Pullman's streets. Pullman's **people.***

But the troops, sulked Averman...*well, the **troops** belonged to President Cleveland.*

The afternoon had been a bloody disaster. Averman poured another Scotch, switching off his surroundings. *A very bloody disaster.* The trains being escorted through the city by the militia had been stopped, as planned...but the federal troops on the trains had fired into the strikers, and Averman himself had seen a dozen men go down. Now, he had received word that Debs himself, and four other strike leaders had been arrested...*Damn!*

Averman, the union's enforcer and Debs's right hand, had never been known as a patient man, and now gave in to a display of his famous temper, throwing the empty shot glass across the small room, where it shattered most pleasantly against a picture of Governor Altgeld. The Governor's weak attempts at preventing the entrance of Federal troops into Illinois, and handling the strikers using the state militia had gone on deaf ears in Washington, just as the local strike had spread into a national one. *The spreading of the strike in late June had been exhilarating,* Averman admitted to himself...the first real demonstration of the national power of a union. *But today's fiasco...*

"Give me another glass," growled Averman to the thin man behind the bar. The man grinned a ghastly grin and complied, just as Averman turned his head to his companion, a burly bodyguard...who was *gone.* And the small room...? *Empty.*

"What the hell...?" stuttered Averman, but only for a moment. The thin man behind the bar was turning toward him with an outstretched arm.

The last thing Averman saw was the man's skeleton smile.

* * * * *

While the horses had the sense to relax and graze nearby, the men of the Alder Grove haying crew took their ease at the end of the long season the way they always did—pitting the Haulers against the Pressers in a baseball game for the official summer bragging rights.

Bud Gardner took his lead from second base, stretching his tired leg muscles as he did so. He was not the only one who was sore; Harlan winced through each half-swing of their team's weather-beaten baseball bat.

From the churchyard that butted up against the third baseline, some of the girlfriends, wives and mothers of the players on both sides took a moment from loading the long tables with food to clap and shout their encouragement to Harlan. "Get a hit, Harlan!" and "Hit'em where they ain't!" echoed simultaneously from a particularly pretty blonde and a striking brunette, and the two girls eyed each other suspiciously.

*Harlan, you're gonna be **really** tired by the end of today,* Bud mused.

As he led off the bag, Bud could see that the sun had almost fallen over the roof of Alder Grove Methodist Church, the understood signal for the end of the game, an odd rule with uncertain origins that sometimes ended a game in mid-innings. *Harlan will be the last batter, so may as well take my chance now.* As the pitcher wound up and corkscrewed a curve toward the plate, Bud exploded from his stretched-out stance and sprinted toward third base. Halfway to third, Bud's hearing registered the satisfying *crack* of Harlan's bat as it spanked the ball into the dusty air. It slammed into the ground just behind second base, but slowed unnaturally as it plowed through the stubble.

Nevertheless, Bud was committed, and picked up steam as he rounded third base. Looking ahead, he could see the massive form of Jed Jensen, catcher for the Haulers, towering over home plate. Bud could tell from his expression that the throw from second was nearing Jed…but so was Bud, and his speed was building to a crescendo as he lowered his head and pumped his legs toward the Norwegian behemoth. Forgetting the throw, Jed smiled as he turned his bulk to meet Bud. Fortunately, Bud had the advantage in momentum, and when his shoulder crunched into Jed's abdomen, he heard the satisfying *oof* of Jed's breath giving way over his shoulder. Both players crashed into the ground, and as Bud toppled over Jed, he just remembered to brush his foot against the empty gunny sack that formed home plate, dragging it with them both as they skidded through the hay stalks.

"Safe!" screamed half the crowd, while the other half let out a moan, seeing that Jed had clearly missed the throw. The neglected ball skittered through the twisted wire fence into the church's graveyard, knocking over odd offerings of flowers until it came to a rest firmly against John McMillen's headstone. Gladys, his elderly mother, smiled and pointed at the ball, exclaiming, "That's my John—never misses a catch!"

Although mirth began to prevail in the churchyard, it took awhile for the ball field to sort itself out. Both teams felt compelled to champion their downed heroes, and although the battle was heated for a few moments, honor quickly gave way to general exhaustion and hunger after a swift-thinking woman began to yank the church bell.

As the dogpile over home plate cleared, Bud looked up to see Jed towering over him, reaching his massive hand down to pull Bud to his feet. "Purty good hit dair, Bud."

Bud shook his head. "Thanks, but with that corkscrewing pitcher of yours, I was lucky to get it past first base, Jed."

"Jed meant when you hit *him*, Bud, just *now*," Harlan threw in, as Jed nodded in confirmation. "And *you're* the king of the corkscrew pitch, Pard. But that roughhousing is gonna make you *sore* tomorrow...!"

"Yeah, but at least I'll be **breathing**, Harlan," Bud shot back. "I noticed that both Rebecca and Martha showed up for the game. Are they gonna kill each other, or just you?"

"What a delightful problem," sighed Harlan. Slapping Bud on the back, he hauled his friend to the tables, which were now crowded with steaming piles of corn on the cob, roasted chickens, and freshly baked breads. On the back steps of the white clapboard church, Bud saw his little sister Daphne staring wistfully at Wayne Hansen, who was mightily cranking an ice cream churn. Bud rolled his eyes at Harlan, who laughed and was about to hand Bud a plate when the low words, "Let us give thanks..." drifted over the churchyard, followed by a hush, and a strong baritone sang out:

Be present at our table, Lord...

Followed by dozens of voices, joining in with...

Be here and everywhere adored

Thy mercies bless and grant that we

May feast in fellowship with thee...

After the "Amen" (sung in three parts, not counting the stray gray-haired altos that wandered off into the weeds somewhere), Bud lifted his eyes and was startled to spot the lanky form of Jeremiah, his oldest brother, carelessly parting the throng crowding around the food tables with his peculiar head-down, hunchbacked stride. Jeremiah always did sport a stern visage, but this evening his dark brown eyes seemed especially intense—it appeared to Bud that he was searching for someone through the hungry host, and Bud felt a sudden wave of apprehension. As he turned toward Bud, recognition sparked across Jeremiah's eyes, and he beckoned Bud with impatient, jerking hand motions.

"Father wants to see you right away," grunted Jeremiah. Bud's stomach fell. He suspected that the immediacy of his father's request was more likely related to Jeremiah's need to please their father than their father's need to see Bud. Six years his elder—and sixty quick-tempered pounds his superior—Bud always felt compelled to respect his older brother's wishes, but he thought of his brother as a bit of a toady, nevertheless. Still, it was a summons that could not be ignored.

With a sigh, Bud turned toward the tables, snatched up a couple of chicken thighs and several steaming biscuits, and reluctantly followed Jeremiah to the wagon. Home was just over a mile away, and under Jeremiah's hands the wagon rolled down the hill and rumbled over the low wooden bridge at Bell Creek. Bud's eyes noted the brown trickle of sluggish water—there had been only thirty hundredths of an inch of rain since mid-June. While this had been tough on the hay harvest, most farmers in this area—corn farmers—were facing a catastrophe. While Stephen Long's description of Nebraska in 1823 as "the great American desert" had been proven largely overstated by the underlying fertility of the soil and the sweat of the first wave of immigrants to the state, seventy-one years later Mother Nature was doing her best to make the story ring true, with acre after mile of stunted brown corn stalks.

As the wagon topped the next hill and left Bell Creek behind them, Bud, squinting into the summer sunset, recognized the familiar outlines of his home through the swirl of dust and grasshoppers kicked up by the rising wind. Cottonwood trees huddled about the southwest corner of the intersection ahead, providing both shade and shelter to a white framed, two-story house with green trim. Horses grazed in the pasture next to the house, and a massive red barn stood opposite it, across a narrow lane that snaked its way down to the farmstead from the roadbed. Bud could see a lonely kerosene lantern inside the barn where Pop was milking the cows—a job generally reserved for Daphne, who was lucky enough to remain at the hay harvest social.

Bud jumped off the buckboard, gulping down the last morsel of chicken, and tossing the bones to Snookie. His latest acquisition, a brown mongrel that was part rat terrier and part whatever came around the barn last, gratefully snatched the bones and scurried off behind the corn crib to some private Xanadu. Turning toward the barn, Bud noticed that Jeremiah was still shadowing him, and rolled his eyes under hidden brows. Part of his mind asked himself, *what could Pop want?* And the other part was afraid he knew the answer.

The latch to the barn door rose easily, swinging open with the soft *creak* that no amount of oil had yet been able to cure. Pop was there all right, at the third stall on his left, humming as he finished stroking the last cow's udder. He seemed lost in thought, not noticing the door open or Bud enter, despite the noise. Bud saw that the pail was only half full—even the cows weren't producing—and his father audibly sighed as he slowly rose from the three-legged wooden stool.

"Pop...you wanted me?"

His father started, his eyes going up in surprise. "Bud!...my, that was quick. Didn't you stay for the social?"

Bud couldn't help scowling as he threw a sidelong glance toward Jeremiah, who was shuffling expectantly behind Bud at the barn door, arms folded. His father smiled tightly, and shook his head.

"Jerry, would you please excuse us for a few minutes?" his father asked. Jeremiah glowered at Bud and sullenly exited, latching the door with a *click*.

His father stood for a moment, collecting his thoughts. Twice he opened his mouth, but as he turned to speak to his son, he stopped, unable to find words. Gazing absently around the close confines of the barn, his father suddenly blurted, "Bud, do you want to take a walk? I could use some fresh air." Bud nodded uncertainly, and followed his father out the back door of the barn.

The sun was nearing the horizon, providing the skies with that long, pleasant summer afterglow that Bud's mother called "cooling time." Bud's father didn't seem to notice—once he cleared the corner of the barn, he immediately set a steady pace directly south, past the vegetable garden and tool shed, striding purposefully. Maintaining a steady pace, he walked directly into the cornfield, and Bud stayed at his side, one row over.

"I didn't mean to drag you away from the social." As he walked down the row, his father's pace gradually slackened, and his palms and fingers reached out to brush the scorched leaves of the corn, gently, as if his touch could heal them. "Clear summer night like this, you should be out howling at the moon." He slowed further, and Bud could see his father's mind turning. "Night like this, I proposed to your mother...." His voice drifted off, and his father absently stopped to check the stalk of one of the larger plants. *It would have been strong—it would have been tall—if heaven had sent just a little rain*, Bud thought.

Bud didn't exactly know what to say, but wanted very badly to say it. Finally, he found the words.

"It's time for me to go, isn't it, Pop?"

Turning slightly away, his father lowered his head, and nodded.

"Larry and Roger left for Omaha today—they are going to try their luck with the meat packers, seeing as how the Bohemians are on strike. Jerry will stay on the south place...with his Margie expecting, I just couldn't..." He paused, and then looked Bud directly into his brown eyes.

"I sent a telegram to my brother yesterday."

Bud was utterly stunned. "But I thought...Gramps says...you and Uncle Zeke haven't spoken..."

"...for thirty years. For a dozen reasons, neither of us has budged for **thirty years.**" He shook his head. "And what happens? He sends an answer back within 20 minutes. God, that man must have a woman in the telegraph office." He managed a twinge of a smile then, shaking his head as if some fond memory of his brother had managed to break free to the surface.

"Here's his telegram..." Reaching in his pocket, his father carefully unfolded a sheet of paper and handed it to Bud. In the fading light, Bud could just make out the message, typed under a Western Union letterhead.

It read:

SEND HIM
Z
817 R STREET
LINCOLN

His father put a hand on Bud's shoulder. "I'll send another telegram tomorrow...with the other boys gone, we'll need your help with the haying...and cutting the corn for silage...figure about four weeks."

Cutting the corn for silage, Bud thought. *That meant no corn crop this year...the stalks and leaves from the unripened corn would become fodder for their hungry cattle.*

"Is it really that bad, Pop?"

His father didn't really need to answer.

* * * * *

Broadway, aside from hosting some of the heaviest traffic in Manhattan, was a communication nexus of the borough, criss-crossed with hundreds of overhead telephone and telegraph lines. Nearly all of them terminated in the tall, clock-towered brick building at the corner of Dey Avenue, with eight private lines especially reserved for the tenth floor. At a huge mahogany desk, where eight of the most modern telephone handsets in the world gleamed under Edison's electric lights in brass and black lacquer elegance, a middle aged man in a custom-fitted gray suit was quietly paging through a typewritten report. He gripped a cigar tightly with his back teeth, at first puffing only occasionally. But as the hands on the marbled timepiece across the room neared nine, his furtive glances toward it increased their tempo, until a white haze of tobacco smoke congealed above his head like a gathering stormcloud.

At ten seconds to the hour, the gray-bearded man could hear the gears in the huge clock tower above his head begin to spin up. Reaching into his pocket to minutely adjust the time on his engraved watch, he started at the clatter of the centermost telephone handset, which nearly coincided with the deep *bong* of the clocktower declaring the hour. Picking up the earpiece, the man announced into the mouthpiece, "Yes, I'll take it. Wait until the damn clock stops ringing, then put him through."

The man placed the earpiece carefully on the desk, took out another cigar, bit its end off, and struck a Lucifer. The cigar flared as the man drew it into life. Satisfied with its progress, the bearded man leaned slowly back into his leather chair, and placed the earpiece to his ear.

"I appreciate your punctuality, Mr. Jay. How did it go today?"

The man puffed silently, and a slow grim smile spread across his face as the telephone scratched and buzzed its answer into his private ear. The clouds from the cigar grew more occasional as the voice droned on, and the man grunted in understanding at odd intervals between the slackening puffs. Finally, the gray-bearded man spoke again.

"Excellent, Mr. Jay. And our plans for August?"

Once again, the man listened and puffed. His face was a mask of intense concentration, punctuated by the occasional grunt of acknowledgement, terminating in yet another grim smile

vii

"Make sure of it." Abruptly, he hung up the earpiece, took two rapid puffs, and picked up the earpiece at the next telephone. Strangely, he spoke to no operator, but his call was connected almost immediately. He straightened slightly as he heard the voice on the other end.

"Beakins here. Mr. Jay reports that his current job is finished and can be ready to begin shortly." A pause.

"Yes, in about four weeks…yes…yes, I'll keep you informed."

As he lowered the earpiece, Beakins drew deeply on his cigar, let out a slow exhale, and reached into his desk drawer. Pulling out a bottle of amber liquid, he walked to a silver tray next to the window, placed two large shards of ice into crystal tumbler from a large silver pail, and filled the tumbler from the bottle. Outside, he could hear the elevated train sliding by, its wheels clattering west. Unconsciously, he lifted his head in that direction, out across the hundreds of miles that separated him from his quarry, in the prairie town where he awaited, unknowing.

Four weeks.

* * * * *

It's strange how quiet this room is now, Bud mused as he gazed out the open window at the night sky, listening to the crickets chirp and a light wind rustling through the dry corn. Larry and Roger's end of the room was vacated, their closet empty, their beds made…*it was unsettling.* So it was with some relief when Bud heard the familiar shuffle of the old man ascending the stairs, completing his nightly round to the outhouse…and to assure all was well in his domain.

"Hey, Gramps," the boy said, turning away from the blazing stars to watch the old man creep up the last step to lean against the frame of his small bedroom door.

"Hey, Peapod," his grandfather replied, out of breath. "You're usually snoring away by now—havin' trouble sleepin?"

"Yeah…thinking about Lincoln, I guess," Bud admitted. "And my uncle, Ezekiel. Is it…is he…is he okay, and all?"

"Haven't seen him for a long time—but yeah, he's okay, Peapod." His grandfather's voice, while strong, might have cracked a little, Bud thought.

The old man and the boy looked out the window together. The corn in the moonlight looked like a stricken congregation in a dying town, standing in rows, whispering together in the rustling wind. Quietly, the old man laid his hand on the boy's shoulder.

"He's more than okay—he's family."

Bud nodded, yawned and bid Gramps goodnight as he turned from his moonlit window to his small bed. Settling in, he pulled the cool sheets about him and let his thoughts turn to Lincoln…and the uncle he had never known…before giving way to sleep.

Four weeks…

Friday, August 3, 1894
11:45 am

There really wasn't any way around it...the wheel was broken, and the wagon wasn't going anywhere.

Harrison pulled a white handkerchief out of the vest pocket of his overalls, took off his brown felt hat and wiped the back of his neck, then his balding brow. The rim of the gray wooden wheel lay shattered below him at the bottom of the steep ditch on the right side of the wagon, with several missing spokes lying a dozen yards behind the rig. The rut next to the broken spokes had been deeper than he had suspected, and Harrison would have cursed—had it not been for his grandson sitting at the edge of the road.

As usual, Roscoe's slightly crossed eyes wandered...this time to a dandelion. He picked it and blew on the seed head gently, watching the white fluff float over the weedy edge and down the steep side of the ditch. A breeze caught the seeds and floated them further on, nearly to the sluggish waters of Salt Creek.

The wagon hung precariously on its three good wheels, tilting toward its missing front wheel and leaning over the ditch like a drunkard over a spittoon. Bags of flour and beans, cans of kerosene, and a variety of other necessities were piled behind in the back. Shaking his head, Harrison edged slowly toward the team of horses, being careful to avoid the soft soil that bordered the top of the ditch, one steadying hand on the shaky wagon box. Murmuring softly to the brown gelding, he gripped its halter and carefully led the team and crippled wagon to the center of the road. As the horses stamped, he had started to unhitch them when he heard the faint soft sound of hoofbeats from the direction of town.

Turning, Harrison spied three riders approaching up the road from the south. In the glare of the near-noon sun, he could make out that the three were dressed in bowler hats.

Not farmers.

Harrison swallowed, walked calmly over to his grandson, and gently placed him on the floor of the wagon. As he finished unhitching the team, he continued to watch the men approach through the corner of his eyes. The largest of the three was within a hundred yards now, and the sun glinted off his gold watchchain—and his nickel-plated sidearms. He rode the large bay horse with a straight back and a calm, proud demeanor. The men behind him wore checkered suits, and bore the hard looks of men who meant business, but Harrison couldn't make out any sidearms. Quietly, he grasped the reins of the now-unhitched horses and led the team away from the wagon and toward the men…placing himself between them and the wagon where his grandson absently played.

With as smile of recognition, the tall man in the lead reined in and dismounted as he neared Harrison. The other two men started to dismount, but kept their places when their leader held up his hand, waving them back. Their horses stamped impatiently as the man in the bowler hat approached the farmer and his team. Standing in front of the farmer, he picked up one of the loose wagon spokes and snickered.

Tossing the spoke to Harrison, he growled, "Hello, Harrison. Reckon you've had a bad day."

"Doesn't look like it's going to get any better, either, LeBlanc." Harrison's left hand tightened on the reins of his team as he fumbled to catch the spoke.

"We tried to catch up with you in town, but you'd already left. You must have heard we were looking for you."

"Can't say I did," Harrison murmured.

LeBlanc smirked skeptically and rolled his eyes. "Right. So, have you had a chance to consider our offer? Seems that a prosperous farmer like you would be interested in…staying that way. And in doing what's right for your family."

"Such as it is," one of the men interjected. "No wife, no son, and one half-wit grandson."

Harrison's eyes shifted uneasily to where the boy was absently playing with a wrench in the bottom of the wagon, and then back to LeBlanc's cold stare.

"Sounds less like an offer, and more like a threat."

"Then I guess you're as intelligent as I heard you were." With his left hand, LeBlanc reached into his vest pocket and pulled out a cigarette; with his right, he pulled a match from his belt and struck it against the holster of his .45 Remington. He lit the cigarette, breathing in the cool smoke, and exhaled slowly, looking at Harrison.

"So, Mr. Harrison—are we in business together?"

Before Harrison could answer, he heard the unexpected sound of a horse to his left, laboring up the steep ditch from the creek bed. At the rim of the road there suddenly exploded a big red roan horse, ridden by a man with a small wagon wheel perilously balanced on the saddle pommel. LeBlanc's men scooted their horses to the other edge of the road, narrowly missing the heavily breathing horse and its rider, a big gray-bearded man dressed in a brown duster. Before the horse came to a stop, the man swung off his saddle and dropped the wheel to the ground between Harrison and LeBlanc. As it rolled and spun to a stop, the man beat his hands against his legs, knocking the mud from his chaps.

"Sorry to take so long, Mr. Harrison. I had to pull the blacksmith from another serious job...he's a newlywed. It's probably not a perfect fit...that's the wheel, not the newlyweds. Hello, LeBlanc. Still shilling for McGee?"

"Hello, Gardner." LeBlanc tried to act nonchalant, but Harrison could see the stiffness under the pretense. "As a matter of fact, I was just relating a fairly generous offer from Mr. McGee...if it's any of your business..."

"If you call stealing corn at ten cents a bushel generous, he's a goddamn saint at eleven. LeBlanc, the only offer your boss ever made was one taken under protest. Take some advice...farmers in this county can do better this year, and they will."

"The Voice of the Grange, huh? Ten years ago, the farmers would have heard a different story, Gardner." His eyes darted to his mounted men, now on his right—his head jerked to the left, and they started to dismount.

"Your men need to stay where they are, LeBlanc." Gardner's voice was level and deep, and the men hesitated, eyeing LeBlanc.

LeBlanc laughed. "That worked pretty well twenty years ago, too, I'm sure. Not today, though..." But as LeBlanc reached for his gun, Harrison chucked the wagon spoke at the gunman's eyes. Startled, LeBlanc dodged the spoke, and Gardner stepped forward to plant a quick right-hand punch on LeBlanc's nose, smoothly pulling LeBlanc's gun from his holster with his left hand as the tall man fell backward. LeBlanc's bowler hat rolled to a stop near the wagon wheel.

Gardner turned, and leveled the gun at LeBlanc's men. "Git!" he barked, and cocked the Remington. "Your boss will be right along." The men hesitated, then finally turned and rode south.

LeBlanc eyed Gardner, and fished a handkerchief out of his suit pocket. As he dabbed at his reddening nose, he smirked, "Couldn't handle me on your own, could you Gardner? This goddamn farmer is going to be sorry he..."

3

Gardner interrupted. "Hold this, Harrison, and go see to your boy." Handing the Remington to Harrison, Gardner said, "Get up, LeBlanc. You're a mean, nitwitted bastard, and you need a lesson from an old lawman."

LeBlanc grinned, stuffed his handkerchief into his vest pocket, and slowly got up. "Jesus, Zeke, I thought you had more sense than this. Why don't you give yourself a chance and ride off? Maybe we can all still do business..."

Gardner broke in. "Maxie boy, when your daddy got drunk and beat on your momma, I threw him in jail. If I hadn't had to let him out, you might have turned out straighter. As it is, I guess it's only fair that you're leaving the straightening to me. Now, fight or git."

LeBlanc rose suddenly, and with a bellow unexpectedly chucked the wagon spoke that lay under his back at Gardner, catching him by surprise. Gardner flinched, and LeBlanc plowed into him like a steam train, knocking him down and rolling on top of him, landing two or three blows along the sides of Gardner's head.

Shit--shouldn't have pissed him off, Gardner thought as his head spun under the blows.

Reacting on instinct, he thrust his boot into LeBlanc's groin, rolled, cuffed his adversary in the right eye, and punched him in the throat. As LeBlanc lay gasping, Gardner got up quickly and got a rope from his horse's saddle. After he tied LeBlanc's hands and got up, he kicked LeBlanc—twice—firmly in the butt, hesitating between strokes. He walked over to Harrison, who had by now managed to back the horses in front of the wagon.

"You sure took your time about that wagon wheel."

Gardner hitched the left horse and strung the traces though the guides. "Saw 'em a half mile off—just wanted to come up quietly. You didn't seem very tempted by their offer."

"Not hardly," Harrison smiled. They worked together quietly for a time, fitting the new wheel to the axle, and screwing on the hub.

"Not a bad fit at all, actually...looks like that blacksmith can do more than just honeymoon," Gardner said.

"Let me ask you a question." said Harrison. "Not that I'm complaining, but what did you boot him in the ass for? I wouldn't expect you to kick a man when he's down."

4

Gardner spit a stream of blood from his mouth, lowered his head to Harrison's ear, and whispered his reply. "Harrison, do you want him remembering that you chucked the wagon spoke at him, or that I kicked him in the ass?"

Harrison grinned and held out his hand. "I take your point," he said quietly. "Many thanks."

"Good. Now, help me with these supplies."

2

Friday, August 3, 1894
10:07 pm

The dimly lit street was pockmarked with deep shadows marking the alleys and the uneven spaces between buildings, broken by an occasional flickering glow under the gas lamps. Its brick surface wavered and rolled, thrown up like a seabed, a product of the winter heave and spring thaw. Bud stumbled over an upturned corner of brick and cursed, barely regaining his footing to avoid a pile of horse turds.

"Shit," he mumbled, then half-smiled. *I must be tired*, he thought to himself, *not to smell **that** a mile off.* For a half moment, the earthy smell recalled a vision of horses harnessed and ready to pull the haymaker, its rake rolling up the dried clover to form a ripple, and men in rows behind the haymaker setting up the hay to dry...

Bud shook his head and shifted his burlap bag to his right shoulder, squinting at the doors hung at irregular intervals between low, brick and white clapboard building porticos lining both sides of the street. The dim numbers over the doors skipped along...807, 809, 813...as the steady clumping of his boot heels echoed along the empty sidewalk. Somewhere, up ahead, tinny music and the boom of drunken baritones flowed out of a lighted doorway along with the smoke of burning tobacco. The horses tied outside swished their tails to ward off the flies, and one of them—a big roan mare with a Spanish saddle—stamped impatiently and lifted her head, calling softly for her master. Bud resisted the urge to pat the horse's neck—a good thing, too, because as he passed close by, the big horse tried to take a nip out of him. As he jumped out of the way, his gaze shifted to the black-on-white sign above the door, advertising BEER 5 CENTS.

And the number under it. 817. 817?

Bud rubbed his eyes, thought again about how tired he was. He had started walking early that morning from Alder Grove, angling southwest over farmsteads and through groves of trees, gathering momentum and swinging into a steady trot as the sun burned the mist off the meadows. He had picked up Logan Creek, crossed the Elkhorn, and followed the familiar roads through Dodge County. By noon, he had made it to Fremont, 20 miles to the south. The train pulled out of town and climbed the river bluffs of the Platte, marking the farthest he had ever been from home. Through his long walk, he had planned to sleep on the train, but his excitement at the sights of the new towns he had heard his father speak of...Wahoo, little Swedeburg, Ceresco...kept him awake with excitement.

But the sun had set before he got to Lincoln, the train being terribly late due to a breakdown just south of Ceresco, and the tangle of streets between the station and this dingy little corner of the capital city near the tracks befuddled Bud's sleepy head.

"I must have the wrong street," he murmured, and re-traced his steps to the last intersection. *R Street...could there be more than one R Street in Lincoln? It's a big town...*

Quietly, Bud walked back to the lighted doorway, and peered into the smoky interior of the barrelhouse. The room was lit with six gas lamps along the long plaster sidewalls, producing smoke that glowed softly beneath the pressed tin ceiling. A Negro chinked and rattled a syncopated tune out of a banged-up piano against the far wall. Men in loose-fitting work clothes sat conversing on stools, leaning their elbows on a long bar that ran along the right hand wall, laughing and gesturing as they tried to convince the bartender and their neighbors of a particularly important point. At a table on his left, two girls in frilled dresses with bare arms dangled cigarettes and talked quietly, glancing at Bud with predatory eyes from behind heavy rouge and mugs of beer. Way off in the corner, a nasal voice spoke softly, punctuated by an occasional chitter.

"You er okay, kid?" asked a deep voice just inside the door. "You er lookin' lost." Bud turned to see a mountainous man in his early 20s dressed in a white shirt and a brown checkered suit towering over him, with long blond hair flowing out of his perfectly aligned derby hat. The Swede, for his part, saw a tall and thin young man with tousled dark hair and whiskey brown eyes, and white teeth that shone even in the dim gaslight.

"I guess I am. I'm looking for my Uncle Zeke...Ezekiel Gardner...I was told he was here."

A smile wrinkled the corners of the blue eyes under the Derby hat. "You er name is Pack maybe, ya?"

Bud looked confused, shook his head. "No, my name is Bud...Bud Gardner." Bud held out his hand. "Nice to meet you." The Swede's smile spread wider across his face, and his hand engulfed Bud's, working it up and down in long, pumphandle strokes. The big man could feel that the boy's grip at the end of his deeply tanned arms was firm, despite his wiry frame.

"Ya? Gardner, huh? Ya dohn't say!" He spun Bud around, and half shoved, half lifted Bud to the nearest end of the bar, where a short man with a carefully trimmed mustache stood with his arms up to his elbows in

7

suds. Seeing the Swede approach, he lifted his hands from the water and wiped them on his apron.

"Hell, Swede, whatevah are you draggin in here now—anothah kitten? Jesus, jes' throw it with the othah ones out back, willya?" The bartender turned his head to the patrons at the bar, and Bud relaxed slightly when he noticed the fastest of winks in his right eye.

The Swede looked crestfallen. "You din't trow out dos kittens, did ya, Amos?"

Amos shook his head. "Uh course ah didn't, Big Swede." He paused for effect, and blurted, "The Chinaman down the street paid me 10 cents a head for 'em. He's makin' some kinda damn noodle dish, and ran outta dog." The patrons snickered, then guffawed as Amos put Big Swede's face through its paces, from crestfallen to hopeful, to angry, and finally to a hesitant smile as he saw the joke.

"Ya, dat's purty good, Amos," he mumbled through his grin, though his eyes still spoke clearly—*You better notta hurt dose cats.* With a broad gesture to Bud, he exclaimed, "See who I brung, yah? He sez his name is Bug Gardner—he's lookin for his Uncle Zeke!"

Bud said quietly, "Actually, it's Bud, with a "d", not Bug."

"Well, Bug, it's a pleasure to make your acquaintance. Mah name is Amos Aloysius Seville. Any friend of Mistah Zeke is a friend of mine—as long as you'ah not askin' for credit." Amos bowed slightly as he stuck out his hand, and Bud noticed its softness as he shook it—but there was a wiry strength in it, too, and a cool toughness to his eyes that bored into Bud's.

Amos smoothly pulled an empty chair over to a nearby table, and gestured for Bud to sit down. "Well, well, anothah nephew of Zeke's...but this time, with a name to match. It's an occasion." With a rapid gesture, Amos swept a bottle of brown liquid and two glasses off the bar, and placed it in front of Bud. "Will you have a drink with me...to the family name? It's not exactly bonded, but it's wet."

Bud hesitated, his eyes cast down, his hands fidgeting. "Mister...Seville, was it? No disrespect, sir, but I promised my mother I would stay away from hard liquor."

A snicker or two emerged from the party of workmen, and a titter from the girls at the table nearest Bud. Amos held up his hand.

"Now this IS an occasion—a Gardner that doesn't drink hard liquor. AND pays mind to his mother." Amos rolled his eyes toward the ceiling,

8

and smiled as he curled the ends of his greased mustache. "No hard liquor...you must be Methodist folk. Now what do you think she would say to a beer, Mr. Gardner?"

"Well, she probably wouldn't hold with that, either, sir...but I never actually promised about beer, and it would suit me just fine—thank you."

"Then Mr. Swede, you may bring this fine young man...a beer. The CLEAN glasses are under the bar, if you please. And one for yourself, for bringing us such a progeny."

As Swede filled two mugs and began to sit down, a brown blur streaked out from the darkened corner of the room and jumped on to Swede's lap. As it reached its paws out toward the glasses of beer, Bud could see that it was a huge raccoon. Despite an odor that successfully rose to challenge the combined reek of cheap tobacco and stale beer for supremacy, Swede grabbed it by the collar with one hand, and stroked its lower back.

Smiling, he admonished the chittering creature. "Hey, dere, Skunk! Vat choo tryin' to do, trink the whole bar? Bobber, you better come git dis rodent before Amos shoots it or sells it to da Chinaman."

A slouching figure slowly approached from the dark corner, walking stiffly and muttering through his bare gums and a stubble of gray whiskers. Bud thought he looked to be 90 years old, at least. He spit, and shook his head, but his blue eyes sparked as he reached for the raccoon. "Shit, Swede, nobody would take that animal, not even the Chinaman. Smells too bad to cook, and doesn't do dishes, either." Quietly, he stroked it under its chin until its trilling was low enough to be mistaken for a purr.

"Pees on the floor well enough, I expect, though," Amos said, and shaking his head, added, "Bobber, why do you keep company with that animal, and more to the point, why do you insist on bringing it into this establishment?"

"I'm surprised you'd ask," said Bobber, finally reaching the table, pulling up a chair, and sitting carefully. "He's a mascot, like the little midget what plays for the Southies." Skunk jumped from Bobber to Swede, and pawed at Swede's empty glass.

"Sure drinks beer like the midget," muttered Amos. "Although Skunk is possibly a superior hitter. The game last week was a total loss—the Southies beat the Saltdogs by 21 to 10. You should sign up the coon."

"Speaking of coons, your boy has stopped playing, Amos," one of the men cried from the bar.

9

"How about something we can sing?" said another. "Enough of that cakewalk shit." During Skunk's performance, Bud noticed that the large Negro had gone to pour himself a short beer from the brass tap behind the bar. Now his head turned slightly away from the rest of the group as he ambled back to the piano, and his close-mouthed smile turned increasingly stiff.

Amos rose from the table, carefully placing his beer on the opposite side of the table from Skunk. Walking over to the row of men on barstools, he bowed, and placed both of his hands carefully at his sides. For the first time, Bud noticed the black grip of a small silver pistol protruding from the back of Amos' waistband, facing Amos' left hand.

"Gentlemen, the Professor does not appreciate your referring to him as an animal. And we all know none o' you can sing...especially you, Mister Lee." That caused a chuckle, until Amos' face went cold.

"In future, you will please refrain from this boorish behaviah."

He's not kidding, Bud thought.

The largest of the men at the bar fidgeted, and turned white. "Shit, Amos, we was just kiddin.' Tell the Perfessor we're sorry..." and the talk at the bar turned quietly to other things.

Amos turned, walked halfway to the Negro, and said "The gentlemen apologize, Professor. Please do resume the recital." Almost immediately, the syncopated melody started up again. It was an odd, pitching, swaying kind of music, and rolled out of the piano like nothing Bud had ever heard.

"What kind of music is that?" asked Bud.

"The Professor calls it raggy, or ragged, or somethin' like that," mumbled Bobber, alternatively scratching and swatting Skunk, who was now reaching for Amos' beer. "He says he learned about it in Missouri."

"He's pretty young to be a Professor."

"They jest call him that. His real name is Tom Turpin. He's on his way back to Saint Louis—he ran outta money and is earning his train fare back home. Don't care for it myself, but the young ladies like it."

As if on cue, Amos made as if to return to the table, but instead detoured to where the two whores sat quietly watching the show. He turned to the nearer of the two, an auburn-haired girl with green eyes, and flashed a smile.

"Miss Eugenia, you look especially lovely this evening. And my, my, Miss Maggie, it must have taken you an hour to get into that dress."

Eugenia laughed. "May be, Amos, but it wouldn't take two dollars and two minutes to get her out of it." Maggie scowled and punched Eugenia in the shoulder, feigning anger.

Amos laughed, "Sounds like a generous offer. Shall I convey it to our new friend?" Bud blushed as Amos and the girls turned to him, looking down at his hands again.

"I don't think so, Amos," Maggie said quietly, delicately holding her cigarette between two fingers, her palm upraised at her side. "He ain't had enough beer, and I ain't seen any cash as yet."

Leaning toward her, he murmured, "No, and his mother would hardly approve." With that, he moved back to the table and sat next to Bud. Raising his glass, he said, "Now, good company, where were we? Ah, yes...we were drinking to the young man, and the Gardner name...may you be truly deserving of it..."

"I wouldn't aim quite so low," came a voice from the door. As Bud swung his eyes to the sound, he saw a big gray-bearded man under a lacerated cowboy hat enter the room, dressed in a brown duster pulled over a red shirt and blue dungarees. He paused, looked right at Bud, pushed his hat back, and smiled.

Shouts of "Zeke!" went up from the crowd, and Bud felt a catch in his breath as the tall man waved to the assembly, then strode to the table where Bud and Amos were sitting. He walked briskly but stiffly, legs slightly bowed—as a man that had spent the whole day on a horse, but wasn't about to slow down. As he was always taught, Bud stood up.

"Zeke," said Amos, "May I introduce you to Mr. Bug Gardner...he claims to be another one of your nephews." Before Bud could speak up to correct his name, Zeke cut him off.

"Amos, that's Bud—with a "d"—and yes, he's my nephew all right." Looking at Bud, he quietly held out his hand. "Nice to finally meet you, Bud. How're your folks?"

"Pop is well, Mr. Gardner, and Mother is fine, too. They...send their love."

Grinning, the man removed his hat, and shook his head. "Just make it Zeke, Bud. And it looks like they sent me a little more than that—they sent me you."

Turning to the rest of the group, he said, "Mind if I steal my nephew for a few minutes? Bring your beer, Bud." Zeke motioned over to an unused table near the piano. Bud hurriedly picked up his burlap bag, and dropped into his seat while Zeke poured himself a beer.

"Your father sent me a telegram telling me you were on your way. I have to admit to being surprised to hear from him after so long." Zeke's blue eyes stared at the wall across the bar, and Bud suspected that his uncle was remembering something from long ago.

"Yes, sir," Bud hesitated. "How long has it been since you…and Gramps…and my father…?" Bud's voice trailed off, and he looked down at his hands.

"Over thirty years, I guess. It wasn't the happiest of partings." Zeke's eyes gained back their focus, then locked onto Bud's. "But you must have heard something about that."

"Gramps told me that you and him…he…had a disagreement about the farm."

"That's an understatement, Bud. They say that blood is thicker than water, but money seems to trump it all. I think we sorted it out…your father got the farm, and I got a ticket to Fort Snelling and the Army of the Potomac. I guess every young man has to find his fortune, somehow." Zeke drained his beer, put glass down, and looked at Bud with an appraising eye. "And now, here you are, looking for yours—right?"

Bud met Zeke's eyes. "Yes, sir, I am."

"In a tavern? Times must be very hard on the farm."

Bud stiffened. "Yes, I guess they are…and, I guess I was pretty surprised to find out you lived in a bar room…"

"Over a bar room. Guess beggars can't be choosers, though—especially when it comes to black sheep uncles."

"Okay. *Over* a bar room," Bud said. His temper rose a bit at the interruptions…and the hidden accusation that he was asking for charity. He got the sense that his uncle was pushing at him, prodding him—*was it just to see if he would stand up for himself?*

So be it, then. "So, what the hell difference does that make, especially these days?"

Zeke sat there, arms folded, looking intently into his nephew's eyes. "Go on."

Bud frowned. "I think you know the tally, Uncle Zeke. Farms are folding up left and right, all over. It's the drought, and the times—they can't make the mortgage, not with the crops going under, and you can only shoot so many coyotes at 50 cents a head. At Fremont, I saw fifty men getting into a cattle car, some on the inside, some on top. They said they were going to Omaha, to try and get some of the strikers' jobs at the packing plants. They were all carrying sticks, or knives...they heard that the Bohemians were shooting at the railcars as they pulled into the yard. Four weeks ago, my brothers Larry and Roger were on a train just like that..." Bud fell silent, and took a sip of his beer.

After a moment, Bud raised his head and looked steadily up into his uncle's eyes. Time to level.

"Look, I don't know what you do. I don't know why Pop sent me here. I can work hard, and I'm not afraid to take any job...any honest job...that you might know of. But I won't take any charity. Now, I only want to know two things. The first thing is...can you use me?"

Zeke narrowed his eyes at Bud, but then broke into a grin. "That's a pretty short speech for a high school graduate. I guess the answer is...that depends. Did they teach you anything useful at Craig High School?"

Bud was taken aback at his uncle's sudden influx of humor, but managed to respond, "I can read and write, of course. My mathematics wasn't too bad, either. But you're right—oratory was never my strong suit."

"I wouldn't worry that, Bud—we're in Lincoln, and you can buy a politician for a pint of warm piss. And none of them is as wordy—or as loud—as Congressman Bryan. Talk is cheap...I'm more interested in whether you can think. And of course, play baseball."

"Play baseball?" Bud's voice was incredulous. "You can get paid for that?"

"Depends on how you play it...and whether you win. The Saltdogs—that's our team—have been in the outhouse since the frost broke. They're made up mostly of railroad men—baggage handlers, yard workers, and the like. The opposition is mostly trolley workers. Got a game tomorrow, as a matter of fact, and I don't like our chances much." Zeke thought for a moment. "Your mother says that you hate to lose."

"She's my mother...she'll say anything," Bud smiled, lowering his head at the compliment. *So that's it...Mother has been corresponding with Uncle Zeke?*

"Bud, do you know anything about..." Zeke's words were cut off by the sudden growing silence....and then the complete stillness of the bar. Bud noticed that everyone's heads turned to Big Swede, who stood to the side of the door, and exchanged a meaningful glance with Zeke. Big Swede's massive hands rested casually on a large ax handle. Bud noticed Amos behind the bar, drying beer glasses, but Bud could tell that he watched the door from the corner of his eye. Voices murmured outside, then went quiet.

"Play the piano, Professor," Zeke said, loudly enough to be heard outside. "Looks like we have some guests."

As the piano started to play, heavy boots shuffled on the bricks outside, and two large men dressed in rumpled checkered suits and bowler hats walked slowly into the tavern. They leisurely eyed the assembly—making special note of Swede, Amos, and especially, Zeke—and nodded back at the dark figure behind them. The gaslight revealed a short man, neatly dressed in a gray pinstripe suit and a bowler hat, and looked to be about 50. The man straightened his bowtie, sniffed at Swede—who smiled back at him—and whispered to his men, who began to advance slowly toward Gardner. As they passed Bobber and Skunk, the raccoon chittered and hissed.

"Gentlemen!" cried Amos, as he leapt over the bar, a bottle and glass in his right hand. He landed perfectly several feet in front of the two suited henchmen, and bowed to the thin man standing behind them. "May ah offer you a drink? And a seat, of course." With a single fluid motion, Amos placed the bottle and glass on the bar and spun two chairs directly in front of the henchmen, nearly tripping them. Maggie and Eugenia laughed and clapped their approval. As the two men moved to grab at the chairs, the well-dressed man raised a gloved hand and cleared his throat.

"That will not be necessary, boys," whispered the man. "I will speak to Mr. Gardner alone. Have a seat, and a drink. I will call you if I need you."

As the men slowly lowered themselves to the seats, Amos moved to the side and placed the bottle at a nearby table, allowing the man to pass.

"Have a seat yourself, McGee." Gardner motioned to a chair across from him, and then to Bud. "May I introduce my nephew, Mr. Bud Gardner?"

"My, Mr. Gardner, you do seem to have a large family. A pleasure to meet the young Mr. Gardner, I'm sure."

Zeke smiled. "What brings you here tonight? I left your boy LeBlanc cooling his heels with a deputy sheriff down at the courthouse."

"He'll make bail, Gardner. He wasn't very charitable when he spoke of you." McGee pulled out a cigarette, and lit it carefully with a match.

"It didn't look to me that you were in the business of charity, McGee. Your offer spoke more expressively in the language of profit...even graft."

McGee narrowed his eyes. "Now, now, we needn't be unpleasant, Ezekiel. Business is business, as they say. And the harvest is approaching. I understand that the Grange is negotiating a—nontraditional—freighting arrangement."

"Nothing non-traditional about good business."

"It is non-traditional for *our* business." McGee drew again on his cigarette, and tapped his ash on the floor. "For years, our community has agreed on freighting arrangements and...spheres of interest...regarding the harvest. I wonder what Chicago will think about changes to that arrangement?"

"I can only imagine that, what with the drought and the Pullman strike, Chicago would be happy to get whatever grain it can. That's not my business, though...nor, I imagine, is it really yours." Gardner leaned forward, and spoke in low tones. "It's my business to make sure the farmers in Lancaster County get a fair price for their corn...and are not *interfered* with."

McGee smiled, "Truly, Mr. Gardner? So charitable? And with your family in the freighting business, how could you *possibly* be interested in profit for yourself?" McGee took a last, long drag on the cigarette, ground the butt into the table, and gestured around the room.

"Of course, you also run this fine establishment, so profitable in itself. Complete with a strongman, an acrobat, an animal act...and I am quite sure, a ringmaster." With this, he stood and motioned toward Bud. "All you need is a clown. Perhaps your nephew here is interested?" Bud's face reddened and he started to get up, but his uncle caught his arm. His grip was like a vise, but he managed to smile at the thin man. Zeke slowly rose, and Bud didn't notice any sidearms.

"No, McGee, I believe you hired up the last clowns that were available. I saw your two boys there on the road this morning—they were the ones with the floppy shoes and the baggy pants, from what I could tell of their backsides." The men in the checkered suits, until now busying themselves in their beer, paused in mid-gulp and glowered at Gardner.

15

"But their boss is the biggest clown of all," Zeke went on. "He believes that farmers are fools, and will just keep falling for the same joke, year after year. But you're slipping, McGee. People, even farmers, know a worm when they see one."

McGee wrinkled his brow, clamped together his jaws, and clenched...then unclenched his hands...and relaxed. He took out a pocket watch, snapped it open, but barely glanced at it before snapping it closed and replacing it in his pocket.

"My, my, would you look at the time," said McGee. He made a short bow. "It has been a pleasure, as always, to speak with such a progressive thinker and leader as you, Ezekiel. I wish you much luck in your endeavors...you will be needing it." With that, the short man spun on his heels and walked briskly through the front door, trailed by his two henchmen.

Amos watched the men leave, then walked over to Zeke and Bud with two fresh drinks. "What the hell was that all about?" he asked.

Zeke just shook his head. "Amos, that man was here to do two things—to tell us that he knew what we were up to, and to scare us away from doing it. He was only partially right about the first—has he accomplished the second?"

"Not damn likely," pronounced Amos. Amos raised his glass, Zeke *clinked* it, and they drank quietly for a bit. Bud could tell that his uncle was thinking something over. After a moment, Zeke fixed his gaze on Bud and asked, "You had two questions, Bud. The answer to the first one is— Yes, I can use you. Now, what was your second question?"

"When do I start?"

Saturday, August 4, 1894
6:30 am

Bud woke slowly to the thunder in his head, and to the reverberation of trains. They sounded so close by that Bud thought at first he must have been aboard one of them, an unwilling passenger trapped in a world of smoke and steam. As if through cotton, he could hear the trains hissing impatiently, the steady ruminations of the steam engines and the clatter of the cars, punctuated sharply by an occasional *bang* as the trains were loaded, coupled, and sent on their way, out of earshot.

With unnatural care, Bud pulled off a thin quilt and slowly rolled his body upright onto his small bed, paused, then squinted at the morning light that was forcing itself through an open, unshaded window. He realized with some relief that he was still wearing his clothes from the night before, and a flicker of a smile crossed his lips as he half-remembered a fleeting dream of a blonde girl in a pink frilled dress (*was it Maggie?*) that now danced away as he rubbed his eyes.

Bud got shakily to his feet and shuffled across the wooden floor toward the light, half covering his eyes. Gradually, he opened them just enough to observe the motion of trains in the train yard below. Brakes shrieked, cars slammed into one another, and through it all, the thump, thump, thump...*thump, thump, thump...*

Of the door.

"Coming..." he murmured. *What was in that beer?* His mouth felt like he'd eaten an old pair of wool socks...

Thump, thump, thump...

"Coming!" Bud stumbled to the door and pulled it open, revealing an open stairway and small second-story platform attached to the outside of the building. Through the dizzying sunlight, Bud made out the unlikely figure of a young soldier dressed in a brown uniform, and a smile that could pass for a smirk. The soldier walked inside, took off his hat, scratched his blond hair and grinned, showing white teeth.

"Morning, Bud! Uncle Zeke told me to wake you up, and not to be quiet about it, either. 'Course, I'm the soul of propriety when it comes to hangovers...your first one, is it?" The soldier leaned against the doorframe, and made little circular tosses with his hat that gave the impression of complete relaxation. In an odd way, it managed to put Bud immediately at his ease.

"Not quite, but it's definitely my best effort so far." Bud did his best to straighten his hair and tuck in his shirt. "Did you say, "Uncle" Zeke—then that would make you..."

"Your older, more experienced cousin. My name is John Pack—you can call me Johnny." The young man stretched out his hand and Bud took it, trying to shake it with more strength and confidence than he felt. "Have a seat, Cuz, and I'll pour you a drink."

Bud raised his hands. "Er, I don't..."

"Water, Bud, just water..." Johnny moved toward the white porcelain pitcher and washbowl that was placed on a three drawer oak dresser, the only furniture in the sparse room besides the small bed. In the curved mirror over the dresser, Bud watched Johnny fill a glass of water and hand it carefully back to him. It tasted good, and Bud's hands trembled as he drank it all down.

"Thanks."

"I remember the first time that Uncle Zeke took me drinking," Johnny went on. "About a year ago, when I graduated high school. Woke up in this very same bed here—and so did my three older brothers before me, come to think of it. Guess you could say you've been initiated into a family tradition of sorts. Not one I'd care to repeat...you look like I felt, by the way."

"Like your tongue was covered in cat fur?"

"Right...Amos stocks only the very finest vintages, imported from the highest quality Salt Creek distilleries."

"For a moment when you came in, I thought I had been shanghaied into the Army, and you had come to collect."

Johnny laughed. "Would have served you right. Actually, I'm on my way to cadet assembly at the University, so I thought I'd impress you with my freshly pressed uniform. Though I rarely have the same effect on the Lieut."

"The Lieut?"

"First Lieutenant John J. Pershing...our Professor of Military Science, drill instructor, and personal emissary from Hell. Abandon all hope..."

"...all ye who enter here.' Didn't realize that they taught Milton in Lincoln. Must be more civilized here than I was led to believe." Now that he was waking up, Bud felt his natural tendency to tease coming to the fore.

"This from the educational Mecca of Alder Grove, Nebraska. Where did you pick up your astounding knowledge of English literature, Bud...the local blacksmith?"

"Yes, but he preferred Longfellow—'Under the Spreading Chestnut Tree...'"

"...the Village Smithy Stands.' Bud, you and I are going to get along just fine...but right now, we've got to make it hop—you've got hot grub, a slew of cousins, and—most importantly, my MOTHER—waiting for you at our house, and cadet assembly starts at seven o'clock sharp for me. Where did you hide your shoes...?"

"Darned if I know. Don't even remember how I ended up here last night..." Bud looked automatically about the room, but the paisley wallpaper started his head swimming again. He sat down on the bed and rubbed his eyes. Bud recalled foggily that there had been talk for years about the cousins in Lincoln that he had never met, children of his father's...sister?

"How many cousins?" Bud asked, now joining Johnny in the search for shoes.

"Well, I've got three brothers and four sisters—that's eight of us if you count yours truly...but you're likely to just run into the girls and wives this morning...here they are!" Johnny exclaimed, handing Bud's brown Brogans to him. "I forgot...Maggie usually places them right here under the bed." Johnny tried to hold a straight face as he waited for the eventual reaction...an open mouthed stare...and burst into laughter as he slapped Bud on the back.

As the joke dawned on Bud, he chuckled. "Darned thoughtful of her."

Bud tied his shoes and followed Johnny out the door and down the stairs, both of them taking two steps at a time. They turned and picked their way through the narrow space between the building and a wooden fence, and emerged onto a brick boulevard that Bud recognized as R Street, confirming that the room he had slept in was upstairs of the barrelhouse where he had met Uncle Zeke last night. The bar was locked now, and the windows shuttered, but Bud could hear sounds of a piano tinkling inside. Bud gestured toward the second story.

19

"Was that room…the one I slept in…is it Uncle Zeke's?"

"Thought I told you it was Maggie's?" As Bud's face turned pink, Johnny relented. "It's one of Zeke's. He has a couple of hideouts—he stays mum, and we don't ask."

* * * * *

Zeke woke that morning at dawn with the same "cat fur" tongue that Bud had mentioned to Johnny, but without the resilience of youth. Firmly resolving to stop playing young men's games (at least some of them), he crept out of bed and washed his face, then shaved and determined to untangle his hair.

I keep losing this stuff, thought Zeke, as he looked into the mirror, combing his long gray hair back to cover a thinning dome. *Must be this brush.*

Zeke managed to get his pants and boots on before he heard Maggie stir. He had finished buttoning his shirt and was just placing five silver dollars on the nightstand when she spoke.

"You don't have to do that," she said as she stretched. Maggie propped herself on her elbow, and her curly hair fell to the pillow and around her breasts in long blonde ringlets. "Makes me feel like you're just a customer."

Zeke smiled. "Now, Maggie, you turned down a couple of fine offers last night in favor of my company. Wouldn't be fair to deprive a lady of her livelihood, especially on a Friday night. Payday comes only once a week." Crossing the room, he knelt and kissed her, toying with her hair and enjoying the smell of her for a moment before he rose again and put on his hat. Grabbing his coat, he strode toward the door, half turned to her and winked. "Besides," he added, "I wouldn't pay five dollars for any woman, so it MUST be a gift."

He was already halfway down the hall before he heard the pillow hit the door.

* * * * *

Pointing ahead, Johnny proclaimed, "There's my alma mater."

Striding east along R Street, Bud saw for the first time what must have been the University—a sprawl of brick buildings surrounding a massive five-story gabled structure. Bud caught himself staring again, and had to consciously close his gaping mouth. *Everything was so damned BIG here…*

Tossing his head nonchalantly toward the central building, Bud asked, "What's that big brick monster with the tower on top?"

"University Hall. Most of my classes are in that building, and roll call is just on the other side of it, in the quad." Johnny turned to Bud, and gave him a mock salute. "This is where I leave you, soldier. Just turn south here on 11th—it's on the corner of 11th and J—1109 J Street, okay? Uncle Zeke left word with my folks last night that he will meet you there in about an hour, then take you over to the game."

Bud began to return his salute, then stumbled over Johnny's last words. "Uh… game?"

Johnny grinned and shook his head again. "Cousin, I don't know what they call what you drink in Alder Grove, but we call it **beer** over at Uncle Zeke's, and I advise you to **stay away from it**. It contains **alcohol.**"

As Johnny spoke, the wheels in Bud's head started turning. *I remember Zeke asking about baseball...that was before that weasely McGee character came in...after that...?*

"Now, to remind you," Johnny went on, "You're playing for the Saltdogs this afternoon at one o'clock. Standing in for one of our players? Any of this sound familiar?" Johnny reached out and gently knocked on Bud's head, until Bud held his hands up in surrender.

"Okay, whatever…"

"We call it 'other duties as assigned,'" Johnny remarked, but was suddenly interrupted from the direction of campus by the sound of a shrill whistle. Johnny's mild grin turned immediately to a look of sheer terror. "Shit! Gotta go, Cuz!" and without another word sprinted toward the large building.

For a time Bud stood clearing his head. After a few uncomfortable moments of self-reflection and castigation (*Did I* **really** *agree to play a game this afternoon? Did I really* **forget** *that I* **said** *I would play a game this afternoon...?*), he caught himself staring at the massive edifice of University Hall. It was easily the largest building Bud had ever seen, at least six stories if you counted the tower. Although it was still over a month until classes started, most of the windows were open, and he could hear the sounds of cleaning ladies chattering away inside the building, moving desks and chairs with loud intermittent squeaks of wooden legs against wooden floors, preparing the building for classes. Several large rugs were hung from some of the windows, and Bud saw clouds of dust fall away from them as they succumbed to the *smacks* of enthusiastic

21

women. In his mind's eye, Bud remembered going with Mother to Alder Grove School and washing blackboards with his brothers and sister as Mother and the women of the community tidied the classrooms on Saturday mornings. A squad of painters with scaffolds and ladders swarmed around one of the campus buildings to his right, squabbling in a language that sounded like Czech.

As Bud backed up to get a better look, his mind gradually was made aware of a metallic rumble. His head snapped to the right as he heard the words, "Watch it, Buster!" followed by a bell and metallic squeal of brakes. Bud jumped back onto the curb just in time to miss a brush with a covered rail car of some sort—Bud immediately realized from photographs he had seen that it must be an electric trolley. The driver swore in a language that Bud had not heard before—but managed to gesture in a language that was all too recognizable—before the car curved on rails to the south from R Street onto 11th.

Bud's eyes followed the trolley, and he was once again mesmerized by the scope of the street scene before him. For blocks and blocks, three- and four-story brick buildings lined the brick street, topped by arches, pinnacles, and other frippery. Tall, arched windows marked the second and third floors, and striped awnings covered most of the first-floor storefronts. White telephone poles towered over the sidewalks on both sides of the street, each replete with five cross braces and a dozen wires to every brace. Trolley rails divided the street, where horses pulled wagons, carts, and hacks, stopping and starting at random, making a ballet of sorts at the intersections. Merchants were now hustling about the storefronts to place baskets of fruits, vegetables, eggs, cheeses and other produce onto long wooden sidewalk tables under the spreading canopies.

Checking this time for the hazard of a trolley car, Bud crossed to the west side of 11th street, hoping to warm himself in the rising sunlight as he moved south. As he crossed P Street, Bud was suddenly accosted by a short, balding man sporting a paper hat and a large, handsomely waxed white mustache. Dressed in a white shirt and black pantaloons that were stuck in his boots, he was draped neck-to-knees in a stained red and white striped apron. The little man jumped up from his short stool and gestured elaborately with open palms to a small open brazier next to him, where almonds appeared to be roasting. "Hey!" he piped, "You look hungry, Papageno! I gotta nuts here, hot and gooda than you ever had. The angels, they come down ever morning and kiss my nuts."

There's a picture, Bud thought.

The Italian smiled at the blush creeping across Bud's face, and selecting a single nut carefully with a fork in his left hand, flipped the hot nut into a napkin that had magically appeared in his right hand. The man held the nut out, and Bud took it, tossing it gently from hand to hand until it was cool enough to pop into his mouth. To his delight, Bud found that it was coated in a sweet, salty mixture that exaggerated the crunch of the nut as he bit into it.

"You're right," Bud admitted. "You have *great* nuts."

Bud's hunger now rose in him like a bird of prey, and he reached into his front pocket, where he found a nickel deeply buried, left unspent from the train trip. Handing it to the little man, he watched in fascination as the man accepted it, snapped a paper into a cone, and shoveled a scoop of almonds into it with a smooth, practiced motion.

Handing the cone to Bud, he remarked, "You new around here, I think. I see you walking. You look *all around* to the tops of the buildings, to the trolleys, to the fruit, in the windahs." Smiling, as Bud nodded, he gestured at all about him as he spoke. "You think this is a big? You shoulda see New York City. It's like a hunnert times this a big. It has trolleys that zoom up on the sidewalk just to run a you over. It's a crazy place."

"Is that why you left, Mr...?"

"Verlucci. Vincente Verlucci. You calla me Vinnie, though, everybody does." Bud found that Vinnie's handshake was strong, warm...and oily. "I left to find a bigga place. Nebraska is very big, inna different way, though. Plenty a room, si?"

Bud nodded as he crunched his almonds.

Vinnie pointed his fork at Bud, and looked at him, eyes twinkling. "I think you visiting here, or mebbe you find a job?"

"Finding a job...with family, though, so maybe it's like visiting, too, I guess." Bud admitted.

"Yeah? Well, I know everybody in Lincoln...who you gonna work for?"

"My Uncle...Ezekiel Gardner."

The man's eyes shot up, and started to gesture even more excitedly. "Zeke? You gonna work for Zeke? Zeke is a very good friend a mine! And you say he's your uncle, si? So, what's your name, then? Pack, I think..."

23

"No, it's Bud Gardner. I'm on my way to meet the Pack family this morning."

"Si, si, down on J Street. I know right where it is. You say your name is Gardner, and you're gonna meet all the Packs today? Together? You're gonna need a bigga bunch a nuts." At that, Vinnie pulled out a huge brown bag, *smacked* it open, and started shoveling nuts off the brazier, scoop after scoop, until they nearly filled the bag. He then dropped the bag into another bag and neatly rolled up the top.

"You take this with you, and you give it to Emmy. You say it's from her boyfriend. SHE'LL know who I am..."

"Er, thanks, Mr...Vinnie. Are you sure..."

"You bet your life. No charge for Zeke. Now, you better get going, they a much betta when they a hot."

With thoughts of breakfast now uppermost in his mind, Bud shook hands with Vinnie and accelerated, crossing O—with barely a glance up and down that "main street" of Lincoln—then N and M Streets. There the architecture abruptly shifted from red brick businesses to white clapboard houses and churches amid large yards, with an occasional brick home thrown in for variety's sake. Here and there, horses that were tied to concrete hitching posts would raise their heads as he passed. On reaching J Street, Bud did take a moment to put down the almonds, and glance around as he straightened his clothes. Four blocks to the east, he could see the spire of the State Capitol just covering the rising sun; a block to the west, the Lancaster County Courthouse looked like a miniature version of the Capitol, its red bricks glowing orange in the light of the low morning sun. At the basement level, Bud could make out the bars of the jail cells, and he wondered about the man that Uncle Zeke had sent there yesterday...

* * * * *

"Morning, Ezekiel," Fred said, not even looking up from his copy of the State Journal as Zeke walked in. "See you left some prime horseshit for my boys to clean up after I left yesterday." Fred Miller's feet were up on the desk of his second-story courthouse office overlooking J Street, which was difficult as it was already piled with stacks of papers in short wooden boxes entitled "Jury Summons," "Warrants," "Court Proceedings," and a last amorphous category entitled "Horseshit."

"Guess I know which box to find the paperwork in, then," replied Zeke, gesturing to the last box on the right. "But at least I let your deputies handle it—I know how you love to be home early on Friday nights."

"Right, like you were ever home early on Friday nights when you were sheriffing," Fred scoffed. "I was down on 10th running drunk patrol, as usual, every payday."

"Well, it's nice to know some things don't change much." Zeke looked in the right-hand box, and sure enough, there was a paper entitled "Record of Arrest." Scanning the document, Zeke learned that Judge Lansing wouldn't sit on a bail hearing for Maxwell G. LeBlanc until Monday.

"Guess our boy will be sitting it out for the weekend, anyway," Zeke remarked. "I'll be there, of course, though I don't expect Harrison to make it in."

"Don't expect that it would do much good if he did, anyway, except maybe to aggravate LeBlanc," Fred agreed. "He's got two witnesses ready to swear he was minding his own business on that road."

Putting down his paper, Fred looked over his reading glasses, his blue eyes staring intently under gray eyebrows. "Zeke, why are you stirrin' the pot? Time was that you and farmers were anything but friends. Seems like now you're sticking your neck way out for a bunch of sodbustin' immigrants."

Zeke stared for awhile at his feet, then admitted, "Guess I didn't care much for farmers, or farming, it's true. Most of 'em couldn't read, much less vote in a county election. But times are changing, and people change, too, Fred. That's progress."

Fred shook his head. "There's something you're not telling me...but I guess it'll wait." Leaning forward, Sheriff Miller dropped his voice. "Zeke, you need to be careful. McGee is connected...with some of the biggest sows in the pen. I can't watch your back every minute—and I won't unless there's a damn good reason."

"When I've got one, you'll be the first to know," Zeke held out his hand. "Okay?"

"Fair enough." Fred shook Zeke's hand, smiling wryly. "Say, how about lunch today? My daughter Millie's making her first attempt at chocolate pie, and a man hates to die alone."

"Tempting," Zeke grinned. "But I've got a few errands to run today, and it would help if I were actually breathing." Zeke hesitated, then added, "Going to the game later?"

"Between the Southies and the Saltdogs? Of course…if I recall, your last skirmish resulted in two broken arms and a half-dead umpire. These games between the railroaders and the streetcar companies are mostly what keep me in business."

"Well, don't count out the railroaders today…if you have a little ready cash, you might consider this a tip."

Fred gave Zeke a sideways stare, humor starting to play at his normally stolid countenance. "What are you up to, Zeke…did you poison the opposing pitcher?"

"No one on the opposition, I assure you. But we might have a few substitutions on our side this week."

* * * * *

Knowing he was expected, Bud finished tucking in his shirt, hefted the bag of warm almonds, and hiked across J Street to the door of the three story white frame home with a mailbox that clearly designated it as "1109 Pack." His boots *clumped* up the front steps, and taking a short breath, he knocked on the screen door, which rattled and squeaked under his knuckles. Almost immediately, a voice called out "Coming!" and the door swung open to reveal a middle-aged woman of medium height in a modest brown cotton dress. As she looked upon Bud's features, her eyes arched, her face brightened, and gasping, she leapt through the door, clasping Bud firmly by both arms.

Saturday, August 4, 1894
7:45 am

"I just can't get over how much you favor your father."

Emelia Pack was cooking. *Well,* thought Bud, *not exactly.* There was a word for war (compared to a simple killing), and for a tornado (compared to a dust devil). Bud didn't know the word for the enterprise unfolding before him, but "cooking" seemed pretty puny. Wood-burning and gas-fired stoves wrestled one another for space on the north wall, and both were ablaze with pots simmering, boiling, and bubbling on their surfaces. Four young women and a teenaged girl were busily mixing dough, rolling it out, pitting cherries, and peeling apples, pitching them into scattered crockery at odd intervals. Aunt Emmy was standing at the wood stove, fiddling with a small pan of eggs and bacon along one of the red hot edges.

"Yes, Ma'am. Mother says we are so alike she has to check us from the back for the one with the bald spot. Or wait for one of us to speak—apparently I'm the more intelligent in her eyes, as I share in the Rose blood."

Aunt Emmy chuckled, and scraped the contents of the pan onto a china plate. From his first helping, Bud recalled that small roses surrounded the inside rim of the plate, but were now obscured again by heaps of steaming food. She handed the plate to her nephew, and waved him on as she sat on a stool beside him, a wistful look in her blue eyes. She took a long strand of gray hair and pulled it behind her ear, then patted her brow with a towel she untucked from her waist.

"That sounds like Idey...she was mighty proud of her family. We all knew each other in Corning, of course, before your folks were married. She was just a year older than me, and I think she might have had an eye on my Rufus at one time." Bud stopped shoveling food for a minute and stared, thinking what it would be like to have somebody else as a father. *Unthinkable—the fabric of the universe would surely unravel...*

"But, then Rufus had a taste of my scrambled eggs, and it was all over." Bud nodded—they were soft, but not runny, with bits of bacon in them, and peppered to perfection. Bud paused in mid-swallow again...*how had Uncle Rufus managed to get a taste of Emmy's scrambled eggs while they were courting?*

"Momma, how long should we cook the apples, again?" Ginny was a scrawny fourteen-year-old, tall with mousey brown hair and hazel eyes.

She could easily have passed for Bud's kid sister, Daphne, and chattered away with much the same effect as a mockingbird in a horse stall—nonstop, random, a little too loud for the close confines, but still welcome. She had finished peeling apples, and was now stealing glances at Bud, with very little success at subterfuge.

"Just keep stabbin' 'em until they fall apart, honey. We're gonna mash 'em all into applesauce, anyway." Turning to the bag that Bud had brought in, she remarked, "My, that smells wonderful. Is it an offering for the feast tomorrow?"

Bud turned to the brown bag, now starting to show stains through the second layer of paper. He scooped it up, and felt that it was still warm. As he unrolled the top, the delicious odor of spiced almonds spread over the kitchen, accompanied almost at once by the sighs of the females.

"Almost forgot...Mr...er...Vinnie sent these over for you." Bud stopped short, and Aunt Emelia caught the hesitation in his voice.

"Momma's *boyfriend*!" chirped Ginny.   The two young women laughed and joined Ginny in a chorus of "WooooOOOOooooo's", with added jibes of "Italian men!" and "Better not tell Father!" Bud could tell by the mild smile and absence of a blush on Aunt Emmy's face that this was an old joke. "Mr. Velucci is a dear man, and he certainly does do things in a big way! How shall we ever EAT all this?"

"By starting NOW!" Ginny yipped, and greedily scooped up a handful of nuts. The towel her mother grabbed to snap her retreating backside cracked the air several inches short of its intended mark, and Ginny dropped a few nuts into her sisters-in-law's hands before crunching them in the far corner of the kitchen. She eyed the towel in her mother's hands warily, ready in a moment to scoot out the side door of the kitchen. Seeing the futility of another direct attack on her daughter, Emmy threw the towel nonchalantly over her shoulder.

"I'd try and excuse the roughhousing, but it's only the beginning, I'm afraid, Bud." Emelia handed the bag to the nearest of her daughters-in-law. *Was it Rose? Ruth?* Bud had forgotten her name in the rush of introductions at the door. He had managed to recall that the oldest of his cousins, Jeff, Jim, and Joe were all married, and busy today about town in various family jobs. Their wives, and his cousins Judith and Ginny were surrounding him, now greedily passing around the toasted almonds and making crunching sounds as they chatted in low tones.

Reaching for a handful of the salty sweet confections himself, Bud asked, "Do you have the whole family here for dinner every Sunday?"

"Not every Sunday, the boys and Judy all have to visit their in-laws on other Sundays," answered Emelia. "We get the first Sunday in the month, plus Thanksgiving Day, Christmas Eve, and the Fourth of July. Tomorrow, we're lucky—everybody is planning to make it, plus a few extras...altogether, about 23 people."

Bud looked around, and blurted, "Where do you PUT them all?"

Emma laughed, and pointed to the long oak table that the women were now busily sprinkling with flour. "See this table? We can add twelve more leaves, and extend it the whole length of the kitchen and into the dining room."

Bud shook his head. "Must make for a lot of commotion."

"That's putting it lightly—I keep advising Julia that she should marry a station master, to direct traffic around the Pack switchyards. Today is baking day, and it may look a little crazy, but the real insanity kicks in between Mass and noon tomorrow, when the rest of the cooking starts. I swear, it's worse than the State Asylum..."

For a moment, Bud stood in shocked silence...it was all he could do not to let his jaw drop into the pie dough. *Mass? So his cousins were* **Catholics?** With a new perspective, Bud's eyes darted around the bustling kitchen, and into the dining room beyond. Sure enough, there on the west wall was an unobtrusive wooden crucifix, with the painted figure of Christ painfully bearing the sins of the world. And the silver chain peeking around the collar of his aunt's neck...it probably held another one. *No* **wonder** *we haven't heard much about them over the years. The way that Father feels about Catholics...*

"Now, not another nut until tomorrow, young lady," her mother scolded, glaring at Ginny and making a half-hearted motion toward the towel on her shoulder. "Get started on those dishes, girl."

Ginny pulled her hand away from the bag, frowning, and reluctantly moved to the sink, where she started filling the large basin from a small red hand pump. Bud's own mother had just had a pump installed in their own kitchen last spring, and Bud hadn't missed the trip out to the well every morning and evening. As Bud shoveled in the last forkful of eggs and walked his dishes over to Ginny, he heard the sudden sound of girl's laughter coming in from the front porch, intermingled with the opening screech and closing slam of the screen door. Bud turned to see two young women with swirling skirts stumble into the kitchen. The taller of the two was clad in a paisley skirt and white blouse, and was wearing what looked like a soldier's blue kepi on her head. She was laughing so hard that she was forced to keep a hand on its brim to maintain its position over her wiry brown hair. The shorter of the two was dressed in brown muslin, and had blonde hair that tossed about her shoulders as she laughed.

Through her laughing gasps, the blond girl continued her story, wiping tears from her eyes. "...And I couldn't BELIEVE that he was still going to propose right there in the train station! There must have been a hundred passengers watching him as he knelt down and begged that poor girl not to leave town. There was paint dripping from his hair, his clothes...you'd think that he would have gotten the idea from the first bucket she threw at him."

"So what did she do?" queried the older girl in the kepi, trying to gain some control, but knowing that the story wasn't over yet.

"She did what any intelligent girl would do...she picked up another can of paint and chucked that one at him, too! There he was, covered in one can of black paint, one can of white—and he just kept spinning around, looking at himself, shaking himself off..." she paused, taking a kerchief from her purse and wiping her eyes, one at a time. "He looked like a demented barber pole!"

"What's black and white and red all over?" threw in the other girl, chuckling. "Robert Jensen making a proposal!"

There's not much pity for a man in love around here. But Bud couldn't help joining in the laughter, anyway.

Amid the mirth, Aunt Emmy had tried to interject herself—without much effect. As it began to die down, she shook her head. "You girls are just awful. And I suppose you're going to excoriate this poor lad in the Journal this week, Willa?"

The taller girl took off her kepi and shook her long brown hair, her eyes sparking. "Certainly I shall think about it, Mrs. Pack, but I've already got an article started on the tent revival going on down at the State Fairgrounds. It's nearly as ridiculous, but not as distasteful."

Bud decided to throw in. "Are you referring to Robert Jensen, Miss, or to proposals in general?"

Willa winked at Mrs. Pack, smirked and turned to face Bud. "Is that natural curiosity, or a personal interest, Mister...?"

"Gardner, Miss...but please call me Bud." When he held out his hand, the girl gripped it firmly. Bud noticed the ink stains on her fingers and her sleeve. Her grey eyes twinkled mischievously as they locked on to Bud's.

Mrs. Pack cut in, 'Where are my manners? Bud, this is Miss Willa Cather. And your cousin, Julia. Julia works for the telephone exchange, Bud. And Willa, as you've heard, is a writer."

"That's One Way of Putting it..." said Julia. "That's the name of Willa's column. Comes out on Tuesdays."

"Actually, I'll be writing more in the line of theater reviews this year than short stories. The editors think that will sell more newspapers than my 'meandering observations on the Lincoln scene,' I believe they phrased it. It's all one to me...what with the *Hesperian* and my senior classes, I'll be quite busy enough."

"Am I to understand that you write for the **Nebraska State Journal**, Miss Cather?" Bud shook his head in wonder at the nods all around. "That's a big paper. Must be very exciting."

"Not as exciting as Julia's job." Willa replied. "She generally hears the news long before we do at the paper, don't you, Julia?"

Julia rolled her eyes. "I'll never tell, Willa." Turning to Bud, she remarked, "So, one of my mysterious cousins finally appears...from Alder Grove, isn't it?"

* * * * *

At the stroke of 11:00, Amos Aloysius Seville turned the lock, threw the bolt, and pulled the barrelhouse door open to R Street. The stale beer and tobacco odors seemed to ooze out of the door, slinking down the street. "Fresh air," muttered Amos. "How disgusting."

Stepping out onto the narrow sidewalk, Amos struck a match, lit a small cigar, and waited. Off to his left, he could hear the pitched chaos that was the trainyard; to his right, rifles slapped in close order drill and orders barked from the University campus where the cadets drilled. As his eyes trailed over to the campus, Amos saw what he was looking for, stumbling off the R Street trolley with faltering steps toward the barrelhouse. *Right on time.*

Amos exhaled, crushed his cigar against the frame of the door, and moved inside, leaping lightly over the bar. Selecting a particular bottle of rye, he pulled the cork and placed a small shot glass neatly next to the bottle. Over in the corner, Tom Turpin was hammering random notes repeatedly on the disheveled piano, probing the instrument's interior with a tuning wrench.

"Give it up, Professor," Amos advised. "It's like trying to reinvest a virgin. What's done is done."

Tom smiled. "Now Mr. Seville, you know that every...lady...can stand a little paint."

Before Amos could reply, he heard a shuffle and belch, and observed a squat, familiar figure fill the lower half the doorway, leaning heavily against the jam. As the man removed his rumpled fedora and shuffled toward the bar, Amos made a short bow.

"Welcome, Coach," chirped Amos. "Ah observe that you are as punctual as always, this fine Saturday morning."

"Shut up and pour," the man mumbled, dropping his satchel on the floor of the bar with a *whump* as he ascended onto one of the barstools. From his place behind the bar, Amos observed that the clasp of the satchel was broken, and a section of gray cloth was trailing along the floor, with the word *Saltdogs* written in script across the front. Amos poured three fingers of rye whiskey into the tumbler as he asked, "So, what ah the boys' chances today?" He already knew the answer, but it was important to follow ritual, for the sake of form.

"Shitty," the man croaked after he downed the fiery drink, shaking his head. "You know how it is—half of the team is sleeping off last night's adventures on 10th street, and the other half couldn't hit a baseball if it was hung on a bell pull."

Amos poured another, this time to the top of the glass. "You seem to be contending that all our good players ah drunks...and don't the Southies have the same problem?"

"True," admitted the coach, draining the glass again. "The difference is probably how much more drunk the Saltdogs got last night." On any other morning, this is where Amos would have stopped pouring—but to the coach's astonished delight, his two-fingered 'come hither' gesture was rewarded with another glass.

"Come now, Coach, you have some talented players that don't drink at all—take Frank Crawford, for example. Ah do believe he's hit eight home runs this season, and word has it that he wouldn't touch the stuff."

"There are exceptions to every rule, I s'pose." The short man was now slurring his words, and a little rye dribbled noticeably down his chin as he inverted the glass into his watering hole. "But Frank's never satisfied, always wanting to 'try this', and 'try that.'" The small man gestured extravagantly from left to right, nearly falling off the stool. "Mebbe he should try coaching."

Maybe he should, thought Amos, not for the first time. As bad as the Coach was making it out, Amos knew that the Saltdogs had only one real disadvantage over the Southies, and he was sitting directly in front of him. Unfortunately, as his brother-in-law was the stationmaster of the Fremont, Elkhorn, & Missouri Valley railroad, he couldn't very well be fired from the company team.

He could, however, be coaxed to resign…at least for the day.

Seizing the nearly empty bottle, the coach put it to his lips and had another slug. He then began to giggle, to snicker, and finally laughed until he coughed. "He'd probably teach us to kick the baseball through a pair of uprights!" The coach was now teetering dangerously on the barstool, and the discordant, random and staccato piano notes from the Professor's tunings sounded more and more appropriate.

Amos smiled, hopped over the bar, and gently eased his customer from the barstool to a chair beside the table. Out of nowhere, another glass and bottle appeared on the table beside the short man, and the sound of a cork being pulled popped through the coach's cobwebs.

"Have another, Coach?"

* * * * *

In a small private office that adjoined the stables, Miles McGee straightened the pencils on his blotter, shuffled his papers impatiently, and for the fourth time snapped open his Elgin railroad watch. The office mirrored many that he maintained in and around Lincoln--to the chagrin of the men he controlled. Scowling, he struck a match with his gloved hand and lit the pale cigarette that was perched between his thin lips, allowing himself a long drag while he shook the match out. *The impertinence of that ex-deputy, that…**barkeeper**…. Thinking that a bunch of lumber freighters and tavernkeepers could stand in the way of the established order. If only that damned Masterson hadn't backed up the…what did they call it now? The "Cooperative?" What the devil could that storekeeper be thinking?*

Suddenly, McGee heard the steps of two men shuffling about on the porch outside his office. Crushing out his cigarette, he straightened his black coat, took up a fountain pen and began scribbling a few lines on his blotter as the men burst through the door.

"Beg pardon, sir," stuttered the larger of the two. "We was just…"

"Sleeping it off, most likely," interrupted McGee. "I do not appreciate unpunctuality, gentlemen. It is unprofessional." Sighing, he removed his glasses and rubbed his eyes. After a pause, he asked, "Tell me, Franks...how do think it went yesterday?"

"Purty bad, I guess," mumbled the big man, shuffling his feet nervously. "We was surprised, is all. Gardner got the drop on us." The man shrugged. "It happens."

"And you, William?" McGee asked, turning to the smaller man. "How do you feel about your performance yesterday?"

"I'm pissed, that's what," the young man spat. Whipping aside his coat, he pulled a revolver from his belt. "Say the word and we'll burn that bastard barkeep down, boss."

Glaring at the pistol, McGee spat, "I appreciate your enthusiasm...where was it yesterday, I wonder? Holster that, damn you!" Shaking his head, he turned back to the larger man, and struggled to soften his voice.

"Franks, it appears to be past time to send a message to Mr. Gardner...I'd prefer an oblique message to a lethal one, but either way— deliver it tonight after the meeting. Make it clear—this is not his business."

The larger man's visage gave way to a gap-toothed grin. "My pleasure, sir."

Saturday, August 4, 1894
12 noon

The uniform was too big, it itched, and it smelled like a Charles Witzel cigar. And Bud was just about certain that it harbored hitchhikers.

Twenty-four hours ago, I was getting on a train for Lincoln. Now I'm playing a baseball game in a drunk's uniform, on behalf of a man I barely know, with a team I've never met, for an unknown sum of money. If we win.

God bless America....

For what seemed like the hundredth time, Bud hiked his pants up (this time leaning his hip against a splintered bleacher support in order to help him defy gravity) as he watched the crowd begin to trickle into the park for the game. When Bud and Zeke arrived at the barrelhouse, Amos had managed to scare up a safety pin from behind the bar to address the uniform's...generosity. Its owner was nowhere to be seen, but a loud snore was drifting up from behind the piano, and Bud began a series of shrewd guesses as to how a vacancy had suddenly appeared in the team's lineup. As with the small town teams that Bud had played with for years, the universal rule was that you couldn't play unless you were in uniform...and when appearing in a proper uniform, it was assumed (at least by the opposition) that you were "on" the team.

Unfortunately, this particular uniform had proven to be a trifle short on length and downright magnanimous on diameter. Despite the manufacturer's claims about the pin, though, Bud was pretty sure that he was anything but safe—one good dive for second base, and he suspected that he'd be "out" no matter what the umpire's call.

The ballpark squatted at the corner of 6th and D, just behind the water works and southeast of the railyards, designated "Lincoln Park" by some incurably optimistic municipal worker. Bud, Zeke, and Big Swede had arrived about an hour early for the game, with Zeke and Swede making a beeline with the beer wagon to claim a prime spot behind the bleachers. As the other vendors were still setting up, Zeke had tossed Bud a silver dollar, urging him to "try out a runza with the Czechs," and waving vaguely over toward a wagon parked on the far side of the field, near the privies. Bud fingered the silver dollar now, and decided that he might as well find out what a "runza" was before the other players arrived—and the inevitable introductions started.

The wagon looked as though it might have been painted yellow, once. Between the left hand wheels and a pair of sawhorses that supported a span of one-by-twelves, a young woman shook out a blue and white checkered tablecloth. As she smoothed the tablecloth carefully over the planks, Bud noticed that her dress featured the same blue checkered pattern…and that her eyes were nearly the same color. Glancing up, she flashed a smile and brushed a lock of raven black hair away from her face, tucking it behind her left ear.

"Hello, farmer. Hungry?" She spoke with the crisp consonants of an eastern European, and Bud guessed that it must be either Polish or Czech.

Bud placed the silver dollar on the tablecloth. "Does it show?"

"Of course it does. Your pants are falling down. You must be starving."

"Yep." Bud grinned at his pants, now holding them up with both hands. "But I doubt you'll be able to fill this rig up."

"I think I would need a bigger wagon. Wait here." Walking around the back of the wagon, she quickly reappeared with a large platter of light brown, square yeast rolls. The smell of cooked beef, onions, and cabbage filled the air, and Bud's mouth began to water.

"Bierocks!" Bud chirped, and had to stop his two hands from reaching for them in order to keep his…dignity.

"I have heard the Germans call them that, and the Russians call them pirogies. But around here," she admonished, "we call them *runzas*. And you need a stitch, farmer, or you will not be able to try them. It is a two-hand operation."

With an agility that surprised Bud, the girl scrambled up the front wagon wheel and began to root under the buckboard seat, tossing pliers, hammers, and other tools aside with a series of *clanks*. Grunting gently with satisfaction, she snatched up a brown cloth-covered box and leapt down. As she did, Bud caught a glimpse of ruffles under her checked skirt and blushed, looking down quickly. When he looked up, the girl was already kneeling in front of him, unfastening the safety pin at his waist.

"Er," Bud said. *Eloquence,* he thought.

"Be at ease, farmer, it is *my* needle I am interested in." Smirking, she shoved the (already bent) safety pin between her teeth, and pulled a series of pins out of a red tomato-shaped pincushion that was buried in the brown sewing box, rapidly jabbing them between pinches of cloth around the shrinking circumference of this pants. Bud didn't know whether to be offended by the effrontery, astounded by the efficiency, or frightened at the sharpness of the pins. But in a matter of seconds, the girl was standing, thread in one hand and needle in the other, spool in her mouth. Mumbling through the spool, she took Bud by the arm and marched him rapidly to one of two privies that was nearest to the wagon.

Opening the door, she said, "Shuck 'em. The runzas are getting cold, and I am losing trade." Bud glanced back to her table, and saw that a growing line of men were staring back at him from the girl's runza stand, nickels held out in anticipation. Bud closed the door, obeyed, and handed out the pants. As he listened to her walk back to the stand, he thought to himself, *might as well*, and answered nature's call.

By the diffuse light that flowed through the cracks around the board walls of the outhouse, Bud sat and read the six-inch wide strips of newspaper that were conveniently hung over a horizontal two-by-four. He noted that September corn was up to (an unheard of) 52½ cents a bushel, that the Northwestern line was advertising reduced rates for round trip tickets to Hot Springs and other tourist points, and that Hood's Sarsaparilla offered cures for scrofula, salt rheum, and dyspepsia. Bud was pretty sure that he didn't want to know what these illnesses were, even if it meant that a sarsaparilla awaited the patient. He was just wrapping up the paperwork when he caught the muted sound of conversation coming from behind the outhouse. Craning his head closer to the cracks in the outhouse wall, Bud could detect movement outside, and smelled the sulfurous odor of a match being lit.

"Thankee," muttered the first voice. Cigar smoke sifted through the cracks in the outhouse wall. "You say that a friend from Kearney gave you muh name?"

"Yes, indeed," replied the second voice. "He mentioned that you and he had done a horse deal there, once."

"Yeah, ah knows a few folks out there." Bud couldn't make out the faces of the men, but assumed from his speech that one of them was a Negro. His suspicion was confirmed when he caught a glimpse of the nearer man's dark hand, clothed in a cheap, dirty blue suitcoat, flash past the crack in the wall. As the sound of footsteps thudded softly away, Bud caught the last bit of conversation, "Mebbe we ken talk more about it later...you know 'bout the Hoo Hoo Club?"

The Hoo Hoo Club? Bud grinned. *Must be quite a club...*

Bud's eavesdropping was interrupted by three firm raps on the door, followed by the appearance of a feminine hand clutching a pair of uniform pants.

"Best I can do in two minutes, farmer." The hand skittered back through the door as Bud grabbed at the tossed garment, just preventing its plunge into the void beneath the outhouse. Bud pulled the pants on, appreciating how the folds of cloth were sewn neatly upon themselves, both inside the waistband and down the seat. The garment fit admirably.

Banging the door behind him, Bud walked over to the wagon and stood over a steel washtub that squatted behind the left rear wheel, next to a small coal-fired warming oven. Pointing to the water, Bud raised his eyes at the girl, who nodded quickly and continued to make change for the men in line. Bud rinsed his hands, wiped them, and got in line, eyeing the girl again. She wasn't exactly dainty…just right, Bud decided, with a sort of square-shouldered strength—and he enjoyed the way her eyes sparked.

As he stepped in front of the table, she grasped his hand and plunked a runza wrapped in brown paper into it. The sandwich felt warm through the paper…and so were the girl's rough hands. They lingered there for the briefest moment, until Bud stirred and she jerked her hands away, looking down at her table.

Picking up his silver dollar with his free hand, he held it out to her and asked, "What do I owe you?"

"A nickel—three for a dime."

"Guess now that my pants fit, I'll take just one," Bud remarked.

"I'm low on change right now," the girl replied, waving away the dollar. "Come back and pay later, between innings." Pausing, she added, "Don't drink it all up between now and then, farmer."

Small chance of that, thought Bud. *Enough of **that** for a while.*

"Thanks…and thanks for the stitch, Miss…?"

"Anna. Anna Marie Vostrovsky." Bud reached for her hand, but the stamping of feet and the impatient *hrmphing* voices from the line at his rear unnerved him, so he settled for twitching his hand to his brow, touching his cap. "Thanks, Miss Vostrop…Vosttof…er, thanks, Anna…" Bud stuttered, and hurriedly stumbled out of line.

The sandwich was warm and spicy, and meat juices trickled against his cheek as Bud shuffled his feet gradually toward the dugouts, taking bite after enormous bite. He was lost in thought for the next few moments, chewing and walking, until he felt a hand clamp on to his shoulder from behind.

"How's the runza?" Zeke asked. "And...where's mine?"

Bud sputtered through a mouthful of beef and cabbage. "Great!...but...you didn't..."

"That's okay, Bud," Zeke smiled, hesitated, slyly glancing at the yellowed wagon, then stared through narrowed eyes back at his nephew. "Pretty, isn't she?"

As Bud's ears reddened, Zeke added, "Get any change back? There's no pocket in your uniform."

"Oh, right," Bud stuttered, cramming the last bit of the sandwich into his mouth with one hand, and handing the silver dollar back to Zeke with the other.

Zeke stared at the dollar incredulously for a moment, then shoved his hat back on his head. "Free food...from the *Czechs*? Bud, you certainly make a good first impression..."

"I'll need a nickel to pay her later," Bud said defensively. "She was out of change." Bud hesitated, then added, "She took in my uniform a little, too..."

Zeke looked Bud over, shook his head and chuckled softly. "Had your pants off already, did she?"

As they approached the dugout, Bud could see that the scene unfolding before him resembled as much a brawl as a team meeting, with eight men sharing the same uniform as Bud, all seeming to be convinced that they had the floor. The speeches were animated, punctuated by pointed fingers, shaking fists, hats being thrown to the ground, and other gestures of frustration, all performed while balancing pitchers of beer and lit cigars. Considering the dry condition of the infield, Bud had to hope that none of the cigars would get away from the players. Altogether, they looked a pretty shaky lot, with unshaven faces, red eyes, and unkempt uniforms being the norm, and Bud felt some small comfort in that his own still baggy-in-the-butt uniform was not altogether out of place.

From his back pocket, Zeke produced a small leather glove. Handing it to Bud, he murmured into his nephew's ears, "I'll do the talking." Bud nodded numbly, taking the glove and fitting it nervously onto his left hand.

A smallish fellow with a cigar poking out from under a neatly trimmed mustache gestured toward Bud and piped up. "So, where you been hidin' this Jasper John, Zeke? Under the Barrelhouse with the beer?"

"Glad you asked, Pete." Zeke threw out an arm toward Bud, and lowered his voice a trifle as he gestured the team to close in around him. "This is my nephew, Bud. He's a fine player, and as far as the opposition is concerned, a cousin of the stationmaster." Zeke offered an overt wink, and the more sober of the players nodded in comprehension.

"See that he's wearing one of his 'family's' uniform, despite the alteration," Pete remarked. "What happened to Fats?"

"The Coach is indisposed," piped up a new voice. The team turned their faces to Amos Aloysius Seville, who folded his arms around the two nearest members of the now-huddled team. In contrast to the other players, his uniform was sharply creased, and his hair neatly combed. "He sends his condolences, and hopes that his absence will not be too sorely missed."

"Only by the opposition," remarked Frank Crawford.

"Ah would suggest," offered Amos, "in the unfortunate absence of our coach, that Mr. Crawford fill his position. Any objections?" The players grunted in general agreement.

"Best we get warmed up, then," Crawford offered, and pulled Zeke aside. As he turned and began to exchange throws with Amos, Bud could hear the pair murmur, and occasionally detected the newly-crowned coach nodding his head to Zeke's replies through the corner of his eye.

It wasn't long before Bud's attention was drawn by two cheers, each of which built quickly to a roar. One was from the wagonload of men that was just now tuning around the end of their dugout and into the field...and the other was from the clearly partisan crowd that was hailing them from the bleachers. As the wagon took a turn around the bases, the crowd cheered wildly, and the man seated next to the wagon driver began to bleat out a "TAH-TAH-TAH -- tah-tah-TAH, tah-tah-TAH, tah-tah-TAH!," familiar to the war veterans in the crowd as an *advance*. Bud's practicing team gestured rudely to their competitors as the wagon ripped around the infield baseline, nearly trampling Jake and Pete in front of their own dugout, and digging ruts in the dust as they churned around second. Other than the bugler, the loudest denizen of the wagon appeared to be a child— but on second glance proved to be a midget, hoisting a bottle of whiskey to his throat to the delight of the crowd. As the team pulled to the front of the bleachers and disembarked the wagon, the small man was hoisted onto the shoulders of two of his larger teammates.

In the midst of the pandemonium, Frank Crawford pulled Bud aside, and Bud again felt a vague discomfort at the intensity of Crawford's gaze.

"Your uncle says you can pitch," said Crawford. "We need a pitcher, there is no doubt. How many innings are you good for?"

Despite Bud's nervousness at his new coach's candor, he did not hesitate in his response. "Three innings, at the outside, sir. I pitch a knuckleball, and I'm not much good after that, except for the outfield."

"Very well," said Crawford. "Expect to be put in near the seventh inning, unless we are behind more than three or four runs. Play hard, but leave something in your arm for when you are called." At that, Crawford headed into the dugout and started scratching out a lineup on an Indian tablet with a stubby pencil, licking the lead periodically to lubricate the process.

Saturday, August 4th

Dear Harlan,

It has been a very strange first day here. I arrived in Lincoln late last night, and met my Uncle Zeke. He runs a tavern called the Barrelhouse on R Street, and we came to an agreement that I would work for him, doing odd jobs. One of those jobs, it turned out, was to join a Lincoln baseball team called the Saltdogs. It is composed, for the most part, of railroaders. We just finished a game against a team of mostly trolley workers and, believe it or not, a midget, called the Southies.

The game is played a little different here than in Alder Grove. The pitching line is 60 feet, 6 inches from the plate, instead of 48. Someone told me that it was partly because of Cy Young, who has been striking out too many batters out East at the closer-in distance. This caused me some problems, though it does help the hitters.

The other major difference is the crowd. Harlan, I have never seen so many ill-tempered sons of bitches as the baseball fans in Lincoln. It's bad enough for the players, but it is absolute hell on the umpire. From the moment that man stepped onto the field, the crowd began to throw tin cans, bottles, and even food in his direction. Uncle Zeke says that the man is a Lincoln town policeman named Malone, and he is very tough. He must be, to stand the abuse that was hurled at him (although being a tough local cop may have caused part of the problem, who knows?). The worst are a group calling themselves the Seventh Street Baseball Society. They are a bunch of drunks with megaphones that sit behind a large banner in the top row of the bleachers, so they can hurl hidden missiles over the chicken wire behind home plate at whomever on the field that they despise at the moment. Thanks to them, my vocabulary has expanded quite a bit, though I am not sure where I will ever be able to make use of it.

Our team got first at bat, but I have to admit that we made a poor showing in the first innings. The Southies' pitching was not especially good, but most of our Saltdogs were still pretty hampered by the previous night's festivities. Across the field, I could see that two pretty gals, Maggie and Eugenia, were delivering pitchers of beer to the opposition. That didn't hurt our chances, I guess, but the way things were going, we would need a lot more help than that.

I managed to get a single in the second inning and a double in the fourth, and we were behind 8 to 3. I came in at the top of the fifth. I had never pitched from 60 feet, so I was not very sure of myself. My warmup showed that my fastball was pretty much petered out at the longer distance, so I decided to concentrate on my knuckleball. It worked pretty well, too, with a few curves thrown in to change things up. The beer must have been working on the opposition, because I struck out the side in the fifth and sixth innings. However, I had trouble in the seventh. We had caught up, nine-to-nine, but that damned midget got up to bat and I walked him.

After the seventh, both teams took a fifteen minute break, and I visited a young lady named Anna, who was selling Bierocks at a wagon behind the bleachers. They call them Runzas in Lincoln, and they are exceptional. At her wagon, two of the Seventh Streeters came by and made a few suggestive remarks. I took one of them by the collar and the other one pushed a table over, so I gave him one in the chops. I thought it was going to be a real ruckus until Big Swede, another of Uncle Zeke's friends, came by and drug both Seventh Streeters behind the outhouses. I did not see them again.

I was pretty tuckered, even after the stretch. However, the other team was stuck with a tired pitcher, too, and I smacked a homer in the eighth, driving in two runs. Their pitcher tried the hidden ball trick, but our guys were wise to that, so they hid a spare ball in the tall grass of the outfield and threw it in when one got past the infield. The Seventh Streeters alerted the umpire to that one, though, and we were still ahead eleven to ten at the bottom of the ninth.

I was beat, Harlan. We got two out, but the Southies loaded the bases with three little dinger hits. Then they put in the midget, and I was really ready to throw in the towel. But Coach Crawford came out and advised

42

me to concentrate on hitting the strike zone this time, no matter how slowly I pitched. I looked over at Uncle Zeke, who winked at me, and pointed at a girl in the stands. It was Maggie, and she was smiling at the midget, and he was looking right back at her (I don't blame him). I pitched to him, and damned if he didn't take a swing! The ball dribbled out to me at the mound, I tossed it back to home, and we won the game, 11 to 10.

The Southies' manager was so pissed off at the midget for hitting the ball that he picked him up and tried to throw him out into the grandstand, where the Seventh Streeters would have eaten him, I suppose. But Maggie ran in and stopped him, patted the midget on the back and walked him to the beerstands behind the bleachers.

After the game, I met Mr. Fielding, the stationmaster for the FE&MV, who sponsors the Saltdogs. Uncle Zeke explained how I took his brother-in-law's place after he "became indisposed" (passed out drunk), but Mr. Fielding didn't seem at all concerned about it—in fact, he seemed pretty pleased to have beaten the trolley workers.

Getting close to supper, so I'd better close. Still gotta write Mom.

Bud

P.S. Martha or Rebecca?

Saturday, August 4th

Dear Mother,

I arrived without any trouble in Lincoln last night. Uncle Zeke has had me very busy working for him already. Eating tonight with Aunt Emelia, who sends her love. I hope to send more later. Don't worry.

Please give my best to Gramps and Snookie.

Your son, Bud

Saturday, August 4, 1894
6:30 pm

Aunt Emelia's kitchen still smelled of freshly baked pie, and it was all that Bud and Zeke could do to avoid grabbing a knife off the shelf and cutting out a slice for themselves. "It's for Sunday," was all Emmy would say, so Bud and Zeke settled for half a cold chicken and buttermilk from the icebox.

Out of curiosity, Bud looked around and asked, "Where is everybody? I was under the impression that there were a load of cousins around?"

Ginny piped back, "Saturday is 'Meeting Night' in Lincoln. Father, Jeffrey and James are in the Knights of Pythias, Joseph and Johnny are Oddfellows, and all the wives are in the sister organizations."

"And your sisters?" queried Bud, between bites as he cleaned off a thigh.

"Julia is working the switchboard tonight, and Jill is *courting.*" Her voice lowered to a conspiratorial whisper. "Father doesn't approve—he is a prison guard, and a Presbyterian, and Father says nothing good can come from either of those avenues."

Wonder how Uncle Rufus feels about Methodists? thought Bud uneasily.

Bud was startled out of his reverie by the sound of a tinny, stuttering bell—three long rings and a short ring—that appeared to be coming from the kitchen. After a moment, it began to repeat itself, but was interrupted by the sound of Aunt Emelia's voice, which loudly proclaimed, "Pack residence." Pause.

"Yes, he is here—would you like to speak with him?" Longer pause. "Very well...yes, hold on a moment, and I'll pass along your request." The hallway echoed with the tap of Emmy's approaching high-button shoes on the wooden floor.

"Mr. Sanders is calling. He was wondering if you would mind dropping by the Farmer's Cooperative Association meeting this evening?"

"Fine, fine. Tell him I'll be right along." Emelia hurried back into the kitchen, and could be heard passing the information back along. Just before she finished, she could be heard saying, "You can hang up now, too, Mary."

Bud looked at Ginny in astonishment. "You have a *telephone* in your house?"

Ginny nodded enthusiastically. "Yes, but it's a party line, so twelve of us in the neighborhood have to share it. We're only supposed to pick up when we hear our own ring. Ours is three longs and a short."

Zeke grinned. "Mary Hogan still listening in, is she?"

"Yes," Ginny spat disgustedly. "Every call, no matter whose it really is."

"Well, we all have to get our entertainment somewhere," Zeke offered. Pushing his chair back and rising, he turned his head to the kitchen and chirped, "Much obliged for the meal, Em...Bud, we have a little errand to run at the Farmer's Cooperative meeting."

Emelia came to the door, and for a moment stood in the door way, wiping her hands on her dishtowel. "Ezekiel...a word in the kitchen, if you don't mind...?"

As Zeke made his way into the kitchen, he heard low, but insistent tones emanate from Aunt Emmy, punctuated occasionally by a series of grunts from Zeke. It concluded with an "All right...all right..." from Zeke, who then suddenly appeared in the doorway, slung an old set of saddlebags over his shoulder, and said, "Make it move, Bud."

"Is everything all right...?"

"Everything is fine. We have been given our marching orders, though—and they do not include any more than one beer for you tonight, Mister 'Family Dinner is Tomorrow, so Have Him Home Early.' "

Guess that establishes the pecking order, thought Bud...then paused, letting the statement sink in.

"So, I'm to stay here tonight..?"

"For the foreseeable future, Bud," said Emelia, striding back into the dining room with a determined smile. "You can bunk upstairs with Johnny." She paused, embraced Bud, and kissed him on the forehead. "It's wonderful having you here...now, get along, boys, and mind what I said, Ezekiel."

An evening breeze had finally managed to cool the air when Zeke and Bud walked out the back door and cut through the alley (butted on both sides with family horse stables), swinging west. Bud was still at a walk, but was having a hard time staying in stride with Zeke—at 6'1", his uncle's

45

legs were several inches longer. Bud expected his would catch up, eventually, though...his legs had begun to start slipping out from the ends of his trousers again, as they had managed to do every summer. The drought may have stunted the corn, but it hadn't stopped the family growth spurt that came as regularly as the long summer days to the Gardner boys, all the way into their early 20's.

As they strode toward the railyards, Bud glanced over at one of the concrete obelisks that were parked crookedly on the street corners in order to get his bearings—did a double take—and pointed at the nearest route marker. "Have I missed something, Zeke? We were on J Street, we came over one block..."

"...and now we're on H Street. No, you're not seeing things, Bud," Zeke remarked. "It goes right from J Street to H Street. There isn't any I Street."

"How come?"

"There are a couple of theories on that. One is that Lincoln was built so quickly back in '67 that it was just plain left out by accident. Another is that the capital "I" and the capital "H" look too similar on a city map, and people get confused if the map is turned sideways. That speculation seems to be most popular among the folks who don't read, or know the order of the alphabet."

Bud grinned. "Championed, no doubt, by the Seventh Street Baseball Society. Any other theories?"

"Well, the surveyor *was* a notorious drunkard. But I try and never hold that against a man."

"I never could understand why they put the state capital here, in the first place."

"Most reasonable explanation in the world, Bud—politics. The brand-spanking-new state legislature back then was composed pretty much the same way as it is today—about a third of the legislature coming from the fifty square miles around Omaha, and the rest of it from the other seventy-seven-odd thousand square miles of the state. Omaha argued for the state capital—since the territorial capital was there already—but the rest of the state didn't want to put all that power and money in one place. None of the rest of the state had a claim that anybody would buy, either, though. Leave it to an Irishman to solve the problem."

"An Irishman...?"

"W.T. Donovan, an Irish steamship captain from out east. Seems in the summer of '67 the legislature had narrowed down the potential capital sites to someplace south of the Platte River, just squeezing out the "North Platters" who favored Omaha. So they sent a set of four commissioners to the counties around here to scout up a building site. It was hot then…damned hot, just like today…and after spending a very dry week or so poking around the various counties, they accepted a late afternoon invitation to the Captain's home here in what was then the little village of Lancaster. The way I heard it, "cooling refreshments" were made liberally available to the commissioners—consisting of a case of Irish whiskey brought up from the only icehouse to be found in the county. Little Lancaster started looking better and better to them as the evening wore on. 'Course, the commissioners later claimed that the deciding factor was the potential for developing the salt basin to the northeast of here—our own 'Saltdogs' were named for the pioneering scalawags that turned up here for the free salt. Donovan read the crux of it, though—folks don't generally have any idea about what they want—but they know damned well what they **don't** want. Nobody wanted to vote for an already-established community—somebody else's winning snubbed everybody else. Donovan shut them all up in his attic, patriotically offered to switch the name to Lincoln after our dear late president, and sealed the deal."

Bud chuckled. "Besides, how can you disagree with whiskey on ice in the middle of a heat wave?"

Zeke nodded. "Come to think of it, Washington, D.C. was born the same way—they picked a where-the-hell-am-I spot, named it after a president, and spoiled the hopes of all the big contenders. In Lincoln's case it was a salt creek instead of a salt marsh, but the idea was pretty much the same—but a spiteful consensus is better than none, I reckon. Having seen them both, I allow as I'd have to pick Lincoln—it has fewer skeeters, anyway."

Crossing 5th Street, the pair turned north. Bud admired how the rays of the setting sun lit up the large white grain elevator that was standing next to the tracks ahead of them. As they approached it, they observed several black men stirring in the adjoining lumber yard. Each was ornamented in fine, but eclectic haberdashery, with gold chains hanging from their vests, brushed derby hats, and scarlet and yellow neckties. Turning, the tallest man in the assemblage suddenly started when he noticed Zeke and Bud's approach—but then, as in recognition, immediately relaxed. He tipped his hat to Ezekiel, who raised his hand in return, but kept moving down the street.

"What are those niggers up to, Uncle Zeke?" Bud asked absently. After a moment, he came to the sudden realization that he was walking alone. Turning, he observed that his uncle had stopped a few steps back, standing with his hands in his pockets, looking at the ground, and kicking the dirt in little circles. With a mingled sense of curiosity and sudden unease, Bud turned back and moved nearer his uncle, who was still staring at the ground.

"What's wrong...?"

Looking up and sideways at Bud, Zeke hesitated, then replied, "Just how many black men have you met, Bud?"

Bud didn't need to hesitate...the answer was easy. "One, Uncle Zeke...last night at the Barrelhouse...Amos kept callin' him the Professor."

"Uh, huh," Zeke replied. "You probably aren't aware of this, but they generally don't like being called that. In fact, I've got a few customers— and friends, including Amos—that would take offense in hearing you use the word...so you might as well get over it. The term is 'Negroes', if you have to generalize...but you'll find that people's own names work as well as anything else." Smiling tightly, Zeke started walking again.

Bud shuffled uneasily, then got into stride with Zeke. "So, what are those...fellows...up to?"

Evasively, Zeke replied, "If we have some time after the meeting, I'll introduce you to them. They're certain to be around until late in the evening."

They turned again west onto K Street and crossed two sets of north-south tracks, hesitated as a big 4-4-2 engine and coal tender steamed south directly in front to them, then crossed the last two sets of tracks and continued west. After a few minutes, the houses thinned out, the brick streets turned to whiterock, and they came upon an array of horses and wagons crowded around a solitary white frame house and barn. As they approached it, Bud could hear that muffled shouts were emerging from the open barn door. Quietly standing at the door with Ezekiel, Bud saw that the barn held 30 or 40 men that were seated in wooden folding chairs, facing toward the far wall where a large man was standing behind a set of wooden horseshoe cases that acted as a makeshift podium. The seated men were wearing garments that varied from overalls to Sunday suits, but all wore white shirts and neckties, nonetheless.

The speaker at the front was a plump man of medium height in a rumpled gray suit, with green elastic suspenders that, between their normal heavy belly load and the man's frantic gestures, appeared to be getting a serious workout. His glasses and gray goatee gave his round face a rather bookish expression, but his voice and mannerisms were anything but that of an academic.

"Now settle down!" the man cried, and picking up a ball peen hammer, rapped it on a nearby anvil to punctuate his remarks. "Fred, light some lanterns—thought you boys could make some kind of decision before dark, but guess I was wrong." Flipping his hammer end-for-end in midair, he pointed the handle with authority at a tall man in the front row, and added, "Finish what you were saying, Jorgenson."

A thin, balding man rose, whose overalls, though worn in the seat, still looked to carry a fine crease. His voice bore a heavy Nordic inflection...*probably Danish, thought Bud*...and his hands wrung his weather-beaten fedora as he spoke. "It's time to sell the damn corn! Fifty two and a half cents a bushel...we've never seen it so high, by God! Enough pissing around—let's make the deal and pay off Masterson!" Shouts of "Yes!", but many shouts of "No!" went up from the audience, and the chairs creaked and dust from the barn floor rose along with the small audience of farmers.

The Dane went on, gesturing to a man seated with a small boy that was absently rolling a rubber ball back and forth between his hands, just under the haymow off to the left side of the crowd. "What Harrison there went trew yesterday is yust a beginning you know. We need to tink about our families, too. And we need the sheriff to keep dat damn LeBlanc in the jailhouse!" More shouts of "Yes!" rose from the listeners, and the hammer rang out on the anvil again. In the light of the lanterns, the man behind the podium finally recognized Ezekiel at the back of the crowd. Seeing the hammer handle motion him forward, Ezekiel reluctantly moved through the crowd. As he neared the front, the crowd stirred, and dispersed shouts of "Gardner!" were mixed with a growing murmur that quieted as the speaker raised his hands.

"We all know Ezekiel Gardner here—and what he did for Harrison and his boy yesterday afternoon." More murmurs, mostly of assent this time. Holding out the hammer, the speaker added, "Ezekiel, you have the floor."

"Thanks, Sanders," Ezekiel replied. "Your floor looks to be in pretty good shape, though, so you can keep the hammer for now." Their laughter evidently lifted considerable pressure from the assembly, and Bud moved a little closer to the front, finally sitting cross-legged in an open space on the barn floor next to Harrison and his little boy. The boy's wide spaced eyes and innocent expression indicated to Bud that the boy was probably retarded. Harrison at first eyed Bud somewhat suspiciously, but as Bud reached out to return the lost ball from where it was stuck under a nearby chair, the boy's grin seemed to disarm his...grandfather? *Probably*, Bud thought. Their attention turned back to Ezekiel, who was half sitting, half leaning on the anvil with his arms crossed.

Ezekiel said, "LeBlanc will come up for a hearing on Monday. With McGee's connections, it's a good guess that LeBlanc will probably make bail." Murmurs arose, but Zeke quieted them. "Things are rapidly coming to a head, folks. The corn has never been higher, and it seems to keep going up a little every week, so I can see why many of you would like to hold on a little longer. On the other hand," he went on, "there are a lot of you that don't feel very comfortable staying on Masterson's credit."

"That's right," one of the older men stood and shouted from the back. "How do we know that Masterson will keep his word, and pay us the Chicago prices?"

"Minus 10 percent, Schimmerman!" Another voice chimed in with the German.

"C'mon, we've plowed this ground before, Otto," Zeke replied. "The reasons why Masterson should keep his word? One," he said, holding up a single finger. "—you're using his goods instead of somebody else's. In the long run—that's good for him. Two—" A second finger. "According to your contract, he's making a percent a month on all debts, while he carries you. As long as his own suppliers and bankers don't start shoving him around, he's good as gold. Sorry—for all you Pops out there—make that good as *silver*." Some laughter, as the overwhelmingly Populist crowd— "Pops" for short—elbowed each other, and a few mock "Free Silver!" cries went up from the audience.

Zeke went on, holding up a third finger. "Three? You've got a signed contract with Masterson locked up tight."

"Where are you keeping it, Zeke?" someone shouted from the back of the room.

"Under my pillow, where I keep my ol' bear traps," Zeke joked. Bud could see that the crowd was starting to relax. His uncle's informal, easy way of speaking had a way of reaching an audience that many a politician would envy.

"I know all about that," Otto went on, "but I still wanna know--just how did you get Masterson to agree to all this, Zeke? Corn never went for more than half the Chicago price around here when LeBlanc was shilling for the corn chandlers. Why wouldn't Masterson want more?"

"Look Otto, it's no secret—times are tough for everybody. When the market crashed last fall, everyone was scrambling to find a way to get by. So is Masterson. He knew corn would have to come up in the Spring— nobody guessed it would come up this **much**. So, I just took him over to the Barrelhouse and we talked it over."

"That Maggie girl of yours can be mighty persuasive, I hear!" Some laughter, followed by some fairly intense razzing of the questioner, with "How would YOU know?" being the most commonly parroted jibe.

Otto Schimmerman crossed his arms. "McGee doesn't like it."

"Never has. We knew that going in."

"So what are you going to do?" Otto asked.

Zeke replied, "That's up to you. If you think it's time to sell, I'll close the deal with Masterson, and start lining up the freighters. If not, go ahead and hold on a while longer, and make a little more. But if you want my advice, don't wait too long—things are shifting around, and McGee has already figured out that he needs more help if he's going to play bully-boy. If he gets it…" Zeke's voice trailed off, leaving a slight chill in the room.

"I'm done, Sanders. Where's your hammer?" Zeke said, as he strode away from the podium. He looked over at Bud and jerked his head toward the door. Bud gave the Harrison boy a last pat on the head, sprang up, and the Gardners headed off into the summer twilight.

* * * * *

The two men sat on the unfinished foundation stones, silently smoking tailor-made cigarettes. Two horses were tethered nearby, among the piles of brick and lumber. Unlike University Hall, the new library had been years in the planning, and many months in construction. Unfortunately, the Legislature had delayed funding so many times that the foundation was nearly all that was presently complete. The work crews were scheduled to start again on Monday, in theory. Until then, the library basement, open to the stars, was a fine place to smoke…and wait.

Presently, the larger of the two men took a last drag, threw away the butt, and walked to his horse. He lifted a rifle from its leather scabbard and inspected it.

51

"What time is it, Franks?" the smaller man asked, and pulled a short-barreled Colt from his belt, twirling it absent-mindedly.

Pulling a silver pocketwatch from his rumpled checkered vest, Franks remarked, "Meeting oughta be getting out any time now. Better get set up, Billy."

"Think he'll be coming the way you expect?" the younger man asked, giving his pistol a final spin and slamming it expertly into his holster.

"He generally does." Franks gently hefted the rifle under his arm. "Ready?"

"Yessir," Billy answered, carefully adjusting his derby. "Let's show that bastard who's really wearing the baggy pants."

Saturday, August 4, 1894
9:45 pm

Bud hiked along with his uncle the short distance back into Lincoln, thinking about the meeting. All the local grain elevators were either owned or controlled by the railroads. You either paid their price at the railhead, or, if you arranged for a higher price elsewhere, you paid a steep price for hauling it by rail to your buyer out east.

"Uncle Zeke, does LeBlanc own the grain elevators?" Bud asked.

"No, he just owns a freighting company, Rufus' competition. McGee is the grain chandler—owns or controls all the elevators in the city, and most for miles around. LeBlanc had an 'arrangement' with him by which the price for corn included his hauling the grain. And of course, if he hauled it, he was there for the weighing, and what if the scales, or the moisture tests were a little…tilted…towards the corn chandlers? Why, was that MY thumb on the scale? How could THAT have happened?" Zeke laughed. "Neither of them are too happy about my spoiling their schemes."

As they recrossed the tracks, the sounds of the trainyard gave way to voices, rising in merriment. Looking quizzically at Zeke, Bud was about to speak when his uncle put a finger to his lips and gestured for him to follow. The voices were rising from a set of railroad ties, six feet wide and nearly eight feet high, and a flicker of light was vaguely visible from a crack between two of the ties. As they neared it, a man dressed in splendid attire suddenly stepped out from a pile of two-by-fours in front of them. Bud recognized him as one of the Negroes that was standing earlier in the same lumber yard, and—whispering a quick word to Zeke—the man let them pass.

Climbing the ties, the pair reached the top and gazed down. In the open space below, four men were kneeling down and throwing dice into the corner of the crowded space by the light of a kerosene lantern. Silver nickels and dimes littered the interior space, and with every one or two throws, money changed positions in front of the characters. The man that was throwing the dice was dressed in a dirty blue suit, and his small pile of nickels appeared to be shrinking with every throw.

"Keep that up, Davis, and you'll have to go back to stealing chickens," joked a dark man with a brown tweed suit.

"'Tisn't nothing to me, Jack Brown," replied Davis, who scooped up the dice and made another pass. "My luck is gwon change. I'm gwon find a job with the railroad." Throwing the dice again, Davis squinted, then slumped.

"Boxcars," chuckled Brown, looking gleefully at the pair of sixes. "And I reckon that's as close as yer going to get to a railroad any time soon, Davis." Chuckling, he picked up Davis' remaining nickel. "New shooter."

Zeke and Bud dropped down, dusted the splinters from their trousers, and silently waved to the lookout as they crossed the lumberyard toward the Barrelhouse.

"So, what do think about the local entertainment, Bud?" Zeke asked, as they swung over to 9th Street and headed back north toward the center of town.

"Seems to be a pretty strange place to gamble," replied Bud. "Do they meet there every night?"

"It varies. You can usually find them here on Saturday nights, near the dark of the moon. Or if somebody with real money wants to play a little Chuck-a-Luck. They call themselves the Night Owls, or the Hoo Hoo Club," his uncle replied.

Bud took off his ballcap, and scratched his head. "Hoo Hoo Club? I've heard that someplace before…"

"Really?" his uncle asked, absently. "Here in Lincoln?"

"Yeah," Bud replied, then recalled the source. "I was—er—sitting behind the bleachers before the game—in the, uh, necessary, and I overheard two fellows talking about it. One was a nig—Negro, and was planning to meet somebody else there tonight."

"When I was a deputy sheriff, I collected some of my best information—while sitting," chuckled Zeke. "Whoever it was had better be careful—the folks that run that show would rather keep it away from prying eyes. Did you happen to see who it was?"

"I got a quick look at the coat belonging to the n-Negro, through a crack—it was kind of like the shooter's."

"Coulda been George Davis," replied Zeke. "He does love to talk."

"He was inviting someone to come to the club tonight. I didn't see him, but he smoked a fine cigar."

"Could use one myself," Zeke replied. Their path led through a block of warehouses that lined the street next to the trainyards. Bud remembered getting turned around in this section of town before he found Zeke's place...*last night? Hard to believe it's only been 24 hours*, thought Bud. *Seems like forever...*

* * * * *

From their cover behind a pile of bricks, Franks nudged Billy and pointed, "There he is—meeting musta gone a little long."

"Hurry up," whispered Billy, unholstering his Colt. "While they're in the light."

"Good a time as any," muttered Franks to himself, drawing a bead on the larger of the two figures.

* * * * *

As the Gardners set about crossing into the darkness, the whistle of the departing engine began its sudden, shrill scream and built quickly to a crescendo as the passenger train gathered speed for its journey north through the trainyards on their left. Bud felt a strong urge to crawl into his hat. Distracted, he tripped against the curbstone on the far side of the street. Zeke, kneeling to catch him, felt the crack of a bullet whiz past his ear, and the sudden crumbling of brickdust fall on his hat and neck. Grabbing Bud by the nape of the neck, Zeke hauled his nephew around the corner of the nearest building, then winced as his bum knee went out from under him. Zeke ignored the fire in his knee and reached into his boot, pulling out a short knife. Motioning Bud to be still, he peered around the corner of the alley.

* * * * *

"Damn whistle," grunted Franks.

"He's mine!" shouted Billy, barely audible over the sound of the whistle, and began to climb clumsily over Franks and the bricks. A massive jerk at his beltline stopped him cold, and pulled him back.

"N-n-n-ope!" said Franks. "'Nuther time—they're ready, and we ain't goin' into the light to git 'em." Franks added, "Come on—we delivered the message we were told to." And with that, the pair darted back to their horses and a quick escape.

* * * * *

The whistle of the departing train and the clattering of horses' hooves had died into the distance, and the street was completely silent. Sticking his neck out around the corner, Zeke looked slowly up at the pockmarked brick facade where the shot had chipped bricks. Feeling the top of his head, he shakily pulled away a few bloody gray hairs, whistled, and shook his head.

"Not bad shootin'," Zeke said, now grinning at Bud. "Good thing you're so clumsy, nephew...looks like your stumblin' might have saved me the cost of a haircut—though I'm not sure...it could have just been a warning shot." Reaching down, he massaged his sore knee and attempted to rise. Looking up at Bud's ashen face, Zeke asked, "You O.K.?"

"I...I guess so," Bud nodded stonily. He noted his uncle's pain but was lost in his own thoughts. He tried to catch his breath, but it was coming in gulps, and his thoughts were racing. *What the...who the hell was shooting at them? What the **hell** am I doing here? What the hell...?*

"...am I doing here...?" he repeated softly. "What the hell am I *doing* here, Zeke?" His shoulders and arms were shaking, too, now. Uncontrolled, hot tears were forming in his eyes, and he could feel his control starting to break. He didn't care. Trembling, he swiped his uniform arm across his eyes and his voice, though trembling, too, started to grow as he spoke. "Look, what is this all about, Zeke? Baseball games, and... farmer's meetings, and...and now **shooting?** What kind of horseshit deals are you mixed up in?" He could feel his anger growing now. "What the hell have I gotten into here? You **tell** me, Zeke! Who is shooting at us, for cryin' out loud?"

"Easy, son," Zeke said. "Give a man a hand up." Once standing, he steadied himself on Bud's shoulder with a shaking hand, and turned to limp down darkened P Street, away from the site of the attack. After a few steps, Zeke's arm dropped from his nephew's shoulder, and he clapped his hands together. Rubbing them together, he began to speak in a low, casual tone as he limped down the darkened alley, his stunned nephew in tow.

"This knee hasn't been the same since the war. I remember the first time I was shot at. July of '61, I was a greenhorn private in Company D of the First Minnesota, and after nine weeks of training at Fort Snelling, we felt like we could whip the Johnnies blindfolded.

"They put us all on a long train ride to join the Army of the Potomac in camp around Centerville, Virginia. We heard a pretty respectable ruckus down on Blackburn's Ford, and we found out that threescore boys or so had lost it there, and the rest came back all bloodied up. When our

56

regiment reached the town, it was business as usual—complete confusion, with three other brigades all tied up at the crossroads. I had started thinking that this might not be as easy as the officers were telling us, but our new brigade commander came around and told us 'never to worry, we had the goods on the Rebs, and they would never know what hit them.'

"We marched along the banks of Bull Run for a while, stopping, and starting, all bunched up and then all strung out. Finally, we crossed Bull Run, headed south, at a little church house at Sudley Springs. There, the whole regiment was ordered to drop our backpacks, and we piled them in a huge heap just beside the road. We were told we could come back for them later when we had whipped the rebellion. We kept our cartridge boxes, though, and we filled our canteens. The water was muddy, but cool…I was already so hot in my wool soldier suit that I was covered in sweat outside, but all dried out inside. About the time I got the stopper on my canteen, we heard the sound of shots coming from the hill in front of us.

"You found out today what I found out then—shots *crack* the air when they go right past your head. First time it happened, I thought I'd been hit in the ear. You can bet I looked right hard at the woods behind me, there—but Sergeant Owens was eying me pretty close, so I picked up my canteen and my rifle, and fell in with the rest of the company. About four hundred yards on, we stopped behind a rail fence and started taking aim at a bunch of Johnnies that were taking potshots at us, popping in and out from behind some haystacks. The fence was only two rails, but it felt good to stand behind something. I know I hit one Reb then, maybe two, but I was too busy loading and firing to think about it.

"The haystack caught on fire, and the Johnnies ran back up the hill. When we got to the top of it, we could see that they were running down the far side and up to the top of the next one, a big hill to the south. It was full of smoke, and their cannons were opening up on us as soon as we crested the hill. If anybody had turned around, I would have been right with him. But there was Owens behind me, smiling this time. 'Come on,' he says, 'long as they're runnin', we're chasin.' He pointed at some of the men in other units, and laughed at the way they were squatting and diving and making all manner of trying to dodge the shells around us. Him cackling there kinda steadied the rest of us, I reckon.

"We moved down the hill, and about half way down Sergeant Owens detailed J.T. and me to help a battery haul a 12-pounder up the big hill. By the time we got back to D Company, things had got pretty hot up there. The bullets were cracking like popcorn all around us, and the Johnnies were howlin' to beat the band. We wrangled hard over that field for about an hour, first us scooting forward, then getting thrown back again. 'Bout that time, Sergeant Owens caught a bullet in the leg, and Lieutenant Perkins ordered a couple of us to haul him back down the hill to a brick house along the road that was being used as a hospital. What I saw there made me feel sick to my stomach, and I just about fainted. Surgeons were dressing wounds, and there was a pile of legs and arms in one of the corners. When Sergeant Owens saw that, even he went pretty white. They gave him some water, and I even got two or three swallows, which settled my stomach and made me feel a little better.

"The next thing I knew, there was a howling outside the house. I looked out the window, and I could see that the retreat had commenced. The wounded were being pulled up and yanked along, so I grabbed up Owens. We all commenced to move along at a break-neck gait—horses, wagons, litters, everything was abandoned. Of all the helter-skelter, pell-mell, devil-take-the-hindmost gang I ever saw, that crazy crowd beat them all. Some of them stopped and helped take hold of the wounded, but some would pass by, as much as to say, "They can have you, but by God they won't catch me!" I don't believe there was ever a greater stampede of troops than there was between that house and the bridge back to Centerville. The papers the next day called it the 'Great Skedaddle.' Like you, I wondered what the hell I'd gotten myself into."

Bud and Zeke walked along in silence for a time. As his uncle had told his tale, Bud felt small, and as if his own adventure over the last day and a half were pretty puny by comparison.

"Sorry about that, back there, Zeke…guess I came a little unwound, too."

Zeke smirked, "You've had a long day, Bud, but you've handled yourself pretty well. I know things seem pretty strange to you right now, but just keep playing along…you're doin' fine. Now," he added, pointing across the street, "how about that beer your aunt allowed you?" There, right across the street, was the Barrelhouse…the door was hanging open, the gas lamps were blazing from within, and the sounds of people laughing and shouting rose with the clinky-clank of the Professor's rag music.

"You bet," said Bud.

8

Sunday, August 5, 1894
1:10 pm

Bud was trying to digest an enormous Sunday dinner and keep up with Zeke's long strides. He had five whole dollars jingling in his pocket, his first week's pay from Zeke. He wished his brothers Larry and Roger were here, instead of living in a tenement in Omaha, lined up for scab wages at the packing plants where the Bohemians were striking, and would just as soon shoot them as look at them. Aunt Emelia would fuss over them like a mother hen, too.

Bud smiled at the exuberance of the Pack family. Sundays at his own family's house had always started solemn, and stayed that way through dinner, supper, and evening prayers, with scarcely a word being spoken except to direct chores and correct the wayward. Although an eerie, fasting silence had been kept by all in the Pack house until Mass was over that morning, the chatter had begun directly after the last hymn, and gone on non-stop since then. St. Theresa's, the large cathedral on 13th and M Street had gathered a solemn multitude that practiced strange rituals—finger dipping, kneeling, and Latin hymns, with incense floating over the congregation's penitent heads—then had **really** shocked Bud by spilling hundreds of laughing, gay families into the broad street. Bud had managed to kneel, sit, and stand when shown, and to stay firmly in his seat when the Pack family went forward to communion. *You-ker-ist? Real wine, every Sunday? Father would probably have a fit if he found out*—which started Bud smiling all over again.

Bud had made another startling discovery at the cathedral—a young lady with jet black hair and flashing blue eyes, seated next to two large men in their early twenties that must have been brothers, walking next to her as if they were guarding the princess of Romania. Her dress was white this time, not blue checkered, and her long fingered, clever hands were folded in prayer instead of hovering over meat sandwiches. But after the service, the smirking face he saw half-turned in his direction was clearly the same as the one that had demanded Bud's pants, and given him a much-needed stitch. Bud had swallowed hard at seeing her, but the swirling crowd had parted them after the service, and...*well, she was Catholic, after all. No point in thinking too much about it.*

But he did.

Zeke had been absent from both Sunday services and the dinner table. When Bud had last seen his uncle the night before, Zeke had said that he was waiting around to meet an old friend, and had scooted Bud off home with an escort from his cousin, Johnny. Despite the fact that Johnny snored like a bear in a boxcar, Bud considered him easy company, and found that many of his perceptions about the Pack family were probably being slanted from Johnny's cockeyed, satirical point of view. *Uncle Zeke missed out on a terrific meal,* Bud thought, more than fulfilling the promise of all those smells that he recalled from yesterday's preparations. Bud smiled at the memory of Johnny, who had not stopped stuffing his face with pork chops, biscuits, potatoes, fresh green beans, corn on the cob, cherry pie, and Vinnie's sugared almonds long enough to say "boo."

During dinner, Bud had nearly given up keeping names and faces straight – there was Jeffrey Pack, the oldest, who ran the day-to-day operations of his father's freighting business and was married to Pamela. James was the second son and unmarried. The third son, Joseph, was the family accountant and married to Annette. The oldest daughter Judith was married to Leonard, a jobber that traveled up and down the Platte River Valley, selling hardware. Julia and Jill were unmarried. Julia had joined in the rambunctious conversation on silver, Populism, and William Jennings Bryan, while Jill had sat there silently, playing with her food through the entire meal. When Bud had asked Johnny about her, his cousin simply replied, "Boy troubles." As Daphne was just turning 15, Bud nodded in understanding. There had been plenty of trials, tears and torment over the last six months as Daphne broke in her new boyfriend. Bud smiled. *Poor guy.*

Ginny had been seated next to her mother, clearly so Aunt Emelia could poke, correct, or wrestle her to the ground as necessary. It was evidently a full time job, and Ginny's napkin was a study in how gravity had a stronger attraction for linen propped on the knee of a fourteen-year-old than on any other substance.

Uncle Rufus was a blowtorch of a man—large framed, unreserved, and gregarious. Prior to Zeke's arrival, Rufus had quizzed Bud about what he was doing for Zeke, warning him, "That Zeke...he always has an angle. Don't get me wrong, he's not crooked, exactly—but he has more angles than a house of mirrors." Aunt Emelia had not been happy about her brother pulling Bud away from "family time", but Zeke and Bud had made their escape while her temper was still smouldering.

Bud glanced over at his uncle and wondered what Zeke would ask him to do, besides come with him to Mooney's restaurant.

* * * * *

"Bobber! Get up, you old possum trapper!"

Dimly, the old man perceived the shaking, the noise, and the light—figured it was just another earthquake—and crawled deeper under his grizzly pelt. *Yellowstone...between the earthquakes, the geysers, and the forest fires, a man can't get a good night sleep...*

Amos tried again. "Bobber, your shack's on fire! Get up!"

Wasn't much of a shack, anyway...

"He doesn't look like he's gonna wake up very easy, Amos," Swede said, crouching and contracting his huge frame to avoid knocking over the kerosene lamps, axes, prybars, shovels, and other sundry track repair equipment that hung over his head and to his sides, but only succeeded in knocking over a couple of boxes of nails that were stacked precariously on a shelf behind him. "Sorry, Amos," Swede said, crouching even lower as he tried to pick up the scattered hardware. "Kinda close in here, ya?"

Amos agreed with a grunt and tried another tack. Striking a match, he lit a cigarette and leaned against the doorframe. "Well, Swede, looks like Bobber would rather sleep in today...too bad...ah can almost smell the bacon over at Mooney's. And did ya hear they just made up a fresh batch of scrapple? A big ol' pan of headcheese frying up...well, that's more for us, I guess. Let's go, Swede."

As they turned, Bobber groaned, dropped his feet into an old pair of rubber boots, pushed past the other two, and walked out the door. Swede was stupefied.

"Headcheese? What's that?" he asked, as the pair broke into a trot to catch up with Bobber.

"Recipes vary. Depends on what comes around the corner, what's left over, or what's slowest," replied Amos, striding now to stay alongside the surprisingly spry old fart, crossing tracks in his jingling four buckle boots.

"Uh...I think I'll stick with the bacon."

* * * * *

Mooney's Restaurant inhabited an unassuming white-framed storefront barely thirty feet across that stood next to the St. James Hotel directly across from the train station. Large front windows and a swinging half-door illuminated small square tables that were jammed together at odd intervals, and a long gas-fired grill running down the left-hand side where

61

meals were served nonstop to station passengers. Business was brisk, since there were few eateries open on Sunday afternoon and none so near the station.

Bobber burst through the swinging door at a brisk hobble, head lowered, and swung himself into the nearest stool in front of the long wooden counter that separated the customers from the hot grill. "Gimme a pound a headcheese," he said, jerking a thumb behind him toward the just-entering forms of Amos and Swede. "They're buying."

Jasper Mooney, a graying man with a short cigar, a week-old beard and an apron that held clues to every meal cooked over that period, looked over at Amos for approval. At Amos' nod, he shrugged his shoulders and took a canister from under the bar, scooped up a mass of the multi-hued mixture with a worn metal spatula, and plopped it onto the grill with a hisssss. Immediately, the smell of frying grease mixed with peppers, sage, and garlic hit the room. Bobber rubbed his hands together eagerly, mumbling, "Don't overcook it...yeah...is that sage?...black pepper...oh, gizzards!...and sumthin like... pork, maybe...er, not...?"

Amos shook his head and took a chair near the door (Swede took two, but was careful to emulate the same, nonchalant lean that his companion affected against the pineboard wall). As he waited for Zeke, the small, wiry man absent-mindedly scanned the room, sizing up the customers—an old habit born of necessity that he saw no particular need to let go. Amos felt that his personal philosophy combined the best elements of Franklin (the early bird gets the worm) and his old boss, Mr. Barnum (there's a sucker born every minute)—embracing both industry and limitless opportunity, considering the human race as a whole. He observed that the room was filled by-and-large with faceless, nameless male passengers absorbed in scarfing down the eggs, bacon, and ham sandwiches that Mooney provided. *All those unguarded wallets*...he mused, but did his best to place the thought out of his mind for the moment. In the corner, a young woman in a modest gray dress quietly took the patrons' money between trips to the kitchen, exchanging loads of dirty dishes for clean ones. As Amos' eyes completed his scan of the room, his eyes suddenly lit on a clean-shaven, graying man of trim physique in a brown suit with a beige half-cape slung over his shoulder. For a split second, their eyes met, and then the stranger's dark eyes moved away, appearing to nonchalantly cast about as Amos's had but a moment before.

Ah have seen this man. Where have ah seen this man before?

Deep in thought, Amos entirely missed seeing Zeke's entrance, but it was clearly registered in two other ways—

Swede shouted, "Mr. Zeke!" and promptly crashed to the floor, first one chair giving away, and then the other in its turn, and—

The man in the corner rose, smiling, and strode over to where Zeke and Bud had entered, his hand outstretched.

Zeke grasped the stranger's hand, shaking it, then smacking the man's shoulder with his free hand. "J.T.! I see you found the place—hope the indigestion wears off before the poison kicks in..."

"You always could pick a fine eating establishment, Ezekiel. Like that eatery in San Francisco next to Lucky Lil's?" Bud noticed that the man had gripped his uncle's hand strongly, and for a moment, their eyes locked as if engaged in some unspoken contest. Finally, as if by mutual decision, the pair broke their grip.

"Come to think of it, could explain the lack of domestic animals in the neighborhood," admitted Zeke. Turning to the rest of the group, he announced, "Gentlemen, let me introduce J.T. Lynch, an old...friend...of mine. Shall we all sit down and have a cup? Mooney! Bring us a pot!"

Mooney nodded and scuttled to the large brass urn in the corner, filling a tin pot with coffee, and spilling a set of battered tin cups in front of Bud, Zeke, Amos, Swede, and J.T. When invited, Bobber waved his left hand in the air and then pointed at the grill, never stopping his fork from filling his bearded face. Shaking his head, Amos waved an assent at Mooney, who dropped more headcheese on the grill. Bobber grinned with unbridled avarice.

As hands shook all around and Swede poured their coffee, Zeke went on, "J.T. and I have known each other a long, long time. We served in the First Minnesota Infantry Regiment through the war and spent some time in California afterwards.

"About three weeks ago, I got a telegram from J.T. saying that he might be passing through town this weekend...I took the liberty of asking him to stay a little longer, and he agreed." Lynch nodded quietly, and pulled a silver cigar case from inside his coat pocket, snapping it open. It wasn't a cheap cigar, Bud noticed, and he was pretty sure that the cigar case was not the only flash of silver that his eyes had caught as the stranger's jacket flashed briefly open. The man struck a match and expertly browned the end of the cigar, rolling it between his fingers as he moved his dark eyes around the group, lighting briefly on each person's face as if studying it. When his eyes met Bud's, Lynch noticed Bud was still staring at his slightly open jacket. J.T. grinned, puffed his cigar to life, then placed his cigar case back in his pocket and nonchalantly buttoned his jacket.

Zeke leaned his elbows on the table, and after a pause, went on. "We all knew that it was going to get a might dicey around here once the Grange decided to sell their corn…in fact, it already has." Dropping his voice, those around the table leaned in toward him. "Last night, Bud and I had a little…encounter…with McGee's men. Thank the Lord that Bud was around…I was ready to go screaming down the street and surrender to the first little girl I found." The table laughed nervously, and Zeke went on, explaining the happenings of the night before. Bud was relieved that his uncle left out the part where he lost his nerve, but felt a little guilty about it nevertheless.

"Do you know who it was that shot at you?" asked Swede, draining the last of his coffee, and filling up another cup. "Isn't LeBlanc still in jail?"

"LeBlanc is still in the county jail, though he probably won't be there for long. No, I'd say that his two compadres, Franks and Billy-boy, were probably behind it. And I wouldn't put it past McGee to bring in more help if he thinks he needs it."

"This morning, I rode out to Harrison's place—Bud and I left the meeting a little early, and I wanted to see what they decided. I found out that the farmers have decided to sell the grain—in two weeks, unless the price goes down by two cents before then. If it goes up by two cents, we can sell immediately."

Everyone around the table groaned. "What are dey thinking?" snapped Swede, speaking for all of them. "Are dey crazy? The price of corn has never been higher!"

"Look, the terms of the agreement call for a 2/3 majority to agree before any of the grain can be sold." Zeke countered. "Be happy that they made any decision at all. Of course, anyone can bow out of the agreement at any time—but then the bills and loans come immediately due to Masterson. So far, nobody has bowed out."

"So, allow me to summarize," J.T. offered, as he tapped his cigar ash into his coffee cup. "Our…undertaking…is to defend these farmers, their corn, and the freighters for another two weeks, against an entrenched and determined opposition, until the corn is delivered to the chandler."

"That's about the size of it," Zeke grinned. "We have one advantage, though…turns out Bud here pitches a hell of a knuckleball. We have any trouble, Bud'll just bean 'em into submission." At that, the group chided

Bud without mercy, who found it hard to worry while being slugged mercilessly in his sore pitching arm.

"I did hear a bit about that game, Bud...sorry I had to miss it." Pointing his cigar at Zeke, J.T. chuckled, "I have to hand it to you, Zeke—you sure know how to pick a fight. Didn't you learn *anything* at Gettysburg?"

"Apparently not."

"This man...Masterson, you say? He's the key to the operation, isn't he?" J.T. observed. "Above everything else, he has to be protected, it seems to me."

"That's been Amos' job, here," Zeke replied. "But I understand that he's out of town at the moment?"

"Indeed," Amos replied. "Down in Fairbury, ostensibly talking with some of his wholesale suppliers—but will be coming back into Lincoln on Thursday or Friday of this week." Bud noticed that Amos had a strange, absent look on his face as he spoke to J.T.—as if he were thinking deeply, his mind elsewhere. But a WHOOP! and a sharp crash from across the room drew all of their attention toward Bobber, who appeared to be cradling something in his arms, protecting it and himself from the repeated towel whacks of the gray-dressed waitress.

"GET THAT...RAT...out of here!" The young woman reared back and appeared to be prepared to deliver another blow, when she felt a strong arm of Jasper Mooney restrain it. Skunk skittered out from under Bobber's grip. Scooping a last handful of headcheese into his grizzled maw, Bobber trailed the raccoon out the front door. Frustrated, the girl stomped her foot...just once...slowly uncorked her fists, and bent to pick up the broken dishes. As she turned, Bud saw a flash of dark hair and fair skin peeking out from under her kerchief, and suddenly recognized her.

"That's coming out of your pay, Anna," Mooney growled. "I can't afford to keep you in plates." The girl jerked her head...up and down, just once. She appeared to be close to tears, when she heard the ringing sound of a quarter dollar spinning and dancing around on the griddle...then another...and other...until four of them stopped and sat down peacefully together in the sizzling grease.

"Pardon the rodent, Mooney," Zeke drawled, his face breaking into a smile from across the room. "That ought to account for the headcheese...and the crockery." Bud's face started to beam as well, until he saw the look of fierce anger cross the face of the girl. Picking up her towel and a spatula, the girl crossed the cooking space and leaned over the sizzling grill, expertly flipping three of the quarters into her towel. She crossed the room and spat on the quarters, then threw the towel down at Zeke's feet.

"That ought to cool those off, I reckon," she growled, and Bud saw that her blue eyes were burning with hate. "Headcheese is a dime a plate...and I DON'T need charity from a high-and-mighty know-it-all like YOU, Ezekiel Gardner." Spinning on her heels, she poured a last scornful glance toward Bud, and stormed into the kitchen, her black curls streaming behind her.

"You always did have a way with the women, Ezekiel," J.T. chuckled. "Seems that the young ladies of Lincoln are as perceptive as your other paramours." Dusting his hat and carefully placing it over his long, graying hair, he held out his hand and declared, "I'm in, Zeke...at least until another job calls...sounds like fun."

Zeke looked him in the eyes, hesitated only a fraction of a second, and then shook his hand. "Thanks, J.T. Shall we meet for coffee in the morning?"

"I prefer tequila in the evening. But seeing this is Lincoln, I'll settle for beer."

"I think we can probably do better than that." Turning to Bud, he said, "I have a little job for you tomorrow, Bud. Please be so kind as to meet Mr. Seville at the passenger station...you'll be catching the 7:25 going south." Bending down, he murmured, "Go on back and give my apologies to Rufus and all, if you please...I've got some scheming to do."

* * * * *

Franks shuffled his feet, and tried to decide if it was proper to knock on the door.

"He told us to git here on the double...so don't dawdle, Franks," murmured Billy.

"Shut up, Billy. I ain't...it's just..." With a moment of hesitation, he knocked gently. Surprisingly, he heard, softly, "Open the door, gentlemen."

The door creaked slightly, opening into a darkened room, with only a blue gaslight in the background to light the upper rooms, as all the shades were closed. It dimly illuminated an ornate front sitting room, with a fine davenport and settee, crystal glasses over a small mahogany bar in the corner…and a dark shape coming through the door from the darkened …bedroom?...beyond. The bespectacled man fiddled with his sash, walked over to the bar, and started to make himself a drink, while the visitors shuffled nervously. Franks took off his hat, wiped his feet, and entered, with Billy trailing him closely. Together, they stared at their feet until the silence was broken by the little man.

"You had a busy night, as I've heard it relayed to me," the man spoke in a low rumble. "Did you really take a shot at our friend, Mr. Gardner…a mere *three blocks* from the train station? I want you to stay *away* from Mr. Gardner and his associates, for the time being." The small man absently swirled his glass.

"Yes, sir, but…"

"Emphatically. I will take care of them by other, more…talented…means."

A long silence followed, broken suddenly by the murmur of a woman's voice from the other room. "Mr. M?" it sounded, and Franks thought he could just catch a brief flash of blonde hair as it moved in the shadows of the far room. The small man turned to his guest. "Gentlemen, that will be all, I believe."

Wisely, Franks nodded curtly and, reaching blindly behind him, shoved Billy as he backed out the door.

"What the hell…?" started Billy as the door closed, but feeling a sharp jab in his ribs, finally decided to take his partner's advice.

Monday, August 6, 1894
7:29 am

The station master of the Rock Island depot at the corner of 20th and O glanced at his pocketwatch nervously, then glared again from the "knowledge box" onto the steep-roofed passenger platform that stood outside the ornate brick station that was built in the modern, "Chateauesque" style. The southbound train looked to be ready to depart from the track, and for the third time he stared bullets at its conductor outside, pacing on the platform, and tried to bore a mental image into his brain. *You're late. Get out of my station. This is an express train. It leaves at 7:25 a.m.* **Sharp,** *dammit.*

He sighed...once again, his mental powers were clearly not making any headway with Stannard. *Bullhead. What the hell is he waiting for?*

Suddenly, he heard the clatter of boots on the brick, and two figures flashed by his window. One of them was recognizable as Amos Seville, the bartender at the barrelhouse down on R Street. The younger man, all out of breath, also seemed familiar...*wait, was he that pitcher for the Saltdogs last Saturday? What's he doing with Amos...?*

"Sorry to be late, Captain," Amos Seville said, out of breath. "My young charge here was...misplaced."

"I was at the other station, sir," Bud objected. "I..."

Staring directly at Seville, Stannard jerked his thumb over his shoulder. "Get on the train, willya?" said the conductor, with only the ghost of a smile crossing his lips. "Or R Street may die of thirst...this month."

So, that's it—monthly whiskey run, thought the station master. *Nice of the conductor to hold the train for him.*

Well, actually, he allowed as he watched he two figures disappear inside the last passenger car, *it looks like they'll pretty much make it on time.*

Seeing what he expected to be his last passengers get on the train, the conductor trotted to the engine where the fireman and the engineer were waiting for him.

"Steam up, Mr. dePuis?" he queried, pronouncing it "dePew"—a moot question, as he could see the reading on the pressure gauge from the platform.

"Yes, Captain," the engineer growled. "Been up for **10 minutes now**. Ready **whenever you are**. We oughtta make good time, **once we get underway**."

"Fine, fine..." the conductor said, absently, already setting off back down the length of the train. Waving at Harry Foote, the brakeman that was standing next to the caboose, and receiving a wave in return, he cried, "All aboard!"

"Looks like Bull Stannard is cutting it pretty close today," murmured Bill Craig. The fireman was carefully spreading the coals within the firebox using a long iron rod, then, satisfied, slammed the door closed.

"That's enough of that noise, water warmer," Ike dePuis growled, again. "Sassing the Skipper is the hog driver's job." Moving to the left side of the cab, he leaned out the window and waited for the signal from the conductor, who after only a glance up and down the train, gave two short pulls in the air above his head, signaling the engineer to start the train. Smiling grimly, the engineer gave the cord for the steam whistle two short tugs and starting pulling the bell, signaling "all clear" as the train pulled out.

* * * * *

"I wasn't LATE," Bud repeated, as the train started to move. "I didn't know that there were two stations here in town." Slumping in his seat, he pouted, "I just went to the wrong one, that's all."

"Actually, Mister Gardner, there ah four passenger depots here in town, one freight terminal, and five ticket offices, not counting the city trolley lines, of course."

"I need some coffee," Bud complained, and looked around for a coffee cart.

"This is NOT a Pullman car, Mr. Gardner," Amos countered. "Hot meals, cold hors d'oeuvres, and fine cigars ah not to be found close at hand. However, as you are young, ill-prepared, and appear to have a skull remarkably full of mush, ah will endeavor to accommodate you."

Turning toward the back of the car, Amos signaled to a white man of medium build, who tipped his hat and moved gracefully forward through the rocking train to stand in the aisle next to them. Clasping Amos's hand, he remarked with a smile, "Good morning, Mr. Seville. Is it August already?"

"And a hot one, at that," Amos grinned in response. "So ah thirst must be abated somehow...do you agree?"

"Yes, Amos," he chuckled. "It must indeed."

"But seeing as how it is the *early* morning, ah wonder if you could help us track down a bit of coffee?"

"I believe we can just manage that, Amos, if the water is up," Harry responded. With a surefooted ease, Harry Foote instantly spun on his heel and moved back in the rocking car, flipped open the door, and disappeared in the noise of the space between the cars, adroitly closing the door behind him.

"So," Bud went on, as if to no one in particular, "what are we doing on this train, anyway?"

"Uh...logistics." Amos produced a cigarette and struck a Lucifer, taking a long draw and blowing it out the window. "Lincoln may seem like a happy, thriving machine," Amos continued, "but the strain of life requires a...lubricant...to avoid serious fracture of the mechanism."

"Ah...translation, please?"

"We ah on a beer run, my young friend." Noting that the few passengers in the car were yards away, Amos leaned in slightly and said, "Your uncle has a number of suppliers—mostly out of the county, since the State Department of Revenue is most observant in and around the capital, and Ezekiel prefers to stay on good terms with the Lancaster County Sheriff's Department. This particular supplier is in Fairbury. There ah others...as you will learn over the next few days."

"So...this is illegal, what we're doing?" Bud queried. *Great, now I'm a criminal.*

Amos raised his right hand, and crossed his heart with his left. "Why, every pint comes through a licensed brewery." Dropping his hand, he continued. "However, we do tend to help Fred Krug with his supplies. You might say that these supplies ah a little more...ready to distribute...than most."

"So, we deliver beer to a brewery?"

"A very efficient operation. Beer comes in the rear door...gets labeled, 'Krug,' and goes out the front door, four blocks down to the

Barrelhouse, and directly to the consumer. Horses hardly have a chance to rest. Your Uncle Rufus runs a very capable freighting operation, and doesn't seem to mind night work."

"Well, I guess times are hard," murmured Bud. *But I know what Father would say,* he finished in his head. Turning away from Amos as if to avoid the topic, Bud gazed out the window and thought he could just glimpse the gray stone towers of the state prison that bordered the edge of town on his right. Bud shivered slightly. At that moment, they were passing along a long trestle bridge that spanned a set of two train tracks, separated by a small creek.

And then the country, brown with the lack of rain, enveloped them.

"Hard?" Amos laughed. "Try growing up in Virginia aftuh the War. Ah, Harry...!" Amos exclaimed, as the passenger brakeman returned, bearing a steaming gray tin pot in one hand, and two matching cups in the other. "It looks as if you were able to find us some coffee after all."

"Sure, Amos," Harry Foote replied. "Pardon me, now, but we're braking the train soon in Rokeby, and I'm needed up top."

"You brake the cars from the top of the train?" Bud marveled, and noted through the corner of his eye that the conductor was approaching from the front, murmuring "Tickets, please," to the scattered passengers, waking those that needed it.

"Where else? We haven't installed air brakes in any of the trains on this section of the line. There are a number of larger passenger trains back East that have managed it—and all of them have either more hills, more passenger cars or more frequent stops. The rest of us will have to make do with the way things are—at least until 1903. "

"Why 1903?" Bud asked, sipping his coffee, then heaving a deep sigh.

"Congress passed a new law last year," Harry replied. "It requires all trains to have mandatory safety equipment, including air brakes. We have 10 years to do it. Our president thinks it will break the railroad."

"Tickets, please," said the conductor, and Amos produced two tickets from his vest pocket, which were duly punched. As the Captain handed them back, Bud noticed that his left hand was missing two fingers. "Better get up top, Mr. Foote, and stop jawing with the passengers." he said.

"What happened to your fingers, Captain Stannard?" Bud queried, then inwardly cajoled himself for his impertinence.

"Lost 'em back when I was a brakeman," he replied. "We couple the cars together using two cast iron pins, one for each end of a link that fits between two cars. When we couple up the cars, the link and one pin are in place at the end of one car, and the second pin is suspended above the coupling of the second car. When the brakeman gives the "slow" signal to the head end, the cars are supposed to come together gently. Sometimes we have to reach in to steady the pin—if you don't time it just right, you can get your hand caught, and lose a finger." He smiled. "I won't hire a brakeman with all ten—means that they're too green. The bigger lines are starting to install Jansky couplers—they're a lot safer, because they join the cars up from the pressure of the cars hitting each other.

"Later, gentlemen, I have a train to run." The Captain grinned a perfectly toothless smile then moved easily down the rocking car.

* * * * *

These handcuffs are a bitch to get off, thought the sheriff, as he twiddled with the lock. *God, these keys are getting **smaller**.* The man standing in front of him in the entrance hall of the Courthouse was stamping impatiently, and that wasn't helping the process any, either.

"Hold still, LeBlanc," Fred Miller said as he reached into his vest pocket and pulled out a pair of silver rimmed reading glasses. The cuffs popped into focus, then popped off LeBlanc's wrists.

"How you gonna shoot a bad guy if you can't see him?' asked LeBlanc, rubbing his wrists with a sneer.

"Don't worry, Maxwell," Miller retorted. "I shoot by sense of *smell*. I won't miss you."

"I won't miss you either. Where are my guns?"

"Ask your boss." Pausing, he said, "Do you know what happens to people who leave the county, or otherwise piss off Judge Strode by dicking around when they're out on bail?"

"Let me guess," said Maxwell LeBlanc. "He gets really, really angry?"

"Yep. And then he calls *me*," staring at the young man over his glasses. "And I pull out this here **knife**," doing so, slipping it from his right sleeve into his right hand with a rapidity that stunned the younger man, "and I cut their **balls** off." The black handled little knife, twirling slowly between the older man's right thumb and forefinger, had a blade that glinted with malice along its silver edge.

72

"Uh huh."

"Be a good boy, now, Maxey," Miller said, pointing to the door with the knife.

LeBlanc stumbled slightly, composed himself, and walked into the morning sunshine out the front door of the Lancaster County Courthouse. McGee was sitting in a black shay at the corner of J Street, his gloved hands nervously twiddling the reins. He seemed to be conspicuously not looking at LeBlanc.

"Where are my guns?" LeBlanc said, for the moment completely forgetting his little encounter with Sheriff Miller.

"Back at your freight yard," McGee stated, starting the horses with a sharp shake of the reins. "You won't need them here in town, though. Out of town, possibly."

Wonderful, LeBlanc thought, and rested a hand delicately over his crotch.

10

Monday, August 6, 1894
8:50 am

"So," Bud began, "You were born in Virginia, then?" The coffee had grown cold, and as much as Bud enjoyed cold coffee (versus none at all), it was also…gone.

Amos took a long drag on his cigarette, flicked it out the window, and turned to stare at the boy. "Tell you what," he said. "We'll hold an exchange of information. You first, then me, et cetera."

"Okay," Bud replied. "where did…"

"NO….," Amos interrupted. "**You** first." Pausing to light another cigarette, he squinted one eye and pointed it at his seatmate. "Why did your father send you to your uncle Zeke?"

Bud dropped his head and looked down at his hands. "It's not very mysterious. Our farm…is a failure—at least this year. Dad cut all his corn down and is feeding out the silage to the stock, what little is left. There isn't any money, nor any work at home. Two of my older brothers went to find work in Omaha, at the packing plants. The Bohemians are on strike."

"Ah imagine it's getting pretty rough down there—did they find jobs?"

"Roger did—Larry is still looking. Before I left, I heard that they had hired over 700 men to fill all the slots." Bud looked out the window. "At night, the strikers wait for them at the gate and follow them back to their rooms, and throw garbage at them, and…they call them scabs."

"So your folks sent you to your uncle Zeke. But ah was given to understand that he and your father didn't get along very well."

"I was thinking that it might have been Gramps that made him do it…or maybe my mother talked him into it…" Bud's voice trailed off. "So," he said, changing his tone, "You're from Virginia?"

"Ah'm from all ovuh, Bud, but, yes, ah was born in the Commonwealth," he replied. "A favored son of the South. Born during the unfortunate War of Northern Aggression and Occupation." His cold eyes locked onto Bud's. "My mother was a Leesburg whore and my father was a soldier…most likely a Yankee."

"You don't *know*?" blurted Bud, then, shocked at his own insolence, immediately stammered, "I'm…sorry…that was…I'm sorry, Amos."

Amos turned suddenly, a look of crazed delight filling his face. "It was YOU? At last! FATHER!" and threw his arms around the younger man. Bud started, then, noticing the smirk on Amos's face when he pulled away, finally gave in to a nervous chuckle. Amos simply shook his head.

"Are you SURE you graduated from high school?" Amos added, taking another drag on his tailormade.

"Well, it was a pretty *small* high school..." Bud admitted.

"You sir, are what my old boss, P.T. Barnum..." Amos pulled off his derby, placing it over his heart, "...God rest his humbugging soul..." placing it back in his head, "lovingly termed...a rube."

"I thought he called us 'suckers'," smiled Bud. "As in 'There's a sucker born every minute?'"

"That term was reserved for your run-of-the-mill simpleton...a common mark. You have to work, at least a little, to turn people into suckers. You, on the other hand, Mr. Gardner, appear to be of the 'fresh from the farm, buy this bridge' variety of idiot. A rube."

Pausing, he leaned back and stubbed his cigarette out in the ash tray protruding from the back of the seat in front of him. "To tell you the truth, Bud, Phineas T. was not the sort to call anyone a sucker. It was his rival, a circus man named Adam Forepaugh, who really took the prize in that arena. His show had more animals, more European performers...but his was more of a traveling con game than 'the Greatest Show on Earth.' Forepaugh ascribed the "sucker born every minute" line to Barnum in a newspaper interview, attempting to discredit him."

Amos shook his head, and a small smile gleamed from his blue eyes. "Funny thing is...the Boss never denied making the quote. He actually thanked Forepaugh for the free publicity that the quote gave him. He always said that the people didn't mind a little challenge...a little mystery...as long as they got their money's worth. Like the sign that we always had at the sideshow—'This way to the GIANT EGRESS.' When the people finally found it, they found..."

"A door. A big door, I expect."

"Right. Plus a man with a definition of "egress" on a small card and a 10% discount to the next show. They flocked to get in...and to tell their friends to be sure and see the 'giant egress.'"

"It sounds like you got along pretty well," Bud said softly, not wanting to break the mood.

"Well, you wouldn't have thought so, for as long as he had me cleaning up after the elephants. Do you have any idea how much an elephant shits in a single day? 200 pounds. For Jumbo, it was 350 pounds. So with two dozen elephants..."

"That's a ton of shit..." Bud threw in, finding his feet. "Sounds like an 'offal' job."

"Yes," Amos winced, more at the pun than the memory. "And it was ALL MINE. 'Run away to the circus!' my friends said. 'Get an honest job,' the Judge said. Well, Ah guess he probably did me a favor...it was certainly better than running around with the local urchins on the streets of Washington, D.C. And every twelve-year-old should learn to shovel shit. It...'builds character', P.T. said."

"Funny...that's the same thing my Gramps always says," agreed Bud. "But when I asked him to help, he always claimed to have gotten plenty of character earlier in life, and that now it was my turn."

"Sounds like your Gramps is as full of...character...as dear old P.T."

"So how long were you...uhh..."

"A sanitary engineer? Until ah was nearly seventeen. By then, my specialized training had made me suitable for only two careers...politician, or sideshow man."

Suddenly, Amos leapt to stand on his seat, with one foot on the backrest. "LADEEEEEZZZZZ AAAAAND GENTLEMENNNN....!" he cried, his face beaming. The ten or twelve passengers in the car with him suddenly turned toward Amos, who continued, "Please deye-rect your attention to the front, where you will see the Amazing Aloysius, known throughout the palaces of the crowned heads of Europe as the GREATEST acrobat and juggler of ALL TIME!" Leaping onto the squat, narrow wooden seat back, Amos balanced himself, nearly hitting his head on the roof of the car. Quickly reaching into his left suit coat pocket, and avoiding the pistol grip, he produced three red clay balls, and proceeded to juggle them before the small audience, first in a cross-weave, then in a circular pattern, finally pulling off his hat and letting them fall....

.....plunk....

......plunk....

.....plunk...

...into his hat.

Dropping to the center of the aisle, Amos bowed while the small crowd laughed and applauded—especially Harry Foote, who seemed to be used to this sort of routine from Amos. "Magic!" Harry cried, before the applause started to dwindle. "Show us magic, O Amazing One!"

Bowing, Amos produced a silver dollar from his right coat pocket, making it walk back and forth across the back fingers of his right hand. Suddenly, he tossed it up and grasped it with his left hand. Placing this hand to this mouth, he coughed, and out sprang a lace handkerchief. "Yours, I believe, Madamselle?" he said to a particularly pretty young woman in a gabardine dress, who blushed just a bit when she took it from him, nodding, and placed it in her purse. Placing his hand under his chin, he looked perplexed. "Now where is that dollar?" Suddenly, his face looked as if it had struck upon the answer, and he reached behind Harry's ear, producing it to the satisfaction of the crowd.

"Now don't forget to tip the brakemen, ladies and gentlemen," he said, made a final bow, and sat down next to Bud, to universal applause.

"I can see why Harry called out for a magic trick," Bud remarked. "And, despite my intrinsic nature as a 'rube', I observe that you—and possibly Mr. Foote—are quite a hand at this."

"Well, it never hurts to keep the railroad happy," Amos admitted. "Especially in this line of work."

"Tell me..." Bud said, leaning close to Amos. "How did you manage to get the handkerchief from the lady?"

Amos looked shocked. "REALLY, Mr. Gardner, the magician's code prevents any possible comment along those lines. Nevertheless," he went on, "I WILL say that however it was obtained, it would certainly have been returned...eventually." Grinning, he tipped his hat to the woman, who produced another perfect blush.

"Now, ah believe ah have more than answered your question regarding my particular origin. My next question is an important one...what is your real name, 'Bud?'"

Now it was Bud's turn to redden. Furtively looking around, he lifted the back of his hand to cover his mouth, and whispered something into Amos's ear.

"Oh, my," remarked Amos. "How very unfortunate. My condolences."

* * * * *

77

The sun was well up in the east when Willa Cather and Julia Pack, walking quietly down 11th Street, met Zeke, walking north with his roan mare. It was nursing its right front foot, and before Zeke noticed their presence, Julia noted that he was murmuring quietly to his horse, persuading it to keep moving.

"Uncle Zeke!" cried Julia, and the older man removed his hat, hopped from the dusty street onto the bricked sidewalk, and scooped up his niece.

"Julie girl!" Zeke boomed, and nodded to her companion. "Willa," he said, nodding his head as he lowered his niece.

"Uncle Zeke, you are in serious trouble," scolded Julia, folding her arms in emphasis—but her face gave away a certain degree of inner mirth. "Aside from the fact that you whisked my cousin away from a perfectly delightful feast yesterday, held in HIS honor," she went on, "Mother is anxious that you are leading him down the path of perdition. Is he *really* on a whiskey run? How CAN you be making a Barrelhouse roughneck out of that nice young man?"

"With great care and deliberation, I assure you," Zeke replied, smiling. "I intend to focus his alcoholic adventures on weeknights and Saturdays, with drinking on the Sabbath limited to only half that amount. Consorting with lewd women will be optional, not compulsory."

"You certainly seem to be in high spirits," observed Willa. "Could it have something to do with a certain farmer's organization making final preparations to close their deal with a local merchant of prominence?"

"As always, Miss Cather, the *Nebraska State Journal* seems well-informed." Zeke shook his head. "So are things...a-buzz at the paper?"

"More of a low rumble...like a steam train...ready to go off a cliff." Willa eyed him. "You do realize that there are monied interests in this city that would prefer you to fail—utterly—in this, don't you? How did you manage to put all this together, Mr. Gardner?"

"Am I speaking to Miss Cather, the friend of Julia, or the reporter of the *State Journal*?"

"Oh, don't fret—this story is like dynamite on a burning fuse—no one at the *Journal* is going to come anywhere near it until about 30 minutes after it explodes."

"Hm." Zeke stayed silent for a moment. "Girls...I believe I will need some help, in what I have always believed to be a good cause."

"Is that the cause of the farmers of this county, or of Ezekiel Gardner?" Willa queried.

Zeke shook his head. "I admire your directness, Willa."

"You're in thin company."

"Nevertheless." Gardner stroked his horse's neck, and looked up, squinting in the morning sun. "Gonna be hot," he said, glancing at the girls, who silently stared back. *Nebraska women*, he thought. *No slack whatsoever.*

"Would you believe that it's a mix of both?" he replied, squinting one eye in the sun. "Yes, I'm making a bit—but I'm taking a serious chance—and so is your father, Julie Pack," he said, pointing at his niece. She blinked, but did not lower her head.

Shaking his head, Zeke added, "What we are making—if we pull this off—is nothing like the profit that LeBlanc and McGee have made over the last 10 years—or will make this year. But it might be enough to break them, or at least teach the railroads and corn chandlers that they don't need to push things their way all the time." Hesitating, he added, "Like to hope you think that could be worth a little of your time."

"You certainly are a spellbinder, Mr. Gardner," Willa remarked, shaking her head. "You ever thought of politics as a career?"

"If I did, Miss Cather, I would have run for Sheriff, instead of suffering as a Deputy for 13 years." He smiled. "And isn't it just a little early in the morning for rude talk?"

"I guess it is," Willa admitted. Mimicking Zeke's prolonged wink, she replied, "So…how is it you think I could can I help, Mr. Gardner?'

"That's the spirit." Zeke nodded, once, with emphasis. "Just keep your ear to the wall. You probably hear more rumors than anyone I know, at that rat's nest in the Journal building. Except maybe…" he hesitated, turning toward Julia, "for Julie here."

Julia started. "You don't mean…"

"Now don't tell me, Julie," Zeke cajoled, looking down, "that you've never listened in to any of those conversations that keep those wires humming, sitting there in your spider's web over the Burlington depot?" He looked at her, and mildly smiled. "What I need, is for you to keep an ear open for McGee's line. He's on…"

"I know his number," Julia interrupted. "But Uncle Zeke, you know it could mean my job…"

Walking up to her, he grabbed her hands. "It's in a good cause, I promise, Julie girl." He looked directly in her eyes, and her shoulders sagged.

She nodded. "Just the one line," she said, quietly.

"Thanks," he said, squeezing her hands. "If you hear something, ring me…or Amos, at the Fairbury hotel. Well," he added, quickly, as if uncomfortable with the mood, "I'd like to stay around here all day, but I've got a horse to shoe."

"Uncle Zeke, be careful," Julia said softly, and kissed her uncle on his grizzled cheek.

"Shoot, Julie, I was BORN careful," he replied. And with that, he led his horse, hobbling, up the street.

11

Monday, August 6, 1894
10:35 am

The rest of the trip to Fairbury was uneventful. Unless you counted the cows on the track entering town, and the sign propped in front of them that said, 'SLOW the hell DOWN.'

Bud was within earshot of Stannard when the conductor muttered, "Slow down HELL...I've got a schedule to keep." He burst out of the car with a head of steam, and striding up the track, pulled the sign down. Over the soft, sighing engine, Bud could hear him bedevil the engineer.

"Run the damn thing over next time...you ever heard of a schedule, dePuis?" As Bud watched Stannard walk back to the passenger cars, he saw dePuis make a rude gesture to Stannard's back.

Moving again, the train made the short trip into town without further delay. Bud observed the brakemen swing up like apes to the top of the cars, followed shortly by the conductor. As the brakes squealed, the white frame platform of the Fairbury train station slid next to them and Bud started to get up.

"Just a moment, Mr. Gardner," Amos said softly. "We ah the last passengers off this particular train." After a few moments, Seville tapped his friend's shoulder, and pointed to the rear of the train. Getting up, they moved quickly between the cars to the rear freight car.

Bud's eyes took a few moments to adjust to the light, so he moved carefully, as he was surrounded by reapers and plows—all points and sharp edges. Nevertheless, he was roughly ushered into a corner of the freight car, and yanked down by his companion. "Thirsty?" said Amos, and handed him a silver flask.

"Er, no," stuttered Bud, "thanks..."

"Ah know, ah know," Amos cajoled. "You promised your mother. You do know what whiskey tastes like, don't you?"

"Yes, of course," Bud said, trying to keep the offense out of his voice. *Well, sort of...*

"Good...because the next run is a whiskey run, and the Germans in Scribner have occasionally been accused of...sharp practice. Don't let them sell you horse piss, will you?"

"You aren't coming?"

"You will not have my gentle company to guide you, ah'm afraid…ah've got business here in Fairbury. But ah'll escort you out to the exchange this afternoon." Amos took a sip and closed the flask. "When you taste the whiskey, make sure you spit it out—don't swallow. Grimace, too. Then mention the quality—which is bound to be bad. But it's generally strong enough for railroad men."

Within the next 15 minutes, the train started to move again, and Bud listened to the sounds of Fairbury pass behind them. As the train started to gain speed, Bud rolled over Amos's words in his mind. *Scribner…that's the other side of Lincoln, nearly 70 miles north…my part of the country. The German part sounds right, but whiskey makers?* Bud shook his head. *What other things go on under my nose that I don't know about? Am I really such a rube?*

Sounds like it, he admitted to himself.

It wasn't very long until the train started to slow again. Bud felt it jink to the right, braking suddenly, and, slamming the cars together with a— bang, bang BANG!—it stopped altogether. Looking through the cracks in the vertical slats forming the railcar siding, he saw Harry Foote move to the front of the freight car, decouple it, and heard the train move out. Meanwhile, five or six brakemen went to the back of the freight car, uncoupled the caboose behind them, and laboriously shoved it until it was back on the main line. The train backed up, the caboose was coupled, and the back door of the freight car cracked open.

"Be seeing you, Mr. Seville," came the soft voice of Harry Foote.

"Much obliged, Mr. Foote." The door closed as the train pulled away, and Bud could hear Harry's feet scrambling outside to catch up, sweep up on it, and disappear with the departing train.

"And…now we wait." Amos said.

"Good," said Bud. "Show me how to juggle." Bud could almost hear Amos's head shake.

"Well, let's get out of this car, first." Amos sprung up and held out a hand to Bud, and the two of them threaded their way to the front door of the car, carefully avoiding the farm implements showing off at odd angles, nearly blocking their path. Bud's eyes, once re-adapted to the bright sunshine, noted that the train was already out of sight over a small dip in the land, miles away, and its black smoke column had nearly dissipated. It left a practically spotless horizon, a prairie landscape devoid of houses and

82

farms, only broken by the rails reaching out both directions as straight as a surveyor could make them. Above them, a meadowlark parked itself on the two-strand telegraph line that paralleled the track, and sang its familiar *TWEET-TWEET-tweet-deet-**tweed**elly-deet*.

Amos plucked his three clay balls from his suit coat pocket, separating them, and juggling them absently. "Want some free advice?"

"Uh...on juggling?"

"Yes, indeed... on juggling priorities." Returning back to his first pattern, Amos said, "Like the fingers on your hand—unless you're a brakeman—life has five rules of juggling. First rule—keep it simple. This is the criss-cross pattern. The most complicated pattern won't amaze as much as a well-rehearsed simple one." Spinning the balls faster and faster, and the whizzing red balls became a pink 'X' suspended over Amos's blurred hands.

"Second rule—tenacity works, in forward AND reverse. If it's important, stick with it and don't quit. You'll only get good at anything if you practice. The corollary is, whatever you do, you'll *be*...so be careful what you practice." Closing his eyes tightly, Amos maintained the speed of the balls, and if anything, sped them up slightly.

"Third rule—keep your head about you. There are some very strange articles that can hit you out of nowhere—so be ready." Changing his pattern slightly, Amos arranged for each of the balls to take it in turn to land squarely on his head—where they stayed, as Amos moved about under them to keep them there.

"Fourth rule—stay away from the 'hard stuff'." Bowing slightly, he dropped the balls—one, two, three—into his left hand, and then threw them—hard, one at a time, into the side of the freight car, where they stuck. "We ah only made of clay."

Bud clapped his approval, and Amos bowed, retrieving his juggling balls, now disks. Pointing to Amos's flask, he asked, "Does that go for bartenders, too?"

"Yes, especially for bartenders." Removing the silver flask from his right hand coat pocket and unscrewing the top, he passed it under Bud's nose. "This," he said, "is the last of the coffee."

Bud smelled the flask, shook his head chuckled. "Kinda wondered where that went." After taking a sip of the brew—still slightly warm, with a slightly tinny taste—Bud screwed the silver cap back on to the flask. "So what's the last rule?" he queried. "You said there were five."

"Well, unfortunately, ah can't tell you that one...you ah going to have to discover that one for yourself. Generally, it's a rule you make up after learning a hard lesson. In my particular case, the last rule is," throwing all the clay disks into the air with his right hand, "Have a surprise ready." With a confidence that was clearly born of the second rule, he whipped a small silver pistol out of his left hand coat pocket, and fired three shots in rapid succession at the clay spheroids. Walking calmly over to them, he tossed them to Bud. There was a small hole in each of the pieces.

Suddenly, Bud heard another three shots sound, as if from far away, too late to be an echo. "That's the answering signal," Seville said, pointing with his pistol. On the horizon, six wagons were approaching, each pulled by a team of four mules. "Loading time," Amos said, and pulled three brass bullets out of his shirt pocket, jamming them into their tiny silver cylinders.

* * * * *

"I don't keer what you say, he looks like a Hun," Bobber said, as he shoved the broom around the barrelhouse.

"He's a friend of Zeke's and dat's good enough for me." Swede was crouched low, so low that he was nearly eye to eye with the old man. "Yer missing da dust pan, Bobber." Pointing, he emphasized, "See! It's right in front of you."

"All right, all right," Bobber grumbled, and shoved the pile into the dark shape that was in front of him. *It sort of looks like a dust pan.*

"You're going blinder every day," remarked Swede, walking the dustpan to the side door, and pitching the dust into the alley out back. "You should wear dose glasses Zeke got you, maybe, ya?"

"I don't need glasses to see that Mr. J.T. Lynch is up to something," Bobber said, and spit in the direction of the spittoon.

"You just hit the piano bench, y' know," Swede sighed, grabbing a rag and heading toward the bench that Bobber had just plugged.

"You ain't been with Zeke for near as long as me. I knowed him when he was wearing tin up in Dakota, and way before. He's gotta lot of history with J.T., and there's a lot of it that ain't good."

"Zeke trusts him," Swede countered. "Got Mr. Pack to loan 'em a couple of horses and a rig."

"No, yer wrong there." Bobber said, pointing a finger at the big man. "Zeke doesn't trust 'im, he *needs* 'im. It's different."

"Maybe we don't," Swede countered. "I was watching the courthouse, like Zekiel said, and McGee took LeBlanc off real quiet."

"Back in '19, General Jackson told us somethin' about the Creeks. 'It ain't what they're doing while yer watching,' he says—'it's the "ain't watchin'" part what'll get you scalped.'"

* * * * *

Bud marveled at the efficiency of the loading operation. Soon all of the freighted machinery was unloaded and strewn like children's toys on the prairie surrounding the freight car, and nearly 150 barrels lined the track next to the freight car. Amos took the bung from six random barrels, and dribbled its contents into a little silver cup. He sipped it, swilled it around in his mouth, and, with a tiny wink to Bud, spit it out. His face scowled, his head shook, his mouth mumbled words that sounded like curses...and then he moved to the next barrel and repeated the process. Several of the men seemed to be smiling, and Bud's eye caught at least one open nudge. *They've seen this performance before,* Bud realized, *and they don't give it much shrift.* But then Amos pointed to a barrel, and it was immediately taken to the side and reloaded on the wagon, to the muttering of the men.

Finally, Bud heard Amos say, "Load 'em." In less than an hour, Bud was watching the last wagon disappear over the hill loaded with farm implements. He waited with Amos under the shade of the freight car, trying to figure out which ball should be tossed first—*the one in the left hand? One of the two in the right?* Within five minutes, the balls had all found Mother Earth multiple times, and become a messy conglomerate of sand, sandburs, prairie hay, and track tar—all held together by the original clay. By the time the northbound train arrived, however, Bud had managed to perform four or five criss-crosses before his act collapsed. When he tried to hand the mess back to Amos, Amos held up his hands and shook his head. "They're yours now," he explained. "You dropped 'em."

"You mean you never...?" but before Bud could finish the question, three short bursts from a train whistle sounded from the rise, and Bud followed Amos's gesture, climbing into the freight car, squeezing between the barrels into a slot just wide enough for the both of them.

The smell of beer, whiskey, and oaken barrels was overpowering, and the heat in the freight car was stifling. Outside, the approaching train had finally crawled to a stop, and the brakemen began the tedious task of removing the caboose, moving the train forward, and getting their freight car shoved into the space between by moving forward, switching tracks, backing, pinning and pulling. Amos sat next to him and lit up a hand-rolled cigarette, and its musky smell reminded Bud of the stuff that Gramps smoked behind the corn crib where Mother would not pester him, and he said as much aloud.

"Ah don't know much about Zeke's father," Seville asked. "Tell me about him."

"Well," Bud replied, "His name is Jeremiah, just like my father. He's a farmer, but he left the farm to Father, and ran a store for a long time in Hooper, near Alder Grove, where I live...er, lived, that is," he corrected. "When Grandma died," Bud paused, "about five years ago, he moved in with us."

"Ah know that part," Amos interrupted, "Ah want to know what he's like." The smoke swirling about Amos in the half darkness gave Bud the impression of a magician, or a mystic, or...some sort of holy man, looking for something. Bud saw that he was deep in thought, and wondered at his friend's sudden curiosity.

"Well, he's educated—that is, he believes in education—I don't think he went much past 8th grade. But he's read all his life, and would read to me when I was a kid," Bud explained. "Stories, you know, then...well, Greek mythology and Shakespeare. When I was little, I remember wearing a big hat, and putting a stick in my belt, and we would play parts in the front yard of his house in Hooper. King Lear, and Richard the Third, and...well you get the idea.

"Well, when he moved back with us, he spoke to Father. It was quite a speech—he said that I was to go to high school, and if Father disagreed, he guessed the store in town could just go to the church...or the devil, he didn't care which." Bud hesitated. "I remember him saying, 'we have to give our children a chance to be who they are, not just what we expect them to be.'" Bud paused, then added. "As it turned out, it didn't make much difference about the store. Burned down in '91 before Gramps could sell it. I thought that Father would surely take me out of school...but he left me in...he let me finish." The freight car fell silent for a time, and Bud could hear the engine slowing slightly. They were nearing Fairbury.

"So, you went to high school," Amos whispered. "Did you find it difficult?"

"Really hard. Especially Latin," Bud smiled. "Hic, haec, hoc...conjugating verbs...nominative, accusative, ablative..."

"Dative and interrogative," finished Amos. "All the cases. You must have had a good education." Bud stared at him, open mouthed.

"Don't act so surprised, Mr. Gardner," he added. "Mr. Barnum didn't make me spend my whole time shoveling elephant shit. The bearded lady," he added with a smile, "was especially...instructive."

Oh, my... thought Bud, *that is a very strange...notion.*

Before Bud could completely recover, he was startled to see Amos turn on him, rather suddenly.

"So, here's my question, Mr. Gardner." Amos pointed the stub of his cigarette at Bud's chest, and looked directly into Bud's eyes. "Why do you think that your grandfather sent you, and not your older brothers, to high school?"

Bud stuttered, not prepared for the fierceness that shone in his companion's eyes. "Because...well, maybe it was because I was the only one that wanted to go."

"Well, maybe you were," conceded Amos, "but ah don't think that was the reason. Ah'll leave you with a hint," he said, pausing as the train pulled to a sudden stop, the cars *bang-bang-**banging*** their punctuation. "Your grandfather seems to think that you and your Uncle Zeke have a lot in common."

"Pardon me, but he kicked my uncle ***off the farm***, Amos." Bud blurted. "And he sent me to high school. He treated us completely differently. I just don't get what you're driving at..."

"Just think about it," Amos said. At that moment, the side freight door opened quickly, and the face of Harry Foote appeared. His eyes were wrinkled with impatience, and he beckoned them rapidly with his hand. "Hurry up, dammit," he whispered.

Bud and Amos piled out, and following Amos's lead, Bud sprinted around the back of the caboose to the rear door of the wooden station house. Amos paused, slowed down, and opened the door for Bud. Once inside, Amos walked nonchalantly to the station master's grille, and whispered, "One ticket for Lincoln, please."

"That'll be a dime," the gray-haired man replied, peering over his half-moon glasses as if in recognition, and handed a paper ticket over once the silver Liberty dime slipped across the worn surface of the counter. "Train leaves in two minutes."

"This is where we part ways, Mr. Gardner. Ah have a different…assignment, here in town." Amos stated, handing the ticket to Bud with a slight bow. Reaching into his pocket, he tossed a small cloth bag to Bud. "And here's some beef jerky for the trip. Stay at the station with the freight car until your cousins arrive. If you run into any trouble," he added, "Just throw those disgusting juggling balls at them. You'll frighten them to death."

"All aboard!" cried Stannard, and Amos hustled Bud into the nearest passenger car. Quickly, he scanned the car, and as if satisfied, exited with a small wave. As the train began to pull out, Amos turned and headed toward the hotel, whistling.

* * * * *

Darkness was sneaking into town, the shift change from the nearby yard was turning up, and Swede was doing his best to keep the glasses full, while keeping half an eye on Bobber. Skunk was at his feet again, this time eating sardines that Bobber threw down, one at a time, from a tin can dripping on the bar.

"That stuff smells disgusting, like it's been rotting in a hot shed," remarked J.T.

"That's Bobber, not the fish," muttered Big Swede. "The sardines aren't bad at all."

Quietly, the rest of the group shifted a few feet down the bar.

J.T. maintained, "My boys here say that LeBlanc and his boys haven't been around all day, and that McGee has been in his offices all day. Isn't that right, Rankin?"

"That's right, Mr. Lynch," agreed the black man standing next to him. A big man, Rankin could almost look Swede in the eye—and it was a hard stare that he returned to anyone that held his gaze. Dressed in a dark duster and a brown cowboy hat, he sported a Remington revolver at his hip, and rested his hand on the bump there that protruded from the duster. "He's just been sitting there…even had sandwiches sent in."

Abruptly, murmurs of quiet appreciation and greeting began to filter through the crowd, and Zeke turned to see Maggie entering the bar. She twitched a slight smile at the customers, but then moved quickly to the side door that led to the upstairs room. Taking a last swallow of his drink, Zeke nodded to the group, and muttered, "'Scuse me, boys."

Crossing the room, he climbed the stairs, and hesitated at the first small bedroom that he found on his right. Opening the door quietly, he found Maggie, gathering a few items from her dresser into a heavily embroidered drawstring bag that she had apparently been carrying under her arm. As he stepped into the room and leaned on the doorframe, he said mildly, "Maggie girl! Haven't seen you for a couple of days."

Maggie jumped visibly, then turned and half hid her bag behind her. "Zeke!" she exclaimed, her free hand flying to her chest. "You startled me." Fluttering her hand over her abundantly endowed upper torso, she seemed to regain her composure, and smiled at Zeke. "I had a good customer…" she admitted. "Hope you don't mind."

"Admire your pluck," Zeke replied, and moved to kiss her. As he gathered her into his arms, she hesitated, then pulled away after just a small kiss.

"Sorry, Zeke, but I'm afraid I'm in a bit of a hurry," she stuttered, then smiling, added, "Gotta bill to pay off with Tennebaum. He's…waiting for me."

"Working late," remarked Zeke, then gazed at her bag. "Is that why you're taking your jewelry?"

"Er, yes," she replied. "Pawning it to pay him off."

"Hm," said Zeke, pretending to polish his watch. "Would have thought your new customer could have covered that for you." Staring at her, he smiled mildly. "Can I help?"

"No, no," Maggie replied, patting his hands shakily. "It's all right…I'll be all right."

Outside, Zeke could hear the thump of Swede's clodhoppers hitting the top step, followed by a rumbling *harrumph*. Zeke turned to face him.

"Sorry, Zeke," Swede mumbled, his hat dwarfed in his huge hands, "but you tol' me to tell you when the train was close. Bud, you know, will be at the station in about twenty minutes."

"Thanks, Swede." Turning, he said, "Maggie…" but Maggie was gone, the outside door swinging slightly in the cool night air.

* * * * *

Sixty miles to the northeast, Roger Gardner stretched and wiped his hands. It had been a long shift. By his count, fifty-seven beef carcasses had been laid in front of him, and he had spent the last 12 hours slicing each of them into steaks, ribs, loins, and other cuts. His hands ached from the labor, and several small cuts had appeared on them again. Nevertheless, he took the pen extended toward him by the small man in the thick glasses, and bent to sign the ledger placed in front of him. The accountant removed two silver dollars from a wooden box and dropped them into Roger's hands.

Now, for the hard part.

The entrance gate to the slaughterhouse loomed ahead of him, and Roger saw that the curving wrought iron name that it supported, **Hammond**, was once again dripping with shells and egg yolk. And the crowd outside the gate, was, once again, *ugly*. The Bohemians that had made up most of the original workforce for the slaughterhouses—before the strike—were shouting, cursing, pointing at the scabs massing at the exit of the gate. A meager number of guards—inside the gate to prevent any *entrance* to the plant—not safe *exit*—fidgeted with their clubs. A few unsnapped their sidearms.

As they had last Saturday, Roger formed up into a rough line with the rest of the men waiting to exit. As he waited for the whistle, he sweated.

"Did you see the dodgers that they circulated today?" stuttered a young man behind him. "Stay away from South Omaha…women, stop your men from working at a striker's job…if you cannot, we will not be held responsible."

"Just stay focused," the man next to him said. "If we can get a hundred yards out, we'll make it just fine."

At a minute before the whistle, Roger heard the warning, "Line up." The strikers heard it too, and obeyed. Their front line bristled at least a dozen men who weighed over 200 pounds, big Bohonks, braced for impact. Roger shuddered when he saw the row behind them, growing clubs from beneath their coats. In the last ten seconds before the whistle, things grew deathly quiet.

The whistle cut the air like a knife, and Roger broke for the gate. The man next to him stumbled, and fell directly across Roger's path, causing Roger to trip, and the man behind him to fall over both of them. Above his head, Roger could hear the thrashing, the wild cries, the shots fired over the heads of the rioting mob. Struggling to get up, he was knocked over again and hit his head on the cobblestones. He lay still, curled at the feet of the scuffling crowd and clutching his head until it cleared. Looking up, he saw what looked like a break in the struggling masses between him and the gates. With as much speed as he could manage, he picked himself up, and ran for it.

After several hundred yards, Roger let himself slow down and caught his breath. His head throbbed, but he straightened and jogged through a dark alley a block over in order to enter his rooms from a darkened side street. Scaling a fire escape, he reached the third floor hallway, moved down the dimly-lit corridor, and wearily turned the doorknob for his rooms, where his brother Larry would be waiting for him.

A dark form screaming, "Hovno!" was the last thing he heard before darkness fell about him.

Tuesday, August 7, 1894
8:35 am

D*ear Mother,* Bud wrote. *How are you? I am fi...*

Bud crumpled the paper up and threw it into the seat across the aisle from him.

Dearest Mother, Bud wrote. *Work is very...interesting.* Bud sighed. Crumple...crumple...toss.

Dear Ma. I'm really enjoying working at the bar. My uncle has turned out to be only half the drinker that Father thought he would be. There's an old guy there named Bobber who has a pet raccoon that likes to drink, too. He's sitting next to me and smells so bad that he makes the coon smell good. I met a pretty whore the other day. Her kisses don't taste too much like cigarettes, really.

I'm learning how to juggle.

Crumple...crumple...toss.

Bobber snored, as Bud tried to find inspiration at the end of his pencil.

Dear Mother,

Here's four dollars that I've managed to make in the last week. I'm awfully busy, or I'd write more. Everything is fine. Love, Bud.

Nodding slightly, Bud enclosed the money order that he had gotten at the Post Office first thing that morning along with the letter, sealed it, and placed the two penny stamp on it. Looking out the window to his right, he saw the Elkhorn River Valley slipping past him in the midmorning sun.

Bud yawned. In the last twelve hours, he had arrived back in Lincoln from Fairbury, met his cousins at the Rock Island depot, transported the beer to the Krug brewery on 8th Street, witnessed the labeling operation, and helped steer the beer down the long alley ramp into the basement of the Barrelhouse. The beer was in danger of becoming overwarm, but the sawdust that the farmers had packed between the barrels had helped avoid too many problems. According to Zeke, the railroaders wouldn't know a quality beer from a rank bottle of snake piss, in any case. Bud hoped so...the way things were going, he would probably end up tending bar.

Bobber turned over in the seat next to him, snorted with finality, and woke suddenly. Looking around the passenger car, Bobber smacked his

---

12

Tuesday, August 7, 1894
8:35 am

D*ear Mother,* Bud wrote. *How are you? I am fi...*

Bud crumpled the paper up and threw it into the seat across the aisle from him.

Dearest Mother, Bud wrote. *Work is very...interesting.* Bud sighed. Crumple...crumple...toss.

Dear Ma. I'm really enjoying working at the bar. My uncle has turned out to be only half the drinker that Father thought he would be. There's an old guy there named Bobber who has a pet raccoon that likes to drink, too. He's sitting next to me and smells so bad that he makes the coon smell good. I met a pretty whore the other day. Her kisses don't taste too much like cigarettes, really.

I'm learning how to juggle.

Crumple...crumple...toss.

Bobber snored, as Bud tried to find inspiration at the end of his pencil.

Dear Mother,

Here's four dollars that I've managed to make in the last week. I'm awfully busy, or I'd write more. Everything is fine. Love, Bud.

Nodding slightly, Bud enclosed the money order that he had gotten at the Post Office first thing that morning along with the letter, sealed it, and placed the two penny stamp on it. Looking out the window to his right, he saw the Elkhorn River Valley slipping past him in the midmorning sun.

Bud yawned. In the last twelve hours, he had arrived back in Lincoln from Fairbury, met his cousins at the Rock Island depot, transported the beer to the Krug brewery on 8th Street, witnessed the labeling operation, and helped steer the beer down the long alley ramp into the basement of the Barrelhouse. The beer was in danger of becoming overwarm, but the sawdust that the farmers had packed between the barrels had helped avoid too many problems. According to Zeke, the railroaders wouldn't know a quality beer from a rank bottle of snake piss, in any case. Bud hoped so...the way things were going, he would probably end up tending bar.

Bobber turned over in the seat next to him, snorted with finality, and woke suddenly. Looking around the passenger car, Bobber smacked his

92

lips, wiped his face (it didn't help, noted Bud), and gazed out the window for a few minutes, adjusting to the daylight.

"Comin' up on Hooper," Bobber muttered. "Some good fishing there on the Elkhorn, if you can stand the skeeters."

"Yes, my Gramps and I used to go fishi..." Bud started.

"Course, ain't nothing like the skeeters out on the Snake in '34. Like to carry you off...did see 'em carry off a couple of sheep—might have been the eagles, though."

"Er,..."

"Eagles weren't genrally dangerous, unless you went after their little ones—which the Blackfoots regularly did, just to prove their mettle."

"Ah..." *He's like a damn Dutch clock...just runs faster and faster the longer it goes...*

"Went out with Osborne Russell till '43—fought the Indians, drank with 'em, married, 'em—that's when the fightin' generally started up agin'..."

"Well, I..."

"Know much about yer Uncle, do ya?" The grizzled man stopped and stared silently at Bud with eyes at least a thousand years old, and a directness that shocked him.

Bobber shoved Bud hard in the shoulder. "Whatsa matter, cat got yer tongue?"

"N-no. I'm just delighted to get a word in edgewise." Bud blurted. The old man continued to stare for a moment, then broke into a wide toothless grin. *Well, maybe one tooth, then,* admitted Bud. "What can you tell me about him?"

"A goodly bit...but here we are at Hooper, and I gotta pee." As the train slowed to a stop, Bobber hopped up and swung out the rear door of the small, plain wooden car. Bud admired how well the old man moved as he slipped around the corner of the station to where Bud knew the outhouses were located. He'd had plenty of occasions to use them himself, as the station and its...facilities...butted right up against the pretty little downtown. Two-story buildings with brick facades lined both sides of the broad main street, with horses, wagons and vendors scattered at odd intervals along the sidewalks. Just down the street on the right hand side was a new brick building where a clapboard general store used to stand, previously operated by his grandfather for many years before it burned down. During the summers, Bud could remember helping around the store—sweeping, stocking, and receiving the occasional peppermint for his troubles. Gramps was generous with his grandkids, and Bud was a shadow that was hard for the old man to shake off—not that he tried that hard. When he needed a moment's peace, Gramps would send him down to this station to watch for the morning train, and "see if there's a package there for me." Bud knew the stationmaster here very well...and it worried him.

I'm bootlegging, he thought, and slinked down further in his seat. *This would **kill** Mother...and me, too, if Father found out.* Bud was pretty sure this was **not** what his father had in mind when he sent Bud to Lincoln.

God, I sure hope this is temporary. But if it is, why is Uncle Zeke taking the time to acquaint me with all these supply routes? Does he expect me to do this from here on out? He looked nervously about him, expecting at any moment to see somebody from home that might recognize him, and carry the word back to his parents. *I'd have to come up with some reasonable excuse for traveling through Hooper. With Bobber.*

Oh, well, at least Skunk's not here, he thought, smiling weakly.

Bud was relieved to finally hear the "All Aboard!" sound from the side of the track. Two short whistles blew, and the train started to move forward....but where was Bobber? His ears provided the answer as he heard the old man swearing up a storm at the side of the train, swing up the rear of the car (still swearing), and plop next to Bud, trailed by the conductor, who Bud noticed was limping noticeably.

"We will NOT have that sort of language on this train, Mister," the conductor said sternly, then dropped his voice. "Now just settle down, or you'll have to finish your... business...on another train." Smiling at Bud, he added, "See that your...uncle here...stays quiet, will you, young man?"

"Yes, sir," Bud intoned automatically.

"Good boy," he added, patting him on the shoulder. He spoke a little louder, as Bobber continued to grumble under his breath. "Nice game, by the way, last Saturday. You sure showed those trolleymen. Tickets please," he said, as he limped toward the new passengers, and the train started down the seven-mile trip to Scribner.

"I can see why ol' Flat Wheel was glad to show those trolleymen up," Bobber grumbled. "Back in '90...I think it was August, damn hot anyway...he was conducting on a' inbound when he saw the streetcar company—the North Lincoln Eye-lectric Railway—they was trying to cross the railroader's tracks and expand their lines. Anyways, the streetcar men laid track cross the MoPac, and FEM&V, and Burlington tracks, rippin' rails up and such. Ol' Flat Wheel hobbled down and told the Super for the Elkhorn, and the lawyers for all of them railroaders were there as soon as you can say 'Jack Robinson.' Well, the three railroads, they moved their locomotives onto the tracks right in front of the trolleymen. Then there's a standoff...both sides are swearin' at each other, tradin' insults, mulling around the trains and such. Anyways, the lawyers for both sides finally git the attention of the bosses, and they clear the tracks on both sides, trains and trolleys, and they decide to solve their problems in the courts."

Bobber's eyes danced. The story was upon him, and he was like a bad cook making cheap steak in front of a starving man. "The next day," he went on, "this judge issues a restrainin' order 'gainst the railroads, stoppin' 'em from interferin' with the streetcar line. But by the next mornin,' the streetcar company charges a whole bunch of railroad bosses with disobeying the restrainin' order. Now things get even better..."

Bobber grinned. "That afternoon the sheriff and another deputy, not your uncle Zeke, they were called out to the building site. The railroads had blocked the main and the side tracks...they filled 'em up with locomotives. When the Sheriff ordered 'em to move off the crossing, the engineers and conductors would only move one locomotive at a time, always leavin' one to block the track. So the Sheriff arrested the engineers and conductors, and a skirmish starts up agin' between the trolleymen and the railroaders. It was lookin' to become pretty bloody...so the Sheriff swore in another 20 deputies, and armed 'em all. The Sheriff's men was bout to fire on the railroaders when Zeke shows up, and sizes up the situation. He goes right over to the Super of the trolleymen. He says, 'You, sir, are a complete ass,' and punches him in the mouth! Drops him like a sack of corn meal, right there on the tracks. Then he draws his Colt, and points it die-rectly at the Super's nose. And now ever'body gets real quiet-like. 'You're under arrest,' Zekiel says, and before the Sheriff can move a muscle, he shouts to the fireman of the first engine, 'Now, get this piece of shit off the tracks!'"

Bobber was laughing now. "So, course, the crowd cheers, and the fireman moves the train, and the Sheriff fine'ly sees what's happenin'. So he takes the Super of the trolleymen off to the jailhouse, and gives him a stiff drink, and apologizes and such in the quiet of his own office, you see. And Zeke moves the engines, and the crowd gets dispersed—without bein' shot. THAT," Bobber said, "is your Uncle all over. Don't look at what he's doin'—look at what he's DOIN'. "

* * * * *

"Telegram for Mr. Masterson," the baggage boy said, and handed the envelope on a silver salver to the overstuffed man in the overstuffed paisley chair.

"Thank you my boy," he said, and reached into his bulging vest pocket. Rejecting the dime that first slipped between his fingers, he pulled out a penny, and handed it to the young man, who met Amos's eyes, and surreptitiously rolled his own. Amos grinned, bit off the end of the cigar he had at hand, and asked, "So, what does Western Union have to say this morning, Mr. Masterson?"

Amos had been the on-and-off companion of Masterson for nearly a day now, having met him by "accident" in the lobby of the Fairbury Hotel, ostensibly there to visit a cousin. Masterson claimed to be arranging flour shipments from a local gristmill—but a few inquiries with the baggage boy indicated that his interest was of another sort altogether...and the young lady upstairs didn't seem to be in a particular hurry to leave town. So the man had welcomed Amos's company, and the free cigars and bourbon were a considerable inducement to his companionability.

By Tuesday afternoon, Amos himself was beginning to think that Zeke's intuition had finally failed him. Masterson may have been a skinflint and a blowhard, but Amos couldn't see why anyone would want to kill him—even over a grain deal. But as Amos watched the fat storeowner open, unfold, and read the words written on the yellow message blank, he saw worry and care descend upon his round face, and began to suspect that Zeke had been right...again.

"N-nothing," Masterson stuttered. "Just a bit of business." Rising suddenly, the man stumbled over to a wicker wastebasket in the corner, crumpled up his message, and made as if to drop it in. With a brief glance backward over his shoulder at Amos, however, he hesitated, and at last stuffed the paper into his pants pocket. Taking off his glasses, he removed a handkerchief from his pocket, and nervously wiped them until Amos thought the cheap gold filigree would be rubbed completely off the frames.

"I'm – uh – well, I'm thinking of heading back to Lincoln, my friend," Masterson announced suddenly. "My...business here is nearly done."

Amos nodded, lit his cigar, and puffed it into life. "Well Sir, then perhaps you will join me for a farewell supper? I understand that they are serving Guinea hen and roasted potatoes this evening."

96

Masterson licked his lips, and allowed himself a smile. "That would be...delightful, sir," he replied, "Perhaps you will let me spring for the tip?"

"Certainly, sir," replied Amos. *Better hide the kitchen knives.*

* * * * *

Otto scuffed his feet in the dust of the brick main street just up from the Scribner depot, and folded his hands together under the front of his brown overalls. Winking one eye against the noonday sun, he cocked his head to the young man and his grizzled companion, and asked with a crooked smile, "So...where's Ezekiel, then?"

A lanky man in his thirties with straight black hair and a permanent sardonic grin, Otto looked every bit the farmer, right down to his patched leather shoes and faded fedora. He and his two companions had met the train in town, and it was clear that they weren't in any hurry.

Bud started to open his mouth, but Bobber jumped in. "He's damn busy," said Bobber, "so he sent us to bring out the whiskey. Where is the stuff, anyway..." he mumbled. "I'm getting thirsty."

"Well, we can help you with that, anyway," Otto offered, and pointed to the corner brick building just across the street from the tracks. As they entered the tavern, Bud was struck by the Victorian opulence—the padded mahogany chairs, the brass barrails, the huge mirror behind the hardwood bar. From above the bar, a nearly naked lady reclined and looked saucily out at the patrons, lifting a beer stein. Otto pointed to a half dozen chairs around a table in the corner, scooped a bottle up from the bar, and slid into one of them, uncorking the bottle with a fluid, practiced hand. A mustachioed, balding man in a gaudy vest and a white apron put five shot glasses around the table, and started to fill them, one at a time, moving clockwise around the table, where Bud's glass waited.

Bud's hand dropped to his side, and accidentally brushed up against the bulge in his trouser pockets—the three clay juggling balls, now melding together in the summer heat. His memory flashed back to a yesterday, remembering Amos's words: *Rule three--keep your head about you...*and placed his hand over his glass just as the barkeep started to tip the bottle toward it.

"I'll pass," he said, feeling a lot less confident than he was trying to sound. Raising his eyes to look directly into Otto's, he asked "Where's the stuff?"

Bobber sputtered and coughed on his second drink (his first was gone so quickly that the barkeep had just gone on pouring), looking at Bud as if he had Junebugs crawling out of his ears. Before Bobber could speak, Bud laid a hand on his and added, "We don't have all day, Otto. Train leaves in two hours."

Otto stared at him, intense and silent for a moment, then broke into laughter.

From there on, Bud found, it was pretty easy. Led into the back room of the bar, he found fifty 20-gallon kegs. He copied Amos's routine from yesterday—selecting random barrels, pouring the contents into a small glass, checking the color, swishing and spitting it out, wrinkling up his face. All but one of the eight samples burned his tongue. At this, Bud turned toward Otto and simply raised his eye. Otto sipped it, and shrugged his shoulders. "Bad barrel." But Bud noticed that he gestured for three barrels to be moved out of line, not one. Glancing through the storeroom door back into the gleaming bar, Bud noted that Bobber, meanwhile, was bent over the corner table, his face snoring into his folded arms.

"Load 'em," he barked, in a rough approximation of Amos's confident intonation. Glancing over at Bobber, he added quietly, "And load him up, too, please."

* * * * *

Just down the street from the hotel, the little wooden framed Western Union shack sulked against the train station, both buildings looking like old men that had been standing in the sun too long. As Amos opened the door, the flies rushed out.

Seeing the telegraph operator snoring at the key, he didn't wonder at their sense of urgency. Amos wanted to leave, too.

However, the lack of supervision was a stroke of luck—avoiding the necessity for...manipulation. With skilled hands, he slowly inched the yellow pad from beneath the dirty elbows of the slumbering telegrapher, and drawing it into the yellow light filtering through the dirty window, looked carefully over the surface of the top sheet. Smiling, he drew the stubby pencil from the fingers of the wire tickler, and gently rubbed its edge over the surface of the pad. Block letters now stood out from the page.

Amos straightened, pulled the rubbing from the Western Union pad, and headed for the hotel.

* * * * *

The telephone rang in the upstairs room, and a tinny version of Julia Pack's voice came over the line. "Uncle Zeke," she said, "Amos is calling for you, long distance."

"Please put him on, Julie."

As Zeke waited for his connection, his eyes wandered over the upstairs bedroom that he and Maggie had shared, off and on, since June. Through its open door, Zeke observed that most of the contents of the small closet were missing...Maggie's of course. Their short conversation the previous night was a dead giveaway. She had met another man, and had cleared out.

Well, Zeke thought, *she must have cared a bit about us, or she wouldn't have been so embarrassed last night when I caught her leaving.*

He shook his head. *I always was a damned fool where women were concerned.*

Amos' voice came over the phone. "Zeke?"

"Amos! How's the weather in Fairbury?" Zeke asked.

"Mostly cloudy, Zeke," Amos replied. "Masterson received a telegram about an hour ago. He looked pretty put out when he opened it, and announced he was coming back tomorrow."

"Well, I don't suppose that we can do much about that. Any idea what was in the letter?"

"That's what ah'm calling about. It read, "MASTERSON, REQUEST RETURN TO LINCOLN SOON AS POSSIBLE STOP WOULD HATE TO HAVE ZG INFORMATION FALL INTO RUBY'S HANDS"

"It's signed, 'MCGEE,'" Amos added. "Is Ruby...?"

"Masterson's wife. Damn," cursed Zeke. "How did McGee get that telegram out? J.T. said his men had that covered."

"His men?" queried Amos, incredulously. "Ah thought Lynch was here by himself."

"J.T. brought in two men after you left yesterday. There's a black man named Jasper Rankin, and a skinny white fellah name of Trudeau. J.T. says they are both good men..." Zeke's voice trailed off.

"Doesn't sound like you ah any too sure, Zeke," Amos remarked.

"Well...they do look a little..." Zeke admitted. "O.K., ***damn*** shady."

"So the message got through to Masterson," Amos said. "What does it mean?"

"It means...that McGee thinks he has found himself a wrench," said Zeke. "And he's going to twist some on Clive Masterson." He paused. "Amos," he said, "do you think you could get Masterson to stick around Fairbury for a few more days? I'd like to buy enough time to meet with the farmers..."

Amos considered. "Maybe another day," he said, "If ah had a little help." Quickly, he outlined his plan.

Zeke chuckled. "Well, I'll see what I can do from this end. Be careful."

"You too."

After he hung the earpiece up, Zeke paused for a moment. A sudden thought occurred to him, and he strode over to the small closet. Moving a pair of old boots from the corner, he pried a floorboard up in the corner, and pulled out a small metal box. Dusting it off, he lifted the cover--and found it empty. A cold feeling welled up in the pit of his stomach. He winced, shook his head...and smiled, sadly.

I'm a damned fool, he thought.

Think fast, Gardner...

13

Tuesday, August 7, 1894
6:20 pm

Masterson had to admit that the brandy and cigars at the Fairbury hotel were excellent for such a small town. Between them and the fine supper that preceded them, he had just managed to calm down from the earlier message, bidden his lady friend in Fairbury farewell, and make his own travel arrangement back to Lincoln for the following morning.

"Well, ah'll miss your company, Mr. Masterson, indeed ah will," Amos said. "It is a shame for certain and sure—ah surely would have liked you to meet my cousin." Amos lit his cigar, and offered a lighted match to the older man, holding it to the cigar as well until it puffed into life.

"Really? Well, it's always good to have family around," admitted Masterson. "Is he in the same...trade...as you?" Masterson, though a fallen Methodist, was still a confirmed hypocrite, and as such was reluctant to discuss the tavern business in polite company.

"No, you couldn't be more wrong, Mr. Masterson. SHE is...an actress, and is traveling through from Chicago to start in a new show in Denver. She should be arriving any time on the evening train. Ah was wonderin', would you mind accompanying me?" Amos winked, reached into his coat pocket, and produced a picture.

Masterson stared at it openly until ash fell from his cigar onto the carpet, where it smoldered until he found his voice.

"Uh...of course," he replied, with a gulp. "Anything for a friend."

"Ah KNEW ah could count on you, Mr. Masterson," Amos grinned, rising. "Shall we?"

* * * * *

After the elation of closing his first sale with the whisky distillers of Scribner for his Uncle Zeke, Bud was feeling a little low. The train from West Point through Scribner had been delayed, and it had been nearly five o'clock before the train moved from the small town southeast toward Hooper. Next to him, Bobber was snoring heavily, sleeping the sleep of the dead drunk.

As the train finally approached Fremont from the north, the evening wind began to pick up, and Bud suddenly detected something—a feeling,

101

an electric current, a scent—that he hadn't smelled for months on end—the possibility of a summer thundershower in the making. Full of hope, he pulled the window down on his left—yes, definitely the smell of rain—and looked to the west. Faintly, on the horizon to the southwest, over miles of withered corn, there it was—a thunderhead building. The popcorn cloud was percolating up, already miles high, round and orange and pink, like a sweet grapefruit in the setting sun.

Rain, he thought, joining the hundreds, perhaps thousands that were straining to observe, to coax rain from the same horizon. *Come this way.* **This** *way.*

The train kept moving, and the cool air flowing over the passengers produced a low murmur of appreciation.

"Rain," Bobber murmured next to him, startling Bud. The old man had lifted one eye toward the window, then settled back into his seat. "Goin' south of us, though." Within seconds, he was snoring again.

Ten minutes later, Bud knew that Bobber had called it fair. The sweet rain was not going anywhere near his family's farm farther north in Alder Grove. Bud sighed. *Too late for our corn anyway*, he thought. *But we might have gotten another hay cutting...*

As the train inched into the station and shuddered to a halt, Bud attempted to shake Bobber, to alert him that they were pulling in for a short stop, with an opportunity to drain his small bladder—but nothing that he attempted would stir the aged trapper. Bobber's snores echoed off the walls of the train car interior, and even grabbing his nose only served to shift the source of the snores to his throat. Bud noticed that his fellow passengers had finally given up on dishing him dirty looks, and had cleared a circle of about eight feet in diameter around the pair of them.

"Fremont station," the conductor announced, striding through the car on his way toward the car behind them. "Twenty minutes."

Aiming to stretch his legs, Bud stood in his seat, and waited for the rest of the passengers to leave before making his way out of the rear of the car. Once outside, he reveled in the clean air (Bobber was not so much against the *idea* of a bath, as the execution), and took a moment to glance about him, looking about for the toilet. The city fathers had succumbed to civic pride (and the powerful plea of the railroads) last year to install washrooms with actual flush toilets inside the small station. Bud had pulled the chain on the thunderbox and was beginning to wash up when a familiar voice rang out in the close confines, echoing off the tiled walls. "Bud!"

The young man's face rose toward the door, and the look on his features could have framed the definition of "shock" in most dictionaries of the world, regardless of language.

"Father?"

Bud hardly had a chance to move before his father strode across the concrete floor, embraced him, and asked, "How in the world did you hear?"

"Hear what?" Bud blurted, still trying to comprehend his father's presence here n Fremont.

His father released him, and stared, nearly open-mouthed. "You hadn't heard?" he asked, incredulously. "Then...what are you doing here in Fremont? I thought you were here to meet the train."

"What train?" Bud asked, now totally confused. "Father, what happened?"

"Your brother, Roger." His father hesitated. "Son...he was attacked yesterday in Omaha, when his shift was over at the packing plant." When Bud started to open his mouth, his father said, "He was stabbed in his rooms by one of the strikers...a Bohemian... Larry's coming home, too."

Bud's head reeled. A million questions were spinning around in there, trying to fight their way out of his throat. The winner: "Is he...is he badly hurt, Father?"

"I guess he's had about forty stitches. He was hit in the head, and when Larry found him, he was unconscious. He's lost a lot a blood, but the knife skittered along his ribs, and doesn't seem to have hit anything vital. He'll be in bed awhile. He'll be in on the next train from Omaha, in about an hour." His father hesitated. Two men came into the washroom, and his father took Bud gently by the arm led him to the far end of the platform, under a large cottonwood tree.

"Bud, I...may have been...I was probably wrong when I sent them off to find work—and you, too. I think," he said, haltingly, as if with great effort. "I think you should...I want you to come home with me. Tonight, with Roger and Larry."

Bud stood in stony silence, and tried to form the words. "Father, I'm here doing a job. For Uncle Zeke. He expects me in Lincoln tonight."

"He'll understand, I'm sure," Jeremiah Gardner replied. A cold edge had suddenly slipped into his voice. "What has he got you doing?"

"Uh," Bud stuttered. "Just moving some...stuff from Scribner to Lincoln."

"What kind of stuff?" Bud had seen this look in his father's eyes before—it usually preceded a well-deserved trip to the woodshed. Bud squirmed under his father's glare.

"Boarding in just a few minutes," a passing brakeman said, tipped his hat to Bud's father, and departed.

"WHAT has Ezekiel gotten you into?" his father demanded. The thunderstorm to the south of them picked that moment to BOOM out a warning of the impending storm, and Bud could feel his temper start to rise.

"It's complicated," said Bud.

"Sounds just like your uncle," Jeremiah said, with more than a hint of a sneer. "The more complicated, the better. He couldn't walk a straight line if it was painted down the center of a coal chute and lit up with arclights."

Both men paused. The extreme northern edge of the thunderstorm had managed to just creep over them, and was booming nearly continuously now. Lightning arced in the towering clouds that were still brightly lit by the setting sun, though the twisted spaces under them were dark with the threat of rain.

"Wish this was headed north," Bud said in a small voice.

His father hesitated, then simply added, "Yeah."

A few drops started to hit the dry pine boards that made up the platform, and were immediately sucked into the desperately dry lumber.

"'Board!" cried the conductor, and Bud heard the two short whistles, continuously clanging bell and first huge escape of steam from the cylinder heads that marked the slow departure of the train. Rain started to fall in larger drops, more closely spaced.

"So," his father asked. "Are you coming?" The older man's gaze was stern, but the flash of anger had been released, somehow, by the impending summer shower.

"No, Father...I'm sorry, but no. I have work to do." Reaching into his coat pocket, he quickly removed a letter, handing it to his father. "Please give this to Mother?"

His father just nodded, and accepted the letter, its address now spotting in the falling rain.

Bud held out his hand, and after a short hesitation, his father took it. As Bud turned, his father held his hand for a few seconds, adding, "You be sure to be careful—use your head, boy. Zeke is crafty—but he isn't always wise. Make sure YOU ARE." His father poked him twice gently in the chest, as if to emphasize his last words, then released him.

Bud nodded curtly, trotted toward the train, and swung up into the doorway as it passed. He turned and watched his father wave, his face wet with moisture. Bud swallowed hard, and waved in return, clutching the door rail of the car with his other hand until the station disappeared in a sheet of rain. After about three minutes, the rain stopped as quickly as it had started. Bud wiped his face on his sleeve, cleared his throat, and turned into the car to find Bobber.

* * * * *

It had been 20 minutes since he had met Miss Eugenia, and Masterson was still out of breath. Seated on the front porch of the Fairbury hotel in the company of the young "cousin" of Amos Seville, the grocer was flattered by the easy smile the young lady turned toward him. She was a real looker all right—reddish brown curls, green eyes, and a figure that sent shivers up his spine.

Eugenia, for her part, recognized Masterson as a fairly prominent businessman in Lincoln, and realized that this could be a good opportunity, if handled correctly. Besides, a few days out of that smoky Barrelhouse would do her some good.

Amos admired the interplay between his principals, Masterson fussing over Eugenia, Eugenia shamelessly flirting back. He spoke up, "It's a shame that Mr. Masterson will be leaving us tomorrow morning, for his home in Lincoln." *The setup,* Amos thought.

"Truly?" Eugenia looked at Masterson, a look of distress on her dainty face, followed by a hint of a pout. "I was hoping to spend a few days here, the weather being so pleasant."

There's the hook. Amos turned toward the steward and scratched his nose. Immediately, the steward signaled to the baggage boy, who in turn walked rapidly into the porch, crying, "Telegram for Mr. Masterson!"

Masterson, still trying to make a stuttering excuse for his imminent departure, turned toward the boy, fumbled in his pocket, rejected the dime, and pulled out a penny. Instead of rolling his eyes this time, the boy just smiled and accepted the tip with a "THANK you, sir," and returned Amos's wink while Masterson unwrapped the envelope and removed the

105

Western Union telegraph form. His mouth moved as he read the form, and if Amos hadn't already known the contents, he could have read the older man's lips: MISINFORMED IN MESSAGE YESTERDAY - STOP - APOLOGIZE FOR THE ERROR - STOP - ENJOY YOUR STAY IN FAIRBURY - STOP - MCGEE.

Seeing the confusion on his face, Amos asked in a concerned voice, "Mr. Masterson? Is anything the matter?"

"N-no, no," Masterson replied. "...it looks as though I might be here a while longer myself. My...business...requires me to spend a few more days here, it seems." He puffed out a bit, and rocked on his shoes, smiling at his sly little deception.

The payoff, Amos observed, with satisfaction.

"How LOVELY," Miss Eugenia purred, and flashed a winning smile, first to Masterson, and then, privately, to Amos.

"Indeed!" said Amos, raising his glass of lemonade. "To good business!"

"To good business!" the others rejoined, raising their glasses as well.

* * * * *

The two men were seated on the back stoop of the colored club on 9th Street. "You know, I heered of a man out east a ways," the man said, handing a jar of clear liquid back to his companion, "That got hisself a job jest by savin' a train what nearly got wrecked."

"Sho''nuff?" his companion asked, and motioned to the black man tending the bar. "'Nother round, Mistah barman."

It started about four in the morning with the small, veiled whisper of women's voices, the swish of housecoats across the floor, the carefully silenced opening and closing of doors. At that level, Bud could simply place his head under the pillow and ignore the day's birth, sinking blissfully back into slumber. There was a girl waiting for him there, with raven black hair and blue, blue eyes. Her smile was mischievous, and it was just possible that there was a needle stuck in the collar of her dress. It had been the same dream for the last four nights, now. Retreat seemed like a pretty good idea.

It wasn't long, however, before the day-child's mewing changed—morphing into the clink of pots, the scrape of chairs, the bang of screen doors—until it finally stood up on its hind feet with a *rumble* and demanded to be fed. As if in appeasement, the sacrificial smells of coffee and bacon rose hesitantly out of the kitchen like incense.

Morning started early at the Pack house, and had little pity for those that had returned in the dead of night. Bud had been utterly exhausted by the time that he and his cousin Joseph had returned from storing the Scribner whiskey under the Barrelhouse. But despite the late hour, Bud had been stunned to see a kerosene light propped on a milkstool on the porch of the Pack home when he rounded the corner of J Street. Aunt Emelia was sitting next to it in a rocking chair, her quilted nightrobe bundled firmly about her, the perfect picture of a mother waiting for her errant children. At the sound of their approaching footsteps, she dropped her knitting and wasted no time in hustling Bud and Joseph off to bed.

Now, Em had shifted back into drill sergeant mode, her voice issuing nonstop orders to Ginny and Annette—Joseph's wife—in the kitchen below. Two days' experience had taught Bud that these commands would inevitably result in a continuous flow of bacon, eggs, biscuits and coffee to the workers—who had now started to arrive, would be fed, and then sent on their errands throughout the city and countryside, delivering lumber, stoves, farm implements, nailkegs, leather horseharnesses, sinks, pipes, ladies' undergarments—just about everything you could think of—to the merchants of Lincoln. Everything, it seemed, except grain.

That was about to change, Joseph had assured Bud late last night, assailing his cottony head with an intricate plan while loading and unloading the wagons. If Joseph had anything to do with it, the opportunity to break LeBlanc wouldn't be wasted for lack of organization. Some regular Pack Freight customers had been given special rates to accommodate potential delays in shipment. Extra wagons, horses, and drivers had been recruited from the ranks of farmers having a bad year. Some farmers had agreed to ship their own grain to the waiting Masterson elevator, with a commensurate increase in received price—and risk, should McGee's boys turn against them once again. In the end, all that was needed was a decision by the Cooperative, a signature by Masterson, and the whole shipping operation for 78 farm families—and nearly 200,000 bushels of grain—could begin.

Bud stretched, sat up and scratched his head, surrendering to the inevitable. The sun was forcing its way in under a pulled shade, and the raucous shippers lining up for free breakfast on the porch right under his nose was a cacophony. Despite the ungodly racket it made every morning, however, Bud decided that Rufus Pack was no idiot. Cash was tighter than Dick's hatband, so stretching it with a free breakfast for his workers only made sense. It also assured that any drover still under the influence—and there were plenty of them in Lincoln—would have to show up under the penetrating gaze of the boss's boss. Aunt Emelia had a well-deserved reputation as a generous but tough taskmaster, and if some of the men were still bleary-eyed, they were at least careful to show up clean-shaven and to maintain their silence.

Johnny's abrupt appearance as Bud was finishing his morning toilet was rather a surprise, appearing as he did in full kit. "Good morning, fair cousin," he said, still shaking his head slightly as he dropped a freshly laundered set of clothing on the bed. "Mother says that you are not to step outside this room smelling like a brewery. We have an errand to run." Johnny's voice, always chipper, had an especially mischievous tone.

"I thought you were already at drill," mumbled Bud, wiping the last of the lather from his face. "What will the Lieut say when his favorite cadet is late?"

"We have nothing to worry about there, as it is the Lieut's errand. Now," Johnny said, drawing his sword, and slapping Bud's rump with the flat of it, "Once more into the breach, dear friend—or at least the breeches."

* * * * *

108

"I ain't so sure that this is such an all-fired good idea," said Billy, fidgeting with the silver revolver between his legs under the cover of the train seat in front of him.

"Shut up, Billy," growled Franks. "It ain't like we gotta lotta choice." The three men were seated in the last two rows of the southbound Rock Island passenger car.

From his position at the front of the car, passenger brakeman Harry Foote eyed the three men that had gotten on the Rock Island train with growing suspicion. They were carrying sidearms, which was not so unusual, but the tallest of them sleeping in the back looked a lot like the man that his friend Amos had asked him to look out for. He quickly decided on a course of action, pulling out a pencil and a notebook and scribbling down a few lines. Swinging onto the platform as the train stopped at Rokeby, Harry made a beeline for the small station office.

"Hey, brasspounder!" Harry said flippantly, slapping the paper in front of the chubby young man behind the telegraph key. The stationmaster was clearly out of the office, as witnessed by the operator's stocking feet, which were propped on the desk as he paged through a Sears and Roebucks catalogue. "Get the lead out of your diapers and send this off to Fairbury, willya?"

Ben Rashworth sneered pleasantly, leaned even further back in his chair, and folded his hands behind his head. "Since when do I take orders from a monkey?" using the term universally reserved for all brakemen. After a pause, he added, "A 'hairy footed' monkey," laughing at his own pun. "Anyway, I can't. Strings are off the Johnny ball."

Harry frowned. "High winds last night?" he queried.

"Yep," Rash replied. "Somewhere between here and Fairbury. Linemen are checking for the break now."

"Terrific," Harry frowned. "Hey, try later, willya? It's for Amos."

"I'll see if I can pull a rabbit out of my hat," smiled Rash, happily returning to the women's undergarment section as soon as his friend had left the room.

* * * * *

Following Johnny down the steep stairway, Bud nearly ran into him when Aunt Em suddenly appeared at the doorway, a mixing bowl of biscuit dough balanced on one hip, and a look of deadly earnest in her brown eyes.

109

"Hold it right there, Mister," she barked, pointing a wooden spoon dripping with dough directly at her youngest son's nose. "Just where are you taking my nephew?"

"On an errand...for Uncle Zeke," Johnny stuttered, adding "Ma'am." Usually unflappable, Johnny had long ago learned the valuable habit of respectful subservience, and straightened subconsciously to an attitude of attention whenever his mother's voice was in what Johnny called "full sergeant" mode. "He's 'lent' Bud to us for the day, and we're getting some...supplies...for the cadets. Lieutenant Pershing's orders," he said, then hastily straightening up and adding, "Ma'am."

"Ummm-hmmmmph," she replied, clearly unsatisfied with the answer. "Please wait outside—I need a word with Bud." Johnny knew from experience that this was NOT a request. Nodding his head and snapping up a couple of warm biscuits off the table, Johnny gave Bud a curious, perhaps even piteous glance as he made for the porch.

Emelia motioned to a stair tread behind her nephew, and, stepping into the narrow stairwell with Bud, closed the door behind her. By the dim light falling into the stairwell from a window on the second floor, Bud could see his aunt's stern look gradually fading into a look of concern.

"I got a telegram yesterday morning from your mother, Bud, and I spoke with her by telephone last night," she began. "Why didn't you tell me your brother had been hurt in the Hammond riot? Your mother is sick to death with worry that you didn't come home with your father yesterday."

"Slaughterhouse riot?" Bud asked, dumbly. "Father said he was stabbed in his rooms."

"Well, that's what the newspapers are calling it," Emelia replied. "Your mother said he was followed home and attacked after a big scuffle at the gates of the slaughterhouse."

"How is he?" Bud asked, his eyes dropping guiltily at the recollection of his failure to stay and welcome his wounded brother home.

"Looks like he'll be all right," Emelia said, her hand going out subconsciously to pat her nephew's arm. "His head was cracked pretty good, and I guess he has a mess of stitches and bruises...but if there's no infection, he should be fine in a few weeks.

"That's a relief," Bud admitted with a sigh, raising his eyes to his aunt.

110

"It looks like Larry is already headed back to Omaha to take Roger's old job." Putting down her mixing bowl, Emelia placed her hands on Bud's shoulders and looked steadily into his deep brown eyes. "She says that she wants you to come home, Bud. Any woman that would ride an hour to the nearest town at the crack of dawn, and then scare up a telephone to place a call here is definitely worried."

"Look, I can't do it, Aunt Emelia," he blurted. "I need the work, and my folks need the pay since Roger is out of work...now more than ever. I already sent them four dollars that Uncle Zeke paid me, in advance, for the first week's work—and it's only Wednesday. I owe it to Uncle Zeke—and them—to keep working."

At the mention of her black-sheep brother, Emelia's sympathetic face turned cloudy. "And just WHAT has my brother got you doing at all hours of the night, Bud Gardner?"

"This and that," said Bud with a hangdog expression, using the same weasel-words that Zeke had given him as a job description on that first night at the Barrelhouse.

"Ummm-hmmmmph," Emelia replied, her eyes ablaze. "Sounds like just what I'm going to give your uncle."

* * * * *

It was a delicate task, Zeke realized. He needed the right words, and as hard as words were for him, he searched for them.

"Folks," he started, "I appreciate you comin' in to see me so early, and on short notice. I...I think that the time has come for us to level with each other."

Raymond Sanders and thirteen of the most influential of the Cooperative's families stirred uneasily before Zeke Gardner in the close confines of Sanders' barn—mostly men, with some farm wives and two widows. All in all, they made a fairly small showing compared to last Saturday night's meeting. Even though the sun slanting through the windows into the dusty interior showed that it was only mid-morning, fans and handkerchiefs had already broken out. As Zeke stood before them, hands behind his back, the small crowd stood silently wiping the backs of their necks and generating what breeze they could. The faces staring at him were stern, and perspiring, but their patience appeared to be holding.

Zeke plunged in. "I know that you made a decision last Saturday to wait another two weeks—or until the price of corn went up another 2 cents—but we haven't the time. Our friend, Mr. Masterson," he said, "the

111

founder of the feast, as it were—is getting a great deal of pressure from someone—probably his business partner—to reneg on our deal."

"We have a **contract!**" a small man in a battered straw hat squealed in a shrill voice from the back, pointing a shaking finger at Zeke.

"I guess maybe you've never seen a rich man to go back on his word...but I have," Zeke responded. "It ain't pretty. They bring lawyers. They delay. And by the time you get them cornered in court...the price has gone down." Zeke let that sink in, pushing dirt around with his foot, then went on.

"If you hadn't guessed by now, Masterson didn't exactly JUMP to make this deal. He was pushed into it—he doesn't really **want** to be in it, but as long as there isn't a big wind blowing against him, I think he'll stay with it. However," he said, "Time is short, and I need your help."

"Zeke, we all know that you went way out on a limb to put this thing together, and it's always been about as shaky as a wagon in a whirlwind." The comment came from Eloise Moseman, a graying widow wearing a weathered calico dress and aging ankle-high Brogans. "So, what do you need?"

"Eloise, I need the authority to act as your agent—to get the grain sold, at the current market price—and as quick as possible. Now," he said, looking around, "I know that not everyone is here. But you folks are the drivers of the Cooperative. You have the largest holdings, and when you make a decision, the crowd will follow you. So, please," he said, and the word rang out strangely in the close, dusty confines of the barn, "go to your neighbors. Many of you have church services tonight...talk to them. Corner them for lunch...swing by unexpected. Get your wives involved, for Pete's sake—you **know** how fast they can get the word around." A little laughter at that, and Zeke wound it up. "I wouldn't come to you if it wasn't serious...we need to move as soon as we can. Sanders needs to know from each of you by tonight. I've got a bunch of copies of the agreement here, made out for today's market price—take 'em with you. If you and your neighbors agree, sign this paper, swing the copies by after supper, and we'll start moving the grain as soon as Masterson is back in town."

"When do you expect that to be?" Sanders asked.

"No later than tomorrow."

"How are you going to get to Masterson?"

Zeke smiled. "I've already got somebody with him. They've got a handle on things."

* * * * *

Under the cover of the tablecloth, the young lady's hand was resting on Masterson's knee...and he didn't seem to be in any hurry to brush it away. As a matter of fact, he rather wished that bothersome Mr. Seville, seated comfortably across the table from him, would make himself scarce.

Miss Eugenia, dressed in an oversized white flowered hat and a blue frilled dress with a bodice that left very little to the imagination, sipped coffee from a delicate china cup with her free hand, and smiled winningly at Masterson. His thoughts raced back to the night before, when hours of charming conversation had resulted in a hurried knock at the young lady's door near eleven o'clock. *Yes,* Masterson leered, *this...business trip...was turning out to be an altogether enjoyable experience.*

"Have another scone, Miss Eugenia?" Amos offered as he scooted the nearly empty plate across the table, a secret smirk conveying the question, *Have fun last night, did we?*

"No, no, I couldn't eat another bite, Amos, dear," Eugenia replied through clenched teeth, her eyes widening slightly as if to reply, *Shut UP, you idiot.* "Why, *think* of my *figure!*"

"With pleasure, Miss Eugenia," Amos offered, a remark which Masterson, his overloaded brain working feverishly to offer her a lavish compliment of his own on her appearance, missed completely.

In the sputtering midst of Masterson's ensuing flattery, the baggage boy came by and whispered in Amos' ear. Amos placed his cigar in a silver ash tray before him and said, "Excuse me, gentles...I appear to have a telephone call." His eyes met Eugenia's and flickered to Masterson—*keep him here.*

"Hurry *back,*" Eugenia offered, her eyes pleading—*just kill me.*

The telephone closet off the hotel lobby was cramped, but had a wooden door that would theoretically close if the user stood on his head, didn't mind claustrophobia (or spiders), and preferred utter darkness. Fortunately, Amos' background in the circus was ideally suited to the privacy he required.

"Hello?...Julia!" he said, recognizing the voice of his employer's niece immediately. "What's up?"

113

"Amos..." Julia Pack was talking in a frantic whisper, as if she was in a hurry, but trying not to be heard. "Uncle Zeke told me to call you if I...if I found something that...oh, Amos, I think that something bad is about to happen, and I can't get hold of Uncle Zeke."

So...Zeke was able to convince Julia to listen in on McGee, Amos said to himself. *Kudos to Zeke—that was not an easy task.* Julia was as straight as they come.

"Calm down, Julia," Amos said, as softly as he thought the connection would allow. "What have you heard?"

"Okay...," Julia could be heard taking a deep breath on the other end of the phone. Finally, she offered, "I just connected a long distance call to Miles McGee. McGee said that he needed some more help and, quote, 'please send your specialists,' and that he was 'sending some men on the morning train to retrieve Masterson' and that 'when Masterson comes back, we shouldn't ever have to worry about Zeke Gardner again.' Amos, what did he mean?"

Ignoring the question, he asked one of his own, "Did he say how many men?"

"He didn't say how many, Amos, I couldn't call right away...I had to wait until Mattie...that's the other girl that works this shift...until she took a break..." Soft sobs poured from the other end of the telephone.

"Julia, calm down, all right?" Amos interjected. "Are you sure he said the morning train? This morning?"

"That's what he said, Amos," Julia repeated.

Amos' brain was racing now. "You did the right thing, Julia," he assured her. "Ah'll take it from here. Don't worry...everything will be fine."

"Right, Amos," Julia said, and then abruptly, "MattiesbackIgottago." *Click.*

Amos unfolded himself from the closet, opened the door, and glanced at the clock behind the front desk of the hotel as he rubbed his legs back into some semblance of circulation. *Ten o'clock...that leaves about an hour and forty minutes until our company shows up....*

Come on, Phineas T., a little inspiration here...

*Hmmm...*Amos thought, then smiled. *This way to the giant egress...*

114

Wednesday, August 8, 1894
10:35 am

P.H. Cooper's establishment off 16th and J Street was not the biggest icehouse in the city, but did specialize in providing crushed ice, by the barrel. The crusher itself was driven by an overhead canvas belt that ran in a continuous loop through a small window to a steam engine outside the back door and loading bay. The engine's hissing and puffing could be heard blocks away, and when Johnny and Bud drove their small wagon up the back alley to the loading dock, tying their two-horse rig to the small iron post provided there, the noise and heat generated by the little engine was overwhelming. For a moment Bud considered moving their small wagon, but an impatient tug from Johnny convinced him to just try and get the job done as quickly as possible.

The boys felt the outside heat immediately dissipate when they stepped through the outermost of its double doors into a short interior chamber that was lined like the rest of the building with hay bales. Bud, basking in the cool air, thought that working in an icehouse would be nearly ideal—at least in the summertime. But as the outer door closed and the inner door opened, he discovered that the interior of the building was even noisier than the steam engine outside. The ice crusher itself resembled an oversized metal barrel lying nearly on its side with spikes lining its interior, turning at about one revolution every three or four seconds. The ice fragments ricocheting around on the inside of the crusher sounded like hail on a tin roof—or a hundred tin roofs—until they slid into a wooden barrel through a downspout trailing out of the end of the mixer. In the next moment, a middle-aged man dressed in overalls and a blue sweater lifted and released a fresh ice block with a pair of ice tongs into the raised end of the turning crusher.

Now it REALLY got noisy, with the constant hail sound interrupted again and again by the deep resonant BOOM of the ice block banging around on the interior of the crusher. After a time, the man with the tongs moved over to the boys, who by now had placed their fingers in their ears. When the block had been completely crushed, the man threw a lever, the belt slipped free of the crusher, and the echoes off the building walls—and within the boys' ears—soon subsided.

"I had a couple of students from the U knock that crusher out for me," the man said proudly, nearly shouting, gesturing to the now-silent steel

115

contraption, and digging wax out of his ears. "If you're not deaf when you start here, you will be when you get to July. By August we are all quite proficient at sign language. Anyway, there they are—two barrels of crushed ice. We'll cover them with blankets to keep them from melting."

"Great," Johnny smiled, "please pack ice around the cream and eggs in the wagon as well. I think the sugar and vanilla will keep better away from the ice, so we'll stow those forward, if you don't mind."

"Going to a social, are we?"

"To a cadet drill, actually—and a political speech, possibly."

"I'll take the drill, thanks. Seem to have changed some since I was in the Army."

* * * * *

Amos waited until the phaeton and its occupants disappeared around the corner from the hotel, then burned up the road to the train station.

It had been far from easy. Attracting Miss Eugenia was the first hurdle—luckily, the sun was low and strong enough that his silver ring's flat face caught her attention from across the dining room in the small lobby of the hotel. Excusing herself for a visit to "the Necessary," Eugenia had at first rejected Amos' plan as ludicrous. But faced with the exigency that Amos related to her, Eugenia just shrugged and said, ominously, "This is going to *cost* you, Amos."

Amos didn't doubt it in the slightest. His next stop was the front desk—which wasn't going to be cheap, either.

Within five minutes of returning to the dining room, Eugenia began a gentle soliloquy on how beautiful the day was shaping up to be, how the *bounty* of nature was so...*invigorating*, how she *longed* to go *bare*foot on the hills like when she was a *young girl*, and how it used to it thrill her *senses* to *feel* the grass on her *bare skin*. She tossed in a few coy looks and batted eyes, and Masterson was hopelessly harpooned.

Was it possible to rent a buggy for the morning? A phaeton? Lovely.

For his part, the desk clerk...a wily little Irishman named Manny with a gap toothed grin...found it highly improbable that he could help...create the illusion...that Masterson had left the hotel early that morning. Oh, yes, he *supposed* that he could mark the room as checked out...but the *risk*...why, he could be *fired* for that...

116

Really? The man's *life* was at stake? Well, yes, those *rogues* in Lincoln were bound to do *anything...*

...and the bills were so very *crisp.*

Bursting in to the train station, Amos rapidly checked the timetables. Yes, an early morning train had left for Falls City on the Burlington & Missouri River line...and *yes*, a slow moving freight train was due through the area about a half hour from now, headed in the same direction.

But, *suck an egg*...the freight train was scheduled to leave town too early—about twenty minutes before McGee, or his man, or whoever was coming...would arrive.

As Amos strode toward the stationmaster's office, he wondered if his luck would hold. The stationmaster was a slightly built man whose face featured a balding pate, a graying beard, great looming eyebrows, and the cleverest brown eyes Amos had seen this side of his mentor, Mr. Barnum himself—which was one of the reasons why all beer deliveries happened out of town. Fairbury, as a crossroads of both East-West and North-South lines, happened to also serve as the headquarters for the Western Division of the Chicago, Rock Island, and Pacific Railroad. As such, the stationmaster was physically located right under the noses of railroad executives in the offices that formed the second story of the long building that served as both station and headquarters—though rumor had it that he had been with the railroad long enough to learn how to avoid them. The stationmaster's reputation wasn't exactly that of a martinet—just damned contrary, and not easy to coerce given the best of circumstances.

And Amos was badly in need of an undeserved and immediate favor.

Nathan Brockhurst, unbeknownst to the man that was now seeking him out, had come to recognize Amos as a monthly visitor to his yard, though only rarely stopping in Fairbury. Brockhurst had heard the rumors of bootlegging, of course—he did **live** in this town, after all—but like many others, preferred to look the other way. The locally brewed beer, if it existed, was being paid for. The transportation was lawfully arranged, and people's livelihood depended on it. However, when it came to following the rules in his station, he was resolute. There was the right way, the wrong way, and the Rock Island way—and he was a disciple of the latter.

"Hello, Mr. Brockhurst," Amos said as he walked into the office. "Ah'm Amos Seville, and ah was wondering when..."

"I know who you are, Mr. Seville," the older man interjected, hunched over his desk, filling out a last form of the same sort that appeared to

117

overflow his outbox. Without looking up, he slid a green envelope over to Amos. "I appear to have a gift for you—an Irish Valentine. Just came in from the Rokeby telegrapher—lines must finally be back up."

The station-to-station telegram—arriving on green company paper in a green envelope—was succinct:

NOTIFY AMOS SEVILLE FAIRBURY HOTEL EXPECT THREE UNWELCOME LINCOLN VISITORS MORNING TRAIN STOP H FOOTE

Straightening up in his creaky wooden office chair, Brockhurst's dark eyes blazed at Amos over half-moon glasses. "You got about forty-five minutes until that train comes in. Who's on that train?"

Amos wasn't surprised that Brockhurst had read the message—it was Rock Island property after all, and he had probably taken the message himself. He looked at the steely eyes of the stationmaster, and decided that honesty just *might* be an effective—if novel—course of action. "Three hombres that are after an old fellow at the hotel." *Well, maybe a **little** subterfuge.* "Is the Sheriff in town?" Amos knew full well that the Sheriff was out of town—as he was always conveniently missing around a delivery date.

"No," said the Brockhurst, "we got a drunk Deputy asleep in the cells, though." Looking down at the nib of his pen, he affected to clean its tip. "So, what are you gonna do when they get into *my* station?"

"Well, ah'd just as soon move them along to another station, if you don't mind," Amos grinned, leaning against the doorpost and feigning disinterest. "Saves wear and tear on the passengers, the platform, and the paintwork."

"Humph," the stationmaster grunted. "What did you have in mind?"

"Ever heard of an Egress?"

"Can't say as I have."

"Well, you got one coming in here in about fifteen minutes. With a little help, I think that we could get those three men to take a little trip in it."

* * * * *

In the end, help came in the form of the Fairbury Western Union telegrapher—and a stationmaster in Falls City.

118

"What do you *mean,* he left town?" LeBlanc demanded, his fist slamming down on the reception desk. His face a mask of rage, he grabbed the collar of Manny, the clerk. "Where did he go? Where the *hell* did he go?"

Manny stammered. *Here's where we could lose it,* thought Amos, standing in a dark corner of the lobby, peering around the corner at the front desk using a pocket mirror. His nickel-plated Smith and Wesson revolver was in his left hand, and if any of the three toadies arrayed in front of him reached for their firearms, he knew he would have to use it. Part of him almost wished they would—just to rid himself of what was sure to be a continuing nuisance.

"F-Falls City!" the clerk managed to squeak. "H-he left early this morning...s-said he was g-going to buy some furniture...from a w-warehouse. It is g-going out of business." The clerk strained to reach something under the counter, but LeBlanc held him pinned.

"H-he got a telegram yesterday...I think it's still down here...here, in the wastebasket. Can I show it to you?" his eyes pleaded, and LeBlanc reluctantly let him go with a shove. Amos had to admire the clerk's acting ability. Or his ability to accomplish anything, if his panic was indeed genuine. Either way, the man was playing a dangerous role quite convincingly.

The clerk rummaged around in the wastebasket, and produced a crumpled up yellow Western Union form. Having composed the telegram himself, watched the stationmaster transmit it to a colleague in Falls City, and received it at the Western Union shack next to the station, Amos knew its contents:

CLIVE MASTERSON, FAIRBURY HOTEL

MUST SELL ENTIRE STOCK FURNITURE DUE TO WAREHOUSE FIRE STOP WILL SACRIFICE FOR 20 CENTS ON DOLLAR STOP TELEGRAPH IMMEDIATELY IF INTERESTED STOP M FINCKENOR

There were so many ways that this could fail, thought Amos. The date was torn off the telegram to hide that it was actually sent today, not yesterday—one check at the Western Union would collapse the entire ruse. So would questioning any person in town other than the stationmaster or the desk clerk—Masterson's philandering was the talk of the town, and any citizen of Fairbury would have been delighted to relate details—imagined or otherwise—of Masterson's morning phaeton ride with Miss Eugenia.

But the one constant of these three gentlemen, Amos knew, was their uncanny—even athletic—ability to dodge the obvious, dive in without the facts, and jump to a conclusion.

"When is the next train to Falls City?" LeBlanc asked, a tone of panic now replacing his anger. Amos had been ready for this response, and smiled to himself as the clerk shakily produced a timetable. Pointing to one of the lines, he responded, "There's a freight that was due to leave 10 minutes ago, headed east. But, I didn't hear it leave..."

"Come on!" LeBlanc screamed, and with Billy and Franks in tow, sped out into the dusty street and around the corner. Amos followed at a safe distance, and was satisfied to watch the three accost the conductor of the little rattler, force money into his hands, and climb into one of the freight cars. The stationmaster glanced at the conductor, who in turn signaled the engineer. With a hiss and a rumble, the small train headed east.

Returning to the hotel with a self-satisfied look, Amos skipped through the door and strode to the small bar off the lobby. Reaching behind the counter, Amos pulled out a bottle of rye and two glasses, placing them squarely on the reception desk in front of the clerk. Manny smiled weakly, pulled the cork, tossed it behind his back, and poured liberally. Raising their glasses, the men clinked them together and downed the shots with obvious satisfaction.

In a shadowed alleyway across the street from the hotel, a lone, thin man holding two weary horses had also watched the three men enter the hotel—and, after a few moments, hurriedly board the small train and immediately head east, as if it has been held especially for them. His smiling face was a mask of death.

* * * * *

As their mule labored to pull their laden wagon up Tenth Street, Johnny pointed out some of the various buildings of the University on their right. Bud was fascinated, again, by the size and symmetry of the brick buildings, but also by the stark spaces between the buildings, nearly devoid of trees.

"That's because of the building plan," Johnny remarked. "There have been at least a dozen of them, each placing a different building here or there. The trees, if planted, are thought to get in the way. Of course, the buildings never get funded, the trees never get planted, and we have no trees to kiss the pretty girls beneath."

"I doubt that lack of trees are much of an impediment to you, cousin," Bud jibed.

"How well I ignore you! See that large rectangular hole in the ground?" Johnny ran on, unimpeded by Bud's sarcasm. "That's not a cave...a common dwelling place in Alder Grove, as I understand it...that's going to be the new library. Actually, it's spent the last 2 years *preparing* to be the new library. By the time it's in, we'll probably all be learning by phonograph, and will never *need* a library."

"Well, you'll have a fine place to listen to phonographs then." Bud reasoned, smirking.

"Still ignoring you." Pointing across campus, Johnny remarked, "The large building on the far, southeast corner is the Chemical Laboratory. It was built in 1885. Should have abandoned it in 1886. It smells of rotten eggs and alcohol. So do the chemistry students."

"The one just north of it...see it, there, on the east side of campus? That's Grant Hall. It has the gymnasium, and the armory—it even has a bowling alley. We all take fencing there—even the women." Johnny smirked. "That's the kind using swords, not the kind with barbed wire and leather gloves, as you practice in the hinterland."

"The women take fencing?" Bud retorted. "No wonder you can't get any kisses under the trees."

"What? Excuse me, this is my bad ear. That building on the far northeast side," he droned on, "is the Industrial College. Also called Nebraska Hall. Want to learn how to bang two pieces of metal together? Understand the mysteries of the atom? Study a bug? There's your spot."

"What's that white frame building right in the middle? Just north of the steam plant? University chicken house?"

Johnny rolled his eyes, then spoke in mock hushed tones. "We don't really know what happens in there. Volta Incognito." Johnny made several signs of the cross, then laughed. "Actually, it is the Dynamo laboratory. The electrical engineers meet there, religiously, to speak with their god, Thor."

"Maybe they can put in a good word for...my brother." Bud was so stunned by his own words that he actually gasped, and apologized immediately. "Sorry, cuz...don't know why I said that."

"It's O.K...must have been right there on the surface, waiting for a chance to jump out." Johnny offered, granting Bud the courtesy of looking nonchalantly away. "So, let's deal with it. What happened?"

Bud spent the next few minutes relating what he knew about his brother's attack...and his choice to come back to Lincoln rather than go home with his father. Despite having asked Bud to relate the story, Johnny already seemed to know quite a lot about it—in fact, quite a few more details than Bud had heard from his father, including the fact that the man, when he had attacked Roger, had screamed the word, 'Hovno'—whatever that meant. Probably Czech, they both decided, since most of the striking butchers were Bohemians.

They'll probably have to install a private line between Emelia and Mother just to handle the message load, mused Bud, *if this keeps up.* Clearly, the communication lines between Johnny and his mother were singing right along as well. *I wonder if Zeke knows...?*

Johnny offered, "Your brother was lucky...several of the workers were badly beaten, and I guess the rioters went on to burn down the grain warehouse at the stockyards this morning. Word has it that the governor is thinking about calling out the militia. Course, they're all going to be here at camp next week, so they could easily be mobilized."

"Really?" Bud said.

"Sure," Johnny replied. "It always happens the second or third week of August. Always after the wheat harvest, generally between hay cuttings, and before school—and the corn and spring wheat harvest—starts. 'Course, it's always hotter than hell, but it's the only time we can all get together and not interfere with everyone's schedule."

"So—your cadets—you're going to participate?"

"Of course, you idiot--that's why we're here on drill. We're getting 'Burlington Beach' set up for the rest of the militia as a training exercise. The Lieut wants us sharp—though we only have one company here, and not all four."

"How many in a company?"

"For our Company "J", only sixty-five—it's a small company, of course, because it's a cadet company, and the Lieut is trying to give more opportunities for cadet corporals, sergeants, and lieutenants. The point of the thing is training for leadership."

"I notice that you have an extra stripe on your uniform. Does that mean something?" Bud asked, innocently.

"Yes," and now Johnny straightened, practically preening. "I made Corporal this week..."

"Congratulations!" Bud said, all pretense of teasing his cousin dropping immediately from his voice. Jerking his thumb to the back of the wagon. he asked, "So, we're celebrating?"

Johnny laughed, "Well, we can't very well 'wet the stripe'—the Lieut is completely against spirits in camp. But after two weeks in this heat, the cargo back there will be most welcome."

* * * * *

Fairbury. Endicott. Diller. About the time he hit Odell, LeBlanc was having serious second thoughts about chasing Masterson halfway across Nebraska to Falls City on the rattler freight. The only two things he knew about Falls City were that (1) it sat on the Missouri river, and (2) it had that fat bastard Masterson sitting in it, buying furniture from a burned out warehouse.

But...what if he wasn't?

LeBlanc and his companions had ridden with the conductor in the caboose since their mail stop back in Endicott, and though it had certainly been more comfortable than riding in the freight car they had boarded in Fairbury, it had its drawbacks. Starved for conversation, the ancient conductor had related the background and family details of every brakeman aboard the train, the engineer, the fireman, every package in every freight car, and every station of every town on the line. According to him, Odell was a small town in the southeast corner of Gage County with about two hundred people in it. LeBlanc was quite sure by the time that the train was pulling in that he hated every single soul in it, wished them violent and horrible deaths, and would gladly have thrown the cats and dogs into the same category.

Jumping onto the dusty wooden train platform before the train had even stopped, the three men made a beeline for the Western Union office. LeBlanc fired off a telegram to McGee:

MASTERSON NOT IN FAIRBURY STOP REPORTED HEADED TO FALLS CITY FOR FINCKENOR FURNITURE FIRE SALE STOP WILL CHECK ALONG LINE FOR INSTRUCTIONS STOP

Having seen the telegram sent, LeBlanc left Franks and Billy to wait for a response while he tried to find a telephone in Odell. It didn't take him ten minutes traveling up and down the tiny main street of town to decide that he might have better luck finding ice cream in hell. Disgusted, he headed back to the station, and shortly heard the whistle signaling the freight's imminent disembarkation. Sighing, he hustled his men back to the freight train.

Wednesday, August 8, 1894
11:25 am

A few miles west of campus, a tent city had spring up along the southwestern shores of a small salt lake adjacent to the Burlington tracks. "Burlington Beach" had served as the cadet and militia training ground for several years now, allowing both small arms practice along the railroad right of way, and—as Bud's ears bore witness on their approach—artillery practice as well. Out in the middle of the lake to their right, Bud suddenly saw a huge plume of water erupt. Squinting, he was able to make out a raft with a large tri-colored flag attached, surrounded by what appeared to be the remains of several others. No more than a minute later, the last raft exploded into hundreds of splinters from a direct hit, accompanied by the shattering din of the cannon's report and the cheers of the gun crew on the western shore.

"There goes Missouri," Johnny remarked with an evil grin. "Another victim of our Rattlesnake Boys."

"You have *cannons*?" Bud asked, incredulously.

"Parrot guns, actually," Johnny responded. "Ten pounders—three inch rifled artillery. We received four of them last year, and the Lieut has been dying to give them a go. They're war surplus, of course, but appear to be serviceable."

"*Quite* serviceable," Bud agreed. "Your boys are pretty hard on poor old U. Mo." It didn't take an enthusiast to be aware of the Nebraska's sports rivalry with its neighboring states, especially Missouri, Iowa, and Kansas. But he had not heard the term...

"Rattlesnake boys?" Bud queried.

"I was referring to the gun crew. Haw, Maybelle!" Johnny replied, hauling on the left rein, and encouraging the mule to pull the small, covered wagon away from the road that paralleled the Burlington tracks and onto a lane that led toward a group of trees on the western shore. "The gun captain and two of his men happen to be on the football team."

"So...the football players are called Rattlesnake boys?" Bud asked. "I didn't know the team had a name."

"More of a nickname, actually," Johnny explained. "No one knows exactly who started it. Scoring can happen pretty fast in football, surprising the crowd—like being struck by a snake. My guess is that it got hung on us after a few tough games where we "bit" the opponent and came back from behind. Coming back from behind is a big feature of most of our games. They also call us the 'Antelopes' sometimes—another allusion to speed—but, then there's the Bugeaters..."

"They call you the *Bugeaters*?" Bud asked.

"Only our opponents," said Johnny. "And as a rule, only once."

As the boys drew up to the camp, they pulled up to a young man whose uniform was wearing but a single stripe, standing guard by a fencepost at the gap in a barbed wire fence where the road passed through to the cadet camp on Burlington Beach. He stood at attention, but lowered the rifle and bayonet to a threatening position as the wagon drew near.

"Halt! Stand and be recognized!" The young man was doing all he could to be taken seriously, but Bud would have been surprised if his cracking voice had slipped all the way down to tenor. "Password!"

"Ice Cream!" barked Johnny with a straight face, drawing a grin from the young soldier, who snapped to attention and saluted.

"Yes, SIR!" the soldier said, doing his best to stifle his grin under Johnny's stern gaze. "The corps commander's compliments, and please proceed *directly* to chow, to await further orders."

"As you were, Private," Johnny said in a firm voice, followed by "Giddup, Maybelle," and under his breath, "We'll save you some, Robby."

"Thanks, Johnny," the boy whispered back, snapping to attention and saluting as the wagon passed. Just ahead under the trees, Bud heard a rumble of voices and saw dozens of men jostling one another to find their places before long picnic tables under a broad canvas awning. Each one wore a blue uniform, and whipped their hat off as soon as they stepped under the awning. At seeing the commotion, Johnny immediately stopped the wagon, tossed Bud the reins in a frenzy, and ran to his place under the awning. In less than a minute, every cadet was standing like a statue in front of a tin plate, his hat under his arm.

"Ten-HUT!" a cadet wearing three stripes standing at a head table stood erect, and immediately all of the cadets arrayed in front of him stood to attention as well. Out from under the trees behind the head table, a tall man in a trim mustache and an even trimmer uniform paced briskly to the table, whipped off his hat, and snapped to attention. A bugler off to the side of the group played a series of flourishes, and after the last triumphal note, the cadet in the three-striped uniform shouted, "Cadets of Nebraska—

126

BE SEATED!" Abruptly, each of the cadets took a seat and sat rigidly in front of his plate, except for the tall man at the head table, who still stood erect. For a moment, the only sound Bud could hear was the wind that was gently rippling the canvas.

"*Rifles*," First Lieutenant John Joseph Pershing stated in a clear, steely voice. "You have worked very hard this last week, and you have made good progress. I am almost convinced that your dress parade before the state militia next Monday will not *completely* embarrass the University, the governor, and the entire State of Nebraska—not to mention our company mascot over there." He motioned to a small goat parked under a nearby tree, and Bud saw that the animal was decked out in a red blanket with a huge white "N" sewn on both sides. A soft round of laughter followed, then Pershing continued.

"However, I wish to remind you of a few minor points. First, please recall that the *adjutant* is in complete control of the formation. Your attention will be directed to him—not to your first sergeants, not to me, and definitely NOT to our mascot. When he is satisfied with the alignment, he will direct your captain to put his company at Parade Rest. That captain will take one step forward—only one step forward, if you please, Mr. Johnson—and command, Shoulder-ARMS, Order-ARMS, Parade-REST. You must—and will—respond at the appropriate time for each of these commands—or you may well find yourselves strapped to the very next raft out beyond Burlington Beach, awaiting the pleasure of our new field guns."

"Secondly," the commander went on, ignoring the low chuckles from the picnic tables, "when the adjutant sees each company at Parade Rest, he will signal the principal musician to play a *slow march*. The company will march from right to left in front of the assembled battalions, and then return back to their position. Please remind yourselves that the count of one-two-three-*four* is critical. Although a relatively high number, *four* can be reached if an appropriate effort is applied. If you find this too difficult, please consider applying to the University of *Iowa*.

"Finally," the tall man spoke, waiting first for the laughter to cease, "Once the marching has completed, the ranks are aligned, and the commissioned officers are in their places, the adjutant should command, FRONT, and Present-ARMS. He will then face front, salute the governor, and report, 'Sir, the parade is formed.' Please recall that the governor is a *civilian*, and as such must be excused his humanity, should he stumble, swallow a bug, or slip in the horse leavings while inspecting the formation. You, as military men, are exempt from such grace. Please bear in mind

127

that if just ONE of you loses his composure at such a point, I will PERSONALLY make that person, and the entire company, RUE THE DAY." The chuckling had ceased completely on that note, and for several long moments the commander let that message sink in to the silence of the company under his steely gaze.

"Gentlemen," Pershing continued in a softer voice, "as I said, it has been my great pleasure to serve with you. Because of your fine work, Congressman Bryan has elected to furnish ice, sugar, cream, vanilla extract—and a speech at three o'clock. Our Chancellor and several members of the press will also be present. So...the Rifles will assemble to welcome the delegation. Exercise B, I believe, Mr. Miller," he finished, with a low murmur to the adjutant, who nodded in acknowledgement. More low murmurs from the cadets followed this statement, some excited, others moaning softly at the prospect of...yet another...political speech.

Pershing barked, "Squad B will fall out for churn duty directly following chow. *Rifles...dig in!*"

*   *   *   *   *

According to the loquacious conductor, the only telephone in the Pawnee County seat was currently in the sheriff's office. So when LeBlanc arrived and picked up a telegram at the Western Union Office instructing him to call McGee immediately—one of many identical messages that were undoubtedly strung along his expected route—he was hesitant to carry them out. Instead, he sent Billy, who was not violating any bail conditions, to the sheriff's.

"Can't use the telephone for personal business, unless it's an emergency," Billy said, on his return. "The old fart said there was one in Table Rock, though, since it's on the main line between Lincoln and Falls City. He says it's in the general store under the Opera House." Having delivered his message, Billy flopped into one of the cushioned, cracked leather benches and slid his hat over his eyes.

LeBlanc harrumphed, looked at his watch. Table Rock was the next town over, a short twenty minutes away. According to the schedule, there was a passenger train out to Falls City scheduled to depart within a few minutes of their arrival, while the freight was scheduled to turn toward Lincoln, pulling in by nightfall. At least they could make up some time, and get off this damn rattler.

*   *   *   *   *

128

Chancellor Canfield was a handsome man in his early forties with a full head of wavy hair, a winning smile, and a beautiful daughter. He had just witnessed one of the finest displays of military drill anywhere—by his University's own Pershing Rifles. But the look on his face could barely be passed off as satisfaction. He smiled—sadly—and shook his head imperceptibly.

He was eating ice cream out of a hot tin plate. In hundred degree weather. In a wool suit. With a fork. After a long-winded speech, by a man that set the standard for them.

And he was doing his best to act happy about it.

Someone had misplaced the spoons. It could have been an accident—or, it could have been a campaign "dirty trick" by an anonymous Republican. In any case, the ice cream...well, the cream that had once been icy...was still cold, and sweet, and didn't taste like beans, thought Canfield.

*Well, not **much** like beans*, he reflected. This was an army camp after all, and tin plates had a long memory.

"Delicious ice cream," said Canfield, attempting to stab the last nearly solid lump with his fork, before he gave up and sipped the cream from the edge of the plate. Simultaneously, at least sixty pairs of lips followed suit, under an equal number of hungry, grateful sets of eyes.

"Yes, sir," said Lieutenant Pershing, who smiled inwardly, and joined the Chancellor in sipping his cream. Once again, he appreciated the inherent generosity of the man that stood next to him. Others would have more regard for manners, and less for his boys—but that couldn't be said about Canfield, Pershing reflected. To him, the students always seemed to come first. "I'm sure that the boys appreciate this generous gesture on the part of Congressman Bryan."

"Indeed," Canfield agreed. *Whatever you thought of Bryan's politics, you had to admit that he had an inspired sense for what would play for the public*, he thought. He could just envision the headlines in the Omaha World-Herald, now: 'Bryan Provides Cool Refreshment to Hot Cadets.' Of course, it also occurred to him that the Lincoln Journal, a Republican paper that leaned against its hometown boy would probably counter with something like 'Bryan's Hot Air Ruins Cold Treat for Soldiers.'

For his part, Bud Gardner was not only grateful for the ice cream, he was basking in...that is, on...the only luxury that could be termed *superior* in the entire camp. *Well, maybe **posterior***, he reflected, as he was sitting on a very large block of ice up in the bed of the wagon...and grinning like

129

an idiot. Next to the wagon, a pile of two dozen empty, dripping ice cream churns looked like the discarded remains of a dairy fire department that had used its own product to extinguish the flames. Bud grinned as he saw his uncle riding in on his red roan mare, its black mane and tail flowing freely as he trotted through the now-empty sentry post. Spotting Bud's waving hand, Zeke urged his horse over to the wagon. Bud received a bone-crushing handshake to answer his own, and a toothy grin as a bonus.

"Have to admire a man that can keep a cool head," Zeke remarked as he dismounted. Pulling off his hat, he walked back behind the wagon, where a trickle of water was streaming off what was left of the ice blocks. Filling his hat, he held it under the nose of his horse, which drank gratefully.

"Mr. Gardner!" Bud saw that a well-dressed man with a head of thick wavy hair was hustling over with his hand extended, followed at an ambling walk by Lieutenant Pershing, who was smoking a cigar. Zeke took his hand and shook it, removing his hat as he did.

"Pleasure to see you again, Chancellor," Zeke said. "How did your cadets look today?"

"Excellent, Zeke," Canfield beamed. "Finest corps of cadets anywhere, except...perhaps...at West Point." Pershing approached, nodded his thanks to the Chancellor, and his greetings to Zeke. "So, Zeke...what brings you out here this afternoon? You won't make any progress selling your wares to our Congressman over there." Everyone chuckled...Bryan was a well-known teetotaler.

"Heaven forbid. No, I heard the cannon, and got curious," Zeke smiled, jerking his thumb over his shoulder toward a battered Missouri flag that still hung bravely above the water, held by threads to a flagpole that was leaning at a sharp angle from the wreckage floating out on the lake. "Guess your boys must have figured out which is the business end, Lieutenant."

"Yes, but I'm afraid we've a long way to go before we can be considered dangerous," Pershing grinned. "Many thanks for the help with the shells, by the way."

"Yes, I heard that we were sent the guns without any ammunition. Where in heaven's name did you find the shells, Zeke?" Canfield asked.

"Now, Chancellor, a magician never reveals his secrets." Gesturing toward the wagon, Zeke said, "Mind if I introduce my nephew? Come on down here, Bud."

Bud obliged, a little nervously, his eyes locked on Zeke's mare, which stared back at him with malice. *What did I do to that horse?* Circling carefully around the red beast, Bud soon found himself shaking the hands of the small crowd that had surrounded Zeke. He found Pershing's grip especially strong, and, with nothing to lose—and an inner voice that told him the Lieutenant wouldn't be offended—he did his best to squeeze it back with equal...enthusiasm. Staring into Pershing's eyes, he immediately recognized a likeable man—who loved to compete. After a few seconds, as if by mutual agreement, the pair released their grips.

"Well," Pershing said, "your nephew has a fine grip, Mr. Gardner."

"You should see him pitch," Zeke said, proudly. "He led the railroaders to victory last Saturday. Smart, too—high school graduate, Chancellor."

"Really?" Chancellor Canfield nodded appreciatively. "Well, I hope you'll consider joining the University, young man."

"Yes," Pershing piped in. "Nothing like a good education to round out a man. Given a little encouragement, you might even make a Rifle."

Bud blushed and stuttered, "Thanks...thanks very much. But I'm working with my uncle right now."

"...and I'm sure that's an education, all in itself," chuckled the Chancellor.

* * * * *

The Table Rock Opera House had been built the year before, the last gasp in a series of vain attempts to wrench the Pawnee County seat from Pawnee City. Though they lost, it still spoke great things for the little town, as the conductor confidently stated. LeBlanc was again swinging onto the train platform before the train had stopped, beating it for the little grocery store under the Opera House, about a block from the train station. On his way inside, he heard a band strike up above his head, making it necessary for him to shout to the grocery clerk for the telephone. A small stray dog sat outside the grocery store, cocked his head, and started howling over the music.

It took the grocery clerk a few minutes to figure out what LeBlanc was asking for—the cotton in his ears wasn't especially helpful. "Two bits!" he finally shouted, and pointed to the telephone on the wall.

When McGee picked up his line, he was startled to hear a roaring overture from one of Puccini's operas—played entirely with brass (stringed instruments being scarce in Table Rock), and led by a vocalist that sounded more like a coyote. Over the racket, he could just make out LeBlanc's voice, and suddenly figured out what the call was about.

"There ISN'T any furniture store in Falls City!" he shouted into the receiver.

"I know, it BURNED DOWN!" LeBlanc shouted back.

"No, no! There NEVER WAS a furniture store there!" McGee screamed.

Blessedly, the band upstairs took five, and so did the dog. "SO, WHAT'S HE...doing in Falls City, then?" LeBlanc shouted, then suddenly backed off a normal voice.

"Are you *sure* he's not in Fairbury?" McGee asked.

"I saw the telegram, and he was checked out of the hotel," LeBlanc countered.

"Did anyone see him get on the train?"

"I...I didn't ask," LeBlanc admitted. "I was trying to catch a train myself."

Geniuses, McGee fumed. *Where the **hell** is Masterson?*

"Find out—*now*—when the next train leaves for Lincoln, and when the next train leaves for Fairbury."

"There's a passenger train to Falls City in twenty minutes." LeBlanc offered.

"**LINCOLN** and **FAIRBURY**, you moron!" McGee practically screamed into the phone. During the pause that followed, McGee could hear LeBlanc accost the grocer for a timetable, rustle through the pages, then finally give up and shout the question at the grocer.

"Sir, the next train for Lincoln is in an hour. There isn't another train west towards Fairbury today, Mr. McGee." McGee hated it when LeBlanc started acting polite—it meant that things were really in the shitter.

McGee considered telling LeBlanc to **start walking** to Fairbury, then hesitated. The truth of what had happened suddenly struck him like a thunderclap. If Masterson really was still in Fairbury, someone was *covering* for him—the fat sonofabitch just wasn't *smart* enough to elude anyone. Someone was *gathering* information on who was coming out to "visit" him, and *misleading* his men when they got there.

132

Seville. Shit...that's where he is. Guarding Masterson—leaving false trails for his men to follow. For the last several days, McGee had been sending out-of-work men into the Barrelhouse, with instructions to report on the whereabouts of Gardner, Seville, and his other known associates. Amos Seville had been missing since Sunday. He had been in Fairbury, guarding Masterson—leading false trails—and probably preventing his telegrams from reaching the grocery man.

Sending LeBlanc back to Fairbury was a waste of time, McGee realized. They'd have to think of another way to get to Masterson, or wait until he returned to Lincoln.

"Get home, LeBlanc...you've screwed up again," McGee sneered. Before LeBlanc could answer, the receiver went dead.

For the second time in less than a week, LeBlanc had been chewed out by his boss. His temper, short at the best of times, had reached the breaking point. He slammed the earpiece back into its metal cradle, threw a handful of change onto the counter, and stomped out the door of the grocery store just as the band upstairs started to struggle through the love theme from Puccini's "Manon Lescaut." Outside, the little dog started howling again with the music, and LeBlanc didn't hesitate—he drew his nickeled pistol and shot the animal, nearly missed, and continued firing until the dog was down, his pistol empty. The few people on the street quickly scurried away or turned their heads. Sweating, breathing heavily, and grimacing with satisfaction, LeBlanc replaced his pistol and walked back to the small train station.

*   *   *   *   *

It was late afternoon, and the crowd had begun to thin out. The dishes had been done, and the cadets had returned to their drill. Bud and Zeke were loading the last of the ice cream churns onto the wagon, for return to the dairy where Zeke had borrowed them. Bud shook his head.

"I swear, Uncle Zeke," Bud observed. "Is there anything you can't produce if asked? Ice cream churns? Cannonballs? What else do have up your sleeve?"

"Well, it never hurts to keep people happy," Zeke admitted. "Never know when you might need a favor yourself."

"Did you learn that as a deputy sheriff?" Bud asked, stringing the reins through the rein guides and then tying them to the wagon seat. The silence from his uncle caught him by surprise.

133

"Actually," his uncle finally responded, unhitching his own horse. "I learned the opposite as a deputy sheriff—that the law comes before people's happiness. Been unlearning it for the last three years now."

Not sure that he was on sure footing, Bud went ahead and asked a question that had not occurred to him consciously, but he now realized had been burning within him. "Why *did* you quit sheriffing, Uncle Zeke?"

Zeke looked his nephew in the eye, and paused—as if he was thinking the question over. Finally, he just sighed and mounted his red roan. "It's a long story...maybe I'll tell you someday, Bud. For now, just take the churns back, and return the wagon to Pack Freight. Johnny says he will take the trolley home."

"Are you coming along?"

Zeke shook his head. "I'll pick you up tomorrow morning at your Aunt's house. And then—back to Alder Grove?" Zeke's brown eyes were piercing. "It's what your mother wants, you know."

Before Bud could utter a reply, Zeke interrupted. "Your father sent me a telegram last night from Fremont. He also said you wanted to stay here and work with me." Seeming to busy himself with adjusting the saddle on his mare, he continued, "You could have taken a few days, you know. You can come back and start up with me again when you feel...ready." Zeke let the word hang in the air.

Bud felt obliged to fill the gap.

"I'm ready to work right now, Uncle Zeke," he said. "As much as Mother would like all her chicks at home, I'm only a burden to them right now. Unless," he went on, "You've had second thoughts...?"

"You'll do, boy," Zeke said, gruffly. "If I got rid of you now, I suppose that the railroaders would shoot me. Now, get along with you...I need to speak to the good Lieutenant."

Though he had managed to deflect Bud's burning question—why had he quit sheriffing—Zeke appreciated that it was a very good one. So good, in fact, that it had been on his mind for six years now—three of them while still Deputy Sheriff, before he actually turned in his badge and decided to deal with it. Thanks to Bud, he was chewing on it again when he spied Pershing, writing in a journal at a camp desk under a cottonwood tree. Getting off his horse and tying it to a bush, he approached the young officer, who finally broke his concentration and looked up with a smile.

"Mr. Gardner," the Lieut said, standing and extending a hand. "I see your nephew has hauled off the remains of our celebration. A nice young man, that."

"Yes, sir," Zeke agreed, shaking the Lieutenant's hand, and taking off his hat.

"Have you thought about enrolling him in the U?"

"Well, uh, perhaps in time, sir," Zeke said. "Right now, I was wondering if you could do me a favor?"

"Sure, Mr. Gardner—and please call me John," Pershing offered.

"I'm obliged, L — John. And it's Zeke, by the way. Uh...the Chancellor told me you had finished your degree in Law?"

"Yes, just last year," Pershing remarked. "Why, do you need a lawyer?"

"As a matter of fact, I do," Zeke allowed. "I need some advice on a contract."

"Well, I'm not your man, I'm afraid," Pershing admitted. "Contract law was not my best subject, and I have almost no experience in the actual practice of law...not a member of the bar, either, for that matter. Tell you what, though...the man that shares my rooms is a crackerjack lawyer. Would you like an introduction?"

"Yes, indeed," Zeke admitted, gratitude showing in his eyes. "Thanks...thanks very much."

"Fine, fine," Pershing replied. "Come by my rooms at say, eleven tomorrow. 1213 O Street. My roommate should have returned from the Capital for lunch by then, and you could ask your questions there in privacy. Does that suit?"

"Right down to the ground."

* * * * *

When Masterson and Eugenia finally returned from communing with nature, the horse drawing the phaeton looked nearly as tired as they did. As they pulled up to the hotel, Amos observed immediately that the horse had not had water all day, and was trembling with what was clearly approaching heat exhaustion. Amos immediately slipped the baggage boy a silver dollar, whispering a request to make sure the horse was fed and watered.

As the boy gently grasped the horse's halter, Masterson tipped his hat to Amos, managed a weak smile, and stumbled stiffly out of the carriage, moving around it (albeit at an exhausted, glacial speed) to help Eugenia out. In the few seconds where she was out of Masterson's sight, Eugenia managed a plethora of facial expressions, ranging from an expert eyeroll, to a deadly, sidelong stare thrown *directly* at Amos. Amos gulped. Immediately upon Masterson's appearance at her wagon's door, though, "Miss" Eugenia reappeared, and Masterson's face beamed.

Could they take a bite of supper? Sorry, Miss Eugenia was absolutely *satiated*, she claimed. All she could THINK about was a hot bath—did Amos think that could be arranged?

"Absolutely," Amos stated. In fact, it sounded like it would be *life-saving* (probably his own).

Once they had reached the hotel lobby, Eugenia made her adieus and slipped up the stairs. For his part, Masterson was ravenously hungry, and was more than happy to relate the day's escapades over dinner. Although Masterson's evident leer offered an evening of untold adventures—Amos was pretty sure that he would rather they would stay that way.

"Unfortunately, family business draws me away," Amos said, bowing in apology. "Shall we breakfast, then?" Masterson smiled wanly, and drew away to the dining room. *Grouse tonight.*

Amos waited for Masterson to draw out of sight, then resumed his vigil at the telephone booth in the lobby of the hotel. While he waited, a silver dollar absently flipped across his fingers, from one side to another. About seven o'clock, the call finally came.

"Amos," Julia's voice trembled, and if Amos had not been contortioned by the tiny phone booth into near-numbness, he would have pondered on how that voice could **work** on him. "I intercepted a call about an hour ago from LeBlanc to McGee—I'm sorry, but I couldn't reach you until just now." In a tired voice, Julia related the jist of the call.

"So, we don't expect him tonight?" Amos asked, just to be sure.

"I don't think so," Julia agreed.

Quickly, Amos formed and outlined one more plan for the night—if it worked, he might gain himself a day or two of peace. Outlining it for Julia, Amos felt a bit guilty for drawing his boss' niece even further into the web that they were all weaving—but she was best positioned to make the call, and they both knew it.

"Okay, Amos, I'll try," she promised. "Please...please be careful," she added, and the phone line went dead.

Good advice, thought Amos. *Think I'll take it.*

* * * * *

The Burlington train slipped into Lincoln without the fanfare of a Saturday night. With an underplayed gesture, Fred Miller directed his deputies toward the three outlaws the moment their feet hit the brick platform, and nonchalantly followed his men, his hand grasping a small silver knife that he appeared to be using to clean his fingernails.

"Evenin', Maxie," he said, looking over his eyeglasses as the two burly deputies grasped LeBlanc's arms. An almost imperceptible smile graced his lips. "Told ya not to leave the county."

* * * * *

The long shadows of sunset that had played heavily on the green space between the Burlington and Union Pacific tracks on their journey south had given way to darkness, and the two cousins realized that they were probably not going to be home in time for supper. Somehow, it didn't bother them...they had walked vigorously southward for over an hour until they reached the four hundred-foot Rock Island railroad bridge that spanned the tracks they were following. The boys had accoustomed themselves to long, brisk walks during the evening—a "training" walk, they called it, preparing for the day that they both hoped to join the U.S. Marines. They were now strolling northwestwards again toward home, and the cigarettes they had stolen from the sleeping bum under the bridge behind them tasted cool and sweet.

"Hold it, Lewis," Frank Ryan whispered, halting the pair of them. "Who's that up ahead?"

"I think it's a nigger," Lewis replied, uncertainly.

The man in the blue coat headed south toward them did indeed seem to have dark skin, though in the darkness it was hard to tell for sure. As he approached within a hundred feet of them, the Ryan boys saw that he was carrying a long, strange tool over his shoulder, and a gunny sack under his arm. Uneasy about stealing the cigarettes, both boys dropped them immediately.

"I think it's the same nigger we passed up coming down here," Frank said. "Remember? We came up from behind him."

"Well, it's hard to tell in the dark," Lewis whispered. "What's he doing here?"

Frank and Lewis Ryan knew that a lot of hungry men were out of work and living along the tracks, though they had not seen many this far south of town. Nevertheless, the black man carrying the long tool—kind of a cross between an axe and a shovel—spooked them.

"I dunno, but he's mighty big," Frank stammered. "Lewis, let's get home—we're late."

"Let's cut across the woods, then," Lewis suggested, motioning to their right. Without another word, they crossed the Burlington tracks and slipped up the embankment into the trees, beelining toward their homes in south Lincoln.

Slowly, the black man approached the spot where the boys had left the tracks, picked up the still lit cigarette, and took a long drag, watching the spot where the boys had disappeared into the foliage. He smiled. *This could work out just fine*, he thought.

Near dawn, Bud was still trying to stack the ice cream churns. It was damp, oddly chilly, and the tiny kerosene lamp propped on the wagon seat barely lit the dairy barn. The place stank of sour milk and cattle, but oddly, also like spilled whiskey and stale beer. Deep shadows cloaked the walls, and Bud kept brushing against them, knocking hidden scythes, hoes, and corn knives down on him that had to be replaced before the churns could be stacked. A small boy with vacant eyes played near him in the dust, and Bud had to keep moving him in order to keep the wagon from rolling over him, being pushed by a German farmer in overalls, with Bobber asleep in the back. The churns themselves were heavy, clumsy, and didn't stack easily, falling at the slightest imbalance. *Why can't I do this? Why do I feel so stupid?* He felt that the stacking had gone on for hours, even days...and when his uncle Zeke placed his hand on his shoulder, Bud burst out, "Let me finish this job, willya? I can *do* it!"

But his uncle didn't stop shaking him, and Bud finally gave up, turning toward the light, which seemed to be strengthening. He rubbed his eyes, and blinked at his Aunt Emmy, who appeared to be staring oddly back at him. Slowly, the cobwebs cleared, and Bud found himself in the room that he and Johnny shared. Johnny was gone, and his Aunt's smile seemed a bit strained.

"Well, I'd like to let you finish, Bud, but you said last night to get you up to meet your Uncle. Breakfast is ready downstairs when you are."

"Where's Johnny?" Bud asked.

"He came downstairs a few hours ago," his aunt replied. "You were...restless, so he decided to sleep on the couch."

Bud felt remorse. For many years, he had been reliably informed by his older brothers that he talked in his sleep, although it was generally limited to times of extreme stress. *Well, I guess the last week qualifies,* he admitted to himself.

"I'm sorry, Aunt Emmy," he began, rolling out of the bed and putting on his trousers. "I..."

"No need to apologize, Bud," Emmy sniffed. "Well, come on, Bud...my scrambled eggs are pretty good, but I can't say they improve with age."

Following her down the steep, creaky stairs, Bud was surprised to find that the men usually lined up for breakfast outside the porch had departed, and that the house had settled down to mere post-apocalyptic disorganization. Zeke was pouring himself a cup of coffee.

"Sit down and help yourself, Bud....you too, brother," said Aunt Emelia.

"No thanks, Em," Zeke demurred, but Bud sat right down and made short work of the eggs laid in front of him, still warm, with bits of bacon mixed into them.

"More, Bud?" Emelia queried, never truly happy unless a second helping was forced upon any guest. Bud shook his head and held his hands up, smiling.

"Any more and he'd start to cluck, Em," Zeke remarked. "Bud, seeing as how you've eaten the *whole coop*, I wonder if I could interest you in heading down to the Barrelhouse—I'm headed over to Pershing's this morning, and Swede needs some help with restocking..."

"Go on, Bud," Emelia said, not taking her eyes off Zeke. "Your uncle and I have a few things to discuss."

Oh boy, thought Bud.

Oh shit, thought Zeke.

"Uh, okay, Aunt Emelia—that is, Uncle Zeke...I'll...just be going now," and Bud grabbed his sack lunch, making a beeline for the back door.

"Have a seat, Ezekiel," Emelia Pack said, and poured the coffee.

* * * * *

Franks and Billy felt like they'd been on a twenty-four-hour snipe hunt. Three trains, five disembarkations, and twenty-nine towns later, they were back in Lincoln—and McGee's face barely masked the rage beneath it. But both he and they were quiet now, sitting in a small upper room, with shades drawn against the morning sun. As he had listened to their tale of wandering woe, the small man seated on the plush davenport across the room from them had puffed absently on a small cigar, and stared out at nothing in particular with his icy blue eyes. At its conclusion, with LeBlanc dumped back in jail—again—Miles McGee wrapped himself more tightly in his robes, and frowned, stubbing out his thin cigar.

"I had so hoped to avoid all this," McGee sighed. "Clive Masterson is a fool, but I would have thought he'd have greater sense than to carry this

140

farce to its conclusion." Reaching into the pocket of his voluminous robes, McGee pulled out a single piece of paper, unfolded it, and stared at it. Slowly, his head lifted, and a smile crawled across the short man's face that threw shivers down every spine in the room. That caused Franks' skin to crawl. That dripped with *sin.*

Refolding the paper, McGee said quietly, "Gentlemen, I have some...more proficient and professional...assistance due here tomorrow night. In the meantime, I shall give Mr. LeBlanc his head."

Turning his head to Franks, he said simply, "*Wreck* him."

* * * * *

It was a good question, thought Zeke. Maybe that was why Emelia repeated it.

"Just what are you trying to make of my nephew?" Emelia's eyes stared levelly at her brother over her petite, china teacup, embroidered around the edges with pink roses, while she stirred it slowly with her silver spoon.

When she looks like that, I wonder if she knows how much she looks like Mother? Probably, Zeke speculated.

"I'm not trying to make anything out of him, Em," Zeke said, defensively.

"Well, you're succeeding admirably," Emelia said. Stopping her stirring, she leaned forward, bracing her arms on the oak table. Her brown eyes sparked, and Zeke noticed for the first time the resemblance between his sister and his nephew. Bud had her eyes—and their mother's.

"Just why did you take him on?" Emelia asked.

"I was ASKED," Zeke said, reflexively. "Jeremiah asked me, and I said yes. I'm just trying to help him make a living."

"Tending a bar?" Emelia said.

"It's what I do."

"It's not ALL you do. And now that he's here, we'd be glad to put him to work freighting—you KNOW that," Emelia stated. "Why not let us? It's a better living than you are offering. He could even go to the University...he's certainly qualified...and..."

141

"You know why." Zeke countered, cutting her off. "For the same reason that Father hasn't spoken to you in 30 years...or Jeremiah, for that matter."

"Because I married a Catholic?" Emelia laughed, rising out of her chair. "So, you've become religious, all of a sudden? Zeke, I'm so pleased—do invite me to the Church of the Holy Whore some Sunday, won't you?" Her voice was rising, and Zeke was hardly surprised to see her neck start to redden. *Soon it'll be her face, and then the top of her head will come off. Same old Em.* Zeke would have smiled, if that pesky old feeling of mortal danger and impending doom hadn't cautioned him.

"Now, Em, you KNOW what would happen if Bud's father, or ours, found out that he was working and living with you," Zeke said, calmly. "They'd be down here like a shot to fetch their son."

"I'm not so sure about that," Emelia countered, walking over to the window, and gazing out onto the street. The sun was already hot, and the dust of J Street rose in its slanting rays as the horses passed back and forth between the Capitol and the Courthouse. "Maybe five years ago, when Mother was alive. But, not today. I think that Daddy's...softened some..."

It could be true, admitted Zeke, to himself. Their mother had always been the ultra-religious one, and when Emelia had married—by circumstances, been forced to marry—"one of those fish-eaters" as she'd termed it, the entire family had (in some cases, reluctantly) gone along with her, turning their backs on Emelia and her new faith. All except Zeke...and surprisingly, Bud's mother, who still corresponded, despite her mother-in-law's objections. *But now that their father was alone,* thought Zeke, *things might be changing...*

"Maybe," admitted Zeke. "But I don't see what's wrong with working at the Barrelhouse, Em..."

"Stocking, cleaning, yes," Emelia said. "But buying...and bootlegging?"

"It's all perfectly legal..." Zeke interrupted.

"Legal as long as Fred Miller is the Sheriff, you mean," Emelia countered. "He's made a habit out of looking the other way since you saved his bacon back in '90."

Emelia moved around the table, and sat down next to her brother. Gently, she placed a hand on his arm, and looked into his own brown eyes. "Ezekiel," she said, "You've lived life on your own terms since you were weaned...because it was forced on you, yes, but also because you wanted it

142

that way. Result? You are so cock sure of yourself as captain of your fate that you've got people jumping into your boat, left and right – even when you got no blamed idea what's around the next bend. And sometimes, Zeke, as you know very well, it's a waterfall."

Before Zeke could interrupt, Emelia pressed on, her intense eyes pinning the older man to his seat. "Now, I want you to think **hard** about it. I know you like the boy—but aren't you, on some level, still trying to best Jeremiah—and our father? Be honest—isn't it possible that you are using Bud to get even with them—proving to them that your life here is a valuable one by pulling Bud into it? Yanking him out here to do your bidding on a whim?"

For a moment, Zeke didn't speak—at first he was shocked, then offended, and finally, just pissed off. Emelia saw the signs, his own face reddening, and before he could rise to his feet, she grasped his arm and gently forced him back down into his chair.

"Hear me out, Ezekiel—whatever else our family thought of us, we could always level with each other." Grasping his shoulder, she went on. "You and I have...unfinished business...with our family. I think that Bud could be the way that we can...finally...find our way home again. Please...please don't wreck it...or him."

Zeke looked into his sister's eyes, now tearing up. *Damn, she always knew I was a sucker for tears.*

* * * * *

Having just left the surveyor's office on the top floor, George Washington Davis strode out of the passenger depot of the Burlington and Missouri River Railroad with a full head of steam. His friend met him just outside the ornate double doors, and Davis was livid.

"They don' listen," Davis said, hotly. "Here em 'ah in this new suit a' clothes...railroad clothes!...an' ah' say how ah needs a job—an' they jist don' care."

"Calm down, George," his companion said, patting his shoulder with assurance. "Let's git a cup of coffee, and you ken tell me about it."

Crossing the street, they entered Mooney's restaurant, and took a couple of empty seats in a secluded corner of the establishment near the kitchen door. The pretty young waitress with raven hair took their orders, quickly placed a couple of mugs of steaming hot coffee in front of the two Negroes, and collected their nickels...then returned to her sweeping.

143

Anna Marie was not exactly eavesdropping...but she couldn't help hearing the excitement in the shorter man's voice, noticing his fine blue suit, and his scarred, though handsome face. As they drank their coffee, the taller man kept calming the shorter man down, reasoning with him. Before she was called to another table, Anna saw the taller man put his hand on the shorter man's shoulder, and heard him remark, "It's like ah been sayin,' George...sometimes ya jist gots to *show* people what you ken do."

* * * * *

In the basement of the Barrelhouse, by mutual agreement, Bud moved the whiskey kegs against one wall, while Swede moved the beer kegs against the other. Despite the fact that the whiskey kegs weighed less than half as much, Bud had a hard time keeping up with the Nordic giant. At six feet six inches tall, Swede was the biggest man Bud had ever met, and Bud marveled at his ability to shove, roll, and even stack the 250 lb behemoths...with a smile that never left his tanned face. How old was he? Somewhere in his early 20's, Bud thought—with a young man's strength, enthusiasm, and optimism.

At their first break, Swede pulled up a whiskey barrel, gestured to the one beside him, and pulled out a brown paper bag from behind his barrel, while Bud reached for his own bag from Aunt Emelia. He was about to open it up when Swede opened up his own sack...and Bud sincerely and *immediately* wished that he *hadn't*. The incomparable smell of lye had filled the unvented basement, and Bud's eyes instantly began to water. Out from his sack, Swede proudly pulled a large tinfoil-wrapped package of...

"Lutefisk!" Swede proclaimed proudly. "We normally get this around Crissmas, you know, but we just had da tent anniversary of da Swedish Lutheran Church in Gothenburg, and my mudder sent me some on da train yesterday. It's REAL good."

"I can TELL," Bud said, trying not to gag. Inside the foil was a whitish substance that looked like a cross between jelly and runny mashed potatoes. It offered the kind of stench that would have made even Skunk dive for cover...*not Bobber, though,* Bud reflected. "What the heck is *in* that stuff?"

"Cod, mostly," said Big Swede, "mixed with some lye—it helps keep it from spoiling."

"How can you *tell*? No, no, please put that away, Swede," Bud interjected, when Swede held it out to him, "Enjoy your treat."

144

"Suit yourself," Swede said. "Amos loves it, he does really, ya know."

"Oh, yeah?" said Bud, half-turned away, in part to avoid the stench, in part to protect his roast beef from contamination.

"Oh, yah—he sez he uses it to clean the coal outta the stove when nuttin' else works..."

When Bud turned back around, he saw that Swede's face was absolutely deadpan. However, when Bud started to grin, Swede finally cracked, opened up and guffawed. They were still cutting up when the Professor's head popped into the basement door and asked, "Is Zeke down there and WHAT the HELL is that **SMELL**!?! I am NOT *drinkin'* that...!"

"No, he's not here," Bud said, still chuckling.

"Smells like the Mississippi River at low tide," murmured the Professor. Then louder, "Git up here, Bud, and talk to this fella—he needs to speak to Zeke, fast."

"I'll come too," said Swede, snatching up his lunch.

"Uh, leave the Lutefisk, Swede," urged Bud. "There's an empty barrel to turn over it right over there, and a concrete block to put on top of it, for safety."

* * * * *

Ransom Reed Cable Jr. had his head in a book, as usual. Unfortunately, he was also descending the outside stairway that led from the offices of the Chicago, Rock Island and Pacific Railway, Western Division. So when he managed to put a foot wrong (also as usual), he plunged directly into the Fairbury stationmaster, crossing just then on the platform below. The resulting crash—Nathan Brockhurst happened to be carrying a crate of dirty glasses from one of the sidetracked combination cars at the time—was a prominent feature of the morning and afternoon coffee breaks, both upstairs in the corporate offices, and downstairs amongst the brakemen and engineers.

Nothing like a good wreck to pull labor and management together.

"I am SO sorry," said Cable, apologizing for what must have been the sixth time. Stooping along with Brockhurst, together they were picking up the pieces of broken glass that were spread all over the platform at the bottom of the stairs. "It was all my fault...I just wasn't looking where I was going, and..."

145

"Never mind it, Rance...it's far from the worst pileup I've ever seen at this station," he said. Brockhurst had recognized at once the thin young man in the familiar oversized wool suit, which still seemed to be wearing *him* (instead of the other way around), despite a summer's "fattening up" at Miss Maybelle's boarding house. "When the circus came back into town last year, a certain old yard goat—who shall remain nameless—failed to switch back to the main line after he sidetracked a rattler. So when 'Fireball' Carter came in with a hot box on the circus train, the smoker left the high iron and smacked into the rattler parked there in the hole. The jambusters would have sorted it out right away—if the tigers hadn't gotten loose."

"Tends to complicate matters, I suspect," Cable observed, now laughing.

"Just another day at the Rock, I'm afraid," Brockhurst replied. He raised a finger and shook it at the young man. "Now, you don't have to go telling...upper management...about that—I'm not exactly sure that report made it all the way upstairs, to tell you the truth."

"Your secret is safe with me," Cable said, and Brockhurst believed him. Despite his inherent clumsiness, he had worked hard and made a good name for himself over the summer, never once trading on his family name. "But I'm afraid I already heard about it—from Father himself, to tell you the truth," Cable went on, chucking glass into a nearby trash bin. "Come to think of it, it might have been the reason they sent me out here—it sounded like a lively place to spend the summer."

"And has it been?" Brockhurst asked, throwing the last of the broken glass into the same trashbin.

"A lot more interesting than Princeton," Rance admitted, now looking around the platform, as if having lost something. "But I'm afraid that I'll have to catch up on my summer reading, or I'll be even more behind the eight ball than I already am. Have you seen my book? It's a volume on Ibsen."

"Here's the trainwrecker," Brockhurst said, reaching under the stairs and brushing the dust off its cover. "Hmmm—didn't that fellow say, 'A community is like a ship; everyone ought to be prepared to take the helm?' Sounds like a dangerous sentiment for the son of a railroad president, doesn't it—sure you can stand the competition?" There was just a hint of humor in Brockhurst's peculiar sidelong glance as he held out the book to the young man, and Rance didn't fail to catch it.

Never underestimate an old stationmaster, Rance mused.

"Actually, Father would have wanted it that way—he worked himself up, and he expects me to do the same," Rance said, taking the book, and sticking out his hand. "If I don't see you before I leave, thanks again for the help this summer, Mr. Brockhurst—I learned a lot."

Brockhurst took his hand. "Taking off on the evening train, are you?"

"Yes, at seven...straight back to Chicago, via Lincoln," said Rance. "There'll be a little going away dinner at the hotel at five—are you coming?"

"I'll be home with the Missus by then, I'm afraid. So, good luck, youngster—and keep your eyes open—we have enough to worry about on this line," Brockhurst said gruffly, giving Rance's hand a final squeeze and turning away quickly, hauling off the partially-filled case of still-unbroken glasses to hide what might have been mistaken for a smile, in a face better known for its severity. Despite those occasional, uncomfortable phone calls he had been obligated to take from the young man's father—in which the stationmaster had crustily reported his son's creditable progress from the "bottom up"—Brockhurst had decided at last that, yes, he *would* miss the young man.

For his part, Rance watched the stationmaster hobble gamely off—then, smiling openly, ambled off in his own direction, once again burying his head in his book. If he had not, he might well have noticed the tall man that stood on the platform not ten feet from them. Once the boy had passed, the man dropped his newspaper to reveal a sallow, impossibly thin face with a wide grin. His long strides made a hollow echo on the raised platform as he walked slowly to the Western Union office to send his telegram. Suddenly, a steam whistle on the stationhouse blew. Snapping open his watch, the man confirmed that it was precisely twelve o'clock—*just seven hours to go.*

147

Thursday, August 9, 1894
11:00 am

Ascending to the main floor of the Barrelhouse, Bud found that the middle-aged man waiting for him had a boy about six years old clinging to his knees. The boy gazed up at Bud with a familiar, vacant look and simple face that bespoke a retarded child. *Where have I seen him?* Bud thought. *Somewhere...*

"Hi," the man said, holding out his hand. "I'm Robert Harrison. I met you last Saturday."

Of course... Bud took his hand. "I remember you, sir...from the Cooperative meeting, wasn't it? You're the one that had the...uh, run-in with McGee."

"That's right," Harrison replied. "Bud, isn't it? I need to find your uncle Zeke."

"I believe I heard him say that he'd be with Lt. Pershing this morning, sir," Bud said, and felt a sudden tug at his leg. Bud was surprised to see Harrison's little boy holding up a red rubber ball with faded yellow stripes...apparently the same one that the boy had been rolling around on Sanders' barn floor. A faint but definite smile danced on the boy's lips as his eyes stared up in expectation.

"I see that Roscoe remembers you, too," Harrison said, now, smiling, too. Reaching down, he lifted the boy easily to his shoulders, the boy's mild smile shifting immediately to a wide grin. "Does one of you have a City Directory?"

"Back here, I tink," said Swede, who, having returned from the cellar, now rummaged behind the bar to produce a battered paperback book that read,"Lincoln City Directory, 1893, Nebraska State Journal Printing Company."

"Would you mind holding my grandson while I take a look?" To Bud's surprise, Roscoe moved without hesitation from Harrison's arms into his own, still grinning. In the background, Tom Turpin sat down and started rippling the piano keys, eventually settling on a tune with a cheery ragtime lilt. It sounded only vaguely familiar until the Professor started singing,

"Baa baa black sheep, have you any wool?

Yes sir, yes sir, three bags full...."

Bud started laughing, pointing at the Professor, who grinned and nodded as he rippled a roaring glissando up and down the keys for a big finish. Bud clapped with approval, and to his amazement, so did a beaming Roscoe.

Flipping through the pages, Harrison finally turned to Pershing's name, and read off *1213 O Street.* "Well, we're off, then," Harrison said, then hesitated. Observing his grandson's obvious delight in Bud's company, he took off his hat, shuffled his feet and asked, uncertainly, "Uh...Bud? I know it's an imposition, but...I wonder if you wouldn't mind watching Roscoe here for about a half hour or so, while I run Zeke down? He seems to be getting along fine with you, and I promise to be quick."

Harrison shuffled uneasily, and before Bud could answer, Swede broke in, his huge hands patting Harrison's shoulder. "Sure, sure. Datted be okay, Mister Harrison. Bud chust gets in da way, anyway. Bud, you could take him upstairs to da bedroom up dair, mebbe, ya?"

Bud nodded—he was used to taking care of his little brother and sister, David and Daphne, and Roscoe seemed an amiable enough companion. In any case, it beat rolling whiskey barrels around in a basement filled with lutefisk.

*   *   *   *   *

Pershing's rooms were located above a drug store on the south side of O Street, and as Zeke approached the door at the top of the narrow enclosed stairway, he was surprised to see the door in front of him open quickly, as if in anticipation. Lt. Pershing stood there smiling, and quickly gestured Zeke inside, to a small, immaculately kept kitchen. Pulling the coffeepot from the stove and placing it on the white rectangular table near the window, Pershing and Zeke seated themselves at the two wooden chairs that surrounded it.

As Pershing poured them both a cup, the kitchen door swung open, and a stack of law books with legs stumbled into the small kitchen. Pershing sprang up to steady him, and as the books were peeled away, a slim, energetic man of about 30 stood before him, with hair parted in the middle and ears that stuck out at a perilous angle above his starched collar.

"Hullo, J.J...and this must be Ezekiel Gardner." The young man's hand grasped Zeke's, and his eyes locked onto the older man's, lighting up like an arclight. "Charles G. Dawes. Don't know if you remember me–we met briefly a few years ago. You were helping out on the Sheedy trial, as I recall. Please have a seat. J.J.? How about some coffee?"

"Not sure you need anymore, Charlie," Pershing said, laughing. "You look to be pretty charged up the way it is."

"Hell n' Maria, J.J., have pity! I just ran into Bryan, and I'm ready to fall asleep." Zeke smiled, and Dawes remarked, "Just fooling, of course, Mr. Gardner—W.J. Bryan and I go to the same church, and he was a good friend to me when I was a wet-behind-the-ears lawyer here a few years back. In fact, I think that some of these are actually **his** lawbooks." Flipping open several of the covers at random, he added, grinning, "*Quite* a few, it appears. I'd better return them before I leave, or I'm likely to be editorialized into infamy as another greedy, unscrupulous Republican in that damned paper of his."

"So...you're leaving town, Mr. Dawes?" Zeke asked. Dawes reminded Zeke of an electrical dynamo—bright, energetic and a little unstable—and he could see that he had a fair job ahead of him if he wanted to keep the conversation on a single track.

"That's right, Mr. Gardner—I struck Lincoln right at the top of a boom," Dawes noted. "Then it started sliding. I'm afraid I found that Horace Greeley's advice to 'Go West, young man' was not good short-range pecuniary council. Look how I'm forced to lodge with my old friend here...desperate and destitute....leaving town in total disgrace...a shame really..."

"Don't let him kid you, Zeke," Pershing warned, mirth still flitting across his features. "He's done all right here since '87...he's made some good cases against the railroads, bought a few buildings...even managed to save the American Exchange National Bank last year when a lot of banks were going under. He's only staying with a poor soldier like me because his wife and children are vacationing with family, and he's sold every other asset he's got in town."

"Never believe anything Pershing says, Mr. Gardner—those new cannon have him addlepated." Dawes sat down, leaned back in his chair, and for the first time, his face turned serious, those blazing eyes boring into Zeke's. "Well, enough about me, Mr. Gardner. How can I help you?"

* * * * *

Bud and Roscoe were both giggling by the time they got to the top of the stairs—Roscoe, because Bud was carrying him upside down, and Bud, because Roscoe's laugh was that infectious. As they entered the small upstairs bedroom from the interior hallway, their laughter stopped suddenly. Through the open door across the room, they could see a man on the small second-story platform that overlooked the trainyard, seated on

150

a wooden chair with his feet on the exterior railing, smoking a cigar. As he turned and rose to face them, Bud recognized the man as J.T. Lynch, and relaxed.

Roscoe didn't, and tensed.

"Well, hello, little feller," said Lynch, addressing Roscoe, taking off his hat and spinning it on the tip of his finger before tossing it lightly onto the bed. "Think I must have something for you in here." Patting his vest pockets as if searching for something, Lynch feigned surprise when he slowly pulled a peppermint stick out of his left breast pocket. Roscoe's tension vanished as he reached for the candy. Bud took the candy stick, gave it to the boy, and placed him on the floor of the small room, where Roscoe seemed content to alternatively suck the candy and roll the ball, then roll the candy and suck the ball, all things eventually reaching a delightful, sticky equilibrium.

"Well, I see Zeke has you performing quite a sundry of tasks for him—including babysitting," said Lynch. Sitting back in the chair, he produced a cigar and offered it to Bud, who declined. "Come to think of it, he acted the same way as a sergeant back in the Army of the Potomac—I was a corporal, in charge of babysitting the platoon most days—while he babysat the Lieutenants."

Bud sat on the floor, rolling the ball back and forth with Roscoe. The boy was completely engrossed with the candy and ball. *What was Lynch doing up here?*

"Zeke said he served with the First Minnesota...so you were with them, too?"

"From Alpha to Omega—nearly was the Omega for both of us, too—especially at Gettysburg." J.T. rolled a cigar between his fingers, then lit it and puffed it into life, though his eyes now focused elsewhere. "We were late to the battlefield...missed the first day entirely...marched eighteen miles like hell was on our heels though Union and Taney towns. Hotter than hellfire...Zeke always said then if he ever got out of the War with his skin, he would start a bar just to quench it." J.T. smiled, but the smile didn't quite reach his eyes.

"When we joined the battle, it was to cover a gaping hole left by Dan Sickles. He had sent out his Third Corps to meet Longstreet's Alabamians out in the Peach Orchard and the Wheat Field, which turned into a bloody, brawling mess. Hancock...he's our Corps Commander...comes galloping up to our regimental commander, Colonel Colvill, and points right at our colors. 'What regiment is that?' he yells.

151

" 'First Minnesota,' says Colvill.

" 'Charge those lines!' yells Hancock.

"He needed to gain time, you see," said Lynch, coldly. His eyes blazed, and his voice went grave, and quiet. "He'd already sent for reserves, but he needed five minutes, and we was *handy*. So in we go, our lonely ol' regiment—262 of us, man and boy. With so few men...and *everybody* went, cooks and all...we were still only a hundred yards wide. Afterwards, they told us that it was 1,600 Alabamians, under Wilcox, that we faced. Seemed like more, somehow..."

"Shoulda seen Zeke," Lynch said, shaking his head. "He led the way down the slope until we neared a shallow ravine, and when 'Charge' rung along the line, he smiled over at me, and said, 'Ya wanted to die in your bed, J.T.?' We yelled like furies, running down the near side and crawling up the far side...right into the face of shells, and bullets, grape and canister. I was numb myself...I couldn't believe that it was happening... Sam Nickerson, Jim Ackers, ol' Oscar Woodard...all dropped from the ranks, with the rest of us still pulled forward. Our attack was foolhardy, and savage, and for a while the graybacks kept their distance from us, and emptied a constant, intense fire into our ranks.

"'Course we couldn't hold. But by the time that retreat sounded, they say we hadn't gained five minutes...we'd gained *fifteen*. When we let up our fire and started to pull back, the fire was brutal, vicious. A grievous shot hit me in the back...well, a little lower than that...and Zeke helped me the rest of the way back onto Cemetery Ridge. There were 47 of us...the rest were all either wounded or dead on the field." Lynch fell silent, and for awhile the only sound in the small room was Roscoe, rolling his now hopelessly sticky ball into the bedspread that hung down onto the floor next to them.

"So...you did it," Bud said, quietly, looking up at last. "You won."

"If you wanna call it that." Lynch's icy, returning gaze nailed Bud to the floor. "Do you think that it was worth it? Did who was right or wrong matter to those poor bastards dying in that ditch, calling for their mommas? All that matters is that you *live*. You grab it, and hold on to life. No one is going to help you...do it yourself."

Quietly, Bud said, "What about Zeke? He helped you..."

"Zeke...yeah...the one fellow that I knew I could count on. That is," he said, his features now turning warmer, "except where women were concerned."

152

"I don't think that concerns me too much," said Bud, glad that the conversation had turned to a lighter topic.

"Don't be too sure," Lynch said, smiling slyly, as he lit his cigar. "Had a girl in Leesburg once, name of Penny—that was after Gettysburg, when Zeke and I were reassigned to Custer in the Shenandoah Valley. Found out that your uncle—ladies' man that he is—was sparking her, too. We—had words—and in the end, we both got mustered out and left for points west, so that settled it. Wasn't a woman ever born worth a friendship." Lynch leaned forward, pointing his cigar at Bud. "Don't forget that—especially when he steals *your* best girl."

Not likely, Bud mused, Anna Marie's angry refusal of Zeke's offer to pay for broken dishes springing immediately into his mind. *I don't think they get along....*

Then another thought struck him like a thunderclap. He started grinning like an idiot.

*Holy Cow ... I've got a **girl**.*

* * * * *

"Allow me to summarize, Mr. Gardner." Charles G. Dawes stood up, stretched, and paced about the small kitchen that was now occupied only by Zeke and himself—Pershing having discreetly stepped into the parlor. "You made a contract to sell a great deal of grain to Mr. Masterson, once the Cooperative approves the price. But you can't locate a copy of the document—is that it?"

"Well, there was more than one copy made, but it isn't handy," Zeke admitted. "Could the contract still be executed without it?"

"With the willing participation of both parties, of course," Dawes said. "Is that the case?"

"I'm not sure," replied Zeke. "The party of the second part is...wavering."

Dawes rubbed his chin. "Well, a positive result is still possible, but of course, any conflict could mean a protracted court case. It would be your word against his...unless there were any other witnesses?" he queried.

"None we could call upon," Zeke said, quietly.

Dawes leaned against the doorpost, and gave Zeke a penetrating look. "I'd rather not ask this, but it will come up in court if the contract is disputed. Was the contract coerced in any way?"

153

Zeke was silent, then responded, "Not in any way that the party of the second part would admit to."

Dawes sighed, and shook his head. "It's damned funny business, Mr. Gardner. A contract that depends on a committee on one side, and a wavering rascal on the other. My advice is to get an amicable settlement...as soon as possible, too. I've seen what's happening to the corn prices, and somebody could get...greedy."

"Good advice," said Zeke. "Money can make people do foolish things."

"Or power," replied Dawes, as he began stacking his books. "Hell and Maria...just look at what's happening with the railroads. They represent the most prestigious, fastest growing, highest technical achievement of our age. In the last ten years, the miles of track in this country have doubled, and re-doubled, but the number of actual firms operating and controlling them have reduced to a mere handful. Owning and running a railroad is extremely prestigious...and railroad owners are a very *exclusive* club. Only the wealthiest, and most ruthless, need apply. They are run by powerful men who would stop at nothing to win, including cutting one another's throats. Men like J.P. Morgan, Commodore Vanderbilt, E.H. Harriman...Jay Gould."

"Jay Gould," Zeke shuddered. "I heard he died over a year ago."

"His son, George Jay, is a reasonable facsimile." Dawes sighed. "Men like these are swarming around, positioning themselves as potential buyers of the Union Pacific."

"Union Pacific? I guess I had heard that they weren't doing so well," Zeke admitted. "They're in bankruptcy, aren't they?"

"Yes, they're a wreck," Dawes stated, flatly. "But that's the best time to invest."

A sudden knock on the kitchen door stopped the conversation.

"Pardon me, Zeke," Pershing said, sticking his head into the kitchen, "but you have a visitor. A Mr. Harrison?"

"Ask him in, please." Turning back to the attorney, he said, "Thanks, Mr. Dawes. I'll be in touch." He took Dawes' hand, and shook it warmly, as Harrison and Pershing entered the kitchen. Pershing took half of Dawes' books, and the two friends left.

Turning to Harrison, Zeke said, "So—are you here to give me hell? Or just bad news?"

Harrison said, "Good news and bad news—which first?"

"The bad news of course—this is Nebraska, dammit, not New Orleans."

"There weren't enough votes to carry your motion to sell—we haven't been able to get to half the signatures you requested yesterday—not enough people had heard about it. Those that we did get hold of were pretty much for it, though." Harrison tried to frown, but a smile kept creeping over his features.

"Well, drop the other shoe, dammit," Zeke said. "You're grinning like an idiot."

"Have you seen the paper?" he said, dropping a copy of the Journal on the table.

Under the title "A Wild Day in Corn," Zeke read the subtitle "Sudden Jump Skyward Causes an Uproar in the Pit," and "Every Trader a Buyer and the Advance Over Six Cents" with growing excitement. Following his finger down the narrowly-space column, under the "Closing Prices" it read "CORN—August, 59 ¼ c." Zeke looked up at Harrison, who nodded.

"You read it right," Harrison chuckled, and reached into his shirt pocket, and fingering two sheets of neatly folded white paper. "I have here five copies each of two letters, both signed by Mr. Sanders, exalted and esteemed Secretary of the Cooperative. One is a copy of the minutes from the meeting of August 4, authorizing action for immediate sale of up to two hundred thousand bushels of corn at a market rate of at least 54 and a half cents, minus up to 10% for transport and other expenses. The second is a letter from Mr. Sanders authorizing you as Executive agent for sale of said corn." Harrison held out his hand, and his face went all solemn. "Congratulations, Zeke. You've worked a long time for this. I never asked for it...you know that. But...it's what you said you'd do...and I know that...Bobby and Antonia..." After a pause, he pulled out his handkerchief, and made to wipe his brow—but managed to wipe his eyes in the bargain. "Damned hot in here, isn't it?"

"Thanks, Robert," Zeke said, laying a gentle hand on his shoulder. "Wouldn't have wanted to hear it from anyone else."

"Now," he went on, having given Harrison a chance to recover, "We need to get the word out to the farmers, so they can get started shelling and bagging—the sooner the better." Zeke thought of the magnitude of the task ahead of all of them...and tried not to dwell on the burden of failure. On seventy-eight farms all over northern Lancaster County, corn had been

155

stored for nearly nine months in corn cribs and barns, protected as best they could from thieves, from the weather, from animals, from rot—generally on the cob, in order to keep the corn dry. It would take several days to get the corn shelled, and several more to get the corn hauled—nearly two hundred thousand bushels—to Masterson's scales on O Street.

Zeke smiled. *Time to see what Emmy's boys are made of.*

* * * * *

Roscoe needs a dog, thought Bud.

For the last ten minutes, Bud had retrieved every ball that Roscoe had rolled his direction in the small upstairs bedroom—each accompanied by a giggle—while J.T. Lynch had resumed smoking on the small landing outside the exterior door, seated in a chair, rocked back with his feet up on the handrail. It didn't bother Bud...he was lost in thought.

When had Anna Marie become "his girl?" He had only seen her three times, and twice they hadn't spoken. The one time they had met, she had done most of the talking, and it hadn't been exactly romantic.

Of course, he reflected, *she **had** taken his pants off.*

Bud grinned. *I'm hungry. For **runzas.***

Roscoe looked up, and immediately walked to the interior door, reaching for the knob. By the time that Bud got there, the door was opening...from the outside.

"Hello, Bud," said Harrison, entering the room with a smile amid Roscoe's coos of delight. "I hope Roscoe's been a good companion."

"Not bad," said Bud. "He's done most of the talking, though."

Harrison laughed, and reached in his pocket. "Thanks. Can I...?"

"Sorry, Mr. Harrison. Uncle Zeke overpays me as it is," Bud replied.

"Okay," he said, scooping up the boy, to his coos of obvious delight. "Come on, Roscoe! We got corn to shell!"

Bud straightened the room, listening with one ear to Harrison's footsteps *clump* down the steps into the Barrelhouse, and the slam of the front door. Customers would be coming in soon, and Bud knew that, having had last night off, he was probably looking at a long night of sweeping up. It was hot in the upstairs room, and Bud yawned. The bed looked inviting, and for a moment, he thought about catching a nap. He was only partly awake when Lynch broke his reverie. In a voice that

156

approached sarcasm, the older man quipped, "He's a sweet little retard, isn't he?"

Before Bud could react, the telephone on the wall rang, and Lynch sat up abruptly. Suddenly, a cold look possessed him. "Pardon me, Bud, but I've been waiting for this call."

Bud quietly obliged Lynch and made to leave. As he closed the door behind him at the top of the interior stairs, he could clearly make out Lynch's voice barking, "Jay here."

Later, Bud wasn't sure just why he paused at the top of the stairs. It could have been that Lynch's last derogatory remark about Roscoe still rang sourly in his ears, agitating his suspicious nature. He wasn't exactly pressing his ear to the door...but he wasn't exactly moving, either.

"Yes," the voice spoke. "Yes, he's in position. What train? Are you SURE? This has to be *exact*." A long pause. "Right. Yes, I'll take care of it."

For a moment, Bud thought about moving down the stairs, but his curiosity—and his shoe, which needed tying—kept him pinned in place, squatting at the top of the stairs...though his ear wasn't actually *on* the door, he reasoned. Lynch's side of the conversation carried through the thin paneling into the dark stairwell in a low rumble.

"I'm not terribly certain about the advisability, or even feasibility of this, Mr. B...I normally spend a good deal of time planning an operation before an attempt. How certain are you of your intelligence...? Yes...*yes*, that may be possible. Well, I'll tell you what I'll do—I'll look things over, and call you from Omaha tomorrow. I'll need anything you can get me on the man's habits then...Yes, *yes*...good*bye*."

As the last few words were being spoken, Bud started moving down the stairs. *Omaha?* Bud wasn't sure, but it almost sounded like Lynch was leaving...

Bud, his still sleepy head lost in thought halfway down the stairs, failed to hear the door open quietly behind him.

Or to feel J.T. Lynch's icy stare on the back of his neck.

Or to see the gun, cocked and ready in his hand.

Or to hear the upstairs bedroom door...slowly...close behind Lynch, after he watched Bud blithely descend and close the door at the bottom of the stairs.

Eventually, Bud emerged from the interior stairwell into the main floor of the Barrelhouse, where Tom Turpin was still noodling with the piano. The music, rhythmic and dreamlike, slowly drew the sleepy young man until he found himself quietly leaning his arms on the weatherbeaten upright. Its lacquer finish was cracked, and its top was riddled with circular stains and scars, where hundreds of glasses had been parked over the years. Bud ran his hand over the wounds and stains, and eventually found himself observing the Professor. Turpin's white shirt was unbuttoned and his black bow tie was askew, as if sprung open by the force of his massive neck. In his early twenties, well-muscled, and clearly over 250 pounds, Turpin looked as if he could have easily managed it—but at the moment, his face was blissful as his massive fingers caressed the keys. Opening his eyes slightly, Tom noticed the boy's musings as he absently stroked the splintered piano top.

"It's beat up, all right," Turpin said, his basso voice rumbling. "The harp's in good shape, though. Could use a good tuning, of course—but couldn't we all?" Bud nodded and smiled, as the Professor's deep voice droned on.

"Shows you can't tell from the outsides, can you? Take your uncle, fo' instance. He looks like a man as hard as an old nail, doesn't he? Then he sees me scrounging to come up with a nickel for a sandwich a few weeks ago back at the station. Doesn't give me money—gives me a job. Hard on the outside...not so hard on the inside..." Turpin struck a few more chords, but as Bud was about to agree, a voice startled them.

"Well, there are two sides to that story," said J.T. Lynch. Cigar smoke wreathed about his head. "Yes...he's got a soft spot for folks today, especially farmers—but you should ask him how it used to be. Say, 'round '88 or so."

Walking slowly up to Bud, his voice dropped to almost a whisper, and the grip Bud felt on his shoulder was anything but warm. "See you *around*, boy." Then, the stare turned into a smile, the grip turned into a pat, and with a tip of his hat to the Professor, J.T. Lynch made his exit through the front door, checking his pocket watch, and whistling as he turned onto R Street.

"Now *that* man," said the Professor, "there's but *one* side to *that* story."

19

Sheriff Fred Miller was disgruntled—God, how he hated that man standing on the opposite side of the desk.

Of course, he *was* a *lawyer.*

"I'm sure you'll find the papers *quite* in order," said Hezekiah Kohlman, leaning nonchalantly against Miller's doorframe. His tweed suit was rumpled, his collar was *not* starched, and the fedora he was absently twirling in his hand was the kind of disgrace that a haberdashery would rather burn than market. He smelled distinctly of dill pickles. However, "Heck" Kohlman's greatest pleasure was being realized, and his outward appearance had little to do with it.

He was tweaking the nose of John Law. *Halleluiah.*

"Heck," Fred Miller said, "You are *officially* a burr under my saddle. You know very well that LeBlanc left the county, in violation of an official court order."

"I know nothing of the sort," countered Kohlman. "My client came in on a train that had its last stop within the county. I'm sure he was having a *delightful* day until you unlawfully *sequestered* him in county jail for an *innocent* day's journey *entirely* within our fair County of Lancaster."

Miller looked over his glasses in disbelief. "Heck, are you seriously trying to tell me that they took a train on the Rock Island to Rokeby, walked thirty miles from Rokeby to Bennett, and then took the train in to Lincoln from *there*?"

"The *judge* believed it," Kohlman said. "There is no *evidence* to the contrary."

Fred snorted, reached into his desk, and pulled out a small yellow pad. He wrote a quick note, ripped it off, wadded it up, and tossed it at Kohlman's head.

"Do me a favor?" he said. "Tell LeBlanc I'm sharpening my knife."

Kohlman smiled, lazily extended himself from the doorframe and picked up the wad of yellow paper from the wooden floor. He smoothed out the release, put on his hat, tipped it at the Sheriff, and, still smiling, headed toward the jail.

Amos was *not* smiling. It wasn't the topic of conversation so much as its location—he was back, once again, in that chiropractic nightmare that the hotel called a telephone closet.

"I hear you, Zeke," Amos said. "Get Masterson back, and as soon as possible....Right....right....tonight should be possible. There's a train that leaves for Lincoln about seven o'clock. Yes, we'll get Eugenia to work on him...Yes...Bye, Zeke."

Amos hung up the earpiece, opened the door, and unfolded himself once again from closet's cramped confines. Emerging into the afternoon sunlight, he turned at what sounded like...snickering. There was the baggage boy, grinning.

"What's so funny, Pete?" Amos queried. "Never seen a contortionist perform?'

"Actually, yes," Pete replied. "This is the winter home of the Campbell Brothers' Circus, you know—so we get contortionists, fat ladies, sword swallowers...the works...right here in Fairbury, four months a year. Just never in that telephone closet." Peter motioned for Amos to incline his head, and then whispered into his ear from behind a cupped hand. "To tell you the truth, sir, the manager had that telephone placed into a closet that he figured no one could fit into and close the door—so he could eavesdrop on all the conversations. You've been giving him fits, by the way, not knowing what's going on. But Manny is eating it up with a spoon." Pointing to the front desk, Amos noticed that the desk clerk was indeed grinning, and even offered Amos a little wave in acknowledgment.

Well, reflected Amos, *it does get a little slow in a small town when the circus is on the road.*

When the blood finally started to come back into his legs, Amos headed upstairs. The door to Eugenia's room was closed, but the murmur of voices was clearly audible from the interior. Reaching into his pocket, he pulled out his last telegram form, wrote out his short message, and slipped it under the door. Knocking briskly, he did his best to imitate Manny's high, Irish voice in calling out, "Telegram, Ma'am," then skittered back down the hallway.

Bud was about to return to help Swede with the last barrels in the cellar—lutefisk or not—when Zeke came through the front door of the

Barrelhouse. Bud observed right away that his uncle's face was unusually sunny—as if holding an inner secret that was just busting to get out.

"Hello, Bud! I hear you've been babysitting Harrison's boy," Zeke said, striding over to his nephew and patting his shoulder. "Beats rolling barrels around, doesn't it?"

"Yes, sir," Bud answered, a little guiltily. He'd spent the last ten minutes listening to the Professor's ragtime music, and hadn't quite gotten around to returning to the cellars. "I was just going to head back down and give Swede a hand."

"Ya, but da job is done arready, yuh know," said Swede, coming in through the back door, wiping his brow with a large checkered handkerchief and giving Zeke a secret wink. "It goes a lot faster when Bud is gone, I 'tink."

"Well, I always did suspect he was a shirker," Zeke said. Bud was about to object, until he saw the smirk on his uncle's face...and Swede's.

"I've got a job that ought to keep him out of your way for awhile, Swede," Zeke said, walking over to the bar. Motioning for Bud to pull up a stool, Zeke reached into his duster and placed a small bundle of folded papers onto the bar, including copies of the letters that Harrison had brought him, as well as what looked like a map of Lancaster County. On it, a blue inked line was clearly marked, along with a dozen X's, straggling into the rural countryside north and west of Lincoln. Next to each X was a neatly lettered name. The last piece of paper appeared to have a dozen names marked at the bottom, with what appeared to be a signature block.

"Bud, these are two letters that need to be carried to the farms marked on this map. Read them out to each of the families, and have the farmers sign at the bottom of the third letter—here, next to their names—if they want to sell at the price marked. The corn needs to be shelled and the first loads ready to go by first thing Monday morning. If they want to haul their own grain, have them indicate it next to their name. We'll let them know when they need to deliver their first load to Masterson's scales on Monday morning—it'll save them 2 cents a bushel, but if they're late to the scales, the deal's off. Now, repeat that back to me."

Bud did so, and with a curt nod, Zeke said, "That's fine. Now, you know where I keep my horse stabled?"

"Yes, sir," Bud winced. *God, not that roan mare...*

"The livery man has a horse for you to borrow there—just mention my name. Don't worry—it's not Lily," Zeke smiled. Reaching into his pocket, he added, "You ought to have him back by dark if you get a leg under you. Here's a dime—stop by Mooney's and pick up a sandwich for the road," and flipped it toward Bud.

Mooney's? Bud thought, then grinned...as he recalled who worked there.

* * * * *

"Now, Clive darling," Eugenia said, looking over her glass at Masterson as she sipped lemonade, "I simply must get into Lincoln...immediately...to meet Mr. J. Edgar Owens." Picking up the yellow telegram that had been delivered to her room, the young brunette waved it before her older companion as if it were made of gold. "The Funke Opera House is re-opening in just a few weeks, and it appears that the lead actress in their new production has broken her foot—a horse started, and a carriage rolled over it, poor thing. In any case, the director— that's Mr. Owens—has offered me an audition as Queen Titania. If I failed to appear, my agent would never forgive me...so I plan to take the seven o'clock train to Lincoln tonight."

"That's a shame," said Amos. "Of course, it means that you'll have to give up your role in Santa Fe..."

"I thought it was Denver," grumped Masterson.

"Uh, right you are, dear," Eugenia cooed, and her hand fell lightly on Masterson's knee as her voice dropped to a mere whisper. "I shall miss you terribly, of course darling, but it seems a marvelous opportunity. You can look me up at the Lincoln Hotel, anytime that your schedule allows." Her green eyes sparkled behind her long eyelashes, and Masterson was lost, once again.

"Well, it's time I returned, in any case," Masterson said, pulling out a telegram of his own. "I got a telegram myself today—I have a grain deal that I need to close in Lincoln."

Amos was well-acquainted with its contents—but for the first time in days, he was not the author.

"Funny," Masterson remarked, looking at Eugenia's telegram. "They seem to be written in different hands."

"Well, then, since it's our last day in town, let's...celebrate," said Eugenia, changing the subject as she put away her telegram. "I believe that there's pheasant being offered tonight at the hotel...some sort of celebration."

162

"Apparently, the head of the local militia is going to Lincoln tonight to set up camp," said Amos, puffing one of his short cigars into life. "I've already put our names down as part of the dinner party."

"Why Amos," said Eugenia, "You think of everything."

* * * * *

Bud's dinner looked to be a little less extravagant—but he was hoping that the company would be excellent.

That is, if *she* was there.

Mooney was no less hospitable than when Bud had first met him, last Sunday—but he was no more hospitable, either.

"She left a half hour ago," Mooney said, as he threw another slice of ham on the grill. Made sense—hot ham and cheese sandwiches were marked as the specialty of the day, and the smell of the toasted bread, sauerkraut, and mustard were drifting into Bud's nostrils like a hot slice of home. But Mooney's words had kicked the joy out of Bud, and he had lost his appetite, nonetheless.

"Do you know where she's gone?" Bud asked, with a slice of hope as thin as Mooney's ham.

"She's off for the week—until Sunday, that is," Mooney said, absently flipping the ham, cheese, and sauerkraut onto a buttered slice of bread, which he flipped onto the grill. "Stays in a boarding house down on C Street four nights a week—then Thursdays, she walks home to the farm—up near Crounse. Headstrong," he mumbled, shaking his head. "Shouldn't be walking alone through the trainyard up north there—too many men out of work along the tracks. Good worker, though—easy on the eyes, too. Course," he added, with a devilish grin. "Stephan and Lukas could change a man's mind."

"Stephan and Lukas?" asked Bud, waiting for the other shoe to drop.

"Her brothers," said Mooney, flatly. "Want some advice, kid? Move on—they're Czechs, and they don't like outsiders."

Mooney bagged a hot ham sandwich for the young man while he unfolded his map and looked for Crounse. *Odd name...could it have been named after Governor Crounse?*

After a few moments, he spotted it up in the extreme northeast corner of the county, near Eloise Moseman's place, the last house on the route that Zeke had marked. *Well,* he reasoned, *why not go there first, then work*

163

my way back southwards through the route? It would take the same time either way...

The gray horse that Bud had picked up at the livery was a fine docile gelding that looked to be in good shape, if a little on the slow side. Climbing onto it, he surveyed the scene ahead of him. Seventh Street stretched ahead north, and would eventually run over the tracks and past the banks of Salt Creek until the road led north to...*Crounse? Well,* Bud thought, *might as well ride north and catch all the farms on the way back as catch them on the way up.*

"Giddup," Bud urged, as he headed north to find his girl.

* * * * *

The Fairbury Hotel was sparkling, and extra staff had been hired to handle the large number of guests that were congregated for the evening. A long white table stretched over the entire length of the hotel dining room, spilling through a large archway into the hotel lobby. At one end of the table, a tall man in a blue military uniform was surrounded by a large party of friends; at the other, a young man in an oversized suit was being praised by a smaller party; between them, a middle-aged man was seated next to a beautiful girl dressed in a long white gown and a radiant smile. The large party was exuberant; the smaller party was congratulatory; the smallest party wavered in its loyalty between each, reveling in both.

"I give you...Colonel Charles J. Bills, and the boys from Fairbury!" shouted a portly man at the north end of the table, and the entire hotel rang with shouts of "Here, here!" and "Huzzah!" as the glasses were lifted.

From the other end of the table, a soft-spoken bookish man in his thirties raised a small glass of wine. "Here's to Ransom Reed Cable, Jr... man in his own right."

From what Amos observed, he guessed that the boy was probably the son of a powerful man—and had seemed truly pleased at the suggestion that he had made it on his own. *Well,* Amos mused, *better that than the other way around...pleased at a flattery only won by privilege or family name.* As a bastard that had won his way upward from the business end of a shovel, Amos appreciated hard work—even by the privileged.

On the other hand, his particular charge, Mr. Masterson, seemed truly pleased by flattery, especially by a beautiful girl. *So much the better,* mused Amos. *All the better to eat you with, my dear.*

164

Outside, a tall man waited near the train station, looking through the brightly lit windows of the hotel up the street as he patiently smoked his cigarette.

20

Thursday, August 9, 1894
5:05 pm

Bud's mount wasn't exactly winged Pegasus. But together they did manage to find a sort of slow trot that allowed the pair of them to make up a little time—faster, at least, than the expected pace of a walking girl, while still sparing the gelding. They were carefully preparing to descend the near bank of Salt Creek just north of the Burlington tracks...when he heard a girl's clear voice scream, "*What are you doing? STOP IT!*"

Kicking his horse into life (or at least a higher state of wakefulness), Bud cantered northwest along the Burlington tracks, searching in the direction of the shriek. Worry filled his features. He had seen dozens of vagrants—*bums, why not just call them that?*—hanging around the stations at Lincoln, until they were chased off by the bulls guarding the trainyards into the hobo jungles at the outskirts of Lincoln. So many men out of work...so desperate...

"*No!*" the voice cried out again. "*Put that knife down!*"

Bud's heart leapt into his throat. There was no doubt now—it was Anna Marie.

"Giddup!" he cried, and the gelding moved from a canter to a gallop as Bud urged him between the low shrubs that dotted the space between the tracks and the creek. Following the line of the shriek, he managed to spot a small campfire in a ditch that led from a culvert under the tracks ahead, emptying a trickle of dirty water into the creek about fifty yards away. Dark forms were congregated around the campfire, and the men's murmurs and shouts of rough encouragement to one another didn't frighten him nearly as much as Anna Marie's shouting...because it had stopped.

The gray gelding was wheezing now. Bud had managed to urge him into a sort of a gallop...such as it was...and the boy's hard breathing was beginning to echo that of the old horse when the pair of them rumbled over the lip of the ditch. His heart froze when he spied his worst fear—Anna Marie's raven hair and crouching form, just visible behind and beneath the stooped figures of four ill-dressed men. Several of the men's hands were clearly covered in blood.

With a panicked shout of "Get away from her!" Bud sprang from the saddle and, without losing an ounce of momentum, plowed his shoulder into the largest of the vagrants, a black-bearded giant, well over six and a half feet tall. Their now-combined momentum tumbled them both into the small stream of brackish water at the bottom of the ditch, where Bud disappeared into a thick stand of dry nettles. When he emerged a second later, fists balled, he was ready for what he supposed would be a pitched battle. But he was hardly prepared for what he saw.

Anna Marie...a bloody knife in her hands...

...crouched over a chicken...

"Bud?! For Pete's sake, what are you doing?" From Anna Marie's hand dangled a dripping butcher knife, and below her was a headless chicken with a variety of appendages spread randomly over an old flour sack. Her face was a mask of shocked curiosity, but it was nothing to rival Bud's own. Hers didn't look to stay that way, though, as the faces of the men standing next to her each held the germ of an infectious smirk.

"Well...aren't you...you mean you aren't...uh...in trouble?" Bud stammered, his eyes now toggling between Anna Marie's and those of her grinning companions.

"No, but choo vill be," growled the bearded giant that Bud had tackled, just now dusting himself off as he removed himself from the nettles. "You haf excuse, maybe, for killink poor starving *rolnik*? If you are hungry— you must first **ask**...*stupidy hlupak...rosmyslet si to...*"

"Uh...I'm sorry...I'm really sorry," Bud interrupted, after what seemed like an impossibly long stream of foreign invective, complete with (unfortunately quite understandable) hand gestures, and accompanied by chuckles from the bearded man's companions. "I was following Anna, trying to give her a ride home, and I thought that...that Anna was in trouble. She was yelling, and..."

"Well, what do you expect?" Anna asked, her blue eyes now twinkling above the ghost of a smile, despite the fists she had balled up on her hips. "You bring a perfectly good bird to these...*posetliki*...and what do they do?" Now Anna's gestures started up, miming the words that followed. "They twist it, and smash it, and bruise the meat..." Shaking her head, she kneeled at the bird again, wiped her blade on the flour sack, and returned to cutting it up. "Honestly," she said. "Men are so *helpless*."

With a speed that would have rivaled...well, frankly, his own mother— or any mother in Nebraska, come to think of it—Anna finished cutting up the chicken, expertly separating the thigh from the hip joints and the breast from the backbone at the rib joints. She split and cleaned the gravel from the gizzard using a pail of water that the bearded man had placed silently at

167

her side. Bud smiled at him, but the giant just *humphed*. By the time he had looked back at her, the heart and liver had been separated out as well.

"*Hotovo*...ready for the pot," she said, ducking her hands into the water and drying them on a small piece of cloth she pulled out of her apron. "*Now*, if you would so kindly offer my friend, Mr. Gardner here an apology—we will be on our way, I think," she said, with finality. "He was just trying to rescue me from you...you *psanki*. Frightening a *chlapeček* like that—for shame..." Her half-covered grin wasn't lost on Bud...or the men.

As if connected at their hips, the men cheerfully pivoted in unison toward Bud, dutifully removed their hats, and bowed, saying "*Bohužel...bohužel...bohužel...*" with the large bearded man adding under his breath, "*...stupidy hlupak.*" They also offered what could only be *thanks* to Anna Marie, who held up both hands as if to wave them off, murmuring what Bud took for a "you're welcome."

"Now, if you haven't *killed* your horse, farmer," Anna said, folding her arms and flashing her eyes at him, "Did you say something about offering me a ride?"

* * * * *

By 6:30, the party had broken up at the Fairbury hotel—into several parties, actually, all of them headed to the train station. The sun was setting, and the little Rock Island express train that had just pulled into the station—a "Fort Worth accommodation" consisting of an engine, a coal tender, a combination car, and a standard passenger car bringing up the rear—shone black and red in the rays of the setting sun. The steam rose from Engine 213, and the conductor was familiar to Amos. Having placed Clive Masterson and Miss Eugenia in the rear passenger car, he strode up to C.D. Stannard and held out his hand.

"Evenin', Captain," Amos said, eyeing the polished engine with appreciation. "You certainly have this girl looking her best. She looks like she could fly."

"Evening, Mr. Seville," said Stannard, who grasped Amos' hand, then pulled out and checked his gold watch. "She's a zephyr, all right. Looks like we'll be a few minutes late getting off, though—make it about ten minutes from now. Need to hustle some mailbags down from the head shed," he said, pointing to the Division offices above the train station. He smiled and added, "Surprised you're riding with the passengers—used to seeing you with the freight."

"Now, C.D., you know ah always *start out* with the passengers," Amos retorted.

"Hello, Mr. Seville," piped in Ike dePuis, the engineer. "Lincoln running dry again?" Bill Craig, busy leveling out the coals, still managed to grin, though as the fireman, knew he was not allowed to speak in the presence of the Captain unless first spoken to.

"No chance of that, until this crew gets into town," rebutted Amos. "You boys make sure you drop by the Barrelhouse when you get in—the boss always holds back a bottle of the best for y'all."

"Yeah—just *how* good?" asked dePuis.

"Well, it sure as hell doesn't come from Fairbury," Amos said, tipping his bowler hat at the train crew, who laughed their appreciation. Strolling back to the combination car, Amos swung up its narrow wrought-iron steps into the brightly lit interior. The half smoker, half express car was swarming with passengers, mostly swarming around Col. Bills, who was standing at the narrow bar in a splendid blue uniform that was festooned with gold braid. His boisterous voice played over the crowd as he cheerfully held court.

Harry Foote had been asked by Stannard to pour drinks for the colonel's party. Looking up, Harry noticed Amos smiling from across the car, and shook his head sadly. As the blowhard colonel continued to pontificate about the Omaha meatpackers' strike, the brakeman pointed two fingers at his skull and jerked his thumb to feign a shot to his head. Fred Scott, the tall Kansas baggage master, leaning against the doorframe of the "express" shipping/baggage room that made up the forward half of the combination car just a few feet from Harry's station, noticed the gesture and snickered noisily.

"Fred," Harry whispered to his lanky co-worker, "Get me out of this, willya?"

"Can't leave the express area, Harry, you know that," Fred whispered back, nudging his elbow into Charles Cherry, a postal clerk from Kearney who was now making regular express runs along the Rock Island line. Cherry's spreading grin did not exactly look sympathetic.

"Come on, Charles...we mustn't distract Harry from his *important assignment*," he laughed, pulling Cherry with him into the baggage area, waving and saluting before they locked the door behind them.

Amos quietly departed through the rear of the combination car, stepped over the gap, and opened the door to the passenger car that brought up the rear of the train. The travelers assembling here were less verbose, but still milling around—all except, it seemed, for Masterson and Eugenia, who were snuggling in the last row of the passenger car, Eugenia rolling her eyes in a brief moment when Masterson's were averted. *The bill she is going to present to Zeke*, pondered Amos, *may just break the Barrelhouse...*

As he made to sit down in the row across the aisle from his charge, Amos observed a small party of businessmen out on the platform that was milling about Mr. Cable—the young railroad executive who, Amos had gathered from the dinner party at the hotel, was about to return to his home in Chicago. Waving a last goodbye to the departing group, Rance Cable slipped into the side door of the passenger car from the platform and placed his carpet-sided valise in the overhead luggage rack. He had only just slid into his seat at the front of the car when a tall man dropped his newspaper and stepped swiftly across the narrow aisle to take a seat beside the boy. As Amos watched from the rear of the car in curiosity, the hauntingly thin, sallow-faced man spoke but a few words to Cable. After a few heartbeats, the young man, his face registering shock and surprise, stood up in unison with the thin man. Pressed unnaturally close together, they turned to the side door opposite the platform, and exited the train onto the track side of the train, where the unlikely pair slowly made their way across the side tracks and disappeared into the brush opposite them.

Amos, his interest now piqued, had half-risen to see what was afoot...when conductor Stannard's sharp voice cried from outside, "All Aboard!" Shaking his head at the strange circumstances of the young man's exit, Amos settled back down...to what he hoped would be a quiet ride into Lincoln.

* * * * *

"Do you make a habit of rescuing young maidens, farmer?" Anna Marie Vostrovsky set a good pace, and Bud's borrowed horse, not yet recovered from his unexpected gallop to the site of her "rescue," was doing his best to stay even. So was Bud.

"When we met at the game...last Saturday?...you felt compelled to correct the behavior of a couple of *hlupaks*," she went on, and though she was looking down, Bud swore that her face still wore a shadow of a smirk. "So, you are a hero, then?"

"If I was," Bud replied, "I would not have needed my large friend to bail me out." It was true—if Swede hadn't hauled the Seventh Streeters away by their collars last Saturday, Bud would have been in no condition

170

to finish the game, much less rescue a young maiden. "Just as you bailed me out tonight. Tell me," Bud asked. "What is a hlupeck?"

"It is pronounced *hlupak*," Anna said, now grinning. "You would say, 'idiot', I think."

"Well, I felt like one," Bud agreed. "But I didn't expect you to be screaming at a couple of...were they Czechs?...about how they cut up a chicken. Where did they get it, I wonder?"

"From me, of course," Anna sniffed. "Jasper Mooney let me have it at a very good price—it would have spoiled if he hadn't." Anna walked silently for awhile, then added, "Times are hard. Those boys aren't so bad, you know. They just need work."

"You've met them before, then?"

"You think I go around giving chickens to strangers?"

"I don't know—you give *stitches* to strangers," Bud observed.

"I considered it my moral obligation to the crowd," Anna admitted. "Those pants were so loose that someone was bound to be embarrassed— even if it wasn't you. So," she went on, "however did you get into such a position?"

"That would have been Zeke—you could say I got drafted," Bud said. "I know it sounds strange, but I had only gotten into town the night before, and that was the first job he gave me."

"So—you work for Ezekiel Gardner?" Anna eyed him suspiciously. "I thought I saw you in Mooney's last Sunday—were you with him?"

"Yes, Anna—I work for him," Bud said, and cringed at his expectation of Anna's reaction to what he must say next. "He's...he's my uncle, Anna. My name is Bud...*Gardner*."

"Oh...I see," Anna said, and the sigh she let out was audible. "Well, I appreciate the offer of a ride, Bud...but..."

"Anna...I saw what happened between you and Uncle Zeke last Sunday," Bud blurted. "What's going on between the two of you? Did he...did he do something...wrong...?"

Anna started to walk faster. Though she wouldn't look directly at Bud, even a sidelong glance at her convinced him that the storm clouds were starting to gather. "Ask your Uncle, Mister Gardner," she said, coldly. "You won't hear it from me."

171

Her pace, now a determined one, at first caused her to stretch away from him, and the dust kicking up from her whirring boots actually began to cloud her from his view. Bud was unsure how to proceed. He felt the moment, the girl, their friendship...all slipping away from him. But somehow...he really...

Suddenly, a thought occurred to Bud, and he pulled at the gelding to speed him along. After a few minutes, he managed to catch up with Anna and match her, stride for stride. For a full five minutes they walked together, and the gelding cantering behind Bud made the only sound, with an irked *neigh* and an intermittent shake of his head.

"Anna," Bud finally said, softly. "Have I ever told you about my brothers?" The girl, her face a cloud, didn't look at Bud—but her pace might have slowed, slightly.

"I have four of them," Bud went on, looking down at his feet as he matched Anna's pace. "Jerry is the oldest—he's still at home with my parents. So is David, my younger brother, along with my sister Daphne. Larry and Roger are a little older than me. They moved to Omaha about six weeks ago, and Roger took a job with the Hammond packing house." Anna Marie stopped suddenly, then turned toward the boy, who faced her openly.

"There's been some...trouble there. Maybe you've read about it in the papers?" Bud asked, and at a slight nod from Anna, went on. "Three days ago, a striker from the packing house...stabbed Roger when he got back to his apartment. He was waiting there in the dark for Roger to come home. When the man struck, he apparently said...a word. I think it was '*hovno.*' Do you know what it means?"

"It's Czech...it means, 'Shit.'" Anna said, looking away slightly, then turning her eyes back to Bud. "Did...did your brother...?"

"He's back home. There were a lot of stitches, but the infection looks to be under control. He'll be all right, the doctor thinks, with time."

Anna's blue eyes were piercing, questioning. "Why did you tell me this?"

"I don't know, exactly," Bud replied. "Most of the strikers are Czech. We figured that the man that stabbed my brother was Czech, too," he said, adding, "Like you."

"You must hate the Czechs, then," Anna said, quietly. "Me, included."

"I don't know why," Bud said, looking levelly at her, his voice now as still as hers. "I mean...*you* didn't stab him."

Anna looked down, and brushed a lock of dark hair behind her right ear. Her head gave a short nod. Bud got up on the horse, and reached down to Anna. Taking her hand, he braced against the stirrups and swung her up behind him.

* * * * *

The sun was setting, and Zeke, for his part, was also riding the roads. But his road differed fundamentally from those that he had sent his nephews trekking with copies of the grain deal throughout Lancaster County earlier in the day. It was steel, and his ride involved a train, inbound from Omaha. Approaching the capital city from the east, he could just make out the triangular heart of Lincoln against the setting sun, its vertices formed by the Capitol, University Hall, and the huge stand pipe down by the waterworks.

Asleep in a secluded corner of the brick MoPac platform there slumped a lean, gray, coil of a man. The sounds of the approaching train did not wake him, nor did the furry pillow under his arm that *chittered* when it recognized Zeke swinging off the car. Unlike many of the vagrants that would normally be "escorted" from the station property for sleeping on its benches, Jefferson "Bobber" Davies had earned his snoozing spot through a combination of odd jobs, extreme age, and the patronage of the man that approached, now pushing his hat onto the back of his head and smiling through his graying beard.

"Wake up, you old possum trapper," Zeke said, lightly tapping his boot against the old man's. "It's way too early for hibernation."

"Whiskey and taters," mumbled Bobber, still half asleep.

Zeke smiled, and leaned his mouth close to the old man's ear. "Chow time," he whispered.

Bobber stood straight up, causing Skunk to scramble off the platform altogether, where he sat peering expectantly at Zeke from behind a trash barrel. Bobber, for his part stood smacking his gums and giving Zeke a remarkably similar look.

"O.K., a quick stop at Mooney's, then," Zeke laughed, but then turned suddenly serious as the pair of them crossed Seventh Street to Mooney's place. "So, did you follow her?"

173

"You ain't gonna like it," Bobber mumbled, not pausing as he pushed his way through the swinging doors of the establishment and sat at the gas-fired grill. "She's at McGee's."

Of course, thought Zeke, his worst fears now fully realized. *It all fits.*

Zeke flipped two bits at Mooney, and sat lost in thought as Jasper served the old man. After Bobber plunged through two heaping plates of hot, but largely unidentifiable sausage-like substance, he finally pushed back from the grill, belched in satisfaction, and picked up a toothpick. Having few teeth, it didn't take him long to finish his dental hygiene—after which he felt human enough to add a few details.

"She's been coming and going there since Saturday, Zeke," Bobber muttered. "Seems to spend the rest of her time over at Miller and Paine's picking out new duds and such." Shaking his head, he added, "Osborne Russell wasn't an eddycated man—not many of us out in Blackfoot territory in '41 were—else why would we be there? But he had him a sort of 'trapper logic.' Went something like, 'Never offer honey to a bear, a drink to an Indian, or a secret to a yaller-haired woman.' So...what you gonna do, 'Zekiel?"

Zeke seemed lost in thought for a moment, then turning suddenly toward Bobber...grinned. "Give her another secret, I reckon."

* * * * *

The sun had long set by the time that Bud and Anna finally reached her family's farm just south of the small Czech village of Crounse in the northwestern corner of Lancaster County. As it turned out, Anna was in no particular hurry—she reported to Bud that she often got back after dark on Thursday—so the pair of them had managed to stop by each of the twelve farms on Bud's list and gather nearly every signature that Zeke had requested, leaving messages for the two families that had been off visiting for the evening, and skipping Robert Harrison's home west of Woodlawn, who had already signed the letters, according to a note from Zeke.

Their encounter with Eloise Moseman, the last stop on the list, had been, well, sweet. A sturdy widow with slate gray hair wearing a pair of her husband's old dungarees and Wellington boots, she was returning from the barn with a pail of milk when the pair of them rode up the short lane. Eloise had recognized Anna immediately, of course—though not a Czech, she was a neighbor—and the pair of them had started chattering along like magpies, briefly forgetting Bud's presence altogether. When Anna had introduced Bud, she had stuttered slightly at his last name, then fallen silent. Eloise, for her part, had acted surprised, then...oddly touched. She

174

had gently laid her rough farmwife fingers on Anna's smooth cheek, murmuring, "I am so glad that you are opening up to friendship, Anna." *Did she know something of the trouble between Anna and Zeke?* wondered Bud. *Judging by her reaction to my name, probably. I wonder how common that knowledge is? Time to pump Bobber and Swede for some information, I think...*

The ride had been a pleasant one, though it was difficult to gauge each other's reactions to their dialogue while seated on the horse. Bud had always felt that facing forward on the same horse was a poor forum for deep conversation, and Anna must have agreed, because they kept it pretty light. Bud ended up doing much of the talking, chattering on about his parents, grandparents, siblings, and their little community of Alder Grove—set up along the banks of Bell Creek in speculation of a railroad line that never appeared. He stayed mostly clear of the subject of his uncle, and his long estrangement with the family, though. Bud felt he was in deep water there where Anna was concerned, anyway; and besides, the why's and how's of his family's breakup were still a mystery to him.

Anna's own discourse revolved mostly around her little town of Crounse, since most of the talk of her family and their past seemed to be off limits to Bud. Her little village was also set up along the banks of a creek as well—actually, at the confluence of two creeks—in hopes of being placed along yet another railroad that did not materialize, and probably never would. Apparently, it had been named after the first governor of Nebraska in a fit of state pride, and the tightly knit Czech community helped each other with the planting, cultivating, and harvest. For miles now, Bud had been curious to see how the crops were doing in this part of the county. However, the sun had set, and the moon was not cooperating—though gibbous and high in the southern sky, it lay behind a dense cloud cover for the time being—another cloudy night that was failing to produce rain.

As it turned out, his other senses were evidence enough.

All around him, assaulting his nostrils like a distant symphony in the ears of a once deafened man, the sweet smell of damp earth, of green, ripening corn—stand after stand of it, rows and acres and miles of it—sprang upon the farmer within him, and held him in his saddle with the force of its utter unreality. His shock deepened as the slight evening breeze picked up suddenly, transporting the rising sound of the wind singing and rustling its way through the thousands, millions of green, healthy stalks and leaves.

His emotions nearly overcame him. *All this drought,* he thought. *Every county, every state for five hundred dusty miles in every direction--- how was this miracle possible?*

"How is this *possible?*" the question echoed from his racing mind to his lips, as Bud reached for the small kerosene lantern that had been fastened with twine onto the right hand D-ring of the rented saddle. The pressure of a small hand placed over his own temporarily squelched his curiosity.

"Irrigation," she said. "We're a busy people, Bud." Sliding off the back of the horse, she turned to him. The moon chose that moment to force its light through the clouds, revealing Anna's face, smiling faintly. If Bud had been able to turn from it, he would have seen the miles of irrigation ditches that led from the dams where the streams met at the little town of Crounse.

But he didn't look away.

"I get off here, Bud," she spoke softly. The moon and the evening breeze played over her raven hair, her eyes shone out at him. "And we don't need the lantern, though my brothers would be...very, uh, *excited*...to meet you, I'm sure. But I'm also pretty sure that it can probably wait...a while, anyway."

He thought hard about kissing her. There in the moonlight, she deserved kissing. But in less than a moment, she had already turned to walk up her short lane. Watching her depart in the moonlight, Bud was not disappointed. The pressure of her hand, and the smile that had lit her face....*it was enough,* he thought, for now, and he turned his gelding back toward the barn and home, grinning at the vibrant life that now surrounded him.

* * * * *

Amos, at that moment, was not grinning. Yes, his charge, Clive Masterson was blissfully in the company of Miss Eugenia, now taking refreshment in the combination car just ahead of the passenger car—where Amos now reclined, smoking a cigarette, and uncharacteristically, worrying about the young man that had so surreptitiously been hurried from the car just minutes before the train had departed. *Why had the thin man fetched the boy?* His mind raced back to the exchange, his eyes absently drifting to the overhead luggage bin, where...a carpet bag sat.

Belonging to the boy...What was his name? Ransom Reed Cable...yes...his friends at the dinner back in Fairbury had called him

176

'Rance.' *Well,* thought Amos, standing, stretching, and strolling over to the luggage rack, *time for a little scouting expedition, ah reckon.*

Nonchalantly, he reached up and pulled down the bag, placing it on the seat next to him. At the clasp of the bag was a small keyhole. Rolling his eyes, Amos reached into his vest pocket and pulled out a small leather packet, opened it, and coolly selected a long, thin sliver of spring steel with a hook at its end. Within two seconds of placing it into the keyhole, the bag was open. Smiling with satisfaction, Amos replaced his lockpicks and reached casually into the bag. *Clothes...a book—ah, Ibsen...a rather nice cigarette case...and there it is,* he thought, pulling out a fine leather wallet.

Filled with bills. Large denominations.

Replacing the billfold...reluctantly...and replacing the bag, Amos slowly lowered himself back down into the young man's seat, and frowned. Rich as the young man might have been, no one left a wallet with that amount of cash in it, unless he was forced into it.

* * * * *

Ike dePuis was not grinning either. At Rokeby, they were still a full five minutes behind schedule, and with only twenty minutes left to go into Lincoln, he inched the throttle up a notch. "Pour the cobs to 'er, Bill," Ike said, and Bill Craig, his fireman, shook his head. There had been repair work recently completed on the road up ahead of them to smooth it out, suffering as it was from the heat and heavy traffic of summer. It had been especially needed on the trestle that spanned the UP and Burlington lines just south of Lincoln. *All for a few mailbags from the head shed,* he muttered to himself, shovelling more coal into the firebox.

* * * * *

"We must be making nearly fifty," mumbled Harry Foote, looking out the window of the combination car, his face edged with worry. "Pretty fast for this stretch, wouldn't you say, Captain?"

C.J. Stannard, reluctantly breaking away from a very pleasant conversation with a beautiful auburn-haired woman turned to Harry and spoke quietly, "Now, Harry, there's no need to worry the passengers." Looking over the compartment, he glanced at his watch and let out a slight *harrumph.* They were late, and that fool Ike DePuis was trying to make up time on the worst section of the track. He snapped his watch shut and turned to Col. Bills and his party. "Sir, we'll be arriving in Lincoln very shortly, please find your seats in the passenger car."

177

The Fairbury delegation obediently moved with Harry Foote's assistance, leaving a sleeping Clive Masterson and a relieved Eugenia behind in the combination car. Amos smiled at the brakeman as he entered the passenger car, and, once Col. Bills was out of the line of sight, Harry and Amos rolled their eyes in unison.

"Taking care of that lump up in the combination car and listening to that blowhard with the toady chorus is enough to make a man start drinking again," Amos admitted. "Is he all right up there?"

"Masterson?...sleeping like a baby," said Harry. "The young lady makes a fine...escort."

"Eugenia...yes, she's had a lot of practice along those lines," Amos stated, matter-of-factly, then voiced the question that had been bothering him since Fairbury. "Do you see those empty seats up front? A young man took the one on the left back in Fairbury—his bag is still up there in the luggage rack." Amos pointed to the carpet bag, and Harry nodded. "It's curious. Almost as soon as he got on the train, a thin man seated across from him—there, in that seat on the right—got up and appeared to...remove him...from the train. Do you know anything about either of them? The boy's name was Ransom Cable."

Harry's jaw dropped, and Amos could see that he had hit paydirt.

"*Ransom Cable* was on this train?" Harry said, shocked. "Amos, that's impossible. Ransom Cable...is the name of the president of the CRI&P. Amos, he *runs* this railroad." Shaking his head, he added, "You said, it was a young man? Couldn't have been him, then."

"Ah believe that ah heard him introduced in the Fairbury hotel as "Ransom Reed Cable, Jr.""

"Oh, shit," said Harry, which were the most appropriate words he could have uttered as the train slammed into utter darkness, accompanied by the scream of brakes and the sound of hell itself being unleashed.

178

21

Thursday, August 9, 1894
9:17 pm

The moon had taken its sweet time about it, but had finally managed to break through the clouds skirting over the dry farmland south of Lincoln. It was now lighting up the rails that ran under the wheels of Engine 213 far more effectively than its weak kerosene "box" headlight could, and Ike dePuis looked upon it as a sign of good luck—he was making up lost time, and with a little more of it, they would only be a few minutes late getting into the capitol. The Chicago, Rock Island & Pacific Engine 213 with its tender, water, and coal weighed in at a whopping 84½ tons, but for all that...she was a *greyhound.*

Ike dePuis had cut his teeth on older model, smaller steam engines from the Civil War era, which had suffered cracked boilers, fractured drive trains and other vibration-induced breakdowns from rattling along the ever-changing, superheated and frostbitten tracks of the old Chicago, Kansas and Nebraska Railway—until 1891, that is, when the CK&N railroad was incorporated into the rapidly-expanding CRI&P. The new owner had infused the hard luck railroad with more roads, better crews, and most importantly, better equipment. The upgraded engine that was now driving the two car, local "Fort Worth Accommodation" was a case in point—it had bigger cylinders, a larger boiler, and a bigger firebox than previous models. A New York Central 4-4-0 No. 999 had just the previous year earned a place in history when it reached a speed of 112.5 mph while pulling a similar four-car Empire State Express between Batavia and Buffalo, N.Y. *Of course,* Ike thought, *that engine had 86-inch driving wheels, instead of the 62-inch wheels on our girl, and higher pressure cylinders.* But he patted the boiler case in pleasure, and thought about what a shame it was to waste such a fine engine on local service. He longed for a chance to really open her up...*maybe on one of the Platte River runs,* he mused.

Bill Craig shook his head again. He'd been partnering up with Ike as his fireman for years now—long enough to know when Ike was in one of his 'git-outta-my-way, I'm-driving-this-train-to-home' moods. His experience was considerable in its own right, sufficient that—when the two of them were alone—Bill felt brave enough to offer a little friendly advice.

"Better slow this hog down, Ike," warned Bill. Having just leveled out the coals for the final few miles into Lincoln, he hung up his shovel on the wooden wall of the cab, and wiped his face to clear away the coal dust. "Haven't they been workin' this section of track? The trestle and the state pen are comin' up, and..."

"All right, all right," harrumphed Ike, taking Craig's advice and inching down the throttle a tad, but still mumbling something like 'smoke agent' under his breath. Leaning out the cab, he took a last long breath of the cooling night air that rushed past him before he crossed the trestle over the UP and Burlington tracks, and entered the outskirts of Lincoln, where he planned to throttle her down in earnest. *Nights like this are what railroading was all about*, he mused, *when the miles skate under your trucks, and the rails stretch out ahead of you like silver ribbons, to a warm bed in a good hotel...*

Had he later been given an opportunity to explain his next few seconds of action to a board of inquiry, Ike dePuis would have put it all down to reflex, and the trained eye that twenty years on the rails had given him. Given the speed of the train and the generally poor lighting from the engine's single yellow headlight, he should in reality never have caught the slight misalignment in the right hand rail just a few yards into the bridge, about 50 yards ahead. If Bill Craig had been called to testify later, he would himself have voiced his astonishment at the speed at which the engineer nearly simultaneously cut the throttle and hit the brakes, while yelling, "*Down the sand...!*"

Unfortunately, neither of the men would be testifying, because these were the very last words that either of those humble men would ever utter on this Earth.

The testimony would have been superfluous, in any case—even a hard-nosed Rock Island board of inquiry could hardly have blamed the wreck on its engine crew. Fifty yards of warning only left the men about three seconds to react and apply the brakes to a train that weighed over 120 tons, traveling forty-five miles an hour when it hurtled onto the trestle. No brakes ever devised would have stopped that behemoth, and even at forty miles an hour—a slightly more reasonable speed given the conditions that night—their reaction time would have increased by less than half a second had Ike chosen to slow her down.

When the small right wheel of the forward truck fell off the gap in the rails, the engine's right wheels ran along the ties on that side, while its left wheels, amazingly, stayed on the left rail—that is, until its right wheels hit the end of the next, still fastened, exposed rail—squarely—about 30 feet down the track. The resulting shock was so severe that it jogged the entire eighty-odd-ton engine and tender to the left, spreading the left rail and gradually nosing the engine toward the left side of the trestle.

With the train rattling and slashing its way over the ties for the next two hundred feet—where the engine and tender finally left the track and plunged into the dark abyss—there were no good options for Ike and Bill. Forty-five miles an hour and forty-odd feet above a pitch black, rock- and rail-filled gully—even if they had used the next three seconds to leap from the train, their chances of survival were slim. Once they rode the engine over the trestle edge, they were effectively nil.

Careening freely through the night sky for a fraction of a second, the engine, still nosing left, crashed onto its left side directly onto the nearer set of twin train rails that ran through the gully below—those happening to belong to the Union Pacific Railway. Immediately, the boiler burst and the firebox ruptured, spraying thousand-degree coal and live steam into the collapsing cab, instantly incinerating Ike and Bill. Fortunately (if it could be considered that way), the wooden structure of the cab had already crushed the men, rendering them insensible to the red-hot coals now pouring over them. The engine exploded with a *crack*, throwing steam hundreds of feet into the sky, and its head turned to the northwest until it almost paralleled the UP tracks. However, it had not yet come to a full rest when the coal tender, uncoupling from the engine as it went over the edge of the trestle, followed its mistress to the UP tracks below. The thirty-ton rectangular tender, consisting of a coal bunker surrounded on three sides by a massive "U"-shaped water jacket encased in pig iron, rolled a hundred and eighty degrees on its long axis like a bullet, eventually landed squarely on the engine, its twisted machinery joining the blazing heap, its trucks exposed in the moonlight.

The fates of the two in the engine were now sealed, leaving only the crew and passengers in the two following cars for the stars' consideration. One of those stars was probably a lucky one, because after the engine slammed onto the exposed end of the rail, the shock of the impact shattered the link and pin coupling the coal tender to the combination car, divorcing the two rear cars from the engine and her companion. With only one-fifth of the combined momentum of the engine and tender, the still-joined combination and passenger cars hit the gap at the end of the trestle and immediately jumped the track, careening to the left, off the trestle and directly over the steep slope. The combination car, with its two crew and nine passengers, rolled onto its back and slid down the bank, stopping only when it hit a small shelf about six feet from the bottom of the gully—its steel wheels, axles, and eight tons of iron truck landing with a sickening *crunch* as it crushed the flimsy wooden body of the car and its human cargo. The rear passenger coach, its pin and link to the combination car also giving way under strain as it jumped the track, slid down the bank until it rested at a perilous angle against the combination car. Mercifully, it was still upright, though leaning to one side on trucks that were either crushed beyond recognition or buried in the soft dirt.

Strewn all about the cars, thousands of burning coal embers eerily lit the gully, setting a myriad of small fires to the grass, then the pitch-covered trestle, and creeping unstopped toward the passenger cars themselves. Steam rose hissing from the wreck of the burning engine, covering the gully in a thin spreading mist, though which the moon shone its impassive face.

The faces of the only other two witnesses to the wreck were far from impassive. One was shocked, unnerved, and sickened—the other was grinning from ear to ear, as its owner hiked with determination toward his rendezvous in Lincoln.

*　*　*　*　*

Walter Seidell was milking his last cow when the concussive crash of the wreck rolled into his barn siding, rattling its windows, and causing his cow to kick over the pail that the farmer had carelessly left too close to its hind legs, spilling milk all over his pants. Walter cussed, snatched up the pail and hustled to the barn window, from which he saw the glow from the engine fire in the gully a few miles down the track. He was close enough to hear the Rock Island train go by every night, as well as the Burlington train that he knew would come by about a half hour after that. He wasn't sure of the exact time, or which train was involved—but the only explanation for such a crash and glow was a train wreck.

"Lew!" Seidell shouted as he trotted toward the house, still carrying the milk pail. His son, nearing ten years old, met him there, carrying a small kerosene lantern and fastening his overalls, having already headed off to bed.

"Did you hear it, too, Pop?" the boy asked, stifling a yawn. "What was it—thunder, you reckon?"

"Train wreck, I believe—see that glow?" his father said, pointing southwards, past the barn and toward the tracks. "Let's go see—they may need a hand."

As the pair hustled through the backyard toward the glow around the bend of the tracks, Lew swung over the small lantern and noticed that his father's trousers were soaked.

182

"What happened, Pop?" Lew said, pointing to his father's pants.

"Oh, that damned Jersey knocked the milk over and tried to drown me when she heard the crash," Seidell grumbled, then seeming to realize that he was still carrying the milk bucket, flung it back toward the barn before the pair of them hopped down the embankment, into the gully and onto the tracks, heading south.

Later on, Walter Seidell recalled wishing that he had thought to bring the pail, after all.

* * * * *

Another quarter mile up the track, Old Man Saxton and his son, William, were also headed from their adjoining farm toward the sound of the crash, absently carrying the axe that they had just used to dispatch a prairie rattler (which had scared Mother Saxton half to death in the spring house, lurking there just behind the peach preserves). Bill Lonsdale headed over from his farm just south and west of the wreck, as did a dozen other denizens of the small farms that surrounded the tracks south of Lincoln.

To the downtown residents in the capital more than four miles away, the sound of the wreck was not much more than a distant crack-crack-*crack*, as if a ragged volley of distant rifles had been fired. However, the growing fire on the horizon was clearly visible, and a number of its more curious citizens took off to investigate.

And they didn't come much more curious than "Crazy" Charlie Raymond. A part time hackman and full time town character, Charlie had positioned himself facing north on Seventh across from the passenger depot, hoping to pick up a fare from the incoming Burlington train (unlikely), a whore (a potentiality), or a stiff drink (an inevitability). From the second story of the St. James Hotel next to Mooney's restaurant, a young lady was sitting on her window sill and having "words" with Charlie when she spotted the glow on the horizon to the south.

"Looks like a fire," she speculated, and an electric spark lit the hackman from within. Charlie was a sucker for a good fire. Meaning to turn his hack around in a wide arc and head back south on Seventh, he whipped his harried black nag into a trot...and nearly ran Zeke and Bobber over as they emerged from Mooney's.

"Hold 'er up there, Charlie," Zeke said, gripping the reins of the horse in order to spare Bobber from being bowled over. "Where's the fire?"

"South of t-t-town!" stuttered Charlie, pointing. Zeke turned, and seeing the glow on the horizon, looked at his watch. He felt yet another

183

sinking feeling in the pit his stomach. *The Rock Island train was due in about ten minutes...*

"Charlie, wanna earn a fare?" he queried. "I need you to drop ol' Bobber here at the Rock Island depot—and then we'll go and check out that fire."

* * * * *

Although his left shoulder throbbed with pain, Amos Seville was practicing his contortionist act again—but this time, more than an overheard phone call was at stake.

The wreck had been a perfect nightmare of sound, smell and motion, but not of sight—the gas lamps at the front and back of the passenger cabin, supplied by large tanks under the frame of the car, had gone out immediately at the shock of the first crash. Amos was left mostly to guess at how he and most of the passengers had tumbled their way to the front of the passenger car, along with wooden seats, assorted luggage, and a gas-fired stove that had broken free of its moorings near the center of the car. It was this stove that was causing Amos to wedge his bruised body into an impossibly tight space between it and the splintered wooden left wall of the car, in an urgent attempt to free the large man that was moaning under its full weight against the front wall. The moanings seemed to be growing softer in the darkness, and Amos suspected why—the sweet, sickly smell of gas was all around them there in the semi-darkness, with only the light of the moon filtering through the smashed coach windows.

"Come now, Colonel," Amos said, encouraging the trapped man as best he could through gritted teeth. "No sleeping on duty."

With his back and head braced against the cool, cast iron of the stove, Amos finally managed to sneak a knee and one of his feet underneath him, placing them squarely against the wall of the car. With a nod of thanks to the gods that it was summer and not wintertime, Amos heaved and steadily expanded his wiry frame against the cool, massive stove. The pain in his left shoulder grew to a sharp crescendo, and Amos labored to control his breathing, trying not to choke against the gas, grateful for a slight breeze that wafted in through the broken window above them. Gradually, the stove began to budge—slowly at first, and then rolling suddenly to the side with a *crack*. Beneath it, the Colonel, groggy with gas but still conscious, responded to Amos' tired urgings, and half climbed, half stumbled through the side window of the passenger car, followed closely by Amos. Sprawling next to the car, the pair lay gasping for breath in the cooling

184

night air, with sounds of other passengers moaning and coughing about them.

* * * * *

Though Amos had labored mightily to free Colonel Bills, brakeman Harry Foote was the true hero of the hour. Unlike many of the passengers, Harry was not immediately knocked unconscious by the shock of the passenger car jumping the track and careening down the embankment. Seated at the back of the car, he and Amos had wound up on top of the heap of humanity and flotsam at the front of the car after the wreck. Amos had been groggy, but Harry had shaken him until he was fully awake, then immediately started to work at freeing the other passengers. The need was urgent—although there was no fire in the passenger car—as yet—the smell of gas from the ruptured tanks under the car filled the darkness with a sickly, ominous odor. Harry had the presence of mind not to light a match, despite the lack of light all around him, and managed to move two women and a boy through the windows, waking the men and encouraging them to free themselves where possible. When he saw that the passenger car was empty—there were a number of injuries among the fifteen passengers that had escaped, but no fatalities, it seemed—Harry turned his attention back to Amos and Colonel Bills. To his relief, he saw in the light of the moon and the burning engine that the pair lay beside the wrecked car, catching their breath. For his part, Amos noticed as Harry approached them that the young brakeman was limping.

"Amos, you all right?" Harry asked.

"Banged my shouldah a mite," Amos said, sitting up and wiping his eyes, which still stung from the gas, and testing his stiffening limb. "That's the end of ah juggling act on this line for awhile, ah fear. How's the leg?"

"'S alright," Harry said dismissively, kneeling beside Colonel Bills. "And the Colonel here?"

"Well, he was able to get out of the car on his own steam, but ah can't speak for him now—that gas was pretty thick in there," Amos said, then actually jumped in surprise as the Colonel sat straight up and coughed, rubbing the last of the stinging gas from his own eyes.

"It was thick, alright—but I'm tolerable," the Colonel said, weakly. "Though I can't say I would have been, without your help—Amos, is it?" He thrust his big hand toward his rescuer. "I won't forget your kindness, and if you should ever need anything..."

185

"No time for that now," interrupted Harry, a look of impatient determination on his young features. "We need to some help for these folks. I saw a colored man a few minutes ago—one of the local farm hands, I guess. He had a lantern, and I sent him to flag down the Burlington freight. It should be coming by in just a little while, and we can't chance adding another wreck to this one."

"Ah should think *that* would be signal enough," Amos said, gesturing with his good arm to the base of the trestle, which had begun to burn. He was still dizzy from the gas, his throat was parched, and his shoulder hurt like hell now.

"Maybe," Harry said, and pointed northwest along the UP and Burlington tracks. "Colonel, the penitentiary is just over a mile away up the tracks there. Do you feel up to finding us some help?"

"Certainly," the Colonel said, immediately struggling to his feet.

"Good. Contact the police, the railroad..." said Harry, and looking about him adding quickly, "...and the fire department. Tell them that we'll try and flag down the Burlington or the U.P.—whichever is coming into Lincoln next—and send in the survivors."

"Right," said Bills, rising unsteadily to his feet. As he staggered up the tracks, Amos noticed the small, supplicating form of Jay McDowell peel itself from the bank where he had been laying, and catch up to the Colonel, steadying him as they carefully made their way past the burning wreckage of the engine toward Lincoln.

"Now," said Harry, holding a hand out for Amos as he wearily stood. "We need to check out that combination car for survivors, and get..."

"The combination car...Oh, gods...!" exclaimed Amos, his head finally clearing as he got to his feet. "Eugenia!"

Stumbling down the bank, Amos' mind reeled at the sight of the car—or rather, what was left of it. Resting upside down on a small shelf about six feet above the bottom of the gully, the car's massive steel wheels and undercarriage had smashed the wooden frame into the soft soil of the embankment, leaving only a few feet of the sides of the car still visible in some places, and in others—none at all. A small fire had broken out, and was slowly spreading from the side of the car facing the gully to the rest of the wreck. Amos tried to focus, to think, but despair had begun to creep over him. *Masterson and Eugenia—neither had come back to their seats in the passenger car...so they were both in there—under that, somewhere...*

Yet, not all were despairing. On the far end of the car where the express room was originally located, a farmer named Sexton was wielding an axe on the wooden frame, while his grown son and a few other farmers cleared the wreckage away. Inside, the head of the baggage master, Fred Scott, was visible, and through the steady chops, Amos could hear the cheerful old farmer reassuring him that, *no*, he wouldn't be allowed to burn to death. Next to him, a shorter farmer apparently named Seidell kept murmuring, "If I'd only brought that bucket—there's a pond just down there a piece...just a little water would do it..."

Around the corner of the car from that group, Harry had reappeared, and was now trying to rescue the postal clerk—Cherry, who was pinned under some wreckage—from the growing flames. Cherry's voice was rising near panic level, threatening to spiral out of control as the flames started to inch toward his legs. Amos was just about to help Harry out, when he heard it—faintly from the interior, at first, then clearly—a woman's voice, carrying from the smashed passenger portion of the car into the night air through what used to be a...window?...now half obliterated by smoke, half buried in the soft dirt.

Dirt that Amos was now frantically digging through with his bare hands, then a broken plank, then...*yes, ah believe ah could just squeeze in, with a little luck.*

Hell, he corrected himself, as he tucked his head into the gloom, his banged up shoulder now straining against the shattered window frame...*if we'd had any luck at all, we wouldn't be here.*

"Eugenia?" he spoke into the darkness of the car. Nothing was distinctly visible, but Amos had been required to clear away shards of wood, seat cushions, metal brackets—and a very sticky-soft, heavy object that Amos was trying his best to forget entirely. His body was now wedged into the car beyond his knees, and it occurred to him that there was now very little hope of turning around and crawling back out the way he had come in. But that thought flew out the transom of his mind when he heard, softly, not five feet from him, a tired little girl of a voice whimpering...

"Amos?"

"Eugenia," he said, relief and hope now flooding into him. "Just hold on another minute, darlin'...ah'll light a match." Amos smelled for gas, and satisfied that there was none present, struggled to reach into his right front vest pocket for a lucifer. "Care for a cigarette?"

187

"None a' your hand rolleds, if you please," Eugenia said weakly, and as Amos lit the match, he saw her...there, but a few feet away, her green eyes staring directly at him through a mask of blood that was flowing from her auburn hair.

"Can you move towards me?" Amos asked.

"No...my skirt's caught, I think, and it's a tight squeeze," she said, faintly. The wrecked car was filling with smoke now, and though her face was only five feet away, Amos could barely see Eugenia through the fading match.

"Well, unfasten your skirt, darlin'," Amos said, lighting another match. "And ah'll grab you...that is, ah'll pull you out. No time for modesty now."

"Pretty common request lately," Eugenia muttered, and even managed a slight sneer. As she struggled with her clothing, Amos wiggled and inched closer to her through the smoke, while holding the match out ahead of him. Forcing his breathing to stay steady, he banged his feet sharply against the window frame, hoping to be heard outside the burning car. In the fading light of the match, Eugenia had managed to stretch about six inches closer to him, and extending his arm, he had almost reached her outstretched hand...

When something grabbed his arm—from the side—and the match went out.

"Get me out of here!" a husky, desperate voice shouted. Turning his head, Amos saw the broken form of Clive Masterson through the gathering firelight, his face a mask of fear. "For God's sake, I'm trapped—get me out of here!" Glancing down at Masterson, Amos saw that it was true—the grocer was pinned under a heavy beam, which itself was holding up much of the weight of the truck that had crushed the car. As Masterson struggled in the growing light of the fire behind him, Amos saw that the entire structure was dependent upon the strength of it—moving the beam was impossible, and even if accomplished, would bring the steel ceiling down on all of them.

Masterson's shout cost him a coughing spasm, and for a moment, he released Amos' arm. Amos immediately reached out and grasped Eugenia's hand—she appeared to be free now, but was wedged so closely between the remains of a train seat and the side of the car that she could find no purchase to move forward on her own.

At his feet, Amos felt the first tugs of help arrive. "Amos!" Harry Foote's voice echoed into the car. "Is that you?"

"Yes, damn it!" Amos said, his face playing in the firelight. "Pull me out, for God's sake. There's a woman in here."

"No!" Masterson screamed, grabbing Amos' coat again. "Me first, not the goddamned whore!" The fire was licking around Masterson's legs now, but even as he screamed, the man still held firmly onto Amos' coat.

"Sorry, Masterson," Amos said, reaching his free left hand into his coat pocket, wincing at the pain, at his obligation...and what it would mean. "Ah'll do what ah can for you."

Outside, the sound of the shot was muffled—to all ears but Harry's— by the sound of the crackling timbers. As he pulled with all his waning strength, Harry saw the legs, hips, and finally, the head of Amos appear though the shattered gap in the car. Flames were licking around the window frame, singeing Amos' clothes, face and hair—but he maintained his hold on something.

"Grab my shoulders and pull, Harry!" Amos urged, the car in flames around him as he turned his legs and braced them against the timbers. A delicate hand was grasped in his, and with Harry's help, he pulled a woman, unconscious, from the inferno, the remains of her blouse and pantaloons in smoking rags about her. Amos fell backwards, gasping for breath, and Harry picked up the woman—such a tiny, burnt thing—and laid her a safe distance away up higher on the bank as the fire in the car mushroomed, roaring into the night sky. He felt the woman's pulse and her breathing—nodded, patted her hand, then returned to Amos.

"How is she?" queried Amos, as Harry helped him up the bank. Together they sat next to Eugenia, and Amos took her hand with a worried look.

"Burned, but breathing," Harry replied, shaking his head and seating himself next to Amos to catch his breath. "That was a damned brave, silly thing for you to do, Seville. What if I hadn't come along to pull you out?"

"Awfully glad you did, old sport," Amos said, putting Eugenia's hand carefully at her side, then taking his flask from his pocket and offering it to Harry. "Ah imagine Cherry is, too. Who else did you get out of there?"

"Just Fred Scott, the baggage man—that was mostly the doing of those farmers over there, though," Harry said, taking a swig of the cold coffee as if it were the sweetest water, then pointing the flask at the men still clustered around Fred Scott. "Fire was commencing to lick up his legs,

189

and had burned his trousers and shoes completely off by the time they got him out. It was a close thing."

Harry handed the flask back to his companion. "Amos..." Harry asked, hesitantly. "Did...did you happen to see C.D., that is...Captain Stannard in there?"

Amos shook his head, numbly. Harry trembled and lowered his head, fighting away the urge to sob. Instead, his voice grew very, very quiet.

"Ike and Will are gone too, I guess. Ike was from Council Bluffs, over on Fifth Avenue. He has a wife and a child, a daughter. Will Craig...he left a wife and four kids. Captain Stannard lived in St. Joe with his wife...he has—had—two grown sons. One lives in New York, and the other is chief clerk for Standard Oil in St Joe. His wife has been visiting at Ike's house in Council Bluffs, and we had supper there last Tuesday...pot roast, I think, and potatoes..." His voice trailed off. "They were all like brothers to me..."

Harry realized that he had been silently sobbing for over a minute when Amos finally coughed, lit a thin brown cigar, and held it out to him. Harry sniffed, and then nodded. He took a long drag and handed it back, wiping his eyes on his grimy sleeve. To change the subject, he pointed up the U.P. track. There, several horses and nearly a dozen people could be seen approaching them, lit by the fire from the wrecked engine, the combination car—and now the trestle, which blazed away over their shoulder.

"Gonna have a lot of company, it appears, and there's gonna be a lot of questions," Harry said, picking up a dirt clod and throwing it at the burning wreck. "Newspapers will have quite a time with it, I suppose..."

"Speaking of which," Amos interjected, looking Harry in the face. "Ah wonder if you could possibly...uh, minimize our role in this, Miss Eugenia and myself? I don't suppose you could leave us out altogether, as passengers, but, well, we have a...rather checkered past, and ah am afraid neither of us would care for...the publicity, much. It would be a kindness, ah think, if you mentioned that you just found us with the other passengers in the rear coach."

Harry looked at him levelly. "I'll do that," he said, "if you can honestly tell me that what you did in that car a few moments ago...all of it...was for mercy."

Amos met his eyes, and nodded.

Thursday, August 9, 1894
9:50 pm

Just up the bank on the Rock Island tracks, Saxton, Seidell and their sons were standing around, hands in their pockets, talking quietly in a semi-circle as farmers are wont to do when gathering in groups of three or more. This time, instead of the condition of their crops, or their animals, or their barns, they were discussing the rescue that they had just participated in, and—as they would have done if the topic *had* been their crops, or their animals, or their barns—they were doing their best to be duly, but not quite noticeably humble. Surveying the flaming wreckage of the engine, tender, and combination car in the gully below, and the smoldering ruins of the trestle before them, it wasn't too difficult. If it had been other men, it might have made them talkative...excited... even giddy.

But they were, after all, Nebraska farmers. A fire and a train wreck couldn't hold a match to a good, soaking rain.

"Can you believe how torn up these tracks are?" Walter Seidell remarked, matter-of-factly, kicking a twisted rail that had been thrust up at the end of the trestle and now pointed toward the stars, looking more like the frayed end of a knotted ball of twine than steel.

"Sure is," said Lew. Having had ten years to practice, he mimicked his father's hands-in-overalls stance with perfection, and now mirrored his father's rail kicking with similar accuracy.

"Those ties look like someone was plowing crossways through old furrows," remarked Saxton, his foot exploring a splintered tie.

"Sure does," said Seidell, prodding the same tie with his foot, his hands still in his pockets.

"Sure does," said Lew, his own toe taking its turn.

A pause.

"Yep, sure is a helluva mess," said the elder Saxton.

"Yep," said Seidell.

"Yep," said Lew.

"Something's funny here," said William Saxton. The younger Saxton, in his 20's, had spent enough time living near the tracks and consorting with railroad men (in taverns, coffee shops, and other places of ill repute that he was sure his father would rather not know about), so he had come to understand the structure and nomenclature of the roads, was now crouching at the end of the trestle, and pointed to the space where two rails met. "Where's the fishplate?"

"What's a fishplate?" asked Lew. His curiosity had been roused sufficiently to shift his habitual echo-target from his father to his neighbor, and now perfectly mirrored William's posture as he examined the track.

"It's a piece of steel that ties the rails together," William explained. He got to his feet and backtracked along the wrecked train's path to an undamaged section of track. Finding a pristine joint, he pointed again—this time to a piece of metal with four bolts securely tying one rail to another, two for each rail. Lew trailed behind him, followed gradually by the older farmers. "See this? It bolts the ends together."

"Sure does," said Lew, nodding vigorously.

"Yep," said Seidell.

"Yep," said Saxton, folding his arms and nodding in approval. Nothing else needed to be said; his son was obviously a genius.

On a roll now, William moved back to where the rails had first parted. "How about that? The fishplate isn't broken here—there isn't any sign of one at all. Look around for it, Lew...see if you can find it." With his sharper, younger eyes, Lew didn't take long.

"Here it is!" he said triumphantly, picking it up out of the grass, no more than 10 feet away, and holding it up in the moonlight.

"And here are the bolts...and the nuts, it looks like," remarked William's father, matter-of-factly, from a spot not four feet off the tracks. As he held them out to Walter, he added, "Not a mark on 'em." Walter nodded, and the two farmers' eyes met in a dawning understanding.

"And look at this, willya?" said William, triumphantly. From off in the weeds on the same side of the track, he lifted a long iron bar with a strange clawlike hammer on one end. "Bet you can't guess what this is used for..."

"Pulling spikes, I'd guess..." Seidell said, now pointing himself, straight down at the tracks. "Right outta those perfect little square holes in those ties there..."

"We'd better put these back right where we found them, and go tell Mr. Foote," old Saxton sighed. He had seen Harry at work during the rescue, and had tremendous respect for the young man's fast thinking and raw courage.

"Yep."

"Yep."

"Yep."

* * * * *

"Crazy" Charlie was ready to GO—but his fare wasn't—quite. He was sitting in his hack outside the knowledge box, the glassed-in personal domain of the stationmaster, local poobah of the god flamed C.R&I.P. railroad—a Rockhead—in the capital city of the hottest, driest, muscle-headedest, lead-buttedest state in the godforsaken Union.

However, a fare is a fare, he reasoned, *and it wasn't every day that somebody would pay you to go see a fire.* So he sat there—fuming.

Zeke himself was growing more antsy by the minute, too—and the fire was only part of it.

"I can't understand it," Jim Rider muttered. His company hat was off now—and his long, combed-over gray hair had long ago left its gleaming, carefully prepared resting place for points south. His gaze peered intensely at the Regulator clock ticking against the wall over gold-framed glasses, then shifted its focus through the windows toward the glow on the southern horizon, and mumbled, "Bull Stannard would never bring a train in this late...he'd rather die..."

Thinking about what he had just spoken, his eyes met Zeke's in shock, then turned to stare at the floor as his voice trailed away.

"I'll check it out," said Zeke, and turning to Bobber, added, "Hang around for a bit, won't you, Bobber? They might still come in."

Bobber nodded shortly, then turned to the station master and asked, "Who's the fattest man in this here office?"

The conductor started, then said, "Uh...John Price...why?"

Bobber gave him the hairy eyeball. "Where's he sit?"

The conductor pointed to a corner desk, where the old prospector moved like a shot, and began to rifle its drawers. Opening the lowest one, he paused, smiled nearly toothlessly, and said in a high, happy voice, "...*cook*-ieeeeeze...!"

193

Outside, Zeke jumped into the hack, and said to his driver, "Whip 'em up, Charlie. Let's make tracks."

He didn't have to tell Charlie twice...hell, he didn't have to say a thing. Charlie smiled as he obliged.

He *liked* fires.

* * * * *

Time had passed—thirty minutes or more since the train had derailed. Enough time for the excitement and adrenaline of the wreck to give way to weariness, and despite the terrible light and heat of the fires raging about him, Harry Foote felt it *utterly*.

Up on the bank, where Amos sat quietly with Eugenia, fifteen injured passengers were doing their best to cope under the limited ministrations of the farmers, townsfolk, and their wives who had managed to find them so far by the glow of the wreck's fire. There were a number of broken bones, several back injuries, and some of the wounded passengers were most certainly bleeding internally. Harry's lack of medical experience nagged at him, but there was little he could do but make them comfortable until help arrived. *Where the hell was that fool, Bills...?*

To top it all off, about ten minutes ago, four of the men that had helped rescue Fred Scott had excitedly cornered Harry while he was fetching a lantern from a Negro—the same man that Harry had spotted when the brakeman had first emerged from the wreck of the passenger car. Harry had found the man wandering from injured to injured, and from townfolk to farmer, stuttering in agonized amazement, the lantern still unlit. The rescuing farmers had interrupted to report that they had found a crowbar, a fishplate, and other evidence that supported the theory of a deliberate train wrecking. Harry could only rub tired fingers over his closed, weary eyes, nod his head curtly, and quietly thank the men for leaving things as they'd found them. *Well*, he thought, as the men left to "guard" their find, at *least the railroad won't fault poor Ike, and Bill, and C.D....much good it does them.*

Doing his best to think about the work ahead of him instead of those wretched bodies, Harry lit a splinter from the fire of the combination car, brought his lantern to life, and went to the rear end of the passenger car to look for his fuzes in order to signal the Burlington train when it came. Fire was racing from the front of the passenger car to the rear when he finally located them in a box under the back end—it had taken a little digging— when...he heard a *whistle.*

There it was...

Hurrying back down into the gully, Harry had just managed to light one of the round railroad fuzes when the Burlington rattler rolled into the gully, its little freight engine pulling its two cars through the burning trestle at a slow, wondering pace. Spotting Harry's signal, its conductor—an experienced man named Jim Lawson—urged the engineer to back the engine down, and as the train came to a stop, recognized the signaling brakeman.

"Harry!" he shouted, "What the hell happened here?"

"Come over and help us for God's sake—we're smashed up," Harry said. "We need help with the injured."

"Sure thing," said Lawson. "Come on, Red." The big engineer nodded, and together they climbed out of the cab and moved to the two flatcars behind them, clearing space for the passengers from the Rock Island wreck.

When Zeke arrived with Crazy Charlie in the hack, the transfer of the passengers to the flatcars was already underway. So were the interviews. Two reporters from the Journal and one from the Lincoln Evening News were haranguing a short man with a loud, shrill voice and hair that looked glued into place.

"Name is Jay McDowell. M-c-D-o-w-e-l-l, like the general, you know? Me and the Colonel were the first ones out of the passenger car," Jay piped, and then having second thoughts about how many witnesses could dispute such a tall tale, pointed to a young, haggard-looking man in a Rock Island uniform. "A-after that brakeman, over there, a' course...the fella standing next to the Colonel. We helped rescue the passengers, then got on down to the prison to call you good folks...and the police, of course..."

While Jay's tales were still spinning into the nubby pencils of the reporters, Zeke took a silver dollar from the pocket of his duster, and held it out to Charlie—to no effect. Charlie was completely mesmerized by the fire—those tall, mushrooming flames that now poured from the trestle, dwarfing the flames that now licked around the red-hot iron frames of the engine and combination car, their wood and coal having already burned down to a fraction of their former glory. Shaking his head, he placed the coin in Charlie's pocket, and strode over to the young man in a scorched brakeman's clothing who was conversing quietly with the tall Colonel in the blue militia uniform—men both known well to Zeke.

"Anyway, we got back as soon as we could," the Colonel was explaining to Harry. "We contacted the Rock Island by telephone, and they'll be sending a train down with a tanker and men to fight the fire on the trestle any minute. They said they'd also contact the police and fire department, and get what other help they could."

"Like the newspapers?" the brakeman asked.

"Actually, I'm pretty sure that the railroad would rather the press stayed away from this one...but you can't keep a newspaperman from a fire like this," Zeke said, walking into the light of the trestle, and holding his hand out to the brakeman. "Hello Harry...you look like the devil himself..."

"That's about the size of it," Harry said, taking it.

Zeke hesitated, then asked the question that had brought him here at a zephyr's pace. "Where's Amos?" The seven words Harry uttered in reply offered more optimism than Zeke had dared hope for.

"Up there," Harry replied, pointing to the bank. "On the bank, with Eugenia."

Zeke tipped his hat to Harry, nodded at the Colonel, and broke into a run.

* * * * *

Nathan Brockhurst, master of the Fairbury Station, was sitting in his office, enjoying a cigar at the end of a long day when the telephone rang. Sighing heavily, he leaned over the desk and picked up the receiver. His posture changed appreciably as the Lincoln stationmaster unfolded his story; Nathan sat up straight, then he stood, and finally he began to pace slowly, back and forth across the small room, as far as the cord would reach, the earpiece held close to his ear.

"O.K., thanks, Jim. Keep me informed," he finally said, shortly. "I'll round up the ticket agents and baggage handlers right away—we'll have a good list of the passengers together within the hour. Meanwhile—we need to know the names of all the passengers that are picked up—living and...otherwise." A pause. "Yes...yes, I'll inform Chicago."

Brockhurst hung the receiver up slowly, debating about whether to wake the division chief. *The chief was a good man,* he thought...*but no, this had become personal.* Taking a last puff of his cigar, he ground it out on the edge of his desk, and picked up the receiver again.

"Hattie? It's Nathan. Yes...yes, it was very bad news, indeed." Nathan rolled his eyes at the ceiling, recognizing yet again the three major forms

196

of communication in Fairbury...telegraph, telephone, and tell Hattie. No need for a town newspaper...they had an *operator*. "Hattie, I need you to set up a person-to-person call to Mr. Ransom Reed Cable...Senior. His address is Chicago...25 East Erie Street. I think you'll find him on the Lincoln exchange." A pause. "Yes, *immediately*. O.K....just ring me when you have the line set up. I'll be running around the station here, but I'll hear it eventually. Thanks, Hattie."

Hustling out the door, Nathan's mind spun with the dozen things he must do—starting with waking the baggage men that had loaded the train, and tracking down the stationside passenger brakeman that would have taken the final passenger count on the doomed train. Lincoln would also need every spare tie, rail, and track crew that he could lay his hands on. But *gods,* he thought, *that telephone call...**that** was going to be the hard part.*

* * * * *

Back in Lincoln, the Rock Island station master rubbed his eyes. Prior to the telephone call, Jim Rider had spent a half hour hurriedly organizing a train that was just now pulling out of the station, carrying a crew and twenty gandy dancers, each having been roused reluctantly from their sleep. They looked rumpled, and sleepy, but strangely on edge as they boarded the flatcars, heading down to the wreck site with their shovels, cats claws and hammers to repair the burning trestle. Admittedly, it was a hastily assembled gang, and they were being driven by the engine that would have carried the morning train to Fairbury...but with the trestle half-destroyed, there wouldn't be much use for it. Jim knew that there were at least a dozen things that would be needed (and remembered the moment that the train was out of sight), but time was critical if even a portion of the trestle was to be saved—especially if the fire department was late. It was a long way from city water to the wreck site, and it would take every water wagon in the capitol city to put out that pile.

Rider wearily gave a last, short wave to its conductor, then turned back into the office, intending to get his yard clerk, John Price, to dash off a message to the other railroads in town. He already knew that he would need the services of a crane mounted on a flatcar in order to move the wrecked engine, and that it would probably need to come out of Omaha...maybe even St. Joe or Kansas City. *Better get permission from the Burlington or U.P. to move the flatcar to the wreck site*, he thought...*the sooner the better, before some bigwig in a head shed somewhere gets it into his mind to overrule local "cooperation" to score "points" against the Rock. With all this wrangling over the Union Pacific,* he realized, *it might be better to contact them first, instead of Burlington...*

"Wake up, mud hop," Jim said, shaking the chair gently until the straw-haired boy raised his head from the desk. John Price was a heavyset, good natured kid, awakened from a sound sleep, as all the rest, to deal with the emergency at hand.

"Yeah, Chief," John's eyes were sleepy, and his face was imprinted with the faint, reversed outlines of the ink from the blotter he had been snoozing on—otherwise, he looked like hell.

"Get hold of the U.P. offices—ask for the stationmaster—his name is Bert Hendricks. I need to speak to him...move, boy."

John nodded, and as he picked up the receiver from his desk phone and asked for the operator, he reached absently into his bottom desk drawer, fumbled a bit, then peered into it, confused.

"Hey," he asked, to a mostly empty room. "Who took my cookies?"

Thursday, August 9, 1894
10:30 pm

"Whatt did I tell them?" Chief Robert Malone stood at the top of the bank and gestured to the mass confusion demonstrating itself below him in the gully. Two water wagons were being dragged in what looked like circles around the smoldering wreck by panicked horses, while a myriad of men in various stages of uniform ran after them, heaving lines from three steam driven pumps that were waiting, unmanned and stationary, near the base of the blazing trestle. "I said, 'Mayor, I could always use more wagons, more pumps, more horses, but mostly, I could use more *trained* men.' What does he give me? More *volunteers.*"

His brother, Detective Frank Malone of the City Police Department shook his head and smiled. "Well," he said, his derby pushed back on his head, "I'm sure your boys will get it straightened out eventually..."

"Before the damn trestle burns to the ground, I hope," the Chief mumbled, taking off his red helmet, wiping off the sweat on the rim with a handkerchief, and finally placing it back on his head. "You'd better get to work, too, little brother..."

"Right you are," Malone said. Pulling his derby tight over his brow, the smaller man scurried down the steep bank, nearly crashing into a Negro that was having words with Crazy Charlie, the hackman. Without saying a word to excuse himself, Malone strode with determination into the gully, while the black man glanced at the detective nervously, produced a dollar, and urged Charlie into his hack.

For his part, Malone made a beeline toward the crowd of men that were congregated around the engine. A conspicuous man in a Burlington uniform stood before him, and Frank asked, "Pardon me...uh, Conductor, is it? Who is in charge here?"

"Well, if you mean, 'who's in charge of loading the survivors'...that'd be Zeke Gardner, over there," Jim Lawson replied, pointing to a tall, bearded man in a duster who was just now handing an unconscious woman up to a wiry, mustached man waiting on the flatcar.

"Yeah, I know him," Malone said, frowning. Straightening his hat, he stepped around the flatcar and marched up behind Gardner, who was adjusting a blanket on the prostrate woman up on the car. Malone had just raised his hand to tap the large man on the shoulder when he was interrupted.

"Hello, Malone," Gardner said, his back still turned as he adjusted Eugenia's blankets. "Kinda figured they'd send you out here. You always seem to get the messy ones."

"And you always seem to be *around* the messy ones," Malone countered. "So, what can you tell me about this, *Deputy?*" The city detective spoke the last word as if referring to a disease, or a small animal of the family *Rodentia.*

Gardner turned and looked down on the detective with a benign smile, pushing his hat back.

"Now, Detective, I would have given more credit to an investigator of your caliber—I haven't been a deputy for quite some time," Gardner said, wryly. During his long service as a deputy sheriff, Zeke had witnessed on many occasions the antagonism between the Sheriff's Department and the City Police—and Malone was one of the chief practitioners of the art of the snipe. He also knew that Malone hated anyone but his brother calling him by his first name. "You oughta think about quitting yourself, *Frank*—it's very liberating."

"No, thanks," Malone spat. "I'd rather arrest scum than serve them cheap liquor."

"Well, if anybody knows about scum, it ought to be you, Frank," Gardner admitted, then pointing over to where Harry Foote was leaning against the engine. "If you're looking for a man with answers, he's right over there. Rescued nearly everyone on this train—everyone that could be saved, that is. And," he said, pointing to Saxton and Seidell up on the opposite bank, "You'll likely want to talk with those farmers as well. Seems they've found some interesting hardware in the weeds, up there off the tracks."

"Obliged," Malone said, reluctantly, then gestured to the injured on the flatcar. "I'll need to speak to the passengers, here, too."

Two short whistles blew from the Burlington engine, followed by "'Board!"

"Sorry, Frank—afraid you'll have to catch these folks in the morning," Zeke said, swinging up onto the train as it began to move.

"Don't call me 'Frank'...*Deputy*," Malone griped. Zeke touched his hand to his hat, and watched the detective turn his attention to the brakeman while the train pulled slowly away. Zeke shook his head and sighed, then squatted down in the flatcar next to Eugenia. Amos was kneeling on her other side, gently holding her hand. Normally buoyant, his friend looked fagged out, like a three-day-old rubber balloon. Worry creased his features, but Zeke knew better than to ask Amos about how he was holding up.

"Was she unconscious when you found her?" Zeke asked instead, directing his attention to the prostrate girl between them.

"Nearly," Amos said. His gaze stayed fixed on Eugenia, and his voice was still and low. "But still lively enough to give me hell."

"You saved her life, the way that Harry tells it," Zeke remarked, matching Amos' quiet tone. "And that you asked him to keep that out of the papers."

"Ah can only hope so, on both counts," Amos agreed, but then added, "Did he say anything else?"

"He mentioned that Masterson was dead—and that you couldn't save him," Zeke replied. "A pity, that."

"Yes...yes it was," Amos admitted. "All the more so...because ah'm afraid ah had to help it along, there at the end." He took a moment to look up and stare into Zeke's eyes, gently resting his hand on his coat pocket until he saw the understanding dawn in his friend's eyes, then turned back to Eugenia, adding, "Ah'm sorry, Ezekiel."

Zeke dropped his eyes as well, but his mind—habitually—focused on the practical. "I assume you had the sense to shoot him in the heart— they'll recover those bones, you know, and a bullet hole in the skull would be pretty hard to explain."

The ex-lawman detected a short nod from Amos out of the corner of his eye, then turned to stare silently out at the moonlit gully that was passing under the train's wheels. There were only a few miles left to Lincoln's Burlington station, but the train was pulling at a snail's pace in order to spare the passengers, and the deep *clack* of the wheels rolling at sparse, even intervals over the gaps between the rails was like a funeral drum. So much had been lost this night—more than even Amos knew. But looking about him at the misery of the passengers in the glow of the fire that raged behind them, the despair that Zeke had briefly felt was now turning into something harder—and ultimately, he knew, more useful.

"It wasn't your fault, Amos," Zeke said, steel coming back into his voice. "I just hope you saved a few rounds for the bastard that did this— 'cause its *comin'*. And it ain't gonna be pretty.

"So's my bill," said a weak voice from the bed of the flatcar, "and it ain't gonna be pretty, either."

Zeke pushed his hat back and started to reply...but it appeared that Eugenia had already dropped back off to sleep, so...he just nodded and patted her hand. Knowing what she had risked—for nothing, as it turned out—words didn't seem sufficient, somehow.

And Amos' grin was broad enough to speak for the both of them.

*   *   *   *   *

Thursday nights invariably found Mr. and Mrs. Ransom Reed Cable Sr. at the Chicago Opera House. This night, Miss Emma Calvé, a striking French operatic soprano had performed the lead role in Carmen, and the critics had considered her acting ability, stormy personality, and dramatic intensity all as extraordinary. Mrs. Cable (as usual) was thrilled—Mr. Cable (as usual) mostly played with his watch.

It was therefore nearly half past ten before their carriage rolled up Erie Street, and Mr. Cable was able to finally escape from Mrs. Cable—and French Opera—for the sanctuary of his blessed study. However, in addition to the crystal glass of Cognac and fine cigar that habitually graced it at this time every evening, the silver platter that was placed before him also featured a brief note from his personal secretary. It read:

August 9   10:12 p.m.

Person to person call requested immediately by Mr. Nathan Brockhurst. Urgent.

Fairbury Station, C.R.I.&P.

Cable's blood turned to icewater. *Rance was on his way home from Fairbury...today.*

Waiting only until the butler left his study and closed the door behind him, Cable instantly picked up the telephone on his desk. Peter LaRue, his personal assistant (never asleep where this particular telephone was concerned), answered within seconds.

"Peter, please arrange a return telephone call—immediately—to Mr. Brockhurst of the Fairbury Station." Cable hesitated, and then queried his secretary. "Did he mention why he called?"

"No, sir. But it sounded extremely urgent."

"I'll wait."

* * * * *

Crazy Charlie was miffed. His new passenger from the wreck site, a Negro named George Washington Davis, had produced a silver dollar for the ride back to Lincoln while he was watching the trestle fire from the gully, its flames licking the heavens as they leaped from support to support. Between Davis' fare and the dollar he had received to go out to the fire, Charlie now had enough money to buy forty beers, a week's lodging, or a fine whore...

...but he sure hated to leave that fire.

Oh well, he thought, trying to be philosophical, *the fire department was there now—they were bound to figure out which end of the hose was which and put the damned trestle out eventually.*

*At least, I could **talk** about the fire.*

"So," Charlie said, "Some fire, huh?"

"Yeah, sir, it surely was," Davis said, absently. He had been staring off into the night, as if deep in thought. But the query had flipped a switch in the man somehow, and a sly smile crept over his face as he added, "'Course, tweren't nothing like the wreck itself...'"

"Was you there for the wreck?" Charlie asked, incredulously. "How far away was you?"

"Well...I was right there...in the *passenger* car...why, I'm mightily lucky to be alive. Yes, sir, I was sittin' right there next to Mr. Harry Foote, and, uh, him and me got most of the passengers out, I reckon, savin' them, souls and all, from the flames..." Davis was cranking now, and went on to tell about the position of the cars, the bodies that had been dragged out, and the tremendous fire of the trestle. Charlie loved a good story...whether it was true was generally beside the point. However, something about the way Davis kept shifting around, looking up, then back to gauge the hackman's reaction to the story made Charlie suspicious that a good part of the story was utter hogwash. However, he made it a policy never to contradict a paying customer—not to his face, anyway.

"By gods, man, that's amazing!" Charlie obligingly marveled, absently checking his horse's speed. "Bet it made one almighty crash when it happened."

203

"Well, the engine did—the rest was pretty mild by comparison."

Mild? Charlie thought. *In that **passenger** car? Something was screwy about this story...*

Charlie was nearing the turn off of north 27th back west onto O Street. The colored club where Davis had asked to be dropped was only minutes away, so Charlie guessed that it would be safe now to ask a few innocent questions.

"So, what was you doing on that train? Was you off visiting folk away down south? " Charlie asked, conversationally, and Davis hesitated before he replied.

"Yeah, that's it, sir. Off visiting friends. I picked up the train in Rokeby and rode in with Mr. Harry Foote. That's how I come to be there..."

Bullshit, thought Charlie, but couldn't resist leading him on a bit more. "See you lost your coat—was it burned up in the fire?"

Looking about him as the hack slowed to a stop, Davis said, "Yes, sir, it musta been...it ain't here."

The soft glow of gaslight streamed through the open doors of the rundown clapboard building at 9th and P streets, and Charlie could see the confused look on Davis' face when he climbed out, looked around once more for something that was missing—probably the coat, Charlie guessed—then thanked the hackman, and walked into the club.

Charlie waited until his fare got inside, then smiled thinly, shaking his head.

"And they call *me* 'Crazy'," he muttered, as he turned his hack back toward the Burlington depot, and a painted girl that might or might not still be sitting in the window of the St. James Hotel.

* * * * *

Bud Gardner, after a very long ride home, was still pretty much floating.

But you couldn't float and still find your way through the streets of Lincoln at night, Bud recognized, so he turned his attention from blissful thoughts of Anna Marie to finding his way across the tracks of north Lincoln, urging his very tired horse through the tangle of streets around the four train stations that terminated the steel rails like knots at the ends of a shoestring. He couldn't help noticing the glow in the southern skies, and wondered what was on fire south of Lincoln.

Shrugging to himself, he urged the gelding back into a trot, and soon spotted the lights of the Burlington depot as he turned south on 7th Street on his way back to the livery. A train was waiting there, ready to depart...as were an unusually active crowd of people. On a whim, Bud stopped, hitched his horse to a handy post, stretched, then walked into the station. All about him, people whirled about in agitation...firemen, policemen, hospital workers, and railroad workers...*gods*, thought Bud, borrowing a phrase he had heard Zeke use a dozen times, *they must have double shifts running.* No one appeared to be especially interested in the departing train, nor did they want to miss what was happening...but to Bud's eyes, **nothing** was happening...yet. *What's going on?* he mused.

Near him, a tall, thin man in a black tuxedo and a woman in evening wear were talking in hushed tones, part of what looked like a cluster of theatre goers. Bud moved over to them, thinking to ask what was happening—when a light hand touched his shoulder.

"Willa!" Bud said, delighted to see the young journalist, now returning his warm handshake. She, too, was dressed up, wearing a fine green silk dress with a ruffled hem and a matching hat. "You look swell...looks like you've been out on the town."

"Working actually. I was covering a production at the Lansing for the Journal...'Fanchion, The Cricket'...with a capital 'T', pronounced 'Thee' no less," her voice briefly registering in a broad falsetto with a lofty Eastern accent as she pronounced the title, then dropping back to her natural alto as she chuckled and shook her head sadly. "Nothing like a good train wreck to liven up a really bad performance. Trust me, the production is better off without **my** review..."

"Train wreck?" queried Bud, smiling. "It was that bad..?"

"No...well, yes, it was that bad...but I meant that the production was interrupted at the intermission with *news* of the train wreck. The entire theatre emptied to come down to greet the survivors...I must not have been the only one looking for a quick exit. Word is that they are coming in on the Burlington..."

"A train wreck...is that what this is all about?" Bud gaped.

"That's the word," said Willa, looking around Bud's shoulder, and nodding as if to draw Bud's attention south. "Here comes the train, now."

Bud turned, and sure enough, a slow-moving train was approaching the Burlington station from the south, blowing its whistle with a succession of short bursts to indicate that an emergency existed. As it crept up to the platform, the crowd heaved forward, until they were finally met by a line of city police, their white gloves held up to stop the surge. Willa, for her part, took off her hat and reached into her purse, pulling out a small card with the word 'PRESS' spelled boldly upon it, and a small pad and pencil.

"Pardon me, Bud, but I've got some snooping around to do." And placing her hat under her arm, Willa squeezed her way through the crowd to the oldest cop, a big, gray mustachioed fellow who, recognizing her even before her card was visible, motioned her through the line and let her pass.

For the next few minutes, Bud intensely watched the buzzing activity on the platform along with the rest of the crowd—baggage busters, brakemen, hostlers, and even switchmen had been called in to help. Despite the glare from the engine's kerosene headlamp, Bud could make out that several ramps were being set into place to bridge the gap between the flatcars and the platform. Across these, the injured were moved first, some under their own power, some being carried on stretchers by the burlier baggage men, each showing much greater care—even tenderness— than any luggage owner would have previously thought possible. Behind them, the folks that had helped the injured slowly disembarked the train— and Bud gaped.

"Zeke!" he yelled, trying to be heard over the drone of the murmuring crowd, for the tall man in the rumpled cowboy hat and duster could be no other than his uncle...*and was that...Amos?*. While Zeke seemed oblivious, engrossed in lending a slightly built man...yes, he was sure it was Amos...a hand crossing the ramp. However, Willa, who was standing more closely to the police line and speaking with the conductor, heard Bud's voice, looked over to where he was motioning, and quickly waved back her understanding. In a few moments, she had gotten Zeke's attention, and the two Barrelhouse boys were on their way over to Bud. Brushing his way through the crowd, Zeke interrupted Bud's questions with an order.

"Bud, take Amos here back to the Barrelhouse, and fix him up in the upstairs room, won't you? Miss Eugenia prefers a hot bath and a quiet room at the Lincoln Hotel. Meet me there in the lobby at seven a.m.— sharp. Get along, now," and without another word, Zeke turned back and caught up with the slow procession of the injured, walking next to a wagon bed with a prostrate form bundled within.

Bud, frustrated in his attempt to extract information from his uncle, turned to Amos. However, though he had his left arm tied into a sling, he was still able to hold up his right hand in silence.

"Ah'll answer all your questions, Bud, ah assure you...but first—well, frankly, ah need a cigarette, and the station sundry store is still open, ah believe" Bud opened his lips to offer help, but Amos batted him gently down again.

"Sorry, Bud, but they have a *special* brand for me," Amos interjected, adding, "Just wait here on the platform a bit—ah'll be back in just a few minutes."

As Amos ducked into the station, Bud watched the last of the cargo being removed from the train. Those final bundles—consisting of blankets wrapping odd shaped forms—produced conjecture, then pity and revulsion after a human hand was spotted hanging at an odd angle from one of them, and the smell of burned flesh became suddenly evident. After the last of the corpses were moved—with what reverence the Burlington workers could offer—to waiting wagons, the crowd rapidly thinned out.

"All aboard!" the conductor's voice cried out, and two short bursts from the steam whistle of the departing steam engine pierced the night, an anticlimax to the arrival of the injured from the wreck. "All aboard the Burlington Special to Omaha, Des Moines and points East...!"

Maybe it was a glint off the silver watch—perhaps Bud caught some other vague visual cue—but without warning, he found himself suddenly gazing at J.T. Lynch, not ten paces away, standing by the step of the last passenger coach, holding his watch impatiently and waiting for...someone. That someone wasn't long in coming. J.T.'s worried gaze gave way to sudden relief, and Bud followed it across the platform to...a black man, hustling toward the car with a satchel under his arm. Bud recognized him as a man named Rankin from their single meeting at the Barrelhouse, and his blue suit with gold buttons somehow gave Bud the impression of a railroad official. But his demeanor did not. A wild look was present in the man's eyes—a kind of ecstatic, feral euphoria that made Bud recoil somehow—yet he couldn't look away.

"Thought you were going to miss the train, Mr. Rankin," J.T. observed, motioning around with his free hand while he shook his man's hand with the other. "The station is in a real fine turmoil—better get aboard." Rankin grinned ear to ear, and was about to follow his boss aboard the train—which was moving now, slowly north—when Lynch stopped, and turned to stare directly at Bud. Rankin turned as well. For a

207

split second, it looked to Bud as if Lynch was going to step down from the platform...but at that moment, Amos stepped out of the station, and his eyes met those of J.T. Lynch. There was something utterly familiar about that face, and what passed between them in that split second was not quite recognition, yet stronger than déjà vu—and it caused Lynch to hesitate for a moment, as the train continued to crawl away from the platform.

The moment passed. Motioning Rankin to move up into the car, Lynch followed him and stood on the step, then reached into his vest and slowly pulled out a cigar, still facing the pair of them. His teeth flashed a smile as he bit the end off, then spat it onto the platform in Bud's direction.

"Be seeing *you*, Bud," he said, adding "Give my best to your uncle." With a final nod, Lynch walked up the stairs into the moving car.

Bud stood there motionless, with Amos several paces behind, both of them watching the train pull away. Bud had been uneasy earlier in the day, when J.T. had left the Barrelhouse. He was even more uneasy now. *Why was Lynch leaving? Hadn't he promised to help Zeke and the farmers?*

For Amos, the spark of recognition started to flicker, and then to flame as the train picked up speed. Some old memory—something far in the past, but important—was nagging at him, planting him as firmly on the Burlington platform as his mind was now planted in the past. There it was...

...his mother, having drunk herself into a crying jag—again—was staring at a silver frame that she held with both hands. Suddenly, the frame exploded as her mother threw it against the shabby walls of the Washington rowhouse.

"Why did he just leave?" his mother was wailing. "The miserable, selfish bastard..." and her face disappeared into her hands, immersed in waves of sobs. Amos, only six, walked over to the photograph. Under the broken glass, there was a photograph of two Union soldiers, staring solemnly at the camera. As he reached for the picture, his mother came up behind him, snatched it out of the shards of shattered glass, and tore it in two, separating the soldiers. She placed one of those halves carefully in a drawer—the other she dropped, with deliberation, directly into the burning logs of the fireplace.

In the few years that followed while he was still with his mother, Amos recalled stealing over to the drawer and examining the photograph many, many times. He carried it with him now, and though the image had changed over the years, Bud could probably have recognized the soldier—

208

in fact, Bud's own likeness to the man in the photograph, at his age, was striking.

But it was the other man—the man in the burned half of the photograph—that now filled Amos' thoughts. Because he had found him—he had recognized him—at last.

"You okay, Amos?" Bud said, gently. Amos' eyes had gone all strange on him, and Bud's confusion was nearly complete. "Don't you think it's time we got on home?"

"Home?" Amos said, blankly. "Yes." He allowed himself to be led for a time, through the ornate station and onto 7th Street. But when Bud tried to urge him onto his horse, Amos shuddered as if he had awakened, suddenly, from a dream.

"Come on, Bud," Amos stated, his voice evening out. "I need a *drink*."

* * * * *

The icewater that once ran in the veins of the President of the Chicago, Rock Island, and Pacific Railroad was boiling now, and Nathan Brockhurst of the Fairbury Station was seriously considering early retirement.

It looked at the moment as if he was going to get a little help.

"So, no one **knows** where my son is? *No one?*" thundered Ransom Reed Cable, as he paced back and forth in his immaculate study, straining the limits of the cord that ran from his lacquer black and gold desk phone to the mahogany paneling, surrounding hundred-year-old books. At the moment, Cable would have traded all of it for an answer to the question burning in his mind. "Where the hell is he? What kind of operation are you running down there? *Was he on the train or not?*"

"All I can tell you, *sir*," said Nathan, doing his best to keep his temper down, "is that he definitely purchased a ticket, and got on the train. However, one of the jugglers—er, sorry sir, *freight crewman*—swears he saw your son get off the train just before it left the station here. No one else has seen him here in town since then...but we'll be able to check more thoroughly in the morning..."

"And he was *definitely* not one of the rescued there in Lincoln?" Cable interrupted. It was his son, and, *dammit*, he raged, *I will not accept this.*

"We have a preliminary report from the police," Brockhurst said. "He was not named as one of the wounded that got off the train in Lincoln." *Of course*, thought Brockhurst, *that could be bad news as easily as good news.*

209

There was a long pause at the Chicago end. For a moment, Nathan thought that the great man, whose mellow voice had conversationally checked with Nathan all during the summer regarding the progress of his eldest son, was going to blow a gasket. But the next sound that Nathan heard...well, it could have been a tiny burst of static on the line...or it could have been a *sniff.*

"Keep me informed, please, Nathan," said the great man, finally. His voice sounded as old as Methuselah. "I'll be ready for a telephone call at this number all night, at any time."

"You might as well get some rest, sir," Nathan growled, softly. "There probably won't be any more news until the rest of the night shift is rounded up, and we check the hotels..."

And the coroner has identified the bodies, he thought, then went on, "...that'll be dawn, at least, sir."

"Thank you, Nathan," Cable said, "And for God's sake..."

"I know, sir," Brockhurst interjected, tiredly, "Keep it to myself." He wiped his brow. "I'll be here if you need me, sir."

"Thank you, Nathan," Cable said, and then the line went dead.

*   *   *   *   *

About seven miles southeast of Fairbury, two men sat in an abandoned animal shed that had once been a remote part of Rock Creek Station. As a well-frequented stop on both the Oregon Trail and the Pony Express, Rock Creek Station may have reached its peak of notoriety in 1861, when Wild Bill Hickock shot his first two (of many) men—ostensibly for threatening him—but more likely for calling him "Duck Bill," due to his oversized nose. The history of the station that surrounded them as a killing ground delighted one of the inhabitants—a tall, gaunt shell of a man, who reclined calmly, slowly sharpening a straight razor against a long leather strap. The other man, bound hand and foot and dumped unceremoniously on a stinking bale of straw next to the other man's horse, had no idea where he was. The only sounds he had heard in the last two hours was the threat made to him by the man on the train, the thud of a sap colliding with his head...and now, what could only have been a razor sliding back and forth across a strap.

Blindfolded and gagged, he only knew two things, really.

That death had never been closer.

And that he wished he had never gotten off that train.

210

Friday, August 10, 1894
6:05 am

With nothing to do until the morning, the elder Cable had decided to keep the news from his wife, giving her one full night's sleep—perhaps her last for some time—and resigned himself to spending the night in his study next to the telephone. In short periods between waking to the echoes of a telephone—that hadn't really rung—his own dreams had become a purgatorial review of all the wrecks under his tenure as President of the C.R.I.&P., which had, before this, been nothing more than a red mark on a ledger sheet. And as he slept, the ghosts of those men and women had come to visit him. Some had come to taunt him, their skulls grinning...some had simply shaken their ghastly heads, and turned their burned faces sadly away. On the one occasion that the visitor had been his son, he woke screaming.

Now just after six, the telephone rang again. Scrambling out of his nightmares to answer it, he scrambled into another one.

"Mister Cable?" the voice asked on the other end of the telephone. It was a genteel, well-educated New York sort of voice, Cable decided immediately, having heard the same from many of the men that sat around the table of his boardroom.

"Yes?" he replied, irritably. "Look, I need to keep this line free, I..."

"I can understand that," said the voice, softly, "Because your son is missing, and you must be terribly distressed."

"Who *is* this?" Cable demanded immediately. The man's words carried the confidence of an experienced poker player that held a lot of powerful cards, and they filled Cable with a sense of panic that he was trying hard not to allow control over him.

"I appear to be the man that saved your son's life, Mr. Cable, from a very extraordinary death—and now holds it in his hands."

A silence followed that lasted either 25 years or three seconds, depending on where you were standing. *It's a negotiation*, Cable realized, as cold sweat ran from his temples and trickled down under his silk shirt. In his life as a railroad executive, he had experienced very few circumstances where an assertive tack, however contrived, would fail as an opening gambit. However, this was no ordinary business dealing, he realized—so his tone was as cool and controlled as he could manage.

Mostly, it came out as worried, and extremely tired.

"What is it exactly you want of me, Mister...?"

"You can call me Mister 'B', sir," the voice obliged. "And I want very little, really, considering the stakes at hand." In a few short sentences, the voice at the other end of the telephone made his demands, while Cable wrote furiously on a pad of paper at a side table. At the end of his monologue, the caller paused, and his voice dropped almost an octave as he slid the final words across the miles.

"Mister Cable, I hope that the recent tragedy in Lincoln convinces you of the *serious* nature of this request," the voice hissed. "Follow my instructions, and your son will be released unharmed in just a few days. Unfortunately, the same cannot be said of many aboard your company's train. Make sure, Mr. Cable, that your son does not join them, in the end."

And before Cable could reply, the line went dead.

Years later, the senior Cable would describe that moment as the most harrowing of his life. He was shocked, frightened, and cornered, and thought that his entire world was falling around his ears.

For about 20 seconds. And then he was just plain *pissed off.*

"Peter!" he thundered into his receiver. "Get me Nathan Brockhurst!"

* * * * *

Amos Seville and Bud Gardner waited in the lobby of the Lincoln Hotel, and watched as the massive grandfather clock near the registration desk turned seven, then 7:15...then 7:30...then 7:45. On an overstuffed couch, Amos yawned. Seeing him, Bud yawned. Reacting, Amos yawned again.

Bud closed his eyes before another volley was fired.

The yawns were natural—both had slept fitfully. For Bud, the dreams had been delightful—filled with a raven-haired girl who was just *begging* to be kissed in a green cornfield, under the moonlight—until he woke up in an agreeable sweat. For Amos, the dream was also recurring, but not nearly as pleasant—two men in a torn photograph, Zeke Gardner and J.T. Lynch, who had continued to spin and juxtapose, until they blurred into a nightmare.

Just after the clock struck eight, Zeke finally appeared. Uncharacteristically, Bud's uncle looked hurried and preoccupied as he approached the pair of men at a fast walk, the heels of his cowboy boots echoing as he strode across the polished oak floor.

"Sorry I'm late, men," Zeke said, abruptly, waving them onto their feet. "Let's take a walk."

Throwing each other a short glance of guarded curiosity, the boys got up and quickly followed Zeke out onto P Street—and into the maelstrom beyond the normal chaos of a Friday morning. The U.P. and C.R.I.&P. currently had their main southbound rail line squarely blocked four miles south of Lincoln by a burned engine, an overturned tender—and several dead Rock Island crewmembers. Meanwhile, the Burlington route was busily trying to arrange trains for southbound freight and passengers. And thanks mostly to milkmen, newspaper boys, church women, and other early rising purveyors of "the word," both O and P streets were now acting as a magnets for a surprisingly broad slice of humanity that feasted at the altar of the goddess of *Rumor* and her consort, the minor god of *Perverse Curiosity*. They streamed down the hill now, walking the tracks, too curious to be turned away from a chance of witnessing the largest train wreck that had ever happened in the state, the claimer of at least eleven lives, if the rumor was to be believed.

"Sure are a lot of folks headed down to see the wreck," Bud remarked casually. As the threesome waited for the traffic to clear across Ninth Street, Bud's gaze longingly followed a wagonload of gandydancers as they turned down the hill with the rest of the human tide.

Zeke glanced at Amos, who smiled, and jerked his head mildly toward the station as if to agree with Zeke's unspoken suggestion.

"You got those forms with you, Bud?" Zeke said, nonchalantly opening his watch and adjusting the time to match the clock on the tower of the post office across the street. Bud reached into his shirt pocket and handed over a dozen neatly folded forms, each having been signed the night before by a farmer along Bud's trek north of Lincoln. Zeke examined them, nodded, and finally added them to a thick sheaf of what appeared to be identical forms in his duster's inside pocket.

"Looks like it's gonna be a long day," remarked Zeke, offhanded. "But it's pretty clear this morning. So, I guess if you want to grab a few hours off, Bud, feel free. Just be back at the Barrelhouse by noon."

Bud's eyes lit up. "Thanks, Uncle Zeke," he said, and turned to head down the hill.

"Hold on, Pard'," interrupted Zeke, and while Bud backtracked, his uncle reached into the deep outside pocket of his brown duster and produced a small notebook. With a stub of a pencil, Zeke wrote out a short note and ripped it from the notebook, handing it to his nephew.

"The U.P. is taking a crane down to the wreck site this morning to move the Rock Island engine off their tracks. Give this to the stationmaster—he's a man named Bert Hendricks," Zeke said. "He's sending a crane down in the next twenty minutes or so—see if he'll give you a ride. And **don't** be late this afternoon."

Bud grinned, held up the notepaper, and spun on his heels to follow the tide downhill to the station.

Zeke's faint smile was short-lived. Turning to Amos, his voice was low. "We don't need Bud for what we're about. How's your shoulder?" he asked, eyeing his partner's sling.

Sensing what Zeke was getting at, Amos awkwardly pulled the sling over his head, and carefully placed it in his left, lower coat pocket. Stiffly, he reached up to his chest and tapped the slight bulge in his right upper jacket pocket. "Quite good enough to handle LeBlanc, ah'm sure," he replied. "Ah assume that's what we ah at this morning?"

Zeke glowered as he set a steady pace across Ninth Street, east along P. Doing his best not to meet Amos' eyes, he growled, "Masterson was the key to the deal with the farmers. McGee knew it...so did his man, LeBlanc." Stopping, he turned to face his friend.

"Somebody wrecked that train, Amos. Without Masterson alive, the grain deal will most likely fall through, even if..." his voice trailed off.

"Even if the actual signed agreement was available?"

Zeke's eyes flashed as he jerked his head to face Amos, who smiled and shook his head.

"Zeke, you really shouldn't play poker...especially with a Southerner. Your face is easier to read than a newspaper at noon."

Zeke shook his head, too. "Any more observations?"

"Beyond the fact that Lynch left last night?"

Zeke looked astounded. "How did you find out? I looked everywhere for him. They said at the hotel that he checked out yesterday."

Amos nodded curtly. "Bud and ah saw him leave on the westbound Burlington right after we came in last night. Looks like he ran out on us,

214

all right." Trying to sound nonchalant, he added, "Any idea where he went?"

"No idea," replied Zeke, taking off his hat, and scratching the long graying hair underneath it before placing it back on his head. "I don't get it, Amos—first he jumps at the chance to come give us a hand—and just when it starts to pop around here..."

"He's gone," Amos replied. A strange light came into Amos' eyes, but Zeke seemed too preoccupied to notice.

"So," Amos said finally, trying to work the stiffness out of his left shoulder—and the gun hand that it was attached to. "Who do we go after...McGee or LeBlanc?"

"Where McGee is, LeBlanc isn't far away," Zeke said. "Let's move, Pard."

* * * * *

The disassembled crane was a cacophony of beams, hinges, levers, counterweights, and pullies, roped onto a flatbed car around a small, percolating steam engine that wreathed the entire, teetering assemblage within a hissing fog. Considering the track repair tackle that also overflowed every inch of remaining space aboard the flatbed, the conglomeration taken as a whole was impressive—the bastard offspring of a civil engineer's uncertainty and a tracklayer's expedience, birthed in the dark of the night under the jaundiced eye of a baggage buster. Arranged to travel "first" down the southbound track, the flatcar carrying the crane was followed by a carload of workers and a U.P. engine whose impatient engineer had kept blowing the "emergency' signal even after they were far out of the railyard, trying to keep the chattering pedestrians *off the damned tracks*. Consequently, they crept at less than five miles an hour, and Bud could hear the engineer cuss from three cars away.

Crowded into a corner of the slowly moving flatbed between a pile of ties and a barrel of railroad spikes, the young man was happy to be included in the "work party" at all. His job, according to the stationmaster (who had looked at Zeke's note, nodded once, and handed him off to the train's conductor), was twofold: (1) to keep the crane operator from falling out of the train, and (2) to keep from falling out himself. There was no pay, no return ticket, and no apparent duties once he got there. The stationmaster had only said, "Get the operator there, and he'll take care of the rest."

215

However, the crane operator—a fat little man named Leonard K. Johnson, who the stationmaster referred to as "Leo"—being thoroughly drunk, was currently making duty number one quite a challenge for poor Bud.

"Yessir, shook me out of a dead sleep at four this morning," Leo repeated for what must have been the fifth time in as many minutes. His striped Burlington hat was askew over his long, graying hair, his overalls looked to be on inside out, and his slurring words were accompanied by yet another grand gesture that managed to upset his marginal stability, once again nearly rolling him out of the slow-moving flatcar.

Man needs a crane operator himself, observed Bud, as he snatched him again by the straps of his overalls and hauled him back from careening over the edge of the car.

"Only crane car in Nebraska," he went on, once his wandering center of gravity had re-established itself beneath him. "Just finished up a nice little trestle job at midnight, and us boys was havin' a little celebration over to the Palace. Yessir, by God, the Rock's gonna pay pretty for this job."

"So, you think it was wrecked on purpose?" Bud remarked, trying to focus the man on the job at hand.

"Hell, yes—just stands to reason. Ain't you never heard of Round Pond?"

"No," Bud replied, grateful for any topic that didn't involve drunken celebrations at the Palace or potentially life-threatening gestures. "What about it?"

"Another chapter in the Railroad Wars," Leo intoned behind the back of his hand, conspiratorially, as if the barrel of rail spikes were spying on them. His breath, Bud noticed, would have made an onion weep, and his spittle was equally charming. "'Bout a year ago, the gov'ment opened up the Cherokee Strip in Oklahoma to them Sooners. Afore that, Rock Island and the Injuns decided on a station along the old Chisholm Trail through the strip, and called it Round Pond. Well, the gov'ment—and some says the other railroads—got it into their head that the county seat had to be in another spot four miles further south along the line—and they called *that* 'Round Pond.' Rock Island says 'no, we aready gotta Round Pond Station' at 'tother place, and when the gov'ment says they have to stop for the mail at the gov'ment town, the Rock jest puts up a mailhook to pick up and deliver mail through a bag, without having to slow down."

"Ever see a mailbag actually *work* in a high wind?" Leo asked, his eyes now registering some glimmer of coherence through the alcoholic haze. "Hell, that state's near as windy as this one. I heered that one day the wind stopped—ever'body fell over. Anyways, the Rock kept tearin' the bag with their hook, strewing the letters all over the track, not even slowin' down. The Round Pond folk passed laws, tried to flag down trains, put dummies on the tracks, and then wagons, logs—didn't seem to matter."

"Well, last June, the Round Ponders got fed up, tore up about a hundred yards of track and wrecked 'em a freight train. Nobody was killed—that time—but when the Rock rebuilds the line, they *still don't stop the trains* in the gov'ment town! Purty soon the Ponders were taking potshots at trains passing through, and 'bout three weeks ago, one of 'em blew up the tracks. Another one sawed through a trestle just down the road at Enid, there, and finally wrecked 'em another freight train."

"So, do you believe that they was—er, were—here and wrecked the train?" Bud asked, trying hard to ignore Leo's contagious slang, and bring his own language back to a high school standard that wouldn't make his English and Latin teacher, Miss Stransky, openly wince.

"Well...the gov'ment sent in troops—they're squattin' all over the place down there now. So why not move up here and keep up the mischief? When yer mad, yer *mad*. The thing is, though," he said, lowering his voice to nearly a whisper again. "Ask yerself...was it all jest the townsfolk? Or was somebody else takin' advantage...*whoa*, that's what I call a *wreck*."

Looking down the track, it wasn't hard for Bud to make out where Leo was staring. Ahead of the slowing train, a tableau of carnage lay strewn from one bank of the gully through which they were passing to the other. In the foreground was the wreck of the engine itself, still smoldering over a bed of hot coals, and surrounded by an already sizeable crowd of bystanders, many of them in their finest Sunday clothes. On the right hand side and up the bank, the massive iron frames of two wrecked passenger cars that had burned to their trucks sat stranded like picked-over carrion, while behind it all, men were crawling like ants over four hundred feet of half missing, half burned trestle.

"Well, time to get to work," said Leo, cheerfully. Springing down from the flatcar like a child in a playground, the fat little man gestured to the carload of workers behind the flatcar and shouted, "Charlie and Jim! Get that counterbalance unstowed! Get the booms laid out, Rich!"

217

Bud shook his head in wonder...what had happened to Leo? *Just get him there,* Bud had recalled the stationmaster saying. *Guess he wasn't kidding.*

* * * * *

The Jefferson County Sheriff had reluctantly returned to his office after having been pulled out of an early morning fishing session by the man now standing across the desk from him. His Vulcanized waders were dripping all over his threadbare faux-Persian carpet, and he wished like hell that he hadn't come back...but it had little to do with ruining the rug.

It was just supposed to be a routine week, Sheriff Langston reflected, in what had in recent years become a very quiet county. An especially good week to take off fishing, too, as a certain shipment of beer had needed to be loaded south of town, and that *always* made for good fishing—north of town. Up until now, it had been a good business working with the Barrelhouse boys—shipments made regularly that livened up the local economy, making needed cash available to the local farmers (with just a little extra profit for him and his deputy, of course).

As long as the Rock was looking the other way, that is.

But at this moment, the Rock was looking directly at him, and the Sheriff was feeling exceptionally shrunk around his lower regions. He didn't think it was due to the cold waters of the Little Blue River, either.

"So, there was a passenger taken off the train before it was wrecked?" Langston stuttered as fumbled to remove his gear. "Isn't that a **good** thing?"

Nathan Brockhurst was standing directly in front of Langston's desk, his arms folded and his head shaking as he watched the sheriff try to hop out of his soaking wet gear. As he had tried—repeatedly—to explain to Cable, Langston was a certified idiot, and any actual help that the Sheriff could offer would be purely accidental. But orders were orders.

"No—it was a *kidnapping,* Langston. Someone took Cable's son—get it? The train was wrecked, and it might, or might not be connected. But either way my boss, Mr. Ransom Reed Cable, Sr., President of the Chicago, Rock Island, and Pacific Railway, wants someone to look into it...*now,* and *quietly.*" The last two points were emphasized by very strong fingers that *thumped* into the center of Langston's desk.

Having finally freed himself from the waders, Langston sat his soaked white longjohns down in the arch-backed chair behind the desk, and *humphed.*

218

"Hellfire, Nathan, I ain't no detective, and I ain't got none on my teeny little force, neither...jest me and Jasper, and he's drunk in the cells behind me." To emphasize the point, he jerked his thumb to the cells behind him, where a low buzzsaw could be heard working away intermittently. "I go nosin' around, and I'll jest get ev'erbody all riled up."

"Well, you better light a match under somebody," Brockhurst warned. "Cable wants *results*. If he ain't happy, you're not gonna last very long around Fairbury—especially when I inform him about your little bootlegging operation with those Lincoln fellahs."

Brockhurst had intended to include the last statement as an empty threat—he actually had little reason and no real intention to blab on the beer connection, especially when the local farmers were in such need of cash. But the mention of them made Langston's face light up.

"Hey!" the Sheriff said, excitedly, his carpet squishing below his feet as he stood. "One of those fellahs—Zeke Gardner is his name—was a deputy sheriff for years up in Lincoln. Maybe he could, you know, help...on the QT, like."

Brockhurst nodded. He'd met Zeke Gardner on previous trips to Fairbury, and his man Seville had seemed capable enough in getting around those Lincoln ruffians a few days ago. Surely, anybody with an ounce of experience would be better than this idiot.

"Get him."

Friday, August 10, 1894
8:05 am

Somehow, Bobber knew he would be along.

Jefferson "Bobber" Davies was born in 1801 in Nashville, Tennessee, on the inauguration day of Thomas Jefferson. He had served with Andrew Jackson and David Crockett in the 1819 Indian War, and despite having spent extended periods of time with future politicians in a tent through extended, inclement weather conditions under his own free will, he felt he had lived a good life. He had also known Zeke Gardner sufficiently well over thirty years, man and boy, to predict his future movements—especially when his friend was pissed off.

Watching Zeke march up P Street with Amos in tow, Bobber reflected again on how much the two men resembled one another. For years, he had been fixated with the notion that Amos might be a long-lost progeny of Zeke—but seeing J.T. Lynch creep his way back into their collective lives over the last week had thrown considerable doubt into his calculations.

Amos is a good kid, Bobber thought. *So much like Zeke...but there's a definite streak in him that loves to cut corners—and to brood. Like J.T...*

"Mornin,' Zeke," he said, as he stepped out of the weak shadows of the eternally ascending concrete stairs of Journal Building. "Reckon you're lookin' for someone."

Zeke had been caught looking alternatively surprised and exasperated many times by Bobber's unexpected appearances over the years. Today was no exception, though he tried his best to appear unfazed. Amos, on the other hand, was only three years into their collective relationship, and still had tacit permission to be, at least moderately, surprised.

"Bobber." Zeke said, doing his best to adapt to—yet another—abrupt appearance. "You had any sleep?"

"Nope. Air's too dry. Snot builds up, makes it hard to breathe."

"Ah." Zeke had known for years that Bobber's sleeping habits were...eclectic. He had been known to skip sleep for days at a time, then sleep non-stop for what seemed like days more. "Sorry I abandoned you at the station last night. Things got a little...hectic."

"I 'spect so..." Bobber replied. "They was plenty hectic around the station, too... 'specially when LeBlanc showed up. He was lookin' for Masterson."

Zeke's brow shot up, and then wrinkled. "How do you figure that?"

Despite the hectic stream of traffic moving in and out of the Journal Building, Bobber managed to settle himself onto a corner step, and his popping knees sounded like a gun's hammer being drawn back. "'Cause I heard him talking to his 'shadows' about it—Billy Tidmore and...uh, does Franks even *have* a first name? Anyway, he was bragging about what he was goin' to do when "Fatty" got back into town—that he had been turned loose, like, and wasn't gonna hold anything back."

"So..." said Zeke, as the truth finally dawned on him. "LeBlanc couldn't have caused the wreck..."

"...because he expected the train to arrive." Amos finished for him. "Where is he now?"

"Well," said Bobber, pulling an onion and a small knife from his tattered shirt pocket. As they were both well-accustomed to this process, Zeke and Amos each took a generous step backwards as Bobber cut the white bulb into quarters, and quartered each slice again. For years, Bobber had claimed that eating onions helped him breathe, and who could argue with the effects? The man was ninety-three years old, for Pete's sake. But the side effects were often—colorful.

Greedily slipping a sliver of onion into his mouth, Bobber pointed the small knife back over his shoulder. "LeBlanc spent most of the night in a whorehouse back in the alley there. 'Bout seven this morning his 'shadows' came and fetched him to meet up with McGee and Heck Kohlman, up the street there." Bobber pointed up P Street with his little knife, as he slipped another slice into his mouth and started gumming it to death. He offered a reasonable facsimile of a grin despite his obvious lack of teeth. "He's real tired."

"I imagine he won't be much good until later in the day," Zeke remarked, managing a weak smile. Placing a hand on Bobber's shoulders, he said, "Thanks, old man. We could have made a pretty big mistake, there, if you hadn't..."

"Don't jump to conclusions, Zeke," Bobber said, curtly, pointing his little knife at the tall man. "Pissed off confrontations—with guns—are for dumbasses. You know better than to make a play like that. Hell," he added, softly, "You'll wake everybody up."

221

"Right, boss," said Zeke, grinning now. "What do you suggest we do?"

"Hell, I know what *I'm* gonna do—try and get some sleep, snot or no."

Amos smirked. "Well, if we have an hour or two, ah'd like to check on Eugenia, Zeke," he said, wincing as he placed his left arm back into his sling.

"You do that, Amos—you'll find her in room 211," Zeke said, giving him a curt nod. "I'm going to talk with Mr. Charlie Dawes—my guess is that Miles McGee isn't letting any grass grow under Heck Kohlman's feet. They're gonna force payment of those past due accounts, now that Masterson is dead. Looks like we need a good lawyer."

"Contradiction in terms," Amos remarked.

"Generally, but not in this case, I think," Zeke replied. "I'll meet you back at Emmy's for lunch—she says you need a good meal after all you went through yesterday."

"Emmy's a peach," Amos admitted. Over the three years that he had known Zeke, he had more than once observed a glint of cold suspicion in the eyes of the family matriarch where Mr. Amos Aloysius Seville was concerned—caused, he suspected, by his 'colorful' past, and any potential negative effect it might have on her family...especially the girls. But apparently, word of his actions in rescuing both Miss Eugenia and Colonel Bills, despite their lack of 'official' publicity, had made its way to her ears, and had warmed Emelia Pack up—a bit, anyway.

"See you at noon, then," Zeke said, setting off toward Dawes' office at a brisk, leg-stretching pace. Having already decided to make sure the weary Bobber got safely back to his toolshed before he set off to find Eugenia at the Lincoln Hotel, Amos turned back down P Street at a much more leisurely tempo, his pace matching Bobber's.

After a block or so, Amos' curiosity got the better of him. "By the way," he asked as the two of them descended the hill into the Haymarket district, where the railyards and Bobber's welcome mattress awaited. "Where were you when you heard all that talk from LeBlanc, back at the station? He's usually pretty good at smelling out a spy." Bobber had survived the Creeks, the Blackfoot, and a hundred other tribes out west— and Amos felt he could always use a few tips.

"I was jest sittin' there in the outhouse, eatin' cookies, mindin' my own business when they came up and banged on my door. Not to worry, though...I farted real loud, and started mumbling—they moved right off."

222

"Very effective," said Amos, forced to appreciate yet another of the many side effects of Bobber's onions.

"Usually is," said Bobber. "Care for a slice?"

* * * * *

Heck Kohlman turned another page in the big red ledger before him, mumbled something about 'riotous disorder' in the accounts, and 'not being a damned beancounter, you know.' He wrote a signature at the bottom of a page, folded it neatly into three parts—being careful to expose the name of the farmer on the upper, visible third of the page—and slammed it on top of a pile of twenty others.

McGee paid little attention— he was muttering instructions and directions into the telephone. After a satisfied grunt, he replaced the receiver, and rubbed his hands together. Life was very, very good, and he was about to accomplish two things that he had been looking forward to for some time—(a) make a LOT of money, and (b) rubbing Zeke Gardner's nose in it while accomplishing (a).

"How long, Mr. Kohlman, until you think that the bills will be fully prepared?" McGee asked.

"Some time this afternoon," the lawyer grumped, shaking his head. "It would certainly go faster if Masterson was around to help make sense of this."

"If Masterson was around, Mr. Kohlman, I doubt that we would have this opportunity," McGee countered.

"Can't say I'll miss him," yawned LeBlanc, stretched out on a long wooden bench toward the side of the office, with his hat slipped down over his eyes on one polished arm and his boots crossed over one another, propped up on the other arm. Billy and Franks chuckled, sitting in another corner on wooden folding chairs with another chair between them, playing pinochle. "Though it is a pity that Rock Island stole a night's fun from the boys and me."

"You look like you had plenty of fun without Masterson," Billy snorted, which also got a chuckle out of Franks. "You figure it was the Rock's fault that the train wrecked?" Billy asked, then grimaced as Franks laid out a double marriage in spades. "Dammit—are you cheating, Franks?"

"You'll never know, Billy, and that's an iron-clad guarantee," Franks countered, smiling behind his cards.

223

"Sure it was the Rock's fault," sneered LeBlanc, raising his head slightly to get a bead on Billy under the brim of his hat. "Hell, I heard that some of their crew was working on that bridge not two-three days ago. They probably screwed up somewhere."

Lifting the stack of folded letters from the table next to Kohlman, McGee walked over to LeBlanc and dropped them on his hireling's chest. "Here's a stack of Masterson's bills for about a quarter of the farmers in the Cooperative," McGee said, "I want you boys to deliver them this afternoon, and pick up the rest tomorrow. And give them this message: I'm offering twenty-five cents a bushel for corn—and that price goes down starting Monday afternoon."

LeBlanc groaned as he stood, picked up the stack of papers, and put on his gunbelt. Trying to sound more chipper than a sleepless night would have actually allowed, he said, "No problem. We'll have those farmers lined up in no time."

"Well, as a precaution, I have decided to bring in some assistance. They will start tomorrow morning, recruiting men around town to...assist...in getting the corn in," McGee said, and the disgust showed plainly on his face.

"Hell, boss," LeBlanc objected. "We can *do* this—jest give us a day or two, and we'll have all the help lined up that you need..."

"Just do as you are told!" McGee snapped. Turning to Heck, he said, "At what time are you expected in court?"

"About two o'clock," Heck mumbled, "If I can have a little peace and quiet to finish this."

McGee nodded. The goddess of fortune had smiled upon him, taking a remarkable hand in events—and Miles McGee smiled back at her in satisfaction.

* * * * *

On the third floor of the Burlington depot, within the spaghetti factory of wiring, batteries, and switchboards that called itself the Lincoln Telephone Exchange, Julia Gardner hastily pulled the connection to McGee's line, once again feeling slightly dirty at having abused her position. But the words she had heard had startled her, and she decided that she had to take just one more chance...

Plugging into a well-known extension, she listened as the line buzzed several times with no answer. As she was about to remove the line, she felt a firm hand on her shoulder.

"Not trying to place a personal call are we?" Robert Jensen, the shift supervisor, stood over her, and his smarmy smile gave her the chills, as usual. She had found it exceedingly amusing when he was turned down so publicly a few days ago for a wedding proposal right downstairs in the depot—it had involved a can of black, followed by a can of white paint—but now she was sincerely wishing that the girl had said accepted his offer. For Robert Jensen, his combed over hair and sweaty face notwithstanding, was not a ladies' man.

"No, sir," Julia said, thinking fast. "The other party must have hung up."

"Didn't hear the buzzer on that one, is all," said Jensen, pasting his hair down with a sweaty palm. "Can't be too careful with company funds..."

"No, sir," said Julia, and when another buzzer went off, she was grateful to turn away from Jensen's toothy smile and get back to work.

I'll just have to tell Uncle Zeke—or Amos—after the shift, Julia thought...though she was certain that the news would not be welcome.

* * * * *

Though less than an hour had passed, the lobby of the Lincoln hotel was much busier than when Amos had left it, having had a new infestation—reporters. Amos recognized several of the more lightly wounded passengers from the wreck now installed in the lobby, each of them surrounded by a cloud of buzzing men in brown suits, derby hats, and fluttering notepads.

Just what ah need, thought Amos, and had just turned up the stairs to search for room 211 when he spied Colonel Bills coming down them—for once, without his shadow, Jay McDowell. Bills was clearly favoring his left leg, and Amos recalled that one of the Colonel's legs had been caught under the stove when Amos had rescued him last night. Now in a fresh uniform, his good humor appeared to have returned despite the limp, however, and he grasped Amos heartily by the hand.

"How's my rescuer?" Bills exclaimed, pumping Amos' right arm. As much as Amos appreciated the gratitude—even more so because his wounded arm was his left one—he made an immediate move to stifle it.

"Colonel, ah'd be ever so grateful if you'd...uh, forget my particular part in last night's escape from that railroad car," Amos said. "Ah...*detest* publicity."

Bills gave him a curious look, as if detesting publicity was akin to detesting motherhood or the American flag. "Are you sure, Mr. Seville? I was just on my way to talk with a few reporters..."

"Yes, if you don't mind," Amos nodded. "Ah'm horribly allergic to newsprint."

Bills laughed. "Suit yourself—plenty to talk about besides that, I guess. Have you heard the news about the militia? I just got off the phone with the governor—they arrived in Omaha at five o'clock this morning, and broke the strikers! The Omaha Guards placed a gatling gun on N Street facing east, the Thurston Rifles dispersed under the Q Street viaduct, all the way down to the Hammond packing house—and the packers passed right between them. Two hundred strikers dispersed completely—without a shot being fired. How about *that?*" Clapping Amos on the left shoulder, Bills' roaring laugh managed to cover a moan of discomfort that Amos was not quite able to mask—gods, that shoulder still *hurt.*

Despite the pain, Amos managed to recover enough to congratulate the large man. "Remarkable—an amazing feat of military prowess. Alexander could not have done better!"

"If only we'd been a day earlier—damn strikers burned down another barn full of corn yesterday—there's about five thousand cattle that'll be awfully hungry by next week," Bills said, shaking his head for a moment, then brightening. "But hell, think of the inspiration it'll lend the men here on training!"

"Ah'm sure it will lift spirits at your encampment this week, Colonel," Amos said, offering his hand to the big man once again. "Good luck with it."

"Thanks, Amos—and despite what might appear in the papers, I'm very grateful for what you did for me—I won't forget it." With that, the big man winked, and strode out of the hallway and into the lobby, where he was met with a roar from the milling reporters.

Amos smiled, shook his head, and made his way up to Eugenia's room. Though the door was ajar, he hesitated before he knocked, his nerve temporarily stifled by an unbidden vision—the girl trapped under the burning car, Masterson grasping and pleading, Amos pulling his gun...

226

"Come on in, Amos," Eugenia's voice drifted through the door. "And lend a girl a hand."

Obediently, Amos opened the door and beheld a beautiful girl already washed, pressed and dressed in a lovely blue dress. Amos observed that her hair, singed in the flames of the wrecked combination car, had been bobbed, and the presence of the tub in the corner explained a lot about Eugenia's amazing recovery.

Nothing like a hot bath for making a body feel human again, Amos reflected.

"Well, don't just stand there, get over here and help me close this damn thing," Eugenia said, making short hops and landing her...bustle...on the lid of a massive trunk. "Big Swede brought it over with all my clothes this morning—I think I may have overdone my shopping over the last several months."

"Well, business has been good, ah reckon," Amos said as he joined her in sitting on the lid. "Though ah'll never understand how a woman who can spend half her time out of her clothes can manage to spend the other half buying more of them."

Eugenia clenched her mouth to hide the smirk, and Amos was grateful to receive the standard punch in the shoulder that seemed to accompany all his best-aimed jibes at her—despite the fact that it *hurt like hell* this time. After he recovered, he managed to ask, "So, deah...where ah you off to?"

"Chicago," Eugenia said, finally managing to latch the trunk beneath them. "I need a change of pace...and scenery."

"Can't say as ah blame you," Amos said, standing and offering her a hand—which she accepted, hopping off the trunk and straightening her gown. "I assume that Zeke's been by to settle up?"

"He was very generous," Eugenia replied. "Despite the fact that, in the end, we failed, you know."

"Ah know." Amos looked into Eugenia's eyes, and looked as if he was trying to find words—but Eugenia knew what Amos really needed to hear, and in the end, was merciful.

"Don't get sentimental, Seville," Eugenia said, with an air of diffidence that Amos was *almost* sure was feigned. "I do appreciate you pulling me out of that mess and all last night, but that doesn't mean I want to swap spit with a Virginia Creeper like you. I think we made out just fine, compared to some of those other poor sons a' bitches. So stop slobbering, and give me a hand with this trunk, willya? I got a train to catch."

"Certainly, m'lady," Amos said, bowing, and yanked the pull to call a bellhop.

*   *   *   *   *

The large, open front windows of the Omaha Western Union offices facing Dodge Street allowed plenty of light to enter the room, which was fortunate—there was a great backlog of work to be done, and the ambient light from the south-facing windows made reading the finely lettered copy that much faster and easier. Following the morning riots, the company had brought in another five telegraphers from other shifts and city offices in order to handle the tremendous volume of messages that were trafficking back and forth to the state legislature, to other newspapers, and to home towns all across Nebraska. These extra men were now crammed into the reception area behind small wooden folding tables, crouching over their copy and banging away at their hot keys, attached to wires that strung over the counter to interface with a spaghetti tangle of open-faced circuitry humming softly on the beadboard wall at the back of the office like angry bees.

It hadn't been easy for Lynch to traverse the wire-strewn entrance, crowded with newspaper men, city officials, and more than a few members of the state militia. It had been harder still to convince the shift manager to allow him to use one of the two telephones behind the counter—at the present, these were only to be used on an *emergency* basis by *authorized officials*, he was assured. Despite the oft-voiced preference for the free coinage of silver in this state, however, Lynch reasoned that the paper bills he carried might also carry some *small* value as currency, and was not disappointed to find that they also provided proof of official authority— sufficient to unlock the door to the telephone closet quite effectively. Arranging himself before the mouthpiece, he lifted the handset and spoke to the operator (probably only a few feet from him on the other side of the wooden walls of the closet), and waited for his call to be connected.

"Mr. Jay," the voice said, and despite the thousands of miles that separated them, Lynch could clearly hear the irritation of the man come through the waxpaper speaker in his earpiece. "Your call is a half hour late."

"My apologies, Mr. B," Lynch said, "You can thank the state militia for that delay."

"So I understand," replied Beakins. The evening papers were sure to cover the riots in Omaha to some extent, but having his office on the top floor of the Western Union Building on Dey Avenue lent a person a little more information than the average New Yorker. Staring down at the elevated trains that were traversing Broadway, Beakins exhaled a stream of blue smoke and added, "I have that information you needed. You'll find I sent it ahead, and is presently waiting in a white envelope behind the counter for you—simply ask the staff there for a message for Mr. Jay."

"Are you sure you still need this done?" Lynch queried. "Seems the militia has solved your problem for you."

"The root of the problem is still there, and our client assures me it needs a permanent solution, Mr. Jay," Beakins replied. "Read the information, and telegraph me should you need more time…or resources."

At that, the telephone went dead.

The man's efficient, I'll give him that, Lynch admitted to himself.

Lynch's next telephone conversation was equally short and cryptic. But that was the nature of the game they were playing.

"Three days—Monday night?"

"Monday night."

"And after that?"

"We expect to turn the package loose—unless we are instructed otherwise. Continue to check in every day at noon."

"And if someone tries to retrieve the package?"

"Lose it. And we'll settle for half."

"I understand, sir. Talk to you tomorrow, then."

Hanging up the receiver at the Fairbury hotel, the tall, gaunt man produced a dollar for the hotel clerk, tipped his hat, and was about to walk outside to retrieve his horse when a haggard-looking, gray-bearded man emerged suddenly from the dining room and bumped squarely into him.

"Pardon me," said Nathan Brockhurst, gruffly. "Need to look where I'm going, I guess."

"It's nothing," hissed the thin stranger, who grinned like a skeleton as he tipped his hat once again.

* * * * *

229

It had been a long shift, Julia admitted, but at least the stairs were easy to manage going down. As the youngest telephone operator at the Lincoln switchboard, Julia had been pulling night shifts for the last three months—but the work was steady, and Julia was generally pretty upbeat when she got off. Not tonight, though. She had been holding an urgent message for Uncle Zeke for several hours, but, thanks to Robert Jensen's roving eye, had been unable to reach him by telephone.

Sighing, Julia had nearly resigned herself to trudging over to the Barrelhouse when she turned toward the train platform, and saw...Amos, helping a pretty copperhaired girl in a blue dress onto an eastbound train. Though their words could not be heard, Julia saw the softness in Amos' eyes, and the kiss on his cheek as she said goodbye bespoke a long affection.

Turning toward the station as the train pulled away, Amos was startled to see Julia Pack watching him intensely from under the large brick arch that opened onto the platform. Somehow, he couldn't help looking a little sheepish for the display of affection...

...which Julia interpreted as guilt, of course.

"Mr. Seville," Julia said, tersely. "Have you seen my uncle?"

"Uh, ah believe he will be over to your house for lunch today," Amos replied. Her anger confused him, so he decided to change the subject. "Julia, ah wanted to thank you for all your help with..."

"If you see him before that, please tell him I have a message for him, and will be at our house—it's urgent."

And with that, Julia Pack turned her heels, and left a very bewildered man on the Burlington platform.

THE EVENING NEWS

LINCOLN, NEBRASKA   FRIDAY, AUGUST 10, 1894

A GHASTLY SCENE

Portions of Four or Five Human Bodies Found Among the Wreckage

The sight that greeted the thousands of curious people who visited the site of the Rock Island wreck this forenoon was one calculated to inspire the timid person with awe, and hundreds that looked upon the revolting scene will recall the spectacle to their dying day. The only evidence apparent that there had ever been any cars there was the bent and tangled strips of heated and rusted iron, and the wheels and trucks that were still half buried in the smoking ashes.

The engine looked as if it had been dismantled for years and left to decay. The woodwork of the two cars was entirely consumed and there was not even any appreciable amount of ashes left. It seemed as if there was not a scrap of wood as big as a man's finger to be found anywhere that had once been part of the train.

Interest in the wreck chiefly centered, however, on the smoking piles of ashes that lay underneath the still heated iron work of the engine and the combination car. On a table formed by a number of sheets of iron that lay just beside what had once been the cab of the engine, with its blackened face turned up at the hundreds of spectators, was a charred skull, to which a portion of the neck was still clinging. All that resembled flesh had been burned away, but the bones of the face and neck were still and intact. No part of a body could be seen near it. Under another portion of the engine, or rather that portion of it that had once been the cab, was another part of a human body, but it was burned so that no-one could distinguish what portion of a man it had once been.

Under a confused mass of iron strips and sheets, and a pile of trucks that had once been a combination car, could be seen portions of at least two human bodies. There may have been more, but they were so charred and consumed that they were indistinguishable, and as the smoking pile was still too hot for dissection there were doubtless others to be brought to view. The big timbers of the bridge were still burning all around the scene, some standing upright and others lying scattered in every direction. About two or three hundred feet of the trestle work was burned away and still burning.

The wreck had been cleaned away from the Union Pacific rails and trains were running over that line to and from the wreck. The Superintendent of the Rock Island was on the scene and had a telegraph established a few feet away from the burning bridge.

VIEWING THE RUINS

Thousands Visit the Scene of the Terrible Catastrophe

The scene of the wreck was visited by thousands of people, whom curiosity to see such an unnatural and horrible spectacle, had attracted thither. Both sexes were represented in the crowds that swarmed about the ends of the broken and burned bridge, obstructed the work of the wrecking crews, gazed with awe, interest and horror upon the upon the few charred bodies that could be seen, and prodded around amid the tangle of iron still smoking and rusted by the fire. At the penitentiary many buggies poured into Fourteenth Street from the roads to the east and west that joined the already long line that had come straight out along the car line. Many bicycles, hundreds of buggies and many on foot ploughed through the thick dust for miles and seemed to feel repaid for their labor as they gazed upon the ruins. There were hundreds of women and children, scrambling around over the sandy banks, over burning timbers, and amidst irons that were still almost red hot, morbidly enjoying for the first time in their lives the smell of burning human flesh. The scene at the bridge was one which will long remain photographed upon the memories of those that beheld it.

Friday, August 10, 1894
10:33 am

"Mr. Bud!" The young man's ears pricked at what sounded like his name being shouted—somewhere—but it was lost in the swarming mob, too faint for him to pinpoint it. In the hour since Bud had disembarked from the train, there had also arrived hundreds of spectators, each of whom was now absorbed in the panoply of the wreckage—as well as that of the surrounding multitude. Like the fire that had once swept across the now-smoking trestle, the crowd's own exuberance appeared to be self-sustaining. Each new member first reacted with shock at the wreck's carnage, but then merged into the collective, reveling at the reactions of the new arrivals that continually appeared on the scene with a sort of amused, knowing, communal shake of the head at the newcomers' astonishment, before absorbing them as well. The wreck had cracked an overfilled dam, and a vast reservoir of pent-up frustrations—stemming from the drought, the economy, the hard knocks of daily living—had all come pouring out of the sea of humanity that now swirled around the smoldering ruins, grimly celebrating that they themselves had not been caught up in the death that now lay scattered about the floor of the gully.

"Mr. Bud!" came the shout again, and this time Bud was able to locate its source—a balding, smiling man with a broad white waxed mustache behind a yellow cart across the gully, surrounded by women and children, each of which was clamoring for something. As he approached, he discovered that the cart was selling...*lemonade*, and that the vendor was...

"Vinnie Verlucci!" cried Bud, reaching the cart just in time to prevent a half barrel filled with ice and pink liquid from crashing to the ground, it having been suddenly knocked loose by a stray child leashed to a startled border collie. The dog barked enthusiastically at Bud, until it finally satisfied itself that it had balanced the sinister forces of the unseen world that dogs are often called upon to bring into equilibrium—then sat calmly down to lick its privates.

"Good catch, Mr. Bud!" Vinnie said, smiling as he filled another two glasses at once with a huge dipper from the barrel, and collected another pair of nickels. To his left, a gray-haired woman and a six-year-old girl, both in matching black dresses and white aprons, worked together at a small sink and table to wash and dry the dirty glasses that the crowd left behind. "You are a one fine baseball player, I think. You are playing tomorrow, yes?"

"Maybe." Bud had completely forgotten that the Saltdogs played on Saturdays...he hadn't even been sure that they played *every* Saturday. In truth, the idea of playing baseball seemed pretty silly with the wreck still smoldering all around them. Deciding to change the subject, Bud whispered behind his hand with a smile. "Where are your nuts, Vinnie?"

Vinnie whispered back conspiratorially, light dancing in his eyes. "Where they always are...but it's too hot, and nobody seems very interested in them at the moment." Grinning mischievously, he added, "Did your Aunt like them, then?"

"Oh, yes...and my cousins, too," Bud nodded vigorously.

"Yes, Vinnie's nuts are famous," remarked a familiar voice, and Bud turned to see the accompanying smirk that he had come to expect from its owner, a young woman in a plain gray dress with sparking, intelligent eyes. "He really seems to get around."

"Thank you, Miss Willa," said Vinnie, his face reddening slightly as he glanced back at his wife, who paused to shake a chubby finger at him, and then shake her head, before she returned to her dishes.

"Miss Willa," said Bud, nodding at her. "I should have known that the Journal's finest reporter would be here on the scene."

"Oh, he's here, somewhere, to be sure," replied Willa, "and likely flattering information out of someone. You really ought to consider journalism yourself, Bud, when you join the University—flattery seems to come natural to you."

Bud's eyes lowered slightly. "I'm pretty sure that University is out of the question, Willa."

"Why, Bud? It's free, you know."

Bud stared, dumbfounded. *Free?*

Willa saw the look of incredulity cross the face of the young man, and went on. "It's true. There are fees of course, for laboratory supplies, and the like...and there are always those minor inconveniences like eating, and sleeping indoors. But there is no tuition...IF you can get *accepted*, that is."

Before Bud could respond, he felt a tap on his left shoulder, turned that direction, saw no one, and turned back rapidly to see his cousin

234

Johnny standing on his right side. Johnny grinned and affected surprise, as if he hadn't been the source of the shoulder-tapping diversion.

"Willa." Johnny said, touching the brim of his derby and bowing slightly toward their companion before Bud could chide him. For once, Johnny was out of uniform, but he still cut a fine figure in a tweed suit. Looking about him, he shook his head in mock bewilderment. "Welcome to the thundering herd, Bud. Quite a sight, isn't it?"

"Never seen anything like it," Bud agreed, soberly. The crane car that he had ridden into the gully was now lifting and swinging away the charred remains of the tender from the wreck of the engine to the side of the track, while Rock Island workers cursed and labored to hold back the straining crowds from beneath the arc of the tender's path. Behind the milling crowd at the lemonade stand, a makeshift repair gang consisting of gandy dancers, yard goats, monkeys, hostlers, brakemen, hobos, and anyone else who the CRI&P could wake, draft, or swindle—swarmed over the smoking trestle with cats claws, sledge hammers, and wrecking bars, laboring to disassemble its southern half before flames could re-ignite its creosote-soaked members and burn its remaining northern half to the ground. On the other side of the wreck, dozens gaped in silent horror, a semi-circle of mourners with hats in their hands watching as the remains of the engine crew were carefully lifted from the engine and wrapped in blankets. A man with a rosary in a ministerial collar knelt near the blankets and started intoning the 23rd Psalm. Those surrounding him picked up and joined in at "green pastures," just as on the other side of the wreck the tender landed with a deafening crash in the weeds at the side of the tracks, amidst Leo's constant swearing.

"It's a cross between a funeral, a construction site...and a circus," Bud concluded, shaking his head.

"And it's only just starting," Johnny added, pointing up the Burlington track. Bud observed that yet another train loaded with trestle supplies and spectators was lumbering in from the northwest, while scores more people were walking down to the wreck along the sides of the track.

Abruptly, Johnny changed the subject. "Willa, did you happen to see Frank Crawford? I heard from Flippin that he was over here at the lemonade stand, and I wanted to introduce Bud to him..."

"We've met," said a wiry man of middle height, appearing suddenly from behind them with a glass of lemonade. "Bud is our star pitcher—which you would know if you had showed up to the game last week, Johnny Pack." With a tight smile, Frank Crawford shook hands all around, and tipping his hat when it came Willa's turn. "Good to see you, Willa—see you're back a bit early from summer vacation."

"Not much to do in Red Cloud, Mr. Crawford," Willa agreed. "Nothing like this amount of excitement."

"Not in Omaha either," agreed Crawford, referring to his own hometown. "Unless you count the militia being turned out at the Hammond Packing House this morning."

Bud froze, shocked at the news. *That's where Larry works...*

"Got a telegram early this morning from my firm back in Omaha....we handle Hammond's business there." Crawford went on, casually taking a quick gulp of lemonade before plunging on. "Seems that about four hundred men moved in about five o'clock, and set Gatling guns up outside the packing house."

Sensing his cousin's consternation—and its source—Johnny intervened with a question that he suspected was burning in Bud's mind. "Was anyone hurt?"

"Don't think so—appears to have calmed the situation right down..."

"Gatling guns have a tendency to do that," murmured Johnny to Bud.

"—which should make our clients here in town feel a lot easier about shipping cattle there." As Crawford carried on about his law firm's business interests in Lincoln, Bud did his best to calm himself. *Train wrecks, knife attacks, riots, militia, bootlegging...*Bud's head swam with the tide of change that had swept over him and his separated family in the last week.

"...so anyway," Crawford went on, finally winding his story down, "After I let our clients know about the developments in Omaha, I met a couple of the boys on the old team for breakfast...and we decided to come on down here to see the elephant. Now, where...? George! George Flippin! Come over here!"

While Crawford continued to wave, the crowd parted to reveal...a big Negro, smiling under a thin black mustache and striding toward the small group. He tipped his fedora to several young men in the crowd who recognized him as he passed and spoke his name. As he joined the group, the massive man straightened his suit and paused to take off his hat, rendering a short bow to Willa.

236

"Miss Willa," he said in a deep, mellifluous voice, and switching his hat to his left hand, turned to grasp the hand of Bud's cousin. "And, it's John...Pack, isn't it?"

"Y-yes," Johnny Pack said, swallowing hard, and for the first time, Bud detected a chink in his cousin's seemingly indefatigable self-assurance. "I've watched you play, Mr. Flippin—with admiration."

"About as much as you can admire a *freight train*," said Crawford, slapping the big man on the back. Flippin didn't speak, but Bud might have detected the faintest hint of an eyeroll. "And I've been on the receiving end plenty of times when this big boy bucked the line—enough to know that moving out of the way is the prudent course of action."

"Bucking for team Captain, too, George?" teased Willa. "The boys like you well enough."

"No, no, Willa, that's George Dern's job," said Flippin, holding up his hands in denial.

"*If* he comes back from Europe," retorted Cather.

"Come now—our *boy* here doesn't want that kind responsibility, do you, Flippin?" kidded Crawford, slapping the big man on the shoulder—and once again, Bud sensed Flippin's silent forbearance.

"Uh, this is Bud Gardner, George," Willa said, changing the subject and gesturing toward the young man. "Bud's quite an athlete in his own right...he pitches for the Saltdogs, and Frank here is his coach."

"Temporarily...temporarily—at least until the firm ships me back to Omaha, anyway," Crawford said, holding up his hands. "And I'm not too sure we'll be having any baseball games for a bit—at least until things settle down."

"You might say the same for football at the U," said Flippin, shaking his head. "We should have heard something about summer practices by now. Willa, you know the Chancellor—can't you get him interested in supporting the team?"

"I'm afraid my connection to Canfield pretty much stops at his daughter, Dorothy, and doesn't extend to football, George," Willa said, placing her hand on Flippin's shoulder. "From what Dorothy says, I think Canfield's pretty supportive of the sport—but the rest of the Regents think it's just gotten too violent."

"Well, all those broken bones last year didn't help," Crawford nodded in agreement. "They'll be some rule changes this year...they might change some minds. But the hard part is finding a *coach*..."

"Whoa, lookout there!" said Johnny, and the group suddenly dived out of the way as a wagon loaded with a half dozen city police officers raced into the gully and scattered the crowd. Up on the buckboard, a little man in a black suit and a stern face barked orders to the blue-suited, helmeted policemen in a high, shrill voice.

"You men! Get up on the hillside and collect that evidence...you'll find most of it marked with red flags near the southeast end of the trestle."

"Yes, sir, Detective," piped another small man in corporal stripes. "You heard him, men—snap to it." Immediately, a gaggle of policemen scrambled out of the wagon and started up the embankment.

Surveying the scene with satisfaction, Detective Frank Malone spotted George Flippin nearby. "Boy!" he shouted. "Hold these horses."

"Here we go," muttered Willa, though only Bud seemed close enough to hear her.

"I don't get along very well with horses, sir," Flippin replied, and before Malone could respond, Johnny stepped forward to grab the reins.

"What a fine set of horses, Detective," Johnny said, cheerfully, patting their sweating necks, and motioning around them with his free hand. "Mind the leavings when you get down, now—seems that these aren't the first horses here today."

As was usual with Johnny, Malone couldn't tell whether he was being trifled with or not—so after he scrambled down, he settled for straightening his tie, taking the reins from Johnny with a *humph*, and looping them around the wheel of Vinnie's cart. As Malone made his way up the hill shouting further directions to the police corporal, Johnny shook his head.

"No wonder Uncle Zeke calls him a pipsqueaking ass," Johnny said.

"Your uncle always did have a gift for understatement," said Willa, grinning. "Now, who's going to buy me a lemonade?"

* * * * *

After checking both his offices and Pershing's rooms, Zeke finally located his lawyer, Charles Dawes in the Office of the County Clerk at the courthouse, attempting to tie up loose ends on several pending cases before

238

he left town. When Zeke delivered the news about Masterson's death in the train wreck, Dawes sat on the edge of an empty desk, and shook his head.

"Do you think it was deliberate—the wreck, that is?" Dawes asked, shuffling his papers.

"It seems so," Zeke said. "There's plenty of evidence to suggest it."

Dawes sighed. "It sounds like bad business, Gardner."

Zeke nodded, shifting his feet uncomfortably. "Can't argue with you there. What's my next move, then?"

Dawes counted off points on his fingers, as if lecturing a first-year law student. "Well, as I understand it, you have a contract to sell grain for the farmer, but no buyer—at least not a live one—and no written contract in hand. Would his wife honor the agreement?"

"I haven't spoken to her—but she's probably in hysterics, and now isn't a very good time."

Dawes nodded. "I agree...but you can expect that she's got somebody looking after the business for her, and that someone will try to collect those debts through a motion for a writ of foreclosure....probably at a much lower price than your original agreement. Any idea who might be representing the opposition?"

"Heck Kohlman, probably."

Dawes' eyes lit up. "Heck, eh? Wait a minute...Scottie?" Dawes motioned to a small man in the corner of the room, who glanced up from a cloud of papers with a harried look. "Sorry to bother you, but have any cases been brought forth this morning on—shall we say—an expedited basis?"

"You mean, has anybody tried to ram their way into court on no notice?" Scott Low replied, holding up a single piece of paper with two fingers, while wrinkling his nose as if it was a piece of rotten meat. "That would be Heck Kohlman, as of about a half hour ago. He meets with Judge Lansing at two o'clock. And no, I'm none too happy about it, but he's been dropping an awfully big name, and he's managed to bump the docket around."

"Let me guess," Zeke said, "Miles McGee?"

"McGee is mixed up with this? Hell n' Maria." Dawes rubbed his eyes. "I take it back, Mr. Gardner—this is very, *very* bad business."

"So...can you see your way to helping us?" Zeke asked, and though he had six inches on the young lawyer, his level gaze was returned as an equal.

"Mr. Gardner, I'm on my way out of town, and I don't need to buy any trouble. *Nevertheless*," he said, interrupting what he perceived as Zeke's forthcoming objection, "Nevertheless, I'd be happy to give Mr. Kohlman a little parting gift, as a sign of my *admiration*. Scottie, I'd like to file a brief...a very *brief* brief...on the part of the Northern Lancaster County Farmer's Cooperative, for consideration by Judge Lansing at two o'clock. Think I could sneak it in?"

"I believe so, Mr. Dawes," the little man grinned. "If you don't mind my watching the fireworks."

"Thanks, men," Zeke said, sounding relieved as he shook Dawes' hand.

"You're welcome—but this doesn't solve a damn thing, you know," said Dawes, wagging a finger at Ezekiel Gardner. "With Masterson gone, it just delays the inevitable. And there's very little that McGee won't do to get his way, in the end."

* * * * *

In the two hours that Bud had spent in the gully that held the train wreck, he thought he had seen everything. When the Most Honorable Congressman Williams Jennings Bryan showed up to shake hands with the crowd and do a little campaigning, Johnny assured him that he *had* seen everything, and went off to get the buggy from where it was hitched in the brush off to the side of the gully in order to take them home.

But there was one more revelation coming.

"Well, here is surprise." The heavily accented voice came from somewhere in the bustling crowd surrounding the wreck of the engine, and sounded familiar somehow, but Bud couldn't quite place it.

"*Stupidy hlupak.*"

Now he placed it.

Four men came striding out of a crowd of workmen, led by the same black-bearded giant that Bud had knocked down just the night before in an attempt to "rescue" Anna Marie Vostrovsky...from a chicken. Bud's mind raced—the men loomed before him, and this time, he realized that there was no Anna Marie to intervene. Bud gulped.

240

But strangely, the men were not scowling, but seemed to be grinning...mostly. Three of them approached Bud, taking off their hats, and gave him the same short, synchronized bow that Bud had witnessed the night before—while the large man simply stood with folded arms, and continued to scowl.

"We have speaking on last night," the shortest man intoned. "And we have deciding that you are with...honor...for helping to Miss Vostrovsky."

"Uh, thanks," Bud said, trying to sound neutral. He eyed the dark-browed giant standing next to the three little Czechs, and bobbed his head slightly, holding his gaze—until the man finally broke into a grin, and his laughter peeled out, shaking the gully. His slap on Bud's shoulder almost knocked Bud to the ground, but afterwards, he tried his best to return the smile through the pain.

"So, you found some work here, then?" Bud spoke slowly, rubbing his shoulder, and trying to imagine how difficult it would be to come to a strange country and learn an entirely new language.

"Yes," the shortest man replied, frowning "but for only the morning time. Work is finished—we get pay now." Pointing over to the north end of the gully, Bud saw where the men were headed—toward a small table where four bits were being handed out to each worker waiting in a lengthening line.

"I wish you luck," said Bud, holding out his hand, not knowing what else to say.

"And we wish you luck, friend of Anna," said the little man, taking his hand with a wink. He murmured something to his friends, who responded with a chuckle and what sounded like additional jokes...at his own expense, he expected. He heard Anna's name mentioned several times, and wondered if he should object—but someone beat him to that.

"What are you saying about Anna Vostrovsky?!" said a voice from his left, and Bud turned to find two men, both scowling like the giant Czech once had—and looking like slightly shorter bookends made from the same mold. Though the larger Czech simply stood silently and refocused his dark brow on the newcomers, the three smaller men bowed, put on their hats, and made to leave.

But the two parting words that the shortest man spoke in Bud's ear frightened him more than the most penetrating scowl of the departing Czech giant.

"The brothers."

241

27

Friday, August 10, 1894
11:35 am

Anna Marie's brothers stood there, hands on their hips, glowering at Bud like massive stone gargoyles guarding the tower of a princess.

"Who were those men, to be speaking of our sister?" demanded the one on the right. His beard, with flecks of gray, indicated that he was probably Stephan, the older of Anna's two brothers. The younger one, Lukas, had no beard and a slightly less intensive glare, but had two inches and forty pounds over Bud—and it all looked liked like muscle to the young man from Alder Grove.

"J-just friends," Bud replied. Once, back in Alder Grove, he had been caught kissing a girl named Heidi behind her father's barn. The old man, coming around the corner carrying a switch, now loomed in Bud's memory...but unlike then, Bud wasn't sure he could simply outrun this particular brand of trouble.

*And I didn't even get to **kiss** Anna...*he realized, and might have actually laughed at the situation if he hadn't been frozen to his place.

The bearded man took a step toward Bud. "We will be deciding on this, I am thinking," he said, in a low voice. "And who are you?"

"Bud Gar—uh," Bud started to say his full name, then recalling Anna's first reaction at it, stopped himself suddenly. "Uh, just Bud," he finished, lamely.

"Well, 'just Bud'—I'd suggest that you keep your tongue in your head, where Anna is concerned." The younger brother had taken a step forward, and was speaking now. Though his English was more refined, his glare indicated that his thoughts weren't. "And KINDLY keep your tramp *friends* away from our sister."

Bud hadn't even a chance to respond before the older brother stalked over to the pay table, followed by the younger brother, who straightened his hat and gave Bud a last dangerous glance before joining him. The young man felt the air leaking out of his lungs, slowly.

"What was *that* about?" queried a familiar voice from above and behind him, and Bud turned to see his cousin up on a buckboard, with Willa Cather seated next to him. Johnny had a familiar smirk on his face, as if he had also caught Bud behind the barn.

"Nothing," said Bud, glumly, as he climbed into the back of the wagon.

"Uh *huh*," said Johnny Pack, rolling his eyes. "Get up, Maybelle—we need to get young Lothario home to lunch. Haw!" And with that, the small wagon left the crowds, the Lincoln police, and the CRI&P to take care of the wreck, the evidence, and the dead still strewn in the small gully, four miles south of the capital city.

* * * * *

Des Moines really does have many positive attributes, reflected the man in the tailored suit, as he leisurely turned over the last page of the *Chicago City News.* Sipping his tea, he took time to admire the way that the morning sun played upon the rich, hardwood paneling of the Pullman car surrounding him, and to luxuriate in the padded leather armchair where he was taking a late breakfast as the train slowly pulled west. *An efficient, clean train station...an excellent restaurant next door to it...fine, mature trees. Yes,* he thought, *on the whole, Iowa had a thirty-year headstart on civilization when compared to...Nebraska.*

Henri Flint wrinkled his nose and *sniffed* as he contemplated the thought of returning to his home state. A small, dirt-floored trading post in western Nebraska along the South Platte River at O'Fallon's Bluff had provided a thorough education in the many advantages of an *Eastern* lifestyle...and in what it took to maintain it. If his father—a notorious drunkard—was required to kill the Indian, cheat the white man, and beat his wife and son in order to manage a meager lifestyle along a mosquito-infested ditch, how much more was a man required to do to maintain a more civilized standard of living along the north bank of the Chicago River.

So...a homecoming, of sorts. Henri sighed, and folded the newspaper with a sort of finality, resigning himself to leaving his beloved Windy City and returning West in the service of his employer. *Well,* he reasoned, *at least it wouldn't be long—and he wouldn't be alone.*

"Cheevers," he said, turning to the sleeping man across the aisle, his heavy mustache buried into the deep leather chair facing Flint. Cheevers' own newspaper had tumbled down around his ankles, his rumpled clothing bespoke a hard night's drinking and whoring in the brothels of Des Moines, and with one exception, he had the entire appearance of a man given over to sloth.

That exception was the gleaming Colt single-action Army revolver that rested in its well-polished holster on the left hip of the sleeping man. Its

243

bluing had worn to a fine brown patina in most places, with the finish almost entirely removed along the raised fluting of the cylinder and the nose of the four-and-a-half-inch barrel, where it had been dragged against the holster, drawn—many times—in the service of its owner. Flint knew that, like the leather where it lay holstered, the gun was oiled well, ready for use at any time—and that the man that carried it, while also well-oiled at the moment, would be equally lethal when he had dried out some.

Smiling with mischief, Flint began to reach across the aisle toward Cheevers' gun, moving as slowly and silently as possible. As the fingers of his right hand inched across the invisible plane that marked the center of the car, Cheevers' gun blurred into his hand, and when it appeared again, was cocked and pointed at Flint's head. As if by magic, however, a cocked derringer had simultaneously appeared in Flint's reaching right hand and now pointed directly between Cheevers' eyes. They opened lazily to reveal mud brown and yellow slits.

"No fair testing a man with a hangover, boss," Cheevers said, yawning. Holstering his gun and closing his eyes, he nestled back into his chair and was soon asleep again—or at least appeared to be so.

"Well, sleep it off, then," Flint said, tucking his derringer back into the pocket concealed in his right sleeve, then lighting a cigar and staring out the window. They would be in Nebraska soon enough, and the man would likely need his sleep, with what was ahead of them.

* * * * *

"Emmy, you've outdone yourself," Zeke announced with gusto from his place at Rufus' right hand. Before the assembled family, empty bowls and platters that had once carried ham, bread, potatoes, and three different kinds of vegetables now lay littered about them, and murmurs of agreement, head-nods and contented sighs surrounding the dregs of the feast confirmed the big man's verdict.

Amos, who had been seated next to Zeke, murmured his appreciation as well. He had surprised himself at how much he had reddened when Zeke had relayed his bravery in the wreck in rescuing Miss Eugenia. He had always sensed a certain level of tension from Emelia in prior meetings, but on this occasion, the pleasure at his company had seem genuine—as if she was willing to open her family to the possibility of Amos as, at least, a friend. He wondered if he had his own recent actions, or Bud's presence to thank for that. *Bud is certainly a breath of fresh air for the family*, Amos observed as he drew more than his fair share of jibes. *That's the true mark of acceptance in this family*, he thought—*the more you are teased, the*

244

more you are loved. Whatever its source, and despite the hard work that they all knew they were facing soon, Amos was relieved to see that people seemed much more relaxed in general.

Everyone, that is, except Julia. Seated at Amos' right elbow, Julia had been oddly silent for the entire meal, never once responding to Amos' attempts at humor, or voicing a sound of any kind, for that matter. She now sat, either staring directly forward or down at her plate, apparently doing her best not to meet Amos' eyes.

Amos thought back on his accidental meeting with Julia as he had bid Eugenia goodbye at the station. Did she disapprove of his friendship with Eugenia? Amos found it hard to think that Julia could be so judgmental of a woman in Eugenia's situation—Julia had always struck Amos as fair, even open-minded, especially of those that had not had Julia's own advantages in life. With a kind of shock, Amos suddenly realized that it hurt to think that he might have let her down in some way. That realization was sufficiently astounding to cause him to temporarily miss the presence of Ginny standing over him with a slice of cobbler poised on a spatula, asking if he wanted seconds.

"No, thank you, Miss Ginny," Amos muttered, and was grateful to hear the sound of Rufus Pack banging on his glass with a spoon.

"Family," he said, "we have a *job* ahead of us." Immediately, the table grew quiet, and the patriarch nodded at his oldest son.

"Well, the way I see it," Jeffrey said, "We have about ten hard days work ahead of us, starting Monday morning. Along with our own twenty wagons and teams, *James* here," now motioning to his own left, "through guile, manipulation, and *larceny*, has obtained another thirty."

"McGee will never miss 'em," James joked, which caused the Pack family to laugh. *Was he serious?* wondered Bud. *Probably not,* he guessed...but according to Johnny, you could never quite tell with James.

"*Wherever* he got them," Jeffrey went on, rolling his eyes nearly imperceptibly, "We have the use of them for about two weeks. Fifty wagons...at a hundred thirty bushels per wagon..."

"A hundred and thirty three," corrected Joseph, ever the accountant.

"Beg your pardon...a hundred and thirty *three*....should be enough to finish the job in about fifteen hundred trips. Averaging three trips a day to each farm—that gives us...*round about*..." Jeff paused to stare Joseph into silence, "Two hundred thousand bushels hauled."

245

"And *no buyer*." Rufus said, bluntly voicing the thought that all those seated around the table had managed to avoid for the entire meal. He turned in his chair, folded his arms, and leveled his gaze at his brother-in-law on his right. "What about that, Ezekiel?"

"We have a **contract**, Rufus." Zeke said. "With Masterson's...loss...we will have a harder time getting the deal sealed, it's true—but despite that, we *will* sell that grain **this week**."

Amos stared down at his hands. Zeke was dancing perilously close to the edge of a lie, and while shading the truth was sometimes unavoidable—*even preferable, on occasion,* Amos reflected—this was *family* Zeke was talking to...

Rufus Pack stared at Zeke for a beat, then nodded curtly and leaned back in his chair. "Well, if we *are* going to finish the job over the next few weeks," Rufus said, clasping his hands behind his head, and interrupting Amos' thoughts, "We're going to need more men...to help with the grinding, loading, unloading..."

"Say what you're really thinking, Pop," Jeffrey said. "It's not the grinding, nor the loading, nor the unloading—it's the **guarding** that we need help with."

James piped in. "Jeff's right, Pop. Every one of those wagons ought to have a driver and at least one man guarding the grain—riding shotgun."

"This isn't 10 years ago, James," Emelia observed. "There's law and order here in the county, now. We ought to contact the Sheriff, and—"

"The Sheriff's got **two men,** Mother," Rufus Pack said, as gently as he could, taking a moment to sip his coffee while it was still hot. "McGee has three to start with, plus however many more he can round up."

Shaking his head, Zeke interrupted. "It isn't the hauling that really worries me," he said. "It's the time *before* the hauling. You can bet your as...uh...bottom dollar...that McGee will have his men out there—no later than tomorrow—harassing those farmers—getting them to sell their grain. An extra man or two at those farms would come in mighty handy right now."

"You'll need them." A quiet voice spoke from Amos' side, and the family turned toward an unlikely speaker, pushing vegetables around on her plate.

"Why do you say that, Julia?" her mother spoke, gently prodding.

246

"Purely by accident," she said, stealing a glance toward her Uncle Zeke, then plunging on, "I overhead a conversation between Mr. McGee and a Mr. Flint from Chicago. Mr. Flint and an...associate...are coming in from Chicago tonight. They're to make sure that the farmers ship with LeBlanc."

Silence descended, but only for a few seconds.

"Well, let's get some men, then."

Bud's own voice had surprised him, and as all at the table turned to him, he did his best to...swallow...and regain it. "There must have been a hundred men working at the wreck today—they *all* needed work."

"Not for the next few days, I suppose," Joseph said, pushing up his glasses. "They'll be busy working on the wreck."

"Not so," said Johnny. He *loved* to contradict Joseph. "Most of them got paid off this morning."

"Well, how do we get them?" asked Jeffrey.

"Simple," said James. "We take them all down to the barrelhouse, and buy them as much beer as they can drink."

"Son, it always does seem to come down to *one thing* to you, doesn't it?" His father scolded, but only half-heartedly.

"*Two* things, actually," mumbled Johnny, in what he thought was *sotto voce*—but the suppressed snickers around the table told a different story.

"*Men*," huffed Ginny, disgustedly—and that single syllable turned the pent up giggles into an avalanche of laughter.

When it finally died down, Emelia Pack spoke up. "The *intelligent* ones around this table—that would be the **women**, *boys*—would like to offer an alternative to James' proposal."

Emelia went on, not waiting for permission to vet her idea. "You'll buy more men with bread than beer, gentlemen. A good meal and a solid offer of a job...that's the ticket to a loyal worker." Turning to Rufus, she asked, "Would you agree, husband?"

Rufus grinned ear-to-ear, patted his ample belly with one hand, and raised his cup of coffee with the other. "Can't argue with thirty years' experience, boys."

"So, you're suggesting a feast?" queried Judith. Judith brought a practical eye and a ready arm to nearly every problem—which was why

247

she was the first person Emelia generally leaned on to pitch in and help with any project. "Where and when? And how do we go about getting these men to come? It's not like we can send out written invitations..."

"Tonight," said Zeke, warming immediately to Emelia's idea. "At the Barrelhouse. Six...no, seven o'clock. Does that give you time to get a spread together, Emelia?"

"We'll manage," said Emelia, "If you can get the men."

"Which brings me back to my second question," Judith said. "How do we get them?"

"Just ask Bud," said Johnny. "He knows the biggest hobo on the tracks."

As Bud...and the rest of the table...gaped at Johnny, his cousin plunged on. "I'm *serious!* I saw Bud speaking to four Czechs down at the wreck this morning—one must have been seven...eight! feet tall. And they were *bowing* to **Bud**."

"Bud...you're a wonder," said Zeke, shifting his gaze to his nephew, shaking his head, and grinning. "And just how did you happen to *meet* this particular giant?"

Bud was tempted to stay silent, but the stares were deafening. The blush was rising from his neck, and had just reached his cheeks, when he blurted, "I...well, I met him through...a friend."

Zeke had a pretty good idea about that "friend"...and that she sold *runzas* from a yellow wagon...but stayed silent on that subject.

Instead, he asked quietly, "Do you think you could get him...and his friends...to help us for a few days?"

Bud hesitated. He hardly knew the men in question—but the men in question probably needed work, and his extended family...well, they needed all the help they could get.

"Maybe," he finally concluded. "I'll try, if you'll help me."

"Hell, Son, that's what we're **here** for," boomed Rufus, chuckling, and then added, "Now, dig in to that cobbler. Mother's got two more pans in the kitchen."

* * * * *

Getting out of that damned barn, thought Rance, *felt good...chains or no.*

Under the shade of the cottonwoods, Rance grasped the little shovel given him by his captor, and covered his feces and assorted strips of newspaper in a small trench behind the animal shed, which had held him since last night. He felt relieved, of course...but wary as well.

"Well, that's fine then," said the thin man, leaning against one of the huge cottonwoods, and his voice sounded almost kindly to the young man from Chicago. "Now, please be so kind as to return to the shed, there."

Ransom Reed Cable, Jr. nodded, checked his pants to make doubly sure they were free of the chains around his ankles and secure around his waist, then flinched slightly as he passed under the gaze of his subjugator. Pausing for a moment, head downcast, he handed back the shovel, then asked, "May I have a bit of water, please?" His voice nearly choked on the words, but his need was great.

"Certainly," whispered the man with the incessant grin, and reached behind the cottonwood to hold out a wooden canteen. Watching the thin man pull the cork, Rance tried not to drool, then gulped the water when it was finally handed over.

"Thanks," Rance gasped, after he had drunk his fill. It had been the first water he had since yesterday's supper. Despite the water, he felt drained. But he decided not to ask for food, despite the desperate gnawing still in his stomach.

"Does he get along with his mother, and his father, he is wondering?" the thin man said, suddenly. The man's strange shift to such an odd topic and speaking in the third person shocked Rance, but after a moment, decided to answer.

"Yes...I guess so," said Rance, deciding not to meet the man's eyes.

Because that man's eyes spoke *death.*

"It is well," said the skeletal man, his pale blue eyes shining in the corner of the young man's gaze, despite its aversion. "Because the boy's life depends upon it." And with that, the man herded Rance out of the sun, back into the barn, and locked his ankle chains to another chain that was itself locked around the sturdy wooden frame of the horse stall...

...and returned quietly to a small milkstool across the dirt floor that separated them, where he sat, slowly and intently sharpening a straight razor on a leather strap.

* * * * *

249

Lunch was breaking up. Zeke's nephews offered hearty congratulations to Amos for the rescue of Eugenia, especially from James—who, Amos suspected, may have been especially grateful for a reason that the Virginian decided would be best left unquestioned.

Although the Packs had done their best to make him feel welcome, Amos had still felt out of place during the meal. The hugs that were exchanged between the family members at the end of it didn't make him feel any better, and when Julia left abruptly—just before the swirling lunch crowd would have swept her Amos' way—he tried not to slouch. *What's going on with me?...*he wondered.

The telephone rang in the kitchen, startling Amos out of his introspection. Ginny ran to answer it...and in a moment, came running back.

"It's for you, Uncle Zeke," she said, breathlessly. "It's Big Swede."

Zeke nodded, and his cowboy boots clumped on the wooden floor on his way into the kitchen. Amos heard a few grunts of affirmation on the party line, the whisper of a pencil scratching against notepaper, and then an ominous *clack* as the receiver was returned to its U-shaped cradle. After a moment, Zeke returned to the kitchen door and crooked a silent finger at the Southerner.

Amos obliged, entered the kitchen, and found Zeke leaning against the counter, arms folded, head lowered in concentration.

"Ah take it that was not some long-lost relative leaving you everything in his will," Amos offered, which managed to elicit a sad grin from his partner.

"Hardly," Zeke said. "That was Swede...he just related a call that he took for me from the Jefferson County Sheriff."

"Willie *Langston*?" Amos asked, incredulously. "Ah thought he had gone fishing...permanently."

"Afraid not—he's got a *problem*—which is now, apparently, *our* problem...at least, if we want to stay in business in *his* county. On your trip back last night," Zeke went on, "Did you happen to meet a young man named..."

"Ransom Reed Cable...*Jr.*" Amos leapt to a conclusion that scratched an itch that had been bothering him since Fairbury, and saw with satisfaction from Zeke's reaction that it had been the right one. Zeke continued to stare in disbelief as Amos went on to explain how he had met the young man at supper, and how they had gotten on the train in Fairbury together.

"Cable disappeared from the train just before it left Fairbury," Amos went on. "Harry Foote and ah were talking about that, just before the train hit the trestle last night, which is why it's still so fresh in my mind, ah guess. A man came aboard—very thin, very...odd—and spoke to the young man just before they both hustled off...less than a minute before the train left the station."

"Langston," Zeke said, "has been *encouraged* by the C.R.I.&P. to find that young man...and he is, in turn, encouraging *us*. So," he asked, "you actually got a look at the man who took him away?"

"Yes, he was tall, very thin, and had a face that...well, it looked like a *skull*," Amos said.

A cold feeling started to creep up Zeke's spine. It was just...*no, it couldn't be...possible...*that he had *seen* that face before. J.T.'s man—what was his name?—*Trudeau*, he decided. He had been gone a full day before J.T. had left—very *suddenly*—

"What's the matter, Zeke?" Amos asked, and Zeke's thoughts snapped suddenly back to the small kitchen. Amos stood quietly by as he watched the gears turn in his partner's head. He had learned years ago that when Zeke looked like this, a plan was evolving.

"Amos," he finally said, "You know what Cable looks like, and the last man seen with him. I wonder...if you'd consider..."

"...going back to Fairbury and see what happened to the young man?" Amos finished, guessing again. He shook his head. "Ah don't know— much as ah love that place...it's a second home to me now, *really*—ah hate to leave you here, with all that's going on, Zeke."

Zeke nodded. "I hate it, too. But we need to keep the good will going down there with Langston and the farmers, if we want to stay in business...and," Zeke hesitated, but then plunged on, "There's something else."

Amos waited, and a tingle started moving up his own spine as well.

"J.T. Lynch had two men working for him. One was Jasper Rankin, a Negro—you probably saw him get on the train with Lynch last night." Zeke took a single deep breath, and continued. "The other man was tall, and very thin—with a face that looked like, well, a lot like a *skull*."

"Did you catch his name?" Amos asked, and now it was his turn to stare blankly.

"His name was Jack Trudeau," Zeke said, "and he disappeared long about Wednesday night."

Amos considered. If the man who left with Cable was really the same man, this Trudeau, he would have a good idea what happened to his...to J.T. Lynch.

"Ah'll go," said Amos. "If you can spare me."

"I *can't* spare you," Zeke replied, "but I don't see as we have a lot of choice." Sighing, he clapped an arm on Amos' good shoulder. "Give it a day or two, then hurry back, if you can. We need you here, too."

Amos nodded. He would obey Zeke, but first—if he found the man Trudeau—he had a few questions of his own that needed answering.

28

Friday, August 10, 1894
1:45 pm

"Train leaves in ten minutes, sir. It's an awfully roundabout way of getting to Fairbury, I'm afraid," sighed the pretty young woman behind the ticket grating as she scooted Amos' ticket and change across the pitted, wooden counter, "but I doubt you'll find a more direct route—not today, at least."

Amos nodded, and naturally began to reach for the tickets with his left hand, when he rediscovered, with a wince, why it was still tucked into a sling. Sighing, he gave up and swept the change and ticket into his coat pocket with his right hand. *Damn,* he thought, *this shoulder **hurts**.* The halting, bumpy wagon ride over the crowded streets from the Pack home on J Street afforded by Zeke and his sister Emelia provided an all-too-physical reminder of his "busy" night. He was convinced that he hadn't broken any bones, but something felt...well, *strained,* and he seriously considered the notion of actually seeing a doctor about it, instead of continuing to tuck his arm into the homemade sling that Swede had insisted on jury-rigging for him the night before.

The Lincoln station of the Burlington line was evidently under a great deal of strain as well, trying to pick up the slack that naturally followed 18 hours of down time, as well as the added load from the C.R.I.&P., which was still out of service where points south were concerned. Amos' patchwork route was forcing him to travel far southeast, all the way to Table Rock, then straight back west in order to get to Fairbury...by suppertime, it was hoped, but barely.

Amos tipped his hat to the young lady behind the grating and walked out onto the crowded platform, filled with impatient passengers who had been waiting for southbound trains since last night, spectators hoping for news from the wreck site, and baggage busters that were doing their best to hustle them out of the way and *load the damn train.* All along his route to the station, the Virginian had noticed extraordinary numbers of bystanders gathered at Lincoln streetcorners, collecting gossip—thicker, if possible, than they had been during the early morning rush. Eleven bodies had been removed from Burlington trains since the wreck sixteen hours ago...*and who knows?,* thought the mob, *maybe more...*so the Burlington platform had become Information Central, and spectators far outnumbered passengers. Reporters—from the *Evening News,* the *Journal,* even the

Omaha World-Herald and the *Bee*—were buzzing like bluebottle flies around a corpse, pencils and pads in hand.

Reaching for a cigarette as he waited for the train, Amos was just about to strike a match, when a voice interrupted him.

"Allow me," said the man, holding out a lit match. Amos observed the stranger—he was a dark-haired, direct young man with a hungry eye—and, recognizing the archetype, accepted the light, realizing the inherent harmlessness of the species.

"Many thanks," said Amos, his face impassive. "Ah don't give interviews, though."

"How?..." queried the man, then smiled and shook his head. "Is it that *obvious*?"

Amos held out his hand and counted off fingers. "Wrinkled gray suit, ink-stained fingers and shirt cuffs, coat pocket bulging with paper, sharp eye, eager to please...or at least to inquire. Ah don't have to be...now, what's his name?..." Amos hesitated, then added, "Sherlock Holmes?...to figure that one out."

"Very good," the man said, tipping his hat. "My name is Evans...and please allow me to add a few...deductions?...of my own." Holding out his fingers, he started counting. "Your name is Amos Seville. You were on the train last night...in fact, you were one of the first off the train after the wreck, but you specifically asked *not* to have your actions...possibly *heroic*...reported in the newspaper. How's that, so far?"

"Ah'm sorry, but I repeat, sir, ah do not give interviews." Internally, though, Amos thought, *Not bad.* And wondered—*who had snitched? Not Harry—Colonel Bills? One of the farmers? It doesn't matter, as long as I keep mum...*

"Yes—as I understand it, you're "allergic to ink.""

Colonel Bills, then, thought Amos, sighing inwardly.

"I'm not interested in reporting your actions on the wreck, Mr. Seville—but I am looking for some answers on a related topic," the man stated. "What do you know about a young man named Ransom Reed Cable, Jr.?"

"Can't say we were ever introduced," said Amos, barely hanging on to the rim of truth on that one, while doing his best to keep his face impassive. "Why? Was he on the train?"

"I believe he was," said the reporter, plunging on. "But it appears that he may have gotten off the train, just before it departed—and now, there is a good deal of concern over his whereabouts. Are you *sure* you didn't see him?"

Where is he getting this? thought Amos, and at that moment, was gratified to hear the train's bell and the conductor announce, "All aboard!"

"Ah fear that the trauma of the wreck has scrambled mah faculties, sir...," Amos said, tipping his hat, and without a moment's hesitation, he stepped aboard the train.

Wendell Evans, watching the man board the southbound train, was at a crossroads himself. As a young—nearly unknown—reporter on the Journal staff, he was constantly the last man given assignments or information. Given this, he had spent the entire morning trying to track down the whereabouts of the lesser-known passengers, and angles on the story that others—with more horsepower—had not yet pursued. By accident, he had caught whispered conversations between C.R.I.&P. workers on queries regarding the location of Ransom Reed Cable, Jr. He had also been steered, through hints and innuendo, to Amos Seville, whom he had happened to meet at the Barrelhouse on a few occasions—and was *stunned* when Seville had suddenly just appeared before him at the Burlington station. So as the Burlington train started rolling south, Evans decided Fate was showing him the way and stepped aboard.

* * * * *

"Maybe we should warn Swede," Bud whispered to his uncle as the wagon rolled to a stop. Juggling a bucket full of brushes in one arm, and a large wooden box that smelled of soap flakes and lye under the other, he went on to observe in a lowered voice, "Aunt Emelia looks...determined."

"Wouldn't help much," said Zeke, filling his own arms with mops and brooms at the back of the wagon, as he watched his sister climb out of the wagon, march toward the Barrelhouse, and swing open the door, which **boomed** against its backstop like the footfall of doom.

From his station behind the bar, Big Swede jumped at the sound of the door slamming open, but was **really** startled by the woman's form that suddenly appeared in stark outline against the blue sky of the open door, hands on her hips, like an avenging angel. Through the gloom, Swede saw that her eyes were narrowed, and her bloused sleeves were rolled up to her elbows like a track crew foreman ready to swing a nine-pound hammer. When her words echoed across the nearly empty space, the few patrons that had stopped by for a bracer over the lunch period—the bar never did

255

much business during the day unless there was a shift change going on at one of the four railroads that operated on its doorstep—recoiled and scurried toward the side exit like beetles from overturned firewood.

"Bud...bring me the *soap*!"

Within twenty minutes, Emelia and her acolytes Judith, Jill, and Ginny had the tables and chairs stacked, the floor swept and the back quarter of the room covered in soapy water, brushes scraping against the flooring planks, and working themselves up the beadboard walls on three sides. When she wasn't barking orders, Aunt Emelia was on her knees operating a worn scrub brush, muttering things to herself that Bud only caught in snatches between his assigned tasks.

"Never seen anything *like* it...sin and *sloth*...nothing but *drunken sloth*...ought to *burn the place* to the *ground*...just bring me a *match*...*Ezekiel*...bringing *Bud* into a place like this...ought to *be horse whipped*...may do it *myself*..." Emelia emphasized her frustration by intermittently plunging the brush into the soapy bucket next to her, and with mighty forward strokes against the floor.

Swede and Zeke had been ordered to remove every sign of alcohol from the room, including the bar itself, and with Bud's help they had already removed the glassware and the barrels through the double doors at the back of the tavern. After Zeke explained how difficult it would be to remove the mirror with etched beer advertising across its top, Emelia settled for covering those areas with a few bedsheets. Having removed the massive wooden bar itself through the back doors—with Swede taking one end and Zeke and Bud struggling with the other—the men stood outside for a breather.

"So, you quit da bar then, Zeke?" Swede said, nervously, leaning against the bar. "You starting a *church*, maybe, yah? This looks like da church mudders at Gothenburg on da first week of May...that's da same week all da men decide its time to go fishing."

"No, Swede, we're not gettin' religion here. However...I guess it *is* time for our young friend here to leave us and do a little proselytizing." Turning to his nephew, Zeke asked, "Ready to make your Czech giant and his friends an offer of work? Or would you rather face your Aunt Emmy's cleaning frenzy?"

"I give up," Bud said, holding up his hands, stifling a laugh, but then turning serious. "I'll give it a try. No promises, though, Uncle Zeke..."

"Good enough for me," Zeke said, adding, "I'll see what men might be hanging around the stations...then I've got a little errand of my own. Have whoever you can find come by for supper at seven—see you here a little before then?"

Bud nodded, and managed to make it around the side of the building before he heard his aunt's voice call out, "Men! Jawing in the backyard, when they ought to be *working*!" He could almost convince himself that he hadn't heard her...and was suddenly struck by an inspiration. Returning to the back of the wagon—being careful not to be seen by Aunt Emelia— he picked up a wooden box about a foot square and four inches deep, carefully wrapped in a towel, and accelerated across R Street toward the Czech camp north of town.

Zeke turned to Swede, who, having seen the writing on the wall, had a gloomy expression on his normally cheery face.

Zeke laid his hand on the big man's shoulder. "Guess that just leaves you here to mind the store, Swede—sorry. I'll make it up to you."

"I should be *fishing*, I tink," muttered Swede, as he trudged despondently back into the bar.

* * * * *

"I don't understand," said Eloise, leaning on her shovel in her vulcanized Wellington boots, and staring quietly at the paper that had been thrust into her face on the dusty porch in front of her house.

LeBlanc couldn't help but grin. *God,* he thought, *this is fun.*

"Well, you can *read,* can't ya?" the big man sneered, shaking the piece of folded paper in front of her nose, his voice rising. "It says here you owe almost three hundert dollars, lady, to Mr. Clive Masterson, late of the Masterson Grocery and General Supply. He...well, **we**...will be here to collect on Monday...in *cash,* or in *corn.*"

Eloise Moseman's veined, calloused hands took the paper gently from the shaking hand, and her cool blue eyes read it carefully under the shadow of her straw hat as LeBlanc yammered on, in what sounded like satisfaction.

"You didn't really think that Mr. God Almighty *Ezekiel Gardner* could actually *deliver* on his promise, did you? Don't make me laugh," he scoffed.

From inside the house, a teapot started to whistle. The farm wife looked up with tired eyes and said, quietly, "Please excuse me for a moment," before she slipped back into the house.

LeBlanc went right on haranguing the elderly woman as he watched her slip out of her boots and retreat momentarily into the darkness of the kitchen, where he heard her silence the screaming kettle by removing it from the hot stove. "You know who you're up against? You'd best be ready to deliver that corn, or your fine barn out there," he said, jerking his thumb behind him, "might have a little accident."

Slowly, the woman came shuffling back, and her small voice sounded from the front parlor as she spoke.

"What I don't understand," she said calmly, her voice growing stronger as she raised the double barreled shotgun behind the screen door, "Is what gives you men the right to speak to an old widow like that."

The twin ten-gauge muzzles were level with LeBlanc's astonished eyes now, and the individual clicks of the hammers being drawn back each seemed to increase the shock registering on LeBlanc's face, and that of his two men.

"**Get—off—my—land**," Eloise said, her face impassive as she stared fearlessly through her unblinking blue eyes. "Or you can take it up with my husband."

* * * * *

"Don't be so upset, Maxie," Billy said, throwing a pebble at a black and white crossbred heifer that appeared to be within range of the road where they walked their horses. He managed to hit it on the rump, and watched in satisfaction as it lumbered off into the field. "Remember what happened at the farm just before this one? How the old man started bawlin'—saying that 'it's all a mistake'—and 'he had an agreement?' He'll be beggin' to sell his corn, come Monday."

"I'll even it up with her, come Monday," grumbled LeBlanc. "But did you listen to the rest of what he said? 'I've got a *signed agreement* with *Ezekiel Gardner.*" The last words were delivered in a sneering, sing-song fashion, as if the man were still on a playground.

"*Bastard...!*" LeBlanc spat, climbing up on his horse. "Come on, let's split the rest of these papers up, and get this over with...I need a beer." Before his men could object, he had split his bundle into three parts, tossing one to Billy covering eastern Lancaster farms and one to Franks for the farms to the west, keeping to those that straddled the West Oak Creek.

Spurring his mount, his men followed suit, and soon LeBlanc was headed south to the next farm. South...toward Lincoln.

* * * * *

Messrs. Miller and Paine had started their department store in Lincoln in 1880, and despite expanding and moving to a four-story building, their store was beginning to feel a little crowded again. In the ladies' department on the second floor, dresses and frocks of every conceivable color hung on the racks, hats jostled one another for shelf space, and pantaloons and other unmentionables filled the drawers lining the walls near the ladies' changing room. Notwithstanding the chaos, however, everyone—even a stiff old ex-deputy like Ezekiel Gardner—recognized that the well-turned-out lady of Lincoln couldn't find a better selection of dresses, hats and assorted folderol than at 133 South 13th Street.

And despite her other flaws, Margaret Troy was well turned out.

From his vantage point under the shadowed portico of the baked goods department just a few dozen yards up the street from the main entrance, Ezekiel enjoyed the smells of the cinnamon buns drift up through the large paper sack that held them, while he watched the crowds milling about. Every year, it looked to Ezekiel that the women's sleeves were getting puffier, the waists narrower, and the bustlines more exaggerated. The hats appeared to be getting bigger, too, and every Friday afternoon, Miller and Paine's ladies department turned out a new selection for the admiration of their weekend lady shoppers. Ezekiel had known Maggie for two years, and in all that time, she never failed to show up with a new hat, or a story about a new hat, on Friday nights at the Barrelhouse. So, considering the new flush of cash that undoubtedly accompanied her newly installed "position" with McGee...

...*and there she is*, thought Zeke, smiling grimly in satisfaction. Maggie looked spectacular, dressed in a navy blue walking suit, with matching shoes, gloves, hat, and—*lord a'mighty*, thought Zeke—*a parasol to boot.* She smiled as she waved to some admirer on O Street—*a man, undoubtedly*—and then swung straight toward his position.

Zeke felt his anger rise as she approached, and immediately moved to swallow it. He had never been the jealous type—he had always viewed Maggie's profession as just that...a profession, and one in which the young blonde had proven especially adept. No, it wasn't jealousy that made his dander rise now, but the realization that his own carelessness had led him, his family, and seventy-eight other families to the brink of destruction—simply because he had followed a sudden urge to share a confidence with

259

the young woman who was now gaily walking his way. He had always had a weakness for pretty girls—there had always been that latent desire to impress them, to woo them—*hell,* he admitted to himself, *to just plain show off.* For at least the fiftieth time in three days, he kicked himself—then took a deep breath and calmed himself for the task at hand.

As Maggie neared the door, Zeke did his best to put on a grin, and then turned directly north into the southbound Maggie Troy. The resulting collision knocked both of them to the ground, and Zeke managed to spill the cinnamon rolls all over the sidewalk through the pre-torn paper sack.

"Maggie!" Zeke said, doing a fair job of feigning surprise and embarrassment as he rushed over to her. "I'm so *sorry!*...I didn't see you coming. 'Aye God, girl, let me help you up."

Maggie, too flustered to object, took a hand from Zeke, who kept smiling and mouthing his apologies as he first dusted her off, then picked up and returned her hat and parasol, all the while expertly guiding her to a nearby bench. The young woman had acted shocked by her sudden encounter with Zeke, but was probably even more surprised by his calm and friendly nature. Now seated next to her, he gestured to a stray dog that was busily snapping up the cinnamon rolls strewn about them, and laughed, "Well, so much for my errand—guess my sister will have to do without her rolls."

"I-I'm sorry about that, Zeke," Maggie finally stammered. "I didn't see you coming, either..."

"How could you?" Zeke said. "We'll just have to chalk it up to one more wreck here in Lincoln. Think we'll make the papers?"

"I doubt it," Maggie said, finally allowing herself to smile.

"That's good—plenty of that going on without our help," Zeke said, grinning. Zeke then went on to ask if she had known that Amos had been involved in the wreck, and to explain a few sordid details, while tactfully leaving out the part about Masterson. Having established the fact that her presence was not the least concerning to him, he added in a hushed, yet still jovial tone, "So, I haven't seen you around much lately—I suppose it's your new client? Must be a handsome rake."

"Er...yes," Maggie said, then decided to try her hand at the saucy tone that she knew Zeke admired most. "You know all my suitors are handsome, Mr. Gardner."

"Flattery will get you nowhere, Miss Troy—ah hell, why lie to *you?* Of *course* it will..." Zeke admitted, grinning, and then stood. "Well, if

260

you've recovered, young lady, I guess I'll make my way back to the Barrelhouse—I've got a lot to do before I leave tomorrow morning." Extending his hand, he waited until she took it, and stood next to him.

"You're leaving town?" Maggie asked, surprised. For a split second, Zeke was sure that saw insight flash into her intelligent eyes, then received the question that he had been hoping for. "Where are you headed off to *now*, Ezekiel?"

"Well, if you can keep it under your hat—and you ought to, that thing's *enormous!*—I've got a little errand in Sidney," Zeke said, with a wink.

"Sidney—isn't that where you lived before Lincoln?" Maggie was genuinely curious now. She had heard plenty of tall tales through the years involving Zeke's wild experiences hauling, guarding, and even retrieving lost bullion for mining companies that had shipped gold from their mines in the Black Hills country, far away in the north through Indian- and bandit-ridden Sandhills, to the main Union Pacific railhead in Sidney, Nebraska, along the North Fork of the Platte River. But in the three years she had known him, she had never known him to actually travel there.

"Yep," Zeke said, doing his best to keep his tone conversational. "I still keep a strongbox out there. I'm afraid that I...well, you know me, Maggie. I misplaced something a few days back, and I just need to run out and fetch me a copy."

As he stooped to pick up a few random bits of cinnamon roll from the boardwalk and toss them into a garbage can near the bench, Zeke covertly observed Maggie's reactions through the corner of his eye. Despite her paint, they were written all over her young features. A flush of relief...that her original pilfering of the agreement was not suspected, he reckoned...and then, for a split second, there was a minute wrinkling of the brow. *Unease*, he guessed—the scheme that McGee had hatched with her assistance to rob the farmers had just gotten a little more complicated.

Inwardly, Zeke marveled...not on his ingenuity at turning the situation around—he was still kicking himself for allowing Maggie to steal the grain agreement in the first place...but at a truism, proven to him repeatedly, and now, once again, here in front of Miller and Paine. *People believe what they want to believe, and see what they expect to see.* Maggie had teased him mercilessly regarding his nearly chronic loss of personal and professional items—misplaced brushes, combs, the odd receipt, even a watch—over the last several years of their...uh, acquaintance...and that experience had made his explanation seem highly plausible to the young woman.

In parting with her, Zeke allowed himself to externalize the little smile that was now spreading inwardly. Taking her hand, he beamed into her eyes.

"I've missed you, Maggie-girl," he said, softly, and a tiny part of him actually meant it. "Do come back as soon as you can, will you?" And with that he tipped his hat, picked up the remains of the paper bag from the sidewalk and headed north. Zeke thought he could almost hear the gears turning in the blonde's clockwork mind as he headed up 13th Street to the Haymarket district.

Friday, August 10, 1894
1:50 pm

"**S**o, what is in this very mysterious box?" asked Rémy, the shortest, and most talkative of the Czechs.

Bud had been apprehensive when he had entered the familiar gully north of Lincoln, off the side of the Burlington tracks, where he knew that the wandering Czechs had made a temporary home, with their rough tents, campfires, and the smells of men...making their living far from the help of their women, trying to be self-sufficient, and failing, ever-so-bravely. Despite their polite—if not exactly friendly—conversation at the wreck site earlier this morning just prior to the appearance of Anna Marie's brothers, Bud knew that his relationship with these homeless workers was little more than twenty-four hours old, and was constructed, for the most part, on Anna's goodwill.

And Anna was not exactly handy right now.

At this, their third meeting, the Czechs around him were starting to grow familiar: Piotr Rémy, a short man who was obviously the spokesman of the group; two other bearded Czechs, Pavel and Alexi Svoboda, two brothers who consistently formed a sort of semi-Greek chorus at Rémy's side, bowing and tipping their increasingly ragged derby hats whenever they were called upon; and Andryev Malý, the "Czech giant" that Bud had tried to tackle in a mistaken rescue of Anna Marie Vostrovsky...although the intended damsel in distress had turned out, in fact, to be a hen.

Bud smiled in anticipation, then cast off the tea towel covering the tin pan to reveal...

Gasps, all around...followed by at least a dozen faces within a foot of the pan, inhaling exclusively through their noses.

"My Aunt Emelia is an incredible cook," remarked Bud, whose broad gestures in removing the tea towel had managed to fan the rising scent of cobbler to the second ring of men, who were now drawing around the first. "Do you have any plates?"

The scurry for tin plates and battered utensils was immediate and universal.

A few minutes later, the men had settled themselves into a circle around the campfire, groaning in the universal sounds of men under the tender care of a rich dessert.

One of the men mumbled in Czech, and the rest murmured in agreement. At Bud's questioning look, Rémy said, wistfully, "Coffee. The men wish they had coffee."

"I may be able to help with that, Rémy," Bud mentioned, trying to keep is voice low and understated. Gramps had often said that the best sale was closed in a whisper, and Bud had his fingers crossed under his dirty plate.

"Mm," Rémy said, carefully trimming a tiny segment of sweet crust with the edge of a suspiciously tarnished fork. "What of which are you speaking, Mr. Bud?"

"Just this," Bud said, eyes locked on his plate. "I have been sent by my family to invite you to a feast in Lincoln. My Aunt Emelia suggested it. There will be chicken, and mashed potatoes, and gravy, and cobbler...and coffee, of course. All are welcome." The boy kept his eyes lowered and listened to the groans as Rémy described each of the courses. But a harsh voice arising from Andreyev broke the reverie of the group, and his harsh stare at Bud hardly needed Rémy's translation.

"Andreyev...wishes...to know what you expect in return for such a...favor," Rémy said, diplomatically, as he still had a bit of cobbler in front of him.

Sensing that he probably couldn't meet the giant's eyes with a lie— even with a translator—Bud decided to level with the big man. "Look, Andreyev...there isn't any obligation. My family needs good workers for a few days, or weeks. If you wish to do the work—so be it. If you only want the food...what's the harm?" Bud hesitated, and then added, "I have seen what you do to chickens here—my aunt has a much better technique."

After the last phrase was translated, the laughter turned from a trickle, to a stream, and after Andreyev's stone face broke, into a mountainous peal of laughter.

* * * * *

By the time that the last probate case was settled at 2:00 p.m., the honorable Judge Ignatius W. Lansing of the Lancaster County Court was sweltering under his robes. As the courtroom cleared, the judge took out a handkerchief and attempted to mop his face and brow, but managed to miss a large drip of sweat that raced down his nose and *plopped* onto his blotter in defiance. Looking rather like a cat that had made an unfortunate rendezvous with a little boy and a deep well, Lansing looked pitifully over his glasses at his clerk, Scott Low, and wiggled his finger.

"Tell me that's the end, Scottie," he said, in a voice he thought too low to be overheard, "and I'll buy the first beer."

"No such luck, your honor," Hezekiah Kohlman said, lazily leaning against the doorframe of the courtroom, and wrapping what could only have been a dill pickle in a white handkerchief. Heck had a well-developed sense of hearing, honed as it had been for years at thresholds, transoms, and keyholes. "But I'll promise to be brief, and to buy beer for the entire court when our business is completed."

"The court can do without your *beer*, Mr. Kohlman, but would be most appreciative of your *brevity*," Lansing stated, as Heck walked up to the bench and presented a thick ream of papers to Mr. Low, who did his best not to snigger as he muttered, "Amen."

"So what have you got there, Mr. Kohlman?" Lansing asked wearily, reaching for the stack from his clerk and placing it on the bench with a *thump*. Overtly, he wound his watch and placed it next to the thick sheath as he thumbed through it. "It appears from the names crossed off the docket here," he said, gesturing to the redlined paper before him, "that a fair number of petitioners have unexpectedly withdrawn, or postponed their cases. How very...*odd*."

The judge's stare was piercing—and Heck did his best not to grin...*gods, I love this job*, he thought. "Two fairly small matters, your honor," he said. "A petition for payment of past due bills...and, a petition for foreclosure in lieu of default."

Gesturing at the thick stack of papers before him, Lansing cocked his head and squinted his left eye at Kohlman.

"It doesn't *look* small," Lansing said. "Just how many *small matters* are we talking about, here?"

"To be precise...seventy-eight, your honor...that is, there are seventy-eight past due bills..."

"Meaning seventy-eight petitions for payment, and seventy-eight petitions for foreclosure," Lansing interrupted, grumpily. "If my grammar school teacher, Mrs. Magnussen, drilled me in my sums correctly, that comes to a hundred and fifty six *separate* petitions. You have a very strange idea of a small matter, Mr. Kohlman."

265

"The cases are very clear, your honor," Kohlman said, rolling on cheerfully, and hoping at the same time to get the judge's attention off his fine watch. "My client, the wife of the late Clive Masterson, and his business partner, *Mr. McGee*, have carried many of these bills for over a year. They have been most patient, but require immediate payment—in cash, or in *corn*."

At the name of McGee—dropped by Heck in a carefully practiced tone that fairly dripped with malice—Judge Lansing fell silent. Lansing was well-aware of the extent of that man's reach in the county...many of his predecessors had owed their appointments to McGee, and even Lansing had been forced to pay homage, if not render actual judgments in his favor. Grunting, he started to make his way through the stack, raining perspiration on every third page or so. In case after case, the small print told a story of a farmer that had been given a little rope, and a little more...only to face a noose at the end of it. About a quarter of the way trough the stack, Lansing sighed. The paperwork before him was in order—at least the petitions for payment...

...and, hell, it was just too hot to argue.

Lansing was about to reach for his pen to start signing orders when a small, strong voice sounded from the back of the nearly empty courtroom.

"Mr. Kohlman, that *corn* has already been *sold*."

The steps of the young lawyer clumping across the floor of the courtroom startled Lansing for a moment, but when Dawes brightly queried, "Permission to approach?" as he was halfway across the room, Lansing had enough presence of mind to mumble, "Uh...granted."

"Hello, Heck," said Dawes, stepping up to the bench. *Ready for battle?* His eyes blazed, as they challenged Kohlman's.

"Hello, Charlie," said Kohlman. *Fire away,* his eyes volleyed back.

"Your honor," Dawes went on (the formalities having been observed), "My clients—the Northern Lancaster County Farmer's Cooperative, constituted of the seventy-eight farmers listed in the petitions before you, and, who are admittedly in debt to Mr. Masterson's estate—have agreed to sell their corn and remit up to the sum indicated on this agreement. In every case, I think you will find that the payment will cover the past-due bills." Dawes passed a copy of the agreement to Lansing, and Kohlman, who fumed.

266

"Objection, your honor," Kohlman sputtered. "This is highly irregular. Has the learned counsel filed a *petition* before the court? Or a counter-suit? He ..."

"As a matter of fact, your honor," Dawes said, offhandedly, "I *did* manage to find a little time, this morning, to file a brief on behalf of the Cooperative. I believe Mr. Low has a copy in his files...?"

"Indeed I do, your honor," Low said, silently reaching into his folder and producing a few thin sheets of paper, which he handed solemnly to Judge Lansing, and—with a wink and a smirk—to Heck Kohlman.

Scowling at the papers laid before him like a housewife who found a snake under her washtub, Heck began, "May it please the court..." But at the upturned hand of Judge Lansing, Heck brought himself to heel and wisely waited for his honor to finish reading before he proceeded.

"Your honor," Heck began again, "This is nothing more than an agreement to allow Mr. Ezekiel Gardner to act as sales agent for the Cooperative...in no way does it guarantee that payment will be made to Mr. Masterson's estate for past bills."

"I disagree, your honor. I believe that you will find Mr. Masterson's name listed in line 12," said Dawes, calmly, "as the intended recipient of the proceeds of the sale, minus expenses, up to the amount of, and even in excess of, each farmer's debt."

"Your honor," Kohlman said, now heating up, "in actuality, this agreement implies that Mr. Gardner will act as a *sales agent* for Mr. Masterson. But they have *produced no record* of such an agreement to buy the grain on the part of Mr. Masterson. It is simply an agreement that stipulates Mr. Gardner's ability to act on the part of the farmers."

"Line 12..." Dawes interjected.

"...is irrelevant. In fact," Kohlman went on, having reached a full head of steam, " If any such agreement *ever* existed, it could only have been verbal...and is now, circumstances being what they are, unfortunately, null and void."

"Objection, your honor," Dawes jumped in. "Immaterial. My client..."

"And frankly," Kohlman interrupted, "We are unaware of any *funds* that Mr. Gardner would have outside of the late Mr. Masterson's estate that could possibly *pay* the sums indicated in this agreement. Mr. Dawes' client is…a *barkeep*, your honor." Kohlman's sneer was both auditory and visible, and Dawes' counter was cold.

"And yours is a criminal, Kohlman."

Dead silence ensued for a half second, while Kohlman's boiler superheated. When its pressure peaked, he snapped, "Your honor, I demand…."

Judge Lansing slammed down his gavel, with marginally sufficient strength to break the thread of the lawyer's arguments, as well as crack the gavel's oak handle. It was not the first casualty of this particular court…proven so when the judge pulled open a lower drawer, dropped in the fractured gavel to join its myriad brethren, and pulled out a spare from another drawer.

"Gentlemen," he said, "It's just too hot." Gesturing at Kohlman with his restored gavel, he said, "There appears to be a set of conflicting documents here, Mr. Kohlman, but it is clear that your *bills* are in order. What is *not* clear is just who the grain belongs to, or who has really agreed to pay for it."

Pausing a moment to stare at the watch before him, Lansing finally turned to Dawes and shut it with a *snap*. "Given the presence of an agreement to sell the grain, however *tenuously supported*, and the *extensive* amount of paperwork presented to us by the plaintiff—not to mention the extreme paucity of the ink in my well—I'm going to give your client until Monday at 9:00 a.m., Mr. Dawes, to produce a document showing an agreement to pay for the grain, along with proof of available funds—preferably in the form of a bank draft."

"Your honor," said Heck, "these bills…"

"Have waited for a year, and can probably wait another few days," Lansing said, wearily. "Case deferred." And with an "All rise," from his clerk, the judge slid off his chair and dripped his way to his chambers, with Scottie Low at his heels.

"We will be happy to comply, your honor," Dawes said to the judge's rising and retreating form, with more confidence than he actually felt.

"You'd better be," murmured Kohlman, shaking his head as he straightened his papers. "You're sticking your neck way out on this, Charlie. You're on your way out of town…what gives?"

"Hell 'n Maria, Heck," Dawes said, "Haven't you ever stuck your neck out in a good cause?"

268

"Not likely," humphed Kohlman.

"Besides," Dawes added in a lowered voice, buckling the flap of his own briefcase. "You and I both know that an agreement to sell that corn to Masterson—or his estate—*exists*—all that is required is to produce a copy. I'm confident that one will appear, on *Monday*."

And having conveyed the central message that he had been urged by his client to deliver, Charles Dawes exited the courtroom and sought out a cool beer.

* * * * *

Lynch was thinking himself that a beer would have gone nicely with the hot bath he was immersed in...but that would have made it seem too much like a pleasure—and this was business.

"Bring me a towel, dear," he said to the Japanese woman that was hovering near him. She bowed, and as Lynch got out of the tub he surveyed the room again, alone, without the girl's eyes on him. Four brass tubs (one currently filled—his own), one entrance. A side room, where there resided a massage table, his clothing and the source of towels.

In a few moments, the kimono-clad girl returned with a large white cotton towel and carefully dried Lynch, and then she guided him to the long, padded table draped to the floor with white linen to begin a patient massage of his feet and legs. After a few minutes, she mounted a small set of two steps and grasped an overhead bar, lightly stepping on Lynch's back. As she worked the kinks out, Lynch reviewed the facts.

The target likes to show up about eight o'clock every Friday night. Bodyguards are stationed outside the door, and no other customers are allowed inside while the target is...engaged. Looking about him, he confirmed that the room featured a heavy, rolling bamboo blind at one end of it, secured with a set of cotton cords at either end. Towels on small wooden shelves lined the walls.

"That'll do for now, darling,'" Lynch said, handing her a silver dollar. "Go get me some more cigars." The girl bowed, and carefully patted him down with the towel, then walked to a small wooden door in the wall, pulled it downwards toward her, and threw in the towel. She bowed and exited.

After the curtain had closed behind the girl, Lynch walked over to the laundry chute, felt along its edge, found the latch, and then peered into it. A smooth vertical shaft about two feet on a side fell away at least thirty feet, ending in complete darkness. Turning, he walked over to the small

269

window, and peered around the rolling bamboo blind into the strong sunlight, where he recognized a brick paved alley behind the window, two stories down. Walking over to his clothes, he pulled out the pocket watch from his vest...*six hours to go*...and snapped it shut.

When the girl returned with the cigars in her gentle hand, she found that the large man had taken his clothes, and left a half-eagle on the massage table.

* * * * *

George Washington Davis had not slept well. At about three in the morning, he had somehow managed to stumble back from the colored club in Lincoln to the farm where he worked. It was a roundabout tour south of town that had led him to within shouting distance of the still-burning Rock Island wreck. Despite his raging curiosity, however, he had decided to assiduously avoid it at the last minute. The long walk, the drinking, and the late hour all should have conspired to throw him into a deep sleep when he finally collapsed into his rope bed at the back of the tool shed where he "roomed." Davis' dreams had been filled with the scream of brakes, and fiery, metallic crashes. So he had tossed most of the rest of the short night, and when his employer—Fred Lonsdale, a farmer with a tyrannical streak—had roused him at dawn and groused at him to set about his chores, Davis groaned, but complied...although at glacial speed.

Davis would have freely admitted that he had never been much of a farmhand. Having grown up in Washington, D.C., he had no inherent love of the land, and animals—especially hogs, with their intelligent eyes, ever filled with malice—made him uneasy. God knew that he wasn't fond of strong physical labor. The fates, luck, the disadvantage of his race—but more than anything else, his innate proclivity to take the easiest route to simple pleasures—had conspired to limit his options for gainful employment.

And so, he slopped the hogs. *Brutes*, Davis thought, *t'ain't nothin' but brutes*, remembering how an especially vicious Poland White, aptly named Satan, had turned on him when he had fallen several weeks ago in the pen. He had only just escaped the hog's ravenous incisors by squeezing through the narrow space between the lowest fence slat and the mucky ground, enabled by his slight build. He eyed Satan now, and the hog stared back with cold malice, as if accusing him before God, its hungry yellow tusks gleaming in the pitiless sunlight.

270

"Stop eyeballin' me!" Davis shouted as he hurled a pail of slops at the hog, purposefully missing the trough and plastering Satan with a load of half rotten cabbage and carrot peelings.

Satan just *looked* at him, the peelings sliding off his marble sides. Davis' stomach sank.

Time for a walk.

* * * * *

Walking alone on the dusty road that paralleled the Burlington tracks back south into town, Bud was trying hard not to be too satisfied with himself, and was failing utterly.

All-in-all, at least twenty men in the Czech camp had immediately agreed to come to the dinner that his aunt, her daughters, and her daughters-in-law were no doubt busily preparing in the remains of the Barrelhouse...and to relate the story to others in similar camps. Grinning, Bud shook his head, and recalled the miracle that the peach cobbler had wrought upon the Czechs. Like the Barrelhouse itself, whose once manly, stench-supported interior had completely surrendered to the onslaught of the Ladies' Aid brush-and-soap brigade, the Czech workers—encamped as bachelors without the pleasure of women's care and cooking for days and weeks—hadn't stood a chance when faced with superior firepower.

Turning about, Bud noted a rider in the distance approaching from the north. He was walking with a light heart—maybe the man would give him a ride back into town. It would be the perfect ending to a very long, but fruitful day.

The man on the approaching horse had *not* had a wonderful day. But as he saw the young man before him, he too, grinned, and urged his horse to a trot, and then a gallop.

Well, well, thought Maxwell LeBlanc. *Lookie what we got here.*

271

30

Friday, August 10, 1894
3:00 pm

Chief P.H. Cooper tried to comprehend the long strings of sentences that blurred together in the crisp typewritten sheet of paper that he held before him, winced, then tracked his tired eyes upward to follow the slight figure pacing back and forth on the thin, worn carpet before his desk. Malone had been speaking non-stop since cornering him at the door to the police offices after his lunch meeting with the Mayor, and was gesturing excitedly to punctuate the importance of each of his points. Sighing, Cooper held up his hands.

"O.K., Frank, slow down, willya? *Now*, you say that this fellow..." Cooper squinted at the paper before him, picking out the easier words, struggling with the longer ones.

"Davis," interjected Detective Malone, "George Washington Davis. He's the man, Chief...he's the wrecker..."

"Just hold your horses, Frank." The mayor, the city council, and most of all, those damned newspapermen had conspired to rob him of what little sleep his wife's snoring hadn't already been taking away these days. Just when he was looking forward to a few minutes quiet to...uh, gather his thoughts (the couch that ran along on of the office walls had over the years become perfectly conformed to a man of his—stature), here was a pipsqueaking political appointee rattling on with a voice that could peel paint.

"Take a deep breath...and a *chair*, for Christ's sake," the Chief growled, gesturing to the couch...*that lovely, inviting couch*. He sighed. "Just walk it through for me."

"One," Malone said, counting on his fingers, standing and ignoring— as usual—the 'settle the hell down' advice from his Chief. "A nigger carrying a lantern was seen by Harry Foote immediately upon escaping the wrecked passenger car. Foote is sure that he was the first one out—so the man had to be within a couple of hundred feet of the wreck when it happened."

"Coincidence," Cooper said, lighting a cigar and leaning back into his swivel chair and shaking his head. "Lots of folk walk up and down that track—could have been anybody..."

272

"Two," Malone smiled as he held up a second finger, once again ignoring the Chief. "Charlie Raymond, a hack driver, gives a ride to a nigger—*carrying a lantern*—from the wreck site back into town to the colored club over on P Street about an hour after the wreck. Davis tells Raymond that he was sitting next to Harry Foote on the train. I checked with Foote—there weren't any niggers on that train, Chief—not one."

"Uh, that wouldn't be *Crazy* Charlie Raymond, would it, Frank?" Cooper laughed. "Just why do you think they *call* him that? I know this character, Detective—we've hauled him in a half dozen times for starting fires—if he's not an arsonist, he's some kind of lunatic. *There's* your probable train wrecker…"

"Three," Malone went on, undeterred. "At the colored club, where we found Davis' lantern *and* his *revolver*, I might add, I ran across a man named Weems, who told me that Davis had told him that he, Davis, had been caught in the wreck, and had lost his coat, together with $200, the sale of one Maxey Cobb's horses, at Kearney. When Weems asked how he came to be on that train, Davis answered that he had tramped across the country to the Rock Island road near Fairbury, and had there taken the train."

Cooper just sat there with his arms folded. He yawned.

"Four…two cousins, Frank and Lewis Ryan, walking the tracks on Wednesday night—that's the night before the wreck—saw a nigger coming back from the trestle. They report that he was carrying a large crowbar."

"Frank, are you seriously saying he pulled up the track on Wednesday night? Doesn't make a lick of sense—three trains ran over those Rock Island tracks on Thursday before the wreck—why didn't one of *them* crash?" Cooper challenged.

"Davis was probably checking the place out, Chief—to see how easy it would be to pull up the rails," Malone explained, the Chief's skepticism causing a defensive tone to creep into his voice.

"What do we know about this Davis?" Cooper queried, satisfied that he was at least managing to shake the cocky little detective's hellfire confidence a bit. "For that matter, who identified him as being at the wreck at all?"

"That's the fifth point," Malone said, the smile now creeping back onto his face. "William Saxton, a local farmer, identified that it was Davis at the wreck site. Saxton says that he picks up odd jobs on some of the farms south of Lincoln, and that he has been the source of plenty of mischief—

273

petty theft, mostly. Saxton thinks that he's probably holed up in one of those farms, sleeping it off today."

"So, we've got the name of a *mischievous* character who was possibly at the bridge just before the wreck, and has been spreading a story…to a lunatic…about escaping the wreck that doesn't quite hold water." Cooper sighed and shook his head. "Awfully flimsy, Frank…but I guess you'd better bring him in for questioning."

Beaming in triumph, Malone said, "Should we get a warrant? I think that Judge Lansing is in session this afternoon…"

"Detective, if you went in there with your 'five reasons,' he'd laugh in your face," Cooper said, bluntly. "Just go find him, and bring him in for questioning. And, hear me good on this, now, *Detective*," Cooper's voice dropped, and sounded ominous. *"Stop talking to the papers until you have an actual arrest.* No need to turn up the heat on a boiling kettle— this city's hot enough as it is."

"Right, Chief," Malone said, spinning on his heels, his face alight. The door to the city police offices slammed behind him, only to be re-opened a moment later by Sergeant Kinney, his blue eyes dancing with good humor.

"So, what did you think of the good Detective's five points?"

"You were *listening*, Sergeant? How unlike you," Cooper chastised in mock tones of disgust. "Actually, it's the sixth point that convinced me."

"The sixth point…?" Kinney queried.

"The one at the end of the mayor's finger," Cooper muttered as he stumbled over to the couch and lay down, kicking off his shoes. "The one that said—find the man or you're fired."

"Yes, sir, that is a mighty powerful point indeed," Kinney agreed, and added as he closed the door, "In conference sir?"

The only response was a rumbling snore…followed by the sound of Kinney's key snapping the lock closed.

* * * * *

The business of Chicago was…business, or at least busy-ness, if the buildings springing up around the corporate headquarters of the CRI&P were any indication. As cursed as it had been a few years ago for allegedly kicking over a lantern and starting the Great Chicago Fire, Mrs. O'Leary's cow was fairly worshipped these days, having cleared the way for an unparalleled construction boom in the Windy City. The ten-, fifteen-, and even twenty-story behemoths under construction along State Street were the wonder of the age, and the bricklayers, crane operators, steelworkers, and carpenters who labored on them, despite their long hours, were some of the best-paid, and by that measure, happiest workers in the country.

Through the broad, arched window of his corporate boardroom, the President of the CRI&P was contemplating the happiness of those workers now swarming over the multitude of construction sites that lined the widened boulevards of his city. In each of those simple lives, personal chaos and squalor might reign—brothers quarreled, wives left, and children...might die. Yet in the blessing of work, there was escape—to purpose, to industry, and even to honor. Certainly to sanity—an anchor that could help stabilize the uncertainties of home life. Kept separate, a man might manage to keep his head above water in one, or with luck, even both of those worlds.

But when those spheres intermingled, intruding one upon the other—as they had just crashed together in Ransom Reed Cable's own hellish life over the last 18 hours—there was bound to be misery in both parts.

"Sir?"

Standing at the sunlit glass arch that framed the west end of his boardroom, Cable suddenly became aware of a gentle tapping on his shoulder, and he broke his reverie to look upon the energetic countenance of Peter LaRue, his personal assistant. Of all of those gathered in the Boardroom, only LaRue knew what had happened to his boss' son—and even he didn't suspect what was about to happen.

"The Board is ready to convene, sir," LaRue said quietly. "Shall we begin?"

"Yes," Cable said, with a determined look. "Let's get this over with."

* * * * *

Saltillo. Roca. Hickman. Firth. Adams. Stirling. Smartsville. Tecumseh. Elk Creek.

Having crept past the Rock Island wreck site, the heavily-loaded Burlington train rocked gently as it crawled through the small towns on its route southeast of Lincoln. Every stop seemed to take twice as long as it normally would have, with two days' cargo and passengers having built up that required unloading from the capital city. The heat, the noise, the smoke, dust and strain showed on the faces of the passengers and crew of the train...with one exception. Amos Seville didn't make it past Roca

275

before his knees were braced up on the chair ahead of him, his body had slunk deep down into his own seat, and his senses were dead to the world.

It had been a long night for the man from Virginia.

At Table Rock, Amos was gently shaken by the passenger brakeman, and herded half-asleep along with the other transferring passengers to the westbound Burlington line.

At Endicott, where he planned to transfer to the northbound St. Joe line for the last seven-mile segment of his trip into Fairbury, Amos finally stretched out of his cocoon and woke completely. Leaving the train, Amos tried to walk off the numbness in his legs, wishing that he could transfer some of it to his left shoulder. Groaning inwardly, he tenderly placed his left arm back into its sling. *Something was really wrong there*, he realized. Despite his lifelong dread of doctors, he had begun to wonder whether he should have taken Zeke's advice and seen one before he left—when he saw a familiar face on the platform, covertly eyeing him from behind a yellowed newspaper. Seville's cold stare caused the man to drop his act, straighten himself up, and walk apprehensively over.

"Hello Mr. Evans," Amos said, lighting a cigarette and taking a long draw before he settled his icy blue eyes on the stranger. "Nice day for a train ride."

* * * * *

Bud was raised a Methodist, which meant that he was essentially harmless. There had in recent years been a number of splits in Methodism—many of the more charismatic of Methodists had become drawn into Holiness movements, leaving the mainline church for their belief that Man could speak in tongues, even in the midst of Holy Service, when the Spirit so moved him. But in Bud's own Alder Grove Church— aside from the annual budget battle—there was very little actual controversy. They weren't exactly sheep—but then again, weren't they to be led by the Good Shepherd? Bud had heard a lot about sin—both original and manifested—but when it came down to it, he had relatively little actual experience with the real article...or in battling it.

But LeBlanc was likely to be a very good teacher.

Only moments ago, Bud had barely registered the sounds of a horse cantering distantly behind him, along with the locusts, birds, and the barely audible rumble of an approaching steam train—all tickling his attention (which was still absently focused on his triumph with the Czechs), but failing to actually engage it. By the time that the sound of LeBlanc's big

276

Palomino thundering behind him finally snapped him from his reverie, it was already overtaking him in a frenzy of dust, sweat and sound. Passing on the boy's left, LeBlanc nudged his knees and urged his horse's massive haunches to swing to the right, sending the young man sprawling against the slight track embankment and its exposed ties, along with Aunt Emelia's cobbler pans.

It was a jarring blow, but far from a disabling one. But by the time Bud's head had cleared, its rider had dismounted his horse, and the both of them were towering over him next to the track, blocking the sun like a pair of dark clouds. Through the seat of his pants, Bud could feel the rumble of the train approaching—a sharp contrast to the pealing laughter of LeBlanc.

"I do believe we've met. It's Bud *Gardner,* isn't it?" the man sneered, and extended his hand to Bud's prostrate form with obvious relish. The young man took one look at that hand—and the wicked grin on the face behind it—and instinctively *knew*—as any child in a playground knew—what was about to occur. Rolling to the side, Bud quickly sprang to his feet, making sure that he stayed out of LeBlanc's reach. Unfortunately, that placed the young man squarely behind LeBlanc's Palomino. To Bud's eye, his own sudden movement, along with the screaming whistle of the fast approaching steam engine, caused the skittish horse to launch a lightning kick—directly, as it happened, at Bud's head.

What he didn't see, of course, was LeBlanc's thumb jabbing his horse in the ribs.

Had the big horse's hoof hit him squarely in the skull, Bud could easily have been killed. As it was, Bud managed to lean away from the hoof, resulting in a solid impact on his upper chest that sent him flying backwards and to his right, where his head hit the rail with a ringing thud. Unconsciousness began its descent; and as he lay there across the steel rails, the approaching engine's brakes started to squeal.

* * * * *

"Gentlemen, I appreciate your attendance on such short notice," Cable began, eying the eight other members of the Executive Board of the Chicago, Rock Island, and Pacific Railway. Powerful and intelligent investors all, most of the men were in their late fifties, smoking fine cigars and dressed in tailored suits. Cable respected them, of course, knew their abilities—even though they didn't always see eye-to-eye. "It appears that we have a quorum…may I have a motion that we dispense with reading the minutes and move directly into new business?"

"So moved," Robert Phelps grunted.

"Seconded," Findley Larsen intoned, always ready to toady for Phelps.

"All in favor?" Pausing a moment for the expected grunts of assent, Cable plunged on. "Gentlemen, I move that we suspend negotiations in the purchase of the Union Pacific Railway. Do I have a second?"

For a moment, the room's silence was reinforced, then shattered, as the voices of the executives—some querying, some angry, mostly surprised—rose to a confused babble.

"*Second!*" Robert Phelps' strong voice boomed across the mahogany table, momentarily silencing most of the discussion around it. Turning to Cable, his face registered utter disbelief. "Cable, I can't believe my ears. After months of argument, is it really possible that you have finally seen things *my way?*"

"Let's just say I've had a change of ...heart...concerning the timing of this move," said Cable. "I grant you, gentlemen, that we have worked very hard over the last several months to establish an...inside track...concerning the Union Pacific. I have, with your support, advocated this position, and believe that when Congress finally does move to allow the Railway to be removed from receivership, we will be in a prime position to move in response, with a winning bid."

As he paused to light his cigar, Cable gazed around the room. The faces surrounding him were not squawking, exactly—were still, in fact, listening patiently, given their proclivity for disagreement. *So far, so good. But which of these bastards do I really need to satisfy?*

"Let's look at the facts, gentlemen," Cable continued. "Agitators, set against us by some party or parties unknown, have been working against us. The message from Lincoln yesterday was clear...someone is clearly willing to wreck the arrangement that we have worked so diligently to establish."

"Why give in to them, then?" said William Loftis, a staunch supporter of Cable's proposals. William looked utterly disappointed, and it pained Cable to take this tack. But this was not business—this was an absolute necessity that transcended it.

"Because, William, time is *not* of the essence where this particular acquisition is concerned. Can we agree that we could wait months, even *years*, before this particular property is finally released by Congress? And by announcing...through the press... to our stockholders and to the general public that we have ceased an active search for Union Pacific ownership, we will have put those forces that are placing us at immediate risk...at bay."

"The point is this, gentlemen," Cable said, propping his arm with the lit cigar on the arm of his comfortable leather chair and leaning back, trying his best to convey a sense of assured confidence that he did not, in any way, feel at the moment. "I believe that the situation is forcing us to...temporarily...remove our formal bid for the Union Pacific. No one— least of all me—is saying that this is the last word on this matter. Think of our stockholders, gentlemen—at this time, will they be more interested in our continued move into uncertainty, or in our confident move into consolidation of our more profitable avenues?"

A swift but brief silence ensued. Murmurs, as usual...glances—some cheerful, as if relieved that Cable had finally seen the light, and some baleful, as if their "boss" had betrayed them—darted Cable's way. But he managed to ignore them...the stakes, he had realized about six this morning, after the call from the disembodied voice that had directed this action...were too urgent to ignore.

"Call the question," Phelps said, a smile of satisfaction clearly evident on his lips.

"Second," Larsen said automatically.

Toady, Cable raged, inwardly. *I hate the hell out of this.*

"The question has been called," Cable said, still failing to show any emotion. "A show of hands supporting an immediate vote on the motion at hand?"

Around the table, the hands showed an assent—as it did for the motion itself, though by a slimmer margin than Cable would have imagined possible.

"Thank you, gentlemen," Cable said, finally allowing a glimmer of relief to show through. *God,* he thought, *am I tired.* "Shall we adjourn?"

* * * * *

It was a hot afternoon...again...and as Fred Lonsdale paused in his chores to grumble about helpers not being much help and to slake his thirst with some cool water, he saw the horse and rider approaching. Lonsdale recognized the horse and rider as Thunder, a fine Hanoverian stallion, and its owner, William Saxton.

"Company, Ma," Lonsdale called out.

279

Taking off his hat, Lonsdale approached the rider, and grabbed for Thunder's reins as the rider dismounted.

"Hello, Bill, what brings you this way?" Lonsdale asked, hoping it was not the rent payment already.

"Is the coffee on?" Saxton inquired, and Lonsdale's heart lifted a bit.

"Well, if it's not, we'll put it on," Lonsdale replied, and the two of them walked into the little farmhouse.

"Coffee, Ma," Lonsdale remarked, and gestured Saxton toward the small room off the kitchen that served as the parlor, while his wife Sarah busied herself with the kettle. The men quietly discussed the weather, the state of the crops and the livestock, until the steaming coffee was ready, at which point Sarah excused herself, calming the fussy baby on her shoulder with a swing to her hips. Lonsdale admired the purpose behind it, of course...but mostly the swing, truth be told.

"Now...Lonsdale," Saxton said, delicately. "You wouldn't happen to have seen that...Negro, would you?"

"Uh...you mean Davis?" he asked, and realizing that few other Negros had made themselves available for part-time work in this part of the county, responded, "Yes...at the moment, he went out on some fool's errand, instead of doing his chores."

"Uh...you're aware of what happened last night, I expect?"

"Well, sure, Bill...I went out there, but not near as early as you, I guess...saw your name in the paper today. Read all about it—but what are you talking about?"

Saxton hastened to explain, beginning with what Lonsdale already knew—the loud crash that he and his father had heard last night, the general carnage of the wreck, the rescue of the passengers—and wrapping up with his recognition of George Washington Davis at the site. Lonsdale's incredulous look grew as Saxton ended with the police's search for Davis...and the thousand-dollar reward, posted by the C.R.I.&P., for information leading to the arrest of the suspected wreckers.

"You think that Davis...that *he*...?" Lonsdale stuttered.

"The reward for information..." interrupted Saxton, with a wink toward Lonsdale, "Is a *thousand dollars*..."

Lonsdale leaned back in his chair, and sipped his coffee. *A thousand dollars. Why, that would...*

280

"I'll split it with you," Saxton said, his eyes still raised. "Shall I fetch the Detective?"

With hardly a hesitation, Lonsdale nodded, and Saxton headed toward the door.

* * * * *

Seated across the aisle from one another on the hard wooden benches of the unadorned St. Joe passenger car that was now slowing on its final northwestern approach into Fairbury, Evans sought for ways to break the long silence with Amos Seville. Their conversation on the platform back in Endicott had been limited to a polite exchange of greetings, Amos being unwilling to give any information, and Evans unable to figure a polite way to extract it.

Evans had not been a journalist long, and his inexperience nagged at him. He was convinced that any number of his colleagues at the Journal would have found a way to get at Seville, hammering away with questions, and dogging him until he broke. But somehow, to Evans, Seville didn't seem to be the type to bully. Instead, he struck Evans as the type that would make a deal—IF the deal was sweet enough. Evans realized, however, that he was holding almost no cards.

Well, maybe one card.

"Wonder," Evans said quietly, "if you'd like to hear a little more about Ransom Reed Cable, Jr...and Senior?"

"Could be," said Amos, staring forward noncommittally.

"Tell you what," said Evans, now also settling on playing it coy. "I have a bit of nosing around to do myself here in Fairbury. Should you happen to show up at the Fairbury Hotel at, say, eight o'clock?—you might find an exchange of information to be...enlightening."

The train had stopped. Amos took a last draw, then glanced in the general direction of Evans. Finally, he said, "Ah hate to cut my options, Mr. Evans, until ah see what hand ah've been dealt. Should a ravenous hunger...for knowledge, or for the hotel's overcooked steak...overcome me, you might well see me there." And tipping his hat, Seville exited the front of the car in search of Sheriff John Langston.

Trying to suppress a smile as he watched Seville's departing form, Evans sat up and headed briskly out the back exit of the car for the Western District offices of the Chicago, Rock Island and Pacific Railway.

* * * * *

The board was nearly spread.

From his preferred post outside the door, Swede shook his head in helpless wonder. Throughout the afternoon, he had watched the regular Friday patrons of the Barrelhouse—good customers, all—advancing on their favorite establishment from up and down R Street, only to cross the threshold...and stop in their tracks, starkly astonished, within three feet of the door. Whether it was the transformed appearance—the entire interior having been scrubbed to, and in many places, beyond the paintwork—the smell of fresh-baked bread mixed with a whiff of ammonia, or the sound of god-fearing women either directing one another or sniffing in disgust at the entering patrons...each of them variously rubbed his eyes, or pulled off his hat, and invariably, excused himself.

"May as well be *home*," said one, stomping off in disgust. Another found out that he should have been—from his wife, standing behind one of the tables.

Swede had done his best, of course, to warn the arriving customers of what they were in for before they entered, as well as to assure the scattering clientele that "it's gonna be back to normal tomorrow, yassir, you betcha." He sighed heavily. Over the last several hours, Swede had been variously wheedled, sweet-talked, and cajoled into setting up tables and chairs, spreading tablecloths, and doing the heavy lifting required by the Pack women and their growing brigade of drafted church women. Worst of all, he had been coaxed into hauling, arranging, and re-arranging baskets of fruit, trays of relish, platters of chicken and cold roast beef, bowls of mashed potatoes, boats of gravy, pans of cobbler and pies—and three massive urns of coffee—while simultaneously being relentlessly scolded by the Pack women and their legions into keeping his *hands off the food, thank you.*

So when Zeke finally approached the Barrelhouse at five-thirty, the first thing that struck him outside the door of his formerly comfortable and disreputable establishment was Swede's arctic blue eyes, now transformed into those of an angry Frost giant.

Whew, thought Zeke, wincing slightly and nodding to his man as he pulled off his hat and hustled through the door. *Gotta remember to **rectify** that situation...*

As he entered, Zeke was nearly as shocked by the Barrelhouse's transformation as his clientele had been. Nearly so, that is, because although the transformation was truly miraculous—he knew the organizational powers of his sister.

"Ezekiel," Emelia said, or rather, announced—from across the room.

Thar she blows, thought Zeke. His eyes tracked over to her, and once again, he marveled at the total transformation of the room. A long series of tables pushed end-to-end and covered with white linen had taken the place of the bar along one wall, and the small, dirty tables that had formed the bulk of the Barrelhouse's seating area had been covered in white. The chairs were still damp from their scrubbing, and smelled strongly of lye soap.

"Hello, Em," Zeke said, beaming as she approached. His sister had a determined look on her face, so as usual, he tried a little levity, jerking his thumb toward the steps that led upstairs through the side door. "Did you manage to take a whack at the bedroom, too? I don't know when the last time was that I changed the sheets up there…"

"Ezekiel Gardner, I wouldn't set a foot up those stairs if Saint Peter came down and asked me himself," Emelia announced, hands on her hips as she glared at him. But eyeing his still-upturned thumb and growing smirk, Emelia finally relented, broke into a grin herself, and shook her head.

"You and the girls do know how to put on a spread," Zeke remarked, nodding about him. "Don't know how I'll ever get my regulars back, though."

"Then maybe this work hasn't been to waste after all," Emelia retorted. Wiping her brow with her apron, Emelia—mercifully—changed the subject. "Any word on how many might be showing up?"

"Well, I must have talked to right around a hundred railroad workers— but when I told them that beer wouldn't be served, I only got about ten or so to agree to come," Zeke admitted.

"Just as well," Emelia concluded, in a matter-of-fact fashion. "Those are the ones you want, anyway."

"Could be," Zeke said, quietly. *Sure don't think the opposition will care much, though.* "Heard anything from Bud?"

"No," said Emmy, and a little wrinkle of worry began to fret at the space between her brows. "I thought he might be with you."

"Hmm," Zeke said, then shrugged and smiled. "Well, he'll probably come in with the Czechs."

"He'd better," Emelia agreed. "He took my best cobbler pans."

* * * * *

Bud's head was still spinning, both with the force of the recent blow and with the scream of the oncoming train, when he felt a strong hand grasp the back of his collar and yank him bodily from the tracks onto the shallow embankment—where unconsciousness finally managed to swallow him.

31

Friday, August 10, 1894
7:00 pm

It was seven, and in twos and threes, men dressed in their characteristic oil-stained overalls and worn cotton caps began to trickle into the transformed Barrelhouse. Many of these former or off-duty railroad men had spent a long day at the wreck, and most were more hungry than thirsty (the thirstier of their brethren having already gone off to patronize other, more accommodating establishments). Swede and Zeke were stationed at the front door to greet each of them—Swede on the outside, his angry blue eyes having given way to his normally smiling visage by the welcome presence of five silver dollars, presented by Zeke with profuse apologies—and Zeke on the inside, ready to take the verbal ribbing that he knew would accompany the transformation of the Barrelhouse. *Yes*, they were in the right place. *No*, there would be no alcohol—just shut the hell up about it, and *eat*. *Yes*, the food was free. *No, there was no obligation—just help yourself.*

In a few cases, half-day workers from the wreck site had already spent a little too much of their limited pay on liquid refreshment, had not gotten the word about the "change in management" at the Barrelhouse, and needed a little active filtering. In most of these cases, Swede's big smile, the shaking of his shaggy blond head, and the presence of shoulders a yard wide did the trick. In one case, a hard knock on the door brought Zeke out, and the pair of them standing shoulder to shoulder before the door—along with the jibes of those trying to get past them—managed to turn a pair of loud drunks away, and toward a more compliant saloonkeeper.

Inside, the Pack women and their sisters in Christ from St. Theresa's stood behind the tables, ready to ladle quantities of fried chicken, roast beef, mashed potatoes and vegetables, coffee and dessert to the men. Zeke had been fortunate here, he realized—his sister's good standing with the Ladies Aid Society and their already nascent plans to do something of this sort for the poor and out-of-work in and around Lincoln had permitted the plan to be carried out much more quickly and efficiently than anyone could have reasonably hoped for. But then again, the milepost marking a "reasonable hope" had been passed a good piece back, and Zeke had been reconnoitering in the rocky area between "slim chance" and "out of my mind" for so long now that his sense of perspective where chance was concerned had probably been severely bent, if not permanently disabled.

As fortunate as he had been in a family that could set this up on such short notice, however, Zeke realized that the dozen or so men that had shown up so far would barely make a dent in filling their manpower requirements for getting the corn shelled, loaded and delivered next week. Although he kept up appearances as best he could—shaking hands, explaining what was needed in twos or threes to the workers who had shown up, and getting positive feedback for the most part—inside the lining of his stomach a cold weight was settling, and dragging his heart down for a good cold swim.

Funny how the sound of polka music can cheer a man.

It started with the echo of men's voices out in the street—a babble immediately distinguishable from English by its odd inflections buzzing with hard k's, ch's and z's—and with the massed rumble of boots on bricks. Before Zeke could get to the door, it had burst open, and a virtual tidal wave of humanity swept into the Barrelhouse—a wave of hungry men, whose obvious delight at the sight of the spread before them filled their faces with joy that needed no translation. At least thirty men had lined up at the tables before Zeke could turn around to count them—and it was difficult to tell who was more delighted—the men, at the prospect of a feast, or Zeke, at the prospect of the men.

The second wave of Czechs was slightly more civilized, most of them at least pausing at the door to take off their hats and nod to Zeke before hustling over to the tables. However, more than a dozen stopped at the door, surrounding a slight man that made a deep formal bow. Raising his eyes to Zeke, he introduced himself.

"So pleased for to make your kind acquaintance," the small man said, and his following half-bow was duplicated by several surrounding Czechs. "My name is Piotr Rémy."

"Pleased to meet you, ah...er...Pete," Zeke finally said, taking the smaller man's hand with a firm grasp. "My name's Ezekiel Gardner, and I'm awfully glad you came."

At the sound of his name, Rémy's face absolutely lit up. His handshake grew more rapid, and, gripping Zeke's hand even more tightly, began to speak rapidly to his companions in Czech, repeatedly using the words "Bud Gardner."

"*Gibberish gibberish* **Gardner!** *...Bud Gardner!...*" the men surrounding him repeated, nodding and smiling to one another.

One clearly used the word "cobbler."

In the corner near the vacant piano—the Professor having been given the evening off—a trumpet, a trombone, and a small accordion suddenly started sputtering out a bright little tune in 4/4 rhythm, to the complete astonishment and nearly universal delight of the ladies that were valiantly laboring to keep up with the rampant demand at the food tables. It definitely wasn't Beethoven. But there's something about a polka that makes a body happy to be alive...and being fed at the same time just makes the heart all that much lighter. Zeke looked at the tables, and though some of the Ladies' Aid were shaking their heads, their covert smiles and tapping feet under the tables told another story entirely.

"You are family of Mr. Bud Gardner, I am thinking," Rémy remarked, trying his best to be heard over the impromptu concert. Zeke nodded.

"I take it you've met my nephew," Zeke said, and after another round of explanations to his companions, Rémy grinned and nodded enthusiastically.

"He brought us very...delicious?...yes, *delicious*...**cobbler**...this day after noon," Rémy said. "He is brave...but forgetting?" Motioning to Pavel Svoboda, he went on, "We found these beside the tracks, on the way to town—he dropped them, I am thinking, on his way to here, yes? Is he here then?"

From amongst the Czechs, Rémy produced a pair of baking pans—dented and battered at a level far beyond Emelia's most strenuous kitchen use. Accepting the pans and looking them over, Zeke's stomach fell once again, and offered the prospect of an icy dive to his heartstrings.

"He's on his way," said Zeke, trying to maintain his optimism.

I hope.

* * * * *

The sunny afternoon had given away to a light drizzle—and if their shared mood was not enough to put a damper on the Cable social agenda, the weather lent Mr. and Mrs. Cable sufficient excuse to cancel the evening out that they had planned with close friends from church. Mrs. Cable managed to maintain a quiet exterior, but in private, was an intense woman—upon learning of their son's disappearance earlier that day, she had looked at her husband with daggers in her brown eyes and simply said, "Get him **back**, Ransom—whatever it takes." And then she had shut herself into her bedroom, refusing all entreaties to open the door.

Cable felt utterly alone, and was starting on his third brandy when his private line rang.

"Good evening, Mr. Cable," the voice whispered, and recognizing the voice, Cable's veins ran with icewater.

"Good evening, Mr. B," Cable managed to say almost evenly, while attempting to pull his heart out of his Adam's apple.

"I must offer my sincere congratulations," the voice uttered calmly, "for your ability to convene a meeting of the Board so quickly. *However*," he went on, in a rising voice, "I must hasten to add that my associates and I are not *satisfied* with the *content* of that meeting."

"In what way, may I ask?" Cable said, anticipating the answer. "I made every effort to stop our impending negotiations for the Union Pacific..."

"Come now, Mr. *Cable*," the disembodied voice interrupted, "We require a *real* cessation of effort towards acquiring the UP, not just a *delay, or a gesture*."

Damn...where is he getting this? Cable raged inwardly, but fought to keep his temper in control. *Who on my Board is a Judas?*

With a supreme effort, he settled on a calm, but weak defense. "Surely, we need to walk before we can run."

"Indeed," agreed the voice. "But you need to *run*, Mr. Cable, and *right now*. You have a *son,* Mr. Cable, who will be *dead in 72 hours* if you undertake another halfway measure such as you attempted with the Board today." Despite the static that generally accompanied a very long distance connection, Cable detected that his adversary's voice had dropped an octave, and turned utterly cold.

And before he could reply, the line—like Cable's heart—went dead.

* * * * *

Bud Gardner's eyes fluttered open, and in the silence that ensued, his still spinning head made a credible attempt to take in his surroundings. It *appeared* to be...an office, or a library, composed of a wooden rolltop desk scattered with papers, a small shelf of leather-covered books, and a reading lamp beside a cracked leather chair. On it, there was seated a large Negro man with flecks of gray at his temples, reading glasses propped upon his nose, and a red leather book spread upon his lap. As Bud tried to sit up, his head started to spin, and his low grunt drew the attention of the man seated in the chair.

"You've had a nasty bump in the noggin, youngster," the man said as he stood, wetted a towel, and then wrung it out in the washbasin beside the raised padded table where Bud found himself. Bud winced as the man patted it against his head, and *tsked* silently a few times before he went on. "You are *clearly* a very hard-headed boy—you're bruised from ear to crown, but your skull does seem to be remarkably intact. You wouldn't be…Zeke Gardner's kin, would you?"

Surprised at the mention of his uncle, Bud tried to nod—and regretted his decision immediately.

"Thought so—at least that's what the railroad men said when they brought you on board our train." Walking over to the small medicine cabinet that hung above the washbasin, the doctor—for the stethoscope about his neck and his white coat could make him none other—proceeded to spoon some white powder into a glass, mix it with water poured from a blue ceramic pitcher, and stir it with a spoon.

Offering it to Bud, the man went on, "So what in the world possessed you to want to take a nap on the track? According to the engineer, if that man on the Palomino hadn't pulled you off…well, more than just your head would have been scrambled."

Bud nearly choked on his headache powder. *Max LeBlanc…pulled me off the track?* Now his head was *really* spinning.

"Uh…his horse kicked me, and I guess I must have hit my head," Bud admitted, after he had gulped down the last of the medicine.

"Hmmm….well, I'd thank the man, if I were you," the doctor announced. "It was a close thing, as I understand it."

"I think I should thank you, too," Bud said, his head feeling a little better, but still foggy. "So…who should I be thanking, again?"

"Dr. Charles Flippin, of Flippin and Flippin," said the big man, smiling and sticking out his hand. "I'm the first one."

"I spoke to another Mr. Flippin earlier today," replied Bud, trying to recollect the circumstances as he grasped the man's hand. "I believe he plays football…"

"That would be my son," said Dr. Flippin, releasing his grip and fishing his stethoscope under Bud's shirt. "He plays for the U. Have you seen him play?"

"No," said Bud, flinching at the cold stethoscope against his chest. "I met him at the wreck just this morning."

Dr. Flippin's face turned serious. "Sent him down to see if he could help—by then, all the bodies had been brought back to the county coroner, and the cleanup was well underway." Dr. Flippin sighed. "Poor folk— what a tragedy…"

Budd nodded, and tried to change the subject. "So, is he the other Flippin?"

"He will be…when he's finished with his schooling, that is. You might say that the sign is a bit *anticipatory*, in nature. He works here already, but will not actually practice until he gets his degree in medicine, of course." Dr. Flippin said, and shook his head as he took off his stethoscope. "Remarkably healthy—reckon you feel well enough to head back to your uncle?"

Uncle Zeke…crap! Bud thought, snapping his head around to look for a clock, and trying to ignore the twinge. Standing on the rolltop desk, the ornate marbled desk clock accused the young man of negligence, pointing to the hour of eight o'clock.

A panicked look crossed Bud's face. "My uncle—is waiting for me. At the Barrelhouse—817 R Street. Could you…uh…point me in the right direction?" Bud asked, sliding off the table and finding, happily, that his feet were cooperating in keeping him vertical.

"Think I might know the place. Tell you what—," Dr. Flippin said. "I'll escort you there. Been wanting to have a talk with your uncle, anyway."

Bud wondered at the last remark as Dr. Flippin picked up his hat. *Was there anyone that Uncle Zeke **didn't** know in Lincoln?*

* * * * *

Henri Flint and Charles Cheevers hadn't really intended to stop by the Barrelhouse before checking in, but it *had* been a long trip, and having discovered how close the station was to the address that his employer had provided for the Barrelhouse, Flint figured that they might as well drop by and have a little look. Flint had always been a believer in checking out the opposition before his judgment was…colored…by an unbalanced set of facts. In the past, Cheevers hadn't done too badly by following Flint's advice, so he had just shrugged and said, "As long as there's beer."

The Barrelhouse wasn't exactly what Flint had been given to expect. Sure, there was music and laughter pouring out into R Street…but a man didn't have to get within fifty feet before he could *smell* the difference. Ammonia, instead of beer? Lye soap, instead of cigarette smoke? Food

290

that smelled like heaven, and clientele that smelled like...*Czechs*. Flint shook his head, then muttered a profanity that bespoke a deeply felt, ill view of both Nebraska ancestry and anatomy.

As they approached the unguarded door, Flint suddenly placed his hand on Cheevers' arm, preventing him from walking into the Barrelhouse, and pulling him aside. From their position outside the open door, they listened quietly to what was apparently the end of a speech from the big man in the duster, who was standing under the gas lamp at the far end of the big room, hat in his hand. Every few phrases, a small man to his left explained the words to the crowd in Czech, who murmured in response.

"So...that's it then," Zeke said, and shuffled his feet as he tried to separate his words from his tangled tongue. "We need your help for the next week or so. The pay is not great, but the families you will live with will feed you, and shelter you. After a day or two, I will return, and together, we will bring the first loads of grain into Lincoln."

"Where are you off to, Zeke?" one of the out-of-work railroad men asked from the side of the room, cheerily, his stomach full of food and his heart full of hope...for the next week, anyway. "Need to replace all the beer these ladies dumped out?"

Laughter ensued, and when the quick translation was completed, more followed.

"Ray, I have a little errand to follow up on—but with my family here," Zeke said, gesturing to Rufus, Jeff, James, Joseph, and their wives, standing behind the food tables. "You'll be in better hands than I can lend you."

Flint suddenly felt a gentle nudge, and after checking its source (accompanied by a lightning, but checked movement to his hidden sidearm), moved aside as a middle-aged black man escorted a young man with a bruised head into the Barrelhouse. As the pair moved into the room, the murmurs following Zeke's speech increased, intermingled with shouts of "Bud! Bud Gardner!" from Rémy and his companions surrounding Zeke. At first, Bud's uncle beamed in relief at seeing his nephew—but then frowned at the ugly bruise that covered the right side of his nephew's face, as did his Aunt Emelia, squinting from her station behind the food tables.

Bud smiled at the calls for his name from the Czechs, and shook Rémy's hand vigorously.

"Sorry I'm late, Uncle Zeke," he said, simply. "I was kicked by a horse."

"It's all good, son," Zeke replied, winking, and waving his assurance to Emelia. "Better late than never."

As the Czechs applauded and the polka band struck up, Flint shook his head, and motioned to his companion.

"Come on, Cheevers," he grumbled. "I need a good clean beer to rinse this sugar out of my mouth."

* * * * *

The steak really *was* a little overdone—it was fine Hereford beef, though, and as he pushed his plate away and lit a cigarette to finish it off, Amos was not complaining…about the meal, in any case. But seated, once again, in the dining room of the Fairbury Hotel, Amos couldn't help thinking about the last meal he had shared here, last night, with Eugenia—who was on her way to Chicago—and with Ransom Reed Cable, Jr.—who was missing—and with Clive Masterson—who was dead.

Amos hadn't thought very much of Masterson while he was alive, and thinking about him dead didn't make much sense—but it nagged at him anyway. Especially since it was he himself who had put a bullet into Masterson and ended his life. True, the fat little bastard was trying to kill him and Miss Eugenia at the time…but it still bothered him…

…though the fact that it bothered him was sort of troubling of itself, actually, because he rarely bothered to think, much, about self-centered little bastards like Masterson. Even if he didn't really do anything but panic under the train, and grab them, and try to kill them…

I'm definitely overthinking this, Amos admitted to himself, and then smiled, remembering the advice he had given young Mr. Bud, five days ago. *First rule of juggling…keep it simple.*

Amos was not surprised, and was actually a little relieved when Wendell Evans sidled up to him and asked, "Mind if I sit down?"

"Please," Amos said, figuring that a welcome journalist was a little like a fairy caught in a photograph—unexpected, unexplainable, probably an illusion, but worth a few minutes of one's time, if only to stare in amazement.

"Looks like you've eaten," Evans began, as he picked a thumb-full of chewing tobacco from a foil pouch in his vest pocket.

"You're eating too, ah see," Amos said, wincing as he watched Evans place the ball of chaw carefully in his cheek. "Nevah understood how a man can put that mess in his mouth, then turn around and eat a decent meal."

"You should talk," Evans countered, smiling around the wad in his jaw. "I might observe that so-called cigarette of yours smells better than a lit rag, but just barely. So," he continued, "You want to share a little information, or complain about nasty personal habits all night?"

"You first," said Amos, leaning back. He was rather enjoying being in the driver's seat, though he expected the payback would be steep.

"Fine," Evans said, taking a deep breath and throwing the dice. "Ransom Reed Cable, Senior, as you may know, is the President of the Chicago, Rock Island, and Pacific Railway. 'Pacific' is the key word, here...Mr. Cable is a big believer in western expansion... and our little Fairbury, believe it or not, is the headquarters of the Western Division of the CRI&P."

"A delightful little town," Amos said. "Very...efficient. Ah once spent an entire year here in just a little over three days."

"Right," Evans continued, wondering if that would have been the *last* three days. "Anyway, according to one very talkative...well, mostly *thirsty*, source at the Division headquarters, Mr. Cable arranged for his son, Mr. Ransom Reed Cable, Jr., to take a job here this summer...a little vacation from Princeton, you see."

"How nice," Amos remarked, "Nebraska makes such a nice change of pace...from New Jersey, in any case. So, what did the young man do to be assigned to the hinterland?"

"Actually," Evans said, removing the chaw, then wrapping it in a separate piece of foil, and signaling a waiter. "He seems to have been a pretty nice kid. Did most anything he was told, so they gave him a pretty nice sendoff before he got on the train."

I know, thought Amos, taking another drag. *I was there.*

"So, he got on the train," Evans said, "And then, the story gets pretty murky. A single baggage handler says he got off the train, just a few minutes before it was scheduled to leave. One minute he was there, and the next, he was gone, out the opposite side of the train from the platform, and into the brush on the opposite side of the track."

"Did he go alone?" Amos asked, innocently.

"According to the baggage man, he didn't," Evans replied, taking a minute to place an order for a glass of wine and a *rare* steak, then continued. "Apparently, a thin man dressed in a black suit was accompanying him. No one knows if it was voluntary."

"Anyone see him since then?"

"Nobody. Not a soul...he's vanished. There have been railroad men watching the tracks, and every CRI&P station up and down the line since the wreck...nothing. And his father," Evans said, dropping his voice, "Is frantic. He has Pinkerton men on the way here, and to Lincoln, and to God knows where else."

"My, my," said Amos, noncommittally.

"*Now*, Mr. Seville," Evans said, leaning in toward his dining companion, "Did you happen to *see* Mr. Rance Cable last evening?"

"Why would you ask that?" asked Amos.

Evans held up his hand, and started counting off fingers. "You were on the train last night. In the same car as young Mr. Cable. And you ate supper here last evening. At this table. With Mr. Cable." Looking over his shoulder, he darted his eyes over to Manny, the desk clerk, then sideways at Seville. O'Manion, for his part, shrugged his shoulders at Amos and smiled.

"I've run out of fingers, Mr. Seville...and information," Evans said, leaning back on his chair. "And, to tell the truth...patience. I'm not *interested* in **your** story—I'm interested in **his**. Now...**give**." Evans flipped the four fingers of his right hand twice toward himself, then quietly waited.

Amos hesitated, then ground out his cigarette.

"You, Mr. Evans, ah a boil on mah butt," he concluded. "But, it's just possible that another set of eyes would help me...address...this situation. The question is...can ah trust you with some very ticklish information?" Amos stared coldly into the eyes of the man across from him, and Evans looked intensely back at him.

"Try me," Evans said, after a moment.

What the hell, Amos thought. And did.

LIKE MARTIAL LAW

State Troops Called to South Omaha to Preserve Order

Men May Now Go to and From Work Without Fear of Assault.

SALOONS CLOSED THE FIRST THING

One Cause of Trouble Removed—Quiet to Be Restored at All Events

OMAHA, Neb., Aug. 10 – "Move on," was the word at South Omaha, and it was pretty generally obeyed. The sheriff and his deputies having failed to restore order, it was decided at an early hour this morning to call out the state militia. The first detachment, consisting of the Omaha Guards and the Thurston Rifles, arrived on the ground about 5:15. They came on two special motor trains. The Omaha Guards were on the first train, and attached to this was the Gatling gun. The Thurston's were in the rear train. Acting Governor Majors, Adjutant General Gage, and J.C. Watson of Nebraska City accompanied the militia. At N street the trains were stopped and the companies marched to the railroad tracks. Here the members of the militia threw their quilts and camping utensils into a box car which stood in waiting.

The Omaha Guards were stationed at the foot of N street, and the Gatling gun pointed toward the east, commanding a clean sweep of the former hostile ground.

The members of the guards were formed in squads, and one section patrolled N street, another the tracks, while the third marched up Railroad avenue as far south as Hammond's packing house. The Gatling crew stood at the gun, prepared at an instant's notice to fire a volley into any strikers or men who might attempt to rise or interfere with men going to work. The Thurston rifles were marched into the Q street viaduct by Captain Scarff and patrolled Q street to Twenty-fourth and Twenty-sixth street to N. As the men passed down the street to work the rifles were stationed along the streets and afforded them a clear and unobstructed path to travel. General Gage appeared on the scene and personally moved some twenty-five strikers who had congregated, but who were quite cowed by the presence of the troops. At various times the men came in squads of three, but were forced to move on. They argued, and in some instances, of their rights as citizens to stand on the corner, but they saw a squad of the militia coming and they were persuaded to leave the place.

At Twenty-seventh and N streets the largest crowd assembled, there being about 200. They were quiet and when one member of the Omaha guards came towards them and requested them to move on they did so without hesitation or argument. The strikers were kept on the go and not allowed to stay or congregate in one place.

A Difference in the Morning

As the men came to work this morning as usual they formed in squads, not knowing of the arrival of the militia. As a gang of about 100 workers in Swifts passed under the Q street viaduct a smothered cheer arose and the men drew a good along breath when the troops were espied at the end of the viaduct. Some four or five strikers leaned over the railing as the men passed under, but did not make the customary salutation of "scabs." They were perfectly quiet. After about 7:30 o'clock, when all the workers were safe at their tasks, both companies of the militia were transferred to the exchange building, where they were allowed to break ranks and rest in the shade of the balcony.

Adjutant Gage is directing the troops, while Acting Governor Majors is on the ground giving orders. Both men refused to even conjecture as to when the troops will be withdrawn, but it is thought that they will stay here for at least two or three days ans possibly a week. About the first order emanating from the military department was for the closing of the saloons. It went into immediate effect. This will help matters by compelling some of the more demonstrative rioters to sober up. The presence of the troops has had a quieting effect, and it is thought that trouble will rapidly subside.

32

Friday, August 10, 1894
8:17 pm

The bucket of water steamed as the young Oriental woman carefully poured it into the tub, while the man sitting in it smoked…and fumed. Another man might have smiled at the irony—Eduard Novak had spent most of the day getting *out* of hot water. Now, though trying hard to maintain an external appearance of relaxation and routine—he had spent every Friday night in this same bathhouse, and he badly wanted to reassure his followers that, despite the circumstances, nothing had changed—Novak's anger at how the day had progressed was probably sufficient to keep the water steaming, even without the tender ministrations of his lovely attendant.

Novak took a deep breath, and considered playing this morning's debacle over again in his mind—but the Bohemian was at heart a practical man, and instead decided to turn a critical eye on his broader actions over the last several weeks, in hopes of charting a future course. The Hammond plant, he and his fellow union organizers had reckoned, had been deserving of a strike ever since the meatcarvers' wages had been frozen, while their "company town" rents had increased. True, his men could have moved into more reasonably priced neighborhoods farther away from the plants, but without the benefit of public transit, the costs would have been considerable. And what gave the bosses the right to raise those rents in the first place?

No, it had been necessary to take action—and action became even more imperative when the Hammond managers had immediately hired scab laborers to fill their jobs at the plant. They had swarmed into the city by the boxcar load, from every little fleabite borough in Nebraska and Iowa that was facing hard times…and there were plenty of them. His men had harassed the scabs from the beginning, of course—but for every man that his men had managed to frighten off, two more clamored to take their place.

"Girl, get towel," Novak said in heavily accented English, stepping out of the tub. The Japanese girl obliged. Gently, she placed the towel around him, and directed him toward the side room, where the man allowed himself to be guided onto the draped massage table, still deep in his thoughts as the woman worked on his tired muscles.

Had it been necessary to order his men to attack, and in two cases, kill those scab workers after their shifts? Perhaps that was the turning point, a few days ago, the point at which the plant bosses and their puppet governor had decided to call the militia out. Did the plant managers really care about the scabs that much? *No,* Novak grunted to himself—the real turning point had been when the grain barns had been burned to the ground. It hadn't affected immediate production, but had ground the purchase of new beef to a standstill, since additional cattle couldn't be fed. *Just one more push,* Novak reflected. *One more fire, or explosion—or maybe a train wrecking, such as they had just had in Lincoln...would have toppled 'em,* Novak concluded. We were so close...

And we'll be that close again. Despite the presence of the militia, the scab workers at the factory could still be targeted—*especially after hours,* Novak reasoned. And their next plan would be to strike at the plant manager himself. Novak's men had been watching his big house, and would soon strike...in a very different way.

The petite woman's clever hands had completed their work, and as such, she bowed routinely and gently urged the man to a sitting position. She lifted his towel and walked it over to the laundry chute...then, after tossing it in, hesitated, as if glimpsing something out of place. With a perplexed look, the girl looked back at Novak.

Novak obeyed his inner impulse of caution—he crossed the room and drew his knife from a small sheath secreted in the sleeve of his coat. Approaching the laundry chute, he saw that the woman was bending into it and pulling out a long, white knotted chord...

Novak's mind ran fast, realizing that whoever had climbed the rope was now likely to be in the room with him.

His turn into the swinging sap could not have been better timed, at least from Lynch's perspective. The lead-filled leather sack landed squarely against the Bohemian's temple, and the man fell onto the floor with a heavy thud. With a lightning backhanded stroke, the shirtless Lynch immediately arched another blow into the skull of the girl, stifling her scream and dropping her to the floor as well. Working quickly, Lynch pulled a short, knotted length of cord from his pants pocket, wrapped it onced about each hand, and tightened the slack around Novak's neck, while jamming his knee onto the center of the prone man's back. There was an ugly *crack,* and in the space of two minutes, it was all over.

With speed, Lynch checked the prostrate girl...*out cold,* he confirmed, and decided without emotion that killing her would not be necessary after

298

all—and would, in fact, waste valuable time. Lynch reckoned that he had only another ten or twelve minutes before Novak's bodyguard would enter the room and check on his boss. Hoisting up the body of the union leader by his armpits, Lynch dragged him to the laundry chute, and unceremoniously dumped him headfirst into the room below, where his head made a strange cracking sort of *splat* when it hit the concrete. Backing into the laundry chute, Lynch took the cord in both gloved hands, and re-tested its knot against the steam pipes that were running under its frames inside the lower doorframe of the chute, before finally trusting it with his whole weight.   In under a minute, he had lowered himself sufficiently to land with a plop on Novak's body, waiting to cushion his descent in the deserted laundry room.

I found some luck there, Lynch thought in satisfaction. The laundry had been deserted in the afternoon and evening hours during his afternoon reconnaissance.   Since the laundry was operated by the same girls who plied their trade two floors above—it being a standard arrangement that allowed maximum utility of labor—it was deserted when the girls were busy in the bathhouse or the other rooms adjoining them…making the laundry room an ideal place to wait for his target until the man was ensconced in his bath. He had been mildly concerned, of course, over some of the details of his plans—being able to maintain his stealth in climbing the rope during his ascent through the tin-covered laundry chute, the exactness of the target's schedule, and the strength of the cord (stolen from both sides of the rolling bamboo shade). But he had a very good escape route in case of discovery, and when that did not happen, it was only a matter of waiting under the draped massage table until the massage girl left the room before he—***introduced*** himself—to the unfortunate Mr. Novak.

Why had the girl chosen to notice the rope at that moment? It had hung there all afternoon and evening, Lynch mused as he hoisted the body of the Bohemian over his shoulder in a fireman's carry, and turned toward the narrow door of the laundry room. *I must have left it disturbed in some way after the climb—left it conspicuous in some way, not hanging straight down against the inner wall of the chute as before.* Cracking the door and peeking out into the interior hallway of the basement, he was satisfied that his earlier observations were correct—it was completely deserted—and made his way to the basement window in the room across the hall, through which his hired rig could be seen still patiently waiting in the alley.

Lifting Novak's body to the back of the wagon, talking all the while as if to a drunken friend, Lynch's smile of satisfaction grew into a grin of inspiration. *Wonder if the client would consider a little bonus for how the body will be discovered?*

*   *   *   *   *

It had been a long and much-needed late afternoon and evening walk, despite its troubling undercurrents, and George Washington Davis would probably have turned straight into his cornhusk bed in the Lonsdale toolshed south of Lincoln—but for the sight of the young woman in the stable, milking the lone cow by the light of a kerosene lamp. As he approached, Davis coughed, and the young woman started, nearly spilling the milk.

"George!" she said, breathing hard, and steadying the pail. "You sure startled me!"

"Sorry, ma'am," Davis said, cheerfully, bowing slightly and reaching to remove a hat that wasn't there—Sarah Lonsdale made a man do that. Sarah nodded, but oddly, wasn't smiling. In fact, in the last dim rays of the summer twilight, her face looked a little sad.

"Is there anything wrong, ma'am?"

"Uh, just a moment, George," she said, abruptly. "Stay here, would you please?"

Sarah, not much more than a slip of a girl, was always jumping up to attack any problem, so seeing her snatch up the bucket and speed back to the house with no warning was no surprise—though going around the back was a little odd. Sarah had always been kind to him—hellfire, had always been kind to everyone, even that damn hog Satan, as far as he could tell— so Davis was likely to cut it back her way where a little odd behavior was concerned.

In less than a minute, Sarah returned, hauling a covered platter with...was that...*meatloaf?* As Sarah approached, Davis' mouth started to water, and reached for the offered plate with relish.

"That looks ver' good, Ms. Lonsdale...yes, indeed it does..." Davis said, removing the towel, absently scooping a spoonful of supper into his watering mouth, and craning his neck past Sarah Lonsdale to peer back toward the house and into the falling night. There appeared to be a few buggies pulled up to the house, and...*was that Thunder?* Recognition flooded over him...*Will Saxton's horse.* Suddenly, his stomach fell—just as it had when Davis last ran into Lonsdale's neighbor...accidentally, last night, at the site of the wreck.

Catching the look of mild panic in Davis' eyes, Sarah cast hers downward. "Enjoy the meal, George," she said, quietly, and backed out of the narrow door of the stable, allowing Davis a view of the darkening yard through the red, kerosene-lit frame of the kitchen door. It was full of approaching men, carrying lanterns, and murmuring in the dark.

Well, thought Davis, as he hastily ate another bite of meatloaf, *no choice but to face it now, boy.*

33

Friday, August 10, 1894
8:38 pm

Her story was very hard to believe…lying was second nature to the young woman. But then again, she wasn't very good at it.

"Please help me understand—you say that Ezekiel Gardner "ran into" you downtown this afternoon," Miles McGee said, coolly smoking a cigar in the parlor of his darkened apartment, staring out the window at the arclights of the Lincoln theatre district through the narrow slits of the Venetian blinds, just a block away. "And that he was not *angry* with you for stealing the grain agreement?"

"I've already told you, darling, he believes he *lost* the agreement," Maggie said, dragging on a cigarette, then dangling it languidly as she leaned back on the sofa to reach for a glass of wine on an elaborate mahogany endtable with her free hand. Dressed in a white cotton shift and pantaloons that covered her from ankle to collarbone…*well, almost*, reflected McGee…she was the picture of ease and sensuality. *Very difficult to pull off a lie with this degree of ease*, thought McGee, and most who dealt with him would have agreed that he was a foremost expert in that particular field. *Still…*

"He loses things, Miles," Maggie explained, grinning with an inner glow of self-assured cleverness that most would have agreed that she didn't really possess. "He misplaces combs, watches, hell, even bills and papers, all the *time*. So," she concluded, "when he ran into me this afternoon—with an armload of *cinnamon buns*, for Christ's sake!—he had absolutely no animosity towards me. He believes I'm doing a *job*, that's all," Maggie giggled, then caught herself, and quickly ground out her cigarette. Sidling up to McGee, who was seated in a large leather armchair next to the window, she placed her head on his knee and beamed her blue eyes up at him with a singularly unconvincing smile. "Of course, darling, you know *that* part isn't true."

Of course it is dear—you are as transparent as glass, thought McGee, smiling down at her indulgently and patting her cheek. *Which tends to make your other story believable…*

"So—where is it that you believe he is going to…*retrieve* this copy of the agreement?" McGee queried, staring out the window again at the approaches to his rooms in the street below. *They should be along any time now…*

302

"Out to Sidney," she said, standing and stretching before she sauntered back over to the couch and folded herself into its leather embrace. "He still has friends, and a strongbox out there, at some bank, I think." Once again, her body language spoke of complete, ingenuous honesty.

"Thank you my dear," said McGee, smiling. "Now, if you don't mind, please make yourself scarce for a few hours, won't you? I have a meeting with some…business associates…this evening, and I would like not to be disturbed."

Maggie smiled, raised her glass, drained it, and strolled back into the bedroom to get dressed. McGee's eyes followed her with interest. *A beautiful girl…and so patently dishonest. So easy to read…so…honest, in a converse sort of way.* Picking up his cigar, he looked out the window, waiting for his guests.

* * * * *

The beef had been served, the tableware removed, and the dining room of the Fairbury hotel was mostly deserted. Thirty feet away, Manny O'Manion was leaning on the front desk and hungrily reading the Lincoln Journal, which contained a rousing story about last night's Rock Island wreck up in Lincoln. He was completely engrossed—a good many of the wreck victims had joined the ill-fated train here in Fairbury—a few had even had dinner here that very evening! Consequently, the two patrons remaining in the dining room were of little interest…

"So," Evans said, lowering his voice to nearly a whisper, and attempting, with little success, to keep the note of incredulity out of it. "Am I to understand that you actually *saw* the man that **kidnapped** Cable from the train?"

"Ah saw a man *leave* with young Mr. Cable," corrected Amos. "Ah didn't know anything about any kidnapping until noon today…so ah scooted right on over here to see if ah could help John Langston find the man."

Evans thought that Seville's explanation sounded a mite fishy—that Amos Seville wasn't the sort to come running to help a lawman without an angle—but kept it to himself.

"I'm sure he was grateful for the help," he said instead. "Does he have a plan for capturing our friend?"

"Sure he does," Amos said, drawing on his waning cigarette and exhaling it languidly toward the ceiling. "He plans to throw his hands up and wait for the Pinkertons to arrive." Amos ground out the butt, and added, "Ah hate Pinkertons."

"Can't say I like them myself—get in the way of a good story," Evans agreed. "So, what do we do?"

"We use our heads," Seville said, and dropped his voice even further, causing Evans to lean toward him. "If he's a hundred miles away, or even ten, we don't have a chance in hell of finding Cable—so we ah forced to concentrate on the local area around Fairbury—do you agree?"

"I guess so," said Evans. "But that sounds a little like the man that spent all night under the street lamp looking for a dime—after he had dropped it in the cornfield. He said that—"

"He said that the light was better there—yes, ah *may* have heard that one." Amos interrupted, though Evans admitted to himself that there might have been a *bit* of an amused look on his face. "But things aren't as bad as they might seem. The track has been watched, up and down the line, since about ten last night. There was only one train in and out of Fairbury after that, and the passenger brakeman working the platform—he has *seen* Cable before, hell, everybody in *town* has—swears that Cable was not on the train. Could have left from a nearby town—but if it was against his will, the only way that would happen was if it was unconscious. Looks pretty fishy, and nobody is reporting anything fishy...not at any station within 50 miles, that is."

"How do you know that?" Evans couldn't help asking. *Could be that's why I'm a reporter*, he admitted to himself.

"Stationmasters tend to talk to each other way out here," said Amos. "Do each other favors. The local one is named Nathan Brockhurst—he's a...well, ah'd call him a friend—although he'd call me what ah called you..."

"'A boil on mah butt,' was the line, I believe...but I'm not quoting you on anything, I assure you," Evans said, now smirking. "Couldn't he have taken Cable overland, though?"

"Possible, ah guess," Amos admitted. "But if Cable was kidnapped, he'd have to be hidden in a wagon, or a boat—precious little water around here, ah've noticed—and probably drugged. It's a risk."

"So, let's say he's local," Evans agreed. "Where do we start looking?"

"Well, when ah'm troubled, confused, and generally mystified," Amos said, expansively, "Ah ask *questions.*"

"Believe I may have heard of the technique," replied Evans, exaggerating a sigh. "What did you learn?"

"Seems that someone ran into a tall, thin, skeleton-faced man right here in the hotel, just this morning," Amos said, offhandedly, referring to the conversation that he had completed earlier with Nathan Brockhurst—the first man he had visited after checking in with that worthless piece of...sheriff, John Langston.. As he examined his fingers, he reveled a bit in his companion's surprise.

"And *another* man...who shall remain *nameless*," Amos continued, glancing up and over at Manny O'Manion, still entirely absorbed in his newspaper behind the hotel desk, "noticed that the man had happened to use that telephone, right here in the lobby. Now, ah'm not one to say that 'ol Manny there likes to eavesdrop...but ah happen to know that this particular telephone closet has a door that is *particularly* difficult to close."

"And the upshot is...?" Evans encouraged.

"That it is just possible our friend will show up here again...tomorrow, at noon, to receive a telephone call."

"I must say, it's very...generous...of you to share your story with me, Mr. Seville," Evans remarked coolly, the suspicion (and the tobacco juice) nearly dripping from his lips. "I wonder what you want in return?"

"Oh, we'll think of something, ah assure you," Amos said, yawning, hoping that the stretch that accompanied it would unclench his aching shoulder. "But first, my dear *partner*—ah believe that a good night's sleep is in order. Manny...check, please."

* * * * *

Zeke was surprised to see Bud arrive so late—but even more stunned to observe Dr. Flippin coming in with him.

"Hello, Flip," said Zeke, "Got a minute?"

Dr. Flippin nodded, and Zeke murmured to Rufus, who nodded back and managed to distract the Czechs for a minute or two.

In a dark corner of the Barrelhouse, Zeke asked, in a voice that could barely be heard over the polka music, "What happened, Doc?"

"Bud has a pretty bad bump on the head, but he'll be O.K., I think. As far as I can tell, your nephew here was laying on the train tracks north of town, out cold, and a fellah pulled him off at the last minute. His name was LeBlanc."

Zeke was shocked, but thought a moment. "How do we know that LeBlanc didn't put him there?"

"I don't know anything of the sort—only what the engineer told me. I was sitting in the passenger car when the train stopped, and they asked me to take the boy back to my office. I'm sure that I must have been the only doctor on the train, or they would have asked someone more—easily sunburned."

Zeke smiled. "Thanks, Doc." Pausing, he lowered his voice as he continued, "How's your son doing?"

"He's O.K., too, I think," Flippin's voice rivaled Zeke's for silence. "I just wanted to say…thanks for the help."

Zeke said, "I didn't do anything that your son wouldn't have done, if he'd had half a chance to talk for himself."

"Well…thanks. The City police…"

"Can be very close-minded. It really wasn't anything, and you know that. When a man's wife is accosted on the street—any man would take action."

"Uh...the man's bruises were pretty extensive, Zeke." Flippin observed.

"They'll heal." Zeke's hand was extended, and Flippin took it.

* * * * *

In downtown Lincoln, the Friday night follies had begun.

There were six saloons on O Street between the Burlington station and the Funke Opera House at 12th Street, where the arc-lights made deep shadows behind the clapboard marquee. By 8 p.m., every one of these establishments was full to the rafters with railroad men, tradesmen, sales clerks…and soldiers. Well, state militiamen anyway, in their company uniforms that had lain in mothballs for 51 weeks, and were now freshly brushed to what perfection was possible after a long train ride into the capital. They had been arriving for hours, now, at all five stations, and the recently closed, then re-opened Burlington and UP rail lines south of town had created long, hot delays that only a cold drink could cure.

The treatment was readily available—though not as available as it might have been, given the unexpected closure of the Barrelhouse over on R Street. Nevertheless, hundreds of farmers, freighters, businessmen, barbers, and bartenders, dressed in uniforms that were too big and too small, varying from amazingly gaudy to wonderfully simple, set free of work and the womenfolk—cut themselves loose on the main street of Lincoln, Nebraska, and howled at the moon. They toasted "their" victory that very morning on the streets of Omaha, where the striking Bohemians were put down by their brave fellow militiamen, standing behind Gatling guns along the streets, alleys, and tracks that led to the Hammond plant. Despite the loss of a few grain barns to fire, the men of Nebraska had shown their fortitude, and put down the rebellion of the cursed foreigners!

Or something like that. *Let's have another beer, bartender...*

Henri Flint and Charles Cheevers, searching for a quiet drink to wash what they perceived as Zeke Gardner's pious speechifying out of their jaded ears, had instead run into saloon after saloon filled with a far greater quantity of gas than they had attempted to escape back at the Barrelhouse. *Long live the great State of Nebraska!* Cheevers was just turning to his partner to suggest their departure when a fat young private standing next to him at the bar drunkenly raised his glass in salute and showered him in beer, before falling onto a table of patrons. Drenched to the skin, Cheevers' arm sped to his holster, but a familiar hand beat him there—and held it, whispering, "Just wait."

From the midst of the wreckage, a big man dressed in greasy overalls seated with similarly dressed patrons immediately rose, walked up to the private, and growled, "You militia bastards owe us a beer." His chin was about three inches from the private's face, and his eyes were angry, looking for a fight.

"Easy, son." A gray-haired sergeant was already rising from the other end of the bar, and held up his hands to the man in overalls. "The private here was just a little too enthusiastic, that's all..."

"*Screw* him *and* his enthusiasm," interrupted the big man. "Some of us haven't had work for weeks, mister soldier man...and you peckers come into town, knocking over everything..."

"Easy, Jones," urged one of his companions.

"I *ain't* taking it easy," Jones said, shrugging off his friend's arm on his shoulder and turning on him as the pressure in his boiler reached 100 pounds or better. "We sit out there day after day in that damn tent town, near a hundred of us, sweatin' like pigs, waiting for the railroads to call us in for a day here, or a day there, and never a dime between jobs. And then these bastards come into town, knocking around the only beer we see'd in a month—" The man's eyes could have been filled with sorrow, or rage, but Flint's eyes saw...*possibility.*

307

"We'll pay for the beer, Pard," said the sergeant, evenly, turning to his companions, dressed in similar uniforms. "Boys, show your silver for Private Williams, here—it'll come out of his pay at the end of the week." Under the sergeant's steady gaze, each man in his squad grumbled, dug in their pockets, and together produced about a dollar in nickels and dimes. This action appeared to mollify Jones' companions, who managed to bring the large man back to his table, and signaled the bartender for another pitcher of beer.

"Yep...real *possibilities* here," remarked Flint, grinning as he jerked his head to the door. "Time to find the boss."

* * * * *

Most of the Czechs had left, but Piotr Rémy and his lieutenants, including the looming figure of Andryev Malý, had stayed to speak at length with Zeke, Rufus, and Zeke's nephews, as the women of St. Theresa's quietly settled the disorder of the meal's aftermath. Remy nodded as Zeke laid out the plan.

"Tomorrow morning, then," Zeke said, "you'll meet with Rufus and his boys here, and your men will be assigned to wagons and to farms. We will pay in advance for three days' work, and pay for another four days on Friday. Afterwards—well, we'll do our best, but there are no promises."

"We don't need a promise, Mr. Zeke," Remy assured him. "We need only...a risk?...no, a *chance*."

"You'll get both," smiled Zeke, sticking out a hand. "Good luck."

"We can always make use of good luck," Remy said, "but we need, from what you say, *bravery* too, I think. Like Mr. Bud—you should see him, Mr. Zeke. Yesterday, he fights big Andryev, here, to save a beautiful girl."

All eyes, and a few appreciative voices, turned to Bud, who did his best to crawl into his shoes.

"There's a story *there*, I'll reckon," Johnny threw in, and to Bud's ears, his tone of voice indicated an altogether unreasonable enthusiasm to get to the bottom of it.

Remy nodded. "Yes, he is...he is a *hero*, I think."

"I'm no hero," Bud interjected. "I-I just..."

"A hero is just an idiot with his heart in the right place, Bud," Zeke stated, which seemed to satisfy Remy and the rest of the Czechs, whose smiles relayed from one to another as they murmured their translations around the Barrelhouse. It wasn't the first time Bud had heard himself called a *hlupak* in Czech—and thinking on meeting Anna Marie's brothers earlier in the day, he calculated that it probably wouldn't be the last, either.

* * * * *

Cheevers and Flint missed the unassuming gray door facing 13th Street two times before finally backtracking and finding the entrance to McGee's upper rooms. Faced with a single door at the top of a dimly lit three-story stairwell, they knocked, then naturally assumed their positions on either side of the door jams, hands at the ready near their firearms. A small panel slid aside in the center of the door, and Franks' voice filled the empty landing.

"Who's out there?" the voice spoke, a bit nervously, Flint noticed. *From a position of strength? No wonder that they called us in.*

"Flint and Cheevers," Flint replied, easing his hand off his gun. "We're here to see McGee."

Murmurs from within the room slipped through the door—followed by the sound of the door bolt being pulled back with a jerk that echoed like a shot within the hollow stairwell. Stepping into the more brightly lit space within, the men from Chicago gazed about them, and immediately counted the number of potential adversaries by their guns. As introductions were made, Flint kept a running total. *There was Franks, who had answered the door—a toady, but at least not so stupid as to openly show his arms—bulge in the back of the coat and one at the left breast pocket—a derringer,* Flint guessed. *There was Billy, bristling with guns, enthusiasm, but little intelligence—next to worthless—and there was LeBlanc, clearly the leader of the other two, physically imposing—a bully, by the looks of him, but too emotional to be truly counted upon. All in all, a sorry show,* Flint concluded.

"I'm Kohlman," said a man, chewing on a pickle. *The lawyer, immediately identifiable by sight, sound, and smell,* reckoned Flint. *There's one around every powerful man, like a fly around a dung-heap. That leaves...*

"My name is McGee." A gray-bearded man with silver spectacles propped in front of cold, blue eyes stared back at the two newcomers, utterly confident, and in complete command of everyone in the room, judging the newcomers objectively from a position of veiled power. *Ah, the infamous Mr. McGee.* Flint nodded in courtesy, and Cheevers did the same.

"Have a drink, gentlemen," McGee said smoothly, though neither made a move toward the bourbon that was at hand. "I was expecting you an hour ago—I am informed that the train arrived on time. What kept you gentlemen?"

"Reconnoitering," said Flint, simply. "We dropped by an interesting little gathering at Mr. Gardner's place—the Barrelhouse, I believe it is called."

"Indeed?" McGee said, taking a seat by the window in a large leather armchair, and lighting a cigar. After he had drawn it to light, he asked, "And what did you learn there, Mr. Flint?"

"Gardner was doing his best to round up extra hands—to shell and to guard the corn, I imagine," Flint replied. "He was having some luck—there must have been sixty Czechs in there, and a dozen or so railroad men."

That got LeBlanc's attention. "Seventy men?" he squeaked. "Why, we haven't got…"

"…anywhere near that many," McGee finished for him. "But then again, we've barely started, haven't we? That was to be *your* job, Mr. Flint…rallying additional support for our…little cause, here."

Was? Flint felt a pang of unease wash over him.

"Pardon the interruption…do go on," said McGee, expansively, waving his cigar. "Did you learn anything else?"

"Just that Gardner is planning to take off for somewhere tomorrow morning," Flint relayed. "He told the new men that they would be under the orders of 'his family,' whoever that is, for a day or two, then he would return to get the first loads of grain into Lincoln."

"That cinches it up," said LeBlanc, grumbling. "There's another copy of the agreement, somewhere…"

"It also correlates to a little slip that Dawes made this afternoon at the hearing," Kohlman interjected. "Dawes is confident that there really is another copy of the sales agreement, and that it will appear on Monday…in court."

"There are…other indications, as well," McGee said quietly, thinking back on his conversation with Maggie, then coming to a decision. "Mr. Flint—Mr. Cheevers—I'm afraid we have a small task for the both of you to complete before we can finally turn you loose on your primary task—that is, assembling a larger…organization…against our opposition."

Flint sighed. "It's a shame, Mr. McGee. There appears, from even our short reconnaissance, to be a lot of free labor about—discontented, and ready for a little silver in their pockets."

"True enough," McGee agreed, "And I'm sure that Mr. LeBlanc and his men here will do their best to start organizing it in your absence. But there is really little need to do much until the grain is ready to be hauled—and that will be several days, at any rate. No, the greater task at hand is to recover a particular document from Mr. Gardner before he can bring it into court on Monday morning."

"Wouldn't it be better," asked Cheevers, finally deciding to chime in, "to take care of him before he heads off to…where in the hell is he going anyway?"

"To Sidney, Nebraska, by all indications," said McGee. "About 300 miles west of here. Apparently, Gardner spent a good bit of time out there about 20 years ago, before he took a job here as Deputy Sheriff. And, no, I think that our strategy should be to allow him to retrieve the document before he is…encountered. He may have told his family about its location, and a premature…confrontation…might only delay its recovery." McGee leveled his dead eyes at Flint. "I want that document in my hands, Mr. Flint. Can the two of you get it for me?"

"Well, I'm still not sure you need both of us—I have a lot of faith in Mr. Cheevers' abilities," Flint said, which extracted a brief nod from Cheevers. "However," he went on, "If you wish it absolutely…"

"I do, Mr. Flint," McGee said, cutting him off. "I do indeed."

* * * * *

Trudeau didn't sleep—not much, anyway, and being on almost continuous guard duty for over 24 hours, therefore, had not been much of a hardship. Nevertheless, he was relieved to hear the shuffling in the darkness just outside the light of the small campfire. Though the warm night hadn't exactly called for it, the thin man had kept it burning outside the broken down barn where Cable was now sleeping—the remote site of the former Pony Express Station had little else to draw anyone toward it. As usual, his visitor made a passable imitation of a nightjar before approaching, answered by Trudeau's countersign. The man walking into the light of the campfire had a long rifle in his hand.

"Evenin,' Rankin," Jack Trudeau said, not pausing from his razor sharpening. "Trains must have been running on time."

311

"Yeah, but it's a long walk from Fairbury," Jasper Rankin said, then shook his head. "You could have left me my horse, at least."

"Boss' orders," Trudeau said. "Needed it to transport that little squint Cable in there, and he thought leaving it in Fairbury after this morning's telephone call might look suspicious."

"Well, the Boss is usually right," agreed Rankin. "Any coffee?"

"Help yourself," Trudeau said, still scraping away.

Pouring himself a cup, Rankin shook his head. "There's not gonna be anything left of that to use, if you keep that up."

"There'll be enough," Trudeau said, and his grin danced in the firelight as he stared at the barn where Cable fitfully slept.

34

Saturday, August 11, 1894
6:00 am

Saturday morning dawned with a very different set of sights and sounds than Larry Gardner had become accustomed to during his short tenure in Omaha—"Reveille" sounding from a single bugle, a flag running up a makeshift pole under salute, and the murmur of hundreds of men, encamped about the gates of the Hammond meat packing plant. Swinging into his six o'clock shift with the other "scabs," the sight of the militia lightened Larry's heart like no other sight he had ever beheld, and he fairly sung his way into the plant through its massive wrought iron gates.

No spitting. No catcalls. No eggs, knives, or looks that could kill. No *nothing.* It was so peaceful...goddamned beautiful, Larry decided, and found himself whistling "Reveille" as he checked into the plant, grabbing his (and formerly his brother, Roger's) time chit from the rack and handing it to his shift boss before striding through a side door into the dim interior of the slaughterhouse.

In this part of the building, four long lines of empty hooks hung over Larry's head, and beneath them a trail of blood had dripped on the sawdust leading ominously from the living cattle that were rustling in the pens behind the plant. Larry knew that his first job would be to scoop away the sawdust from beneath the hooks and replace it afresh. From somewhere else in the depths of the plant, Larry could hear the chugging of a steam motor, and without warning, the long chains above his head lurched forward with a clank and a jingling rattle. Larry, as the first worker in this section, found a shovel and wheelbarrow, and was directly under the line scooping up the sawdust when he felt a thud on his shoulder, followed immediately by a heavy weight shoving him out of the way. Having strayed under the lines before when they were filled with beef carcasses, Larry automatically stumbled out of the way into the narrow space between the hooks. *How had the butchers started the line so early...?* he wondered, as his eyes wandered to the carcass that had nudged him...

...and were rubbed in disbelief, followed by shock and revulsion.

It wasn't a beef carcass.

Above his head, the naked torso of a man swung upside down from a single overhead hook, pierced through both Achilles tendons in the same way that a beef carcass was usually handled. The man's vacant eyes were open, his tongue was black, and blood had coagulated along the length of his arms and into his matted black hair. Attached to his scalp—*with a fishing hook?*—was a cardboard sign that clearly read, Be Like Me and Join the Union.

I gotta get out of this town. With a queasy stomach, Larry went to find his boss.

* * * * *

Altogether a very satisfactory operation, reflected Lynch, observing the beehive of activity around the Hammond plant across the tracks at Railroad Avenue through field glasses. Though the militia had all the entrances covered last night, they had failed to consider the steam tunnels under the warehouse—a common mistake, even for practiced police officers. It had been simplicity itself to evade the posted guards and place Mr. Novak on the carcass rack.

Lowering the field glasses, Lynch nearly chuckled, then abruptly stopped. *Almost perfect...except...*

Gardner's nephew. Lynch's good mood immediately soured, as he recalled the events of Thursday afternoon. Was the boy listening at the keyhole when this job was assigned? And what had he heard?

Probably nothing, Lynch admitted. *Probably.* But Lynch knew Zeke—had served with him for years, and knew his qualities, better, perhaps, than any other person did—or longer, in any event. And that knowledge spoke of a crafty, sharp-witted bastard who wouldn't quit until he got what he was after.

Had Bud heard of his move to Omaha? Worse, had he heard of the connection to the Rock Island wreck?

Damned careless of me, concluded Lynch. *Guess I'm gonna need to do something about that boy.*

NEBRASKA STATE JOURNAL

LINCOLN, NEBRASKA   AUGUST 11, 1894   NUMBER 383

CAUGHT A FIEND

Wrecker of the Rock Island Train Placed Behind Bars

HIS IDENTITY IS VOUCHED FOR

Responsible for Terrible Death of Eleven Human Beings

NEITHER DENIES NOR CONFIRMS

Strong Chain of Evidence in Possession of the Lincoln Police

George Washington Davis, the dastardly perpetrator of the murder and massacre, which involved eleven lives and fifteen injured, caused by Thursday night's wreck on the Rock Island road where it crosses the Union Pacific and Burlington tracks, four miles south of the city, has been captured. He was caught by City Detective Malone on the farm owned by the Messrs Lonsdale, situated six miles southwest of the city, at about half past nine last night, and two hours later he was lodged behind the bars of the city prison at police headquarters.

Seen at the Wreck

Thursday night when the catastrophe occurred, and as stated before THE JOURNAL, Brakeman Harry Foote was the first to extricate himself from the mass of debris and burning wood. As he got clear of the prostrate and fallen cars he saw a big black Negro running along the bed of Salt Creek and away from the wreck. He was carrying a lantern and Foote, not seeing the color and thinking that it was one of the trainmen who had escaped and was going for help, called to him that he, Foote, was all right. The Negro for some reason stopped, turned, and came back towards the wreck and Harry Foote saw his mistake. He was too excited at the time, however, to think of anything but helping the persons imprisoned and to this, as before stated, he directed his entire attention.

Two Witnesses

With the awful discovery of Will Saxton, the one who discovered the crowbar and fishplates in the grass, became generally known, Harry had his suspicions aroused, but on searching for the Negro amid the crowd of persons who had gathered he found that the man had utterly disappeared.

The suspicion became a certainty but Harry wisely kept his own cousel until James Malone, the city detective, arrived and to him he divulged the circumstances and his suspicions.

315

Malone carefully weighed every word and pondered upon the discovery. Foote, thinking him a doubting Thomas, exhibited the fish plates, crowbars, bolts, burrs, and the dents in the ties. This almost convinced Malone, but seeking Will Saxton, he got him to tell the story of the find, after doing which he told the detectives about having seen a big Negro also and of the suspicious way he acted, working, and then not working, something thus to be doing, something he disliked.

This convinced Malone that there was something in the suspicion. For an hour he lingered around the wreck, collecting all the data possible. He had been informed meanwhile that the villain had possibly gone to Mr. Lonsdale's place, and thither he drove. No one there had seen him for two or three days, but they were able to tell his name. After waiting around for some time, and with this new point, Malone drove back to the city, where he made inquiries about the Negro, and found that he had paid Charlie Raymond, a hack driver, one dillar to bring him back from the wreck to the city. He also succeeded in finding his lantern and revolver, which he left at the Negros club rooms on P Street, between 8th and 9th street.

The Negros Story

In the course of his investigations, he ran across a man named Weems, who told him that he, Davis, had been caught in thewreck, and had lost his coat, together with $200, the sale of one of Max Cobb's horses, at Kearney. When asked how he came to be on the train, he answered that he had tramped across the country to the Rock Island Road near Fairbury, and had there taken the train.

Malone thought that this was the wildest and most improbable story he had ever heard of, so that more than ever the conviction that he was on the right track was forced upon him. Returning to the police station, he secured his wagon, and returned to the Messrs. Lonsdale, where concluded that he would stay until his game did turn up. At about a quarter past nine o'clock, the villain turned the corner of the stable, coolly whistling. Malone stepped to him with the stereotyped remark, "I want you." The darkey grinned and asked, "Wha' fo?" Malone informed him of the seriousness of the charge, but the villain coolly laughed and refused to deny the awful charge.

When he asked how he came there, he explained that he was at the club rooms when he heard the crash, and that he, with some companions, started out immediately for the scene. It just took Malone one hour to drive there Thursday night and not believing this very improbable, this impossible story, he said, "I want you, anyhow." The fiend made no response, but quietly went with his captor.

On the way to the city Malone, thinking to surprise him, asked: "George, did it make much noise when it fell?"

316

Without thinking, the dastard replied:

"Only when de ingine struck de bottom: the odder didn't mek much racket."

In the minds of the authorities there isn't the least doubt but what Davis is the man who caused the horrible catastrophe. His general demeanor, apparent character, and his refusal to either affirm or deny the accusation all go to confirm the suspicion.

Davis says he was born and until three years ago lived in Washington, D.C., and that since that time, he has lived in Nebraska. He has a record, and is known to have served several terms in county jails.

He was seen the night before the wreck by the Ryan boys going towards the wreck before it happened.

A telegram, asking for his apprehension, from a sheriff in Kearney, was received yesterday.

35

Saturday, August 11, 1894
7:00 am

Zeke Gardner closed the morning paper with a violent snap and gazed out the window in disgust. **George Davis?!?** *Well, the railroads had to find* **somebody** *to pin it on…and Detective Frank Malone seems to be obliging them nicely. Damned pinhead…*

Outside, Zeke observed the shriveled fields of northwestern Lancaster County slipping by as the Burlington train gathered speed. Inside the car, things were little better. This was definitely *not* one of the luxurious Pullman cars at the front of the train—instead, Zeke found himself in something more akin to the bench-seated troop cars that he had grown accustomed to in the War. Zeke's lower back had already become acquainted with a new friend—the third horizontal wooden strake in his backrest, jutting so jovially out of line into his fifth lumbar vertebra, in order to make room for the gas line that ran from the tanks under the car to the heater up at the front. Why the hell they couldn't run that damn line *under* the seat was a question for the ages, or some half-drunk car designer back east somewhere…

Still, he sighed, *there were* **some** *advantages to traveling second class.* Looking about, Zeke found himself surrounded mostly by immigrants— tattered men and women with bundles at their feet and in their laps, and a fair number of them were children. Of course, not all of them were **stationary** bundles, sleeping to the rocking motion of the train—many of them were either bawling at the early hour of their departure or running up and down the aisle, despite the occasional shushing by their parents in a tone of voice that was universally understood, even if their dialects weren't. The cheaper fare that Zeke had rendered tended to draw just this sort of passenger, whereas jobbers, and salesmen—and other "businessmen" of a considerably more dangerous profession—were likely to take more comfortable seating further forward. This served Zeke's purpose just fine—seated in the last row of the last passenger car in the train, he was well-positioned to spot anyone suspicious who might come back to look for him—at least until they changed trains in Columbus to the Union Pacific line for the trip west.

Zeke expected interference on his way to retrieve his parcel—given the hints he had dropped, he'd have been fairly disappointed if it didn't come. Of course, he thought, it was always possible that someone had sent a welcome party on ahead of him to Sidney—though this was the first morning train since he had let "slip" the name of his destination. They could also send him some company from further west, of course, such as Denver. But Zeke's money was on his niece, and the information that she had relayed at noon yesterday, about his "company" coming in from Chicago last evening. Assuming that they were smart enough to tail him from the Barrelhouse...

Just then, the train rocked violently...and over the top of his copy of the *Journal*, Zeke thought he just caught the hint of a large shadow falling across the window of the door that led to the space between the passenger cars up forward, then pulling away suddenly. *Nothing like a little company to lighten a traveler's burden*, thought Zeke, lifting the corner of his mouth under the cover of the newspaper...despite the third slat in his misnamed backrest.

* * * * *

Sitting at the breakfast table waiting for Aunt Emelia to whip up some bacon and eggs, Bud Gardner's back felt fine—but...

"How's the **head**?" Johnny Pack said cheerfully, and **loudly**, as he strode into the kitchen, once again resplendent in full cadet uniform.

Bud groaned. "It feels like hel..." Staring in shock at Aunt Emelia's back as she leaned over the eggs, Bud inhaled his words and changed directions like a politician. "Er...like **help**...would be...welcome..."

Johnny grinned and slid into the chair next to Bud. "Well, if help is what you want, here I stand, fair cousin. I have brought good tidings to you. First and foremost, this afternoon's baseball game has been cancelled—too many railroaders still out at the track. I understand that the Rock Island trestle has nearly been repaired, and trains should run on it later today."

Bud's face wore a look of visible relief—as relieved, that is, as a face can look after it has been plastered all over a rail. Bud recalled his grandfather's wisdom regarding bruises—while painful, at least they had the **look** of being painful. Gramps had often told Bud that there nothing like a good bruise to draw a little sympathy—in fact, as wounds went, bruises generally offered a maximum ratio of sympathy to actual injury. Unfortunately, this particular bruise was still in the "this really still hurts" stage, and Bud was looking forward to moving on to the "it really looks like it hurts, but it's actually just green" stage.

"Second...our cadet corps will be drilling before the Governor and the entire Nebraska militia this morning, and you are cordially invited to attend." True enough, Johnny's hand held a crisp white card, and through his left (unswollen) eye, Bud read, "You are invited to attend, Bud, so get off your butt and come along...before Mom feeds you so much you burst like a tick."

"How kind," Bud said, trying to maintain his composure. *Ow—smiling hurts.*

"Actually, Bud," Emelia offered, carrying a steaming plate of eggs and bacon and placing it before Bud, "We'd appreciate it if you could represent the family—most everyone else is pretty busy with this Grange business this morning..."

"But—I can help..." Bud objected.

"You've done plenty, already Bud," Emily said, placing a hand on his. "Fifty-five men showed up this morning and were assigned to farmers all over the county. Most of them were Czechs—many of them asked about you..."

"Come on, Bud," Johnny said, "There may be some burgeoning Florence Nightingale out at the drill that feels hopelessly attracted to men with disfigured faces. And if the pain gets too much for you, I'll just have my friends shoot you."

Bud remembered not to grin, nodded, and dug in.

* * * * *

"So—did he see you?" Henri Flint was in the club car, and spoke softly, but openly and with a smile, as if nothing in the world mattered except the cigar that he was smoking.

"The odds are that he didn't," Charles Cheevers replied, leaning on his left elbow at the bar at the front of the car, unconsciously leaving his right hand free. "But you can never say for sure."

"Of course." Flint paused for a moment, then shook his head, and leaned in toward his partner. "I don't know, Charlie—this character is pretty smart—maybe too smart. He places himself in exactly a position that you or I would use, way at the back of second class—were we in his situation—and then acts as if he hasn't a care in the world—when we know from what Mr. McGee tells us, everything he has is riding on this trip. I just don't know..."

"You think it's a setup, then?"

320

"It ain't clear t'all to me, Charlie...but let's find out." Flint said, taking a last drag on his cigar. "We'll be in Columbus in about thirty minutes...let's see what this character's game is about."

"Push and pull?" Cheevers asked, with a shadow of a smile crossing his face.

"Just what I had in mind." Flint rose, and headed to second class.

* * * * *

For the second night in a row, Ransom Reed Cable, Sr. had slept fitfully in his library, near the telephone. When the telephone rang, jerking him out of his half-sleep, he picked up the receiver, only to hear the voice that had been needling his nightmares since Thursday. "Good morning, Mr. Cable—this is Mr. B.," the voice announced, and before Cable could react with the questions that were burning within him, the man who held his son's life cut him off.

"I'll make this short. I understand that there are a swarm of private detectives in Fairbury, in Lincoln, and in every little tank town in southeastern Nebraska, out looking for your son. It won't do, Mr. Cable. Even if your son was still being held in the area—and I assure you, he is *not*—he would be killed before they could get within a mile of him."

Cable cursed under his breath. As well as Nathan Brockhurst, the station master at Fairbury, he had told his Western Division chief yesterday about the kidnapping. The man had obviously decided, on his own initiative, to bring in every Pinkerton in three states to search "discreetly" for his son—Nathan hadn't the authority, and certainly wasn't that dense. However...*this "Mr. B" is clearly feeling pressured by the Pinkertons—does that mean they are getting close?*

"The timetable and criteria for the release of your son has changed," the voice said, matter-of-factly. "This morning, you will write a letter to the Board of Trustees overseeing the receivership of the Union Pacific Railroad, notarized and delivered by five o'clock today, with a copy to the editor of the Chicago Tribune. The letter will denounce the Board as a group of nefarious rascals, in the pay of several large Eastern railroad holdings. You will also renounce, publicly, any interest in the acquisition of the Union Pacific, for all time. If this is done, you will see your son safely home tomorrow—if not, you will not see him again."

Stunned, Cable's mind leapt ahead to the consequences of this act—not only would such a move effectively cut him off from any fair, future consideration in bidding for the U.P., it would make him the laughingstock

321

of the industry. The stock of his own Chicago, Rock Island, and Pacific Railroad would immediately plummet, making him another target for buy-out—perhaps even more attractive than the U.P.

"Well, what say you, Cable—do you agree to these terms?"

Cable closed his eyes, and bent his head in submission. There really was only one answer.

"Yes," he said, finally. "Yes…I agree."

"Excellent," Mr. B said, happily. "Five o'clock, then, Mr. Cable. And get rid of those Pinkertons." With that, the line went dead.

Cable's face transformed immediately from a mask of worry to towering rage. He slammed the telephone receiver down on its ornate hook, then picked the entire handset up and flung it across the room, where it made a delicious crash against an electric lamp. Immediately, Peter LaRue—always within earshot, night and day—came rushing into his boss' private study.

"Mr. Cable?" he stuttered. "Is anything wrong…?"

"*Everything* is wrong," Cable snapped, and went about relaying the results of the telephone call to his private secretary. LaRue nodded, sensing the struggle going on in his employer.

"So, you plan to write the letter, then?" LaRue asked, understanding well how Cable's compliance would affect his business.

"Yes, dammit," Cable growled. "I'll write the letter—but I'll be damned if I'll pull out the Pinkertons. The men holding my son won't do anything until the letter is delivered—I'll give them until then to see what they can find out."

LaRue nodded his head, and went to fetch paper.

* * * * *

Amos Seville had meant to rise with the sun, but either the sun had decided to get up early, or Amos had slept in about two hours longer than he had intended.

He expected that the latter was the case.

Groaning, Amos dressed, managing at last to stuff his swollen left shoulder into a shirt and coat. Checking his pistol, he found that six thirty-two-caliber shells were seated safely in their chambers, and then reluctantly shifted the gun over to his right-hand pocket.

The walk to the Fairbury stable was a short one, and a cigarette along the way helped to ease him into some semblance of morning normalcy. The manager of the stables was sweeping up when Amos approached him.

"Ah'd like to rent a horse, please suh," Amos said.

"Sorry, partner," the stable manager replied, leaning on his broom. "Just rented the last two horses we had."

"How...unfortunate," Amos said, with a last drag. "Any idea where a man might inquire further?"

"You might ask *me*," Wendell Evans said, from behind him. Amos turned, and saw that the reporter held two saddled horses, one black, though graying around the eyes, and one brown. Though neither was exactly winged Pegasus, they didn't appear to be *quite* ready for the rendering plant, either.

"Mr. Evans," Amos said. "I observe that you have once again *wormed* yourself into my business."

"Our business," Evans said, patting the neck of the black horse. "Where are we off to this morning, then...partner?"

There wasn't much to do except wait until noon to see if the "skull-faced man," as Evans had begun to describe their adversary, decided to show up for a hypothetical telephone call at the Fairbury Hotel, so Amos Seville and Wendell Evans decided to grab a good breakfast. The hotel served a fair lunch and a good dinner—but for breakfast, the pair led their horses to Smitty's, which seemed to be the place most frequented by locals (always a good sign). The biscuits were pretty tasty, Amos judged, even by his standards. Evans seemed to be enjoying them, and was absently wiping his mouth with a handkerchief that looked like something one of the Barnum clowns used to pull out for exaggerated sneezing gags. But despite the quality of the food, Evans' face fell when he got hold of the morning edition of Lincoln Journal.

"They've found the man that wrecked the train," Evans said, glumly. "A Negro named Davis. It says here that he was seen at the wreck, and before the wreck with tools, and…it appears that he has a record of theft in the county."

"Perfect…just perfect," remarked Amos, shaking his head. "Do they mention anything about a potential *motive*?"

"Uh, no, actually," Evans replied. "But I imagine that it could have been theft."

"Anything about looting the bodies of the dead after the wreck?"

"Certainly not," said Evans, looking up from his paper, curiosity now covering his features. "So…you believe they have the wrong man?"

"Evans, if they have the *right* man, why ah we *here*?" Amos asked. "Think about it for a minute. The Chicago, Rock Island, and Pacific Railroad lost an engine, two passenger cars, a tender, and eleven lives two nights ago. There's bound to be a lawsuit brought by the families for negligence…unless…"

"Unless they find the culprit—any culprit—that wrecked the train," Evans said, following Seville's train of thought. "But, why Davis?"

"He's *black*, you idiot," said Amos, bluntly. "And he's handy, with a record to boot. A bigger record than they ah letting on, if mah memory serves."

"You *know* him?" Evans asked, now truly engaged.

"Ah've met him," Seville said, his voice dropping, leaning forward to look Evans in the eye. "He's *not brilliant.* He likes to drink, and to gamble, and to have a good time—and he doesn't think things through to their logical conclusions very often. And he's been in prison...served a few yeahs at the State Pen. He's also a regulah down at a little organization they call the "Hoo Hoo Club," round the corner from the lumber yard."

"So...Davis is *innocent*?" Evans queried.

"Ah didn't *say* that—ah said they hadn't figured out a *motive*," Amos interjected, then added, "Davis may be involved, or may not. But he's certainly handy..."

"Well, if that's the case, we may still be on the right track."

"*May?* Ah'm sorry, Evans, but are you *asleep* this morning?" Amos asked, the incredulity dripping from his words. "Have you *completely* forgotten about young Mr. *Cable*?"

Evans' eyes grew wide, then refocused. "My God—I'm an *idiot*."

"We finally agree on something, Mr. Evans." Amos leaned back in his chair, and watched the gears in Evans' brainpan accelerate.

"Cable was the target all along. The wreck is...was...a diversion."

"It's worse than that, Mistah Evans." Amos added. "It's likely to have been intended as an *incentive.*"

As Amos' last observation hung in the air, the door to Smitty's swung open. Two strangers in neatly tailored suits and bowler hats entered the room, sat in the corner, and scanned the room with a critical eye before ordering. Amos' eyes closed, and his head shook. *Damn.*

"What's wrong?" asked Evans.

Exhaling, Amos uttered, "Pinkertons."

* * * * *

Columbus, the sleepy little county seat perched on the north bank of the Platte River, was the last stop on this branch of the Burlington line. As the train pulled into its little depot on the east side of town, the conductor finally reached the last car in second class and announced, "End of the line, folks. All off for Columbus or the Union Pacific Railway."

325

Zeke Gardner groaned, rose, stretched, and…waited. The immigrants in second class were organizing parcels, tickets, wives, husbands and most of all, children—not a task for the fearful or the hurried. As the car cleared, Zeke checked his watch, saw that he had at least an hour until his train left for points west, and as he descended the stairs of the car to the platform, decided that a good breakfast…or at least a little Irish coffee…might be in order.

Disdaining the offer of a hack, Gardner walked west from the Burlington Station in order to stretch his legs, and was pleased to learn that the two-story frame Bucher Saloon was still standing a couple of blocks south of the U.P. station, patiently waiting on a fire that hadn't quite come yet. Seventeen years ago, more or less, Zeke remembered having a drink…all right, several dozen drinks…there with an old friend, whose long, wavy yellow hair had shaken back and forth as he blathered on about the splendor of the West, and how, as an Army scout, he had witnessed it from his ranch in North Platte clear up to the Rocky Mountains. Zeke had listened, bragging in turn on the splendor and riches of the Black Hills, and remarking on how the Army always seemed to be asleep or absent without leave when Black Hill gold was shipped down south to Sidney, as it was constantly assailed by the Sioux, and other persons of not inconsiderable nuisance. His cohort had assured his fellow patrons that Gardner must have been mistaken—observing that the Indian menace was now no longer a concern—thanks to the *Army*—and proceeding to regale Zeke, the Bucher brothers, and the entire tavern (of course) with the tale of how he— as an *Army* scout—had scalped Yellow Hand at Warbonnet Creek in the northwest corner of the state, in revenge for Custer. At that point, Zeke recalled observing that Custer wasn't particularly worth avenging, being a thick-headed braggart, a politician and, worst of all, a poor shot. Hot words, a general melee, and distressed furniture were the result, of course—followed after a time by cool beer and renewed good fellowship…

Gardner smiled. Youth was good—actually, while it lasted, it was *glorious.*

Joseph Bucher was standing behind the bar, wiping glasses when Zeke came in and sat down on a hard pine stool, his duster nearly sweeping the rough board floor. Bucher had been a stoic seventeen years ago, and time hadn't altered him much—so his only comment on seeing Zeke enter his establishment was, "You gonna break any more of my furniture?"

"Not today—unless Cody's around," Zeke intoned, trying his best to mimic Bucher's deadpan delivery. "You gonna hit me in the head with a table leg?"

"Cody's in New York, so I reckon you're fairly safe," he replied. "I had to replace that wallpaper over dere where you put Cody's head tru it...and a table, four chairs, some glassware, too."

Zeke leveled his gaze at the bartender. "Your wallpaper wasn't all that interesting."

Bucher narrowed his eyes, and the staring contest went on until the side of Bucher's mouth finally quivered, and broke into what passed for him as a crooked grin. Clearing his throat (what passed for a laugh), he placed a cup of coffee in front of Zeke and turned away to finish his dishes.

The coffee, though good, was even better with a nip of bourbon in it, and Gardner was almost entirely lost in nostalgia when another man—a bit shorter, darker, and younger than Zeke—took the stool next to him and ordered a coffee, too. He had the look and smell of *city* about him, with a fine tweed suit and brushed hat, but it was his steady, piercing eyes that immediately raised the hackles on Zeke's neck.

"Morning, friend," Henri Flint said. "Saw you trek over from the Burlington train."

"Didn't realize I was so conspicuous," Zeke said, with full recognition that any stranger that called you a friend...wasn't.

"Well, from the beeline you made from the train, I figured you must know where the best breakfast is. It's true everywhere I travel—find a local, and they know right where to eat—or drink, as the case may be. I'm Henri Flint, by the way," said Flint, sticking out his hand.

"Zeke Gardner," he replied with a short nod, shaking the man's hand, then turning his head to face his drink and eye Flint through the mirror behind the bar. Finally, he added, "So, you're a traveling man."

"Oh, yes—coast to coast. But my home's in Chicago these days."

That figures, Zeke thought. *So where's the other guy?* Gazing through the mirror, Zeke peered into the street, and after a few moments, was finally able to spot a large man in a derby hat through the large front windows, leaning against the telephone pole.

"So, is this home for you, then?" asked Flint, staring at his own cup with a nonchalant manner that Zeke had begun to genuinely admire.

"No, no...I'm from Lincoln," Zeke said. "I'm headed out to Sidney...I have an errand to run. Be back tomorrow, though."

Flint laughed, "Been on a quite a few of those "flash trips" myself...here today, gone tomorrow...whoops! Back again! Such as now...headed right back to Lincoln myself, after an errand of my own."

This last statement shocked Zeke—*back to Lincoln?* Though he did his best to hide his confusion, he could feel the blood drain from his face, and his neck was burning.

Finishing off his drink, Zeke said, "Well—gotta catch my train. Good luck..."

Flint raised his hand in a half wave, then watched as Gardner left the bar. After a few moments, Cheevers came in and sat in Gardner's chair, not cold yet, and started to raise his hand to order, but Flint grabbed it.

"You have a train to catch," he said, matter-of-factly.

"Aren't you coming?" Cheevers queried.

"You can handle him," Flint said. "There's no reason for both of us to go. I believe that Mr. Gardner may have been alerted to our presence, Charlie, and is leading us on a merry little chase, to tell you the truth...though how merry could *Sidney* be, for Christ's sake?"

"So...you want me to..." Cheevers queried, already knowing the answer.

"...carry out our orders from McGee regarding Mr. Gardner. If he heads out to Sidney after his piece of paper—which I rather doubt, now—I'm sure you'll have no trouble in retrieving it, and...dealing with the situation. I intend to take care of our *original* orders—back in Lincoln." Standing, Flint headed to the door, calling back to his partner. "Be careful...he knows he's being followed...he's not a rube."

Cheevers sneered and muttered under his breath, "If you say so." With a last longing look at the beer taps behind the bar, he rose reluctantly and headed to the door after his partner.

Joseph Bucher wiped the last of his glasses, glanced at the money that Gardner had left him on the bar, then allowed his eyes to trail through the front windows after the men that had just left his tavern.

"I'd be **real** careful, whoever you bastards are," he muttered to himself, tucking the silver into his apron. "I don't think you seen what that Gardner fellah can do to a room."

* * * * *

328

In spite of its reduced circumstances, the U.P. still managed to operate at least one Pullman car on routes west along the Platte, and having learned firsthand the numbers and nature of the opposition, Zeke saw no further reason to secret himself in second class. Sitting in one of the Pullman car's leather chairs next to its broad windows, directly across from the 'knowledge box' of the U.P. offices, Zeke had a fine view of the station platform, and was completely absorbed in looking it over when he was approached by one of the porters.

"Can I get you anything, sir?" Despite the recent Pullman strike and its dire consequences, the porter was the model of decorum, complete with white gloves and a winning smile.

"Some coffee, please, George," using the name by which all Pullman porters were referred when on duty, given after George Pullman, their employer. 'George' bowed slightly and left Zeke to his thoughts. With only about ten minutes before they were to depart, Zeke had to decide—soon—on his course of action.

This is not going exactly as I'd hoped, Zeke reflected. It was always a risk, of course, but his hope was that the men that had been sent from Chicago would follow him out to Sidney, instead of organizing an active opposition in Lincoln. It was clear from his confrontation in Bucher's saloon that at least one, and probably both, of the men from Chicago were wise to his ruse.

Flashing back, Zeke experienced one of the old urges that he had often felt as a deputy back in Lincoln in those last months—the overwhelming hopelessness, the desire to lower his head and get quietly drunk. But, somehow, recalling his experiences with Robert Harrison, his son, his daughter-in-law, and most of all, their little boy—strengthened him, as always, so he fixed his eyes ever more firmly on the platform outside his window.

He was not—entirely—disappointed. Out on the platform, the large man Zeke had seen in the railroad car, and outside Bucher's saloon (there was no hiding a tub like that one) was walking with determination down the platform, finally swinging into the first class car behind him. There was no indication of Henri Flint, the man who had introduced himself so openly in Bucher's saloon.

Zeke had a decision to make—go out to Sidney as planned, dragging the second man from Chicago along with him—or stop, turn around, and aid his family in Lincoln with the defense of the farmers and their corn against Flint, and their allies.

It was the trust he had in his family that made up his mind on the matter.

Out his window, Zeke signaled to the man sitting in the glassed-in 'knowledge box', saw the signal returned from the brass pounder sitting behind the telegraph key across from him...and turned just in time to take his coffee from George.

37

Saturday, August 11, 1894
10:35 am

It hadn't been easy to get the faded yellow lunch wagon set up in time—at 10:00 a.m., the exhibition drill by the Nebraska Corps of Cadets had been scheduled to begin two hours earlier than the baseball games that she normally served in Lincoln on this day—and out at Burlington Beach, they were farther away from town, causing Anna Marie Vostrovsky to have to start that much earlier. Nevertheless, the crowds were much larger here, and a part of Anna congratulated herself on her business judgment in choosing to set up here instead of at the baseball field.

But a larger part of her was less than happy about it—because a certain young man was expected to pitch for the Saltdogs that afternoon. And that part was finding it hard to concentrate.

"Uh, *Miss?*..." urged a impatient voice in front of her serving table, and Anna shook loose her stare to discover that over a dozen customers were standing, stamping their feet nervously and murmuring in a queue before her, hoping for a hot sandwich before the exhibition started in earnest.

Hlupek, Anna scolded herself, and accelerated her one-woman operation. Between heating the already baked Runzas in shifts and manning the change table, Anna was as busy as a one-armed paper hanger...and judging from the line growing before her, was falling further behind by the minute. The next step would be to start selling cold Runzas—which was likely to earn her a lot of scowls, if not lose her hungry customers.

In the distance, a succession of political speeches had been rumbling on for a good while now, an immediate precursor to the military drill—the "cost of the soup," as her sister would have said. However, they were finally winding down, and though Representative Bryan, the last to speak, could be counted upon for a good fifteen minutes' exposition on any topic or occasion, that time had long passed.

Busy as she was, however, the familiar, repetitive work paired with Bryan's unending voice managed to cast Anna's mind adrift again, this time turning toward her sister. *What a team they had made,* she recalled. For years after their parents' deaths, they had worked the wagon together—Anna heating and hauling the sandwiches, Antonia charming the customers out of their nickels. Her laughter was as ready as it was

331

distinct—ringing out 'like a silver bell,' her late parents had said when they were little girls—and it mixed well with her oddly accented teasing banter, often inspiring the customers to find a little patience when the lines were long—like today's.

Before Anna realized what was happening, her present loneliness and the happy memories of a few years ago had conspired to bring her to the brink of unexpected tears. For a moment, they hovered there before her eyes, threatening to flood out, balanced on the merest pinpoint of emotional control. Blinking and swallowing hard, Anna scolded herself once again—*come, Anna, now is not the time*—and noticed suddenly that she was down to one warm sandwich left on her serving table. This led in turn to a chain of further realizations—that there was a set of sandwiches that was probably scorching on the warming racks…that another set that needed to be rotated in…and that the murmuring before her had turned to a rumble. Panic and exhaustion were just beginning to turn the tide against her fragile self control…when a familiar, cheerful voice spoke softly from just behind her.

"Looks like you could use some help—got an apron?"

Anna started, delighted to hear the one voice she had most wanted and least expected—but was shocked as she whirled about to find that the young man's normally handsome face was wearing an ugly bruise all over its right side. Her hand extended toward it, pulled back, extended again to touch…then fell at last to her side, her face blushing in embarrassment as she continued to stare, wide-eyed, at Bud Gardner.

"What…?" Anna began to ask.

"I prefer working the front, thanks," Bud said, smiling while he wrapped a white towel from the table around his waist. "That is, if you don't think I'll scare away the customers. Come on—you get the next rack, and I'll get these folks taken care of—let's see if we can knock this out before my cousin starts marching."

Anna stammered, but then just smiled, wrapped her arms around Bud's neck, and gave him a quick hug, bumping his bruises in the process. Before Bud could say 'ouch,' the girl had disappeared behind the wagon, and it was Bud's turn to gape, as the joy of the embrace swept into him.

Bryan was still speaking, but now the crowd heard a competing voice, filled with power, emanating from a small yellow wagon off to the side of the grandstands. "One for a nickel, three for a dime—come on folks, step right up and get your Runzas…!"

Parr's Hardware loomed ahead of them just off the main thoroughfare of Fairbury, its white wooden façade and neat gray crenolated trim managing to give the building a sedate, dignified look that belied its description by Amos Seville as the 'Grand Central Station of Gossip.'

"Sounds like heaven to a reporter," remarked Evans, smiling.

"Which reminds me, Mr. Evans," Seville said, turning on his companion. "For the next hour or two, you are a *nail* salesman. Are we **communicating?**" Evans nodded as the pair opened the heavy wooden door to Parr's and walked to back of the store where the...fertilizer...flowed freely among six graying, balding farmers, all clad in overalls.

"Amos!" Jim Copeland exclaimed. "How's my favorite *nail* salesman?"

That line won a round of laughs...every one of the men around the table knew the business that Amos engaged in, and a few of them were even his suppliers. The cadre chimed in like a Greek chorus: "You up here buying or selling?...How many kegs on this shipment, Amos?...I'll take mine in a tall glass..."

"It's a wonder, Amos," Copeland chuckled. "Every time some mischief happens, you're not very far away. Looks like you got clean away with that train wrecking up in Lincoln, though."

"Don't let on, Jim," Amos replied, in a stage whisper behind the back of his hand, "Think how thirsty those poor Lincoln folk would be if ah ended up in the pokey." Motioning to Evans, who had been standing in the shadows behind him, he continued, "May ah introduce Mistah Evans? He also happens to be a...*nail* salesman."

On first sighting Evans, the men's easy bantering dropped immediately to a stony silence—but at Amos' quick introduction and expertly upturned eyebrows, the atmosphere around the table seemed to ease somewhat. Evans—not dense to the sudden coolness in the room—caught on immediately, and added, "Having tried the...*goods*...that Amos has been bragging on, I thought I'd better drop by and give the man a little competition."

"Now hold on, Evans—don't forget we ah **partners**," Amos retorted, jabbing the man in the ribs, and seeing this, the men around the table once again fell into ease, ribbing Amos in return: "Competition never hurt *anyone*, Amos...Ya gotta watch yer partner, Amos—they can be worse than *wives...*" and so forth, until the joking died a bit, and Amos felt the room was ready for another turn in the conversation, toward something perhaps more useful.

"So," Amos said, straddling a chair backwards and leaning his arms gently on its cane back, "Did you lose any Fairbury boys in the wreck the other night?" As fine as joviality was, Amos had learned from long experience that the juiciest gossip—and most real information—was derived from the solemn spaces between the jokes.

"One," said Doc Connelle, observing how carefully Amos had laid his arms on the chair, and the wince that had accompanied it. As the other men regaled Seville and Evans about the poor Fairbury grain man that had been killed in the wreck and the flock of Pinkertons in the town, Connelle rose and dropped a casual hand on Amos's sore shoulder as if making to depart. Feeling Amos start in pain under his hand, Connelle dropped his lips to the Southerner's ears and whispered, "Come see me in my office after you're done here."

Given the lead story in the morning papers—familiar to all, since the Lincoln Journal had just arrived by morning train and was now spread out over the tables before them—that a Negro had been captured and detained for the crime up in Lincoln, most thought that the joke was on the Pinkertons, having been sent from Chicago just in time to see the Lincoln boys sew up the case. Others thought something else was up—there was a lot of talk about a missing passenger, and one of the gathered men, a retired railroader, claimed that a picture of a young man was being discreetly circulated among his former workmates down at the trainyards, though no names were being used.

Russ Hazard, one of the more cantankerous of the lot, remarked, "Well, as long as they're scouring the county, maybe they'll manage to scare off some of the vagrants...the Sheriff and that drunk deputy of his sure as hell won't."

"Vagrants?" asked Amos, his ears perking up, recognizing that the word might have a synonym...such as *strangers*...which was of particular interest to him. "Having trouble in your part of the country with vagrants, Russ?"

"Yeah, I s'pose so," said Hazard. "There's somebody been camping out at Rock Creek Station...seen the cooking fire for a couple nights running now."

Amos was familiar with the former Pony Express and Oregon Trail waypoint six miles or so southeast of town...having once reconnoitered it as a potential transfer point for, *uh*, nail deliveries. Back then, it had been remote enough for his purposes, but too far from the railroads to be of any real utility, so he had decided in the end to cast it aside in favor of a place just off the tracks. Now, his mind led him back down the road to the barns and outbuildings that were scattered about that abandoned property, while his intuition led him toward a last, understated question.

"Since when, did you say?"

"Thursday night, I suppose," replied Hazard, offhandedly, and turned the conversation back once again to George Washington Davis, with several pointing out how difficult it would have been for one man to pull off, while others, including the railroader, making veiled suggestions as to the need for *someone* to get jailed or caught in order for the railroad to escape *liability*. Throughout this verbal wrangling, one man seemed to be unusually quiet...but despite the pain in his shoulder, was grinning from ear to ear.

Bingo.

* * * * *

There were only two people left in front of the Runza wagon when the bugles of the Nebraska Corps of Cadets blew assembly, amidst a cheering crowd. These last customers immediately decided to forgo lunch in favor of the show, Anna and Bud were left to catch their breath for a few minutes.

"Whew," Bud exclaimed, pulling the towel up from his waist and wiping his brow. Momentarily, he forgot his injury and winced slightly when he patted the towel over the bruised and tender right half of his face. "Is it like that **every** Saturday?"

"This was more hectic than most," Anna Marie observed. "It usually takes a few hours to sell twelve dozen sandwiches—this time I, that is, **we**, did it in about 40 minutes."

After she placed the last empty Runza pan in the wagon, Anna brought out a sign that said 'Closed' in bright red script, and hung it on the wagon in front of the serving table. As she turned to face him, Bud noticed that Anna had a small basket and canteen dangling from the crook of her left arm—and that the other was extended to him.

"Looks like we have two or three sandwiches left—would you like to watch the parade with me?" she invited, and seeing Bud smile (ouch) in agreement, gestured with her head to the wagon's seat. "There's a quilt up there."

Bud grinned even wider (ouch again), gathered up the quilt, and took Anna's hand. Later on, he noted that it was warm (probably from the pans), and still a little dusty with flour—but at that instant, it put Bud in mind of a machine he had tried last year at the Burt County fair. For a penny, it would run an electric current into your hand from a large copper knob that you would grasp and adjust. It was advertised as a cure for all ills, most especially arthritis, though most folks would try it just to see how much current they could take before letting go. When he grasped Anna's hand, Bud thought that the voltage was probably all the way up, though he decided after a few seconds that it was really just a very pleasant buzz— and that there might be something to the curative powers of electricity after all.

Together, they walked over to a spot under the cottonwood trees that bordered the small salt lake at Burlington Beach, several hundred yards from where the troops were assembled, and spread the quilt. In the distance, the drums were beating, and small figures marched in lines before Governor Crounse, Representative Bryan, Mayor Weir, and several hundred assembled militia officers and men, all standing at attention—not to mention nearly a thousand spectators scattered on blankets about the prairie. The cadet band struck up as he and Anna unwrapped the Runzas from their wax paper, and competed to see who could name the tune first. Bud managed to make a lucky guess right away as "The Liberty Bell," but the "Washington Post March," "Semper Fidelis," and "The Gladiator March" all went to Anna.

"You sure know your music, Anna," Bud remarked, taking a swig from their shared canteen, trying his best not to get any crumbs in it. "Do you play?"

"My brothers do," she remarked. "They play in the town band. In Crounse, everyone is very fond of Sousa's marches. Stephan plays the trumpet, and Lukas plays the sackbut."

"Uh, excuse me…what's a sackbut?" A million images were tumbling through Bud's mind, none of them resembling an instrument.

"I think you call it a trombone," Anna giggled. "The other name is Czech, I think, or perhaps French."

"That explains it, then," Bud remarked, then added, conversationally, "Stephan…is he the tall one? Lukas must be the younger—his English is nearly as good as yours…."

"You've met my brothers? When did you meet—" and then stopped, staring again at Bud's bruise. Jumping quickly to her feet, her voice rose even faster. "Did *they* do that to you? I will *kill* them!"

"No, Anna…wait, that was…" Bud rose and held his hands up, trying to interrupt. But Anna Marie was already pacing back and forth on the blanket, her arms motioning wildly, moving to the music booming from the cadet band, which Bud recognized, appropriately, to be "The Thunderer." The stream of Czech issuing from her, though completely unintelligible and a bit frightening, was nevertheless colorful, and her face had grown quite red and flushed by the time that Bud was able to get a word in edgewise.

"Anna, you don't understand…a *horse* did this to me. Not your brothers—it was a *horse*."

Anna looked into Bud's eyes, confused for a moment. As she cooled down, the blood drained away from her cheeks and neck, and she slowly knelt on the blanket…where she promptly put her face into her hands. Her shoulders shook with the effort of bringing her emotions under control.

"I'm sorry, Bud…" she said after a moment, while Bud quietly sat beside her. His arm was around her shoulders in a brotherly sort of embrace, and Anna Marie leaned into him. "My brothers—they meddle in everything I do. They scowl at Mr. Mooney if my tips are low…they glower at Mrs. Tatum, my landlady because they don't like me staying anywhere but at home. They try to bully me into giving up the lunch wagon. You think *my* temper is bad! Stephan and Lukas are very protective, since…" Abruptly, Anna stopped. She turned her face up to Bud's, and let out a long sigh, and finally blurted out, "Since my sister, Antonia…she died."

Bud could see the tears shining in her blue eyes and felt like he'd gotten another kick in the chest. Abruptly, he said, "I'm so sorry, Anna…" then added, "You want to talk about it?"

"It won't do any good—what's done is done." Drying her eyes, she said, "Bud, are you sure you should be here, with me? When they find out about us…being together…"

Bud squeezed her in the shoulder and grinned as he pointed to his face. "It could get *worse* than *this*?" he asked, and Anna finally had to join him in a grin. She reached for his hand, and their eyes met. Bud was close enough to marvel at the flecks of gold mixed in with the blue of Anna's eyes, but there was something else in her eyes, too.

He bent toward her and murmured, "It'd be worth it." As Pershing's new artillery thundered in unison, Bud pressed his lips to Anna's...and there was that crazy arcade machine crackling away—again, turned all the way up.

38

Saturday, August 11, 1894
11:25 am

"So, what's in the sack?" Doc Connelle asked, winding the rope about his hands, and nodding his head toward the burlap bag that Amos had carried from Parr's hardware—in his good right hand—as they had walked to his office.

Damned physicians, groused Amos. *Always want to talk with you when they were torturing you—might as well be a dentist.*

"Supplies," groaned Amos, feeling the rope tighten about his left wrist. Bracing the front of his body against the edge of the nearly closed door, his left arm was extended through the crack between it and the doorframe, terminating in a short rope in the firm grip of Doc Connelle. Amos' shoulder was in considerable pain at the moment with the mere effort of fully extending his arm, and looking into the determined eyes of Doc Connelle bracing his right foot against the doorway, Amos was unwilling to start any sort of deep conversation.

"This may sting a little," Connelle warned, his eyes on Amos' dislocated shoulder. "Ready?"

"R—," was all Amos got out before his left arm shot away from him. He heard a *snap* from his shoulder, felt a volcano of pain, and then mercifully, the world went black.

* * * * *

Six blocks away in the lobby of the Fairbury hotel, Wendell Evans was re-reading the State Journal article on the capture of George W. Davis, the purported train wrecker, in Lincoln last night. Every minute or so, he paused to check his watch, and grimace. There was still thirty minutes until noon, the time when Amos thought that the gaunt man, possibly named Jack Trudeau, would be coming into the hotel to make, or perhaps take a telephone call. Evans admitted that the theory was thin—but it was the only lead they had, and did his best to repress a sigh and focus on the newspaper, in hopes of gleaning any additional facts he could about the wreck.

At the far end of the room, a well-dressed Negro quietly entered the small sitting area that composed the front end of the lobby, bought a newspaper from the luggage boy, and sat down to read the same story about Davis' capture. Had Evans been able to see the man's face behind the paper, he would have seen the wolfish grin grow until it spread from ear to ear.

* * * * *

Henri Flint swung off the train before it came to a stop at the Burlington platform in Lincoln, and headed directly for the Western Union on the south side of the station. The public telephone inside the door of the brick building appeared to be in use by a little man who was sitting on a high stool and barking "No, dammit!" repeatedly into the receiver. Flint was unconcerned—he didn't trust telephones—you never knew who could be listening in. Instead, he waggled his finger at one of the Western Union boys, a thin waif with an eager look under the polished brim of his hat.

"Take a message over to the theatre district for me, boy?" Flint asked, and waited for the grinning messenger to get the nod from his supervisor, an older man in a string tie and a black vest in the corner that took turns swatting flies and fanning himself with the swatter. Aside from the screaming little man on the telephone, it was clear that business was right slow at the moment—so, unsurprisingly, the boss inclined his head, probably reasoning that the three other boys standing around could deliver messages should the end of the world approach.

Nodding back at the supervisor, Flint reached into his pocket and placed two bits on the counter next to the boy, then slid another quarter down its length to the boss. The older man inclined his head once again, and then resumed fanning himself. Flint bent to the counter to write out a message to a man he knew would not be happy to receive it. *Oh well*, Flint thought. *Better to get forgiveness than permission, in this case.* He had a job to do.

"No, dammit!" screeched the little man, "Aren't you *listening*?"

Flint winced (thinking, *can't see how that man actually **needs** a telephone*) as he wrote the recipient's name and address on a Western Union envelope, then scribbled down a note on a blank sheet of paper offered by the boy. It read:

Mr. McGee,

I have returned to Lincoln. Cheevers is trailing Gardner to Sidney, and has that task well in hand, I assure you. I am determined to follow my original orders from Chicago. Please send any available men to LeBlanc Freight for organizing. Will check in tomorrow, or as required by the circumstances as they emerge. LeBlanc will know where to find me.

Flint

340

Stuffing the note into the envelope, Flint dropped it and the silver into the outstretched hand of the boy, who tipped his hat and scooted out the door. Flint followed, but slowed perceptibly as he reached the man on the telephone.

"No!" The little man's screech had turned into a wail. "No, no, n-"

"Yes, dammit," Flint muttered, hooking his foot under the stool and sweeping it out from under the little man in a single fluid movement as he ambled toward the door. Flint did not stand around to witness either the crash or the subsequent laughter from the Western Union boys, though he admitted to enjoying the sound of both as they receded behind his quick-marching feet.

* * * * *

It had been a terrific parade, Bud admitted to himself. *I'm sure it was...or I would be, sure, I'm sure...that is, if I had actually seen it.*

Bud had spent the last five minutes, once the music concluded, floating ten or twelve feet over a blue and white checkered picnic blanket. Now, leaning on one arm, staring into the blue, blue eyes of Anna Marie Vostrovsky, Bud was way past smitten—he was *smote.*

"Cousin!" shouted Johnny Pack. Striding toward him from the direction of the parade ground, Johnny was almost on top of the pair when he suddenly grasped the significance of the scene before him on the blanket, and then braked so abruptly that he nearly fell on his face into Bud's lap. Johnny was about to change direction when Anna Marie rose, urging Bud to his feet as well.

"I am Anna," she said, shyly extending her hand, not exactly sure what the young uniformed man before her had actually observed occurring on the blanket just minutes before—but recognizing him as *family*, and therefore of extreme importance.

"Charmed," Johnny Pack said, clicking his heels together and bowing, brushing his lips over Anna's hand before releasing it with a smile. "I can see that my cousin Bud here is far luckier than he is handsome. Bud, my compliments in finding the most beautiful blind girl in Lancaster County— I hope she enjoyed the parade, if only for the music."

"Uh, thanks," said Bud, nervously, as Anna tried without much luck to hide a grin. Privately, Bud was wondering what he'd have to do to get rid of his cousin and get Anna *back on that blanket*—but he did just manage to remember his manners, and his reason for being here. "Great parade," he mumbled.

341

"Thanks—now, aren't you glad you came?" Johnny asked, innocently.

"Johnny Pack!" hailed a familiar voice, and the boys pivoted, grinning in recognition of Willa Cather ambling toward them. Willa's eyes grew large at the sight of his massively bruised face.

"Bud!" Willa gasped. "What in the world did you do to your face?"

Johnny had been waiting to ambush his cousin on this one ever since spying Willa's approach. "Bud is from Alder Grove," he quipped. "He's learning how to eat with utensils. He's started with a spoon—we're afraid of what he'll do to himself with a fork."

Bud's faced cracked with a grin (ouch, again), as he mumbled something about a horse kicking him amidst the laughter. Willa's eyes flicked from Bud, toward Anna and back again...but the boy's eyes missed their cue, having already turned back to the young Czech girl, who was gazing back at him with a sad little smile.

"So," Willa said, clearing her throat and trying not to roll her eyes at the moony look on Bud's face. "Who have we here?" Before they could react, Willa extended her hand to Anna. "Never mind, boys—I'll introduce myself. I'm Willa Cather, and if you have the temerity to hang around either of these two, you're either very brave or a lunatic. Nice to meet another of the breed."

Anna smiled and took Willa's hand, introducing herself, and trying to return its firm grip. Though taken a bit aback by the young woman's forward demeanor and bright, searching eyes, the handshake was as warm as it was strong, and the eyes more friendly than fierce...so Anna found herself warming immediately to the young woman from Red Cloud.

"So, where's Julia?" Johnny said. "I thought the two of you were inseparable on Saturdays."

"Well, frankly, so did I, Johnny," Willa replied, and a hint of worry crossed her brow. "I was coming by to ask you the same question. I stopped by her work this morning at eight—Julia usually meets me after her evening shift, and we have breakfast—but her shift supervisor said she had gotten permission to leave a half hour early. I was hoping you'd know where she was."

"No, I haven't seen her, either," Johnny admitted. "But don't fret— she's a Pack, and we're just like bad pennies—we always turn up, eventually."

"And that," Johnny abruptly added, turning toward Bud, "Unfortunately for you, dear cousin, is why I came searching for you—it's time you turned up somewhere useful." Unfolding a piece of paper from his uniform jacket, he intoned, "Bud Gardner—assigned to Robert Harrison, Woodlawn. Father says you can pick up the horse you let a few nights ago from the stable—or you can take Uncle Zeke's horse..."

Folding up his list, Johnny explained. "Between family, our own freighters, and the men we recruited last night, he's assigned at least one man to every farmer—two to those living farthest out, like Eloise Moseman. We're supposed to help get the corn shelled as quickly as possible, and come get him at the freighting company if there's any trouble. He's got a dozen good men there ready to come running should we need him."

"So," Bud said, his head spinning slightly from Johnny's sudden new directive as well as Anna's proximity (*oh, does she smell **good**,* he thought). "If someone comes to harass us, we're supposed to just run *away?*"

"*You're* supposed to run away, Bud...and fetch help. There's *another* man there to stay with Eloise. In your case," Johnny paused, unfolding the list to read it again, then squinting at the strange spelling. "It's Andy...uh...Andreeyev Mal..."

"Andryev Malý," said Anna, recognizing the name and interjecting it with an understandably perfect Czech pronunciation. "I think that Bud calls him the 'Czech Giant'?"

Hoo, boy, winced Bud. *First, Zeke's killer horse, then a man that owes me a walloping. This just gets better and better...*

"That's the one," Johnny said, cheerily. "Father said that since Bud had already humbled the man in battle, there shouldn't be any trouble."

No trouble, Bud grumped. *He'll kill me without any difficulty at all.* But then another thought occurred to him, and his face brightened as he turned to Anna. "Hey, that's up near your place, isn't it? Uh, maybe I could walk you home first, then..."

"No such luck, Cuz," Johnny said, placing a hand on his cousin's shoulder, and leaning in to speak *sotto voce.* "Father was very specific about this, Bud—we are all to get on out to the farms as quick as we can— no dawdling. Uncle Zeke sent a telegram earlier this morning—there's a man from Chicago that's heading into town today—he says we need to be ready for trouble."

343

Bud was about to object, when Anna unexpectedly weighed in. "It's all right, Bud...I have to bring the wagon back into town, anyway." And in a gentle whisper, she added, "Family first, yes?" As Anna's blue eyes blazed into his own, he wasn't entirely convinced that her heart was in her words—but he softened, at least for the moment.

"Well, uh," Johnny said, interrupting, in a rare struggle to find the right words. "I think Willa and I will go...inspect the, uh, Parrot guns...yes, Miss Cather?"

"Of course, Mr. Pack," Willa replied, taking his arm as well as the clumsy cue to make their exit. "There's nothing like a good Parrot gun." And, mercifully throwing a few quick nods as farewells, the pair departed toward the dissipating crowd around the grandstands.

"Look," Bud said, turning to Anna. Gently, he took her hand, and looked into those blue pools of water that beamed back at him. "I can at least help you take the wagon in...it's kind of on the way to the stable, after all..."

It was a half truth, they both realized, but at Anna's quick nod, they walked back to the wagon.

* * * * *

It was five minutes to noon, and Wendell Evans was growing restless. Amos was supposed to join him ten minutes ago—*where the hell was he? And where was the gaunt-faced man, Trudeau?* Wendell shook his head, and glanced nervously over to the telephone booth again. *If he doesn't show up, we've got nothing,* Evans fumed, and then noticed that Manny O'Manion, the hotel clerk, was reaching for a buzzing sound beneath the dark wood of his lobby counter across the room. Manny nodded and signaled for the baggage boy, who immediately started a rhythmic cry of "Telephone for Mr. R? Paging Mr. R..." as he paced about the hotel lobby and dining room. Almost immediately, the black man in the sitting area put down his paper and said, "That's me, son," produced a nickel, and walked briskly over to Manny. O'Manion directed him to the telephone closet. Despite considerable gymnastics, its door was finally left ajar as the man took his seat and lifted the receiver.

Great, Evans griped. *Now we'll never get to see who takes that phone call.*

* * * * *

As he approached LeBlanc Freight and Livery, located across the tracks just south of the five Lincoln railroad depots, Flint was pleased to

344

recognize three men loitering on the porch that he had met the night before at McGee's. His encounter with Maxwell LeBlanc had clearly pointed to him as the leader of the other two toadies on the porch, Franks and "Billy"...*did the boy even have a last name?* If the men hadn't so conveniently presented themselves, Flint had planned to seek them out. *So much the better.*

When Flint came within a hundred feet of the house, LeBlanc, who had been leaning back on a chair with his boots on the porchrail, got to his feet and stared at the tall man now walking up the front steps. The look on his face passed from incredulity to a sneer in less time than Flint would have thought possible—and made him wonder if the man was more deadly than he appeared. *He'd almost have to be,* Flint reasoned, *to back up that snide demeanor of his...*

"What are *you* doing back here?" LeBlanc scoffed. "I thought you were trailing Gardner out West somewhere..."

"Plans have changed," Flint stated simply, smiling and assuming a friendly posture, hands in his coat pockets as he leaned against one of the posts supporting the porch roof. "Cheevers is still after Gardner—I'm here to work with you on the farmers."

"I think **we** can handle the farmers," LeBlanc snapped. "And anybody that sticks their nose into our busin..."

LeBlanc was momentarily interrupted...apparently, there was a gun up his nose. Anger almost immediately gave way to surprise, which was gradually followed by fear. Flint continued to smile, but the intense look in his eyes was far from friendly. Billy and Franks were rooted to their spots, incredulous as to how the man had managed to produce a weapon with such *speed.*

"Appears to me that *your* nose is in *my* business," Flint whispered, his face inches from LeBlanc's. However, once he was convinced that the lesson had been taken, he slid the weapon, a .32 cap and ball Police Special, back into its concealed pocket in the right sleeve of his jacket, and added almost cheerfully, "But I can use a man with spirit. Let's sit down inside and talk."

LeBlanc eyed Flint, and the fear on his face considered a turn toward malice, but contented itself in the end with resignation. He pulled out a handkerchief, and as Flint moved into the office, LeBlanc shoved the still shocked Billy and Franks in behind him.

* * * * *

345

The telephone call between the Negro and the unknown party was fairly brief, but it was sufficient in length to raise Evans' suspicions, and then finally convince him that he was an *ass*. Like so many that he himself had chided, Evans had failed to see the invisible—the Negro now completing his call—as an actual person. In this case, a person that may be in collusion with the gaunt man named Trudeau in the kidnap of Rance Cable, Jr.

After the black man hung up the phone, he went to tip O'Manion and appeared to Evans to be making a short survey of the room. Apparently satisfied, he ambled casually through the front door of the hotel, and stepped onto the porch for a moment, where he rolled and then lit a cigarette.

Where's Seville? Evans asked himself, followed by another, more practical question—*should I follow this man?*

It wasn't really a fair question for a reporter, Evans answered himself almost immediately, as he observed the black man step off the porch and cross the street, turning at the corner. With as much stealth as he could muster, the reporter walked quietly out the front door, and followed his lead.

And, emerging from the shadows in the alley across from the Fairbury hotel, another man followed his.

39

Saturday, August 11, 1894
12 noon

On the night before, Flint had seen dozens, possibly even hundreds of disgruntled, out-of-work men congregating outside of Lincoln, waiting for a job, an opportunity, or some other…situation…to arise. "Have-nots" were naturally resentful of the "Haves," and Flint knew from experience that, given the right encouragement, they would make remarkably efficient tools for motivating the farmers to separate from one another, and eventually, their grain. Once, that is, two factors were neutralized: law and leadership. And for that, Flint planned to use the instruments he had at hand—namely, LeBlanc and his men.

Turning to LeBlanc, Flint asked, "Who else have you got?"

LeBlanc's reply was negative, and hinted of evasion. "My business operates on a…contractual basis, Mr. Flint. We draw on men as the need arises. Those we have are busy with other duties."

Flint easily read the lie on LeBlanc's face, confirmed by the averted vision of his toadies, as well as the state of the freight yard—there were dozens of wagons lined up, now unused. The whole setup bespoke an operation that was, until recently, much larger. Where had the workers gone?

Of course. The answer hit him like an arclight—*the men had gone to work for the rival Pack freighting company.* The Packs, according to what he had learned from McGee last night, were related to Gardner somehow, who held the contract to haul the Cooperative's grain—*something like, what, 200,000 bushels?* At two or three cents a bushel for freight, that came to a tidy sum. With a deal like that on the horizon, there were weeks of work ahead of the freighters, at good wages…and Pack, whoever he was, must almost certainly be easier to work for than this man. *So, the best freighters are gone,* Flint concluded, *and the rest are overworked and disgruntled. They'll drive LeBlanc's wagons, but they'd rather pour piss out of a boot than do this man's dirty work—especially against a rival freight company that might hire them someday.*

"I see," Flint acknowledged. "Well, there are other options."

"Do you mean the men out on the edge of town?" Billy said, excitedly. Flint's demonstration of speed on the draw had impressed Billy, and he was eager to return the favor. "We....uh, we...we went to the camps this morning."

LeBlanc confirmed, "This morning, we went to the hobos west and south of town. There's a couple hundred of 'em by now—they need jobs, and I figgered that we'd need 'em to drive the wagons and push the farmers. We bought us two cases of cheap hootch and left it with 'em this morning."

Flint looked at incredulously at LeBlanc—*I appear to have underestimated this man*, he admitted to himself. *He's a bully, to be sure—but he sees what needs to be done, and does it.*

On the other hand, Flint warned himself, *he could just be a mean little bastard.* He began to nod his head...slowly...and grin.

Either way, fine by me.

"Well done, Mr. LeBlanc," Flint said. "You say you know some of these men...would they be the men with grit? With the guts to make a little money?"

"If they don't have grit, I ain't much interested," LeBlanc said, now coloring up with considerable self-pride at Flint's unexpected acclamation.

"Very well," Flint said. "I have two jobs for the three of you. First, I need you to bring the men out in the camps with grit—the leaders, the ones that can move men—to the barn over here....within the hour, if possible. We'll need to borrow a few wagons to bring them here."

"And second?" This time it was Franks, finally speaking up. *Franks is a watcher—more careful,* Flint judged. *Loyal to LeBlanc, certainly. Steadier, perhaps.*

"Second, we need to throw a little scare into the farmers, I think," Flint said, almost playfully. "According to my sources, a certain man—one of the leaders of the Cooperative—got you into a spot of trouble last week. Seems you were just making him a friendly offer for the grain, and a man named Gardner attacked you for it...."

"Harrison," LeBlanc smiled wolfishly. "I think I know just what you have in mind."

* * * * *

"Ladeeeez and gentlemen!" The stocky man was elegantly dressed in a red tuxedo and top hat, and wore a bemused expression—as if he was getting away with a lie, and that every person grinning back at him under

the big top not only knew it, but actually suspected that it might be at their own expense...and didn't give a damn.

"Welcome to the Greatest Show on Earth! Comprising of a World's Fair, Immense Museum and School of Marvelous Mechanism, A Score of Imported Royal Stallions, and a Grand European and Native Circus, all combined in One Vast Undivided Show!"

The crowd roared, of course, and Amos had to agree with them—no matter how many times he heard the spiel, he never tired of it—P.T. always made it seem so personal and fresh. At the top of the center pole at the platform that led to the high wire, Amos dried his sweaty palms and surveyed the crowd below as he waited for his cue. Below him, he could clearly make out the faces of his family—there was Ezekiel, and Aunt Emelia, Uncle Rufus, and his cousins—Bud, Johnny, Jeff and James—and especially Julia. They waved at him, and with a quick nod and a smile, he started out on the tightrope, the huge pole he carried lending him lateral stability as he walked out over the sawdust floor eighty feet below him, without a net.

All seemed to be going fairly well, but when he got out into the center of the tightrope, he found his attention briefly drawn back to the crowd. There below him, the food and fake jewelry vendors were busily hawking their wares—and yes, right on cue, there were the clowns as well. A pair of them appeared to be working a "chasedown" in his family's section, zigging and zagging in and out of the rows. Holding a huge gun, the "chaser" kept aiming his gun at the target clown, nearly pulling the trigger, but holding off at the last minute as the gaunt-faced "target" clown dodged behind yet another audience member. At last, the gaunt-faced clown settled on his "gag" target, and the chaser's blunderbuss, loaded with flowers, leveled at Julia.

But a half-heartbeat later, as J.T. Lynch pulled off his orange wig and grinned straight up at his location—Amos knew, too late, that the gun was not loaded with flowers. From the center of the high wire, Amos leapt at the man, but his descent was slowed to the speed of molasses as he helplessly watched Lynch gun down Julia...then Zeke...Emelia...and finally, P.T. Barnum himself before the gun swung toward his mother...

Amos awoke with the smell of ammonia in his nostrils and a scream half-formed in his throat, choking on both. About him, Doc Connelle's cramped office swam back and settled into his vision, and the fever dream of his family's death faded into the jewel-toned wallpaper.

"Take that crap out of mah nose," Amos griped, leaning up from the small paisley couch on his left elbow…and noticing, for the first time in 39 hours, that it **didn't hurt**—before it collapsed back underneath him and he cracked his head on the claw-shaped wooden arm.

"Careful!" Connelle warned. "Your shoulder is back in its socket, Amos, but the muscles are weak, and you'll need to treat it gingerly. Frankly, it's a miracle, given the time since the wreck…"

"How long was ah out?" Amos interrupted, still grouchy—and despite the warning, struggled to back to one elbow as he looked about the room. *Wasn't there a clock in this damned place?*

Connelle eyed Seville with suspicion, and then fished out his gold watch with an audible sigh. "Twenty-five minutes past twelve. You were out for about an hour while I examined your…"

Amos leapt off the couch, grabbed his hat, and headed for the door at a dead run.

*Shit, **shit, SHIT.***

* * * * *

Miles McGee tipped the young man who was extending a message toward him, dismissed him, and quietly closed the door to his rooms in the theater district. He crept softly past the sleeping form of a nearly naked young woman draped over the couch of his parlor, and made himself comfortable at his oak desk, the light from his shaded windows barely enough to illuminate his work. His silver letter opener found its mark in the corner of the envelope, and shortly the man's aging blue eyes were racing over the handwritten note from…***Flint?!?***

Maggie visibly stirred at McGee's cursing—mostly in Irish, erupting from across the room—but it had been a late night, and after a few moments, she fell back into an alcohol-induced slumber.

McGee fumed. *Flint had been **ordered** to follow Gardner to Sidney…but then again,* he reasoned, *he had been brought here, as his specific request, to bolster LeBlanc's freight organization and shove the farmers back into the status quo.*

As his temper cooled, McGee poured himself a whiskey and pondered the scenarios that presented themselves. *I could track Flint down and **force** him to go West, if I pressed the issue, I'm sure.* Flint, however, clearly preferred to put his reputation on the line in service of his original objectives. If he failed—*well, the blame would go to Flint. If he succeeds,* *however,* McGee reasoned, *I would be credited with asking for him in the first place.* **Win-win**, he finally admitted to himself.

"Rise and shine, girl," McGee announced, roughly slapping Maggie's backside as he strode past her on the way to his desk. He yanked the blinds up and let the afternoon sunshine pour onto the couch where she lay. Now it was the girl's turn to groan and curse, though more softly. *A fine-looking girl,* McGee reflected...*maybe I'll send her to one of the houses in San Francisco when this is all over...*but then thought better of it. *Best to close off the loose ends...witnesses can always have a change of heart.*

* * * * *

Amos rounded the corner, slowing to a trot when the Fairbury Hotel came into sight. *The gaunt man—he could still be on the telephone,* Amos told himself, trying to control his rising panic as he slowed to an amble, and made a quick survey of the hotel's front porch before darting to its side. There, under the cover of a low-hanging willow, Amos crouched down to peer through the lower corner of the large dining room windows, across the jumble of diners' legs and into the lobby where the phone closet was located. From his vantage point, Amos could just make out that the door to the closet was closed—*a bad sign. Nobody ever seems to close that door when it's in use except me.* Once more, Amos cursed his decision—*why had he agreed to let Connelle look at his arm? Gods,* he thought, *ah never felt pain like that before—how can it hurt more to go back into place than when it came out?*

Amos shook his head—*stop drifting, dammit,* he muttered to himself—and gazed back into the hotel lobby. From this position, Amos could see no sign of Evans, either.

Seville debated going through the kitchen entrance to avoid being spotted—it was possible that the gaunt-faced man, if he was still inside, could recognize him from the train. Amos had weighed that possibility before the pain of that doctor's visit had rendered him unconscious. For that reason, he had originally planned to hold the horses and watch from the alley across the street—Evans was to have followed whoever emerged from a discreet distance, and Amos would have followed Evans. Now, time was of the essence, and Amos had to gamble that his position at the back of the train on the night of the wreck had rendered him invisible to Cable's gaunt kidnapper.

Strolling into the front of the hotel, Amos wore a pleasant, unworried expression—the same practiced one he wore, long ago, up on the high wire. Scanning the lobby, Amos' first observations from the side window proved to be solid...Evans proved to be nowhere in sight, and the telephone closet was as empty as a freshly dug grave. Still smiling through gritted teeth, Seville approached O'Manion at the front desk.

"Manny!" Amos hailed. "Seen that shifty Evans character around?"

Manny smiled, and nodded his head. "From the way you scooted away this morning, I thought you might have wanted to get rid of him."

"Depends on the day, ah reckon." Amos replied, scowling, hands in his pockets. *Ah got all the time in the world, Manny. Now hurry up, willya?*

"Yeah, he was here until just a few minutes ago...asked if I'd seen you—seemed real worried about the time, checked his watch a couple of times—then scooted right out the front door and down the street to the left there. He was awful preoccupied."

"Oh, yeah?" Amos said. "What about?'

"He was following a black fellah. Just made a telephone call, and walked right out—with your man hot on his heels, as they say. Couldn't have been half an hour ago..."

Like a lightning strike, Zeke's words came back to Amos, the truth crackling into him with the force of 20,000 volts.

J.T. Lynch had two men working for him. One was Jasper Rankin, a Negro—you probably saw him get on the train with Lynch last night...the other man was tall, and very thin—with a face that looked like, well, a lot like a skull...his name was Jack Trudeau.

But none of this reflected an iota in the face of the man from Virginia—for which P.T. himself would have delivered a thunderous applause.

"Well, ah'd best see what he's gotten himself into," Amos said, tipping is hat. "Thanks, Manny." With that—he strolled to the door and down the street to the left...but as soon as he was out of sight of the hotel's big front windows, ran like the devil was after him.

And he, like Evans, also picked up a shadow.

* * * * *

For most of the warmer seasons in the last seven years, Anna (and her sister before her) had been renting her horse and wagon from the same livery, picking up mostly prepared Runzas from a bakery in South Lincoln, and taking the rig to the various sporting events around Lincoln. Generally, it was rented and returned much later in the day, after a hard athletic competition of some sort; but on this day, it was a few minutes before one o'clock by the time that Anna found her way back to the livery—and this time, it was with a companion.

The sign above the lane to the livery read "LeBlanc Freight and Livery." On reading it, Bud blanched—he recognized immediately that he was heading into the lion's den, the hated rivals of the Pack family, who would be stunned to learn that he was here. But the company was delightful, Bud was eighteen, and the world looked to be tamable by sheer audacity....so the young man ducked his head and followed his heart into the stables behind the front office. Fortunately, no one appeared to be in the front yard when they swung the yellow wagon around the back.

"Anna!" An old man dressed in overalls was standing at the far end of the stables, bowing and gesturing to the open double doors as if to a returning princess. Anna cried out "Gee!" and spun the horses to the left, directly into the open doors. With an equally authoritative "Whoa!" Anna brought the horses to a halt, and the old man closed the doors behind her. Stall after stall trailed off into the distance to their left, filled for the most part with mules of various sizes and shapes. Theirs appeared to be the only wagon in the stable, and their hostler the only one in view.

"So, how was business today, little Anna?" the man queried, lifting the girl by her waist to the ground. The man's face was a mask of delight, and Anna seemed completely comfortable around him—which brought Bud's anxiety level down several notches as well.

"Pretty brisk today," she responded. "I had good help. May I introduce Mr. Bud G—, uh...well, this is Bud. Isn't it a fine day?" Anna's quick change of subject put Bud in mind of a horse salesman he once knew back in Alder Grove who had avoided mentioning a horse's obvious blind eye by directing the buyer's attention to the gathering storm clouds on a summer's day—finally adding that since the animal couldn't see half the dangers surrounding him, it was sure to be twice as sturdy in adverse conditions.

"And this is Mr. Raleigh LeBlanc, Bud—a gentleman in every respect, the brother of the *prior* owner." Anna's introduction was enough to warn Bud that the critical issue of family was involved here—sacred to Anna and a minefield to be avoided if possible.

"Which means, Mr. Gardner," the man said, shocking both Bud and Anna with his insight into Bud's true origin, "That my nephew inherited the stable, and I got the broom." Raising a specimen by its handle, the man returned to leaning on it.

Before Bud could interject a question, the man added, "Heard your name thrown around a lot lately, mostly by the men that were leaving for your family's firm. Nice little business Rufus Pack has, there…a lot of good men moving over to it these days. Didn't know you were taking up with our Miss Anna, here, though." The man's old eyes moved to Anna's face, and Bud saw real pleasure here—as a grandfather might see in a his grown-up granddaughter.

"Well, I…that is…uh…" Bud stammered, but was mercifully saved by Anna.

"Mr. LeBlanc isn't at all like his nephew," Anna announced. "He's always been a good friend to the farmer."

"Better lookin' too," Raleigh interjected with a playful smile, then allowed himself a serious moment. "Truth is, Bud, my brother married a woman that pampered their boy his whole life. Let him run wild, she did. Not that my brother was worth a damn either—he had a mean streak, just like our father. Anyway, after my brother died, Maxie's mother handed the freight and livery over to him. He was already hip deep in some kind of nasty business with Miles McGee by that time—with no idea how to run the business…"

"And too much pride to ask his uncle here for help," Anna threw in, then, as if emboldened by Bud's presence, added, "I always wondered why you stayed on…?"

"Why, to rent you a lunch wagon every Saturday, Miss Anna!" Raleigh jibed, then added, "And for the horses, of course. Always did prefer that end of the business." As if on cue, one of the horses harnessed to the lunch wagon whinnied for their caretaker.

"Love to talk more," interjected Raleigh, "But I need to take care of these girls, here." With considerable speed, the elder LeBlanc removed the halters, tack, and traces from the two horses, and then guided them along a narrow passageway in front of the stables to their stalls at the other end.

"Seems a nice fellow," said Bud, not knowing how to take the existence of a friendly member of the LeBlanc family.

"Yes, he's a dear," said Anna. "As he was saying, he rented this wagon to me and my sister Antonia for a long time…since I was eight, guess. When his brother died, he left it to Raleigh, plus a dozen or so horses and a shack behind the stables. As Raleigh said, Maxwell got the rest of it…you have met him, I think."

"Er, yes," Bud confirmed, touching his bruised face.

"They do not speak, as a rule," Anna said, "But I understand that Maxwell directed Raleigh to stop renting me the wagon last year—and Raleigh told him to—well, that the only practical answer to his nephew's attitude involved a policeman, a lawyer, or a match."

Bud laughed, reflecting how many arguments *could* be settled by a fistfight or a fire, and was about to suggest that they unload the rig when the sound of a wagon entering the freight yard was heard, accompanied by raucous singing. Within a few minutes, a set of double doors opened up a few bays down to their left, and a wagon full of singing men entered at considerable speed, the horses stopping only inches from the stable wall.

"Whoa!" the men all shouted together—over a dozen were dressed in dirty, tattered clothing. They were accompanied by three men that Bud recognized—LeBlanc and his two toadies (Bud forgot their names)—and another that Bud did not know—a man of medium height with an air of authority, at least over LeBlanc and his men. All four of them were currently busy getting the tipsy men out of the wagon, and had not noticed Bud and Anna, as yet anyway.

"Anna," Bud said, levelly, "Let's get into the wagon, okay?" Bud's senses were alert, and Anna did little but nod her head before she followed Bud into the back of the wagon, where they hid and listened among the heating pans and various Runza litter.

40

"Gentlemen," Flint said, softly. "Times are hard, are they not?" Standing in the freight wagon before a half score of rough-looking men, the man's voice was consoling, his hands outstretched. Bud Gardner had taken a course in rhetoric at Craig High School, and from his place of concealment—forty feet away in the bed of a lunch wagon with Anna Marie Vostrovsky—he suspected that Flint, despite his revulsion at the topic, was a master of the subject.

In point of fact, the man put Bud in mind of a circuit-riding pastor he had once heard come though Alder Grove. Like many a revival leader, Flint had led the spectators into the barn in song, ringing out such favorites as "The Strawberry Blonde," and "The Man on the Flying Trapeze," instead of "Shall We Gather," of course, after which he immediately sent the 'ushers'—LeBlanc and his two cronies—out of the barn. Bud had heard the three men get on their horses and ride off, which focused the gathering on Flint alone. Mounting the wagon as the last chorus was finished, the man had issued forth a booming salutation to his "congregation," welcoming them to "the most prosperous freighting business in the West." He had then gradually lowered his tone, becoming first conversational—"Things have certainly changed in the last few years, haven't they?"—then, questioning—"Doesn't anyone realize how hard it is for a working man these days?"—before reaching a somber tone of complete empathy. "And how hard it is for our *families*? Where is the *justice?*"

Here it comes, Bud said to himself, identifying the emotional question in the speech for what it was—a coiled spring. His stomach fell—Bud took no pleasure in recognizing the delivery pattern as a familiar one, but his teacher would have been proud—it represented danger to the farmers, and possibly even his own family.

"Where is the *justice?*" Flint bellowed, and the men surrounding his wagon murmured. "The prices go up, and up, and no one seems to care. These landowners—with corn in their barns, ready for shipment—do they care? Do they offer a poor man a decent wage, or even a *meal*?"

"No!" shouted the men, almost in unison. Through a crack in the side panels of the wagon, Bud spied that a fair number of them were holding pint bottles of reddish liquid. *Probably weren't all that interested in a meal at the moment.*

"Well, I do gotta hand it to these farmers around here—they're pretty sharp, for **foreigners**." *There's another classic technique,* Bud observed. Mr. Jacobs had taught him that blaming "the other" was a classic motivation technique—but was generally used only if one was sure of one's audience. Had Bud been with Flint earlier, he might have an even greater appreciation (or disgust) for the man's abilities—every man standing in front of him had been hand picked as at least a third generation American.

Flint smiled inwardly, though his voice now grew in pitch, volume, and fervor—he knew, from experience, that he had them. "They **refuse** to pay their bills. They **break** an agreement with an **honest man** here in town—to sell their filthy corn to a higher bidder. So now, this honest man is calling out to **you**, men. Make this **right,** and make these foreigners **pay!**"

The congregation roared in approval. Flint opened his wallet, and pulled out dozens of greenbacks.

"Five dollars right now, for each of you, and a dollar for every man you recruit. Every man that can handle a horse and wagon gets two dollars a day, starting tomorrow—but every man that can handle a gun, gets **ten** dollars—**tonight**."

Another roar. Anna looked at Bud, and fear was in her eyes. She started to whisper, but Bud put his finger to his lips, and reached out his other hand, gently placing it over her mouth.

In the midst of the cheering, Flint gave more details. "Bring your men to the barn here at sundown. Meanwhile, take four wagons back with you—you'll find they are well supplied with food...and **drink!**"

More cheers erupted, and one man shouted out from the crowd, "Hey...where's Maxy-boy? He's the one who started all this..."

"LeBlanc and his boys are already **busy**," Flint announced, magnanimously. "They're going to visit one of the ringleaders—a bastard by the name of Harrison."

Bud and Anna locked her eyes on one another, and each of them swallowed their hearts. Harrison—*Robert Harrison? Gods,* thought Bud—*I was supposed to go there. Right away. To protect him...*

Unbidden, the thought of Harrison's little grandson, Roscoe, came to him—rolling his ball back and forth to Bud at the Barrelhouse on the day of the wreck. Now, he and his grandfather were facing three sadistic men with guns. He and Anna were here together—what they both wanted—but because they were, others would face those men without his help. The guilt began to roll over him in waves, and looking at Anna, Bud saw that it

357

was the same with her. As the cheers went on in the barn about 40 feet from them, Bud was possessed by a single urgent desire.

I gotta get outta this wagon, he thought, wildly. *I gotta help.*

* * * * *

The finely dressed Negro was stopping *again*, Evans observed with chagrin, this time bending down at the street corner to tie his shoes. As smoothly as he could, Evans sidestepped into the recessed entrance of a brick haberdashery half a block behind the man, feigning to admire the men's hats, while keeping an eye on his quarry through his reflection in the store window. Since leaving the hotel, the black man had walked several blocks, then paused to buy a newspaper—strolled a few more blocks, then stopped to wind his watch…and was now tying his shoes. Evans was no expert in the art of surveillance, but this man's stop-and-go behavior was starting to spook him. In their passage from the hotel, each man had been accosted once by a man announcing himself to be private detective—a Pinkerton—and shown the likeness of a man that fitted Cable's description.

How I **wish***,* Evans had said to himself, having turned the prying detective away with yet another negative response. *Then I wouldn't have to* **track** *this character.*

Since leaving the hotel, the pair had been steadily moving southward down E Street, past the downtown, and finally through Courthouse Square. Now, they were nearing the towering grain elevator at the edge of town across the segment of the CRI&P track that led to the next little town of Endicott. They were nearly out of streets, Evans recognized, and despite the fact that he had dropped his following distance to over a block, he had become increasingly convinced that continuing to follow the man directly was unwise. The reporter had parked himself under a tree across the street from the tracks and was seriously considering giving up the chase, when his target walked across the tracks and directly into the large, open door of the grain elevator. He didn't walk out.

Evans waited five minutes. The freight yard surrounding the stark tin-clad tower was absolutely still, as was the small glass-enclosed office that butted against it, its Venetian blinds drawn completely against the sun, with a large "Closed" sign propped between them and the window panes. *Was the young Cable being held in the grain elevator?* As the seconds ticked by into minutes, Evans' innate curiosity struggled against, and finally broke, his sense of caution…he eventually admitted to himself that he just **had** to see what was going on inside that building.

With a slight sense of foreboding that was clearly overwhelmed by his insatiable curiosity, Evans crossed the tracks. A strong wind had risen with the day's temperatures, and now that he had left the shelter of the town's buildings and trees which lined both sides of E Street, the loose dust of the freight yard stung his eyes, and he stumbled as he crossed the tracks. A door to the small elevator office stood on the nearest corner of building, and when Evans reached it, he stood in its recessed frame, taking advantage of the shelter it offered from observation. Reaching into his pocket, he had just pulled out a paisley handkerchief and was wiping his eyes—when he suddenly felt the door give way from behind him, and a snakelike grip, unbelievably strong, slammed him onto the wooden floor of the office. Evans' head thumped against the pineboard wall, and before he could recover, the door to the office had banged shut, and the figure was on him. As he tried to rise, something thin and sharp was pressed against his neck, and he flinched—but then held his body rigidly still, as the hovering voice whispered to him.

"The Pinkerton doesn't move," the man hissed. "Or the Pinkerton will die."

Evans complied—having never had a knife at his throat, he found it an amazingly effective argument—and didn't object to being called a Pinkerton, either. *There are a lot of Pinkertons around—maybe he's afraid of them,* his mind raced, grasping for a hope, however slim. His fear went up another notch, however, when it occurred to him that anything that the man pinning him down found even remotely dangerous would be seen—and dealt with—as a threat.

"See you've met my shadow," a deep voice observed as the door of the little office opened, then closed. Though his face was being pushed firmly into the floorboards, Evans recognized the shiny dress shoes and gray slacks as belonging to the man he had been following.

"The Negro makes a jest," Evans' captor replied, in a hoarse voice somewhere between a whisper and a wheeze. "My partner *is* a shadow."

"I see that you picked up my signals well enough," the black man said, ignoring the jibe.

"And what signals did Mr. Jay send?" *The gaunt man had a grip of iron...he must be all muscle and bone,* thought Evans...but his struggles quieted some as he waited for the black man's response.

"He doesn't like the odds," the Negro replied, kicking Evans in the belly. The reporter's body recoiled in pain, and he barely could make out his attacker's words as he struggled for breath. "Too many of these sons of bitches around, and our guest's father has no plans to remove them. The boss says half-price is still a respectable profit, and I agree with him. We are directed to wait until five—and if the boss hasn't joined us by then, our orders are...to dispose of him."

"Sounds like a pleasurable task," the other man replied, as Evans gasped. "And that gives considerable time...and latitude...to deal with this gentleman."

"You've got that sound in your voice again," the man's partner muttered, and to Evans, just catching his breath, his voice sounded disapproving. "But we don't have any time for games, Trudeau...I'd advise you to be quick about it."

His name is Trudeau, Evans noted, trying to focus. A thin man— probably the man that took Cable. *Oh, Holy Mother...is he going to kill me right here?*

"The Pinkerton's hands shall be tied, and then Mr. Rankin will return to camp," Trudeau murmured, almost dreamily.

"The elevator man might come along any time," Rankin added, his voice now urgent. "Or a yard worker."

"This elevator and yard are closed today," the man with his knee in Evans' back replied, languorously nodding his head toward the "CLOSED" sign whose bottom edge protruded from under the closed window blind. "As Mr. Rankin knows very well...having chosen this rendezvous himself, in case of pursuit."

Evans heard a deep sigh, as if in resignation, and then felt his hands being bound tightly behind him with a thin cord. He was terrified—but even more than that, he was ashamed. He had obviously been lured here, completely duped, and was now bound and helpless before a man who was pressing a straight razor against his neck.

Unbidden, a memory flashed into Evans' mind. When he was a boy, his father had a way of getting a hog to cooperate when slaughtering time came around. A couple of weeks before the event, he'd come out to the pen in the morning carrying an apple. He'd hand the apple to the hog, who loved his treats; and each day got to expect them at the same time, waiting with slavering chops. Every day, his father would begin to hold the apple higher, so that the hog would have to stretch up to get at it...then higher still, until the creature was standing against the fence, straining up to reach the apple. On the appointed day, his father appeared with the apple, but also with a straight razor. When the hog stretched up to get his treat, one swift, smooth stroke of the razor severed his carotid artery, and the hog bled out... quick, clean, no fuss. In a similar way, Evans realized with revulsion that he had greedily swallowed tidbits of information about Ransom Reed Cable, Jr., and followed them...here, to this small coffin of an office...and to the edge of a straight razor.

As the door closed behind the Negro, Evans was startled into the realization that he was left alone with Trudeau, and terror bit into him even more sharply than Trudeau's knife. The man was astride him with his knee in Evans' back, breathing heavily, and with each of Evans' breaths the razor shifted a little against his throat, stinging as it cut against fresh skin. *When it digs its way through to the carotid,* Evans realized, *I'll be dead in seconds.* Though he did his best not to give into it, he discovered that he was trembling, and, yes, to his shame and disgust, that he had urinated. Through the corner of his eye, Evans saw a thin, white hand reach down to touch the moist floor, shifting his knife not an iota as his did so.

"This Pinkerton," the man mocked, "Isn't pink at all, is he? He's quite yellow, it must be thought. He appears to leak."

The taunting comment caused a little flame of anger to ignite within Evans—at being called a coward, at his state of physical submission, at his utter humiliation in having urinated...and at Trudeau's maddened, taunting manner of speech. It involved almost no personal pronouns, Evans observed with irritation—no I's, me's or my's—delivered for the most part in the third person, and...disembodied, somehow, as if he was describing what was happening to another person, not himself. Evans had a sudden urge to taunt the man in return—to mimic him, to gain a little of his self-respect back—and perhaps to be a real reporter for the first time, in his last moments of his life. Evans decided that there wasn't much to lose—after all, he would probably be dead in a puddle of pee in a few minutes anyway—might as well enjoy a last fling at the bastard.

"Mr. Trudeau is being careless. The Pinkerton's bloodstains on the floor will raise questions, won't they?" Evans queried, trying to achieve the same taunting, languid tone that Trudeau used, despite being held down. "What will happen when it is discovered? The Pinkertons are already looking for Trudeau—he was seen taking Cable off the train. Will they start searching in this direction? What if they are searching for the Pinkerton, even now? Yes, yes, Trudeau is being very, very careless..."

For a moment, the odd little wager that Evans had made with his own corpse seemed to pay off. Evans' mocking soliloquy was interrupted as he was spun around and rewarded—if you want to call it that—with his first good look at Trudeau's face. Evans was struck immediately by his captor's eyes, black and alert, and his stupefying grin, framed by narrow lips that were pulled away from tall, yellow teeth sweeping nearly from ear to ear, the whole giving an impression of wild, grotesque joy. The man's breath was sour, and his body was shaking and wheezing...*was the man actually laughing?*

He doesn't seem to be at all bothered to find out that he had been seen leaving the wrecked train with Cable. In fact, Evans realized in dismay, *this man was actually **enjoying** the conversation...*

"Yes, there is...an *accord* here," he said, with what sounded like relish. "Another location is needed."

Climbing onto Evans' prostrate form and pinning his shoulders down with Evans' upturned face between his knees, Trudeau folded his straight razor carefully and placed it into his right coat pocket—from which he immediately withdrew a small tin can with a screw lid. From his left coat pocket, he withdrew a handkerchief. Holding it at arms length as Evans struggled with his hands tied beneath him, Trudeau soaked the handkerchief in the clear liquid, then quickly brought it down onto Evans' nose and mouth. Evans' last memory through the heavy, sickly-sweet haze that followed was of Trudeau's intense eyes and wheezing laughter, as the man tied the end of a long coil of rope around his legs.

* * * * *

The sermon was over, the speaker had left the pulpit, but the congregation was still visiting.

As far as Bud could tell from his vantage point in the wagon bed, Flint had moved outside and was shaking his new hirelings' hands as each of them left the stable and boarded the wagons, which had both been moved and were now waiting outside. However, about a dozen of the men were still hanging around inside the stable, enjoying the cool shade as they sipped at their pints.

Meanwhile, Bud was beginning to panic—*when are these guys going to break this up?* Anna was restless as well—both had been in the wagon for over twenty minutes—twenty precious minutes, wasted in a wagon, knowing that LeBlanc was on his way to the Harrison farm, looking for trouble.

"That Mr. Flint sure is a fine fellow," remarked a man with a fractured nose, in an even more mangled pair of overalls. "Sure will be good to be working again."

"Sure...work's fine...but it's the side benefits I'm interested in," remarked another, and through a knothole, Bud could see him holding up his pint...which garnered a laugh from the rest of the crowd.

"Okay, boys, there's more where that came from," rang Flint's voice from outside, adding, "Get up in the wagons, now."

Thank God, Bud thought...they're leaving. It was true—outside the stables, "Camptown Ladies" had gone up, and the last of Flint's men was just taking his leave of the stables when another pair of voices could be heard arguing, their deep voices emerging from the other end of the long stable. In the dim light of the stables, Bud couldn't recognize the men, or understand what they were saying—the language they were speaking was not English—but it mattered little to him at the moment. Flint's men had left, and it was time to *go*.

As he started to rise this time, however, it was Anna's hand on Bud's arm that restrained him, and her finger on his lips urging him to silence. As the arguing pair of men drew nearer, Bud caught the look of panic in Anna's eyes…and then, his eyes widened as well, recognizing that this was a threat of a different kind, altogether. At that moment, the wagon's tailgate at their feet came crashing down, and Bud Gardner and Anna Vostrovsky found themselves staring up at two very large, very *unhappy* faces.

"Jste čubčí syn!" the taller man bellowed, and from where Bud was sitting, Stephan Vostrovsky's blazing eyes looked ready to ignite his bushy eyebrows. Together with Lukas, Anna's older brothers each laid a pair of massive hands on one of Bud's feet, and in a moment, Bud experienced a short flight followed by a sudden—and painful—negative change in altitude.

"Zastavení!" Anna yelled, and quick as lightning, sprang out of the wagon to Bud's aid—until she ran squarely into Stephan, who, with what was clearly a practiced motion, wrapped both arms around her, holding her firmly from behind while Anna flailed helplessly away. Lukas, meanwhile, brought his two massive hands down to Bud's shirt, lifted the boy to his feet, and slammed him into the stable wall, knocking the wind out of him.

"Mr. Bud…*Gardner*, I presume," Lukas said, pronouncing the boy's last name as if it were a curse. "What do you think you are doing *with…our…SISTER?!?*" The last three words were emphasized with a rigid finger thumping into Bud's chest. It occurred to Bud that the blows would have been pretty painful if he were actually *alive*, but he kept the thought to himself, along with any response to the massive man's questions…his ability to draw breath—and to expel it in formulating actual words—had momentarily deserted him.

Lukas had drawn his right arm back and was about to deliver a massive blow to Bud's already bruised face, when two solid clicks sounded from behind him, and the entire Vostrovsky family turned to see Raleigh LeBlanc, with a shotgun half-raised in the direction of Lukas.

"Let go of the boy, Lukas," Raleigh said, nonchalantly. "He looks bruised enough."

"Stay out of this, Raleigh," Lukas warned, without moving his fist either toward Bud or to his side. "He has it coming."

"Well, let's hear about it, then. Tell you what," Raleigh offered in a friendly voice, without actually moving the shotgun. "If I think he's harmed Anna in any way, I'll let you finish what you started."

"He didn't harm me at all," Anna objected, shaking loose of Stephan's grip only after Raleigh's side-by-side ten gauge barrels half-turned in her older brother's direction. Fear and anger were equally mixed in her blue eyes, but she refused to let herself cry. "He just rode home with me from the cadet assembly."

"So I heard," Lukas interjected, and the anger was hot in his eyes, as well. "From our neighbors. Oh, yes, Anna," he went on, turning to his sister, "By the time word got out and we showed up, your little picnic with Mr. Gardner was quite the scandal—half the *town* was there. When we heard who the boy was, naturally we came after you...and we find you here, in the back of a wagon."

Lukas turned to Raleigh. "You do know who this boy *is*, don't you? And what his uncle did to our *sister?*"

"I've heard things," Raleigh admitted, noncommittally.

Now it was Lukas' turn to fight back his emotions, and his voice broke slightly as he responded. "Ezekiel Gardner killed our...Antonia."

To Bud, who was just recovering his breath, the words were like being hit in the solar plexus. *Zeke killed Anna's sister?*

"There's more to it than that, Lukas," Raleigh replied, but his eyes were not unsympathetic.

"There has to be *more*?" Lukas said, his anger rising again, and as he turned to point at Bud, the boy could never recall seeing a man in more deadly earnest. "We *told* you, Gardner, only *yesterday*, to *stay away* from our *sister*."

Bud wanted to object, but Lukas' words regarding his uncle had left him utterly speechless. Anna, however, was not.

"Bud is not his uncle," Anna objected. "He has been a...a *friend* to me, and I have a *right*..."

"A *friend?!?*" Lukas scoffed, followed by a short sentence to his brother, Stephan...who definitely saw no humor in his brother's words. "Anna, you were *kissing* the boy in *public*."

Anna was no liar, and she knew better than to refute the truth. "You are not my father, Lukas," she said quietly, which she appeared to repeat in Czech, for Stephan's benefit.

"Zbývá ani jeden, holka," Stephan said, quietly, and even he looked distressed.

Bud asked the next question without thinking. "What did he say, Anna?" Seeing the girl's reaction, he instantly regretted it.

"He said...he said, 'There is no one else...little one.'" With that, Anna's composure finally melted down, and she turned her sobbing face toward a dark corner of the stable, her shoulders heaving. The males in the room were instantly silent—arguing in front of a crying girl wasn't right, no matter what language a man spoke.

"I think you should *go*, Mr. Gardner," Raleigh LeBlanc said, firmly, then softened a bit as he lowered the hammers on his shotgun, one at a time. "This isn't a safe place for you, you know."

Bud nodded, but as he headed for the large stable door, Lukas' hand shot out and firmly grasped his shoulder as he passed by. What he had to say was short and to the point, and he had already released Bud before Raleigh could react with his weapon.

"I *won't* tell you *again*, Gardner."

Bud nodded once and left the stables behind him, his heart broken and his head confused—except for one thing: He *had* to get to Harrison's. He moved immediately into a trot, and then gave himself over entirely to the power of his young legs—and the wind blowing into his face from the north, filled with the smell of impending rain.

There was a storm coming.

41

Saturday, August 11, 1894
1:00 pm

Amos Seville was steadily moving southward on E Street toward the tracks, the last known direction taken by his reporter friend, Wendell Evans, according to Manny—but that had been three-quarters of an hour ago, and Evans was nowhere to be seen. However, what was visible directly ahead of him was clearly a private detective, stationed at the corner, accosting passers by with a piece of paper—undoubtedly, a picture of Mr. Ransom Reed Cable, Jr.

Amos' dislike of Pinkertons had stemmed from a series of run-ins with the nationwide organization of private detectives during his circus days with Mr. Barnum. They most commonly showed up when something went missing in a town that the circus had just visited. Most notably, one of his best friends—a sword swallower of incredibly varied talents—had left Boston with...a trophy...that had been fairly won, but whose husband had seen it as otherwise. Amos' point of view was along the lines of "finders keepers," but Pinkertons were uniformly less understanding about the complexities of illicit affection. However, as Seville had observed another pair of the professional busybodies on the corners to the right and left, he was just planning to put his head down and soldier on when another though occurred to him.

"Pardon me, sir," the mustached gentleman in the bowler hat said to Amos as he drew near. As the bootlegger from Lincoln had expected, the Pinkerton produced a picture of Cable. "Have you seen this gentleman...?"

"Hmmm...maybe," Seville said, acting interested. "Might have seen him a few days ago, here in Fairbury." Perceiving that the words were drawing a smile of interest from the detective, Amos continued. "I think he might have been with a friend of mine, who just passed this way a few minutes ago—about so tall, dark haired? Was following a black gentleman?"

Unwittingly, the Pinkerton looked directly southward, then quickly back to Amos. *That's it—he continued south,* thought Amos. Before the man could respond verbally, Amos quickly covered his tracks...he didn't want the Pinkerton's attention, now that he had his information.

"Wait—no, he was with another man, at a supper, I think—last Thursday...yes, at the hotel," Amos hastily added, then reached into his pocket for a small pencil and a notebook. "Is he missing, sir? I'm a

366

reporter from the State Journal. Is this connected with the wreck, in any way? Could I get a quote, sir, from your organization…?"

"No, sir," the Pinkerton stuttered, tipping his hat. "Thank you for your information, sir…I believe we know about that supper." And tipping his hat, the Pinkerton hurriedly walked up the street to the north.

Seville smiled, turned, and continued southward at a trot. Had he looked behind him, he would have seen the Pinkerton tip his hat once again, and accost the person following Amos at a discreet distance.

* * * * *

Bud was a superior athlete, and could walk for many miles when the need arose (which in rural Nebraska, was not uncommon). However, he was surprised to find himself panting by the time that he had jogged the 10 blocks to his uncle Zeke's stable. *Nerves,* Bud realized. Dual hammer blows of shame—over his own failure to go to Harrison's farm to protect him when asked, and his uncle's reported murder of Anna Marie's sister— were conspiring to work his respiratory system into a frenzy. *Killing a woman? No,* he thought. *No, that just can't be true.*

Johnny had told him that waiting for him in the stable were two horses—the slow, steady nag that he had ridden two days ago in collecting grain sales agreements from the farmers…and Zeke's own roan mare. Lily was not what you'd call an endearing animal—every time that Bud had gotten within range of her teeth, she had tried to bury them in his flesh— but she was *fast*…and speed was needed.

Burch, the farrier, seemed to be expecting Bud, and when Bud described what he needed, Burch led him to the stalls. With a crooked grin, he extended his hand, palm upward, to the gray nag, and then to the Bitch Demon…and waited for Bud's choice.

"Saddle up the roan," Bud said, with resignation.

"*You* saddle her," the farrier replied. "I'll hold her head."

* * * * *

The dark places are always so much cooler, the gaunt man repeated to himself, as he made the last few adjustments in his captive's bonds, then quickly added to himself, *and they are nothing to fear.*

Trudeau's mind was floating now, but also racing—rapture at his role of the captor was intermingling with a focused concentration on his work. *Yes,* he thought with pleasure, *it is time to teach a **lesson.*** Years ago, as a young boy on his father's farm, his fear of the dark had been discovered. His older brothers had reported it to their father—an educated widower and

367

confirmed drunkard, whose resolution of this problem, as with all those presented by his youngest son and murderer in childbirth of his beloved second wife, had been harsh. In this case, Trudeau had been forced into a windowless cellar, with nothing but a bucket of water for company...or so he thought.

The dark had been terrible, but upon discovering the large black rats that made the cellar their home as well, something came unhinged in the boy. After an hour of screaming, and several more fighting sleep and the ever more brazen advances of the rodents toward the water bucket, Trudeau's mind had arrived at a curious way out of his fugue state of panic. The boy somehow managed to remove his subjective self from his predicament, observing it as if it were a stage play that he was witnessing, and in fact, narrating. *The narrator*, to the boy's thinking, understood all and could not be harmed by the events of a story as it unfolded. The boy that emerged from the cellar was changed—from that moment, Trudeau saw himself not only as a narrator, but as a type of teacher...one whose lessons often dealt in the harsh consequences of crossing him or his employers. .

An application of smelling salts roused Evans from his heavy, chloroform-induced slumber, and as his eyes took nearly a minute to adjust to the dim light surrounding him. Finally, he perceived a large, dimly lit rectangle above him though a dusty mist that smelled oddly sweet. He tried to speak, but he found he lacked the ability. His head couldn't quite make sense of it yet. As his eyes became used to the light, he perceived that he was lying head downwards on a steeply inclined surface with hard edges pressing into his legs and back every few feet. Surrounding him were faint, rhythmic grinding sounds...*was there machinery somewhere near?* Blood was rushing to his head, causing his ears to pound.

"The Pinkerton wonders where he is," a voice sounded from near him. "He may even believe that he is dead. But, assuredly, he will rise."

At the sound of that voice, Evans came immediately to his full senses. He was in a darkened, slope-sided space surrounded by the remnants of corn—*a grain pit,* he realized, part of the grain elevator where he had been bushwhacked—with the dregs of last year's corn surrounding him. He was lying head downwards on a long—*ladder? No, a grain conveyor...*feet pointed up.

If he had, earlier, been close to panic under Trudeau's knife, he entirely crossed the line now, and a muffled scream washed into his gag. His nose was clogging with the dust—in a few moments, he was sure he would choke to death.

And then the world screeched and thundered into mechanical anarchy, as his feet began to rise away from him. Within the space of a few seconds, he saw that he had moved up the conveyor several feet into a narrow chute, much darker than the room that he had previously been held in. Into the claustrophobic, confined darkness he shot, the dust biting into his lungs like fire, his head banging against one of the regularly spaced, shallow metal buckets on the chain-driven track that was forcing his body skyward.

Frantically, Evans attempted to free himself from his bonds. His hands were fastened behind him as if encased in concrete. But his legs, though bound at the ankles, did yield to his efforts to swing them—a bit—from side to side. In a few seconds, he found that he could roll his entire body, and decided that he could have actually dropped off the conveyer—if he had not been surrounded by four wooden walls of the grain chute, three feet apart.

Sweat poured from Evans as he strained his body to look forward, where he perceived a dim rectangle of light stretching above and beyond his prostrate form, growing gradually as he neared it on the rattling, shivering grain conveyer. Breathing was getting a little easier now, but the growing rectangle before him raised his level of anxiety nearly as high as his altitude. Frantically, he swung his feet to the walls of the grain chute slipping past him, but they could find no purchase...and then, there was no wall at all. With a scream that could be heard by no-one, Evans felt his feet dangling freely as the conveyer slipped underneath him on its return journey to the pit where it had begun, followed by the rest of him, tumbling into the void of the tallest portion of the nearly empty elevator.

For a fraction of a second, Evans felt himself plunge feet first into space, until his body slammed into an inclined metal surface, slid several feet—and once again fell into open space. This time, his ankles and legs wrenched violently, back toward the top of the grain conveyer, and the grain chute he had just left, pulled by a rope that had remained attached to the conveyer, coiled in one of the grain buckets that had supported his back and legs as it had dragged him to the top. His body inverted violently, whipping his head down and forward, and straining every joint from his ankles to his neck as his body swung in a wide arc. In the midst of the dizzying change of attitude, Evans heard two distinct sounds—that of the machinery in the grain pit dying away, and that of a man stumbling rapidly up what sounded like a set of wooden stairs. Though Evans' view was inverted and dimmed by the pain of his wrenching tumble from the grain chute, the light streaming from the overhead windows through the dust of the elevator clearly showed that he was suspended fifty feet above a shallow, inclined pile of corn.

And that above him, a man was now standing on a narrow platform near the top of the grain chute, smiling, with a razor in his hand.

* * * * *

Amos trotted down E Street, passed the courthouse, and after a few blocks found himself facing a deserted portion of the CRI&P railyard surrounding the grounds of the Fairbury Mill and Elevator. Seville was intimately familiar with this area, having reconnoitered the wooded island and river area behind the mill as yet another potential site where "supplies" for the Barrelhouse could be obtained. A long concrete dam ran across the Little Blue River, and propped on it was a large iron wheel that slowly turned as the water fell over the dam. In his mind's eye, Amos could envision the 300 yard long steel cable that ran from the dam on the other side of the mill to the machinery inside it, used to operate grain conveyers that moved grain from the collection pit to the elevator for storage. The grounds were deserted now—the elevator was probably tapped out, nearly all of its contents having been sold long ago as the prices had skyrocketed. Hence the silence—or near silence, Amos noted. From somewhere deep within the elevator, machinery was rotating...*who started that up?*

Amos' eyes scanned the grounds—there was no motion except that produced by the afternoon wind—and then to the elevator itself, a rust-streaked tin structure with windows in a small cupola at the top, standing stark against the painfully blue sky. Casting his eyes about, something nagged at him. *There's something out of place here,* he thought. The office windows were closed with sun-bleached Venetian blinds, a "Closed" sign was in the window, and...*what the hell?* There, plastered against the office door by the west wind like a heathen flag, was a multi-colored handkerchief—a twin, if not the very same that Evans wielded at breakfast.

Amos crossed the tracks at a run.

370

Saturday, August 11, 1894
1:14 pm

At the corner of the small, windowed office that butted against the Fairbury elevator, Amos slowed, retrieved Evans' gaudy handkerchief, and slipped silently up to its closed door. Satisfying himself that there was no sound within, he carefully tried the handle—and found it locked. However, marks of a struggle were clear all around the door, and several sets of footprints appeared to lead back and forth to the office from the woods that lined the riverbank behind the elevator. For a moment, Amos pondered whether he should follow the tracks—until the rumble of machinery running inside the building began to slow, and then die. The open door to the slant-roofed, wagon-sized freight entrance loomed to Amos' right, butted against the side facing away from the tracks. Although the mechanical sounds had stopped now, Amos thought he could still detect the faint sounds of movement inside. Stiffly, Seville reached into his coat pocket and fished out his .32 revolver, placed it into his left coat sleeve, and crooked his left arm to keep it in place. *No need to go scaring the elevator man...if it is the elevator man...*

Inching up to the freight entrance, Amos took off his hat and peered around the corner into the slant-roofed interior. Immediately before him was the slope-sided pit in the floor where grain was dumped out of wagons after it had been weighed. Its large iron doors, normally locked and flush with the level of the floor, were standing open now, exposing a ladder on the wall that led down into the pit. Leaning over its edge, he noted that the pit was empty, except for the conveyor mechanism and a good deal of dust on the floor...

...which had a whole lot of footprints in it. Though it was no longer moving, the dust was still floating down the conveyor chute, and the handle that engaged it had apparently been sheared away from its restraining bolt.

As these realizations sank into him, Amos noted a faint sound. It seemed to be coming from far away, high up in the windowed cupola where the loft of the grain elevator distributed the grain from the conveyor to the six large wooden storage cribs. Amos was familiar with the layout of this type of grain elevators, a standard design that spanned many prairie towns. It was considered good sport among his suppliers—often as not under the influence of their own merchandise—to take a "bucket ride" into the loft to get a bird's eye view of the town. Built into the roof of the conveyor housing was a set of steep stairs that also led into the loft, accessed by a door in the wall to his left.

Amos cocked his ears. *Yes, there was a voice in the loft. What the hell was going on up there?*

Amos was tempted to open the stairwell door to the loft and investigate…then hesitated, and instead, climbed the ladder down into the grain pit. He stepped around the wide, canvas belt, now stationary, which when engaged would start the conveyor moving. Behind the grain conveyor, a small, inconspicuous wooden door was embedded in the wall. On it was a sign that read:

No Smoking

No Lanterns

No Matches

Scratched into the paint of the door below the sign, someone had added, "No Shit." Reluctantly, Amos allowed his revolver to slip down into his left hand from his coat sleeve, and then placed it back into his coat pocket.

As gently as he could, Amos gripped its knob with his right hand and turned it. Opening the door, he found himself in a narrow access corridor between the grain cribs, a dizzying space that extended all the way to the peak of the elevator cupola. From seventy feet up, six windows in the loft emitted a soft light that sifted its way back down through suspended grain dust, criss-crossing grain chutes and support columns to where he stood. He listened. Faintly, above him, he could now make out words…tantalizing, as they were so nearly intelligible, yet still just out of reach. A premonition shivered through him, followed rapidly by a decision.

Stepping lightly out of the access corridor back into the grain pit, Amos reached out for the conveyor handle, and pulled it downwards until it locked into the slot marked "engaged." Immediately, the drive belt and grain conveyer started to turn. Amos stepped lightly back through the door into the access space between the cribs.

Although Amos had engaged the conveyor to attract the attention of whomever was in the loft, his action had several unexpected side effects— the first of which could have been disastrous. Wendell Evans, hanging head down at the end of a long rope, nearly unconscious, suddenly felt himself moving *upwards.* Unable to see his predicament clearly or to warn anyone of it in any case through his gag, his feet nevertheless moved toward the overhanging edge of the grain chute that had dumped him into the crib where he found himself. Although the chute had allowed his

372

passage downward, it that was not designed to drag a man back through it feet first, and would likely break the man's legs rather than smoothly continue to drag him upward. Fortunately for Evans, the second effect was for the rope, which was tied to one of the returning buckets on the bottom of the conveyer, to get tangled in the chain drive. Immediately, a shriek emitted from the conveyor, which threw its chain off the sprocket and the canvas belt in the grain pit off its drive assembly as well. The entire mechanism ground to an immediate halt, though the drive wheel, still engaged to the long cable that led to the dam on the Little Blue River, kept spinning maniacally.

Amos had considered two options when he had turned on the conveyor—the first was to wait for whoever was in the loft to come down and turn off the conveyor, then burst out of the access corridor and get the drop on whoever it was. But it also occurred to him that if Evans was anywhere in the building, he'd be up in the loft—so when he discovered a ladder on the side of one of the grain cribs, he took the second of the two options: rapidly, he started to climb.

He was about halfway up when he heard, over to his right, the sound of someone creeping down the stairs that ran along the top of the inclined grain conveyor between the walls of the access corridor. *No one up to any good is going to be moving that quietly,* Amos thought.

Including me, he admitted to himself, and picked up the pace of his climb to the elevator loft while maintaining his stealth as best he could. When he ran out of ladder, he cautiously pulled himself up through a square opening. It opened into a narrow catwalk that ran between the three grain cribs on each side of the huge structure, flanked by a fifty-foot plunge into darkness on either side. The silence within this eerie space was broken only by the shuffle of his feet, the cooing of a few pigeons—and an odd, intermittent bumping that appeared to be coming from the interior of the nearest crib.

Leaving the catwalk, Amos grasped one of the roof trusses and carefully edged out onto the narrow wall between two of the cribs in order to get a better view of their interiors. From there, Seville saw that a rope led from the grain hopper in the floor of the loft into the nearest grain chute, from whence it plunged into the nearest crib. Following the rope downward about ten feet into the darkness of the grain crib, he met the inverted eyes of Wendell Evans, which were filled with a strange mix of terror, urgency, and relief.

"Hello, Mr. Evans," Amos said softly, immediately stooping to a crouch over the reporter suspended in the crib.

"Hello, Mr. Pinkerton," came a hoarse whisper from his right, followed by the impossibly loud *clack-click* of a pistol being cocked.

Damn, Amos thought. *Whoever he is, he's quiet as a tomb.*

"Know anything about grain elevators?" asked Amos, rising slowly to face the voice, still balancing precariously on the narrow walls between the cribs. "They ah not especially fond of open flame. You must have seen the signs at the entrance."

The thin man pointing the gun was standing a couple of dozen feet away from Amos on a steep stairway that surmounted the wooden box containing the grain conveyor. The man looked about at the dust suspended in the air, and smiled a skeleton grin that would have caused a corpse to shudder. Abruptly, he uncocked and holstered his gun with his right hand, while with his left pulled a metal object out of his coat pocket. As he flicked it open, the light flashed against the shiny blade of a straight razor. His blazing blue eyes shifted to the rope that ran down to Evans' helpless form dangling in the grain crib, and for a split second gleefully caught Amos' gaze before the thin man hurled himself up the stairs.

Amos himself had begun to move at the moment that he seen Trudeau brandish the razor. There was only one purpose that could be served by it, and Amos knew he had a scant few seconds to save Evans from a headlong plunge into the darkness. Leaping to the grain chute, Amos straddled it, bent his knees and grasped the rope.

This is likely to hurt a bit, Amos thought, and had just managed to snake a single twist of the rope around his right arm and begun to brace himself when the tension behind him disappeared completely under Trudeau's straight razor. As Evans' dead weight hit the end of the rope, Amos concluded that his personal pain estimate might have been a bit understated. The strain was tremendous, but by supporting the bulk of the weight with his right arm, he just managed to avoid the pop in his left shoulder that he knew would end this struggle, and probably Evans' life. As the rope parted, Amos pulled at the loose end with all the strength this left arm could muster, doing his best to simulate how it might depart from Trudeau's view if it was being pulled by Evans' own weight. With a speed and dexterity that bespoke half a lifetime's worth of training as an elephant handler, a tent jockey, a magician's assistant, and a dozen other circus jobs where his livelihood depended on how he handled a rope, Amos swung the free end in a large overhead arc, then whipped it suddenly down and around the free end of the grain chute. When it had completed an entire circuit of the chute, Amos released the section he was holding with his left hand and grabbed at the free end once again, looping it through the loop he had completed…

...and ducked just in time to avoid a crushing blow from Trudeau, wielding a grain shovel that *whooshed* as it narrowly missed his skull. Amos stumbled backward and let go of the rope, which whizzed away from him, pulled by Evans' limp body into the void. There was no more time to worry about it, however—Trudeau was at him again, bringing the shovel down with a maniacal laugh and a *clang* that shook the rafters, missing Amos again by only inches.

Amos was astonished by the speed and stealth of his adversary—he barely had the time to roll away and onto his feet before Trudeau's shovel crashed into his left shoulder, sending an electric jolt of pain through him. Amos tripped on one of the grain chutes on the floor of the catwalk—and thanked St. Barnum for his intervention, as the shovel missed his head for a third time. Flailing out with his legs, Amos managed to kick the back of Trudeau's own—which collapsed his knee and caused him to topple over. Amos' second kick went for Trudeau's balls.

First rule, thought Amos. *Keep it simple.*

Unfortunately, Amos missed, but did manage to connect with Trudeau's solar plexus, which caused a slight break in the man's relentless attack. The Virginian spun to his feet again, this time casting about for a weapon. None presented itself. There was the gun in his pocket, of course, but that alternative presented the same problem to him that it did to Trudeau—a no-win situation.

Wait a minute, he thought. *Where did Trudeau get **his** shovel?*

Amos spun on his heels and headed for the stairs, followed hotly by Trudeau. At its top, he jogged to the side to miss the wooden casing that surrounded the conveyor—and saw that several more were hanging there, right on the casing.

Second rule—tenacity works.

Amos grabbed a shovel and whirled to find that Trudeau was swinging an identical grain shovel at his legs from a few stairsteps down. As the men circled one another, shovels in hand, Amos decided that he would have laughed at the ridiculous situation he found himself in—if the light in his Trudeau's eyes were not quite so mad.

"The Pinkerton is quick," Trudeau's voice finally creaked. "And that is how he will die."

Trudeau swung, Seville countered, and the incessant, rhythmic clang of their shovels meeting rang through the entire structure. At one point, Trudeau switched to hold his shovel with one hand, and in the other his razor appeared, swinging at Amos' throat, and leaving a red line on his cheek as it narrowly missed.

Third rule—keep your head about you, Amos murmured to himself.

Amos' shoulder was on fire again, and every swing that he made, on defense or offense, was increasingly mired in molasses. If it was simple gunplay, or if his shoulder wasn't injured, he reasoned that he could hold his own—but as it was, the show was winding down, the audience had made its judgment, and the cast was slowly packing its bags. So it was little wonder that, in parrying another near miss from Trudeau's razor, Amos felt the hard steel of his adversary's shovel clip his forehead. His head spun, and all he could think as he went down was his fourth rule: *Stay away from the hard stuff.*

Amos reached for his gun—if he was going to go down, he might as well take Trudeau with him—but Trudeau was on him like a mad dog, his knee pinning Amos' gun hand against his chest as he grasped his revolver. Trudeau's breathing was heavy, and his face loomed over Amos' own as he placed his razor over the Virginian's throat.

"Goodbye, Mr. Pinkerton," Trudeau hissed.

"Drop the knife," a small voice quavered from behind them. "He isn't any Pinkerton."

Trudeau turned slightly, keeping the razor steady at Amos' throat, but still allowing his intended victim a glimpse of the stairs, where they both beheld a blonde girl with a *very* large .45 Colt swung in their direction. Despite her quivering hands, Julia's brown eyes burned with pure determination. Amos couldn't have been more surprised if one of the pigeons fluttering around them had turned into an angel and leveled the Sword of God at Trudeau's throat.

"That gun will burn us all down," Trudeau hissed, the light of madness still intense in his eyes as he turned still further to face the girl. "She must be insane."

"Look who's talking," said Amos, taking advantage of the split second of distraction provided by Julia to twist away from the razor. Rolling, Amos grasped at the shovel next to him and saw his gaunt assailant lunge toward his throat …when the world exploded.

The gun's muzzle flash was a fiery torch, and broke one of the nearest windowpanes with its cracking report. But fortunately, the grain cribs of this particular elevator were far from being full, and the dust, though annoying, was nowhere near the critical concentration that would fuel an explosion. Though its flame was enhanced, the gun's report was unable to sustain itself.

Nevertheless, it proved more than effective against Mr. Trudeau.

The gaunt man's hand grasped at his right hip. He spun once, then crashed through the thin rail over the middle crib on the east side of the elevator. Amos darted to the side of the rail where Trudeau met his fate, and looked over it to see the thin man fifty feet below, sprawled over a pile of moldy grain.

Rule five, he thought, staring back at Julia with admiration. *Have a surprise ready.*

Saturday, August 11, 1894
1:43 pm

"Who was he?" Julia asked.

He's an ugly corpse, Amos thought, staring at Evans' cocked limbs, now limp and free from the rope that had held him suspended over one of the grain cribs. Evans' face was beet red from having hung upside down for half an hour, and his hair was matted with blood where his scalp had banged against the side of the grain crib following his 20-foot fall (until the rope at his ankles stopped his plummet, thanks to Amos).

"His name was Wendell Evans," Amos replied. "He was a reporter...or wanted to be."

"And...the other man?" Julia said, hesitating before she added, "The man I...shot?"

"Ah think his name was Trudeau," Amos murmured, becoming suddenly aware that Julia was staring off in the direction of the grain crib where Trudeau's body had fallen. Her expression was vacant...lost in her own thoughts. *Might have a little to do with killing a man,* Amos chided himself sarcastically. His urge was to cross over to her, put his arms around her...to comfort her. But it was his fault she had gotten into this in the first place. So, instead, he spoke softly and watched her through the corner of his eye.

"Ah you...ah you going to be...all right?" he stuttered quietly.

Julia looked up, blinked twice at him, then seemed to come back to herself. "I will be...at least, I think so." Suddenly, her brown eyes bored into Amos' own. "What was he doing with...Mr. Evans, was it?" Julia asked, earnestly. "And why was he trying to kill you...well, **both** of you, Amos?"

Amos caught himself noticing again...and always, it seemed, at an odd time...how extraordinarily intense Julia's eyes could be. His first sight of them, three years ago in Lincoln, had come at a delicate time for him—and diverted the course of his life in ways Amos did not yet fully understand. P.T. Barnum had died that spring—the circus showman who had taken him on as a child, put him to work scooping elephant shit, and acted as the only "father" he had ever known, really. Following his death, Amos had no wish to stay with the show and work for Bailey, the domineering bastard who had been the operating force behind the show for the last several years—so the Virginian had packed his meager belongings and travelled to Lincoln. In his pocket was a torn photograph with a name on the back of it, portraying a grinning soldier. In his own mind, "E. Gardner, 1 Minn." was a man who had either left his mother, broken her heart, or both…and was, most likely, his own father.

Tracing the location of the former sergeant from the records and recent correspondence of the First Minnesota regiment (kept as part of the records of the Grand Army of the Republic in the what had once been Ford's Theater in Washington, D.C.), Amos had eventually made his way to Lincoln, a bustling capital that in 1891 had been riding an economy whose bounds appeared to be as limitless as the prairie that surrounded it. When he mentioned Zeke's name to the stationmaster, Amos had been directed to the Office of the County Sheriff, and who had in turn directed him to the Pack home. Amos recalled on that short walk being unsure whether he was looking for an embrace or a target for the .32-caliber argument that he carried in his pocket.

Whatever his original intent, the stunning seventeen-year old girl who opened the door changed everything.

Yes, she had said, *E. Gardner lives here—when it suits him. He's my uncle, Zeke.* It was Julia's eyes, then as now, that had left him thunderstruck—intelligent, curious, warm, and welcoming as she had taken in the compact man standing before her. *The chip on my shoulder must have been as big as a boulder back then,* Amos reflected. *But she just smiled, and asked me in to tea…*

And thus had begun the balancing act—*a strange thing,* Amos reflected, *considering I had just **left** the circus.* Zeke had taken to him right away, of course, openly having admitted to knowing his mother…but to nothing else…and Amos had not elected to push the matter further, although many times he had later wished that he had. Zeke had immediately taken him into partnership into a new business venture—the Barrelhouse—and the family had accepted him as the son of a "friend" of Zeke's from Virginia. The unspoken suspicion of their relationship placed both a kinship and a barrier between Amos and the Packs…for there, at every gathering, was Julia—her big brown eyes always turned toward the newcomer. *In friendship, yes…but was there more? Could there be more? It was unknown, unknowable…maddening…because if he **was** accepted as a family member, then Julia was as well, and….*

Amos' meandering thoughts were broken by the touch of a small hand resting upon his, and he started, visibly, as he tried to remember where he had left their conversation before wandering off into the undergrowth of his memory.

"Trudeau? He was mixed up the train wreck, ah think. Ah guess he thought we were Pinkertons," Amos replied, his head turned away slightly before gathering his thoughts and meeting the eyes of the girl who had saved his life only moments ago.

"Look, Julia," he added, firmly, "Ah appreciate what you did a little while ago, but…girl, you need to get on home. There ah bad men about, and…"

Julia's brown eyes flashed again, and she crossed her arms in indignation. "Oh, *really,* Mr. Seville? Well, I wouldn't have known if you hadn't **told** me. Gracious, perhaps I ought to think about carrying a *firearm*…"

Amos' retort was interrupted, mercifully, from an unexpected quarter—a groan, arising from the sprawled form that lay between the two of them.

"How's a man to get any sleep around here?" Wendell Evans muttered.

Julia's hand leapt to her mouth, and as Amos scrambled to Evans' side, he couldn't help blurting, "Evans! You're alive?"

"Don't jump to conclusions," Evans said, his eyes fluttering open to meet Amos' own. "Bad journalism."

"Ah reckon you're right about that," Amos grinned. "Ah withdraw my observation."

"What happened to Trudeau?" Evans asked, raising himself on one elbow, then wincing and rubbing his right leg with his free arm. "The last thing I remember is slipping down this chute here, and there he was standing right above me, mocking me in that corkscrew speech of his…"

"Do you remember the grain conveyor starting up?" Amos said, withdrawing a silver flask from his pocket and handing it to the reporter. Wendell gulped, then winced as if to say *"Coffee?"* before handing it back and responding.

"You mean the **second** time—after I was dangling in that damned pit? Yeah—nearly broke my legs when it yanked me up—slammed my head against the side of the crib…guess that was the last thing I remember." Looking around, he said. "Can I take it that was your doing? And that since he's not around, you killed him?"

"*Now* who's jumping to conclusions?" Amos queried, and pointed behind Evans' back to Julia, who had quietly been tearing a strip from her petticoat, and was about to begin bandaging the man's head when Amos drew attention to her. "There's our rescuer."

Evans tried to turn around, winced, and thinking better of it, decided instead to lie down on his back again. Any attempt on their parts to thank

Julia over the next few minutes were silenced immediately, and with a deliberate, steady hand the girl bound Evans' head, urging the reporter to "sit still" until she was satisfied that the bleeding had stopped.

"We need to get him to a doctor," Julia said. "And then get the sheriff, I guess."

"The doctor, ah agree with," Amos said. "But the Jefferson County Sheriff is as useless as tits on a boar hog." Catching himself, he added, "Uh…beg pardon, Miss Julia."

"Well, what about the Pinkertons, then?" Julia asked. Before Amos could answer, Evans interrupted.

"We don't have a lot of time. Trudeau—ol' skull face—has a partner. A black fellow, a real dandy, name of Rankin. He was the one that took the telephone call…"

"I know—Manny told me about it at the hotel. What about him?"

"He said that their boss told him to "dispose" of Cable at five o'clock—unless he showed up before then with other instructions." Evans managed to rise onto his elbow, then winced and rubbed his right knee. "How much time does that give us?"

"A little over three hours," Amos said, checking his watch. "If they're where I think they are, we'll need every minute of it." He shared the information about the "vagrants" seen at the abandoned Rock Creek Pony Express Station by the farmers holding court over at Parr's that morning. The look in Julia's eyes was not what Amos would exactly call convinced.

"It's the only lead we've got, Julia—and if what Wendell has said is true, we don't have much time."

"Who is this 'Cable' fellow? And why is he so important?"

"He may be the reason that the train was wrecked. The man you shot may have kidnapped him, and the other man…well, I think he could have been one of the wreckers. Look, Julia," Amos was trying to sound calm, but the situation was urgent. "We've got to get help for Wendell, and I've got to get moving."

"I could go with you," Julia offered.

"Wendell needs you," Amos said, flatly. He rose, and helped Julia to her feet. "Ah need you to go get Doc Connelle…he's just up the street. As soon as you can get Wendell settled, get hold of Nathan Brockhurst—only Nathan, understand? And send him to meet me at Rock Creek Station."

Julia bowed her head, nodding once.

As Amos turned to go, Julia grabbed his arm with her left hand. In her right was the Colt, which she held out butt first.

"Better take this," she said, still looking away. "I'm not gonna be there to save you next time. You will **be careful**, Amos…won't you?"

Amos wanted to look into Julia's eyes, but settled for patting her arm. "You bet."

As he made for the stairs, Amos dwelled upon Evans' words…*Cable would be killed at five…unless their boss showed up with instructions. Julie's deception was a necessary evil—waiting*

Well, Mr. Lynch, Amos thought. *It looks like we just might meet again, after all.*

* * * * *

For the most part, the road to Harrison's farm north of Lincoln wound along Oak Creek. It was familiar to Bud, since he had travelled over a good bit of it in order to deliver the grain agreements just two days ago— but not at this particular **velocity**. Lily, the red roan mare beneath him, was tearing up the miles at a pace the young man would never have believed sustainable, while simultaneously trying to unseat him. Bud had urged the mare to cut through two pastures in order to shave a few miles off the road, and each time Lily had jumped the low fences with an exuberant lurch and an extra kick. In crossing Oak Creek, Lily had jinked suddenly to run Bud under a set of low branches, followed by a hitch to the left that would have certainly thrown a less determined rider. But despite her cleverness and bad temper, Lily was determined as well, and seemed intent on reaching their destination at the fastest possible clip. Three times Bud had slowed the horse to a trot in order to rest her, only to feel her burst suddenly into a racer's pace just when he had allowed himself to relax.

Lily…could the name be short for Lilith? Bud wondered. His grandfather, as much a student of the classics as the Bible, had told him the story of a female demon of that name who had supposedly tried to force her intentions on Adam before Eve was created. Bud decided that Zeke had heard the story as well, and applied the moniker to this red demoness.

Well, Bud thought, *maybe it's time to make a deal with the devil.*

"Lilith," Bud announced. "We've got about three miles to go. Burn up this road, and you'll never have to carry me again." The mare snorted in response as it turned to cross another pasture, responding to the pressure of its rider's knees and reins…all the while watching for her opportunity.

* * * * *

382

"Your cobs are piling up pretty good there, Robert," Eloise Moseman warned, shifting Roscoe from her right to her left hip. The boy gurgled and reached for the straw flower on the farm wife's hat, flipping its brim up to expose her light blue eyes to the relentless afternoon sun before Eloise plucked the flower off and handed it to the smiling boy. It was true—the corn cobs emerging from the mechanical sheller had formed a nearly perfect pyramid of jumbled brown cylinders in the bottom of the wagon that Robert Harrison was standing in, but its apex was threatening to clog the output of the mechanism.

"I know, Weezy, I know," Harrison grumped from the back of the wagon, where he was shoveling yellow ears of corn into the feeder end of the mechaniism. "Just a few dozen ears to go, then we can start the cleanup."

"Good…'cuz your infernal machine there is running out of steam," Eloise warned, motioning over to a small steam engine that was popping and hissing as it labored to drive the sheller.

"Yeah—startin' to run low on water. Need to watch that—can seize up and raise six kinds of hell if it runs dry," Harrison remarked as he threw a half dozen more ears into the hopper. There, a maelstrom of metal teeth peeled the kernels from the cob and slid them down a chute into another wagon parked adjacent to the one Harrison was standing in, where they stood piled like yellow nuggets of gold in the sunshine.

Eloise had spent the morning keeping an eye on Roscoe and helping out with the shelling. It was common for neighbors to help one another out with jobs like this, and Eloise and Robert had lived within sight of each other's home places for twenty years. When they both lost their spouses to influenza a few winters back, the pair found themselves spending more and more time in one another's company, helping with the chores…and the loneliness. A few of the neighbors thought they ought to just go ahead and get married—but neither felt a need for it, and with no grown children to shame them into it, they found their balance and their comforts where they could—without all the fuss of involving the church.

With most of their neighbors in the Co-op busily shelling their own corn, neither Robert nor Eloise expected much in the way of help in this particular task, and were just leaving the breakfast table to get started when they heard a knock on the kitchen door. Cautiously opening it, they were surprised to see a bearded giant of a man—at least six and a half feet tall—and his small Czech companion, with a letter from Zeke Gardner introducing them as farm hands. Two dozen eggs and a gallon of coffee later, the men dropped their clothes and blankets in the small "soddy"—the original Harrison sod home that now acted a bunkhouse for harvesters, threshing crews, and the occasional farmhand—and pitched into work.

A good thing too, for Eloise needed both hands this morning keeping the little boy away from the machinery. True to form, seeing Eloise's attention turn to the mechanism, Roscoe squealed and stretched his hands out toward the rotating belt that led from the engine to the spinning drive wheel of the sheller—but Eloise had him firmly in hand, and prevented the youngster from getting anywhere near the sharp-toothed gearing.

"Looks like Roscoe's got you pretty much played out, too, Weezy," Harrison observed, smiling as he pushed that last of his corn into the hopper. "Now, where are those Czechs off to?"

"They asked where to find the necessary," Eloise replied, adding quietly, "Pretty good workers, wouldn't you say?"

"Yeah," Harrison admitted—then after a pause, "Good people."

Eloise reached over to Harrison and patted his arm. It was quite an admission, given what Harrison had been through six years ago, and Eloise smiled inwardly at the changes that had been wrought in the man. Amazing what being a grandfather could do to you...

"Well, what do you know? Two of our favorite people." The voice behind them dripped with sarcasm, and though it startled them both, Harrison knew who it was even before he turned around.

"Three," Billy Tidmore sneered, grinning to LeBlanc and Franks, seated beside the other two riders on his sorrel pony. "Don't forget the retard."

"Oh," LeBlanc said, his eyes leveled at Harrison. "You can bet I surely *won't.*"

Eloise tightened her grip on Roscoe and glared at the three men, whom she had last seen just yesterday—over the sights of her shotgun. The loud, even chugs of the steam engine and the mechanical rattle of the corn sheller had completely covered the sound of their approach.

"Ma'am, you don't seem very happy to see us," LeBlanc said, his hand resting on his holstered sidearm. "That's a mighty fierce look for somebody without a shotgun to back it up..."

Eloise started to move forward, but Harrison interrupted, placing himself between his neighbor and the men. "You men get off my land," he barked. "You're not welcome here." His angry eyes flicked from face to face of the three men, then to the grain shovel in the bed of the wagon.

"You don't want to do that, Harrison," LeBlanc said, his voice dropping an octave. "We're here to deliver a message, and you don't want anybody...anybody else, that is...to get hurt..."

384

Reaching into his vest, LeBlanc pulled out a wrinkled piece of paper and tossed it on the ground at Harrison's feet, who continued to stare stonily at LeBlanc, trying to keep his composure at the scene unfolding before him—readying himself to grab the shovel when it did.

"That's an agreement to settle your debt with the estate of the late Mr. Masterson," LeBlanc said. "You just sign that, and, if you're *lucky*, we'll be on our way."

"Nice of him to have the corn ready for us, eh, Maxey?" Billy remarked, pulling his pistol from its holster and spinning it. Franks had just started to laugh…when the lights went out. For Billy's part, the *clang* that he heard in response to his jest seemed odd, and by the time that he turned his head and caught the image of the little man finishing his swing at Franks—a dark giant had sprung upon him and pulled him to the ground.

Harrison had done his best to draw LeBlanc's attention as he had spied the Czechs advancing on the riders from behind the barn, their footsteps covered by the very same machinery that had allowed the riders themselves to steal up to the wagon without notice. LeBlanc had missed the Czechs' approach as well, but his horse had caught the glint of Remy's shovel just before it had connected with Franks' head. Panicking, the horse swerved and knocked Harrison and Eloise to the ground before taking off with his rider at a buck. Scrambling for Franks' rifle under the feet of his big bay, Harrison yelled, "Get her into the soddy, Remy!"

Remy nodded and half herded, half carried a dazed Eloise to the sod house, only a dozen yards away. Nearby, the huge black-bearded Czech had wrenched Billy's gun out of his hand and was swinging a massive haymaker at the slim outlaw's head. Barely ducking in time, Billy wriggled away and was headed for the barn when the first crack of gunfire snapped at the air around the Czechs' head. Harrison had a hold on Franks' rifle now, but instead of returning fire, he grabbed the massive Czech and shouted, "Into the soddy!" The men had just managed to make it into the makeshift bunkhouse when a hail of gunfire smashed against the door behind them, sending wooden splinters into the room.

After bolting the door, Harrison took a station at one of the windows and asked, "Is everyone all right?" In the dim light around him, he did a rough count…and then felt the ice form around his heart.

It came to Eloise at the same time, and her voice was a whisper. "Roscoe."

"I think you mighta *forgot* somebody!" a voice came from behind the wagon. As Harrison peered through the grimy pane, he saw to his horror the form of a small boy suspended over the hopper that housed the spinning teeth of the shelling machine. LeBlanc was smiling, hidden for the most part by the wagon and the body of the shelling machine, and he had to shout to be heard above the machinery.

"Better get out here before I lose my grip," LeBlanc added, and smiled as he lowered the crying boy just an inch to emphasize his point. "He sure does like to wiggle."

Handing the rifle to Eloise, he said, "If he doesn't hand over Roscoe, you know what to do." Eloise made as if to object, but seeing the look on Harrison's face in the streaming light of the dusty room, she simply nodded. Cocking the rifle, she stood at the window and watched her man unbolt and open the door. The noise from the engine had reached a screeching pitch. The squealing unnerved LeBlanc, who appeared relieved to pull the boy out of the hopper and step away as he reached for his gun, still grasping the boy in his other hand. She had watched Harrison make his first steps into the yard toward LeBlanc…

…when a reddish blur crossed in front of the windowpane, kicking up dust as it leapt over the wagon entirely, directly at Roscoe and LeBlanc. As the horse—for that's what it was, winged Pegasus though it might be—hurtled to the ground on the far side of the wagon, it crashed into LeBlanc and threw him to the ground, with Roscoe still firmly in his grip. The horse stumbled and rolled onto its side with the momentum of the crash, and its rider—a thin form just visible through the dust, staggered to his feet…just as the engine's check valve gave way.

Through a small copper valve mounted on the side of the boiler, a large cloud of venting steam was pouring into the yard. In the cover of the steam and the dust from the flailing horse, Harrison, who had a better view of what was happening than Eloise, ran out to Roscoe, snatched him up, and then stumbled back toward the soddy, yelling, "Bud! Come on—get *in* here!"

Still stunned from his fall, Bud was engulfed in a strange world of his own, surrounded by dust, steam, screaming horses and the curses of angry men. He had somehow managed to stagger to his feet and was now stumbling toward the red roan horse that had carried him here with the speed of a summer storm. The anarchy in the farmyard didn't seem to faze him in the least, and he murmured, "Can't lose Uncle Zeke's horse…she's a runner…he'd kill me…"

The mare was on her feet now, spinning in circles, bucking, and kicking out at LeBlanc at the same time as she snapped her teeth at Bud's outstretched hand. The horse's teeth closed on empty air, however—instead, Bud felt a massive hand on his neck jerk him off his feet again. He had been dragged several feet out of the bright sunlight of the yard, and was surrounded by thick dirt walls before he could turn to see his attacker—a big Czech, shaking his head as he smiled under his beard.

"*Stupidy hlupek*," the giant intoned, slapping Bud on his shoulder as a rain of bullets shattered the windows of the soddy.

Saturday, August 11, 1894
4:25 pm

This has got to be one of the stupidest damned stunts ah have ever tried, Amos muttered to himself, for what must have been the fortieth time in as many minutes. Trudeau's gelding was skittish. It had resisted being led the six miles from Fairbury, then, suddenly scenting its camp and its equine companions as they approached Rock Creek Station, had nearly broken free. Now, it was refusing to stand still and allow itself to be to be tied to one of the sturdy cottonwoods that lined the creek banks.

"Stand still, dammit—you'll be free soon enough," Amos muttered as he put the finishing touches on the knot that secured the horse's reins to the tree trunk, and made a few last adjustments to the other contraption that was also wired there. The horse gave a final neigh of disapproval, causing Amos to wince and look nervously over his shoulder to the south. Just a half mile downstream, the twin camps of west ranch and the east ranch of Rock Creek Station lay waiting like a coiled serpent, and Amos was having second thoughts about his proximity to it. His careful approach from Fairbury had allowed a good view of the west ranch from the higher ground on the west side of the creek, and he was fairly sure there was no one camping in the ruins of that ranch. The east ranch lay in a hollow, however, amidst trees that were difficult to penetrate with the binoculars he had brought with him from Parr's hardware store. Amos knew that he had to be close enough to the east ranch for the sound of gunfire to attract the attention of its denizens, but he had no idea whether there were one or a dozen men there guarding Rance Cable, Jr.—or if there was anyone there at all.

Amos sighed and turned to finish his work, fighting back the second thoughts that had dogged him since leaving Julia and Evans in the care of Doc Connelle back in Fairbury. Though none of them knew exactly to what part of the sprawling Rock Creek Station Amos was heading in such a hurry. Evans knew that he was after a bad character, and Julia could sense his nervousness. They had both urged him to wait and get some help...but Amos had smiled, explaining that he just wanted "a look around"—and had galloped off anyway, trailing Trudeau's horse. At the time, he had reasoned that his familiarity with the area and ability to approach with stealth were the keys to trying this damned fool thing out in broad daylight. A posse would make too much noise and take too damned long to implement—and the timetable that Evans had mentioned for Cable's "elimination" at 5:00 made waiting until dark a practical impossibility.

Amos looked at his watch…it was nearly 4:30. Reaching up to the tree trunk, he adjusted a small knob on the ticking mechanism held there with bailing wire, pulled a knob…and cantered down the west bank of Rock Creek. Swiftly, he leaped across its slow-moving, gurgling waters—running low but not quite dry, despite the drought—and struggled up the opposite bank to his waiting mount. Climbing into the saddle, he swung away from the bank for a dozen yards or so through the scrub oaks, pine thicket and Russian olives that he hoped would provide cover for his approach, then turned downstream, carefully picking his way through the trees toward the East ranch.

* * * * *

At sixteen minutes before five o'clock, Jasper Rankin checked his watch for the second time in the last five minutes. He removed his derby hat and fanned himself, shaking his head before replacing his watch. While it was somewhat cooler in the half dugout/half barn in the old east ranch of the station than it was outside, it was still damned hot, and his partner's absence was not exactly helping to cool Rankin off.

From the start of their partnership together three years ago, Rankin had admired the calm (some might say cold-blooded) efficiency that Trudeau applied to his work. He had actually found Trudeau's occasional slip into "third person" interesting…and even a little comical. In the last several jobs, though, both Rankin and his boss J. T. Lynch had noticed a gradual increase in the number of episodes where Trudeau slipped into his "narrator" mode. Trudeau was spending more and more time finishing off his targets, drawing out what would otherwise have been a speedy process, sacrificing efficiency and professionalism for…well, for pleasure.

Rankin sighed, got up and looked out the door toward the bridge that led to the dilapidated buildings of the west ranch across Rock Creek. It provided the only easy approach to the buildings where Rankin, Trudeau, and their "guest" were quartered. Squinting against the western sun, Rankin saw that no one was on the bridge or the road leading to the Station. Trudeau was truly late now, either still mesmerized by his "work," or worse—goddammit—perhaps even caught by those Pinkertons that were crawling all over Fairbury. Even if he did return, it was starting to look like Lynch might have to make good on a private remark he had passed to Rankin following their last job in Pullman City, to "terminate" their partnership, unless Trudeau's condition improved.

Behind him, stretched out on the wreck of an old rope bedframe with his hands and feet tied, Ransom Reed Cable Jr. thrashed again. About an hour ago, he had come out of his chloroform-induced slumber, and following a short trip to the open trench outside that was serving as a privy, had started to plead again for his release. Rankin had casually whacked him across the face with a pistol, but when that failed to shut him up he had tied and gagged the boy and thrown him on the bed. Rankin admitted to himself that the young fellow had held up pretty well until this afternoon, but it looked like the lack of sleep and Trudeau's leering, rambling whispers through the night were finally taking their toll. Cable's eyes were looking increasingly panicked, wide and white with fear.

Just as well to have him tied and gagged, then, Rankin thought, *if the boy was feeling feisty.* In about fifteen minutes, it would make it a lot easier to tie his body on his horse and dump it into the creek...after he cut the kid's jugular vein, of course. He was just thinking about where he had put his knife down—probably outside the cabin where he had skinned a jackrabbit last night—when a shot rang out.

Immediately, Rankin snatched up his rifle, and peered across the creek to the approach from the Fairbury road. No movement, and Rankin was just calculating that the shot must have been within a half mile or so...when Trudeau's horse appeared, running down the hill from the northwest, through the west ranch, and across the bridge—until it came to a stop near where Rankin's own horse was tied.

Rankin hesitated...then swore.

"Damn the man...what's he gotten himself into now?" Rankin grumbled as he crossed the yard and tied Trudeau's horse to the hitching post, noticing in passing that one of the reins was shorter than usual. Rifle in hand, Rankin swung into his own saddle and headed toward the bridge. In less than a minute, he had crossed it and disappeared around the bend of Rock Creek.

From out of the treeline to the north, Amos Aloysius Seville crossed the yard of the east ranch at a sprint. He couldn't believe his luck. The shot from the kludged mechanism he had wired to the tree—an alarm clock with its external hammer tied to the hair trigger of Julia's .45 Colt—had its muzzle touching the tied reins of Trudeau's horse. Miraculously, it had actually managed to free the beast, falsely indicating Trudeau's proximity to Rankin when the horse followed its instincts and fled back to the east ranch. Amos was unsure whether the scheme would work at all, and was just about to take a shot at Rankin in the doorway (at over a hundred yards, a risky shot at best with a handgun), when the rigged .45 had gone off.

As Amos neared the door of the dugout barn, he patted the flank of Trudeau's horse and drew his .32 revolver. Halting momentarily outside the doorframe of the barn, he ducked his head into the darkness of the interior. He saw open tin cans, refuse...and a bound figure, lying prostrate on a raised bed. The boy was alert, and his eyes registered confusion as Amos crossed the room. When Amos pulled out and flicked open his knife, the boy's eyes went even wider, and he began to thrash about on the rope bedframe.

"Easy, Mr. Cable—ah'm here to git you out of heah," Amos said, attacking the bonds at the boy's feet with his knife, and then his hands. Slipping off the boy's gag, Amos was embarrassed to hear, "God bless you," followed by a heave and a great trembling sob.

"Time enough for that later," Amos interrupted, grasping the boy's shoulder and lifting him to his feet. "Can you travel?"

"Just *watch* me," Cable said, rubbing his wrists and wiping his eyes with his sleeve. The eyes, Amos saw, were now transforming...becoming hard, galvanized.

Amos moved swiftly to the door, saw the yard was empty—then crossed back, pressuring Cable to follow. Amos didn't hesitate at the door, urging, sometimes almost dragging Cable across the yard to Trudeau's horse, who glared at them with its ears laid back.

"Can you ride?" Amos asked. He did not wait for Cable's answer, and his eyes were not on the boy, but were fixed on the bridge as he helped Cable into the saddle. "Ride south," Amos instructed, sternly. "Follow the line of the creek for a mile or so—there's a farmer with his place right along the creek. Tell him that Amos sent you, and that you ah in need of help. Stay there for an hour or two—ah'll come for you. *Now*, dammit!" And with that, Amos slapped the rump of the skittish horse, which headed off, following the line that Amos had directed.

Amos himself began to leg it north across the hundred yards of open ground to his own horse, waiting back in the trees. He had covered about half the distance when the *crack* of a bullet split the air next to his ear. In the fraction of a second that followed, his mind blurred into motion, registering

—the sound of the shot, off to his left—

—the horse hooves thundering over the bridge—

—the recognition that it was Rankin—

—that he was carrying a rifle—

—the hopelessness of covering the open ground to his horse—

—and the immediate need to cover Cable's escape.

So, Amos drew his pistol, and *charged.*

As he began to fire, a fair part of Amos thought, *all right, ah take it back...**this** is **definitely** the stupidest damned stunt ah have ever tried.* But in addition to scooping elephant shit and selling tickets to the geek shows, Amos also had a stint as a trick shooter as part of P.T.'s sideshow. He learned that a rifle is an incredibly difficult weapon to shoot accurately from horseback, especially at a gallop toward a moving target with the horse's head directly in the line of sight. The prior trick shooter whom Amos was replacing—an old horse soldier with Jeb Stuart who had recently become a part time tent jockey and full time drunkard—told him that most cavalrymen preferred to make use of a saber or a revolver on horseback, and generally dismounted to employ his rifle, as it requires both hands to aim and reload it.

It hadn't taken long for Rankin to realize that the shot and the return of Trudeau's horse had been a diversion. As he was galloping back, Rankin had been surprised to see Amos running across the yard of the Eastern ranch, and now was even more shocked by his reckless charge. He swore and considered his options, which included dismounting the horse and plugging the man—but his opponent was armed, and coming on fast. In the end, he spurred his mount and dropped his rifle alongside of its straining head, leveling it at the crazy son of a bitch running straight at him. Rankin was just squeezing off a round when the man suddenly dodged to his left, crossing in front of his horse.

The charging horse loomed above Amos like a locomotive, and the big bore muzzle of Rankin's rifle, rising up from the horse's flank, was as large as a cannon. Amos watched it swing against the horses head before it flashed, just as he had extended his pistol toward the horse's head and pulled the trigger.

Amos never really liked horses, anyway.

As his big rifle went off, Rankin heard the crack of a returning shot…just before his horse and saddle tumbled out from under him like a barrel over Niagara. One of the horse's front hooves smashed into Amos' hip, spinning him out of the way of the initial crash, which was spectacular—tearing up the prairie sod, first with the force of the original impact, then with the churning of the horse's flailing death throes. Another hoof lashed out, clipping Amos in the temple…and the lights went out.

* * * * *

Amos awoke to a spinning universe, a ringing head…and a sun that was definitely further down on the horizon. As he attempted to move, all the pains of the last three days were dropping him calling cards, waiting in the parlor to be introduced. *Trains, horses, shovels—ah wondah what **else** is gonna fall on mah head?*

Groaning, he struggled to his feet. His head still buzzed, but it was clear from the red sky…what he could see of it…that some time had gone

392

by. He rubbed his eyes, and surveyed the carnage. There was the dead horse that Rankin had been riding, blood from its head wound staining the ground not a dozen feet from where he stood. But...there was no *Rankin. Anywhere.* Amos scratched his head—thought better of it...*it hurt*—and puzzled. *Was Rankin alive? If so, why am I?*

Turning around—he noticed that something else was wrong ...*where the **hell** was the saddle? And the rest of the tack? The halter...hell, even the **blanket** was gone.*

Amos started to shake his head—thought better of it...it *hurt*—then stumbled his way back to the dugout barn. The light in the barn was dim, but there was no doubt.that Cable's ropes, the empty tin cans, the clutter from two days living...even the slit trench, outside...all of them were **gone.**

What in the name of Aunt Ethel's unmentionables...?

Amos was beginning to become convinced that he had dreamed the whole thing—when he spotted a silver glint in the wreck of the rope bed, highlighted by the last rays of the setting sun. Reaching into it, he pulled out his knife. Folding it carefully, he walked out of the barn and moved toward where he had left his horse.

The creek was quiet as Amos moved through the trees. Sure enough, his mount was waiting there, just as he had left it...neighing softly and stamping its feet. Amos patted its neck, and was about to swing up into the saddle in order to return it to its barn in Fairbury, when a twig suddenly snapped behind him. Amos whirled about, and instinctively reached for the pistol in his vest...which wasn't there.

Facing him, having stepped out from behind a large cottonwood, was J.T. Lynch...holding a dry, medium-sized twig that had just been broken in half. His face was neutral, until he reached into his coat pocket, and pulled out Amos' nickel .32 revolver...and then he grinned.

It was the sort of grin that Amos imagined he had seen before...many times, but most often reflected in a smooth pond, or perhaps in a store window as he passed by.

Or maybe even in a bathroom mirror.

"Missing this?" Lynch asked, and tossed it casually to Amos.

Amos caught the small Smith and Wesson pistol, broke it open, and saw immediately that the bullets had been removed. He began to understand what had happened to Rankin, the saddle, the tack, and all the evidence of the camp. Other realizations also started to wind their way up his brainstem from where they were lurking, and the shivers that accompanied them were based on emotions that Amos was barely able to conceal. However, he managed to just reply, "Much obliged."

Lynch reached into his other coat pocket. Amos did not flinch…if this man wanted him dead, he would have been very capable of it while he had been unconscious a few minutes back. From his pocket he pulled a silver case, which appeared to contain a half dozen cheroots. Lynch held out the case to Amos, and as badly as he wanted a smoke right now, nevertheless declined.

Choosing a small cigar from the case, Lynch eyed Amos quietly as he lit it with a Lucifer, then rolled his fingers over the open flame of the match to put it out. "Thought we might have a few words," Lynch said, puffing the cigar into life.

"Communication is a wonderful thing," Amos replied, moving slowly to a nearby tree, folding his arms as he leaned against it. His left hand, slipping inside his jacket and hidden from view by his right arm, touched the handle of the knife he had placed there not ten minutes ago…free from the search that Lynch had obviously performed while Amos was unconscious.

"Fancy little trick you pulled there with the alarm clock," Lynch remarked. "I'll have to remember it. Don't know if I would have relied on it under the circumstances, though."

Amos nodded, trying not to appear disturbed in any way…but the man's knowledge had been uncanny, and only had one explanation.

"Ah was a little desperate, to tell you the truth," Amos admitted, adding, "So…you were watching then?"

Lynch nodded. "I followed you from Fairbury. Got in about four hours ago. Looks like you were a mite busy there, too."

"Indeed ah was, sir," Amos said, "Thanks to your man…Trudeau, was his name?"

"Among others." Lynch eyed Amos, almost coldly now. "You cost me two good men, Mr. Amos Aloysius Seville."

"Did I?" Amos asked, a dry smile curling at the corners of his lips. "Sounds to me like you didn't do much to warn your man Rankin away from his little encounter with me…what, about an hour ago?"

It was Lynch's turn to nod an acknowledgement. "Very astute, Amos," he replied, and he chuckled now, softly. "I just wish you'd finished the second job as well as you did the first."

Amos' composure broke slightly, and he couldn't stop passing a quizzical look to the man facing him in the fading light.

"Oh, Rankin survived his little encounter with you...that's a certainty," Lynch said. "He came around and got to his feet about two minutes after you killed his horse. Looked pretty angry. Picked up your pistol...would have shot you with it, too."

Lynch took a long draw of his cigar, looking deeply into Amos' eyes. "I shot him, of course. But you already guessed that part, didn't you?"

"I had my suspicions," Amos said. "One less man to split the fee for the train wreck?"

"Train wreck?" Lynch laughed. "Why, Amos, you know who performed that nefarious act—it was Mr. George Washington Davis of Lincoln, Nebraska. It said so in the paper this morning."

"Assisted by your men."

"Perhaps...but I was with your friends at the Barrelhouse at the time— your friends...Zeke's nephew in particular...can witness to that."

"Oh, come on, Lynch," Amos scoffed. "Anyone with a brain in Lincoln that has ever met Davis knows that he isn't the kind of person to come up with something like this. Your men put that man up to it...and probably helped him do it. Rankin, at the very least." *And that's the reason,* Amos suddenly realized, *why you wanted him **dead**.*

Lynch narrowed his eyes. "It could be argued so...but I assure you, Amos, that George Davis was there, that very night, pulling up spikes and tearing up the rails of the CRI&P."

Amos had no response to that. Davis was a born follower—he blew with the wind, and the man before him had bent the man to his purpose like a willow in a hurricane. Instead, he changed the course of the conversation. "So, why are you here?"

"I'm here to make you an offer, Mr. Seville." The words hung there as if suspended by the cottonwood branches themselves.

"You seem to be able to think on your feet...might say you came by it naturally. Take your mother, God rest her soul. Times were hard during the war, and she was a survivor...so are you."

Amos bristled...the man was speaking of his mother as if he *cared* for the woman. "And my father?"

"Yes, I thought you'd come to that. Do you know who your father is?"

The directness of the question caught Amos off guard. "I'm...not sure."

"Have you narrowed the possibilities?"

"Yes," Amos replied. "My mother had a picture of two men..."

"She *kept* that? My my..."

Amos went on. "She tore it in half, and kept Zeke's side."

"She always was sentimental," Lynch replied.

"And burned yours."

A shadow crossed Lynch's features. "We had a falling out, you might say."

"So, what's the answer?" Amos was having a hard time staying neutral.

"What's *yours*?" Lynch asked.

Damn. This man had an extraordinary talent for changing the direction of a conversation, Amos observed. "What do you mean?"

Lynch's eyes narrowed. "I *mean* that I am in the market for a new partner. Interested?"

Amos did his best to hide his revulsion, and jerked his head back toward Rock Creek Station. "Your idea of partnership looks a little questionable. Where's Rankin?"

"Where he can't possibly cause any more trouble," Lynch replied. "I've had my concerns with both Mr. Rankin and Mr. Trudeau for some time, I assure you, Amos."

"And Cable?"

"Well," Lynch said, with just the hint of a smile. "I guess you'll just have to call that one the fish that got away...in a way, that is."

"I don't understand."

Lynch looked directly into Amos' eyes with a stare that was both dead, and tempting. "Join me, and you will."

Amos shifted his left hand, and got a better grip on his knife. "I don't think so, Mr. Lynch..."

"Pity. Fine Virginia tobacco," Lynch remarked, inhaling deeply. "That state certainly spoiled me."

"So, is that it, then?" Amos pressed. "You plan to just walk away from this whole fiasco?"

"What fiasco?" Lynch said. "I've got a happy client, Mr. Cable has his son back, and you..."

"Yes?"

"You get to *live*, my boy...if you can keep your mouth closed. If not? Well, my associates might just have to make a little visit to that pretty niece of Zeke's."

Lynch's eyes moved a fraction of a second before his hand did, but the gun was out before Amos' hand had cleared his lapel pocket.

"Think it over." Lynch's eyes were hollow pits, and Amos slowly extended his hand and dropped the knife. Without a word, Lynch gestured with the pistol, and Amos moved in the indicated direction, away from the knife. Lynch walked over to Amos' horse, and swung up into the saddle.

"Stay healthy, son," Lynch said, and spurred the mare into the gathering darkness.

45

Saturday, August 11, 1894
7:15 pm

"I was just sayin' that I think..." Franks said, crouching behind the barn. His head hurt like hell, his rifle was missing...out there forty yards ahead of them, in the sod house, with Harrison...but he still had his sidearms. Unfortunately, that fact didn't seem to be lending him a lot of confidence at the moment.

"There's where you made your *mistake*, then, isn't it?" LeBlanc snapped. "I do the thinking around here...not you."

"We could try around the back again..." offered Billy, looking bleakly at the two shot-out windows facing them, and the solid log door.

"That sod is a foot thick around the other three sides, and the roof is the same," growled LeBlanc. "So just shut up about it."

Why are we here, again? Franks wanted to ask, but stopped himself again. He knew why—LeBlanc had been humbled, and he was going to exact his revenge on Harrison and that woman...*Moseman?*...that had stuck a shotgun in his face.

We were supposed to just throw a scare into Harrison...and now... Franks shook his head, but said nothing. Again.

"Look," LeBlanc said, harshly. "It'll be dark soon, and we'll make our move then. Keep them off guard—just keep on firing through the windows. Shut up and stay cool."

In this heat? Franks muttered to himself, but loaded his weapon again.

* * * * *

"It ought to be in about an hour now," Harrison said, cycling the ammunition out of his rifle, counting the rounds, and re-inserting them. Through the corner of his eye, Bud was silently counting along with him.

Four.

"You think they come when it is night, then?" Remy asked, nervously, his English more stilted than usual.

"Yes, I imagine so," Eloise said calmly, helping Roscoe move the small herd of "cows"—made out of a box of matchsticks they had found near one of the bunks—from one side of their corral to another. She, Bud and Andreyev Malý, the big Czech, had conspired to surround the boy in a protected corner of the soddy, devising a number of games to keep his mind off the fact that the six of them had nothing to eat or drink for the last six hours, and that occasional potshots into the wall of the soddy kept intruding every now and again.

These games for Roscoe are probably doing even more good for me than they are for him, Bud thought, nervously. Thinking back on Saturday a week ago, where he and his uncle had eaten brick dust after a rifle shot in a dark alley near the train station—probably fired by these same men— Bud reached a conclusion: *I do **not** like being **shot** at.*

"Guess I'm glad now that we never tore down this old soddy," Harrison said. "Both of the windows face the yard, and they'll never burn us out of this pile of dirt."

*Burn us **out?*** Bud thought. *Wonderful...*

"You never throw **anything** away, Robert," Eloise said, absently checking Roscoe from venturing out of the "corral" again. "That's the main reason I haven't said yes, you know...I don't want to clean out that mess you call a **house**."

"I could always move in with **you**," Robert said, his eyes smiling, even while they kept a watchful eye on the yard.

"***That'll*** be the day," Eloise shot back...but her eyes were smiling, too.

"Forgot how homey this place used to feel," Harrison said, ignoring Eloise's jibe. "Cooler than the house, too."

Yeah, Bud thought. *A dirt floor, grass walls, a sod ceiling, and a few scorpions for pets. Wonder what he charges for rent.*

A bullet **cracked** in through the left window, thudding into the wall opposite, where it joined a number of its brothers. The right side of the rear wall had gathered a similar swarm behind its own window.

"The first years...they were good ones here, Weezy," Harrison said, ignoring entirely the shot of a moment ago. He seemed to be lost in thought, as his eyes wandered about the yard from the shelter of the left window. "Lots of hard work, a' course...first just Tillie and me, and then with the kids coming along..." Harrison's voice trailed off, and in a while the man took off his glasses and wiped them, along with his brow and his eyes, with a once-white handkerchief.

Bud turned to Eloise. Over the last several hours, he had admired her pluck—being held with their backs against the wall for hours had not seemed to bother her. At the same time, he had sensed the gentle sort of way about her, one that invited a confidence...

"Mrs. Moseman?" Bud asked quietly. "Did you know Anna's sister, Antonia?"

At first, Eloise seemed to ignore the question, brushing the dust from her apron after a long afternoon of wrangling with Roscoe. The young boy yawned. "Hand me Roscoe, Andreyev," she said. "Let's see if that old rocker in the corner still works."

Checking the windows first, Eloise lifted the boy, who didn't resist, and gently carried him over into the dark corner by the far bunk. "Come along with me, Bud" she added, as she climbed into the rocker. It creaked under their combined weight, but the sound was comfortable rather than strained—like a harp that had been tuned for just this purpose. Eloise gestured to the bunkhouse bed beside her, and as the young man from Alder Grove climbed into it, he listened as the old farmwife sang, "Bi-i-i-i yo....B-i-i-i yo....Bi-i-i-i yo..." A monotonous, yet comforting pair of lilting syllables that soon had Roscoe off to sleep—and Bud halfway there himself when Eloise started to speak.

"Robert and Matilda...Tillie, he always called her...moved here in '65, right after the War, before Lancaster was called Lincoln...before we were even a state. They built this sod house, then got busy growing corn and children. They had three; but two of 'em—Ben and Martha—they went down with the whooping cough. So, they were left with little Bob...Robert, Jr., that is. They loved him, doted on him...and sort of spoiled him, I guess you'd have to say. Verne and I didn't have any children of our own, so we adopted all of the children in the neighborhood. Bob was one of our favorites."

"But there was another—a dark haired, blue-eyed little girl from the new Czech settlements, a few miles north of us—name of Antonia. She showed up on our doorstep one morning—she couldn't speak a word of English, but held up two little fingers, and bounced her hand until we figured out that she had followed a rabbit over the two miles to our farm. We took her back home, but first made sure to feed her—so, like any intelligent stray, she kept coming back."

"Her parents were sweet, but they had their hands full with a pair of boys, and a brand new baby named Anna—I believe you may have met her, Bud—so when we offered to have her over now and again to teach her English, they were grateful. She learned—quickly? My God, that girl around books was like a fire around dry prairie—then taught her sister and two older brothers herself. She even managed to teach her mother and father a few phrases—before they died, that is, about ten years back...when Antonia was sixteen. And that would have made Anna..."

"Eight, I think," offered Bud, and Eloise nodded.

400

"About this time, Bob Harrison, had grown into an eighteen-year-old—and you know how they can be. Strong in the back, and even stronger in the head. Ready to take on, and take down the whole world. Constantly on the scrap with his father..." Eloise pointed over into the corner toward Harrison, who seemed lost in thought, his eyes scanning the gathering darkness. Then she went on, her voice now not much more than a whisper.

"If his father said white, he'd say black. He'd laugh when scolded, scream at the drop of a hat...he was just another person altogether around his parents than he was around anyone else. Finally, they had just about enough of him, and "encouraged" him to find some work outside their own farm, as long as he was around for the heavier work. Mostly, he came to live with us...and that's how he got to know Antonia."

"He hadn't met her before?" Bud asked. "She was only a few miles down the road..."

"Well, I don't know how you were raised, but Tillie was a German, and raised by her people to hate the Czechs over in the old country. So the Harrisons never had much to do with our new neighbors to the north, and until Bob moved in with us...neither did he."

Eloise grinned. "But, oh, my...how *that* changed when he met Antonia. Before long, it all came to a head at a picnic that Verne and I held here in the spring of '87. We had every farm family in the neighborhood there...except for Robert and Tillie, and a few of the Czechs...and it ended in a proposal—of marriage, that is."

Eloise leaned her head even closer to Bud. "Well, you can guess how Robert and Tillie reacted. You could hear the argument way over at our house, a mile away. A lot of "not fair"s" and "cut off's" in the air. But that wasn't the worst part. The worst part..."

"...was telling her brothers." Bud finished, and Eloise nodded, wisely.

"I gather you've met?"

"Unforgettable experience." Bud said sourly, but added. "Please go on."

Eloise nodded and stood up, gesturing for Bud to get off the bed, where she laid Roscoe, now dead to the world in slumber. Bud took a place at Eloise's feet in the corner, and listened enraptured.

"So, here they were...two young people, completely smitten, both smart and hard working, who had managed to alienate their families altogether. They got married by the county judge—that was *well* received...by both families, I'll tell you. And the only course they had left

401

to them was a hard one—they found a man willing to let them share crop on a broken down farm that was about ten miles east of here. That soddy made this one look like the state Capitol. We lent them one of our mules, and they went to work on forty acres with a broken-down plow and no cash. Of course, the landlord ran a store, and offered credit…"

The light hit Bud at once. "Masterson?"

Eloise nodded. "He was very generous—at first. Tools, food, cloth, seed… needful things. But after a few months, Masterson started to make a few…requests. First, it was labor from Bob on other farms…a task here and there. But it grew, until the young man was supplying free labor half the week, just to make payments on the equipment that he had gotten from Masterson. Then…there were the things that he asked of Antonia. He needed a few odd jobs done in his store, then some laundry, and then…"

The farm wife's whisper drifted off…and Bud was left to his own imagination. Suddenly, a large part of him didn't want to *know* the rest of the story…but he was committed now.

"Well," Eloise said, suddenly resuming, "One day, Antonia came home from Masterson's big house, crying…and wouldn't *stop* crying. And from that day forward, there was no more "extra labor" for Mr. Masterson…from either of them."

The rocking chair creaked quietly in the corner.

"By the time that autumn came, the corn stood tall…but so did their debt to Masterson. The crop came in…and went out, barely making a dent in what they owed. And Antonia…well, she was with child, of course—due in January. When Verne and I last visited Antonia, it wasn't just a few pullet hens that we brought them…it was an offer from Robert, Bob's father—a plea, really—that they come back here and live with them. Antonia had told me earlier that the rent was three months late, but she and Bob were still stubborn, as well as optimistic…in the corner of their soddy, there was a small Christmas tree, hung with tin foil stars…though there wasn't much under it. "

"We stayed overnight, and left them on December 13—an unlucky day, because on our way down the lane, we met a man with a hard face. It was your Uncle Zeke, wearing his Deputy's badge. He tipped his hat to us, and when we asked him what was wrong, he told us that he had a paper to deliver from the county court—a 30-day eviction notice, signed by Judge Lansing. Back in those days, your uncle was a different man, Bud—he was rigid as a fence post when it came to enforcing the law. God help me…Verne and I were actually grateful to see him…that it meant that the couple would finally go back home and be reconciled with Bob's parents."

402

"I'll take it from here, Weezy," a gentle, deep voice said, and Bud turned to see Robert Harrison standing behind him in the waning light. He placed the rifle down on the bed, and motioned to Andreyev and Remy to keep watch at the windows. They nodded silently, leaving the other three seated around Roscoe, who started to snore quietly.

"That was one lonely Christmas," Harrison said, "But Tillie and me, we were hopeful, too, Weezy. If Masterson hadn't foreclosed, we might even have asked him to. We wanted those kids *home*. So, we dropped letters in the mail saying how much the neighbors missed them, we sent a telegram inviting them over for fritters on New Years Eve…we even sent the pastor over. Everything but go ourselves. You see, Bud, we were still too proud to knuckle under and admit we were wrong to oppose the marriage…even though it was pretty clear then that they were strong, and meant for each other." The light was low, but not so much that Bud missed Eloise's slow nod.

"We learned later that Bob had spent the whole 30 days breaking his back, working for everyone, anyone that would employ him. It was an impossible task – there just weren't any jobs paying more than a dollar a day in Lancaster County, and Bob and Antonia still had to eat. He even spent a few nights working for the U.P.—trying to come up with the fifty dollars it would take to keep them there. Thirty days later, it was January 12. It had been cold in the days leading up to it, but it was so lovely that morning—by the time Zeke rode up, it must have been fifty degrees. Bob held out forty hard-earned dollars, still short. But even if he'd had all fifty, Zeke would still have had to turn him out….the debt was to Masterson, not the county…and so Zeke served the papers, and helped them load the wagon. Antonia's labor had probably started by then, but she didn't breathe a word of it in front of Zeke. By one o'clock, the kids were headed west, to our place. Zeke headed back south, to town."

"Wait a minute," said Bud, suddenly alarmed. "Did you say '88? January *twelfth???* Oh, gods…"

"That's right. In about an hour, the temperature fell from fifty degrees to twenty below. The wind whipped up, and snow started scream down from the north. By two-thirty, the snow was so thick that you couldn't see six feet in front of you. Between the wind and the cold, and the wet snow…well, that mule…that mule just plain gave out. And when it fell, it tumbled straight into the ditch, and brought the wagon in right after it, spilling everything. Antonia must have told Bob about the baby being on the way…she obviously couldn't travel. So Bob found Antonia's steamer trunk…her "hope chest"…and wrapped Antonia in a blanket, then turned the whole trunk over her, and went to find the closest house, or some kind of shelter…" Robert coughed, and Eloise reached over and patted his arm.

403

"Pa said it snowed three feet that day," Bud mused, so caught up in the story that he forgot for the moment where the story was going. "There were kids stranded in a schoolhouse…was it over at Mira Valley…?"

Eloise nodded, placing an arm on Bud's own. "A teacher saved some seventeen kids by stringing them together and leading them a mile away to her boarding house. But in Plainview, another teacher tried to move three kids to her own house seventy-five yards away…and they all froze to death."

"And so did Bobby," Robert said abruptly, swallowing hard. "He never made it. Lost in the snow. But, he saved Antonia…that is, at least she was found alive the next morning. The spokes of her wagon wheel jutted out of the snow bank, and they found her under the steamer trunk. She'd lost a lot of blood, and the cold…"

"She lived long enough to deliver her baby, Bud," Eloise said…and laid her hand on Roscoe.

"They come," growled big Andreyev. Harrison snatched up the rifle, and moved quietly to the window.

46

Saturday, August 11, 1894
7:45 pm

"Just how sure *are* you about this information?" Albert Dillon queried in the semidarkness. He placed a cigarette in his mouth, but as he bent to reach for a match, Fred Miller grasped his hand.

"I wouldn't do that, Al," Miller said. "Think about what those hands smell like."

Dillon gulped, then nodded in the waning twilight. His hands and his clothing both reeked of coal oil.

"I think we can trust her," Miller said, reaching into his pocket and pulling out a small knife with a black handle, which he used to clean his fingernails. "She seemed pretty distraught when she came in the office. Not as upset as her brothers, though."

"They certainly weren't far behind her...and she *did* seem pretty eager to get the facts out before they swept her out of the office," agreed Dillon. "What do you think of that other story she told? About the boy?"

"It'll have to wait...we'll check on it after we've settled here," Miller said, shaking his head. "Yes, I think she can be trusted. She's honest, and a hard worker, even if a little stiff-necked...like her sister was."

* * * * *

Zeke Gardner occasionally found himself reminded that one of the few interesting features of advancing age was its ability to allow a man to stand in two places at once—in the present, and also in the midst of a memory that rivaled the present in its vivid texture. He was struck again by this realization as he stepped onto the Sidney train platform in the gathering twilight. While he drank in the homely little cow town laid before him, he simultaneously compared it, as if in a stereoscope, to the bustling rail town of two decades ago. Back in the day, Zeke had worked to protect the gold shipments that traversed the no-man's land from the Black Hills to this, the nearest railhead two hundred miles to the south—when Sidney had been home to three hotels, twelve saloons, an even greater number of bordellos, and an Army post that frequented all of the above. For nearly a decade, Sidney had been the bawdiest boomtown in the West, fueled by cattle, gold, and greed—and had created a boot hill expansive enough to prove it.

Standing now on the lonely wooden U.P. platform in full view of that hill, Zeke was struck by a related question—which vision was the confounding one? Was it that recollection breaking into today, or the scene before him that broke into his memory? Both of them were equally true, he guessed, because both were real—though his friend Bobber had assured him that the earlier memory would become the "truer" reality in the end.

Zeke chuckled. Bobber himself had been a large part of these memories here in Sidney. An ex-mountain man composed entirely of iron muscle and bone, he had been hardened and shriveled by time to the consistency and utter utility of a dried pea—he wasn't anything very fancy, but he'd see you through. Then in his seventies, Bobber had ridden shotgun with him on many a ride into Sioux country, wanting only the simplest of pleasures—his beer, his bacon, and his beans (having given up the last "B," *bordellos,* a decade ago).

It was the train's whistle, signaling departure that finally broke into Zeke's musings. Having picked up the mail and dropped off its three passengers, there was no reason to dawdle in little Sidney—the last gold had all been shipped years ago. But there was still treasure in Sidney to be had, of a sort—*though it could be even more dangerous to recover than Black Hills gold,* Zeke reminded himself. *Well, better get to it.*

As he waited for the slow-moving train to pass in front of him, Zeke placed the small valise that he had brought with him on the train platform before him. Opening it, he slowly withdrew and uncoiled an ancient article of leather and iron—his cap and ball army revolver. The holster's original flap, marked "US," had been cut down years ago, and much of the gun's bluing had been worn to a dull silver after years of use. Buckling it about him, he sighed—it had been years since he had felt its weight on his hips, the need to carry a firearm having been left behind with his badge of office. *But I have to see this through,* Zeke reminded himself. *I owe it...to her, and to them.*

The train having passed, Zeke strode purposefully toward the tavern across the tracks along Rose Street. As he did so, several watchful pairs of eyes were upon him, each looking forward to their meeting with different degrees of intensity—but there was little doubt that the most intense pair belonged to the large man who now walked out from the shadow of the train station, and followed Gardner at a discreet distance.

* * * * *

Flint should have been satisfied. After nearly four hours of haranguing and a little outright bribery in the form of three demijohns of passable whiskey, he had been able to round up about forty out-of-work men from the north end of Lincoln, who were now vigorously shouting tavern songs in the back of four freight wagons. And as they pulled into the front yard of LeBlanc Freight, Flint saw that a crowd of at least another twenty appeared to be waiting for him there in the darkness, outlined in the light of a single kerosene lamp. *Well, looks like the wagon we sent south did produce a few more men after all,* a part of Flint mused. *A good start on a mob.*

But something nagged at him.

As the wagons pulled in toward the porch, two sudden observations struck the man from Chicago, despite the loud and raucous company surrounding him in the back of the last wagon. The first of these was the odd silence of the men waiting on the porch…no singing or laughing, and no glowing pipes or cigarettes, either. And the second—a strange, heavy odor as they crossed the halfway point of the lane.

The hairs on Flint's neck went up. Succumbing to some wild instinct, he jumped from the back of the last wagon as the first wagon slowed to a stop, far outside the dim circle of light provided by the kerosene lamps. Retracing the tracks of the wagon, Flint reached to the ground where the odor was strongest. Bringing his finger to his nose, a thought struck him…*coal oil*…just as the flash of a kersosene lantern from the porch struck the ground at the front of the first wagon with the speed of a summer storm.

With an audible *phoomp*, an intense yellow fire leapt both directions from the smashed lantern, creating two flaming arms that quickly raced in a spreading circle around the terrified wagon teams, the horses screaming and bucking within their harnesses, the men tumbling in confusion from their wagons. The fiery arms continued to trace twin arcs around the interior of the freight yard, the coal oil feeding the blaze with an unbelievable speed. Realizing that he was about to be cut off from escape, Flint sprinted for the outer gate and dived through the converging flames, barely avoiding their colliding rage.

Through the flames, Flint watched in helplessness as the men he had brought from the camps outside of town were first run down within the blazing circle, then handcuffed, and finally hauled back in twos and threes through a gap in the ring to the porch. There, an old man stood in the light of the spreading yard fire, whittling with a small knife while another man, his badge clearly visible in the firelight, took down the names of the captured men. Others brought out horse blankets and buckets of water to beat back the flames. When Flint heard the first clangs of a firebell approaching the yard entrance here where he stood, he suspected it was time to *exit.*

Hopping the fence surrounding LeBlanc's yard, Flint took a moment to stare at the municipal fire wagon burst into the chaos and race in a circle around the fire, spewing water until it began to succumb. Sighing once, he turned away and began walking calmly down the street with his hands behind his back, reviewing the how the tide had so rapidly turned—and his options.

Clearly, it had been a perfect ambush. The law had somehow discovered the exact time of the meeting, and had acted on the information. And that meant only one thing.

Someone had been...indiscreet. And that someone would most certainly pay.

* * * * *

The first shots erupting from the yard came in a volley, ripping in through the open windows of the soddy just inches above Bud's head. They thumped once again into the dirt walls behind him, and rained even more dust into the already choked room.

"They are moving!" Remy screamed from the other window. From the scant light left to them, Bud watched the little Czech produce a flask of whiskey from his coat pocket, which he uncorked and then sipped as well as his shaking hands would allow.

Guess Uncle Zeke must have passed around a little of the product last night after all, Bud thought. *Wonder how he got it past Aunt Emelia...*

"I know," Harrison growled, next to him. In response to the shots, he had fired once in return, and for a moment the yard was quiet. "One of 'em is behind the wagon now. I think he is probably sneaking around the side of it, but it's too damn dark to tell for sure. If I could see them, and could get a clear shot..."

No chance of that, thought Bud. *There's not enough light out there....*

Glancing over toward the bed, Bud saw the box of matches, most of which had been split and whittled into little cattle and horses for Roscoe, who, amazingly, had fallen immediately back to sleep after Eloise had snatched him into the nearest corner. A silly thought sprang to Bud about striking them and sending the herd of them stampeding out into the yard, lighting the wagon on fire and...

...and the pieces all fell into place.

"Remy!" Bud whispered, urgently. "Give me that whiskey!"

"Bud, for shame..." Eloise started to scold, but Bud was not listening—he had already raced across the soddy. Rummaging through the little Czech's jacket, he produced the bottle as three more shots cracked the air over his head.

"Vat are you doink, Mr..." Remy began to stutter.

408

"Greek Fire!" Bud barked, running over to the bed. He took out his jackknife and ripped a section of cloth from the dusty coverlet, then dropped the knife and unknotted his shoe, yanking out the shoestring. "I read about it in *Harper's Weekly.* There are all kinds of theories about it...but one of them was simple alcohol, in a flask, covered in a flaming cloth. They were thrown by ballistas..."

"What is ballista?" Remy asked, watching Bud in nervous fascination. "Do we have one?"

"No," said Harrison. He was doing his best to keep his attention out in the yard, but there was a new note of excitement in his voice. "We do have a *pitcher,* though."

As Bud started to wrap the cotton cloth around the bottle of whiskey, he was surprised to find Andreyev suddenly kneeling next to him. Quickly, the big man took the bottle from Bud's hands and sprinkled a little of the mixture on the cloth, corked the bottle, then handed it all back to Bud. As fast as he could, Bud wrapped the cloth around the bottle and tied it with the shoestring, while Andreyev felt around for the matches. It was nearly pitch dark in the soddy now, and Bud could hear the large man mumbling "hlupek" to himself...until, abruptly, he was again kneeling next to Bud, shoving the box of matches into his hands.

"Be careful, Bud..." Eloise urged from her corner.

"Try to get it inside the wagon, Bud," Harrison said. "It's full of cobs. I'll cover you while you throw..."

Bud nodded, then realizing the futility of the gesture, thought to reply, "Ready." Harrison raised the rifle to his shoulder as Bud stood behind him...and as he lit the match to the cloth, together they both fired. Bud's shot had barely left his hand when the whole cloth flared into life, and the young man could feel the heat scorch him as it departed. Thirty feet away, the bottle smacked into the side of the wagon, broke...and the wagon side burst into flames.

Beneath it, immediately visible, was the crouching form of LeBlanc, drawing a bead on Harrison...but the older man fired first, and was immediately rewarded with a cry of pain from beneath the wagon. LeBlanc rolled and scurried backward just as a flaming board from the wagon fell between them. Harrison thought to follow up with another shot—LeBlanc was visible, and a shot was possible—but instead, he held his fire.

He had one bullet left.

The wagon blazed, illuminating the whole yard before them, and when the cobs in the bed of the wagon caught, the fire became an inferno. Next to the wagon, the fuel lines leading to the steam engine that ran the shelling machine were beginning to smoke.

"This could get right interesting," was all that Harrison said. And in a moment, it did, when the fuel oil tank blew.

* * * * *

Watching Franks dress LeBlanc's wound behind the barn, the explosion of the boiler's oil tank was the last straw for Billy Tidmore. Without a word, he got on his horse, and before either of his partners could bellow at him to stop, Billy had spun the horse to the north and left at a gallop, being careful to keep the farm buildings between him and Harrison's rifle.

"Might not be such a bad idea," Franks said. "They'll see that fire for miles, and somebody's bound to come by and investigate."

LeBlanc swore. His shoulder felt like hell, and what was worse, he had gotten nothing for it but more trouble. He had half expected Flint to come in with a gang of men to finish the job—maybe fire the house...but now, there were five people in that soddy that could identify them...

He sighed.

"Shit," he finally said, and grabbed the reins of his horse.

* * * * *

Stepping into the Palace Bar, Zeke felt many eyes falling on him...but the green eyes at the end of the long, curly maple bar were the ones he was most interested in.

"Well, look what the cat dragged in," Sally smirked, pulling one of the taps until the glass beneath it overflowed with beer. Expertly, she dumped the foaming head before sliding it in front of Zeke.

"Evenin', Miss Sally," Zeke drawled, tipping his hat at the barmaid. Her shortish, brunette hair was graying now, but the eyes beneath had a light and a fire that Zeke had come to appreciate years ago.

"Zeke, 'Miss' Sally went through the door 20 years ago, and I ain't seen her since," Sally replied, shaking her head and smiling as she filled another glass under the flowing tap. "What you see is what you get."

"Promises, promises," Zeke countered, and when Sally slid the beer down to him, he raised it toward the woman, then wagged his finger at her. Rolling her eyes, she slapped a dishtowel over her shoulder and moved on down the bar until she leaned close to him.

410

"How the *hell* are you, Ezekiel?" the woman said, with a tenderness that seemed out of place with her tough exterior.

"Tolerable," Zeke replied, darting his eyes around the bar. "You got my telegram?"

"Yep," Sally replied, expertly lighting a cigarette, then dangling it from between the fingers of one hand while she reached into her bodice with the other. From it, she produced a yellow Western Union form that she tossed on the bar.

"Do you still have that box I mentioned?" Zeke responded, taking another sip of his beer. Behind him, he could hear the double doors of the saloon swing open with a creak, and a check in the mirror confirmed his suspicions.

"I shouldn't," Sally said, looking down, then returning Zeke's gaze. "I ain't a safe deposit box, ya know."

"Yer better than that, Sally old girl," Zeke countered, looking at his hands, recalling the trust that was forged years ago in tougher times. His gaze returned to hers. "Is it here?"

"Yeah, it's here," Sally said, but as she began to move, Zeke grasped her hand, speaking softly.

"Just put it down at this end of the bar, will you please? You might clear out the area first, though, if ya don't mind." His stare was fixed, and its meaning was unmistakable.

"Where is he?" Sally murmured, and when Zeke's eyes darted toward the other end of the bar, Sally speedily copied the move, sizing up the situation.

"You sure ya know what yer doin'?" she asked in earnest.

Zeke winked in response...but his smile was gone.

"Yer outta yer mind, Gardner," she said simply, but she moved away, first slopping half a bucket of water on the bar and then wiping it down, then cajoling the nearby patrons toward 'better tables in the corner.' After they moved away, muttering, she reached under the bar and carefully placed a lonely gray steel box at the far end against the wall. Zeke got up from the barstool, and had just reached it when he heard a deep voice intone, "That's about far enough."

Turning, Zeke observed that a large, bearded man was smiling grimly at him, casually leaning on the far end of the bar with his hands clasped at chest level. Chairs screeched in all directions from the pair as they locked eyes on one another, clearing nearly every table along the bar, with the lone exception of an old-timer over at the far end near Cheevers with his face on the table, snoring in his cups.

"What's this about...?" started Zeke, but stopped as the man at the other end raised his finger and waved it back and forth, as a schoolmaster might correct a small child.

"I think you know, Mr. Gardner," said Charles Cheevers, his eyes so utterly confident that they came off as bemused. "Why don't you slide that box on down here to me?"

Surveying the room, Zeke had to admire how his adversary positioned himself perfectly for a gunfight. Leaning with his left side against the angle of the bar, Cheever's right hand was free to draw, while Zeke's gun hand was still on the bar—and his sidearm was partially blocked beneath the lip. Even if Zeke was faster—*and I'm not*, Zeke admitted to himself— Cheevers could still duck and dive to his left behind the corner of the bar, allowing himself cover for a second shot.

"Take it easy, Mister," Zeke stalled. "Whatever it is you want..."

"No." The bemused look was gone now, replaced with dead eyes. "The box. *Now.*"

Zeke was no fool. Nodding, he reached for the box...and suddenly flipped it open, grasping the handle of the pistol that was hidden among the papers there. But through the corner of his vision, he saw that his adversary's gun had already cleared its holster, and in the fraction of a second he had left to live, he realized that there was nothing—absolutely nothing in the world—that he could do to stop the hand behind it from pulling a trigger before he did.

In that same split second, having cocked the hammer and nearly brought the gun level, Cheevers knew it too. So it was with a sense of complete astonishment that the gunman felt the unexpected shock of the rising barrel as it collided with a wiry, withered forearm. In a flash, he recognized that it belonged to a torso—not sleeping, but rising from the adjacent table—and met the ancient, grinning eyes of Bobber Davies. As the gun struck the aged bone, it snapped the forearm like a dry twig, angled toward the rib cage of the old trapper...and went off.

Seeing the scene play out before him as if in a dream, Zeke had nearly cocked his piece when he saw Bobber's arm dart out...as he had hoped and half expected...but was barely able to squeeze off the round after he saw Bobber's body recoil from Cheever's first shot. Whether it was emotion at the thought of Bobber being hit, or the hopes of keeping his shot wide of the old trapper, Zeke's own shot drifted right. It struck his adversary in the left shoulder, and he could see that the Chicago gunman was already lining

412

up for his second shot…when Cheevers' head exploded into non-existence. Sally lowered the shotgun as Zeke threw down his gun and darted to Bobber, whose flowing blood was soaking into the sawdust covering the floor of the Palace.

47

Saturday, August 11, 1894
7:55 pm

Amos had arrived at the Lang farm far later than he had hoped...his leased transportation having been unexpectedly appropriated by J.T. Lynch. So when the Lang brothers spotted a man approaching on foot, silhouetted in the darkness at the end of the lane that led to their farmstead, Russ and his brother Charlie approached with caution, their rifles shouldered.

"W-who's out there?" Charlie stammered.

Leaning against the Lang's rusty mailbox, Amos didn't speak, but whistled a few bars of the chorus from "It's a Hot Time in the Old Town Tonight"—then struck a match, illuminating his face as he lit his cigarette.

"Easy, Charlie," Russ said, lowering his rifle. "It's gotta be Amos."

"Yeah," his brother agreed, recalling the whistle and the tune from their fairly frequent visits to the Barrelhouse in recent months (working the occasional roofing job in Lincoln as needed), where the Professor had played the song over and over at their request. Smirking in the darkness, he added, "Nobody else has cigarettes that stink as bad as his."

"We were starting to worry about you," Russ said, jerking his thumb behind him toward the small white frame house. "Your friend what's-his-name in there said you'd be right behind him."

"How's he doing?" Amos asked, walking rapidly toward the porch.

"See for yourself," Charlie replied, gesturing to the farmhouse. There on the porch in the light of the half moon was Ransom Reed Cable, Jr., soundly snoring in the big porch swing, creaking softly as it rocked in the light evening breeze. He didn't stir at all, even when the three companions walked softly onto the porch and stood next to him.

"He wouldn't go inside," Russ murmured. "He just kept looking for you, until he dropped off."

Two days of torture surely takes it out of a man, thought Amos, wondering if claustrophobia would be a side effect that would plague the boy for years, or if a good night of sleep would solve the problem.

"Dead to the world, isn't he?" Charlie quipped.

"Close—too close," Amos said. Speaking softly, he gave the Langs an abbreviated story about the boy's kidnapping at the old Rock Creek

Station. However, he left out most of the details—including the the boy's name and that of J.T. Lynch. Despite his stated willingness to ignore "the one that got away," the man was still very much in the neighborhood—and his threat regarding Julia was one that Amos planned to take seriously...at least until the girl was safely home. *Then we'll see...*

From the end of the lane, the sound of horses' hooves broke Amos' reverie. They did come, after all, Amos thought. The note he had left at the Station had finally been discovered.

"Let's get this boy to Fairbury," Amos said, and nudged the sleeping Cable until he awoke with a start, panic in his tired eyes—followed by a flash of recognition, and a look of genuine relief.

* * * * *

It was a lonely place, but that wasn't Zeke's choice—it was Bobber's—*and it would be the way he wanted it.*

A few miles north of Sidney, the ex-Deputy Sheriff of Lancaster County leaned on his shovel, breathing hard, his hours-long labor finally at an end. Gazing at the cold moon, he was just enjoying the final movements of a long symphony of memory, composed of themes encompassing the long history that he had shared with Bobber. Zeke had *certainly* met him at least twice while serving in the Army of the Potomac—Bobber being a wiry sergeant of volunteers from the new state of California when Zeke was a green-behind-the-ears recruit from Minnesota. Years had gone by, and suddenly, there he was again, in Deadwood, riding guard on the gold shipments to Sidney. Bobber's health then was not good, not bad—just stable, like a mule that lived to pull, and the longer he pulled, the better he pulled. For all of the following years in Lincoln, Bobber's understated presence had been a back door into the secret ways of Lancaster County—never seen, always seeing, and always backing Zeke's play...even in January of 1888, when Zeke's decision to follow his orders and evict the Harrisons on the eve of the blizzard, with such bitter consequences, had estranged him from much of the county he had served.

Zeke had questioned his own actions, of course, more than even his most vocal second-guessers, and in his own mind, had come up wanting. If he had not stopped to check in with the office, if he had made better time through the snow in his return journey with Bobber to check on the couple, if he had disregarded orders entirely and not turned the Harrisons out at all...? The list was endless, as was the merciless criticism Zeke had heaped upon himself.

In the end, it was Bobber who had come up with the solution to Zeke's anguish...and the key that would turn his life into something salvageable.

"Zeke," he had said, a delicate letter dangling from his withered hand, "Every man needs somethin' to live for, to offer up. Fer me, it's been helpin' you—and now, it's yer turn. Here it is—right in front of yer face. You go to Harrison, boy…and you make it *right*."

And so, the conspiracy—for Zeke, to help Harrison, serving a penance that as a non-believer he never would have believed possible a few years earlier—for Harrison, to take his vengeance on Masterson—and for them both, to help a tiny circle of farmers find their way out of a cycle of overwhelming greed and poverty. And, just maybe, give a little meaning to the death of two young people…who did not deserve to die alone in the cold.

Bobber, now lying under six feet of Sandhill sod, was the key. For although it was Zeke who had discovered Antonia Harrison next to the overturned wagon under her own hope chest—and had gotten her to the warmth and safety of a nearby farm in sufficient time to deliver her child— it was Bobber who had discovered her husband…and the letter. There was no way to tell how long Bob Harrison had known of its existence. Perhaps only minutes, an hour at most…probably discovered when he turned the trunk over, emptying its contents to offer some protection to his wife. Written in her hand, it had been a plea for Masterson to reconsider his decision to evict them, reminding him of his "scurrilous behavior" on the day she had left his service. It had been returned, with a hand-written message scrawled at the bottom that "teasing whores have no right to request a damn thing."

For the thousandth time, Zeke wondered what had been the effect on Harrison in those few minutes he had left to live, after he had discovered the letter. Was he furious? Certainly, with Masterson…but with his wife, for not confiding in him? Zeke guessed that *worry* had probably been the overwhelming factor in his mind…with his wife slowly freezing to death, along with his child…

Of course, Masterson had no idea how much the girl had talked to Zeke prior to her death…but Zeke had made damned sure that Masterson *thought* it was enough to convict him of rape, and worse…of murder, in turning the girl out in a blizzard.

Hence, the grain agreement.

Standing over Bobber, Zeke marveled at the old man's choice of a final resting place, confided to him years ago. A sandhill in the middle of nowhere, it had been out of a pit on this very spot that he and Bobber had dug several million dollars' worth of gold bars, stolen from them on the Deadwood Trail in '73.

416

"You said that it was the most expensive hole you had ever seen," Zeke said, his voice choking now. "And as good a place as any to be shoved into."

There was so much to say.

But Zeke guessed what Bobber would have said, back in his prime, as a trapper with Osbourne Russell back in '38, in the Rocky Mountains fighting Blackfoot, as a sergeant in the Army of the Potomac…or even now, standing next to his protégé in spirit and rich memory.

Get on with it, willya?

Thrusting the shovel deep into the pile of sand at his feet, Zeke added, "Thanks, Pard."   And mounting the rig he had borrowed from Sally, he turned south toward the train that would take him back east at dawn.

* * * * *

"You look beat," Amos Seville murmured to the reclining patient next to him, finishing his story as the grey dawn seeped through the windows of the Western Division headquarters of the Chicago, Rock Island, and Pacific Railroad, though he himself had seen even less sleep—at least in the last 24 hours—than the boy.   Amos felt every bruise from his encounters with Jack Trudeau—the madman—and his partner, Jasper Rankin, a heartless scoundrel. Both of them had nearly killed him.

But I wouldn't have traded places with Cable, he reflected, observing the boy's hollow expression.

"In a manner of speaking," Nathan Brockhurst agreed, arms folded as he watched Doc Connelle apply the last clean strips of gauze to the boy's myriad razor cuts. "But not beaten."

Connelle's other patient, Wendell Evans, nodded from his chair in the corner, where Julia Pack was serving coffee to the men in turns from a battered pot. It had taken the girl what seemed like forever to locate Nathan Brockhurst yesterday afternoon and send a party after Amos, and Julia's relief on seeing the men return safely with their charges a few hours ago was still visible on her face.

"Those men were nightmares, Rance," Evans said, sipping his coffee as stared into the boy's eyes. "I should **know.** I'm sure your father will be proud you came through it so well…"

"Speaking of which," Brockhurst interrupted, rocking forward from his desk, littered with yesterday's piles of hurried correspondence from Chicago, and every point along the Rock Island line. "I'd best get a telegram off to Mr. Cable…"

417

"Ah wouldn't do that just yet," Amos said, quietly, turning to Connelle. "Doc, would you excuse us for a moment?"

"In for a penny, in for a pound, Amos," Julia said, laying a hand on Amos' shoulder. Her eyes bespoke of her trust in Doc Connelle, and in a moment, Amos relented.

"Go ahead and tell them, Mr. Evans," he said, nodding to the reporter.

"When I was with those...*men*," Evans said, suppressing a shudder, "They spoke about your father's plans to keep the Pinkertons on the case here—even though your father had been warned against it by whoever was paying for your capture."

A look of realization was dawning on Cable's features. "So that means..."

"Someone close to your father was telling those cutthroats about his plans," Brockhurst said, harrumphing as he sipped his coffee from a battered tin cup. "Somebody at the very top, I'd guess. Figures...how else would they have known the precise day when you were going home...?"

"So I can't *go*?" Cable said, a worried look descending again on the tired features.

"Sure you can," Amos said reassuringly. "We just need to be a little quiet about it."

"That's right. In fact, we're leaving today," Evans announced, walking stiffly over to Cable, and patting him on the shoulder. "I'm going with you—and we're not going to tell anyone about it—even the Pinkertons."

"All the way to Chicago?" Cable said, hope filling his eyes.

"That's right, Mr. Cable," Amos said. "Ah'm sure Nathan here can arrange a swift passage, and ah'll have a good friend of mine meet our train there in Chicago." Meeting Amos' eyes, Nathan nodded his assent.

"Who is he?" Cable said, suppressing a yawn, and for all the world looking as if he would fall right back to sleep in his chair.

"It's a *she*," Amos said, a crooked smile creeping into the corner of his mouth. "Her name is Miss Eugenia Livingston...and ah'm sure she'll take *good* care of you until your father contacts you."

Cable nodded, and the smile on Amos' face was about to spread into a grin...when it was scorched into oblivion by the searing pain of the coffee cascading from Julia's hand into his unprotected lap.

* * * * *

418

The train wasn't difficult to arrange, and soon a 4-4-0 engine, a coal and water tender, a second class sleeper car and a caboose were assembled from the oddments Brockhurst could scrape up from the roundhouse. The orange sun was just peeking over the horizon when the short train was ready to depart from the Fairbury station. Cable was already bundled in and snoring away again—one of only four passengers—bound on an (until recently) unscheduled special, direct to Chicago, by way of Lincoln.

While Julia and Doc Connelle helped Evans onto the platform, Brockhurst waggled his finger at Amos from under the awning that covered the yardmaster's office. As Amos approached, the old man extended his hand.

"I guess I was right in pushing the Sheriff to get hold of you," he said, gruffly. "Not bad work for a bootlegger."

"Please, Mistah Brockhurst," Amos objected, "Ah prefer the term 'venture capitalist.'"

"Well, you've shown good judgment, and a fair bit of grit, whatever you call it," Brockhurst admitted, then gazed seriously over his glasses, meeting the eyes of the man from Virginia. "But I can't say I agree with keeping Mr. Cable in the dark about his son."

Amos' eyes dropped to his feet, scuffled them on the platform, then met Brockhurst's gaze. "Well, ah can't say ah like it much, either—ah imagine he's pretty tense by now. Any ideas?"

"I have *one*," Brockhurst replied, a slight smile on his face. "You might call it a back door approach."

As Brockhurst shared his idea, Amos grinned and finally nodded. It was a good plan—good enough to add a request. The station master nodded in his own turn, and with a final wink, Amos strode over to the waiting sleeper car. At its steps, Amos extended his hand to help Evans up, who took it with as much vigor as he could muster—which wasn't much.

"Well," Amos stated, "Wouldn't surprise me to see you get a newspaper job out of this, after all, if that's what you really want, partner. Cable is likely to be pretty grateful to the man that brought his son in."

"Possibly," Evans groaned, slipping into one of the triple-stacked beds that lined the dark interior of the car, "but not by telling *this* story."

The whistle sounded twice, signaling the imminent departure of the little train. Amos was about to extend his hand to Julia to help her aboard when Doc Connelle spoke.

419

"Don't know if I could have taken what those two men took from that monster," Connelle said, shaking his head. "If that man had anything to do with the wreck, I'd better hear about it—I won't stand by and let an innocent man in Lincoln hang for another man's act."

"You have my word on it, Doc," Amos replied as he shook Connelle's outstretched hand. Watching the physician disappear around the side of the station house toward his home in downtown Fairbury, Amos stared into the sun…and yawned.

"You could use some sleep," Julia said, her eyes full of the man from Virginia as she made her way up the narrow stairs to the car where Amos stood. Without a single whistle or call from the train's hand-picked (and very discreet) conductor that might wake the still sleeping town, the train slipped away with its four passengers.

"So could you," Amos said. Glancing at the train's interior and then back at Julia, his raised eyebrow was subtle, but still visible. "Upper, or lower?"

"One more word out of *you*," Julia warned with a hint of a smirk, "And I'll fetch another mug of coffee for that lap of yours…"

* * * * *

Flint was not fond of early mornings—especially Sunday mornings—and he suspected Miles McGee wasn't either. But Flint had long ago observed that there never was an appropriate hour for bad news to present itself, and that most men in power would rather have it quick and to the point, so they could deal with the consequences at hand. Having eluded capture and laid low for most of the night from the sheriff's posse, Flint felt confident that he was not being actively pursued as he reached McGee's upstairs apartment in Lincoln's theatre district. As he reached for the doorknob, however, he was surprised to suddenly see it swing inwards, and fast as a striking rattler, instinctively pulled and cocked his sidearm.

"Put it away," McGee said quietly, his back already turned as he walked away from the door and took his seat next to the window. Its heavy velvet curtains were drawn closed, but the morning sun lit the seam between them, and a sliver of light fell across McGee's features. He had obviously slept very little.

"My sources inform me that your *legendary* skills at organization and coercion may have been…a bit overestimated," McGee said flatly, his pale eyes turning first toward the window, then settling on Flint. Flint's confidence didn't often allow him to feel uncomfortable, but he was approaching it now.

420

"Well, we did have a bad night," Flint said, holstering his gun. "Did your sources happen to say just who informed on us?"

"According to one of the deputies, it was a young Czech girl...think that her name was Ann, or Anna...with some hellacious last name, mostly consonants. What does it matter?"

"It is my experience that examples, even unproveable rumors, tend to get around," Flint said. "And that makes our job that much easier next time."

"I'm not worried about next time—I'm worried about *this* time, Mr. Flint," McGee pulled a cigar out of the inside pocket of his smoking jacket, bit off the end, and held a match to its tip until it flamed into life. Languidly, the old man took a deep draw, then turned his gaze back to Flint...who was experienced enough in dealing with men of power to know when to wait for a question instead of filling empty space with idle chit-chat.

Besides, thought Flint uneasily, *this man has a shoe to drop...*

"Am I given to understand that you expected a telegram from your associate, when he had recovered the grain agreement from Gardner?" McGee asked, as if he already knew the answer.

"Yes...and I have received no such message." Flint replied, coolly. "But that doesn't mean..."

"Your man Cheevers is dead, Flint," McGee said, flatly. "I have a source in Sidney that said Gardner and a barmaid shot him down in a tavern there last night."

Flint was shaken to his core. *Cheevers...dead? That man was as fast as me...maybe faster...*

But the only external sign Flint gave was his right fist flexing and relaxing as he stared at his boots.

"Damned shame," Flint said, finally. "Need that agreement."

McGee simply nodded.

"Any word...from your *sources*...on when Gardner will return?" Flint asked.

McGee shook his head. "Not as yet—could be back as early as tonight, though—and *has* to be back with that agreement by tomorrow at 9:00...to appear in court before Judge Lansing."

Flint nodded. That checked with what Gardner himself had told him, back in the Bucher Saloon in Columbus yesterday morning.

"I'll check in at noon, today," Flint stated, putting on his hat. "He can't get back before then. Meanwhile…"

"Are you *still* thinking about that girl?" McGee chuckled, shaking his head. "You have an overdeveloped sense of vengeance, Mr. Flint."

"Just thinking practically, Mr McGee," Flint replied. "It has its utility, as I said."

"Very well," McGee said, rolling the cigar between his fingertips. "I'll make a bargain with you. I'll give you the information you want…the girl's name, where you can find her, everything…if you'll do me a small favor in return."

Flint's arms folded and his left eyebrow went up. "Which is?"

McGee nodded toward the bedroom. In the shadows, Flint could make out that a carpet had been clumsily rolled up…and that a dainty hand dangled limply from within one of its open ends.

"That rug needs cleaning," McGee said.

48

Sunday, August 12, 1894

8:10 a.m.

For Ransom Reed Cable, Sr., isolated in his huge, dark paneled personal library on Erie Street in downtown Chicago, it had been yet another sleepless night—worse by far than the last two. Since five o'clock yesterday afternoon, he had been expecting a call announcing the release of his son—or the discovery of his death. Cable was unused to second guessing his business decisions regarding the CRI&P—once made, they were made—and even his cantankerous board members were wise enough not to contradict him, at least to his face. But his decision yesterday to keep the Pinkertons on the case, even after he had been warned off by his son's kidnappers...

A cold, immobile cigar was clamped between Cable's fingers, hovering over a corresponding hole in the arm of his stuffed leather chair, next to an unfinished supper on an adjoining endtable. He was deep in thought, possibly even half asleep when the door to his library opened...and he was instantly alert.

"Yes, Peter?" Cable's voice was neutral, but LaRue detected the strain behind it.

"No news as yet, Sir—but...Mrs. Cable asks you to join her for breakfast," LaRue replied, expecting to have his head bit off. Cable had left strict orders not to be disturbed except in the case of a long distance telephone call.

Instead, Cable stirred from his chair. "Very well, Peter," he sighed, placing his extinguished cigar in a nearby ashtray. "Stay close to the telephone, won't you?"

"Indeed, sir," LaRue said, and watched carefully as his boss moved down the hallway to his wife's rooms.

He's nearly broken, thought LaRue, doing his best to keep a smile from crossing his lips. *He's made decisions that no Board in its right mind could agree with...or pardon. If this doesn't satisfy...I don't know what will.*

* * * * *

For the third time in as many minutes, Bud Gardner rubbed his eyes and fought back a yawn. The boom of the organ, the choirboys chanting in Latin, and the sheer alien pageantry of the Catholics preparing for their service at Saint Theresa's—the second he had ever attended—would normally have been enough to keep the fascinated young Methodist alert.

But it had been a very long night.

The Harrison farmyard had been quiet for at least 20 minutes before the old man had cautiously swung the pockmarked door of the sod house open, satisfied at last that LeBlanc and his men had truly left. Zeke's horse, Lilith, standing placidly outside the corral that held Harrison's horses, had been the only surprise waiting for them—snorting softly and actually walking up to Bud when the boy appeared in the glowing light of the embers from the burned-out grain wagon.

By the time that Bud and his large Czech companion had made their way from Harrison's place to the little town of Malcolm along the Missouri Pacific tracks just north of Lincoln, it had been nearly ten o'clock. It had been past eleven before the young man from Alder Grove had managed to awaken, and finally convince the sleepy stationmaster to telephone the Sheriff in Lincoln. To Bud's surprise, Sheriff Miller was still awake. As soon as Bud had mentioned that Max LeBlanc and his men had pinned them down on the Harrison farm all afternoon, Miller had said that he'd be right out, urging the boy to wait at the Malcolm station for him.

Another hour went by, and sure enough, a steam engine, tender and freight car appeared, backing up the track from the direction of Lincoln. Through the steam pouring from the cylinders of the little engine, the door of the freight car opened suddenly to produce Miller and two other men on horseback. After a short discussion with Bud, the Sheriff had ordered him back to Lincoln with the train and a scribbled message, asking him to drop it off at the courthouse on his return—then turned with his men to tear up the road to Harrison's, with the Czech trailing behind on Harrison's mule.

Four hours of sleep, thought Bud, fighting another yawn. *Ought to be enough*—but when Emelia had awakened him at seven—scolding him slightly for having come in after three in the morning—he had found it difficult to keep his eyes open, despite the teasing that Ginny and Johnny had mercilessly piled upon him as the family prepared for Mass. Bud was ravenous, but no breakfast was forthcoming, of course—Mass, he learned, was to be taken on an empty stomach—and the Runza he had shared with Anna Marie at lunch yesterday seemed an age ago.

Anna Marie. There it is, Bud admitted to himself—*the reason that I volunteered to get help, and to return to Lincoln, and to get to church on time.* Though he had not shared his experience at Harrison's with any of the Packs as yet, he wanted the girl to know—by his presence at church, if nothing else—that he was all right. But as yet, with only moments remaining before Mass was to begin, she was nowhere to be—*wait a minute. There at the back...*

...was a dark-haired girl in a white linen dress. Bud's breath caught in his throat.

She was kneeling between two immense men—her brothers, of course, giant bookends that guarded the girl like a slim volume of perfect poetry—that were now busily scanning the room with lowered brows. To Bud's relief, their glowering stares had landed squarely upon the Packs, ten rows ahead of him. He, however, had managed to duck and just miss their gaze—having excused himself and Ginny at the last moment, as the Packs could not quite squeeze the two of them in at their row. Finally, noting that the heads of the two brothers lowered to their hands, Bud slowly leaned his head back, trying to catch Anna's eye.

Half way through the homily, he managed it—and was rewarded with a start and a smile, which Anna barely stifled in time to prevent the boy's discovery across the church by her towering and watchful companions. When the congregation kneeled again a few minutes later, bowing their heads at the transfiguration of the host, Anna committed a venial sin—by raising her hand over her head and tugging downwards sharply, once. Bud puzzled...then, suddenly, understood the gesture.

* * * * *

Iphegenia Cable had experienced the same horrific three days that Ransom himself had lived through, and when summoned to breakfast, Cable firmly believed that he would find his wife withdrawn into a shell, wringing her hands over her missing son, yet marginally following the breakfasting custom that Sunday morning dictated. So Cable was completely taken aback when he walked into the large dining room and saw that Mrs. Cable was once again surrounded by her beloved copy of the Chicago Tribune, drinking coffee and eating scones with the same detached indifference that Sunday mornings usually lent the Cable home.

"Iffie!" Cable exclaimed, then failed to find the words to follow.

"Ransom," she said, taking a sip from her steaming cup without lifting her head from her paper. "Blessed Sunday."

"Blessed Sunday." Cable's reply was as automatic as it was incredulous. Seating himself at the opposite end of the table, he numbly helped himself to a scone with butter while staring at his wife. When he had last seen her, she was racked with tears, crying in the darkened confines of her room. Now, it was as if the last three days had never happened. *What in the name of Shakespeare's ghost was going on here?*

425

"There's a telegram on the salver there, next to you," Mrs. Cable announced, lifting the section of the newspaper before her in order to cover her porcelain features. "As you can see, I've excused the servants, and am acting as natural as the situation allows."

Puzzled now beyond forbearance, Cable reached for the Western Union telegram placed there, and read:

FAIRBURY NEBRASKA

12 AUGUST 1894

IPHEGENIA CABLE

25 E ERIE STREET CHICAGO ILLINOIS

YOUR SON IS SAFE AND ON WAY TO CHICAGO STOP SOMEONE ON MR CABLES STAFF MAY BE BEHIND RECENT MISFORTUNE STOP IMPORTANT TO ACT UNAWARE OVER NEXT FEW DAYS BUT DO INFORM MR CABLE OF COURSE STOP FEEL FREE TO CONTACT ME BUT DO NOT REPEAT DO NOT USE NORMAL MEANS INCLUDING TELEPHONE STOP TELEGRAPH ME IMMEDIATELY VIA BEN RASHWORTH ROKEBY STATION STOP GODSPEED

NATHAN BROCKHURST

Standing, then sitting, then standing and pacing, Cable excitedly reached the end of the telegram and violently suppressed an urge to scream in relief and delight. Instead, noticing that his wife's newspaper was visibly trembling, he walked over to her end of the table, kneeled, and tenderly placed her head against his shoulder. The lurching sobs were silent, as was the joy they shared.

After the space of a few minutes, Cable gave his wife a final squeeze, then announced loudly enough for the servants to hear, "I must go to the office this morning, Iffie. You *do* understand?"

Drying her shining eyes on a lace handkerchief, Mrs. Cable replied, "Of course, dear. I shall make your apologies at Sunday Services, of course."

"Thank you, dear," Cable said, making for the door…and the nearest Western Union office. His own eyes were not watering—but blazing.

* * * * *

Bud nudged Ginny. When he murmured a request for her to move, he got an elegant eyeroll, followed by a sharp whisper as she moved out of the way.

426

"Hope she's worth it," she hissed, with the hint of a knowing giggle. Ginny had obviously been watching him more carefully than he had suspected. "Momma will *skin* you if you're up to hanky panky *in church.*"

Bud nodded his thanks, then hurried to the back of the church and into the narthex, where two men were standing quietly. Focused on Anna Marie, he barely noticed that one of the men was wearing a badge of office, and that the other, a dark-haired man of middle height, watched him with intense eyes from under a derby hat as he passed. Halfway down a back set of stairs, Bud stopped...and waited. At the bottom of the stairs, the church's single indoor toilet waited—operated by a long chain that required a strong tug—the rendezvous that Bud thought must have been intended by Anna's hand signal.

In two minutes, he was sure he was wrong...but soon after, the organ piped up and the congregation began shuffling to the communion rail. Five minutes later, he heard the approach of two small feet on the wooden floor of the narthex above—and, suddenly, Anna appeared at the top of the stairwell. Bud's stomach flipped, a grin rising to his face. Motioning to her, they met at the bottom of the stairs. In the next minute, Bud and Anna committed yet another venial sin—an act performed often in church, though usually at the end of a wedding ceremony.

Anna's head fell to Bud's shoulders, her arms still around him. "I was so *worried* about you," she sighed. "You headed right into trouble, you..."

"Hlupek?" Bud offered, awkwardly patting her shoulder. "I'm all right." There was so much to say, he realized—but at the moment, their embrace was just too...mmm...to interrupt with rambling explanations.

"There is little time," Anna said, suddenly lifting her sky blue eyes to stare into his. "My brothers...*listen.* Could you...could you meet me at my boarding house? It's on G Street, 715 C. Three o'clock?"

Bud had barely managed a nod when the sound of large feet *clomping* above them, across the narthex and toward the top of the stairs, spurred Anna into immediate action. With breathtaking efficiency, the Czech girl shoved Bud through the open door of the toilet and slammed the door behind him. As he caught his breath, he faintly heard Anna's voice chattering in Czech, moving up the stairs, followed by gruff responses that could only have been her brothers.

Bud listened, then grinned, remembering how they had met. *She has a definite thing for toilets,* he said to himself. Opening the door, taking the stairs three at a time, he hurried to take his seat before the service ended.

* * * * *

427

How sweet, Flint said to himself at the top of the stairs as the boy rushed past him. *Young love.*

Deputy Dillon had been very helpful, and despite his confidence that the man was already in the ample pay of Miles McGee, Flint dropped a twenty-dollar gold piece in the man's hand. Pointing out the girl who had spoiled his plans last night had been helpful—but the juicy story that followed had been even better. Based on the deputy's information, along with the little tryst that he had just overheard at the bottom of the stairs, a new plan was rapidly forming in his mind, like a clay vessel on a turntable.

So, Flint reasoned, *this girl Anna Marie is the sister of someone Gardner betrayed—and the whole town knows about it.* As he whistled his way out of the back of the church, he committed the overheard conversation between the boy and the girl to memory...and grinned like a schoolboy.

What a wonderful opportunity.

* * * * *

Julia's mother is...scary, Amos sulked.

The hack driver, "Crazy" Charlie Raymond was nearing the State Prison now, on a roundabout route that had first led them from the Rock Island station to the Pack residence, with Julia in tow. Wendell Evans and Rance Cable had boarded an eastbound to Chicago less than an hour ago, and Julia had insisted on waiting for their train and wishing them goodbye before returning home. She seemed to have grown somewhat fond of Evans, in a motherly sort of way—*maybe it was natural,* reflected Amos, *considering that she had helped pull him, heel first and half dead, out of a grain elevator.* As jolly as the parting had been, however...the greeting given them by Emelia Pack, just returning from church, was a far cry from cheerful.

If there is such a thing as cold steam, Amos reflected, *Emelia Pack has cornered the market.*

As Raymond's cab had pulled away from the front porch of the Pack house, the only words Amos had overheard were "Julia Mary Elizabeth Pack, if you think you can just waltz back in here..." before his jab finally registered with Charlie's ribs sufficiently to race the hack toward the courthouse.

The Lancaster County jailer, had been helpful, as usual—offering cold coffee, old stories, and a crooked brown smile that reeked of tobacco—but not when it came to what Amos was really after. Amos' true objective had apparently been moved—twice—once to the City police cells, then late last night to the more secluded cells of the State Prison. These had

428

occasionally served as an overflow for Lancaster County, and the plethora of vagrants pulled in last night that were bulging the cells of both the County and City jails certainly made the transfer a reasonable one. In this case, however, the state cells also acted to isolate the prisoner from the flood of reporters who had all wished an interview with the accused train wrecker, Mr. George Washington Davis.

And to Fred Miller's way of thinking, isolation wasn't a bad idea…because Davis was a *talker*. He happily nattered on to anyone who asked him about how he had been on his way to Lincoln from Fairbury, in the company of the heroic Harry Foote himself, when the train had wrecked on Thursday night. Or did he run to the train wreck from the Ivison Club three miles away, and appear in time to help Harry Foote rescue the passengers? Miller had heard the story both ways, and more— and had actually been relieved, Amos discovered, to be rid of the feller. Miller claimed Davis gave him a headache, and reporters gave him the runs.

"So, what cock and bull story did that Davis boy blow up *your* skirt?" Charlie Raymond queried, exposing a gap-toothed grin under his shaggy mustache, then shook his equally shaggy head.

"*I* was the one that brought him back from the wreck that night, you know. Without his jacket—the one they found at the wreck site. His story then was that he had got on the train at Rokeby, and was sittin' next to Harry Foote when the wreck happened. Then flagged down the train to help carry out the survivors. That boy," he concluded. "Is so pleased with the attention he's gettin', he doesn't even know that he's drowning in his own lies."

The state prison was an imposing destination in South Lincoln that boasted a brick edifice, tall towers, a myriad of guards…but allowed visitors on Sunday, with permission of the Warden, of course. Waving farewell to Charlie at the west gate, Amos seriously doubted that he would be able to obtain that. But he maintained a thin hope, which he found, surprisingly, standing at the north gate.

"Good to see you, Mr. Hill," Amos said, approaching the blue-suited guard at the gate, a man of medium build and red hair, recognizing Amos immediately and extending a hand.

"Amos!" he said, surprise in his voice. "Back already? Why aren't you at Sunday dinner with the rest of the Packs?" Scotty Hill had been sparking Jill Pack for some time now, and was intimately familiar with her family's friends and acquaintances, though his progress at gaining an invitation to Sunday dinner had been painfully slow in coming.

"For the simple reason, ah suppose, that ah am not a Pack," Amos said, smiling. "Though ah understand that one of us has begun to hold hopes in that direction."

"Have to get past her mother, first," Hill said, sourly. "Emelia Pack can be…"

"Formidable," finished Amos. "Stay with it, old man—you might beard the lion…err, lioness, yet."

"Time will tell, I guess," Hill admitted, cocking his eye at the Virginian. "Now—what in the world brings you out here on a Sunday afternoon, Amos?"

"Came to visit a fellow, Scotty," Amos admitted. "And before you reach for that clipboard of yours—ah should tell you that ah am not on the list."

"Hmph," Hill snorted. "So, who is this lucky recipient of the famous Seville charm?"

"George Davis, Scotty."

Scotty's eyes bugged, and he sputtered, "You know I can't…"

"Ah have to see him right now, Scotty." Amos interjected.

"But…"

"Look, it's important," Amos insisted, putting his hand on Scotty's shoulder. "So important, that ah'm willing to risk ah friendship on it. So, what do you say that we spare Miss Jill the gory details of some of your…shall we say, nocturnal activities? Surely, ah'm correct in assuming they ah all in the past, am ah not? Why, I'll even provide, free of charge, one sparkly new alibi—to be used on the day and date of your discretion." Amos' eyes leveled with those of the guard.

Scotty's face fell. Then the young man shook his head and half-grinned.

"Dirty pool, Amos."

"Mah word of honor, Scotty." Amos said, raising his right hand. "A matter of life and death."

"Hmph," Scotty snorted again, with a hint of resignation.

"Twenty minutes," Amos said.

"Ten," said Scotty, scowling. "And if I hear you threaten me with that "nocturnal activities" business again, Bub, I'll clock you."

430

"Fair enough," Amos said, and followed Scotty through the squeaking side gate of the Nebraska State prison.

Sunday, August 12, 1894
1:02 pm

The narrow stairwell leading from the west gate to the basement of the Nebraska State prison which held G.W. Davis was poorly lit and a little dank, considering the drought that was plaguing most of the state. But then again, the lowest tier of cells *was* 30 feet underground, and the water table, this close to Salt Creek, was rather high.

At the bottom of the stairs, a corridor lined with cells—some filled, some not—led to another uniformed guard standing his post. Scotty Hill saluted, and muttered "Ten minutes, chum." The guard returned the salute, shook Amos' hand—deftly accepting the five-dollar gold piece concealed within it—and walked back down one of the side corridors, whistling.

Inside the cell facing Amos was a handsome colored man with intense brown eyes, about five and a half feet in height. He was seated in his cell, "reading" the pictures in a *Harper's Bazaar*, when his face suddenly turned to Amos, and broke into a grin.

"Amos Aloysius!" he exclaimed, rising to his feet and stretching his hand through the bars to meet Amos' own. "Ah nevah thought to see you comin' round heah..."

"Well, there's no accounting for taste, is there George?" Amos joked. "We handsome men of the District have to stick together, don't we?"

It was true of course—both of the men had grown up in the narrow back alleys of northeast Washington, D.C., playing, thieving, and escaping the confines of the law. When he had come to Lincoln a few years back, Amos' nocturnal excursions had eventually led him to the "Hoo Hoo Club," and a reunion of sorts with one of its most loyal (and invested) benefactors—the slightly older George Washington Davis, recently released from the Nebraska State Prison for robbery. They were not close—but Davis had the sort of easygoing demeanor that endeared him to almost all he met—even the prison guards. The warden, it was said, had Davis' picture hung in his office, showing off his striking good looks to the casual visitor like a prize heifer.

Davis grinned and nodded as Amos leaned in, his head against the bars, and his voice dropped to a murmur.

"Ah came here to tell you that a friend of yours has unfortunately passed away—an unfortunate fellow by the name of Jasper Rankin," Amos

432

stated flatly, staring intensely into the other man's eyes. Indeed, it was the very reason he had come to the prison, to see Davis' reaction to the news for himself—Davis was a horrible liar—and as he did so, Amos watched the truth unfold before him, like dominos falling.

Recognition of the name.

Relief.

Hope.

Amos was disappointed, but not surprised at Davis' reactions—they clearly indicated that he was in this thing up to his ears—but **hated** the last emotion…because he had to shatter it.

"As bad as that news is—there won't be a funeral, George. Because no one can find the body—*or any evidence that the man ever existed.*"

Amos watched the tumblers slowly turn in the man's mind, working out his position with every click, his emotions plain for anyone to read. While there was no one left in his mind to fear—and a man like Rankin would have been able to put the very fear of God into a weak-willed man such as this—there was also no one left to **blame.** Davis was left firmly holding a bag that he himself had willingly filled with a skunk, though the animal in question had been handed to him by another man. That man was dead now, and the bag was firmly tied to Davis—and no one else.

Slowly, Davis lowered himself to the bench, staring off through the adjoining cell walls—row after row of cages, constructed of flat steel bars forming endless riveted squares, trailing into the darkness—and let the knowledge of his fate settle on his shoulders.

"Ah am very sorry, George," Amos said quietly. He nodded to Hill, standing next to him.

"Let's get out of here, Scotty."

* * * * *

Swede Jorgenson was normally a cheerful man, but fortune had turned south on him, and as he sat out back of his beloved Barrelhouse—closed, as it was Sunday—he dwelled on how badly things had gone in the last forty-eight hours.

It was almost more than a good Lutheran could bear. First, his beloved bar had been taken over by church women on a Friday night—just when a thirsty Nebraska militia had come into town!—scrubbed it, and turned it into some kind of combination soup kitchen and recruiting station. He had been promised that the bar would be back in business on Saturday, but with Zeke out of town and the church ladies claiming squatter's rights, feeding every vagrant that had heard of the opportunity—and Jesus God, there were plenty of those—who was he to object? Yes, he weighed 250 pounds and could pick up a young heifer under each arm. Who cared? It was a bunch of church women, for cat's sake. And that was *damned scary.*

It was enough to make a man want to take up drinking, Swede reflected.

Sitting on the back porch of the Barrelhouse, stroking the kitten he had found abandoned here just a week ago, Swede surveyed the long, beautiful mahogany bar of the Barrelhouse that now laid abandoned in the backyard, along with its companions—gilded mirrors, bottles and barrels of fine whiskey, chandeliers, tables and chairs—and shook his head.

Well, he thought. *At least it couldn't get much worse. Zeke and Bobber will be home soon.*

And then the Western Union boy came by—and he saw that it was *already* worse. Blinking back the tears, he read the telegram again.

Zeke would be in at five o'clock, and would meet Swede at the station.

And Bobber—wouldn't.

Swede lowered his head, and let the purring of the kitten cover his sobs.

He was just reaching for a handkerchief, when he suddenly—a fraction of a second too late—became aware of a presence behind him as the kitten in his lap hissed. Immediately, Swede felt an unyielding, icy circle of pressure at the base of his skull, accompanied by the four distinct clicks of a Colt hammer being drawn back—and knew enough not to turn around.

"Pleasure to meet you, Mr....Jorgenson, I believe?" Flint said, snatching up the telegram from the porch, where it lay next to the big man. Reading it, Flint nodded in satisfaction...McGee's sources within the Western Union were good, and their abilities to delay a telegram long enough for Flint to follow the messenger were equally commendable.

"Let's take a little tour around your fine establishment, shall we, sir?"

* * * * *

As Amos and Scotty Hill began their ascent from the basement cells, Amos spied a nattily dressed figure that he thought he recognized, checking in with the guard at the top of the stairs of the Nebraska State pen. D.B. Courtenay was a lawyer who specialized in civil cases, and Amos had often seen him hanging around the Courthouse. But he had rarely seen him mix with the criminal class—he looked out of place and even fussier and less comfortable than usual, if that was possible. Looking up at where Amos was staring, Hill started and grabbed Amos' elbow, stopping them while both were half hidden in the dim stairwell.

"That's Courtenay, Davis' attorney—one of them, anyway," the guard stated, nervously. "It's a good thing we finished when we did, or my nuts would have been in a wringer."

"Can't have that, can we...what would Miss Jill think?" Amos rejoined, then asked the obvious question. "Davis has *two* lawyers? Who's the other one?"

"I forget. They both appeared at the start of the inquest yesterday—I don't think they like each other."

It was news to Amos that an inquest had already begun, although it didn't exactly surprise him. *But why would Davis pick a lawyer like Courtenay who specialized in civil cases...?*

The answer struck him like a firebell. *Of course. Courtenay was being paid for by the families of the victims, not Davis—if they could prove that Davis was innocent, they could sue Rock Island in civil court for negligence,* Amos reasoned. *Ten to one that Courtenay was also responsible for arguing the civil suit. But who was this other lawyer...?*

Amos's curiosity must have been telepathic, because at that very moment a larger, potbellied man appeared at the top of the stairs, and an argument immediately ensued between himself and Courtenay.

"That's the man, right there," Scotty whispered. "His name is...uh..."

"Colonel Philpot," Amos said, trying to keep a neutral tone in his voice.

"Yeah—that's *right*," Hill replied, eyeing Amos in the dim light of the stairwell. "Know him?"

"Know *of* him." *Dammit,* thought Amos. *Davis can't say no to* **anyone.**

As it turned out, Courtenay brushed past the two of them on his way down the stairs as if headed for a fire. Philpot, for whatever reason, had decided to take a chair at the top of the stairs and wait for his "partner" to finish with Davis. When Amos and Scotty reached the top of the stairs, Philpot was smoking a fine cigar.

"Afternoon, Amos," Philpot said. "Visiting some of your suppliers?"

"No, Colonel—one of *your* clients, actually," Amos said, watching a scowling Scotty Hill out of the corner of his eye as he hurried out the door to resume his post.

435

"Indeed?" Philpot said, his eyes flickering to Hill and chuckling. With an exaggerated groan, he rose from the chair and motioned outside with the cigar. "Care for a turn about the prison yard?"

Amos nodded, and managed to ignore Hill's presence at the door, though he was almost sure he had seen Philpot wink at the guard.

"So," Amos said, trying to be nonchalant, "What brings you to this case, Colonel?"

"The money, of course," Philpot answered candidly. "A settlement with Rock Island? Could be worth thousands. Question is...what brings *you* to it?"

Philpot's direct nature didn't exactly surprise Amos—Philpot had a reputation of going after the "big fish"—the railroads, the department stores, the banks. Amos speculated that his presence on Davis' defense, similar to Courtenay's, probably had less to do with getting his client off than milking the CRI&P for a large settlement.

"Me? Well, sir...ah am a friend of Mr. Davis. And," he added, "in possession of information that could materially aid your client."

"Do tell," murmured Philpot, twirling his cigar between his fingers.

"For example," Amos went on, "Were you aware that Mr. Davis did not act alone?"

"Well...*if* he was involved in any crime at all, it is clear that he was not the type to plan it and execute it *alone*—any jury can see that the man is a simpleton. That observation, by the way, will likely play a large part in his defense," Philpot observed, then asked, "It *is* clear that he is frightened. Are these...alleged...conspirators pressuring him to keep silent?"

"Not anymore," Amos said, laying his cards on the table. "The man that assisted him is...*corpus morituri.*"

"*Fortuna malis*...for *him*, of course," Philpot observed. "But as far as my client is concerned, it is hardly relevant. It was bad track maintenance and operating negligence that led to the deaths of those unfortunate passengers, not foul play at all..."

"*What*?" Amos couldn't help interjecting.

"Certainly," Philpot continued, gesturing with his cigar as if to a jury. "The track repair crew had been there at the trestle just days before, but were called off to another job before they were finished. The engineer that night was proceeding at an unsafe speed, according to several witnesses. The engine's brakes had been proved faulty just days before. Shall I go on?"

Amos' mind played back over the last week, and realized that he could confirm several of these points himself. But they were facts, not *truth, dammit.*

"Ah'm telling you, *sir,* that there was foul play," Amos rejoined. "There were men that *coerced* Davis..."

"And just how, Mr. Seville, is *that* supposed to help my client?" Philpot countered. "He would be just as guilty if he was the mastermind as the stooge. And just as *dead.* This is a capital offense, sir. The defense of my client is paramount—your 'truth' as you see it—is ancillary."

"But..." Amos began, then stopped. The man was infuriating. "You're doing this for *personal gain,* you damned vulture..."

"Certainly," interjected Philpot, staring intently at Amos. "But that doesn't mean that I'm *wrong.*"

Amos paused, his head spinning. *What was best for Davis now? The truth? Or a good defense?* Sighing, a sense of resignation overcame Seville.

But there was *one* more point to make.

"Ah don't know how you wheedled your way into it, Philpot, but this is your case now. You'd better give it one hundred percent...for your client, not for you," Amos warned, coldly. "Ah'll be watching, and ah have a very, *very* long memory."

"I'm planning on it, Mr. Seville," Philpot replied, jovially. "The higher the percentage, the higher the profit."

* * * * *

Sunday dinner at the Pack house was over, and Bud – although thankfully well-fed – was relieved...finally...to be free.

First had come the interminable telling, and re-telling of his experience at the Harrison farm. There was no avoiding it—Piotr Remy had shown up at the church after services, full of praise for Bud's brilliant "rescue" of Harrison's grandson, charging in on an insane horse, then coming up with the "Greek fire" idea that had finally stopped the siege by LeBlanc and his men. In the light of day, it all sounded impossible, and brave, but Bud knew the truth...that it was all just some random confluence of luck, and nerves, and...and he was too tired to sort it all out.

"Look, this is all well and good—but we still have a lot of grain to move." Ever the practical leader, Jeffrey Pack shook his head. "And do we even have a *buyer*?"

"Zeke comes back into town tonight," replied Rufus. "His telegram didn't say anything about the agreement—but I'm sure he wouldn't be coming back without it..."

The conversation had descended then into the details of the grain move, which would begin tomorrow morning, after a day of rest. What teams would go to which farms, and which farms after that, and after that...it was all too confusing to Bud, who asked to be excused, and went upstairs to take a nap.

On his way up, Bud spotted Julia through her open door, sitting on the edge of her bed. She had been suspiciously absent from the dinner, and was eating a plate of food that had somehow been secreted upstairs.

"Sounds like you're quite the hero," Julia said, smiling between bites of mashed potatoes.

Bud blushed, then met her eyes. "No, I wasn't," he stated flatly. "I was late. I was spending time with..."

"Anna Marie?" Julia interjected, meriting a stare from Bud before she grinned and went on. "Do you think Ginny can keep *any* secret, especially when it comes to a *girlfriend*? She was up here with this plate not twenty minutes ago, and told me about your little rendezvous at Mass before the roast beef was even cool enough to *eat*. Now," she continued, patting the bed beside her. "Come tell your cousin, the other reprobate in the house, what's *really* been going on."

It was funny...*maybe the Catholics have it right after all,* Bud thought. That twenty minutes of confession, of sharing what he had heard in LeBlanc's barn, his meeting with Anna's brothers, his revelations about his Uncle Zeke, his upcoming rendezvous with Anna this afternoon...it had all felt so good to get off his chest. Julia had listened, poked at her food, nodded, and finally offered a little advice.

"You can't change the past, Bud...Uncle Zeke says it, and I believe him. But you can do your best today, and every day, and maybe...with a little luck, it all evens out." Patting his hand, Julia looked up, and her brown eyes were bright patches in the room, even though the sun was intense.

"I know one thing...if you can find love—or a way to redemption, it's all of a piece—then you follow it...right through hell, if you have to. Anything less—and you'll be breathing...but you won't be *living*."

* * * * *

His nap had been delicious...nearly two hours of sunny, uninterrupted sleep, with a hint of a breeze coming through the open window. At the end of it, Bud had even managed a bath—Aunt Emelia had produced a few pails of hot water, hauled up from the kitchen. So on his way to Anna's, he felt clean, rested, jubilant…and with every step, the excitement, the *butterflies* of meeting his girl.

Bounding up the stairs to the upper rooms of 715 G Street at a few minutes till three, Bud's excitement peaked as he knocked on the door to Anna's room. The door swung open, and…

…there on the floor, in front of him lay Anna Marie, her body resting at an unnatural angle on the cheap Oriental rug that was tacked to the floorboards of the small parlor. Bud rushed to her, kneeling at her head. Her hair was matted with blood. Panicking, Bud raised his head and looked around the room.

"Nighty night," said the dark figure that loomed over him, swinging an object that he didn't recognize before the lights went out.

50

Sunday, August 12, 1894
4:05 pm

By Zeke's calculations, he had travelled over 600 miles by rail in the last 36 hours, seen the death of a good man, and had only the contents of his saddlebags to show for it. In his mind, it was a damned poor trade.

Having changed trains at Columbus, he was only about an hour north of Lincoln. *Time to stop trying to nap*, he told himself…it was useless anyway, too many things churning in his head…and to take coffee instead.

Shifting in his chair, he thanked George, the Pullman porter, as he took his cup, then leaned back in his leather armchair and felt a strange weight pressing into his hip. A progression of Colt model revolvers had been fairly constant companions in his life from '61 through '91, when he had finally hung up the last of them along with his badge, and it felt strange to have the last of these jammed into his hip joint again. But Mr. Flint—if that was his real name—was sure to be waiting for him in Lincoln, unless Rufus Pack and his boys had somehow nullified him.

Somehow, Zeke thought, sipping the steaming black liquid from his cup*, that doesn't seem very likely.* He could only hope that the man Flint had not caused the kind of mischief that Zeke had narrowly avoided in his partner, Cheevers, now lying in Sidney's Boot Hill—or Bobber, lying in his own Sandhills grave, north of town.

* * * * *

Amos yawned and stretched his legs, banging his knees on the wooden bench seat in front of him. The streetcars operating in Lincoln left a lot to be desired when it came to comfort, and Amos was more than happy to disembark at its northern terminus, just a quarter mile or so from Burlington Beach. Ignoring the sneer that the operator gave him—Amos *was*, after all, the partner of the man that had taken them down several pegs just a few years ago, not to mention a member of the railroaders' baseball team that had kicked the trolleymen's collective asses just 8 days ago—he disembarked and made his own tracks toward the sound of gunfire.

Having seen the precision drill of the University's Pershing Rifles on more than one occasion, the militia's sloppy formations, ill-fitting uniforms and not-so-sharpshooting at their encampments along the shore were, well, less than impressive. And he was clearly not the only one who thought so, as the sergeants' nearly constant screams, the officers' glum head shakes—and at least one smirk—clearly indicated. The smirk just happened to belong to one of the three officers designated to judge the competition between militia companies, and that man—Lt. John J. Pershing—was clearly doing his best to be...constructive... in his comments. For the fourth time he could be seen crossing out and rewriting the notes he was jotting in his Indian tablet.

"Lieutenant," Amos observed, glancing over the Lieutenant's shoulder, "you appear to be searching awfully hard for the right words to describe this fine exercise."

"Diplomacy," Pershing responded, now clearly trying not to crack a grin, "was never my long suit."

"One does have to appreciate a man that knows his limitations, yet still endeavors to overcome them," Amos drawled. Pershing laughed, and after the men casually shook hands, Amos informally asked, "Have you seen Colonel Bills?"

"Mess tent," Pershing said, pointing toward the shore of the small salt lake, then audibly groaning as the men from Scottsbluff tangled their parading company into a flailing knot of green and brown.

"Lord," he sighed, returning to his notes, "Gordias would have been proud of that one."

Tipping his derby, Amos decided to take advantage of the temporary confusion in the ranks, and quickly crossed the parade ground toward Burlington beach, where a large canvas tent was belching smoke through a stovepipe jutting through its roof—or trying to, at any rate. Tossing aside the flap, he noted that considerably more smoke was coming out of the open flap than the stovepipe, and that although it was difficult to actually *see* Colonel Bills in its interior, location was not an issue—he found he could easily navigate by following the bellows of the commanding officer, bawling out the cook.

Amos' eyes adjusted enough to spot the commander of the militia encampment—the same man who he had first met three days ago, under a gas heater in a burning train. It didn't take long for the big, boldly uniformed man to recognize the man that had rescued him that night.

"Amos!" Bills said, stretching out his arm. "So good to see you here...thinking of joining up?"

"No, suh," Amos replied, "Ah still have hopes for the Confederacy, and expect to be called any day now."

Bills laughed. "So, what does bring you here?"

"A favor—perhaps to both of us," Amos said. "Care to go for a walk along the lake and discuss it?"

441

It had taken nearly an hour, but with the help of Deputy Albert Dillon, Flint had managed to secure and carry the large Oriental rug down the stairs of Anna Marie's rooms and into the freight wagon that waited in the alley, liberated earlier in the day from the LeBlanc freight yard. The rug, which had formerly concealed the unfortunate Miss Maggie, now performed admirably for secreting the tied and gagged forms of Anna Marie and her young admirer.

It was all just too rich, Flint thought, shaking his head in amusement as he secured a tarp over the carpet in the back. *Everything runs around in a circle in these incestuous little tinpot prairie towns. The man I need to take down and the girl I want to make an example of are connected, both by a girl that Gardner is supposed to have killed through neglect, and by the girl's little lothario here.*

"So, where do we take them?" Dillon said, breaking Flint's reverie. McGee be damned—scanning the streets nervously, Dillon seemed intensely interested in getting this job over with.

"To the Barrelhouse," Flint said simply, then gestured to the horse that was tied to the back of the wagon—yet another midnight "requisition" from LeBlanc Freight. "But first, I need a place to hide my friend there."

"What do you want to do at the Barrelhouse?" Dillon said, ignoring the last request as he climbed into the wagon and gathered the reins.

"Never mind," Flint replied, observing, "You don't want to know anyway. Just watch the street. If you see Gardner come, signal me and let him in. Anybody else, send them off. When it's over, you drop me at the horse and report finding this stolen rig—understand? Now—where's a good place to put this horse?"

Dillon thought a moment, then whipped the team up. "Brickyard."

When Zeke's train pulled into town, the aging ex-lawman grabbed his saddlebags and swung onto the Burlington station platform before it came to a complete stop, cutting quite a romantic figure—then swore in pain as he grabbed his left knee, and limped to a bench at the side of platform. As he sat on the bench, rubbing his sore knee, his eyes wandered over to Bobber's shack, and a different kind of pain assaulted him. He thought of words he would have liked to have said to Bobber before it was too late. *Well, not just Bobber. My mind keeps making promises my body can't seem to keep. But keep them, I will.* As the aches subsided, Zeke opened his watch—5:25—then closed it. *No sight of Swede,* Zeke frowned.

442

I need to check on Lil, anyway...might as well ride the rest of the day, Zeke said to himself, and limped through the Burlington station to 8th street. Charlie Raymond was not there, though his rig was tethered across the street in front of Mooney's (instinctively, Zeke looked at the upper windows of the hotel next door—shuttered—and thought he understood...Charlie had found his fares for the day). So, sighing, Zeke stumped the six painful blocks to 1127 M, and was rewarded with a whinny as he entered the stables.

"She's glad you're back, Mr. Gardner," Don Burch said, "And so am I—she's a handful when you're away. I swear she knows when you've left town...she's *twice* as bad."

Zeke smiled, and patting her neck, produced a shrunken lump of sugar from his pocket.

"Lil," he said, looking her over. "Good old girl. Saddle her up, will you, Don?"

"Your nephew calls her Lilith," Don said, nonchalantly placing a blanket over the mare's back. He had long ago learned to treat horses with a firm, constant hand—fewer surprises led to fewer kicks and bites. "She doesn't actually seem to *hate* the boy."

"Lilith, eh?" Zeke had long ago forgotten the moniker he had originally given the mare, when she couldn't stand Zeke either. *Shows we were both taught classics at the same knee,* Zeke thought, and for a moment allowed himself to remember the long talks he had held with his father over the Iliad, and the Odyssey, and his fascination with its hero. *The wanderer...how he had wandered, these years...and wondered how the old man, self taught, would feel about his grandson starting at the U?

Well, he thought, *we'll see...*

Throwing his saddlebags over her rump, he mounted Lilith and headed for the Barrelhouse. *Tomorrow will tell,* he thought, *whether we all make good on our promises.*

* * * * *

In the basement of the Barrelhouse, Bud Gardner woke with a headache that could have powered all the trolleys in Lincoln. He reached for his head...and found that his hands could not move. *Why won't my eyes open?* he thought...then discovered, by blinking them, that they *were*. His mouth was dry—filled with cotton, and his breathing was...entirely through his *nose*. The light was very dim...just gaslights, he guessed, turned to near nothing...and with a little time, he made out the curving wooden walls surrounding him on every side.

I'm in the basement...of the Barrelhouse, Bud realized, *and my hands are tied. Feet, too. The last thing I remember...*

The panic rose in him as he recalled the prostrate form of Anna Marie, bleeding on the rug in her rooms. Wiggling in a new state of near panic, his head **thumped** into a barrel. A few seconds later, stars having cleared, Bud took a moment to calm himself. *My jackknife—which pocket is it in? I don't feel a lump...* Then it came back to him with a shock. *I used it to cut strips of cloth from the bed last night...in the soddy. Oh, God. I must have left it in the soddy last night.*

Fighting back a rising tide of panic and the self-rebuke, Bud struggled to think clearly. *If I'm in the Barrelhouse—where am I exactly? There are four gaslights down here...yes, I can see at least two of them, across the room...and...there's a crack of light around the door to the basement. So, judging from where the lights are, I'm...nearest the wall with the bourbon bottles...*

With slow, deliberately planned movements, Bud managed to roll from his side onto his back...then by exertion and an almost full extension of his legs, onto his tailbone. His feet were too close together to balance or attempt to stand, but...drawing them under him and thrusting back out again...he managed to push himself a few inches, bumping the barrels on either side. One of them, the one on his right, rocked considerably, as if empty. Nudging it again with his shoulder, he thought after a few rocking attempts that he could actually knock it out of his way...which he did, on the third try, the barrel clattering over with a hollow **thump**-*thump-thump.*

Bud was rewarded with an overwhelming **smell** of spoiled fish and lye.

Lutefisk, Bud realized...*oh, Lord, had Swede actually **listened** to him when he suggested putting it under a barrel three days ago?* The smell was past painful, tearing up his eyes and causing him to have to concentrate hard on his breathing. Silently, he willed the effects of the smell away until his head cleared, and he could continue scooting toward his goal past the barrel that had been removed. There on the wall behind him was the shelf of brandy bottles, kept here where it was cool. Rocking back on his hands, Bud managed to lift his heels and move them a few inches closer to the shelves, using his butt as a fulcrum. By transferring his weight back and forth between tied hands and feet, Bud finally managed to get his feet against the shelf...and *shove.*

The shower of glass, brandy, and bourbon surrounded him like exploding grapeshot, and would have woken the dead—if there were any around to wake. For a moment, Bud stood very still in order to sense whether someone was coming. Hearing no one, at least for the moment, he picked around the floor with his hands, and finally found what he was looking for—a shard of glass about six inches long, probably from a bottle neck—and, patiently, started to saw at the rope that was tightly bound around his hands.

With every stroke, he sent out a prayer for Anna.

* * * * *

Spotting Al Dillon lounging around R Street naturally raised Zeke's curiosity—he suspected that Dillon probably had better things to do with his spare time than leaning on the Barrelhouse hitching post on his day off. Even more curious was Dillon's reaction when he spotted Zeke, mounted and approaching on Lilith—there was a strange little double take, then a wave, followed by a rapid departure before Zeke was close enough to give him a hard time.

Well, thought Zeke, as he carefully dismounted and snatched up his saddlebags, *every man has his secrets, I guess.* His left knee still hurt like sin, but Zeke managed to baby it as he crossed the sidewalk, reached for his key and tried the lock…which turned out to be open.

So, he reasoned, *Swede must be inside.* If Zeke hadn't known Swede so well, he would have suspected that the man was sleeping it off, since, having heard the lock turn, Swede hadn't met him at the door. But as Swede never drank to excess, Zeke suspected that the big man was busy inside getting the Barrelhouse ready for business tomorrow. If true, Zeke was grateful—his business had suffered since Emmy had converted the Barrelhouse to other purposes. But as things would be settled in court tomorrow, it would be good to have a place to celebrate.

Although the afternoon shadows were lengthening fast, Zeke found the interior door to the upstairs rooms without concerning himself with turning up the gaslights on the wall. Trying not to wince with each step as he stumped up the stairs, he heard the loud, rhythmic sn-o-o-o-res emanating from within the room at the top of the stairs.

"Just as I suspected, Swede," Zeke said, grinning as he thrust open the door, "Sleeping on the j—"

The pistol pressed at the back of his head would have frozen him in his tracks, if the sight in front of him hadn't shocked him already. There, lying face down on his bed, was a girl whose hands and feet were each bound on a short lead to one of the spindly wooden posts at its corners. Her raven hair was matted with dried blood. Revealed under a blouse that had been ripped down her back, her shoulders moved with barely visible regularity under her shallow breaths, impeded as they were by the gag she wore. Her eyes were closed—and for a moment, Zeke closed his, too.

445

"Hello again, Mr. Gardner," Flint chuckled, snatching the saddlebags out of Gardner's right hand and throwing them in the corner. "Nothing like a good, deep snore to put people at their ease, and invite them right on into a bedroom."

Shit, thought Zeke, wearily. *I'm really getting old.*

"Have you met Miss Anna, here?" Flint asked, conversationally, now removing the ex-lawman's gun from its holster and cocking it, then placing it against the small of his back. "I understand you may have known her sister."

"I know her," Zeke said, his mind reluctantly recalling the little girl crying at the bedside of her older sister, Antonia, lying at the Harrisons the day after the blizzard and the birth of her son. In the other room, her two brothers were loudly arguing with the sheriff for Zeke's arrest. Most vividly, he remembered wanting to reach out his hand to the little girl, to comfort her...and then pulling it back. He hadn't the right.

The sight of her, here—a pawn of a wealthier man, hurt and helpless, just like her sister had been—would have turned his stomach, but it was already cold as a stone.

"You *should*," Flint continued. "The story, as I understand it...do correct me if I'm wrong, won't you?...is this: you killed this girl's sister, though neglect, or duty...or both? Perhaps...but a lot of the town didn't see it that way, did they? So, you've been trying, since then, to make it "right" somehow with them..."

"You must be from Chicago," Zeke interrupted. "You sure talk a lot."

"Almost done," Flint said, cheerfully. "Want to make sure the rumor that gets spread is accurate. So—where was I? Oh, yes, *motive*. Unfortunately, you are a lustful man, Gardner. Everybody knows that— that's how you lost the original copy of the grain agreement—to a woman...that's how people are telling it, anyway."

"So, being a *lustful* man," Flint went on, in a reasoning tone, "I think you really did *want* to kill her sister. Yes, that's it...you turned her into the blizzard on purpose, since you had gotten her...*pregnant.*"

Flint's taunting voice now was tinged with audible glee at the web he was spinning. "Tsk, tsk, Gardner. And, here you are, once again, *molesting,*" Flint shoved his revolver into the back of Zeke's head, "—her little *sister.* You really aren't the sort of man that anyone should trust, are you? Oh, almost forgot...take your pants down, please."

Zeke, briefly startled at the suddenness of this final command, began to speak. But Flint interrupted, cocking the gun that was pressing against his

446

lower back, and spoke through his gritted teeth. "Now, how would you like me to include your nephew in this little scene of ours? He's tied up, in the basement—seems he's been sparking this girl, too. Runs in the family, I guess. If you want him to *live*—and not make this a mutual homicide, on both your parts, for the benefit of newspapers, at least—**drop** your ***pants***, Gardner."

In a sickening flash, Zeke realized that—with his willing cooperation or no—implicating Bud was exactly what this man intended. *He plans to kill me, rape and kill the girl, and kill Bud on top of all of it. Then he'll arrange it so it looks as if I was caught in the act and killed by my own nephew in a fit of some sort—who then turned the gun on himself, I suppose.* Maintaining his control and tensing for action, Zeke reached for his belt buckle, planning to drop his gun belt, then his pants...then reach for the knife he kept in his boot. The odds were long, but...

"I only want to know one thing, Gardner." Flint's playful tone was gone...*he's all business, now*, Zeke observed, moving more slowly with the buckle of the gunbelt, waiting for his move. *This last question is why I'm still alive.*

"Just how did you get the drop on Cheevers, out in Sidney?"

"I had some help," Zeke admitted, stopping for the moment, hands on both ends of his now loosened gunbelt. "A friend of mine grabbed his hand when he went for his gun."

"Thought it must be something like that," Flint said. "You can take a bit of satisfaction to the grave, Gardner—if we had both been out there, or here, things would have been different..."

Zeke was never, later, able to tell just what had occurred first—the door bursting open from the outer stairwell that led to the backyard, or his dropping to his knees and whipping the gunbelt around Flint's legs. Both moves were life-saving—as neither led to Zeke getting his head blown off or boring a new orifice into his backside—but then again, neither was effective. The gun that emerged from the open door blazed into the room—but Flint had already disappeared, stumbling into the interior stairwell. The dark figure at the door crossed the room in four leaps, and fired down at the departing figure of Flint—just missing him, and burying three forty-four slugs in the floorboards of the Barrelhouse as Flint streaked around the corner of the doorway.

Zeke looked up, and the resulting shock at the identity of his rescuer went all the way to his boots.

* * * * *

447

Down in the basement, Bud had barely gotten through the ropes that fastened his hands behind his back when three *holes* suddenly appeared in the floorboards over his head, each accompanied by a loud *crack.* Bud ducked instinctively, and noted that three corresponding holes had appeared in one of the barrels next to him. Tilting his head at an odd angle as if puzzling at his luck, he had just managed to shake off the shock of the three near misses and attack the bonds at his feet when the acrid smell of gas froze him, momentarily, in mid knot. Looking up, he thought that the gas smell...*yes—oh, shit.* In the dim light of the gas lamps across the room, Bud could see that one of the rounds had produced a hole in a pipe that ran between the floor joists.

I'm lucky to be alive, thought Bud, accelerating his efforts to free himself. *Lucky, lucky, lucky,* he chanted, mentally, over and over again, until the ropes finally let go. He was up like a shot, and had taken his first full step to the door...when he tripped over a large, blond figure, lying motionless on the floor.

Swede.

Panic rising with the thickness of the gas all about him, Bud wondered how much time he had before the gas lamp across the room ignited the whole of the basement into a ball of flame. Holding his breath, Bud grasped Swede's massive form under the armpits and heaved, then heaved again...inching his way to the basement door.

* * * * *

J.T. Lynch shook his head. "You never did have much luck with women," he said, ungagging the girl as Zeke stumbled to his feet.

"No luck at all," Zeke agreed, rebuckling his belt and looking for his gun. "What the hell are *you* doing here?"

"You're not going to like the answer," Lynch said, feeling the girl's neck, then nodding his head at the pulse. "I was following your nephew. Planning a nice quiet homicide, to tell you the truth...he had been unfortunate enough to overhear a little conversation I had with my employers back on Thursday before the wreck. When he went to visit his girl, I saw them both taken here by that fellow Flint, and followed them here. Figured for whatever reason, he would do my job for me, and I wanted to make sure...then you arrived, and fouled everything up."

Zeke listened in growing astonishment, both at the heartlessness of the killer that had once been his friend, and the unvarnished honesty Lynch shared—because he still was. *I haven't drawn on Lynch in years,* Zeke thought, *but*...

448

Lynch straightened, then nodded his head at Zeke's holstered gun and gazed into his eyes. "I gotta hope that saving your life will keep you from drawing that, Zekiel."

"Later," Zeke said. "Is the girl all right?"

"Yep," Lynch replied, then jerked his head toward the window as the sound of a freight wagon being whipped down R Street floated through it. "You're about to lose this fellow."

"Not likely," Zeke said, moving unsteadily up the outside stairwell. "Help me navigate these stairs....I'm banged up some."

"I noticed—your knees again, I'd guess." Lynch lent Zeke an arm, noting, "Your nephew is tied up in the basement. I could stay here while you..."

"Not likely, times two," Zeke said, hitting the bottom stair and limping toward Lilith. "I want you where I can see you—but if we lose Flint, we won't sleep very well tonight..."

"*You* won't," Lynch corrected. "I plan on being long gone."

"Help me git on my horse, then get yours," Zeke said, irritably.

"I'm afoot—and what makes you so damned sure I'm coming with you?" Lynch queried, making a cradle for Zeke's weak leg, then boosting him up.

"Thirty years of experience," Zeke said, shaking his head, then pointed at Lynch. "You're a bastard, J.T., but you never ran from a fight. Now, git on behind me." *And I hope Lil bites your ass*, he thought.

"Hmmph," was all Lynch said as he climbed on Lilith, narrowly avoiding the mare's teeth. Together, they whipped Lilith down the street after the freight wagon, disappeared now around the corner of 10th street.

* * * * *

Bud had just managed to drag his heavy burden up the barrel ramp leading up from the basement and open the door at the top when a *whoosh* filled the basement, followed a split second later by the heat wave of a dull explosion. Bud hit the ground outside, and a second later was up again, dragging Swede a few yards into clear space. He listened to the crackle of flames start to fill the basement as he undid Swede's bonds, then removed his gag and slapped his face until the big man reached some semblance of consciousness.

"I tink you can stop dat, now," Swede said, groggily, after an extremely potent whack.

449

"Good," agreed Bud. "Now, let's go find some water—the Barrelhouse is on fire."

Swede looked—gulped, and exclaimed, "Dat kitten—she's in dere! – No, wait...*dere* she is..." A little mottled ball of fur trotted toward him, mewing prodigiously as Swede scooped her up to his chin, stroking her with a degree of tenderness unbefitting a Norseman.

"Good...now put her down—we need to find some water..." Bud said. Turning back toward the Barrelhouse, though, he saw that smoke was pouring out of the basement and the first floor. Within seconds, flames reached the exterior walls, and began pressing upwards to the second story. "On second thought, maybe you better go get the fire department, Swede."

"They're right around the corner," Swede said, still holding the kitten as he ran to comply. Bud was just looking for a bucket in the jumble of furniture that had been moved out of the Barrelhouse, when the girl's scream from the upstairs room finally overcame his shock over the explosion and fire, and back into the reason for why he was trying to escape the basement in the first place. In less than the time it took his mind to say "*Anna*," Bud had launched himself up the smoldering stairs, three at a time.

51

Sunday, August 12, 1894
5:15 pm

*W*here the hell had **he** come from? Flint fumed as he whipped the team to a start, steering the freighter east onto R Street from their hiding place behind the Barrelhouse. *And where is that damned deputy...? The idiot was supposed to a **lookout**, for the love of...is everyone in this godforsaken state a complete **incompetent**?*

As Flint urged the lumbering horses into a gallop, he glanced backward, noting that no one seemed to have followed him out of the tavern—as yet. Forcing himself to calm down even as he whipped the horses harder, he reflected on the narrowness of his escape.

If I hadn't had that room's door already propped open...

*Just who **was** the hellion that came though the window?*

When I get my hands on that deputy...

With a scowling heave, he slowed, then turned the massive rig south onto 10th street, giving one last glance back toward the Barrelhouse. *Yes, dammit...they're coming,* he noted, observing two figures approaching a horse that had been tied outside, just before they were blocked from his vision by the intervening buildings as his team turned south.

Cursing that he had not seen their horse outside the Barrelhouse and stolen it himself, he scanned the street ahead of him. As he had expected, it was practically deserted on a Sunday evening in this business quarter of town. With the suddenness of a summer storm, Flint reached a decision...and, in turn, for his .44 Winchester rifle from beneath the springboard seat. Cocking it, he spun on the seat, abandoning the reins and giving the team their heads while he took aim at the approaching horsemen, now a mere half block behind him across the empty Haymarket square, and Flint's single shot at the head of their mount found its mark. Screaming furiously, the flailing horse threw its riders onto the brick pavement, and Flint laughed as he picked up the reins.

* * * * *

I should have expected that, Zeke cursed to himself as blood and hair exploded from the scalp of Lilith. *Another screw up.*

Turning with the falling, wounded horse, Zeke managed to get his foot loose of the left stirrup and catch himself—then realized with a jolt of excruciating pain that this was the leg he had been favoring all evening.

Fortunately, part of his weight landed on Lynch—who didn't look as if he had been done any favors. Lilith for her part, didn't fall over, but scrambled up immediately, careening off the street altogether, turning onto campus and bucking toward University Hall.

"Get after him, dammit..." Zeke muttered to Lynch, the white pain stabbing up from his knee. "I'll be along."

Lynch looked down, as if making up his mind about something—then looked into Zeke's eyes, nodded once, and ran down the street after the rumbling freight wagon, now nearly two blocks away down 10th Street.

* * * * *

Bud Gardner's entire right side felt the heat of the flames radiating thorough the walls as he ran up the exterior stairs to the upstairs bedroom of the Barrelhouse, where the screams of Anna Marie Vostrovsky were pulling him like a magnet. Yanking open the door at the top of the stairs, Bud winced—dense smoke filled the upper half of the room, and the lower half was hazy...but not so hazy that Bud missed the form of the girl struggling on the bed, pulling at the bonds that held her arms at the bedposts.

For the second time today, he cursed himself for leaving his jackknife in the soddy last night. *Sure could have used it **here.***

Crouching, Bud was at a loss for how to announce himself, so when he began working at one of the knots at her feet, Anna instinctively kicked out at his touch—then turned to see that she had walloped her rescuer on the one side of his face that *wasn't* already a massive bruise.

"Bud!" she gasped. "I am so sorry...I..." Anna's explanation collapsed into a coughing jag. Bud's eyes watered, and as he worked on her bonds, he decided not to risk talking and to concentrate on breathing instead. It took Bud some time to free her leg, and when he had finished, he moved to her left arm...reflecting that he should have started with her hands, so she could have helped him. The knots were taut—tighter now after Anna's struggling. The smoke was thickening, and as Bud looked at the door, he saw the first flames creeping to the top of the stairs. Fighting panic, he returned to the knots—so tight that Anna's hands could clearly be seen as having turned blue in the smoke.

Frustrated and half thinking to alleviate some of the smoke—perhaps even get some shards of glass to work at the knots—Bud aimed a kick at the window behind the bed's headboard, but in the haze instead thumped a glancing blow against one of the curly maple spiral posts that held Anna's bonds. Surprisingly, it cracked—and Bud's second kick busted the left one free. Jumping across the bed and Anna's exposed back, Bud started kicking at the post holding Anna's right arm, as flames began licking past the doorposts of the tiny bedroom and running up its interior walls. With her freed left leg, Anna half rolled and started kicking at the post binding her right leg to the footboard. Choking, they both finally managed to break the stubborn posts. Two of the bonds slipped easily off the tops of the broken bedposts, leaving Anna with only her left arm still tied to one of them. They were surrounded now, with the fire completely cutting them off from both exits. Even the window was blocked by the now burning bed.

"Get down, Anna," Bud said, backing both of them into the one corner of the room that was not yet burning, shoving a set of pillows and a set of saddlebags out of the way with his shoes. Striking the wall behind him, Bud heard a hollow sound—and spun to see the outline of a narrow door.

"Into the closet!" Bud shouted over the crackle of the flames, opening the door and half urging, half shoving the girl into the darkness. Closing it behind him, Bud knew that he was simply delaying the obvious—but could think of nothing else. Breathing hard, he felt despair clawing at him. The door was growing hotter, and the smoke was pouring under it—when he felt Anna slug him and heard her cry out, "Vyhlizet do...look up, *hlupek*!"

Wearily, Bud raised his head—and made out the dim outline of a polished steel doorhandle in the closet roof, winking at him through the gloomy haze and orange light of the fire, now licking at his heels under the frail wooden door.

* * * * *

Piloting his trolley east up the hill from the Burlington Station, Richard Lee reflected on how much he liked working Sundays—his runs around the circuit were generally quiet, mostly ferrying well-dressed folks to evening services or picking up the odd passenger, few and far between on the Sabbath. Early in the planning process for the Lincoln Streetcar Company, the city fathers had originally frowned on the proposal for the trolleys to operate on Sundays, but gave in as the city and the accompanying horse traffic grew to a level such that if trolley operators weren't paid, street cleaners would have to be. Times being what they were, trolley traffic had slacked off some, and Lee had heard "the word" that the streetcar service on Sunday would soon be cut to eight cars. So Lee was determined to enjoy the Sunday runs while they lasted, and often found himself chatting with his regulars—which on this occasion was his single passenger, Garnet Lehl. Seated up front next to him, Garnet was a soft-spoken, small-gray haired woman in Sunday finery, consisting mostly of a large handbag and an even larger hat.

Lee had just reached the top of the hill at 10th Street at when a pair of wild-eyed sorrel horses pulling a freight wagon suddenly materialized from seemingly nowhere, veering in from his left. The scowling driver was whipping the team and screaming obscenities as he bore down on Lee. Mrs. Lehl screamed, and so did the trolley brakes as Lee pulled them for all he was worth. For his part, the driver of the freight appeared to be trying a belated right hand turn down P Street, but the heavy wagon rolled, smashing into the side of the electric car, throwing splinters over the brick pavers and dragging the left hand horse onto its knees, then its side.

Lee felt the trolley rock with the shock of the wagon, then land back on its tracks. Stunned, he saw the driver of the freight leap out of the wreckage, a rifle in his hand.

"Move this thing back down the hill—towards the tracks there," the man muttered, jabbing the rifle into Lee's spacious midsection as he boarded the streetcar. The man's eyes were drawn to the southeast, as if thinking ahead—*perhaps laying out an escape route,* Lee realized. Nodding once to Garnet as if to reassure her, Lee moved quietly to the controls at the other end of the streetcar, and had started disengaging the brakes when he heard an odd clicking sound from behind him.

"Anarchist!" screamed Garnet. With burning blue eyes and tight lips framing her lined face, the spinster slowly raised the cocked Colt's dragoon that she had just pulled from her purse. The huge gun loomed and swayed in the trolleyman's direction, wavering back and forth in Garnet's unsteady, but determined hands. Lee's reaction was a shocked disbelief— Flint's was to cross the car and grab the barrel, twisting it away just as it went off with an echoing blast, black powder smoke filling the car.

"Get off my car...Madame," Flint said as he grabbed up the struggling woman by her starched collar and dumped her unceremoniously onto the cobbles. As the streetcar began lumbering back downhill, Lee was far too busy to notice the well-dressed man running toward them with a pistol drawn, or his obvious chagrin at being left behind—this time, by a trolley.

Damn, Lynch said to himself between heaving breaths, holstering his weapon and feeling the stitch growing in his side as he approached the broken wagon and team. One horse was lying on its side, and the other was lame.

That's twice this guy's gotten away from me, Lynch muttered inwardly, turning down the hill after the trolley. *And it's starting to piss me off.*

* * * * *

Lilith wasn't happy, either. The bullet that had grazed off her skull had also torn a fair sized chunk of her left ear off as well, and her usually nasty temper was...well, *unusually* nasty. When she had finally bucked herself out and Zeke had tracked her into an alcove against University Hall, she actually bared her teeth at his approach.

"Easy, girl. I know it hurts," Zeke said, reaching into his pocket and extending a few shriveled lumps of sugar in his open palm...hoping that she'd take them and not his fingers. She glared at him at first...but after a moment, bowed her head into his waiting palm, and, when finished, nuzzled his cheek. Murmuring to her quietly, he had managed to wipe away most of the blood from her scalp when the firebell at Engine House No. 1, just a block away at the corner of 10th and Q, started clanging urgently, causing Lilith to start again.

With Lilith's reins firmly in his hand, Zeke leaned his head out of the alcove, and saw the smoke rising furiously from...*the Barrelhouse.*

Shit, shit, shit. In less than a moment, all thought of chasing after Lynch and Flint fled from his mind, along with his own and Lilith's hurts. Swinging up into the saddle, Zeke's only thoughts were of the young girl he had left tied up and his own nephew, in the basement of the burning building a block and a half away down R Street.

* * * * *

It was a close thing. At first, the ceiling door to the attic was stuck, unhinging and swinging down only when Bud hung his entire weight upon its handle. Then, the bedpost that Anna was dragging behind her got stuck in the rungs of the ladder that unfolded from the door leading to the attic. But in the end, the pair managed to stumble up into the smoky rafters of the Barrelhouse, and across the attic to a wooden-ribbed vent at the end of the building. Through its slats and the smoke that was pouring up the sides of the building from the flames below, Bud could make out the cluttered backyard of the tavern. Squatting down, Bud kicked at the vent, but made little progress until Anna sat down and kicked with him in unison. At that point, the pine boards gave way, and a hole large enough to crawl through gradually appeared.

"You'd better jump," Bud said, looking down urgently. "Or I could lower you..."

"You first," argued Anna, extending her arm, still tied to one of the bedposts. "Here, take hold of this, and..."

"*No*," Bud said, more firmly. "You just grab..."

"Well, for Pete's sake, *somebody* jump," a voice boomed up from two stories below. "Come on girly...I catch you, I tink." Through the smoke,

Bud saw a massive blonde man gesturing to the both of them, his tree-trunk arms held out in invitation.

"Don't have to tell *me* twice," Anna said, and without another word, flung herself into the void, her torn dress fluttering about her like a pair of shredded angel wings. Bud scrambled to the hole in the attic wall just in time to see Swede catch the Czech girl in his arms—along with her flying companion bedpost in his right eye. Swinging her down and wiping the blood from his brow as if swatting an insect, Swede was just gesturing gamely to Bud when the flames suddenly leapt up the side of the building, forming a flaming barrier between him and safety.

Nothing for it now, Bud thought, *but to do it quick.* Backing up, Bud got a running start, covering his face just as he flung himself headlong through the burning hole. Uncovering his eyes, he had only a split second to realize that he had overshot Swede completely.

But not his Uncle Zeke, behind him.

Or Lilith, the horse he was sitting on.

Or the stack of Barrelhouse tables and chairs, piled behind all of them.

The crash was spectacular, but not fatal. Many of the chairs they landed on were left in splinters, however, and the chandelier propped on top of them was probably not salvageable. It also managed to confer on Bud a good kick from Lilith as he and his uncle emerged from the wreckage. However, to the small crowd of townsfolk that had gathered behind the burning tavern, it looked like a rescue, and drew a round of applause.

"Good to see you, Bud," Zeke said, extending a hand to his nephew, and gesturing to Anna, now draped in a large suitcoat that offered by one of the men in the crowd. "Looks like you'll go just about anywhere to find a pretty girl."

"Yeah," Bud said, taking his uncle's hand and rubbing his bruises with the other—which included pretty much every square inch of him by now. "Guess you know where I got *that.*"

Zeke flashed a half smile, and was about to get mounted in an attempt to pick up what he knew would be a cold trail back to Flint and Lynch when a team of four horses brought a red steam engine and a half dozen firemen to the front of the building, to the delight of the crowd gathering there as well. Staring out across the yard at their attempts to hook the hoses to the pump, the smile suddenly dropped from Gardner's lips, and he spurred Lilith over to a man standing alone across the street under an elm tree, who was holding his head, pacing back and forth as he watched the fire.   Dismounting, Zeke limped a few steps toward the man…and connected with a massive right into the deputy's gaping jaw.

"Dillon," Zeke uttered through clenched teeth, looming over the deputy. "You let me know where Flint is, and I'll let you breathe for another hour."

McGee and Flint's general stooge here in Lincoln thought about denying, delaying, and explaining…but he had already gotten walloped twice—once just now, and earlier by the man that had gotten past him and joined Zeke in the Barrelhouse upstairs. Caught red-handed acting as lookout for Flint, Dillon had worked with Gardner for enough years to have seen the look on his former colleague's face before—and know what it meant. His shoulders fell.

"Try the old brickworks, up against the tracks," he mumbled. "He's got a horse stowed away there."

Zeke nodded, and hobbled back to Lilith. "If you're smart," he said, swinging up, "You won't be here when I get back."

If you get back, Dillon thought, watching the ex-deputy tear down R Street. Then the man reflected—it didn't matter who lost this match-up— it was probably best to leave town for a while, and headed for the stable where his horse was kept.

* * * * *

When "Crazy" Charlie Raymond heard the firebell start clanging away right over at the fire house on 10th Street, he leapt from the bed of the pretty whore he had been sparking, put on his boots and shirt, grabbed his pants, and headed for the door. Tumbling downstairs and out of the St. James, he saw his hack tied right where he had left it out front. Smiling, he scanned the skies and put his nose in the air, hopefully, as he struggled to put his pants on over his boots. *Off to the east—maybe the north? Hell, I'll just try the fire house—God knows they'll never put a fire out in this drought—and if it's here in town…hell, we could see a whole **block** go up.*

Cackling and rubbing his hands together, Charlie untied his horse— who had been known to find fires by smell alone, for sugar cubes—hopped into his hack, and whipped his two-wheeled rig around. A streetcar was coming down the hill—Rich Lee looked to be the driver—and Crazy Charlie waved at the man, waiting impatiently for the car to pass before he whipped the hack toward the station. Strangely, the car seemed to be coming the wrong way down P Street. Stranger still, the car didn't make a left turn onto Seventh—instead, the car slowed, stopped, and after a medium-sized man in a bowler and a trim black mustache jumped off, Rich hustled over to the controls at the uphill end of the car and hot-footed it

457

back up P Street to the east, looking for all the world like the canary that had escaped the cat.

As the mustached man approached, he flagged the hackman, and Charlie noticed that he was carrying a rifle—casually, holding it by the barrel with its stock balanced on his shoulder. Charlie was oddly tempted to whip his rig onward...after all there was a *fire* going on. But his hunger for a fare was stronger, and as the man climbed in, he dropped a five-dollar piece onto the seat beside Charlie—enough to catch any hackman's attention.

Smiling, the man asked, "Do you know the old brickyard on 6th and L?"

"Sure," Charlie replied. *Five bucks for a six-block trip?*

"Make it move," the man said, nervously glancing up the street. "And you can keep that."

With a crack of the whip, Charlie urged his horse into a trot, headed south on 7th. Looking to his left, he noticed another well-dressed man a half block up P Street, jogging downhill toward the cab. The man reached under his coat pocket—then stopped, appearing to think better of it. Charlie shrugged and snapped the whip over the horse's ear again. *A short fare, a fire...and five dollars to finish what I started a half hour ago,* Charlie mused. *Lovely.*

* * * * *

Lynch watched Flint get into the cab, and despite his wish to put a slug into the man...and the cabbie...and his **horse**...he leaned over, placed his hands on his knees, and watched Flint once again race away. Other than the cabbie and the trolley now lumbering back up the street where he had just run...there was no other transportation on the street.

Lynch took a deep breath, walked to the bottom of the hill, then turning left onto 7th, observed that the hack was still visible a few blocks ahead. Taking one more deep breath, he started to jog again, doggedly following the hack.

Where's a horse when you need one around here?

It could have been the firebell in the distance...it might have been his heavy breathing, or even his exhaustion, but the sound of the horse approaching from behind was completely hidden from Lynch until the one-eared red roan mare was nearly parallel with him. Turning, Lynch was shocked to see Zeke Gardner reaching down to him...so much so that he was nearly late in grasping his outstretched arm and swinging in behind him.

"He's headed towards the brickyard on 6th and L…just in case he hits *me* this time," Gardner remarked.

"What makes you think I'm interested, now that you're back?" Lynch asked, still out of breath.

"The man took a shot in your direction," Gardner replied. "There is not a chance in **hell** you'll let **that** go."

Good point, thought Lynch, watching the hack turn the corner, two blocks ahead.

52

Sunday, August 12, 1894
5:36 pm

With every turn of his hack's wheels, Charlie was growing more dissatisfied with his current fare. Not only was he getting further away from a damned fine fire, the passenger sitting next to him kept looking backwards, as if someone was following them. It was…*unnerving.*

"Faster, you idiot," growled the man after they turned onto L Street. "Give him the whip again."

"The fire's in the *other* direction, dammit—this one was over with *months* ago," Charlie muttered under his breath, but instead of cracking the whip, he pointed it forward with a measure of relief. "There's your stop up ahead, mister."

On their left a large wooden shed faced onto 6th Street, its peeling white paint and broken windows testifying to its years of neglect. As bad as it was, the clay shed had clearly fared better than its brothers, a one-story moulding house and a two-story drying house, whose burned timbers and partially standing walls still stood as testament of what must have once been a mighty fire. To the west, a row of squarish brick kilns with arched roofs and open, rusting steel doors squatted with their backs parallel to the tracks, and faced the central burned buildings that once made up the nexus of the brickmaking operation. To the north, four more, larger circular kilns also stood like abandoned brick beehives in front of a stout fence, forming a solid "L" to the north and west. As it was summer, Charlie knew that there would be little activity here until the fall, when the Lincoln Brickworks, now out of town, would perform some of its overflow operations here. Until then, it was as abandoned as any weed-filled vacant lot.

This had been a damned fine fire, *too,* thought Charlie Raymond as he reined up to the corner where the decrepit clay shed stood glowering, as if offended at being so neglected. He was about to elaborate on that particular conflagration to his passenger—when, turning, he saw that the man was gone, already running up to the clay shed, leaving no trace but the promised five-dollar gold piece on the seat beside him. Shaking his head, he now did choose to use his whip—and turning his rig around, he was startled to recognize the familiar figure of Zeke Gardner, spurring his horse in the direction that he had just come.

*His own damned **tavern's** on fire,* reflected Charlie, amazed, but now focused on nothing but the smoke off to the northeast. *And they call **me** crazy...*

* * * * *

In Bud's opinion, the crowd that milled around the burning Barrelhouse could be split into at least three factions. There were the merely curious, no doubt drawn by the spectacular sight of the towering bluish flames pouring out of the disintegrating tavern, fueled by the potent barrels of brandy and whisky in the basement. Standing in small groups at a safe distance across the street, this group tended to quietly admire the brilliant display offered to the town on a tranquil Sunday night, as if a free fireworks demonstration of "The Last Days of Pompeii" had shown up a month early for the State Fair.

Then there were what looked to the young man like temperance folk. Their smiles were smug, riding incongruously on what appeared to be normally sour faces, but now glowing with open satisfaction that the wrath of God had finally visited itself on this place of SIN. Their clothes were of a more somber tone, they tended to clap, and one even held a sign condemning "Demon Rum." Within ten minutes of his escape from the burning attic, Bud noticed that two pastors were each attempting gather their own small crowd of the faithful across the street, glowering occasionally at one another when his rival's volume rose above his own.

And then there were the patrons of the Barrelhouse—they were the quietest, one or two even brushing away a tear.

Bud himself was fascinated by the firefighters—four teams of them, orchestrated in a ballet—of sorts—though Bud suspected that the choreographer could have been a lot happier with the results. A few firemen wrestled with the cobweb of lines that ran from the hydrants up on the corner to the pumps—some manual pumps, while others regulated small steam engines—and many others manned the lines that ran the discharge hoses, keeping adjoining buildings wet, while only a few attempted futilely to put out the flames in the Barrelhouse.

"Bud?" The boy turned to find big Swede tapping him on his shoulder, snapping him from his reverie…and flicking his eyes to his left rear, where a familiar, small man was sadly watching the fire aside a huge bearded man, even larger than Swede.

"We are so sorry," Remy said, simply, the little Czech's battered hat wringing in his hands. "It is so sad…"

"You help Anna," Andryev Malý interrupted. His English was extremely limited, but as he was standing next to Anna—still wrapped in a

461

blanket, her eyes beaming at Bud—the young man gathered that there had been some conversation between the two of them. *Anna was a friend of his*, Bud remembered, and it seemed an eternity ago that he had "rescued" the girl from the clutches of the Czech giant…and a half-butchered chicken.

"Yes, I suppose I did," Bud said…a half second before a white-hot jolt of light exploded through his head, his eyes rolled up, and his world devolved to the vision of another large Czech standing over him—his angry eyes blazing as fiercely as the fire consuming the Barrelhouse—and Bud's world blanked completely out.

* * * * *

Lilith, breathing hard, had a temper up. Still carrying two big men, she was running flat out, bleeding from her missing left ear, and the horse they were chasing—a miserable gelding that smelled as bad as its owner—had left a trail of turds for her to run and slip through at the last corner. So when she felt the sting of the whip that the approaching Crazy Charlie had intended for his own gelding (his inaccuracy with the instrument was a legend among Lincolnites), she did as her temper dictated—and, spinning to the left, threw a sideways kick at the oncoming horse. Satisfied at the connection, Lilith re-focused on the man her master was chasing—and not on her passenger, who was losing his balance and sliding off her back due to the twisting blow she had just delivered to the escaping horse and hackman.

Feeling the tug of her reins, Lilith slowed, but the damage was already done—the man that had been bouncing on her rump slid to the ground, and Lilith had the satisfaction of feeling a hoof kick the man on the way down. Her master was dismounting her now, and while he kneeled with her other passenger at the corner—a shot *cracked* over her head. Backing up, Lilith inadvertently stepped on the prone man—before bucking twice and cantering down the street.

Zeke, for his part, grabbed his prone colleague by the collar, and had just managed to drag him behind a concrete municipal horse trough when another shot cracked around his ears, throwing cement dust into the air. From the clay shed, not thirty yards away, a mass of pigeons fluttered wildly from the upper set of windows.

"Can you move?" Zeke queried Lynch, while trying to pick out Flint's position. *That shot definitely came from the direction of the clay shed. Gotta move…try and keep him off balance.*

"Not right now," Lynch grunted, not knowing whether to grab his ankle, which had been stepped on—or the other part that Lilith had kicked as he had slipped off her rump. Both parts hurt like hell, but only one was apparently broken—either way, though, he was stuck here…for the moment. Instead, he grabbed his pistol, aiming it into the air. "But I can make some noise…"

"Fine. Keep an eye on the street frontage here," Zeke said, motioning south along 6th Street. "If he takes off on a horse…"

"You know me, 'Zekiel," Lynch said, grinning as he pulled his second gun, laying it behind the trough, where it was handy. "I love to shoot at cavalry…'specially when it's retreating."

"Cover me, then—start with that lower window on the end, and work your way north," Zeke ordered, waiting for a nod from Lynch, then sprinting (as well as a fifty-plus man with a bum knee *can* sprint) across the open space as soon as Lynch let off his first shot. Fortunately, the building was close, because Zeke didn't think he had the steam to pull this off after a long run. Forgoing an approach to the door, Zeke instead headed for one of the tall windows…smashed through it, and rolled to a prone position behind a mound of dried clay, spraying three fanned pistol shots into the black interior.

Above his head, pigeons fluttered as dim beams of light from the setting sun streamed through the dusty interior. As his eyes adjusted and the smoke cleared, Zeke saw that the shed was abandoned. Fresh tracks in the dirt floor pointed to another door, opposite the fractured window where he had entered, leading to the interior of the brickyard. Wiping his stinging cheek, he felt the trickle of blood—probably from a glass fragment—as he stumped back to the window. From there, he signaled Lynch with a hand gesture that he was alive, and his intention to rush the opposite door. Lynch signaled back, and Zeke braced himself for another run.

As Zeke was blasting away inside the barn, Flint smiled and settled into his firing position. He was satisfied that it was a good one, having scouting the brickyard earlier for exits and defensible positions. Should things go south on him, his horse waited for him in cover behind the building. Quietly levering a cartridge into his rifle, Flint kept one eye on the door, and a second eye on the corner of the shed along the street—either of which could produce Zeke. *He likes to rush the situation,* Flint had observed from Zeke's entrance, and when the door from the shed slammed open, Flint was pleased that his calculations had proven correct as he opened up.

* * * * *

463

I sure have gotten hit a lot this week, Bud woozily reflected. Lightheaded, it occurred to him: *It's a little like Latin...just as repetitive, but less painful.*

As his eyes opened, he was rewarded with the sight of two large men standing over him, shouting in a foreign language.

He thought, *Oh, look...two large men standing over me, shouting in a foreign language. I wonder if they'll hit me.*

It was in this philosophical, almost third-person frame of mind that he watched the two men's heads suddenly smash into one another, then separate, divided by another huge form, even larger than the other two.

"Hlupeks," the large shadow spoke in disgust...and then Bud was too busy sputtering to observe much, as he tried to avoid inhaling the well water that was dumped over his head.

"Bud Gardner," a familiar voice spoke. "Ah believe you ah the luckiest, unlucky person ah have ever met. Please do inform me if you get run over by a streetcar, and ah'll arrange a poker tournament. Y'all can stand next to me."

"Amos," Bud sputtered, his senses only beginning to come around. "The Barrelhouse is on fire."

"Many thanks, Mistah Gardner." Amos knelt, his hand resting on the boy's shoulder. As Bud opened his eyes, he saw a massive grin cross the face of the Virginian as the man's eyes flickered to the massive fire towering over all of them. "Ah shall inform the State Journal."

Bud's response was drowned out by the four men and one girl standing over him, all shouting at one another in Czech. Looking up, he saw that Anna and her brothers were furiously squabbling and pointing at one another, restrained by the giant Maly and little Remy (assisted by Big Swede), who threw in as best they could. Following a particularly shrill response from Anna, Lukas, the younger of the two brothers turned to Bud.

"What were you doing in that...place...with our **sister**?" he shouted in English, pointing to Anna. Bud was speechless for a moment as he viewed Anna for the first time since her rescue. Disheveled, covered in ash, dress torn, hair singed and matted with dried blood, with a rope still hanging from one of her arms, and bleeding from a myriad of small cuts from splinters she had taken while escaping the attic. *No wonder they clobbered me*, Bud thought, now putting the pieces of the last few minutes together.

"He was saving your sister's life," Remy replied, hotly. "Your own eyes and ears tell you this. Listen to Anna—she is honest. Listen to her." The miniscule Czech followed with a short burst of narrative in his native

464

language, intended, Bud supposed, for her bigger and older brother, Stephan.

Lukas interrupted, sounding unconvinced. "So, Mr. hero—why did you take her there to begin with? That is what I want to know."

"I didn't take her there," Bud said, standing now. "We were both taken there by another man...from Anna's rooms..." As soon as he uttered the words, Bud knew he had blundered—but he stood up straight and tried not to flinch from the volcano that he saw was about to explode from the man in front of him.

"What were you doing in her rooms?" Lukas shouted, and his lunge toward Bud was barely checked by the massive Maly.

"I went to meet Anna there—it was wrong," Bud said, quietly. "But I didn't mean for this to happen. I'm glad she wasn't hurt..."

This time, it was Anna that interrupted, and her voice was steely. "The man took me by force—and tied me upstairs. He was trying to make people think Ezekiel Gardner was...hurting me. I heard all of this, tied upstairs, but was too frightened to move. Gardner went after him, with another man. When the building was set on fire—after they left—Bud came to rescue me."

In the short pause while Remy translated, Anna moved closer to Bud, examining by firelight what was until a few moments ago the unbruised side of Bud's face, now swelling quickly from her brother's blows. When she heard that Remy had finished talking, she turned to her brothers and laid her hand on Bud's shoulder.

"This is a good man. He is my friend. So is his uncle. What happened to Antonia was not their fault. Now," she said, simply, eyeing the crowd that was just beginning to trickle into the backyard. "We go home."

With a final squeeze, she released Bud's shoulder and walked resolutely through the adjoining backyard, away from the gathering crowd, her brothers, the Czechs, and the Barrelhouse boys...including Bud. She did not look back...but Bud was suspicious that it was because she did not want the men to see her cry. Almost immediately, her brothers relaxed, and Maly and Big Swede released them. With a final angry glance at Bud, the men stomped after their sister.

Bud watched them go—then found a mostly unbroken chair and sat down to watch the fire. Amos gave him about thirty seconds of privacy before he found a chair next to him.

"Where did Zeke go, Bud?" Amos asked. "And who was with him?"

465

Before Bud could answer, both of the men suddenly stood up and skittered behind the protective cover of the stack of furniture and alcohol that was sprawled in the middle of the Barrelhouse's backyard, just before the horse and hack—streaking in from the adjoining side yard, tearing up what little turf was left—skidded into the chairs where the two of them were just sitting. Piling out of the hack, its driver stood agape at the towering blue-and-yellow flames. The smell of alcohol, the feel of the flames—Charlie Raymond was in heaven. Quietly, Amos and Bud walked over to where Charlie stood, picked up their chairs, and sat on them, silently watching for a few moments until Amos decided the question just couldn't wait.

"Ah repeat, Bud," Amos said, insistently. "Where's Zeke?"

"I don't know," Bud said, shaking his head. "Anna just said he ran off with another man after the people that put us here. I don't know who was with him, or who he's chasing."

"He damned near killed my horse over at the old brickworks, that's where he is," Crazy Charlie said in a near monotone, apparently mesmerized by the flames. Bud and Amos exchanged a surprised look.

"You *saw* him, Charlie?" Amos asked, incredulously.

"Just *said* that, didn't I?" Charlie snapped, his reverie of the boiling flames temporarily broken. "Carried one fellah from the train station to the old brickworks not ten minutes ago, and Zeke and his friend—riding on that damned fire-eatin' mare of his—showed up about a half minute after I dropped him. Don't know why they were in such a damned hurry to see an old fire, when there's such a *fine* one right *here*....uh, no offense Amos...condolences, uh course," he added quickly.

"None taken," Amos said, then reached into his pocket and pulled out a five-dollar gold piece, flipping it once into the air and catching it before Charlie's eyes as he nodded his head over to the horse and hack next to them.

"Charlie," Amos asked, "Would you mind terribly if ah take her for a little spin, while you watch this fine fire?"

* * * * *

Flint was fast—he had already fired two shots at the shadow behind the slammed open door of the clay shed before he caught the trace of movement at its corner nearest the street. As it was, he barely had drawn his head back in time to dodge the bullets that slammed into the singed siding that surrounded him. Reflexively, he rolled along the catwalk that supported him, then deftly rose just enough to draw down on the second, prone figure that had fired from the corner of the shed. With his second

466

shot, he was satisfied to see the figure roll away with what looked like a solid impact, then turned back in time to spy the other figure racing out of the door, firing at him on the run as he ducked behind a brick kiln.

* * * * *

That *hurt*, Lynch said. The world reeled once or twice while he fought to clear his head. Reaching behind him, he felt the blood oozing into his hand and down the back of his trousers, and automatically, he backed into the plank wall of the clay shed to apply direct pressure to the wound. It seemed to be mostly superficial, but the passing bullet had grazed the outer surface of his backbone, and the intense pain threatened to buckle his knees. Along with the pain in his ankle, it was all that Lynch could do to cock his second piece, keep his eye on the street from which Flint might escape...

...and hope he was still conscious when Flint made the attempt.

The bullet zinged above Zeke's head as he ducked behind the brick kiln. Even given the distraction that Lynch had offered him (at his own urging through the signals at the shed's broken window moments earlier), Zeke was impressed at the nearness of the thing. *Flint was damned good*, he thought again, pausing to reload his pistol. *He was able to silence Lynch's covering fire and still almost take my head off.* From behind the kiln, Zeke moved slowly to its other side. *Can I reach the next kiln? Or attempt to go back into the shed? Was Lynch still active, unhit by those rounds fired by Flint? Could he offer another distraction?* Zeke thought about calling out to Lynch—then thought, *if the call isn't answered—I'm the only target Flint's got left to worry about...and he'll* ***know*** *it.* A knot settled into Zeke's stomach, and in a moment, he started to climb the steeply slanted back side of the kiln.

When I get to ***hell*** *for trying to pull this* ...Zeke grabbed suddenly at a loose brick as he ascended to the open hole in the top of the kiln. ... *the Devil is going to have one helluva laugh at my expense*...

* * * * *

The faint *clang* that echoed from the interior of the kiln could only have one source, and Flint was nearly ecstatic to hear it. Something had bumped up against its steel door ...from the inside.

Flint glanced to the corner of the clay shed—still no motion—then slowly turned, and made his descent down the stairs of the drying shed, his eyes flicking, waiting for the least motion. Once he had reached the level of the brick yard, he gave one fleeting look to the corner and back door of the clay shed—*still* no sign of motion—then tiptoed to the nearest kiln.

467

Edging to its side and then behind it, he saw what he expected—there was no Zeke Gardner lurking behind it, or any of the kilns—leaving his adversary just where he wanted him—inside the kiln. Pausing just a moment, Flint moved to the kiln door behind which Gardner lay waiting...and froze.

The sound of a pistol cocking at the base of his neck was like the crack of doom.

* * * * *

Unlike the man who was under his sights, Ezekiel was not given to explain his actions for the sake of gratification—so Flint was unlikely to find out how he had crept through the loose boards in the fence behind the kiln, around the west side of the lot, until he had come up behind Flint. Only a lawman of fifteen years experience in this town would know where the Lincoln kids were to be found stealing bricks from the interior of the brickworks, and use their same escape method himself. And loose bricks, tossed into open holes in the roofs of kilns made a very satisfying *clang* when they met with the interior of a steel door.

"Drop the gun," Gardner said forcefully, nudging Flint at the base of the neck with the barrel of his Colt. The man's low, strong voice clearly meant business—and Flint hesitated only slightly before he dropped it straight to his feet.

"Now, kick it away," Gardner said, and as Flint started to move his feet, Gardner felt the blow to his right knee, and his right hand spun out of alignment with Flint's skull before his Colt went off.. In the haze of pain that followed, he found that he was crumpled, disarmed, and grasping his knee in the dust of the brickyard—with Flint's form towering over him—before he knew how it had happened. Flint's smile over the sights of his cocked pistol was the last thing that Gardner saw...

...before it dissolved in a haze of blood.

* * * * *

"You certainly took your time about it," Zeke said, turning up the controls that fed the gas into one of the long, horizontal kilns at the west end of the Brickworks. The gas made a very satisfying *hiss* as it fed the fires within. There wouldn't be much left inside within a very few minutes that could be identified. Which was just the way Zeke wanted it—not only would it raise some well-deserved uncertainty on the part of his adversaries regarding the location of their hired man, it would avoid any potentially embarrassing questions from his former colleagues in law enforcement regarding the goings-on at the Barrelhouse and here at the Brickworks this evening. He knew the Vostrovsky family...well. They were not given to offering free information to someone outside their community. The fire at the Barrelhouse was undoubtedly due to a gas leak—*which was true*, Zeke mused—and the shooting here at the Brickyard? Target practice…with the evidence burned at the end of the session in the interest of…cleanliness. *Also true.*

"I was right on time, saving your ass, as usual," Lynch said, though weakly. He was sitting on a pile of bricks, keeping direct pressure onto his backbone—but his grip was slipping, as were his eyelids.

"I suppose we gotta get you to Doc Flippin's, then," Zeke said, and was just reaching down to assist Lynch, when he heard the light click of a .32 caliber pistol cocking behind them both.

"Don't bother," Amos said. "He's only got one place to go from here…and that's *hell*."

The voice had come up unawares to either of the men—but then again dragging a body, setting it into a kiln, and starting up the fires could be noisy work. It meant business, and both Zeke and Lynch froze at the sound of it…though it extended to the soul of only one of them.

"Well," Lynch said, wearily. "If it isn't the prodigal son."

"More like the prodigal *father*," Amos observed, his gun held steady at Lynch's back. "*You're* the one who left and came back *unexpectedly*. Which reminds me…which of you actually *is* my father?"

Zeke and Lynch exchanged looks, and then Zeke replied, "There is no way to tell for sure—but your mother always thought it was Lynch, here. She hated him for that, and herself, too. I always thought it was the best work you ever did, Lynch. Tell you what—I'll fight you for him."

"I've taken my swing," Lynch replied. "He's not buying."

Amos didn't flinch. "His men wrecked that train, Ezekiel. He's guilty of at least eleven murders…we need to turn him in."

"And what happens to Davis when you do?" Lynch shot back, his voice even, though weak. "He's going to be as dead as I am. And what proof do you have? Hell, I was with Bud—he can give me an alibi…"

"You killed your own men," Amos said. "Ah was *there*."

"Prove it," rasped Lynch.

A pause ensued as Lynch and Seville eyed one another…and when it broke, it was Ezekiel who spoke.

"He saved my life, Amos." Zeke said, simply. "And I hate to admit it…but he's right about Davis. Whatever you decide to do…you should do it *now*, not in the company of the sheriff."

It was a long moment, but the soft click of a small pistol being uncocked accompanied an even softer voice as Amos spoke.

"If you're here in the morning, Lynch—ah'll assume you'd like me to *pull* this trigger."

Zeke replied, "I'll escort you to the station, Lynch—by way of Doc Flippin's. I think you can make the Burlington Special—hope you don't have a problem with the general direction of 'East.'"

* * * * *

By the time that Zeke returned from the station, he found Amos, Bud, Swede, Crazy Charlie, and a small group of townspeople still standing around, watching the embers of the Barrelhouse slowly sink into its basement.

"Anybody bring marshmallows?" he said, cheerfully.

The crowd looked at him blankly, as if in shock.

"Come on, folks," Zeke said, chiding them. "It's only a *bar*."

Snickers grew around the fire pit, eventually replaced by low, normal tones of observation and astonishment at the destruction. As they murmured among themselves, Bud drew closer to his Uncle.

"When you were out West, Uncle Zeke," he asked, earnestly. "Did you get a copy of the grain agreement?"

Zeke paused before he spoke, vacantly staring into the fires with the rest of the crowd.

Pointing at the smoldering ruins, he said, "I left my saddlebags in *there*, Bud."

470

53

Monday, August 13, 1894
7:28 am

"Rise and shine, Mistah Gardner." The voice nudging through his dreams was definitely NOT that of Anna Marie—and so Bud decided to ignore it and attempt to chase down Anna one more time. In the light of the burning Barrelhouse, Bud could just make her out at the limit of his vision, walking off with her brothers into the dark prairie. As fast as he ran after her, she and her brothers retreated, grower dimmer and dimmer…

"GET UP, BUD!" This time, the volume attached to the Southern drawl would probably have been sufficient to wake the young man—if the pillow slamming into him from across the room had not already accomplished that. Groggily, Bud sat up and rubbed his eyes. At once, the pain of yesterday's bruising at the hands of Anna's brothers came flooding back to him. Lifting the pillow, he threw it back at the grinning face of Amos Aloysius Seville, leaning against the doorpost, already dressed, dapper, and prepared for the day.

"Coffee?" Bud grunted. Last night as he had entered them, Bud had noticed that Amos' rooms, though small, did come complete with a small kitchen—and knowing Amos' love of the beverage, Bud was hopeful. Amos' rooms were a marvel in other ways—steam heat, for example, and even a few electric lights. But the most amazing feature was the central reason why Bud had been asked by Amos (and directed by Zeke) to this place instead of being sent back to the Pack residence—namely, the availability of hot, running water, on demand. A central, gas-fired boiler kept hot water constantly available to all 30 residents of the building, and though it was generally difficult to come by on wash day, that was generally not a problem after midnight, when Bud had shown up and been able to take an immediate, hot bath. By the time he had gotten out of the tub, fresh bedclothes were waiting for him—plus the clothing waiting for him now—a gift delivered to Amos' doorstep from some member of the Pack family.

Amos laughed and shook his head, replying, "It's in the kitchen, Mister Gardner—ah'm afraid the butler is off duty this morning, so you'll have to get it yourself."

*You'd think from that **smile** of his that there hadn't been a fire yesterday at all,* Bud mused, blinking and trying to focus on the small alarm clock beside his bed, which read half past seven. *And that he didn't have a care in the world.*

"Your Uncle Zeke…now, there's a *real* addict to the blessed bean. Like to take your head off before he gets his first cup," Amos remarked. "It must run in your family. I'd say that you are very like your uncle Zeke, in a number of ways…"

"You mean, it isn't limited to our surly manner before we are caffeinated?" Bud queried.

"Your grandfather must have thought so…" Amos said offhandedly, examining his fingernails.

"You said that once before," Bud replied, recalling his first excursion into bootlegging with Amos, only a week ago today. "But I still don't understand—he treated us completely differently. He forced me to go to high school, and Zeke was practically thrown out…"

"I'd say your gramps appears to have a good eye for people that can take a challenge—and he tends to throw them at people he thinks can take it. Your uncle and your dad couldn't stand each other—who do you think was the more likely to succeed on their own? I'm guessing that you and your brother Jerry are in the same boat—who was the more likely to handle the difficulties of high school?" Amos let the observation hang, then added, "The toughest roads often make the toughest horses—and the toughest men…"

"If they don't kill them in the process…" Bud observed.

"What's life without risk?" Amos asked, then added, "And if you're late, you'll be facing some. Coffee's in the pot on the stove in the kitchen—there are some eggs there on the counter if you want some—just make sure you clean up afterwards. I've got an errand to run. The court convenes at nine o'clock. If I were you, I'd be there early—it might not go the way we'd like, but in any case, it should be quite a show."

Bud recalled something about that coming up yesterday at Sunday dinner—but a lot had happened since then. "Where are you off to?" Bud asked, following Amos into the kitchen and pouring himself a cup as he watched Seville grab his hat, and head for the door.

"Got a telegram early this morning—I'm to expect a long distance telephone call, of all things, and I'm headed over to the telephone exchange to receive it."

"Oh…well, say "hi" to Julia for me," Bud said, with a wink…then ducked again as Amos took a swing at his head with his bowler. "Where's the call from?"

"Chicago, I believe," Amos replied, straightening his hat and headed for the door. "There are a number of possibilities…Oh, wait a minute.

472

Almost forgot," he said, stopping short of the exterior hallway. Reaching into his pocket, he produced a white envelope, and handed it to Bud.

"Your aunt left this with your clothes last night," Amos said, dropping it on the table, touching his hat…and headed down the stairs outside his rooms at a run.

Bud looked at the envelope, lifting the flap—it wasn't sealed. Had Amos looked at its contents? Bud wondered, then shook his head and smiled…of course he had.

Unfolding the paper, Bud scanned Emelia's note. *Well, this explains part of Amos' conversation this morning.*

Whistling, Bud pulled a skillet down from its hook above the stove, and placed it on the gas stove, sipped a bit more coffee, then checked the heat. Satisfied, he cracked a few eggs and dropped them in the pan, thinking about his aunt's note. She had obviously been excited to get the telephone call from his mother yesterday, relating the "surprise" she had gotten within Bud's note. More of a shocker than a surprise, he thought. Especially for Zeke. Well, nice to know you can count on family in a crunch, I guess. Whichever way this court case goes, this fragmented family looks like it's on the mend.

* * * * *

God, I hate the telegraph. Once again, Cable unlocked the door to his library, and walked to the window to open the shades to the morning light. *It's so damn **tedious**.*

For most of Sunday afternoon, Ransom Reed Cable, Sr. had been sitting in a darkened, private corner of the nearest Western Union office, working closely with a single-key operator who had absolutely nothing to do with the C.R.I.&P. On the other end of the line was a young man in Rokeby, Nebraska, sitting in a very small room that jointly served both as the local Western Union office and the Rock Island depot—next to a man well known to both, Mr. Nathan Brockhurst.

Back and forth, the oblique questions and answers flew, each side avoiding giving over too much direct information, because neither of them could be sure who was listening all along the line between Chicago and Rokeby. A telephone would have speeded the process…but in bits and pieces, the picture of what had happened, and who was behind it, finally took shape. Through Sunday evening and on into the early hours of Monday morning, he had acted on that information, and now, back in his study just as the outside sounds of the Monday morning Chicago rush to work had begun sifting through the windows of his Erie Street mansion, he waited for the signal for his plan to be executed.

473

Anderson, his ancient butler, knocked gently on the door, and when beckoned to enter, nodded once, significantly, in Cable's direction. Cable nodded in return, and as Anderson closed the heavy oak door, sat in his large leather chair. Lighting a cigar, he sighed, then lifted the telephone earpiece on the endtable next to him. When the extension in the other room picked up, Cable said into the mouthpiece, "Peter? Please bring your pad in here—I need you to take some dictation."

Peter LaRue had a concerned look on his face when he entered the room—the boss had been out for hours now, and it was not like him to be so secretive. And that bemused look on his face...?

"Shoot, Mr. Cable," Peter said, expecting a serious memo to one of the Division chiefs, or perhaps the Board, shaping them up. *Good information*, he thought...*his client would approve.*

"This one goes to the Station Master, Hinckley, Minnesota...find the name from the Chief of Operations, can't you, Pete?"

"Certainly, Mr. Cable," LaRue replied. *What the hell was this...?*

"Dear Sir. I understand that with the extreme conditions of drought in your area has come a continuing circumstance of dangerous fires breaking out in the forest regions surrounding the station. As you know, our railroad controls most of these timber holdings, and it is of utmost importance that these regions, and our track operations, be spared the loss that the spread of these fires would cause. As such, I have directed that a special squad of fifty firefighters be placed under your direct command. The bearer of this message, Mr. Peter LaRue, will be one of these brave volunteers. Be sure to utilize them to good measure, protecting the holdings of our company to the maximum extent possible. Sincerely, etc., etc."

A chill flashing up his spine like the opening of an icehouse door caused Peter LaRue to drop his pencil and stop taking dictation at the mention of his own name, then stared up at his boss. Cable was staring back into his eyes with a loathing that would have caused even an innocent man to cringe.

"What's the trouble, LaRue?" Cable asked, gesturing with his cigar. "Forget your shorthand?"

"I—I don't understand, sir..." LaRue began.

"Of course you do, LaRue," Cable interrupted. "You were one of the few who knew my son's date of departure, months in advance. You were the only man who knew I kept the Pinkertons on the case, even after I told the infamous "Mr. B" that they would be called off. The men who held my son knew that, as early as two hours after I stated it. How would you explain that, Peter?"

Peter opened his mouth, then closed it, got up from his chair...and walked rapidly to the door of the study. As he pulled it open, he was immediately confused—the doorway was still completely blocked...

The huge Negro standing before him was dressed in a blue uniform, with three gold stripes on each of his sleeves. LaRue couldn't have gotten through the door with less than a steamshovel...and unfortunately, he didn't have one.

"LaRue," Cable said, without turning toward the door, "Meet Sergeant Truett, your new boss—formerly of the U.S. Army Corps of Engineers. The sergeant is a specialist of sorts—many sorts, actually. But in your case, he will drill you in firefighting techniques, and deploy with you and your new comrades—his comrades, that is—in Hinckley."

"But..." LaRue began.

"Now, don't thank me...yet...for sparing your life, LaRue," Cable interrupted, standing and walking toward his former personal secretary. "The sergeant and his comrades have orders to obtain certain information from you, prior to your initiation into their squad. They are expected to be very close to you...for some time..."

"H-how long...?" LaRue stuttered.

"I was thinking...for the rest of your *life*, LaRue," Cable said, his face a mask of anger, now only a few inches away from its target. His voice rose, and with every few accented words his fingers pounded into LaRue's chest, sprinkling a cloud of ashes over the man's starched linen shirt.

"*Your* information triggered the *deaths* of eleven *people*—*most* of which *died* by *fire*. Your traitorous *mouth* caused the *kidnapping*, and attempted *murder* of my *son*, you sonofabitch. You are going to *talk*, then *train*, then fight *fires* under supervision of men whose race you condemned to take the *blame* for it all—until you *die*, LaRue. Sergeant," Cable said, coldly. "Take him *out.*"

"Sir." the sergeant replied, in a voice that froze LaRue's soul, as he grabbed the secretary by the back of the collar.

"You can't be *serious*!" LaRue screamed as the burly sergeant dragged him down the hallway. "No!...I'll talk...I'll tell everything I know!"

"Yes, you will," Cable muttered to himself, taking his chair once again and picking up the telephone receiver. "You bet your life on it, you will."

Though it had been some time since he had attempted it without Peter's help, Cable remembered that dialing "O" brought Margaret, his personal operator on the telephone.

"Margaret?" Cable asked. "I need to make a call to Lincoln, Nebraska. Yes. A person-to-person call, Margaret to…" Here, Cable unfolded the last telegram sent to him from Nathan Brockhurst.

"Amos Aloysius Seville."

* * * * *

By the time that Bud had cleaned up his breakfast mess and arrived at the Courthouse, it was quarter past eight—and he was glad that he had arrived early. As it turned out, the County Coroner, F. D. Crim, had taken over the larger courtroom number 1 to conduct the inquest over last Thursday's train wreck, and reporters were already standing shoulder-to-shoulder in the hallway. From what Bud could gather, George W. Davis was expected, along with his two lawyers, at any moment. The bickering between the two rivals had proved highly entertaining, the arrest of Davis over the weekend was sensational, and when Bud found himself outside the door to tiny courtroom number 2, he found it almost entirely full…of farmers. Not a single reporter seemed the least bit interested in this obscure civil case…

And that would suit McGee just fine, Bud realized. Around the embers of the Barrelhouse last night, Bud had learned pieces of what had occurred without his knowledge over the last few days. None of the weekend's activities—the attack on Harrison, the recruiting and arrest of the vagrants in McGee's cause, Zeke's fight with Flint…even the fire at the Barrelhouse—had appeared in either the Journal or the Evening News. Willa had been right when she had observed that the story was like dynamite on a burning fuse—no one at the *Journal* was going to come anywhere near it until after it exploded—and apparently it had not gone off with enough force to counter McGee's interests as yet.

It was eerie…and Bud was convinced that it was not a good omen. If McGee could hide all those activities, how much power did he have with the *courts?* Bud wasn't sure whether Judge Lansing was elected or appointed…probably appointed, as a District Judge, which was supposed to make him less susceptible to external pressure. But Lansing also had to *live* in this community—and McGee seemed to be able to cast a very long shadow…without anything touching him. LeBlanc and his men were rumored to have left town. Flint was missing, too. But there always seemed to be another thug on the way to help a guy like McGee…

Finding a spot in the far corner, Bud eyed the crowd. With just three rows of "pew" seating, there was only room enough for about twenty spectators, and it appeared to Bud that nearly every seat was taken. Robert Harrison and Eloise Moseman were on the other side of the room, nodding when they spied Bud. Zeke was seated up front, behind the farmer's lawyer, Mr. Charles Dawes, and when he turned and saw Bud, he gestured for the boy to join him. Bud hesitated for a moment, then moved forward to the end of the bench next to Zeke. On the other end of the long bench, seated behind a man eating a pickle—obviously Heck Kohlman, the opposing lawyer—was a well-dressed man in a gray beard and an older woman, dressed in black, behind a veil. When the bearded man turned toward Bud, his pale blue eyes sent a chill through the young man.

"Who--?" Bud started, but was interrupted by Zeke.

"The older man is Miles McGee—yes, *that* Miles McGee. Don't stare. The lady in black sitting next to him is the wife of the late Mr. Clive Masterson. The reason she is dabbing her eyes with that handkerchief is that she is very concerned that she'll be forced to buy a lot of grain at a fair price, due to her husband's idiocy regarding young, powerless women."

Bud, having heard the story, felt his ears burn. "I sure hope it works out that way."

Zeke shook his head. "I'm sorry, Bud…but there isn't a chance in hell. Her money is safe as in the bank. And *that* is *ALL MY FAULT.*"

Bud stared at his uncle and sucked air, shocked at his words. He was about to ask what he meant…when the entire court room turned toward the clerk.

"All rise," intoned Scott Low, the clerk of the District court. "And pay heed to his Honor, Judge Ignatius Lansing. Let all who have business before this court come forth, and they shall be heard."

The scowl on Judge Lansing's face as he entered the courtroom was difficult for Bud to read—it could have belonged to a man who had been forced into listening to a wealthy man try and get away with murder, or to enforce a contract to deliver horseshit to starving children.

Or both.

"Be seated." Scott Low intoned as Lansing took his. "Case 94-918, Northern Lancaster County Farmer's Cooperative versus the estate of Clive Masterson. The plaintiff is represented by…"

"Let's cut to the quick on this," Lansing said, wearily, looking over at Dawes, the plaintiff's attorney. "Charlie, can your client produce a document, signed by the late Mr. Masterson, mandating the sale of the grain from your organization to him or his estate?"

"No, your Honor," Dawes replied. "We cannot."

477

Kohlman grinned, exposing a trace of dill pickle where he was sucking it behind his gum, and turned it toward McGee behind him, who nodded in acknowledgement, as if confident in the outcome all along. He patted the shoulder of Clive Masterson's widow, who may have been crying or laughing, but either way, the uncontrolled staccato made Bud's already turning stomach even sicker.

The farmers in the room let out an audible groan. There would be no crop this year, and last year's now was in the hands of Mrs. Masterson—as were their farms themselves.

Lansing shook his head, and gripped his gavel. "Well, Charlie, I have no choice but to…"

"Just a moment, your Honor," Dawes said, rising. "May it please the court, might I refresh the Court's memory on its written ruling last Friday?" While Lansing nodded, Dawes reached onto the nearly barren table before him and picked up the first of three pieces of paper that were placed there in a perfect, parallel row. Kohlman stood to object, but Lansing raised a finger, and forced him to listen without interruption.

"To whit: The Cooperative shall produce a signed agreement for the sale of grain by those individuals with outstanding debt, enabling payment of all outstanding bills to the estate of Mr. Clive Masterson." Dawes handed the paper to Scott Low, who nodded to the judge as he passed along the copy. "Is this an accurate representation of the Court's order?"

Lansing nodded—he had not only trusted his clerk to know the facts of the case, he had trusted Scottie to draft the actual wording of the Court Order, for his signature. As he passed it to Kohlman, a nasty grimace passed the man's features, as if the ice cream he had been expected had just passed through the south end of a northbound mule, and he was the one left holding a spoon.

"Then, your Honor, I hereby produce a signed document from the Hammond Packing House, Incorporated, agreeing to the sale of the entirety of the corn production from the Cooperative, at the published price as of last Thursday from the Chicago Board of Trade, some fifty-three cents a bushel!"

A stunned silence, then a roar went up from the courtroom that rivaled the blast from the cannon Bud had heard only days ago. The farmers around them stood, shouting, dancing, pounding one another's overalls. Bud joined them, turning from face to face, and in his joy saw Harrison and Eloise embrace, and then kiss one another. Facing his uncle, he saw a man who was smiling, too, but silent, inclining his head and passing a slow wink to his nephew.

Meanwhile, a furious-looking McGee looked as though he were going to make Kohlman take a bite of that mule-processed ice cream sundae.

"Order!" Lansing shouted, pounding his gavel, but Bud suspected that it was half-hearted, having seen the scowl replaced by a look that could only have been relief.

Eventually, the thunderous sound abated, and Dawes went on. "Apparently, your Honor, the Hammond Company suffered the loss of several barns, full of corn, to fire during the last week's unrest in Omaha. They require immediate shipment, and agree to pay all outstanding bills by members of the Cooperative to the Masterson account by close of business today. Following weighing and testing of the grain in Omaha, the balance of the payment shall be made to Mr. Ezekiel Gardner, executor of the grain agreement, for distribution to the members of the Cooperative. A binding contract, your Honor." Passing the document forward to the clerk, Scott Low looked it over, smiled at Dawes, and shaking his head, whispered to Lansing, pointing at something in the agreement.

"Mr. Dawes," Lansing said, apparently trying to stifle a grin himself. "This is highly irregular. The date on this agreement in last Thursday, the ninth of August—the day before our last court date. Are you telling me that you had this agreement in hand on that date, and led this Court to believe that there was a grain agreement with the Masterson estate at the same time?"

"Your Honor," Dawes elaborated, "We did not have this agreement in our physical possession with all signatures on the ninth or tenth, and believed in good faith that the Masterson agreement could be produced. However, the fire last night destroyed our last copy of that agreement. Note that the countersignature, accepting the agreement from Hammond Packing, is dated on Sunday, the twelfth—last night—when we learned that no copy of the original agreement could be produced."

As Lansing read over the agreement, Bud turned a questioning look to his Uncle, whose voice and eyes dropped. "There was never any copy of the agreement, Bud," Zeke admitted. "I just needed to get Flint and his partner out of town for a few days, and chasing that agreement seemed to me to be the best way to do it. But Flint was too smart for me…or I overstretched myself, one. Seems I do that a fair bit these days…either I'm slowing down, or my luck doesn't stretch as far as it used to, maybe."

Zeke's eyes rose, and leveled with his nephew's. "It almost cost you your life, Bud. I'm very sorry for that."

Bud registered the apology, but ignored it for the time being—he was too full of questions. "You…you had the Hammond agreement all along? When did *that* happen?"

"On Thursday afternoon, just before the wreck. I read about the loss of the grain warehouses in the papers, same as you, and got hold of Frank Crawford. He represents the interests of Omaha stockyards here in town, remember? Well, he was able to put me through directly to Hammond. They were on the ropes, Bud, and would have to pay the full Chicago price to any provider. Our offer was the first on the table, and with Crawford's help—they took it."

Bud nodded, remembering Frank Crawford's brag about being involved with the stockyards when they had met George Flippin at the wreck site, last Friday. But he was still troubled.

"Then why did you countersign the Hammond agreement just *yesterday*?" he asked.

"If the Judge looks carefully at that agreement, he'll see the countersignature line was added in a different ink than the original agreement.—last night—Dawes' idea. It's just as valid, and the story gets Dawes off the hook with the Judge…" Zeke's whispered explanation was broken several times by pats on his back from farmers behind him.

"This agreement appears to be in order, Mr. Dawes." Lansing put it down on the desk and picked up his gavel. "The Court finds for the Plaintiff, the Northern Lanc…oh, hell, the Co-op wins. Case dismissed."

Another cheer from the courtroom went up, and Bud couldn't help feeling that the newspapermen in the other courtroom had completely missed the biggest story of the day. He looked over to gloat at McGee— but the man had apparently disappeared, leaving his lawyer to handle the defeat on his own.

* * * * *

Outside the courtyard, the joy was palatable, but brief—the farmers had grain to move, *dammit*, and it was time to get to work. After the handshakes had exhausted themselves, Zeke sent Harrison and Eloise to get the grain moving toward Lincoln, and was left alone. Quietly, he descended the back stairs of the courthouse where his horse was tied, and was about to exit the large doors when two very, very large men came out from behind a hidden enclave at the bottom of the stairs, and held Zeke's arms. His surprise was total, or nearly so—it became complete when a gray-bearded man stepped through the doors from where he had been waiting outside, smoking a cigar. McGee's blue eyes blazed into Zeke's own with a malice that Zeke knew would not ever be quenched…except in one way.

"Mr. Gardner," McGee stated simply, inhaling, then exhaling a cloud of bluish smoke into his rival's face. "You are a burr in my butt."

480

"Many thanks, Mr. McGee," Zeke replied. "for recognizing my greatest talent."

"That agreement…it doesn't *mean* anything, you know," McGee went on, waving at the two goons that held the ex-deputy. "I can hire hundreds of these sorts of men. They'll wreak havoc with your shipments to the railhead. And who will ship the grain, I wonder? No one in this town, I assure you." Smiling, he concluded. "You have merely delayed the inevitable, Gardner."

"I'm sorry to tell you this, McGee, but you'd better get a little more axle grease for that sore ass of yours." Zeke replied, as a smile crossed his features. "If you had bothered to stick around for the end of that court scene up there, you would have learned that our friend Mr. Dawes petitioned the Judge to allow the militia to guard the grain traveling to the railhead over the next week, as an exercise. It seems, that since they are in town, they need something to do besides let the Pershing Rifles show them up in drill, and their Colonel, Charles J. Bills, requested that the judge give his consent for them to act as special deputies of the court—just in case they are trifled with."

As much as he enjoyed McGee's look of shock of the last bit of news, Zeke enjoyed the next part even more, as he added, "And who will ship the grain? Why, the C.R.I.&P.—that's who—at the order of Mr. Ransom Reed Cable, president of the railroad, himself."

Despite the size of the men restraining him and the growing anger in McGee's face, Zeke's satisfaction was complete when he saw McGee's lawyer descend the stairs behind him and stand glowering next to him. "Just ask ol' Heck here—he's a pickle-eatin' sumbitch, but he knows enough to stick around for the end of a court case, you sneaky bastard."

McGee looked as if he were about to explode, but Heck's nod had a strange effect on him. He deflated, somehow, like a rubber balloon—then found a slight smile again. Shaking his head at his men, he nodded once at Gardner as they dropped their grip.

"Round one to you, Mr. Gardner," and walked silently out the doors with his men.

* * * * *

By evening, the first loads of grain had already reached the railhead, and the line of Pack freight wagons hauling them stretched from the C.R.I.&P. station at 20th and O all the way north to Z Street. Zeke sat with Amos and Bud at the station, and took a moment to speak with each farmer loading sacks that his produce would be weighed at scales in Omaha in the presence of Swede Jorgenson, a trusted agent of the Cooperative. They also

481

managed to hand each soldier accompanying the wagons a small gratuity before they were let off duty by their commander—a liquid refreshment from the last bottles that had been saved from the Barrelhouse.

Bud didn't think it could get any better than this—but he had two more surprises coming. And for a moment, he thought that the first was going to lead to more bruises—though he was unsure where anyone could possibly put them.

From behind them all, two large, surly men emerged and tapped Zeke on the shoulder. They were familiar to him from several years ago, when they had accused him of murder, and they looked little less serious now. As usual, it was Lukas who spoke.

"Gardner," he said, simply. "We hear your Cooperative is taking orders for more grain delivery—is that true?"

"Yes...yes, indeed!" Zeke said after a moment of hesitation, temporarily transfixed by this turn of events. "But—it's so unlikely—after all, there is a drought..."

"We have a good crop this year," Lukas interrupted. "Ask your nephew—he has seen it."

Bud was eventually shocked into speech himself by the stares from Anna's brothers.

"Y-yes, I have," he admitted. "A very fine crop—hundreds of acres, by the look of it."

"But, how...?" Zeke queried, but Bud interrupted before Zeke could answer.

"Irrigation...miles and miles of it." Bud stated, recalling the moonlit rows he had marveled at on the night of the wreck—just before he had...almost...kissed Anna Marie. "They are very good farmers, Zeke—and given the drought, this could carry the Co-op into next year."

Zeke nodded, and slowly raised his hand, extending it to the men who at one time might have killed him rather than take it. When Stephan, as the oldest, did—it was as if a great weight had lifted from the ex-deputy's shoulders. For his part, Bud stood gaping at his uncle, grinning like an idiot—until he heard the rumble of a voice—and saw a hand was extending to him as well. Startled, he saw that it belonged to Lukas, whose own eyes were wary, but held a hint of respect. As he took it, he saw the grinning forms of Remy and the Czech giant, Maly, standing in the background, Remy's arms clasped and lifted over his head like a champion.

As the men departed, Bud's second surprise descended upon him like a thunderbolt.

"Bud," Zeke queried, out of the blue, "Have you ever given any thought to attending the University?"

Bud was speechless (which was just how Zeke wanted it), so his uncle went on: "The Barrelhouse will be out of commission for awhile. Hell, the Cooperative will be enough to keep me busy for some time, anyway—and your aunt and I would like to keep you out of trouble, as well. The entrance exams are in a few weeks—feel up to it?"

Bud gulped—it was twice as much as he could hope for, and ten times what he had expected—*but that was Zeke all over, wasn't it?*

"Yes, sir," he said, trying and failing to keep the tears from welling up from within him. Glancing over his uncle's shoulder, he knew that it really wasn't the last surprise of the evening, and was all the happier for it. "I really appreciate it…and know just who can help me study."

"Oh?" Zeke said absently, shaking hands with yet another farmer, "Who's that?"

"Me, son," Gramps said, and when Zeke turned to face his father, the embrace that followed made every man on the platform reach for his overalls, and the handkerchiefs secluded there.

Epilogue

NEW YORK TI

September 2, 1894   All the News That's Fit to Print

RACE FOR LIFE WITH FLAMES

How Engineer Root Brought the Limited to a Place of Safety.

ST. PAUL, Minn., Sept. 2—The town of Hinckley, Minn., seventy-five miles from St. Paul, on the St. Paul and Duluth Road, with a population of from 1,000 to 1,200, was wiped out of existence last night by a raging forest fire which swept down upon the doomed village. The loss of life is variously estimated at from 100 to 400, and it is almost certain that the loss will equal 200. It will be several days before the full extent of the disaster can be known. The death list increases every hour.

One of the most thrilling events was the experience of the train which left Duluth at 2 P. M. Saturday for St. Paul. It was the limited passenger, the best train on the road, and was crowded with passengers. The smoke from the forest fires was so dense that lamps were lighted in the cars. The woods on either side were lashed by fiery, hot breath of the pursuing flames, for a stop would have been fatal to all on board. It was a four or five mile run back to Skunk Lake, which is little more than a mud hole, the mud and water covering not more than an acre. The train had gone but a short distance before it was surrounded by the devouring flames, hot blasts of flame struck the coaches, setting them on fore in places and breaking the windows on both sides. The baggage car was soon a mass of flames, which streamed back over the tender and engine, setting fire to the engineer's clothes and scorching his face and hands. On either side of the engine there was a stream of flame, but never for an instant did Engineer Root Flinch. To remain was apparently certain death for him, but could he hold out for four miles the passengers might possibly escape. To have deserted his post would have been death for all on board. Back of him stood his trusty fireman, who occasionally poured water on him.

A mile or two from the lake the coaches were burning above and beneath. On board, the passengers became panic-stricken, and it was

486

"Ransom, that paper is a week old," Iphegenia Cable observed, her own face buried in her beloved *Chicago Tribune*. She sipped her coffee, and buttering another scone, smiled as she sniped, "And from the wrong *city*."

"Apologies for offending your table, beloved. A friend sent it to me from New York."

As Cable poured sugar over his grapefruit and cut into it, a hint of a smile tugged at the side of his mouth as he re-read the block lettering scrawled across the top of the newspaper page:

THE SQUAD MADE IT OUT. YOUR MAN LARUE DIDN'T.

CONDOLENCES, TRUETT

"Some article that a *real* paper didn't pick up?" his wife teased. Since her son had returned to Chicago a week ago, her old humor had returned with a vengeance. "Hard to believe…"

"Yes—an obituary," Cable observed, then scowled. "Iffie, if you have *one* more scone, Rance, Jr. and I will have to carry you all the way to Service."

Iffie stuck out her tongue, but retracted it suddenly, covering it with her napkin when their ancient butler poked his wizened head in the doorway.

"Sir…Madame…the young Mr. Cable wishes to be announced. He is accompanied…"

"Send him in, Anderson," Cable interrupted, snapping his paper closed. Through the ornate walnut door a tall, energetic young man walked in, unrecognizable from the shadow that had rolled into Chicago just a few weeks ago. Walking over to his mother, he kissed her gently on the cheek, then crossed the room to his father and shook his hand.

"Well, son," his father beamed, "You are looking the picture of health. Must be this fine Chicago *air*," he joked. The "fine Chicago air" was so humid it would have been easier to drink than to breathe. But although his son smiled at the sarcasm, the elder Cable knew that there was more than his humor behind it, and grimaced as he thought about the shoe that was about to drop.

487

"Mother," Cable said, with a nervous excitement, "With Father's permission, I have invited a good friend of mine along with us to Services this morning. May I make an introduction?"

"Let me guess—is it the mysterious Mr. Evans I've heard so much about, since you came back from Lincoln?" Mrs. Cable asked. "I thought he was off on assignment—or have they given him the church beat at the *Tribune*? How horrid—"

"No, Mother, you're right—Wendell is very busy with his new job—thanks to Father. He sends his best from San Francisco—he's covering earthquakes out there, I understand."

A long trip, mused Cable, Sr., bracing. *He could have stayed here in town—there's one due in about 30 seconds.*

"Mother," Rance Jr. announced, "May I introduce my friend, Miss Eugenia Livingston."

From behind the ornate door a buxom, auburn-haired girl in a fine new dress and a very tall, feathered hat stepped in, curtsied slightly, and smiled winningly at the younger Cable, who beamed back in adoration. Mrs. Cable nodded back at the girl, but her pasted smile could not hide the steely glare behind it—and the first quivers of what was shaping up to be a tremulous day.

All in all, Cable thought, *it might be better to be in New York…*then thought better of it. *No,* he reflected. *I'd guess not.*

* * * * *

As Mr. George J. Gould stepped out of the Western Union Building onto the sidewalk lining Broadway, he glanced up at its massive clock tower, opened his own eighteen-jewel Waltham watch, and scowled. The huge, ornate clock face hanging twelve stories above him was undoubtedly beautiful, but was not only late—again—it had stopped completely. Again.

Damn, the magnate fumed, *does nothing **operate** around here?* He had arrived a half hour ago for a surreptitious Sunday morning meeting with one of his "operating" executives, Jeremiah Beakins—a man who had infamously served with his father, Jay Gould for many years—but was now curiously absent. The meeting had been scheduled over a week ago, as Gould needed yet another "little task" performed by one of Beakins' "specialists." And not only had he failed to show up, no one had seen the man since Thursday.

*The man is a notorious **bounder,*** Gould seethed. *He's probably sleeping it off somewhere.* For the hundredth time in the 21 months since his father's death, the eldest son of the man slandered by the *New York Times* as the "quintessential robber baron" saw the organization that his father built shifting about him. So many wolves nipping at his heels, and those of the Missouri Pacific, the Texas Pacific, the Western Pacific...and even the Western Union. So many operations that his father had started seemed to be falling apart—and even the efforts of operatives like Beakins didn't seem to be able to shore them up...

Well, the man sighed, *at least there's Guinevere.* Smiling inwardly, he thought of the afternoon he had planned with his mistress and her beautiful little girl, his daughter Jane. Born out of wedlock, it didn't matter a damn to George—her smile lit him up...*like a business deal used to light up Father,* George mused. *Maybe that's the difference between us...*

Snapping his watch closed and shaking his head, Gould came back to reality and looked around for his carriage. It did not appear to be waiting for him at the front of the building, here on Broadway. He craned his neck—was it parked around the corner, on Dey Avenue? *Wait—there it is.* Approaching down Broadway, an unmistakable black lacquer carriage with gold fittings and red satin curtains pulled up to the curb. A Negro footman stepped off the rear and pulled open the door. Gould hurried toward it, removing his hat and absently handing it to the footman as he passed, then took his accustomed seat as the door slammed behind him and the carriage pulled away. Inside with the drapes pulled, Gould allowed his mind to drift again to his mistress, Guinevere Jeanne Sinclair, now only a twenty-minute ride away. He was just nodding off when the carriage came to a sudden lurching stop, the door swung outwards...and a huge shadow of a man entered.

"Stay still or I'll burn you down," a deep voice uttered, and as the door banged shut, Gould caught sight of a pistol before his vision was lost again to the darkness of the coach's interior. Panic rising in his throat, Gould had started to sputter an objection when he felt the pistol barrel poking his belly and forced himself to be silent. The carriage was starting to move again when his vision finally returned, and he stared across to see a large Negro—his footman?—smiling in the dim red interior.

"Take it easy, Mr. Gould," the black man said, cocking his revolver for emphasis. "I just have a little message to deliver," he added, flicking open a folded piece of paper with his left hand. "And then I will take leave of your delightful company." In a steady baritone voice, the man read the note now before him in the half darkness, and the bile in Gould's throat rose with every fact laid before him.

489

Mr. Gould,

I am pleased to inform you that your employee, Mr. Jeremiah Beakins—the organizer of the recent Rock Island wreck in Lincoln and kidnapping of my son, with your consent—is dead. So is Mr. LaRue, your informant in my organization. The man standing before you performed both acts (at this, a slight nod of the head from the Negro), and is perfectly capable of repeating them, so read carefully:

Your father was one of the toughest, conniving bastards that I or anyone else had the displeasure of knowing, but at least he understood the Cardinal rule. Families are off limits. You broke it. So, should you or anyone else in your rotten clan ever try to touch one of mine again, I'll see to it that your own beloved ones will make the payment—starting with Guinevere and Jane Sinclair.

I've talked it over with Morgan and the rest of the fraternity, and we agree, Gould. You will repay all expenses for the wreck, provide settlements for the families of the dead, and for the legal defense of that poor bastard your men cornered into pulling this job.

And you will keep that pimply face of yours out of my sight, preferably forever.

Cable

When Gould finally looked up, the black man rapped on the roof of the carriage, tipped his hat, and jumped out before it came to a complete stop. For the next few minutes, Gould sat stunned, shaking uncontrollably within its dark, blood-red walls. *Morgan—J.P. Morgan, and the rest of the* **fraternity.** *A fraternity that to which he did not belong—and now, never would.* All that planning, and scheming, and positioning to succeed where his father had failed—to take over the U.P., the only railroad his father had ever failed in, working in ways that he thought his father would have approved—had led directly to his downfall.

Gould rubbed his eyes, and sighed. He had almost worked up the courage to look outside when his carriage door cracked open, revealing the freckled nose and brown eyes of Jane Sinclair. Recognizing her father, she opened the door fully, and scurried into his shaking arms.

* * * * *

490

As the pie was passed, Rufus Pack, at long last, asked the question of the day.

"So, how do you think you did on the entrance exams, Bud?"

Bud Gardner rolled his eyes and tried to ignore the question, focusing instead on the slice of cherry pie in front of him—it was a fine piece of pie—but the growing murmurs and encouraging jests around the table caused him to blush, then break into a grin, and finally, to hold up his hands in surrender.

"I think I did...okay," he said, and when no peace followed, added, "It wasn't easy, you know. The Latin was the worst part—I was rusty, and Miss Stansky would have cut her throat at how I conjugated...."

"Bud! Please!" Johnny Pack interjected. "Leave out this talk of conjugation ...it's a *family* dinner!"

Although Johnny's brothers hooted him down for his rude sense of humor, he was certainly correct regarding the dinner, Bud reflected. And it had gotten considerably larger in the month since Bud had first joined it, now encompassing not only Zeke as a regular attendee, but Scotty Hill (seated next to Jill), Gramps—having visited now for nearly four weeks— and Amos Seville, seated next to Julia, among others. Strangely, even though it was now well understood by everyone in the family that Amos was the son of an entirely—well, almost entirely—disreputable character, the stigma of his potential parentage by Zeke had been dispelled, and he was now seated regularly next to Julia. On this day, Ginny had twice spied them holding hands under the table—though she was leaning toward not tattling about it...yet, anyway.

"You know, I think that you must not have done *too* badly," Willa Cather murmured, coyly. Another "special" guest at the expanded Pack table, Willa spoke with some authority—as returning senior at the University and in town early, Willa had acted as a proctor at the entrance examinations. She was on good terms with Professor Wilson, who was grading the exams.

"I mean," Willa added, nonchalantly, "Professor Wilson didn't exactly run screaming down the hallway, as he does following most of exams he is forced to grade." She stood, solemnly, then raised her glass of lemonade. Bud sat in wide-eyed, paralyzed suspense.

"I give you Bud Gardner, newest student at the University of Nebraska!" The applause had started, and Bud was just beginning to break into a grin, when his grandfather stood and raised his hands for silence. Though his face was naturally gruff, Bud saw a telltale smirk growing in the corner of his mouth, and braced himself.

He could say anything when he's like this, he mused. *And usually does.*

"Ladies and gentlemen," Gramps said, his own glass raised (not lemonade, as he was seated next to Zeke). "As my grandson is the first Gardner ever to go to college, I would be pleased if we could toast him by his given name."

Bud's eyes bugged, and rose to object, but was slammed back down into place by Johnny, seated next to him.

"Hear, hear!" Johnny cried.

"About time, too," Rufus agreed, adding, "Everyone, fill your glasses!"

Milk, lemonade, wine, and a few drinks even stronger sloshed around the table as Bud cringed. With a silent pleading, he cast his eyes toward his grandfather...but it was too late, now—the glasses were filled.

"I should explain," Gramps rumbled in delight, "that I am particularly proud of my grandson, and of his name—which I suggested, based both on the classical hero I always expected he would be, as well as on his mother's maiden name. And so, a toast—to Achilles Rose Gardner, newest student at Nebraska U!"

A roar of approval accompanied Bud's complete embarrassment, especially after Johnny threw in, "Achilles...A. Rose Gardner? Gramps...that's *terrible!*"

In the midst of the tumult that followed, however, a small hand slipped into Bud's, and a set of perfect lips whispered into his ear, whose touch of a Czech accent and tender warmth made the thunderous teasing worth bearing.

"Congratulations, my hero," Anna Marie murmured, and the gentle squeeze of her hand turned the cacophony of jests into a tumult of triumph.

A Note from the Author

This was an amazing period in Nebraska history, as noted in "The Real People and Places of Barrelhouse Boys" appearing at the end of this book. The week of August 5, 1894 really did include a train wreck in Lincoln and riots in Omaha's Hammond packing plant, put down by the state militia, which was training in Lincoln. The newspaper articles included within these pages are as accurate and complete as space (and my limited ability to transcribe) will allow. The book's conversations involving such historical personages as "Blackjack" Pershing, Willa Cather, and "Hell 'n Maria" Dawes are mostly supposition—but are based on historical references (as far as they go). I would have loved to have met any one of them.

Barrelhouse Boys is my first novel, and could not have come into being without a great deal of patient assistance from family, friends, librarians, and historians. I am especially indebted to:

- The staff of the Nebraska State Historical Society, particularly Mary-Jo Miller, Matt Piersol, Pat Churray and Linda Hein.

- The history department of the University of Nebraska, especially Professor Timothy R. Mahoney for his first-rate website on gaslight era Lincoln (gildedage.unl.edu).

- The staff of the UNL Library, especially Peterson Brink, for their generous access to their fascinating collection of photos, yearbooks, and other memorabilia from 1894.

- The Chantilly and Centreville branches of the Fairfax County Public Library, who obtained Lincoln newspapers of the time from the Library of Congress.

- Russell Lang for his excellent works on the history of Alder Grove and the neighboring "big city" of Craig.

- Steve Evans and Tad Styker, for their editing skill and unflagging support.

- My family and colleagues for listening to me rant about this for four years.

Most importantly, I wish to thank Miria Finckenor, her husband Jeff, and their children Erich and Ruth for lending me Miria's time, tenacity, skill and enthusiam over the years that it took to assemble this "monster." Without her, I'm sure this book would never have come to pass. Thanks, Miria!

The Real People and Places of "Barrelhouse Boys"

Prologue

Alder Grove was established in 1869, a time when a railroad's mere contemplation of a rail line through the wilderness yielded them land grants, allowing them to sell land and establish communities even in places where the railroad never quite made it. Alder Grove was built on that sort of speculation, and at one time boasted a hotel, blacksmith, store, post office, and school teaching through 8th grade, even though the railroad never arrived. Alder Grove Methodist Church (at left), erected in 1880, still stands and is attended every Sunday by the faithful. John McMillen rests in its small cemetery there.

Chapter 2

Tom Turpin was one of the first composers of ragtime music and is credited with the first published ragtime music by an African-American. It's a fair conjecture that he worked his way across Nebraska in 1894 as he floated around the prairies following his failed gold mining venture with his brother, a few years earlier in Nevada. He did finally make it to St. Louis, to open his own saloon and continue writing ragtime music.

Chapter 3

University Hall was constructed shortly after the University of Nebraska's founding in 1869, an impressive but structurally unsound behemoth built of wood and sun-dried bricks in what its builders termed the "Franco-Italian Style." This beacon of learning also dazzled young pioneer children, who would mount huge ash heaps in the back of University Hall to view skeletons in the state's first museum.

Chapter 4

Willa Cather was 20 years old in August 1894, preparing for her senior year at the University of Nebraska, where she helped with the student newspaper, and which she had edited the prior year. She is shown at left in her beloved kepi at her desk at the State Journal, for whom she covered the local Lincoln theater scene. After moving to New York, she wrote about life in Nebraska in such books as "O, Pioneers", and "My Antonia," and won a Pulitzer Prize in 1923. Photo courtesy courtesy Philip L. and Helen Cather Southwick Collection, Archives & Special Collections, University of Nebraska-Lincoln Libraries.

Chapter 5

Frank Crawford was coach of the University of Nebraska football team for the 1893 and 1894 seasons. In 1894, he led Nebraska to its first ever conference championship. Though he coached George Flippin for two years and used him to great effect on the gridiron, his personal bias was such that he overturned the team's decision to make George Flippin their captain.

Fred Miller was sheriff of Lancaster County from 1893 to 1895, and deputy sheriff for many years thereafter.

William T. Donovan was key to the selection of little Lancaster as Nebraska's state capitol, Lincoln, which happened pretty much as Zeke described it.

Chapter 6

The University Library where Franks and Billy Tidmore laid their plans to bushwhack Ezekiel Gardner was still in the construction phase in 1894, having stood for years, half built due to lack of funds and Chancellor Canfield's anxiety to assure that the hasty construction that had doomed University Hall was not repeated. Now Architectural Hall, it is the oldest remaining building at the University of Nebraska.

Chapter 9

The Rock Island Depot still stands on the corner of 20th and O, now operating as a bank. Erected in 1892-1893, this beautiful sandstone and brick structure was added to the National Register of Historic places in 1971.

Chapter 9

The Rock Island train crew described here are all real people – conductor C.D. Stannard, fireman Bill Craig, engineer Ike DePuis, and brakeman Harry Foote. With eleven dead, the wreck of the Rock Island train, shown at left and on the back cover of the book, is still recorded as the largest mass murder in Nebraska state history, only rivaled by a 2007 Nebraska mall shooting, which left nine dead. The four hundred foot bridge over the Union Pacific tracks, though half burned, was repaired in little more than a day. Photo courtesy NSHS.

Chapter 12

The Fremont and Elkhorn Valley railroad still operates excursion trains from Fremont to Hooper on the old FE&MV line. Mel's Bar in Scribner is the scene of Bud's first experience in dealing with Nebraska whiskey makers, among whom the author is proud to include his respected grandfather, Otto Pribnow, Sr.

The conflict between the North Lincoln Electric Railway and railroaders of Lincoln happened pretty much as Bobber described it on August 25, 1890.

Chapter 14

Long before he became known as "Black Jack" for his command of heroic African American troops at San Juan Hill, Lieutenant John J. Pershing was instructor of military tactics at the University of Nebraska in Lincoln from 1891 to 1895. He also taught at West Point and led the American Expeditionary Forces in WWI. The first U.S. general to be named General of the Armies (George Washington was given the honor posthumously after World War II), he was considered a mentor to Dwight Eisenhower, Omar Bradley, George Marshall, and George Patton. The Pershing Rifles, America's premier undergraduate military fraternal organization, had its start under Pershing's tutelage at NU.

Chapter 15

William Jennings Bryan, also known as "The Great Orator," represented Nebraska in Congress from 1890 to 1894, with failed bids for Senator in 1894 and President in 1896, 1900 and 1908. Besides being the epitome of garrulous politician, he is probably best known as the prosecutor in the Scopes Monkey Trial. For twenty years, his speeches and writings were at the forefront of political thinking for the Democratic Party.

Chapter 16

James Canfield was chancellor of the University of Nebraska-Lincoln from 1891 to 1895. He and his daughter, Dorothy, were great football fans, championing the rough, new sport despite the opposition of the University's Board of Regents. Credited with a large increase in the student population, he also obtained funds for the new Library, which still stood unfinished in August 1894.

Frank and Lewis Ryan were actual residents of Lincoln, whose unsure recollection of the Negro they had met at the bridge the night before the wreck led to many hours of conflicting testimony at the trials of George Washington Davis.

Chapter 17

George Washington Davis was born in 1855 in Washington, D.C. and appears to have drifted West in the 1880's. In February 1889, he was convicted of robbery, and was released from the Nebraska state penitentiary in June 1892. Arrested in August 1894 for the Rock Island train wreck, his first trial in March 1895 resulted in a "hung" jury, unable to unanimously conclude that he was responsible for the train wreck. Though Davis was silent at his trial, several fellow prisoners testified that the normally talkative Davis had told them there were other wreckers involved, but that he would never mention their names for fear of his life.

Tried again in November 1895, the jury's unprecedented verdict of second (instead of first) degree murder indicated their continuing discomfort with his sole guilt. Commuting his sentence in May 1905, then Governor John Mickey commented on Davis' release form that "diligent and close consideration has led to the conviction that all ends of justice have fully been served, and to grave doubts as to the guilt of said convict." Davis was paroled to Joseph McNamara, a farmer in Beemer, Nebraska, and from there slipped from the pages of history into obscurity. Photo courtesy of Nebraska State Historical Society.

Chapter 18

Charles G. Dawes practiced law in Lincoln from 1887 to 1894, and was known to be a good friend of John Pershing. He was later vice president under Calvin Coolidge, winning the Nobel Peace Prize in 1925 for his plan to stabilize the German economy while still paying their WWI reparation debt.

Samuel Nickerson, James Ackers, and Oscar Woodard were all sergeants of the 1st Minnesota who perished on the second day of the Battle of Gettysburg, just as J.T. Lynch described it.

Chapter 22

Ransom Reed Cable was the president of the Chicago, Rock Island, and Pacific Railway Company from 1883 to 1898. The Cable mansion still stands at 25 East Erie St. in Chicago, now headquarters for a financial firm.

Chapter 23

Crazy Charlie Raymond was a real hackman in Lincoln. Col. Charles J. Bills of Fairbury was the Regimental Commander of the Nebraska militia. Fred Scott of Horton, KS was the baggage master and Charles H. Cherry of Kearney was the postal clerk on the ill fated train (their injuries and rescues were as accurate as the author could make them). George and William Saxton and Walter and Lew Seidell, all of Lincoln, were local farmers that were instrumental in helping rescue those trapped in the wreck (photo above, courtesy NSHS). All of the above testified at Davis' two trials.

Chapter 24

The Lincoln Station (left), built by the Chicago Burlington and Quincy Railroad, still serves Amtrak passengers around the clock. The UP and BNSF each share the yard facilities here.

Fire Chief Robert Malone and Detective Frank Malone did live and work in Lincoln in 1894. Were they brothers? It is not known (but it makes for a better story).

Chapter 26

George Flippin was a famous halfback at the University of Nebraska, the first African-American football player at the school and one of the first at a major University in the United States. In 1892, the University of Missouri forfeited a game to Nebraska rather than play against a black man. He went on to become a physician and help his father found a hospital in western Nebraska.

Chapter 29

Ignatius Lansing was elected as a Lancaster County judge in November 1891. Scott Low was clerk of court in 1894. P.H. Cooper was Chief of Police in Lincoln at the time. The Lancaster County Courthouse (left) was torn down in 1968.

Chapter 31

Charles Flippin, George Flippin's father, was a freed slave who fought on the Union side in the Civil War. He earned his medical degree from the Bennett Medical School in Chicago. He set up a clinic in Henderson, NE and a hospital in Stromsburg.

Chapter 36

"Buffalo" Bill Cody did brag about being at the Battle of Warbonnet Creek in 1876, less than a month after Custer's Last Stand. In truth, he killed and scalped a young warrior named Yellow Hair, sometimes mistranslated as Yellow Hand, and claimed it was the first scalp in revenge for Custer. Cody liked to re-enact the duel in his Wild West show, and the dime novels soon embellished the tale even further. Cody's home and "Scout's Rest Ranch" can be seen in North Platte, Nebraska.

The Bucher Saloon (later Glur's Tavern) still stands in Columbus, Nebraska. It was built about 1876 by Joseph and William Bucher, brothers whose family emigrated to Columbus in 1868 from Switzerland. The tavern is the oldest establishment of its type in continuous use in Nebraska.

Chapter 42

The Jefferson County courthouse was built in 1891. Designed by the famous Topeka, Kansas architect J. C. Holland in the Second Empire Style, it is the crown jewel of the county. In The former home of the Western Division of the C.R.I.&P. is now a railroad museum. The "elevator" in which Amos fought was actually a flour mill in 1894.

Chapter 43

Rock Creek Station State Park near Fairbury, Nebraska, was built primarily to serve the stagecoach and Pony Express, but the Oregon-bound emigrants also stopped here to purchase supplies or camp. Rock Creek Station owner David McCanless eventually built a toll bridge here for emigrant families in 1859, charging between 10 and 50 cents per wagon, depending on what he thought he could extort. In July 1861, while stopping by the station to check on the status of his payments, the bully was shot and killed in an altercation by a young James Butler (later to be named Wild Bill) Hickock.

Chapter 44

Sidney, Nebraska was laid out in 1867 by the Union Pacific Railroad and named for Sidney Dillon, its president. Its growth exploded in 1874 when gold was discovered in the Black Hills, and the Sidney-Deadwood Trail opened the shortest freight route to the gold fields from 1874-1881. Its "Front Street," directly facing the Union Pacific tracks (shown at left)— lined with 80 saloons, gaming halls, brothels and boarding houses—helped give Sidney the moniker "Sinful Sidney - The Toughest Town in the Western Frontier." It is now better known as the world headquarters for Cabela's sporting goods stores.

Chapter 49

The site for the Nebraska State Penitentiary was donated for that purpose by Lincoln's "founder" W. T. Donavan. Constructed at a cost of $312,000 using limestone from the Saltello quarries located about twelve miles south of Lincoln, this imposing building originally had a capacity for 320 prisoners.

Colonel Philpot and D.B. Courtenay were the two lawyers that represented Davis at the original coroner's inquest in August 1894. The newspapers of the time made it very clear that they did not get along very well.

Epilogue

George Jay Gould was a financier and railroad executive, the eldest son of Jay Gould, the prototypical robber baron of the nineteenth century, and a one time president of the Union Pacific Railroad. Unfortunately, while George inherited the bulk of his father's fortune following his death in 1892, he did not inherit his father's business acumen. He managed to lose control of most of his father's holdings, and was actually sued by his siblings for the losses they incurred while he piloted his father's empire into a fraction of its original worth. After his wife's death, Gould married his mistress, Guinevere Jeanne Sinclair, and legitimized his three children by her: Jane, George, and Guinevere.

The "hell" to which Cable sent Peter LaRue was a real one. All during the incredibly dry summer of 1894, small fires had been fought around the logging town of Hinckley, Minnesota. On September 1, a sudden temperature inversion trapped the heat and smoke of the fire, concentrating them under the huge layer of cool air above. When two fires south of town fires joined together to make one large fire, their flames burst through the inversion and the cool, heavy air above came rushing down into the fires to create a vortex of flames. When it was over, the four hour firestorm had completely destroyed six towns, and 400 square miles lay black and smoldering. (Photo and text adapted from Hinckley Minnesota website, www.hinckleymn.com)

State Marker Dedicated by Author on 116th Anniversary of Rock Island Wreck
(Courtesy Lincoln Journal Star)

About the Author

Dr. Joel Williamsen is a Nebraska native raised in rural Alder Grove, south of the mighty metropolis of Craig, and a graduate of the University of Nebraska in Lincoln. He has worked as a desgner for the Army on anti-tank missiles, and for NASA as a spacecraft engineer on the Hubble Space Telescope, Space Station and Deep Impact programs. He is now a Pentagon consultant specializing in aircraft and missile live fire test and evaluation.

This is his first novel.

510

Made in the USA
Lexington, KY
07 January 2011